THIN
PLACES

THIN PLACES

A Novel

Marian Musmecci

iUniverse, Inc.
New York Lincoln Shanghai

Thin Places

iUniverse books may be ordered through booksellers or by contacting:

iUniverse
2021 Pine Lake Road, Suite 100
Lincoln, NE 68512
www.iuniverse.com
1-800-Authors (1-800-288-4677)

Because of the dynamic nature of the Internet, any Web addresses or links contained in this book may have changed since publication and may no longer be valid.

This is a work of fiction. All of the characters, names, incidents, organizations, and dialogue in this novel are either the products of the author's imagination or are used fictitiously.

ISBN: 978-0-595-42356-9 (pbk)
ISBN: 978-0-595-86694-6 (ebk)

Printed in the United States of America

Because, as my husband so correctly commented,
I have been writing this story my whole life,
I dedicate these pages ...

to my parents
whose love and encouragement
fostered in me
an almost always optimistic desire to understand why and to know how ...

to my husband
who is also my favorite friend
and whose love for me
lets me be me ...

to my children
who created in me,
because of who each one of them is,
such a sense of what life should and can be
and introduced me to the utterly unbelievable
expansiveness of mother-love ...

and to those other dear ones
who are my family and friends,
who have cared for and about me
and allowed me close enough to care for and about them ...

thank you ...
the following pages could not have happened without you.

Leah: I behave normally and yet my life and its moments no longer fit my definitions.... I live between and within a perceived and a previously unknown world, and yet I am simply me as I have always been.

Father Tom: All over the world, since the beginning of recorded history, and actually even before that, people have noticed that in certain places unusual things have a tendency to happen, not necessarily bad things, just unusual things. In Ireland, these places are called Caol A'it ... translated that means 'thin places'.

May: The ideas I am sharing with you should feel like reminders, like words heard once but not remembered for a long time. The truth will always be like that. You must stay true to who you are.

Malick: In the place where this struggle will reveal itself fully, perspective will overshadow reality.

Michael: We have forever....

INTRODUCTIONS

▼

Morning sun slides through the curtainless window and falls upon me as I try to hold on to the dreamscape as if I can, like an almost napping fisherman, remember to keep a tight grip on the pole, which is connected to deep water by a thin line of consciousness. Work calls to me. The routine of the day-to-day pushes itself up onto me as if it is a fish caught, and I am a way back into the water instead of the catcher. I remind myself I have created this routine as I reach out arms and stretch. Morning sun fills the window now, and I know I must move, become vertical, rise to the occasion of rising-up. Knowing even as I do that within me there is a story unfolding, faded images painted with words from an old soul into a young ear. Grandma May. My brother called her a relentless old witch, but she was not that at all, and when she was not reminding him of his various chores he would sit close to her too and listen to her carefully woven stories.

Papa John called May's stories fabrications. He would say to her, "Bake bread or do laundry instead of telling these tales," but her words drew even him, although he was reluctant to admit it. We called him Papa John because he was not the father who made us; he was the papa who loved us and lived with us. The man who had created us, who had made love to my mother at least twice, had lost himself in Vietnam, had returned but not. He lived in a small cabin surrounded by towering redwoods not far from Castle Rock River. We saw him on holidays and at least two or three other times a year. We called him by his name, Sean. He had deep eyes and a quiet voice, but too often dark memories filled him so completely he had decided to live alone with them, and somehow, despite how young my brother and I were, we could understand how his love for us and our mother and how our love for him could not be a big enough island for him to escape to from his sea of confusion and despair. So he was a traveler in our lives, stopping by to see how we had grown, how our grades in school were, to ask us about our friends and how we filled the moments of our days. We were Sean's to visit, and he did, even after mom remarried.

Grandma May was Sean's mother, but she lived with us because her husband had died before I was born, and "… because family takes care of family, damn it," as Papa John declared often. My earliest memories are of Grandma May's voice and of sitting on her lap and feeling her heartbeat against my back, her heartbeat a drumbeat patterning her words.

"Storytelling is an obligation too, John," she would say to him when he reminded her of her responsibilities. "Storytelling is the fabric holding together now and then, and fabrications they may be, but nothing comes from thin air, I'll be reminding you." She would remind him with her eyes looking into his and with a strong but gentle voice that seemed to sweep away the shadows and the cobwebs in the sharp rooms of reason and logic, so dream and desire could live there too.

✻   ✻   ✻   ✻

I shake my head and find myself still standing in front of the window of my bedroom daydreaming, going back in time trying to find them all—Grandma May, Papa John, Sean, my mom. Only Grant remains in the present now. Distant brother and sometime friend, we only visit by phone and emails. He is only a voice now, except when I go back then he has substance, a form, a smile, tears.

There is a need though to return carefully to old times. They cannot be shuffled like a deck of cards and chosen at random, or one might end up with a handful of memories too dark to hold without dying a bit, small pieces of self relinquished at a time. What is the greatest fear? Not being able to save loved ones in danger. What is the greatest terror? Knowing that.

I lean into the window letting the glass push back against me. It is warm from the sun. It is me that is suddenly cold. Cold from a memory of fire. So cold.

"Mom?" I turn quickly as the small voice calls me back to the present.

"Son?" I say as I look into large blue eyes.

"What were you doing?" I pick him up as he asks and rub my face into his hair. He is warm and smells like the sweetness of childhood; youth and innocence a scent to be truly savored by those who have traveled beyond youth and innocence.

"John Henry, if we do not hurry we will be late, you for school and me for work." He wraps arms and legs around me as I walk from my room to his. We play this holding game often enough for me to know my part. As I bend over his bed to set him down, he holds on.

"Is it a monkey I hold?" I pretend to try to shake him loose. "Maybe if I apply just the right tickle to the situation," and off he goes, bouncing on his bed.

"You're silly, Mom."

"I know. And you are a wise old man who is going to choose appropriate clothing for the season and the day, and I am going to go wake your sister and make us all fresh juice."

"I don't have to be appropriate 'cause I'm only six, remember?" He is on the floor hiding behind the end of the bed with only his head visible above the bright blue and red of his woven spread.

"In that case I am making carrot juice instead of orange juice this morning."

"No, no, I'll dress right. Make orange"

"You have a deal. Thank you, sir."

"No, thank you, ma'm."

"No, thank you …" and it continues as we make our voices softer and softer as if we are traveling great distances from each other instead of me just going into the next room where I enter a land of pale lavenders and pinks. Daughter's room is accented in warm rose with sprinkles of sun yellow, a garden of sorts. She is underneath covers, just soft blond curls on a pillow of violets. I whisper her name into her ear until she stretches out a small arm, "Mary, sweet Mary, little girl Mary…."

Then we baby talk to each other and exchange kisses and hugs until she stands up on her bed and holds my face between her small hands, telling me quite clearly she wants to wear her bathing suit today. So I put my hands on the sides of her face, reminding her it might be a bit chilly since it is only spring we are in, then she makes a song about being in spring, and we go to her dresser to open drawers to find a suitable replacement for her bathing suit. Then I am off to the kitchen to make juice—orange, of course. And another day has loosened itself from the moorings of night's deep stillness; we are afloat and paddling away, trying to find that most sought after current, which will allow the least resistance to our efforts. And I think how glad I am to have another day as the fragrance of fresh oranges and the laughter of my children wrap around me like comforting arms.

*   *   *   *

John Henry has been dropped off at Lane Grammar and Middle School, and Mary and I are driving toward Dayton School. We are on a street lined with trees that have reached their full height and now sweep out toward each other, their branches layered upon each other so only tiny bits of sunlight are thrown down upon the street below. Mary holds out her hands to catch the rays of golden light.

I stop the car before the gates of Dayton School. The gates are massive and ornate in their lace of flowing iron angles, abstractly geometric and yet clearly in the pattern of tree branches. At 10:00 they will be opened to welcome the day and possible visitors, but at 7:30 they are still closed, the gates like hands with fingers interlaced at the end of strong rock walls, wrapping like arms around ten acres of carefully nurtured yet native terrain, with large and small buildings of stone and timber constructed ever so ingeniously, seeming to rise quite naturally from the very terra firma on which they stand. An uncomplicated paradox of sorts, the view comforting and formidable all at once, just like the program it contains.

Dayton School is a boarding school for the rich and troubled, and I am the only full-time teacher who does not live within its grounds. As I enter my code into the keypad by the gate, Mary chimes a small but persistent greeting, "School time … school time…." I take her hand as we drive through the gates. They close again behind us.

*   *   *   *

I turn my car into the small graveled parking lot that is across from the Administration Building. There is no assigned parking, but I always seem to park in the same place. It faces the three giant redwoods standing like king-kinsmen over a rock fountain. The fountain pours down over rocks of different sizes and shapes until it falls finally into a soft waiting pool of water surrounded by a wide sturdy wall of stone made to welcome sitting. I have released the straps of Mary's car seat; she is wanting to run to the fountain, but she knows only I open the car door, and as much as I know she would like to hurry my exiting-the-car ritual, she does not.

And it truly is a ritual. I seldom travel anywhere lightly, and even less often do I transition quickly from one setting to the next. I have many necessary items which do not always fit into the large leather shoulder bag or the briefcase or the backpack, so I must gather them together before traveling from my car to the outside world. The backpack carries Mary's necessary items; the other bags are all mine. My shoulder bag carries photos in plastic accordion bundles, folded bills and coins in a change purse, then there are documents which clearly identify me as me; there is banking paraphernalia, lip balm, a comb, small lotions of different scents, a nail file, pens congregating at the bottom of the bag, and a small note-book for writing myself notes and to-do lists and poetic combinations of words creating images I want to incorporate into larger poetic combinations. There is also at least one small book of poetry or prose, but usually it is the poetry which propels itself into my heart then into my bag where it nestles, I am sure, next to family photos and my keys. Michael, depending on his mood, is either amused by my collection of keys or he finds them grating. As if instead of having them in my bag I wear them like jewelry, and they clank and clink against his nerves. Some of the keys open doors which still exist and some open doors that are no more, and these last keys are the ones that seem to make the most noise for Michael, even in their silence.

These are the necessary items I carry with me almost always, their organization making such sense to me I can, with hand and no eyes, find the item I am seek-ing. Inside my other bag, which could be a real briefcase's somewhat rural distant cousin, are the thoughts and mind-workings of students, who either honor me with their time well spent or dishonor me with poorly edited half thoughts that in their owners' last minute duress to meet a deadline often miss the point of the assignment. In either case, I read the words carefully, trying not to judge the work's content by its appearance nor judge the theme and its development by a lack of precision in word choice. Both can be resurrected, and in student work there is much need for the phoenix of old to rise from the ashes.

But I am daydreaming again, and Mary has her lips and nose pressed up against the glass of the car window. I am pulled again, twice already in one day, back from my mental meanderings to the present by my children, which seems entirely natural since children live so very much in the present. Most children have not yet collected a past in which to rummage like forest creatures who hide their treasures inside trees or small boroughs then check on them often to make sure ... yes, yes, everything is still here.

We are out of the car now, and I walk behind as Mary runs to the fountain. It is still early May; the sky is promising a shower at least and perhaps a rain, but for the moment the sun appears to be bouncing between clouds like a tossed ball and sending out light-sprinkles of its own. Mary runs from sunlit spot to sunlit spot, a run-jump adventure until she reaches the fountain wall, then she climbs up and sits, her head turned toward me, but her fingers already strumming invisible music into the rippling reflection of the sky. Our morning at work has begun.

I sit down next to Mary and am about to ask her a question when the crunching of footsteps on gravel causes me to pause and look past the fountain. "Look, Mary, Mr. Danner is out for his morning walk." Bradley Danner is a tall, broad shouldered man who takes long, even strides and covers much ground with seemingly little effort.

He is deep in thought until he sees us, then he raises his hand and waves, calling out a greeting to Mary. "Mary, Mary, not contrary, how does your garden grow?"

I help Mary stand on the wall and turn toward Bradley. Mary calls out to him her normal reply, "I don't have a garden, Mr. B, you know that."

As Bradley joins us, he picks up Mary and turns in a circle slowly letting her lean back in his arms, then he adds a bit to their garden exchange, "But you will, I believe. Yes, truly, a fine garden with beds carefully filled with oh so fine treats for eyes and taste buds."

"If I have a garden I won't put my bed in it," Mary says as she straightens up in his arms to look into his eyes. "Why would I want to put my bed in a garden? It would get wet, and there are bugs and dirt. I wouldn't put my bed in a garden, Mr. D, I wouldn't."

Bradley, understanding the sincerity of Mary's thinking, stops circling and replies thoughtfully, "You are most correct, of course, a bed would be a poor thing to put in a garden, but I was speaking of another type of bed."

"Mom's and dad's bed is big and mine is little. And Uncle Brian has a waterbed."

Bradley nods his head, agreeing with her logic then explains, "But remember some words have more than one meaning. We talked about 'leaf' just last week. Remember?"

Mary laughs and says, "Oh yes, oh yes. You were coming to dinner. I told you we couldn't put a leaf in our table, but we could put a leaf on our table, and then you told me about a leaf made of wood."

"Exactly! When people plant flowers or other types of plants they sometimes organize them into small areas called beds." He stands Mary back on the wall keeping her hand in his to make sure she does not fall either onto hard ground or into cold water.

Mary's other hand goes to her hair; she begins to curl one of her shoulder length strands around her finger. "Words should only mean one thing, I think."

Bradley smiles at Mary, "Ah yes, it would definitely make life easier, would it not?"

"It would."

"But …" and he pauses for effect, "I fear it might not be quite as interesting. What do you think?"

She smiles again, "I think I need to think about that."

Bradley and I smile as I gather Mary into my arms then ask her, "Would you like to explore a bit before we go inside?" I do not need to wait for her answer; as soon as her feet touch the ground she is out of my arms and off to peer into flowers and dance a bit with the breeze.

"Are you a single mom again this week?" Bradley asks this as he sits down where Mary had been sitting when we first saw him.

"Yes, but only in the sense Michael is not home; in the heart I am never single." I sit down also, and we watch Mary.

"How long have you been married now, seven years? And you still talk like a romantic newlywed."

"Just the facts, Mr. Danner, just the facts. I am simply telling it like it is. Being married to a fireman in this county is a matter of four days on and four off, and you know what they say?"

"I seldom if ever even wonder what the faceless 'they' say or think, you know that."

"Oh, Bradley, do not be a snob."

"I'm a homosexual; I can be a snob when it suits. It goes with the territory. We are notoriously effeminate and snobby and talk with lisps when it will produce the desired effect."

"You are terrible."

"I thought my politically correct label was 'gay'."

"No, in truth, you are terrible."

"In truth, I'm wishing I had half the energy your daughter has." I nod in silent agreement as Mary's boundless enthusiasm propels her first one way then another. I notice the expression on Bradley's face is serious again.

So I ask, "Did we interrupt you earlier? You looked like you were deep in thought when I first saw you."

Bradley puts his head in his hands and sighs heavily, "Being a Resident Advisor is never dull, Leah; it's never dull. We get one fire put out and before we can partake of some brief repast, there is another blaze beginning down the hall or on the other floor."

I respond to his words instead of his meaning, "Fires are like that."

Bradley slowly sits up straight, leaning toward me, looking into my eyes as if he can read my thoughts. "It's bothering you again, isn't it?"

"It is on my mind but not bothering me."

"Let it go, Leah, or call Michael … or go to talk with Father Tom … or—"

I interrupt him, "Stop it, Bradley. I am not going to explode like a bomb or erupt like a volcano or dive off the deep end like some crazy kid who cannot handle circumstances. I have lived with 'it' for twenty years; sometimes the memory just feels stronger."

"Yes, granted, but are you dreaming again?"

"Mom, look!" Mary's excited voice gives sound to the almost silent movie we are watching of her dancing investigation of the plants and flowers and bigger-than-your-arms-can-reach tree trunks. I am grateful for the interruption.

I stand to go to her, but turn to Bradley first, "Please, do not worry. I can handle the past. It is just sometimes the dreams seem more vivid than the memory, but the dream never changes." I pause, looking at him but not seeing him. "I remember how the sky above the fire was so black the stars were gone. They just stopped then started again beyond the area above the blaze. I know now it was only the brightness keeping my eyes from seeing the stars, but back then, and in the dream, I feel as I did, not as I do now, with twenty years to soften the emotions, the fear, the emptiness. I was a child then; the world so unknown. It is strange though; I can remember the firemen's instructions to each other. I can remember Grant's hand on my shoulder. I can feel the spray from the fire hoses on my face and the quickness with which the moisture dried because of the flames and their heat. Grant kept moving me back, but the heat kept finding me. Even the buttons on my shirt were hot." I am watching Mary as I speak, because I know that is part of what I do as mom, but just for a moment, Bradley is gone and I am only reliving a moment I relive often of late, but seldom, if ever, do I give voice to the memory. It feels strange to have the words outside of me all of a sudden, listening to them as I say them they become separate from me, images painted by someone else, but mine nonetheless.

I stand and smile, "Is life just too bizarre?"

Bradley stands also. I have to look up at him, because he is so close, "You're just going to end the conversation like that?"

We begin to walk toward Mary. "Well, I would hate to monopolize the conversation, and you were going to tell me about your own hot spot, were you not?"

"There is absolutely no way I am going to let you do this.

As one of the people involved in the conversation I have certain rights, don't I?"

I laugh and shake my head, "You have no rights at this point in time. I was only rambling on about old news anyway. Mary and I have to have breakfast before class starts. Would you like to join us?"

"Breakfast with you and Mary would be enjoyable, but you and I are having lunch, and we will continue discussing this situation."

"Today, I lunch with my group."

Mary runs up to us and stops, looking into our faces to sense the emotions coloring us like attire no matter how well we believe we have blanketed ourselves. I believe children peruse adults in this manner a lot more than adults realize. "My tummy says it's time for food."

"Then I agree with your tummy." I take her hand as we walk up the wide stone steps leading into Dayton Hall, which is even larger than the two dormitories housing the students. There is a duality to being in its presence. Dayton Hall somehow makes one feel small and, at the same time, safe. Like the other structures on the campus, it is made of stone and timber and glass. The number of windows make it less overpowering, and, once inside, the windows allow a sense of openness to the point I often take a deep breath expecting the cool moisture of coastal air, then remember I am inside a building. I am fortunate to have such a place in which to spend my days.

Mary runs ahead of us once we are inside. The meeting hall occupies over one third of the first floor and, like the stairs leading in, the floor is stone, but once through the doors a variety of richly colored luxurious rugs make islands in the sea of stone. The entire center of the room is open. There are couches and overstuffed chairs and stacks of floor pillows spaced along the walls of the room. Above the furniture, uniformly framed vivid art work, depicting local scenes, draws the eye of even those who frequent the room, but this morning we seem overly focused on a different sense.

There is the magic morning mix of fresh brewed coffee and bacon and maple syrup wafting out of the cafeteria. We are moving toward it with a most singularly directed motivation, born, I must admit, mostly of desire, since we are all too well fed to actually be hungry-hungry. That I thoroughly enjoy these smells and do not drink coffee or eat meat makes me wonder what the attraction is, but I think it may be childhood related and definitely tied to campouts on the beach and all the wonderful smells connected with those experiences.

My own child is already pointing at different items although her head barely tops the shelf on which the trays are placed to be moved easily down the line of food and beverages. Since no one else is in the room yet, Bradley and I can join her without having to stop often for greetings.

"Mom, I want a little bit of everything, okay?"
I say the parent 'thing', "We will see."

✷   ✷   ✷   ✷

Mild morning has willingly opened her misty arms and relinquished herself to the bright daystar. In other words, it is almost time for lunch and my creative writing group. I am hungry for both. Mary and I are passing through the gates of Dayton School, walking toward the large yarded house with a small plaque on the gate announcing discreetly 'Dayton Day Care' and its address '101 Dayton Place'. The house neighbors the school, sharing the shaded street. There are three other houses, two on each side of the street; they are similar in nature but unique in array. Landscaping and window placement differ, and though all have covered front porches there are visual offerings of a variety of natural stone sculptures and/or potted plants with an assortment of seating arrangements in either natural wood or earth tone paint. Only the daycare center has a fenced yard; its fenceless abandon only surrendered due to child-safety issues. Each of the houses is front-shaded by the large redwoods bordering the street. In the backyards all the houses are open to the sun's light with only small bushes and flowers surrounding seating arrangements, some on uncovered decks. Two of the yards have bird baths, and there is a large pole construction swing and slide set in the daycare center's backyard. The sun does not always or often cut through the coastal curtain of mist and cloud, so houses and their owners seek out the occasional bright light of day by limiting the tall trees which are so plentiful to the area.

Mary wants to skip and for me to join her, but I am not a skipper. Michael says I am too-most-of-the-damn-time-serious to involve myself in activities like skipping, and he may be correct. I do not mind running and hiking; I love to walk, but even as a little girl skipping held no allure. "You may skip, sweet Mary. I will watch and enjoy, okay?"

"So be it, mom," and she is off skipping away but staying close at the same time. She was coloring at her small table in my classroom while I was teaching two of Yeats' poems this morning, so she is feeling artful in her language. I smile thinking about my children. Mary is precocious and loves words and puzzles and wild stories about the creation and 'why' of things. She loves to move herself physically and to connect with her physical setting immediately. John Henry was born wise and thoughtful. He is as solid and timeless as stone, yet his heart so fills him it cannot help but shine out of his eyes, allowing one to more than discern his compassion even as he would, by his very nature, rather go unobserved. He will search out the terrain of his environment with his other senses before he allows himself to become a part of it, but his quick humor saves him from being a little watchful academic. His laughter is contagious and experienced often, and he loves to row in his canoe upon the lake and to snorkel and to swim in the ocean.

Mary and I are at the gate now; she waits for me to unlock it, so we can enter the yard then walk the path to the house where her friends wait for her. The owner and caregiver at Dayton Day Care is Crystal Dayton. She is a non-practicing marine biologist and wife to Nathan Dayton, practicing marine biologist and son to Lane Dayton, who is Dean of Admissions and Chief Steward at Dayton School and the son of its founder, Thomas Lane Dayton. Crystal created the day care center after she had her first child, Lane Dayton II, who is now four. Nathan and Crystal had three years of marriage and many deep water exploration adventures before she became pregnant, first with their son, then with their daughter. They approach childbearing and childrearing as they have every other experience they have encountered—with joy and sincerity.

There is, of course, an aquarium in almost every room in the house. The children, who come to Dayton Day Care, usually know a great deal more about all types of aquatic life than their parents in a very short amount of time. The idea that the sharing of passions creates passionate, caring human beings is a Dayton family ideal, and I have found it to be valid not only in my own teaching but in the raising of my own children. Crystal nurtures this ideal well by allowing one student a week to share his or her current or longtime passion with the rest of the children at the day care center, that passion becoming the theme of the week. Sign-ups are filled quickly, and parents are encouraged to be involved in the process. I feel good about leaving my daughter in such a place, and Mary loves the interaction with children her own age.

So after we greet Crystal and say many 'hellos' and 'how-are-yous' to her young charges, Mary and I hug, then I return to the much appreciated sunshine to walk back to my classroom in Dayton Hall. During breakfast Bradley told me what had occurred last night with two of my creative writing group members, so I am quite certain today's meeting will be emotion filled. Each student at Dayton School must choose a family group based on a high-interest activity. Besides my creative writing group, the following family groups, which are created yearly based on student input, are meeting: astronomy, painting, scuba diving, music, technology, photography, science fiction, local history, and community service. The community service family group is a mandatory activity at Dayton School; each student must complete its requirements in order to graduate. It is one of those requirements about which many new students complain, then by their graduation they are praising its merits, so although we, as a staff, are normally more than willing to receive positive and negative input from our students and institute appropriate changes, we believe time is often a more prudent assessor of what programs are beneficial than the sometimes churlish and inconsistent voices of our young ones. Being willing to respectfully listen need not mean abdicating authority or disregarding a respect for experiential based knowledge. Age, along with time well used can be honored attributes even in our American culture where new or youthful often seem portrayed as better. Our student success rate speaks for itself anyway.

I take a deep breath as I enter Dayton Hall, preparing myself for the possible complaints against the numerous rules which were broken last night by two members of my group, then wonder what position the rest of the group members will take. Family business always takes precedence over the common interest which brings us together, so as I walk up the two flights of carpeted wooden stairs, I decide how best to start the discussion.

✳   ✳   ✳   ✳

I like to be in my classroom alone before the students arrive. I like to get a sense of the atmosphere I have created so carefully by a purposeful arrangement and inclusion of the room's contents. Heavy wooden tables and chairs fill the center of the room. There are couches that face each other. One couch has its back against the wall and is underneath one of the wide windows, which invites the sun into my room, and the other couch with a high shelf behind it creates a separate area so I can have more than one activity going on in the room at once. The couches are large and overstuffed with upholstery in a tight weave of varying shades of pale rose to deep scarlet with just a bit of cobalt blue to add a still deeper contrast. On the walls not used by window or shelf or white board there are portraits of writers, bright paintings from different genres, and a world map. Upon the shelves and wide window ledges are several potted plants. My desk sits in the back of the room, facing the student areas, with a short wooden file cabinet on each side. The desk's top is neatly organized and hopefully assures students their work will not be lost or unappreciated. There is a cobalt blue vase of fresh flowers and a family photo taken during Christmas last year. The black phone is mounted on the wall beside the door for easy access for both my students and me. My room is always clean and organized even in the midst of end of semester projects. I find I need physical order to maintain emotional and intellectual order.

This is most likely true because I am not an enforcer of laws. I do not punish. I believe in accountability and discipline, and that is how I maintain order. Lane Dayton, my boss, once told me my students were a bit unruly at the beginning of each year, but by first semester's end they were quite well behaved. So I lead my students into good behavior; I do not force them, because I have never seen force or intimidation do anything to human nature or the human spirit but crush it or incite it to rebellion, and I refuse to be involved in that process. Trust and compassion are the body guards to my discipline program.

I dial Chef Marconi's extension and request the pizza not be delivered until an hour from now, believing it will take that much time to get the family group business completed. I go to the bookshelf housing my poetry collection to find the edition I know contains the poem I have chosen to provide both a distance between the students and the situation and a pathway into the situation. Of course, I have made plans before to direct a discussion only to have those plans fall beneath the stomping emotions of my young scholars and disappear as in the aftermath of any stampede. I recognize the folly accompanying the need for plans, and I do not mind improvising when there is sufficient call, but—I am rescued from the mental pacing of my own thoughts by the arrival of the first of my twelve. As I turn to see Tucker Garrett, who is usually the last to arrive, I think to myself, this is going to be an interesting afternoon if the most basic of our patterns has already been cast aside.

*   *   *   *

"Hey, Mrs. Callaghan," Tucker greets me in his slow Texas style of speaking. He is one of our few students not from California. We have quite a reputation in the state for taking in young students with problems from well-to-do families and returning those students home again or to a university of their choice, either without those problems or with very workable methods to deal with the problems in a long term sense. Tucker's only real problem is he is shy to the point of being withdrawn and incapable of communicating. He comes from a wonderful and caring family that visits him at least once a month, flying in from Texas on the family jet. His younger brothers and sister look a great deal like him with their dark hair and suntanned skin. They are all large boned and muscular, kept in shape by their work on their ranch. Mrs. Garrett is also shy and blames herself because Tucker is her oldest, believing he learned the behavior from her, but Mr. Garrett reassures her this is not so. I do not usually give advice to parents unless I am directly asked for it, but a kinder woman would be difficult to find, so I did mention to her learning to act shy and innate shyness seemed two very different matters, and feeling guilty did not seem to assist people in helping either themselves or others. People are born with strengths and weaknesses. The responsibility of parents and teachers demand we intervene, at times, in both areas to create balance and nurture progress.

"How has your day been so far, Tucker?"

"Well, ma'm, I've been working with Mrs. Franklin on putting together a computer game. Today we sorta filled some holes we had in my programming. I had a great work out then went for a swim and all that sets just fine with me. So, I don't guess I'll be complaining about the day so far." He looks at the door then back at me with an amused look on his face. "I'm sorta expecting things to get a might more interesting in the next few though. What about you?"

"Tucker, I believe you might just be right." Before I can continue, Maddie Braff and Alana Sayles enter my room, arm in arm, smiling and let their book bags drop to the floor loudly.

"It's going to be so good to see Neil and Charlie get what they deserve—"

I interrupt Alana before she can continue, "What is the process, Alana?"

Maddie speaks for Alana before Alana can defend herself, "She isn't actually discussing the details, Mrs. C. She's just pointing out after a year of getting away with everything but murder it will be nice to see justice served."

The girls sit down at the table next to Tucker as I remind them, "I do not believe the gentlemen you named have been breaking rules incessantly. Unless of course, you both want to back up what you have said with facts; gossiping is breaking a rule too. Correct?" I look at them, waiting for a reply, and hear two barely audible 'corrects'. I walk back to my desk to get a new white board marker and cannot help but notice Maddie is trying to calm Alana down a bit. I can normally understand why students are chosen to be each other's roommate, but in Maddie's and Alana's case I cannot find any logic. Maddie's appearance and movements identify her as an athlete. She has long straight midnight black hair she usually pulls back into a ponytail. She seldom wears make-up and has striking green eyes. She is an attractive young woman but not pretty in the conventional sense. Alana shaves her head and wears heavy black liner around her large blue eyes. I have never seen her without her dark lipstick. She has an angelic face despite rather drastic fashion choices. Maddie likes to wear jeans and sweatshirts or t-shirts in a variety of pastel colors while Alana wears quite an interesting collection of long flowing dresses and skirts with lacy blouses all in deep shades of either scarlet red or black, which show off well her shapely but petite figure.

Tucker is looking at them, one then the other, and definitely has something on his mind, but he does not speak. Instead he looks down, reading his fantasy fiction book again.

Alana leans toward him, "Go ahead, Tucker, tell me what's on your mind." There is a moment as she holds his attention when Tucker seems to be trying to overcome his shyness.

"Alana—" Tucker manages only the saying of her name.

"Yes, Tucker?" Alana leans even closer.

But whatever Tucker was going to say will have to wait because in through the door, either singularly or in combinations, walk the other nine of our group, or ten if Valerie's guide dog, Samson, is counted. Chairs are pushed back from the tables, book bags are set down gently or again loudly dropped, and there is not a word spoken by anyone during this very basic and normally talkative entry procedure.

I stand in front and say, "Welcome." There are mumbled responses and some polite greetings returned. I request journals and pens be taken out and ready for use.

"Before we can have any discussion I need to ask if the process has been followed. So please raise your hand if you have followed the rules, not discussing with anyone the details of the situation involving Neil and Charlie." Not one student raises his or her hand, not even Tucker or Valerie, who usually do not allow themselves to be pulled into such situations. "I have to admit I am disappointed. Since not one of you followed the rules, and I believe this is the first time that has happened in our group, none of you are in a position to help clarify the situation. You have each made yourself a part of it. So instead of being problem solvers, you are each and all now part of the problem. Does anyone here believe I am wrong in that claim?"

No one raises a hand or speaks. "I am hoping your response is an indication of your honest understanding of the process guidelines, not just a refusal to respond because you are being sullen. Is anyone here feeling treated unfairly, etc.?" Again no one raises a hand or speaks.

"Then we will start family group in the following manner today. I am going to write an excerpt from Frost's poem "Reluctance" on the board. I would like each of you to respond to the poem based on your own behavior in the situation. You may not discuss the behavior of anyone else; you may only discuss your own behavior. You are not attempting to explain the details of this situation to me; I may or may not read this particular journal entry. Do you have questions?" The room is completely quiet as I turn and write the six lines from Frost's poem on the board.

> "Ah, when to the heart of man
> was it ever less than a treason
> to go with the drift of things,
> to yield with a grace to reason,
> and bow and accept the end
> of love or a season?"

As I walk to my desk in the back of the room I realize if this same level of involvement in a negative situation had occurred in the beginning of the year, when we were still new to each other, the respectful silence which answered each of my questions would not have happened. There would have been bickering, name calling, and casting of levels of blame. I was, I had to admit, looking forward not only to discussion but to hearing the connections they would make to Frost's realization human nature has an exorbitantly difficult time "yielding with grace to reason" or bowing in acceptance to "the end of love or a season."

What is contained in our human nature that so often seems to drive us to a rebellious state? I see as I look around at my student-children that Charlie is struggling to stay composed. He is bent over his journal and appears to be reading the poem over and over but not writing anything yet. His partner in crime, so to speak, Neil, in contrast, is filling the page. These two are not roommates but gravitated to each other early in their stays here as many of our students do who share common behaviors, positive or negative. Both young men are bright; they are both handsome in their features and athletic in their builds; Charlie is blond and tanned while Neil has red hair with freckles across his nose. They both have a tendency to charm many of the young ladies in their classes, but the rule is until a person can be a loyal and trusted friend to his- or herself, he or she is not ready to be someone else's friend, much less romantically involved. Dating has to be approved first by the Residential Advisor of each student then approved by the family group(s) involved. Both boys have been here for over a year; Neil is only fifteen and Charlie is sixteen. At Dayton School dating is not usually approved until the two people involved are seventeen or have completed two full years of the program if they are both residents here. When drugs and/or sexual abuse have been a reason for attendance at Dayton, then dating is not normally allowed at all.

And again, only the younger or new students complain about the dating rules; the others have experienced the benefits of investing their time and efforts in creating healthy, platonic relationships with self and others. Physical intimacy adds a whole new dimension to the multifaceted equation of relationship, and most troubled teens do not even do simple math well in terms of relationship dynamics. In their pasts, many of our students have used sex like a drug or as a means of control, and neither of those are healthy. Coupling this with the acknowledgment that humans are indeed sexual beings allows staff and students to respect the mystery and magnitude of sexual expression as a natural later step in what should be a lengthy process of getting to know another human being.

Family groups allow students to familiarize themselves with the skills and nuances of relationship building. Nonphysical intimacy is a requirement. Students must be willing to reveal who they really are and must be willing to accept who others are, and in both cases, they must do so without judgment. I have found it to be such a bedrock truth that once I get to truly know someone it is difficult not to cherish the person as a person; even people I have found intolerable initially are usually only unbearable surface deep. Michael questions this belief and references Adolf Hitler and people who abuse children. That sort of down-to-earth thinking is one of the reasons I love him and need him; if I can build my idealistic little structures upon his realistic foundations they will stand the test of time and its circumstances, and I do so respect ideas and ideals not blown by breeze or shaken by gravitational pulls.

"Mrs. Callaghan?"

Oops. I have done it again. Gone away. Turned a mental corner, headed out to lala land, and once again been called back by a young one.

"Sorry about that. Is everyone ready? Do you want to stay at the tables or move to the couches?" Knowing each other as they do, they check eyes and take their own tally for staying or going. Chairs slide back and taking only pens and journals the students move to the couches. There is a thick rug on the floor between the couches, so sitting on the floor is also comfortable, and we always manage to make room for each other. In the beginning, when personal space requirements are wider, arranging ourselves in the couch area is a challenge, but we are comfortable with each other now; our legs and arms and shoulders can touch other legs and arms and shoulders. The addition of Samson to our group seemed to make the discomfort period shorter, even though he is quite dignified in his manner and diligent in his duties to Valerie, he relaxes a bit in the couch area, the students finding it calming to have him there.

I am a floor sitter by nature. It is easier to move around on the floor, and I do have a tendency to move around. Additionally, my hands accompany my words. I am constantly apologizing for bumping others with elbows or causing surface damage to skin or clothing with pencil or pen if I place myself between two other people on the couch. It is so interesting how quickly we begin to sit in the same places, so occasionally I have to mix things up a bit and enforce change, but for discussions like the one we are going to have I do not concentrate on sitting positions.

"Would anyone like to read the poem to us?" Without being conscious of it, we all look at Aden, whose voice makes oral reading song like. When we realize what we have done, the tension melts a bit as we smile at each other. Aden reads Frost's words then we are quiet a moment.

Aden is sitting next to Jacy whose sun bleached golden curls, tanned skin and brown eyes only serve to accent Aden's dark blue eyes, fair skin, and straight black hair, but other than that they are similar in their dispositions. They both appreciate literature greatly, diving into it as naturally as seals dive beneath the surface of the ocean's waves, and just as Aden often reads to us, Jacy is often the first to respond to a reading, "Frost is commenting on the very human part of us that wants to go against the expected or the norm, 'the drift of things'."

Neil allows for a moment of silence, making sure Jacy is done, then adds, "Frost connects the desire to be free to choose our own way with the idea we do not give up easily what we feel or have felt. It's like we want whatever we have chosen to continue even if we know the season for it has ended, or we know someone no longer returns our feelings."

Again, we are quiet to see if anyone wants to add to what has been said. I prompt a bit, "Does anyone have a different interpretation of the words?"

Alana taps her pencil on her leg as she comments in her usual manner of throwing out a piece of her thinking unaided by introduction, "Yielding to the inevitable is not necessarily a natural process … like the line from one of Marilyn Manson's songs 'perpetual rebellion with absolutely no push,' we're always in a state of going against the … like the gravity of living … breaking out of the so-called box, ya know?"

Almost without a pause, because they are getting into making personal connections now, Tucker suggests, "Garth Brooks has a line "Nothing ventured, nothing gained, sometimes you have to go against the grain."

Valerie adds to the discussion "One of my mom's boyfriends used to play poker and he taught me to play. He liked to listen to this song by Nick Morris titled 'All In' that reminds me of Tucker's song. One of the lines went something like '... I could fold or play, call or raise, but instead I may throw it all in....' I interpret Frost's poem to mean humans have choices all the time, whether they realize it or not, and choices are sometimes made based on just reacting, going with a feeling, rather than really thinking about the situation and its circumstances."

Charlie speaks now. He has a favorite band and their lyrics may be the only ones he knows, because he never shares lyrics from any other band. "There's a Door's song, I'm pretty sure the title is "The Crystal Ships", and there's a line that fits, 'deliver me from reasons why.' I think we sometimes just do things because we feel like it. Then when things don't go right, we have to come up with reasons why after the fact. We don't want to always think about things before we do them. Frost's poem touches on the part of us that just likes to move in the moment without thinking about every damned thing, and even sometimes, being reactive and going against what we know to be the safe and sound thing to do. Yeah, 'deliver me from reasons why' means, to me, we need to think about the consequences before we act, not after, even though it may be a 'treason to our hearts'."

I decide to get them out of the comfort of lyrics and ask them to think about other aspects of how we define our place in the universe. "Good, now give me something from science."

Tucker, one of the science enthusiasts in our group, often forgets he is shy when there is discussion of one of his favorite subjects, comments, "The second law of thermodynamics claims that if a physical system is left alone, its entropy will probably increase. Entropy is what specifies the disorder in a physical system. It sort of rules out the notion of perpetual motion. So, like in Frost's poem, physical systems will move toward disorganization or from an old pattern into a new one."

I am basically listening to another person speaking a foreign language when it comes to science, but the other science fan in our group, Maddie, is nodding her head in agreement, so I suggest to Tucker he make a visual for the group, and he and Maddie can explain entropy to us at the next meeting. The other non-science minded people in the group voice their agreement, and we move on as I ask, "Can anyone make a connection to mathematics?"

Alana, our artist of intensely detailed pen and ink drawings, is also our mathematician. As I watch the changing expressions on her beautiful face it reminds me of someone going through a file and saying to herself, 'no ... no ... maybe ... no', but then she suggests, "Maybe there's a tie-in, like when deductions are made from assumptions or when axioms are used as the basis for abstract reasoning.

That's pure mathematics in contrast to applied, but I probably would need to think about it more to come up with something specific."

Not being mathematically oriented either, I am fine with her decision to create her own homework assignment, so I say, "Good, you have a deal. Next family group meeting you can share what you find with us." I offer the next connection as I watch Alana make a note in the back of her journal to remind herself either to talk with Mr. Porter, our math teacher or to do some research, "Spiritual or religious?"

"Siddhartha, alias Buddha, is a possible connection," Teri Allenton muses, almost as if she is talking to herself. Like Alana seemed to do, Teri is turning through pages of mental notes from her two favorite study areas, world religions and philosophy. "He started out a rich kid, came to believe, I think when he was around thirty, that life as he had observed it was little more than suffering, gave up his life of luxury, left his wife and young son and hit the road, so to speak, searching for truth. He definitely went against the flow of life as he knew it and broke all the rules of his class."

Angela Pertoni, a devout Catholic, adds, "Jesus is a good example also. He was raised in the Hebrew faith, but around the age of thirty, he also left the comforts of his home to teach it's more important to do God's will through the treatment of others than to follow the numerous mandates of Hebrew law, which as we all know, angered the Jewish leaders of the day. Even after being whipped and tortured, Jesus did not give in or try to save himself. He stayed true to what he believed."

Aden has been drawing perfect boxes on a page in his journal and he continues to do so as he shares, "The Native Americans who lived in this area thousands of years before it was invaded by the Spaniards believed power or energy was neutral and could be used for both good and evil purposes depending on who was using it. So the idea for them, if I'm understanding my reading, was good or evil was manifested based on the user's motivations, and a person was not preordained to be good or bad, which makes the idea of people being driven by human nature complex in that if our basic nature is shared why do we, as individuals, make such divergent choices?"

I am wanting Aden to get a bit more specific, so I recommend he find a particular belief or story to corroborate his observation to connect more directly to Frost's poem. My request is neatly penned within one of his carefully drawn, two dimensional boxes. Then I ask if anyone can relate to the poem historically.

Neil is quick to respond, "I can think of two examples and they both happened during World War II. When the paranoid American officials decided to round up the Japanese and put them in camps, despite the fact most were loyal American citizens of good standing, many of the Japanese young men volunteered to be soldiers. I think it was more than just trying to prove what side they were on; they were young men who wanted to fight for what they believed in. Talk about following your own heart despite the flow of things. Those people lost their homes, their land, and their bank accounts, but still they were willing to voluntarily risk their lives. The other example would have to be the Warsaw Ghetto in Poland. During much of the round-up of the Jewish people few people believed the Jews were being taken to be exterminated, so there was little to no resistance in the beginning. When the Nazis realized they were losing the war they decided to speed up the killing of the Jews. These Jewish people in the Warsaw Ghetto, I think there was something like only a couple of hundred left from having started at forty or fifty thousand, held off the damn Nazis. Russian soldiers finally liberated the town in 1945. I've read the Russians really didn't want to deal with the Jewish survivors because the Russians didn't know what to do with them and were short of supplies. I read the same thing about the American soldiers unsure of how to meet the needs of the Jewish survivors. Can you imagine making it through all those years then being rescued by people who weren't all that sure they could help you? Talk about their will to live. Think about the determination they had to have had, and not just self-preservation either; they had to help each other to make it through." Neil smiles now, "They were what I would call one hell of a family group."

They are watching me because this process of connecting our own personal realizations to cultural 'truths' always ends in the same manner. They know what will happen next even before I speak the words, "Now, bring it back home. Neil or Charlie, without sharing any of the details, what happened last night?"

Neil speaks first, "I wanted to do something that is against the rules, and I got Charlie involved in it too."

I quietly ask, "What was your motivation for breaking the rules, Neil?"

Neil starts to put his head in his hands then remembers to maintain eye contact. "I think I just wanted to do a normal thing ... just go see a girl. She's a nice girl ... from town. She wanted me to have dinner with her and her family. I wanted to go see her. I wanted to do that without getting high first or drinking anything, just have a normal damn night, no bullshit."

He is looking right into my eyes, and all I really want to do is tell him how great that is and drive him to the girl's house, but instead I have to ask him, "Is that possible for you right now?"

Now he does put his head in his hands, "No, because I've screwed up so many times before when I thought I could just do things normally I'd be kidding myself if I thought I'd broken the pattern."

"Neil, look at me. Are you being punished for your past?"

He looks up, "I know I'm not, but it feels like I am. I wanted to see if I could do it this time ... handle things without screwing 'um up."

"Did you handle things without 'screwing them up' last night?"

"No."

"Why not?"

"I guess I'm not ready yet."

"Would you be ready if you had not been caught?"

Neil leans back against the couch, closing his eyes, "I lied. I broke the rules. I got a friend in trouble, so, no, I'm not ready to be without the rules, but I'm tired of 'um."

I ask him, "What is your plan then?"

Neil sits up, looks at Charlie, and apologizes to him for getting him involved then he looks at me, "I have to make peace with my past, not let it have power over my present. I have to create a new pattern of thinking for myself starting right now. I gotta get my shit together, try to make decisions that won't get me or the people I'm supposed to care about hurt."

I lean toward him, "That sounds great, but how are you going to do it? I want basics, the process you plan to make work."

"I'm gonna follow the damn rules," he pauses as he looks down at his journal then adds, "even if it feels like treason."

Charlie stands up and goes to Neil, "I should've tried to talk you out of it, man, but ... well, I didn't; I just went along like I always do. I'm sorry, Neil." Then Charlie turns to me, "I know the talk and what I need to do. I'm sorry to you and the group. I should've been stronger."

I have to cover one more area of the process, so I ask, "Neither of you considered asking permission, or just talking about what you wanted to do with Mr. Danner. Why is that?"

Neil is quick to respond, "He would've just said no. Why bother?"

"Ouch!" is Angela Pertoni's reaction to Neil's statement. This is a technique we use when something has been said that takes away someone's integrity that is not present. Instead of jumping in to defend, we just say 'ouch' and allow the speaker to think about what has been said and to possibly change the statement back into one which is in his or her accountability zone instead of placing blame on someone else. Angela is the best at this, probably because of her own experiences with people in her life throwing blame around instead of taking responsibility for their part in a situation.

Neil nods his head, "Okay, okay, I get it. I didn't trust the process or go to the people in authority over me to seek guidance. I put my own mind set on Mr. Danner and didn't give him a chance." He smiles at me and winks.

I wait to respond until I can discern from the change in his expression he is ready to listen, "The wink did not impress me, Neil, and your words were right out of the book. Any belief in those words?"

Neil almost gets up to reply, and I understand that need because I like to walk and talk also, but he knows to stay seated and within the circle of the family group. "That's just it, Mrs. C, I do believe in the words and in the process, but … damn, I don't even know how to express it; I just don't want to ask permission to do regular kinds of things, but I know I have to come under authority, so I can someday, maybe fifty million years from now, come under my own authority. It's just not that easy to change how I do things, ya know?"

Now I nod my head in agreement with him, "I do know, believe me, Neil. Changing thinking and behavior are long processes, but what is the only way to reach the destination?"

Three or four of my students respond in unison, "Take the first step then continue on, one step at a time, one moment at a time, without turning back."

"You're relentless, Mrs. C," is Valerie's good humored comment.

I say, "totally" as I smile, and then I look at the rest of the group. "Well, we could, of course, discuss the gossiping you all did and Charlie's role, and we still can if anyone feels a need."

Other voices chime in now, a fresh breeze of accountability moving gently through and hopefully clearing out the animosity and frustration of being so young and having to confront personal demons on an almost daily basis while trying to move forward in a purposeful manner and not feel banished from normal living, a difficult balancing act but not impossible when they remember they are not alone. I notice they have all turned toward the door.

We can smell the pizzas before they are carried into the room. I look around at these children who are not mine but who are, and I pray for every step back they seem destined to take there will be at least two or three steps forward. Success, like any skill, is learned and must be perceived as a possibility; I try to make the skill of succeeding the foundation on which all the other skills I teach are based. I silently toast to that with my first bite of cheese pizza.

*   *   *   *

I listen to them, press my ear up against the windowpane separating generations; sometimes I feel a need to tap on the glass and gesture as if I can actually communicate meaningfully there is a steep incline just ahead or a sheer drop off, that just possibly they will need to apply a bit of caution to their momentum, but that is just age speaking to youth, and I am only a warning sign in their peripheral vision. I do not mind at all; these visits from a distance only make me glad I am not their age anymore, but I do appreciate the fullness of their hearts and their sure intent.

Morgan Connally begins speaking, his hazel eyes flashing skepticism. "Monica Lewinsky will get rich because she messed around with a married man. The first Democratic president to win a second term since FDR and Clinton couldn't keep his pants zipped. He balanced the budget, but they're going to impeach him for dishonesty in a time when more marriages end in divorce than don't, and students surveyed from all around the country claim it's okay to cheat on tests and copy homework. There's porn on the Internet a six-year-old can find, some priests are messing with the minds and bodies of their trusting parishioners, and whole villages are dying of AIDS in Africa, but what is really freaking out Americans is a friggin' nonexistent, or at least unjustified, Y2K bug that could upset TV programming or close down the ATM machines for an hour. Are our priorities screwed up, or what?" He leans back in his chair, looking into my eyes. "And it's odd I have a bit of an anger problem? It's like that old movie about one of the world wars and everything is getting blown up, so the regular folks evacuate this little town in France or England, and the people in this insane asylum are forgotten and eventually get out and are running the town and working in the shops when a bunch of American soldiers arrive. The soldiers don't even notice things are a bit off for a while, because the whole damn world's acting crazy."

I smile at him, "I can see your reasoning, of course, but when have two wrongs ever made a right?" He asks what I mean, and I reply, "You gave other people's bad behavior as a rationale for you getting angry. How can one unhealthy choice justify another? How will that solve anything?"

"Like when Hamlet can't decide 'to be or not to be' so Claudius' deceit spreads," Valerie's fingers stop flying over the Braille in the book she was reading as she speaks. "I think if Hamlet had been honest with his people and told them what his father's ghost had told him, then Horatio and the night watchmen had confirmed the ghost's presence, Hamlet could have won the support of his people, removed Claudius from his father's throne and his mother's bed, and righted the wrongs before so many innocents died. Corruption spreads; it's contagious. I agree with Mrs. Callaghan, rationalizing bad behavior only allows for more bad behavior."

"Yes," interjects Jacy, "but you'd ruin a great play."

Shay Weston begins to drum a rhythm on the table's edge; it is what he does before he speaks, so we wait for the words we know will follow. He does not share his thoughts or feelings easily or often, but when he does there is usually a depth and breadth of comprehension unusual in a seventeen year old, so when he does decide to join the conversation, people who know him, no matter their age, actually seem to stop their own reactive thinking processes to listen. "Generation after generation we don't listen and learn; we think somehow it's gonna be different with us, that we'll figure out the problems that no other generation could, but we don't, and they didn't because we'd have to stop being human or change human nature to solve our biggest problems. We'd have to care about how the other guy is doing as much as we care about how we're doing. It's about greed and desire, and there are only so many pieces of the damn pie, and too many people seem to want bigger slices than they need or have. Whoever dies with the most toys doesn't win; we don't even have a clue who wins 'cause we don't know a damn thing for sure about what this life is all about. You have God, you think you know. You have science, you think you know, but we don't know shit except that everybody dies eventually. Why not make the time here ... conducive? Work together and cure cancer, stop world hunger? Shit, no, man, we build a faster engine instead, a fancier car, dig a little deeper for the oil, cut down a few more trees. The crap we do is unending. Until materialism becomes secondary to quality of life, we're screwed. Period."

I do my own little drum roll on the table's edge, "Is that a spontaneous outpouring, or have you been keeping a list somewhere?"

Shay runs his hands through his shoulder length hair to get it out of his face, and I wish he could clear his mind of its troubling thoughts as easily. "I think it's a spontaneous reaction to a crap load of input, but it's equally possible I've been throwing all this stuff together and sort of letting them steep, making one hell of a brew." He pauses, but I can tell he is not done. "Watch the news, read the papers, and how are we suppose to respond? 'Oh, how interesting.' I don't think so. Damn, sometimes it just seems to make sense to get pissed off, doesn't it?"

I return his question to him, "Does it?"

He is not backing down at all. "Yeah, for me, maybe it does." His words are a challenge, I know, but not at me directly; he is just wrestling with his own demons and asking for help without asking for help, probably because he is too angry to ask for help, and therein lies the problem with vicious circles.

Shay is not normally my angry family member; that's Morgan, but they are roommates, and we do get some transference occasionally. Shay is my keep-everything-inside-and-do-not-react family member, so I look at Morgan, who I can tell is more than ready to respond.

Morgan slaps his knee, "Slow down, roommate, you sound like me now instead of you. If you start acting like the angry one, then I'll have to start being low-key and cool, and I don't think I'd be very good at that."

Shay doesn't respond to Morgan's light-hearted attempt to reach out to him. So Morgan tries again, "Okay, okay, I'm an asshole and you're being serious. I'm not making a joke out of it, okay? I mean, it's sort of uncomfortable to be on the other end of somebody being pissed off over stuff that's out of his control. You're making me look at myself, bro, and it's different from when I'm inside my own melon just firing away." Morgan is looking at Shay as he speaks, but only when Morgan is quiet does Shay look up at him.

Shay speaks so quietly we, as a group, unconsciously lean toward him. "It's a black hole sometimes; my head is like … I want to figure why things happen, why things don't happen … why people die, good people, and then these pieces of shit just get to keep going through their days, day after day learning nothing new, just doing the same old crap." He pauses, looking at us one at a time. "I lost my family in a freak accident. I know no one expects me to just forget, but what the hell sense does it all make; I mean, why bother trying to figure it out, but then, how can you not try to make sense of your own life? And sometimes when I try to do that, I just get down, and even with people like you … my friends, it's just so damn dark and … far away. Usually I just sort of shut down, but lately, I feel like fighting with someone or something, which is crazy, 'cause I don't fight."

We are quiet as we think about what Shay has shared. My elbows are on my knees and my chin is balanced on my hands, and I am aware of my own breathing and aware of each person in the circle and of the sunlight coming in through the windows. I am so stilled by Shay's words, so stilled, as if commenting on them would make them insignificant somehow, and I do not want to do that. I appreciate this part of our reaction to each other when a person has shared something at the core of who he or she is; we often respond in silence. We do not offer the person cliché apologies or quick compassion, instead we just sit and wait patiently for that person to work through his or her own emotions. There is no rushing in with fire hoses and axes to put out or break through; we let the flames burn but we, in our silent camaraderie, close the circle so no one gets burned; it is a controlled situation. It is a controlled fire. It is one of those paradoxical situations on which the foundations of most relevant human truths are based. The watched fire can be contained supposedly. It is the sleeping but not dead embers under the ashes of a fire perceived as out which can rekindle themselves and destroy randomly. So, as a family group, we have to be watchful for each other and watchful of each other. We have to be willing to sit and to wait and then be willing to walk through the ashes together searching for any possibility of camouflaged hot spots.

I notice my students are doing what they are supposed to be doing … journaling. I return to my desk and begin the writing of summaries, recording student comments and behaviors for their personal files. I am careful to document changes large and small. It is just the normal routine of my work: literature classes and family group meetings; conferences with other teacher/counselors at the school; the grading of student work; once a week all school meetings; twice a month outward bound activities on the ropes course with another family group; once a month meetings with Lane Dayton, in which I bring my carefully maintained group member files and we scrutinize progress and/or lack of progress; interactions with other faculty members, which make us part of each other's lives beyond our shared school experiences, and monthly family visitation weekend. My work routine patterns my days and sometimes filters into my family life, even though I try to maintain my two worlds so one does not affect the other.

If my work routine patterns my days, my family life is the fabric of my days. I think often I have chosen the pattern and fabric, that I am accountable to my choices, but there are other times when I feel as if I have been laid-out and fitted-with and fitted-to by some divine tailor. I think during those times then that I have a destiny, a path I walk and somewhere deep within me I know the next part of the journey; I can almost see it through the mist of present tense. I stop myself, realizing I have let my thoughts run away with me again.

I am supposed to be doing my end-of-the-week-organizing of my desk. I remember my other-half, sometimes my better half, is coming home today, then I do rush my leave-school ritual a bit. I become the young one with her face pressed up against the present moment, impatient for the next moment to reveal itself like a Renoir painting, just soft colors and a whispered impression of desire. Michael.

*   *   *   *

We are home, and he is, door thrown open behind him, on the deck, then down the stairs. He is picking up children, ours, in his arms and above their smiling faces, in-between kisses, his eyes meet mine. This is home for me: his eyes, his heart, his arms. Mine, all of him during these first moments, before we exchange words and before we have actually touched each other, we touch and linger here, knowing the swiftness with which the first moment after being parted will pass. It is a spiritual place in a physical world; it is souls communing; I am earth to his sky when we touch like this, over and over again through time and beyond time. My heart beats his name; his answers over and over again through a panorama of countless years of wind willing clouds and even sometimes stars across a skyscape of dark and light; we are poet warriors, romantic and fierce in how we love each other, and we know we have known each other since before we had shape or sound.

He is standing before me now. John Henry and Mary are chasing Puppy. Michael and I are almost lips to lips; only an infinitesimal shimmering sliver of breeze is between us as he breathes into me, "I missed everything about you."

I can only say, "Yes" before we are heartbeat to heartbeat, his arms pressing me closer into him, as if somehow we can truly be one being, drawing breath in unison, relational mouth to mouth resuscitation, the first kiss in four days.

"Great, just damn great. Sex right in the front yard, and you have kids who could see you. I'm shocked, really. I'm really shocked." I do not have to open my eyes to put a speaker to the words. Michael and I are just pressing smiles into each other now as we look into each other's eyes. I move back from him, but stay in his arms then look around his shoulder to see his brother, Brian.

I put on my teacher voice to tell him, "This is not sex, brother-in-law; this is greeting each other after being apart for endless nights and days."

"You never greet me that way," Brian says back to me as he picks up one of Puppy's large rubber bones to throw.

I watch as our dog, which outgrew his name years ago, waits for the throw. "You're sick, Brian, truly sick. This is a husband-wife greeting. You need to find a woman to love before you become even more twisted."

Brian throws the bone and off Puppy goes to retrieve it as Brian focuses his attention on me again. "Oh well, some of us don't meet that special person when we're barely out of diapers and make a life time commitment to each other of 'until death do us part' when we're barely born, and have everything handed to us on a silver platter. No, some of us actually have to grow up and search for that special someone."

Michael and I are standing side by side now as I respond, "How can you be barely born? That is an incredibly uncomfortable possibility for both mother and child. I am going to get my things out of the car, and completely ignore you for the rest of the evening. Or, maybe I will read poetry to you all evening and torture you in that manner. I have a new favorite you will truly despise."

Brian yells 'no', running off to where the dog is trying to get the bone out from under Michael's truck. Michael says he will help me get my things, and we begin the debriefing that occurs when we have been separated by time and distance. We talk of John Henry and Mary and of work related events. We talk of local Lane news and of any social plans or family plans we may have. Of course, in a town as small as Lane, social and family events are usually intertwined.

Michael's family is large and Irish and communal in nature. We group often at one of our houses where we make large quantities of food and laughter together. Normally, family gatherings include the extended family which consists of the men with whom Michael and his brothers work and their families. It is a fireman thing, I am told, and since Michael is third generation fireman, it all makes perfect sense. So our debriefings are seldom brief.

I have put my bags away, rejoining Michael on the deck. Mary and John Henry are eating the butterscotch/chocolate chip oatmeal cookies we made last night. We are all watching the crazy antics of Brian and Puppy. Puppy is standing over him pushing the disgustingly dirty bone against Brian's chest wanting another throw. Brian does as Puppy wants then says, "This dog needs a real name. What does he weigh? Over eighty pounds, I'm guessing, and that is not a puppy. How old is he anyway? You got him before you had John Henry, so the dog has to be at least seven, and that is not a puppy—"

Mary interrupts him, "Uncle Brian, if we gave Puppy a different name he wouldn't know it was him we were calling. So, I don't think we should change his name."

Brian tosses the bone away from him and stands up, brushing the grass and leaves off of his shirt and pants then bows to my sweet daughter, "Okay, Mary, you're the boss, I guess."

That is the last statement I hear as I walk back into the house to finish preparing the dinner, which Michael has already started, but I can still hear the background song of their voices and laughter; it is one of my favorite melodies.

*   *   *   *

Night vision. That is what I call looking back through my day and gaining a new perspective. This is a perspective brought on by being relaxed, no doubt, but also due to the fact it is dark outside; the sun has distanced itself from us, so that moon and stars can have their way with us, whispering magic into us the day disallows. Whispers belong to the night and seem out of place in the light of day. Whispers during the day seem conspiratorial; they lurk and linger like shadows long after the words have flown from mouth to ear. But in the night, whispers are transparent crystal chimes moved by the breath of moonlight and shimmering of stars; whispers are quick in their passing back and forth between lovers or between children who should be sleeping but would rather tell tales or document the day's dynamics.

The night is softer than the day. The night welcomes and makes a place for sweethearts and solitary walkers and poets. The night is deeper than the day; sleepers dive into it passing through time and space to find themselves in strange lands where gravity is nonexistent and monsters, despite their appearance, can be kind. Of course, there is that other side of night.

To be fair, night's opaque shroud must be acknowledged, and one must barricade against that aspect of night. Doors must be locked and hearts guarded, sanity protected, small children tucked in, and all across America tiny nightlights, lit like fireflies, fortify against the scraping fingernails of night, against the distance-muffled screams of night, against the sliding of branches against window screens on windless nights. Thoughts which do not bother one during the day can resurface at night and cause sheet twisting sleeplessness—.

"Are you writing a poem in your head?" Michael's voice against my shoulder brings me back from a word journey of images and poetic musings.

I say, "Yes and no, I think," as I turn to him.

"We could make love again if you want," he says with his lips next to my ear, "or I can just hold you until you sleep. What do you want, wife?"

I smile into the dark, "Both sound good to me, what do you want, husband?"

He is up on his elbow now looking at me then at the lighted face of the clock on my nightstand, "I can't believe it, Leah; it's four o'clock in the morning, and you haven't gone to sleep yet. We've got the whole family plus friends coming over tomorrow ... make that today to barbecue, and you're staying up all night again wandering around in that head of yours—"

I interrupt him, pulling him down next to me, "Just sleep, Michael, just sleep, everything is going to be okay. Just sleep."

He sighs next to me, "Will you sleep with me?"

I lay my head on his shoulder, "Yes, I will sleep with you." And like the often obedient wife I am, I do.

*   *   *   *

Morning is sweet and a bit shy at times the way it sort of seeps into the room. This is totally unlike midday's march with its band of bright light playing loud songs. I am in the kitchen making potato salad and spaghettini primavera. John Henry and Mary and I cleaned the house Thursday before we made cookies and cut the fruit for fruit salad, so I do not have much to do before family and friends arrive. Puppy has already gone out and come in again, taking care of his morning business. He is quite pleased at the bits of potato I toss to him now and then as he lays on the kitchen floor keeping me company. I have closed the door to our bedroom; I am letting Michael sleep in a bit since we kept each other up late making love and whisper-talking. Even later he was awakened by my not being asleep, which people who sleep with each other can do. When I read late into the night, he does not truly relax until I have turned off the light and allowed the rhythms of my body to enter sleep mode. Only then will I hear his breathing deepen. It is so interesting to me the ways in which people connect.

But I am distracted from my thoughts by my view. I love the way my kitchen opens itself into the living area of our home. I am not in a small box separated from the rest of my house; there are no hallways in my house either. The front room and kitchen and the master bedroom stretch across the front of the house, and directly off of the front room are the four other rooms: the second bathroom, our office/den combo, John Henry's bedroom, and Mary's bedroom. The house is surrounded by a wide deck which is covered and screened in on the sides and back and is twice as wide and uncovered in the front. There are tall gates opening into the yard off the deck on both sides of the house also. Both John Henry's and Mary's bedrooms have french doors opening out onto the back deck. Michael and I designed this house after we got married, and the quarter acre of land on which the house stands was a present from his parents upon graduation from college. It is ours in every way.

Like the buildings at Dayton School, the construction of the house is in stone and wood and glass. We chose couches and chairs and rugs of earth tones for the living room and office/den, and the second bathroom is in the same colors also.

Cobalt blue accents are thrown about or carefully placed here and there. Our bedroom and bathroom are decorated in forest green and cranberry and bright white. John Henry and Mary chose their own colors as soon as they were old enough to have a preference. We have many windows and french doors, so light is invited in always.

I am finished with my preparations for the day and have washed the dishes. The fresh cilantro, which I cut for the potato salad, has left its fragrance in the air, and the pancake mix is ready to pour as soon as my family decides it is time to rise and shine.

Puppy and I walk out onto the deck to check tables and chairs and to see if the area surrounding the deck and leading down to the lake is clear of children and husband clutter. Castle Rock Lake covers about twelve acres of land and is shaped a bit like a young child's 'c'. It is fed by the rain and by Castle Rock River which flows down from Dayton Forest's highest peak of six thousand and four feet. How anyone can measure the elevation of mountain peaks and be so specific I do not know or understand, but from the Pacific Ocean, which is one mighty boundary of our town, to its opposite boundary of forested peaks, the tiny township of Lane goes from sea level to over six thousand feet in less than a mile. Needless to say, the river gathers quite a momentum in its relatively short but steep descent. Our property is located on the inner curve of the 'c', which we share with three other neighbors each on quarter to one acre lots.

The populations of giant redwoods at the higher elevations and the coastal cypress are much greater in number than the people who live in Lane. At last count we have one hundred and twenty two full time residents, not counting the fifty-six students who reside at Dayton School. Of course, 'the city' is only forty miles north, and we have quite a few weekend and holiday families, couples, and singles who increase our numbers. Another small town is ten miles south; its children attend our grammar and middle school. Like our older young ones, this small town must also bus its teenagers to the high school in the city, but we cut costs by sharing one bus for those Monday through Friday round-trips.

I am watching morning sun light the lake's surface and twice in the last few minutes I have seen rainbow trout jump out of the water in search of their bug breakfast. The sky looks clear, promising a perfect barbecue day. Our rainy season is mostly over now that it is May, so it is definitely the beginning of the enjoy-the-outdoor season. Even the coastal fog seems to have smiled upon our day and left earlier than usual.

I see a quick but gliding shadow pass over the ground in front of me and look up to catch a glimpse of the wide wings of an eagle turning into the breeze to make a low flight over the lake's surface. They are such majestic birds in flight, but a bit undignified when they are tearing apart fresh and not so fresh animal bodies on the side of the road. Of course, being a vegetarian that whole experience may bother me more than others, but even meat eaters cannot find the sight appetizing.

From the door Michael speaks into the quiet of the day, "Feed your man, woman." I turn to see his smiling face. Men are so attractive in the morning. They have soft expressions on their faces; they have not had to go out into the world yet, so they can still be boy-men. With his pajama bottoms low on his hips, his hair standing this way and that, and his toes curling up from the coolness of the still damp deck, he is too adorable not to touch. "Your skin is still warm," I say into his chest as I wrap my arms around him.

"Jesus, Mary, and Joseph, your hands are like ice," he says as he struggles to unwrap my arms from his body.

I look up into the playfully pained expression on his face, "Well, you could be a good husband and warm me up a bit before breakfast—" but before I can finish my invitation, small arms go around our legs then another pair of arms joins those. Our children are up; our day has begun. I move my cold hands to another location on Michael's back to torture him just a bit more, and he whispers in my ear, "Evil, truly evil, women are, you know?"

I look down into small faces and yell, "Pancakes for everyone," and I am greeted with noisy approval.

*   *   *   *

My front deck and yard are full of friends and family, an assortment of coolers, a variety of dogs, lake toys, and folding chairs, and our circular drive is filled with trucks, SUVs, and more civilized forms of transportation too. There are small and large conversations occurring here and there. Some of the men are shouting as they play volleyball, which of course makes my dog and his visiting friends bark, which makes the kids chase the dogs. The air is full. We are having a glorious and loud celebration of life.

I sit at the large table on the deck with my mother-in-law, Katy, and her mother, Matilda, who was married to Thomas Dayton, the founder of Dayton School. Katherine, Michael's father's mother, and Sarah, Michael's older sister, sit with us also. We span three generations, and if that is not a celebration of life nothing is. Plus, we are watching my children and a collection of friends and cousins at play, so four generations are represented at our gathering.

Matilda, in her late seventies, sits with her eyes closed for a moment, and then sensing I am watching her as the other women talk quietly, she opens her eyes, their clear sky blue in such contrast with her loosely bound silver hair. Her voice is soft but vibrant as she speaks, "I wish May were here, Leah; I could listen to one of her stories quiet nicely right now."

I lean toward her, "She could tell a story. I have started writing some of them down, but so many of them are just pieces of stories. I have trouble remembering her wording."

Matilda takes something out of her pocket and hands it to me. "Later, when you have a quiet moment or two, you might want to read this."

I take the envelope from her noticing it has gone ivory with age. The writing on the front I recognize easily. It is my name in May's handwriting. I look up into Matilda's eyes with amazement but do not trust my voice to speak, to question the unfathomable surprise of having something of Grandma May's in my hand twenty years after her death.

Matilda leans even closer to me, "There are two more letters to be given to you, but May was clear in when you were to receive them, and I will honor her trust in me, doing as she asked." She closes her eyes for a moment then opens them again, speaking in a voice cautionary in its tone and careful in its wording. "I know some of what she will tell you. I thought at times of not giving you the letters at all, but I realized the choice was not mine to make. If after reading the first one, you decide to travel the path it will set you on no further, I will destroy the letters if you request it. Or I can entrust them to another for a later time when you might seek the truth they will share with you. It was with great sorrow May realized she might not be the one to accompany you in this ... uncovering of the truth, but she must have known somehow what was coming, so she prepared this letter and the others for you, just in case."

All my senses have gone into high gear. I have slipped the envelope into my jacket pocket without knowing exactly why I do not want to offer an explanation to anyone else for its existence right now. My mind, however, is focused on only one part of what Matilda has said, "How could she have known about an accidental fire, Matilda?"

"About that specifically I cannot say, but she had sensed something that caused her concern. She responded to that concern by writing the letters." She looks to see if we have been noticed in our quiet conversation by the other women at the table, but they are absorbed in their own discussion, so she continues, "You must realize you have a choice here, but once the choice is made, once you decide to open the letter, I do not believe you will be able to turn back or not want to read the other letters. You will change your life by reading them, and in so doing, you will change the lives of your family and others. Do not rush into this, child. Be wary and be aware. May's blood runs in your veins, some of her gifts too, I believe."

I close my eyes, lean back, let my body relax into the chair, even though my mind is moving back and forth through time like a nimble bodied gymnast, twisting this way and that on thin balancing bars of perspective. But in the distance of now, I hear the laughter of my children and my husband's voice raised in a celebratory yell over a volleyball victory, and I know where I belong. I belong here in the present with my family. Yet even as I am acknowledging that priority, I am pulled back into the past, into May's lap listening to her words again, always thinking her stories were just stories, but remembering each tale's call to duty and family, which to May always seemed to be at the heart of every situation.

I shake my head and open my eyes, knowing I cannot make sense of the mystery in the next few moments. I look at Matilda and take her fragile, fine-boned hands in mine and say, "Thank you for carrying this burden for twenty years. You did the right thing in honoring May's request. I will do the right thing in maintaining our life for my family—"

Matilda interrupts me, "I know you will try, dear heart, but your family is involved more than you know." Now she squeezes my hands, "You will be fine, I believe. Trust those God has put in your life, and don't try to make this journey on your own. There is actually more about this situation I do not know than I know. However, I will answer any questions I can once you have read the letter, but I cannot go ahead of May's letters, or give them to you early, so be patient and trust May's plan."

"I will." I pick up my wine glass and hand Matilda her glass. I raise my glass toward her as I say, "To May."

Matilda touches the side of her glass to mine, adding, "To you, dear, to you." Then Matilda turns to the other women and begins listening to their conversation. I stand and walk to the edge of the deck, observing my family and my guests.

At a table near the edge of the lake, Hank, Michael's father, and Patrick, Hank's father, sit and watch first the canoes and small sailboats on the lake and then turn to observe the activities of the men, women, and children who are playing a variety of games. Hank raises his hand to me in greeting; I wave back to him. I notice not far from them Brian is standing with a young woman who he introduced as Cindy, and they seem to be enjoying each other's company. There is another group of women sitting on blankets spread out on the ground, who are the wives of Michael's coworkers. They have found a sunny spot and are playing cards as they watch the younger children to ensure they do not venture out past the knee-deep water of the lake's shore.

Once again on the ground in front of me, a shadow passes so I shade my eyes to look up into the sky. I see an eagle land on the branch of one of the trees just beyond the party's parameters. I watch it watching us, and then I put my hand in my pocket, touching the smooth surface of May's letter. There is a voice in my head wanting me to build a fire to toss the letter without reading it, but that voice is just an incantation from the past, flying on dark wings into the light of day to scratch its talons against the smooth surface of what I know about my life. I am standing in bright daylight, but it feels as if that dark side of night has wrapped itself around me. I am standing in front of a twenty year old fire; I can feel its hot breath flying out against—.

Michael's hands are on my shoulders; he is pulling me into his arms, "... don't leave, Leah...."

I am between two worlds, so I ask, "What did you say?"

"I said, Lady Leah, write poetry later, don't leave me with all these hungry people on my hands." His eyes search mine, "Are you okay?"

In his arms, aware of his heartbeat, aware of his love for me, neither May's letter nor the flames of an old fire can taunt me, so I reassure him, "How could I be otherwise with you here?"

He picks up John Henry, who has just run to join us, "Then feed us, woman; your men are hungry." John Henry repeats his father's words to me, and I laugh with them as we enter the house together to bring out the food to feed family and friends, reminding myself that love and joy are the way to hold back dark flames. So I pray, let the love and joy be strong enough ... as overhead an eagle circles higher and higher.

Chapter ONE

I am flying, like a seabird, from island to island, sometimes with the breeze, sometimes against it, and sometimes so close to the turquoise and emerald waves that I can taste the white spray. While at other times, I am so close to the sun its golden heat pushes me back, flattens me out until instead of a wild winged bird I am just a cut-out, just a black paper shape against a gray background. I am sitting on our bed jumping from idea to idea. I am sitting on our bed, my arms wrapped around my legs which are pressed against my chest with my chin resting on my knees. I am staring at a letter I cannot see in a jacket that hangs on a peg behind our bedroom door. The letter has been there for a week. Michael is at work again but close enough to call, and in through the bedroom window John Henry's and Mary's voices are soft reminders I am not alone.

I am not alone. I have family and friends, and I like my life. What does this letter from the past want with me anyway? What could May have sent to me from way back then that could possibly fit into what I have made for myself in the here and now, and if what she has sent does not have a place—will not fit into the rooms of our house or the shape of my heart or the contours of my thinking—why would I want to fold back old paper and let her words loose? I lay back against the firm mattress that is softened by a thick quilt of cranberry red and forest green and close my eyes. But what if within the letter are words that have a place in me, in my life? What then? How can I not unfold old paper; how can I not trust May to know what is best? How could the storyteller of all storytellers not have a clear sense of timing and a finely etched development of theme? How can I not wonder at the subject? Who are the main characters in her story? Is the conflict internally based, or is there a setting besides my heartscape wherein an external conflict takes shape and creeps through dark alley ways from the past into the sunlight and shadow of the present? Will resolution come at a cost? Who will pay, and how dear will the price be?

But I am not alone. I can hear two pairs of socked feet nearing the bed, and there are small hushed breaths being breathed like whispers that fill and overflow the ear in which they are intended, and I am a good mom, so I will play my part. Weight on the mattress and still I am only my own heartbeat and a bit of breath, and I wonder if they will pounce like kittens or snuggle-up like puppies.

They are puppies, warm from their play and smelling of the outdoors, and I breathe them in deeply as we hold each other and do cuddle moves, arranging ourselves into one another until there is no space between us at all. We are air-tight, or perhaps we are only one shell on a vast beach stretching out in such timeless directions that both sunlight and moonlight sparkle the water. When Michael is home and finds us like this, he wraps around us and becomes our safe cove, and we are still for him for minutes at a time; we are totally content. But then, of course, someone has to tickle or hiccup or rearrange a leg or arm, and then we are no longer a single shell; we are an octopus with many appendages but with the singular goal of capturing Michael, of making him stay with us. But Michael is at work now, and my puppies are tired, and so we are only cuddles today, and as I kiss the top of their heads I think to myself—a nap would be nice now, wouldn't it? And as their bodies relax, the lullaby of their sleep-even breathing serenades me into a peaceful rest.

*   *   *   *

It is a dream I am in, I am sure. I am sure I am in the tight, shapeless confines of a dreamscape. I am running through ageless oaks and just above me a bird flies, but I do not see it except for a shadow on the ground that is always just a bit in front of me. This bird has wide wings and glides through mist so thick and so wet the air itself seems alive and on its breath is an exhalation of fire. What I do not know is if I am running toward the fire or away from it and not knowing does not seem unusual to me. There is no sense of direction or destination; I am only running, or perhaps I am following the bird and have no other purpose, but I am both inside and outside of the dream, and that duality grants me a distance of indifference. Only the running seems to matter, but I have a perception that if I can keep running all will be well, while at the same time I have no wish list of concerns. I am aware that my movement is soundless, as if the thick carpet of moss and the undulating curtain of mist completely shroud my footsteps. Even my heartbeat does not beat in my chest or echo in my ears, and then I realize I have no pulse, and I gasp for air.

The deep intake of breath pulls me back from where I was, and I become aware of small arms and legs wrapped about me. I take another deep breath to steady myself, feeling like I have returned from a long journey. Then I remember why I do not often take naps. Napped dreams are too deep to surface from easily. My heart is still racing, so I listen to the steady breathing of my children, and it soothes me. I have a pulse, and it is slowing down, returning to a normal rate, as I return to the normal world.

Mary moves her head a bit. As I look down into her eyes which are looking up into mine, she whispers, "Mommy, I was running with a bird in my dream." And then my heart is racing again even though I am still.

I try to make sense of her words and ask, "Was it a good dream?"

Mary thinks for a moment, "It didn't feel good or bad, mom." She rolls over on her tummy now and gives me a very grown-up look and judgment, "It was just a dream."

And I cannot help but be charmed by her expression and matter-of-fact tone, even though I do not understand how we could have the same dream. And even as I think that thought another more disturbing one surfaces: why would we have the same dream? Because I am a person who does not believe in coincidence, what others label coincidence often causes me to stop and wonder, to stop and to peer into the proverbial tea leaves to try to read the signs.

"Mom?" Mary has moved closer to me and is peering into my eyes. "I thought only scary dreams were bad."

To reassure her I say, "Yes, that idea makes sense."

And then she plays one of our word games, "I would rather make dollars than cents, mom." We smile into each other, and I hug her with one arm since my other arm is still under my sweet sleeping son's head.

I whisper to her, "Do you dream often?"

She is watching the flutter of shadow and light cast by the afternoon sun into the room, "More lately, I think, but I would have to think about it to be sure."

As casually as I can I ask, "Did anything else happen in your dream today besides running with the bird?"

She ponders my question then answers, "It was foggy, so I couldn't see much."

She will become bored with my questions if I keep asking them, or she will wonder why I am so interested, so I quiet my uncertainty and reply, "That makes dollars."

Mary giggles as John Henry stretches out his arms and says, "You two are noisy." This remark causes an instant reaction. We wrestle each other until they start tickling me and continue to do so until I slide off the bed onto the floor begging for mercy, realizing that as real as my laughter is, just behind it is the haggard and relentless creature called doubt, which I know I will have to deal with sooner than later, just as I know I will have to open May's letter sooner than later. But for now, for this moment, and until John Henry's and Mary's bedtime, I will try to think of neither letter nor doubt.

Instead, we will make dinner together, and then walk down to the lake and back with Puppy so that on the way he can do his night business. After that there is bath-time and read-a-story-time and tuck-in-time and sometimes a thousand-questions-time before the voices of my young ones say goodnight/sweet dreams to me and to Michael (who is far away but not) and to God who, for me, lately, often seems to fall into that same category of far away but not. While inside me, thoughts fly like fingers over lines of poetry as if they are Braille. I am seeking comfort in heart-bound articulations from the past, words I have taken from a page and placed in my heart for their own safekeeping and for my own shelter. From Eliot's Burnt Norton, "But to what purpose disturbing the dust on a bowl of rose-leaves I do not know" there is the question of motivation while in The Eighth Elegy Rilke deems us "… spectators always …" as we travel through our lives. By attempting to understand the purpose of May's letter and Mary's shared dream without actually undertaking action have I not become spectator?

"Mom?" John Henry is wearing his chef hat and pointing a long handled wooden spoon in the direction of Mary, so I will notice she has used the uncooked pasta we are planning to prepare for dinner as hair ornamentation. My daughter has turned herself into an angelic Medusa.

She smiles at me happily as I walk toward her, "Mary, you have created a new use for pasta."

"Do you like it, mom?" She asks me as one of her decorations slips slowly from her hair and falls to the floor.

"I find it original and interesting."

Her hands are on her hips now, "That isn't a real answer to my question, Mom. Do you like it?"

"I have no strong feeling of like or dislike," I pause and get down on my knees to be at her eye level. "Why do I have to like or dislike something? Why can I not just appreciate what you have obviously taken joy in doing?" I turn to John Henry and ask him what he thinks about Mary's creation.

Looking at her he comments, "I like that it's weird and strange and sort of funny, but I don't like it because I don't want to eat spaghetti that's been stuck in her hair." Then he looks at me, "We have more spaghetti, right?"

As I put my arms around both of their shoulders, more pasta falls on the floor from Mary's hair. John Henry and I look at each other and then at Mary as she sighs and says, "I think I need to get the pasta a little wet then it will stay better."

John Henry points behind her where Puppy is sniffing and licking the pasta scattered on the floor. "Puppy is getting it wet for you!" Mary giggles and starts sticking the pasta in Puppy's thick black hair as John Henry tries to get his chef hat to stay on Puppy's head. I am sitting cross-legged on the floor enjoying my trio's antics, being a spectator with no real purpose and not minding at all.

*   *   *   *

My house is quiet. I have a quiet house. I wonder if houses sigh at the end of the day like people do. Houses must be like those items dog owners rub with their hands in order to cover them with their scent so the dog will know to retrieve that specific object from a group of similar objects. Our family scent has permeated the walls. The house has breathed us in. If I were placed, blindfolded, in the center of a circle of houses, I could find mine. I could feel in my bones which house was mine.

Puppy and I walk outside and sit on the deck. We both look up toward the stars. Since the beginning of recorded human experience, people have done what I am doing, and since the beginning of recorded human experience the stars have not been content to simply be watched; they have motivated responses to themselves, twinkled-out truths that have crossed and recrossed cultural boundaries until their relevance is even more documented than the great flood. Whose scent do they wear, these stars, I wonder? Do they breathe us in like houses do, reflect our mind-sets back on us?

I become aware of the feel of the metal and the plastic of the phone I am holding, and I 'wonder' closer to home and think about what I will say to Michael when he returns my call. 'Hey, guess what?' I will say. Or perhaps, 'May sent me a letter, sweetie' would be more interesting. Then again, I could open with 'Mary and I are sharing dreams now.' Puppy is rubbing his head against my arm which is an 'I love you' in his language, so I scratch his chest and look up into the black and gray charcoal rendering of the night sky, and then my eyes seek the lighter but still reflecting darkness of the lake's surface. Stars twinkle there too. No longer lost in the deep cave of my own thoughts, I hear night's sounds: frogs and breeze through leafed branches, and from across the lake a man's and a woman's voices respond to each other, just soft sounds and indistinguishable words. The night muffles, places its dark hand over the earth and softens the intensity of not only human noise, but even the earth's mood deepens, its cadences heard from a distance.

The phone's ring startles me. I had 'wondered' off again. I am racing heart and breathless as I sit and say, "Hello."

I do not call him at work often, so Michael's first question is quick but not rushed, "Is everything okay, Leah?"

"Yes, yes, we're fine. I just wanted to share something with you, and it seemed best to do it now instead of waiting." Because I know him so well, I can see his eyes change, his hand sweeping his hair back from his forehead as he pauses before he asks me to continue. He knows it is that kind of a conversation, not the rushed casual kind, but the proceed with caution kind, as if we are moving from rock to rock across a stretch of an unknown stream with no way to judge depth or slippery danger.

"Okay," he says when he is ready, "tell me."

"Well, it actually all started last weekend when we had everyone over. Matilda and I were remembering May's storytelling, and then she handed me a letter that May had given her to give to me."

I pause to catch a breath, and Michael reminds me of the unforgettable, "Baby, May is dead."

I do not let my words or tone become defensive, "Michael, just wait, please. Let me explain so it will make sense. May gave Matilda three letters to give to me before she died. Matilda said May told her she felt like something might happen to her, and she wanted me to have the letters in case she was no longer here to tell me herself." I pause and wait, so he can take the time he needs to understand what I have said, but he does not take any time at all before he responds.

"Oh my God, now I know what Father Tom meant."

Now it is my turn to be puzzled, "What?"

"Leah, before we got married, maybe it was a week before, maybe less, I can't remember now, but Father Tom came to my parents' house for dinner one night and while he was there, he asked me to take a walk with him. I thought he wanted to talk about marriage vows or sex or … hell, I don't know … priest stuff, but when he started talking it was about your family and that down the road, and that's just how he said it, 'down the road,' I would need to be strong for you, because there was information about your family you didn't know." Michael pauses for breath now, but I do not respond, because I do not have any words in my head. I am in a well, and he is up above calling words down into me that echo and swell and recede all at once. "Leah, where is the letter?"

I can respond to that, "In my jacket ... in the pocket of my jacket, the one I was wearing that day ... last weekend. It is behind the door in our bedroom, hanging on the hook."

He gently asks, "You haven't opened it, have you?"

"No." I am only that one word called up from the bottom of the well, afraid if I say more the dark water I cannot feel but that must be all around me will rise above my shoulders and then my neck and drown me.

Reassuringly, he comforts me as if his words can be his arms and stretch across the distance that is between us now. "It's going to be okay. Together we can handle anything."

I am out of the well and everywhere at once, "I was thinking this morning that even when we are away from each other, you know when we are separated by distance, that we are still in the same moment; we are breathing the same air under the same sky ... do you know what I mean? It is sort of an interesting thought, don't you think?"

His voice is strong now, "Leah, you can't go poetic or philosophical on me, now; do you hear me? You've got to stay right here, right now, and we have to make whatever sense we can about this. I will come home. I can be there in an hour. You're not alone in this; you know that, right?"

I am listening to his words and looking into the high branches of one of the redwoods next to the lake. There is just an outline that I can see, a cut-out darker than the night sky. And once, during Michael's words, it spread its wide wings out and blocked a hundred stars behind it, and I have to wonder is it the eagle from last weekend or the eagle from the dream?

"Leah?"

"Yes, Michael, I am here. I will not go away. I know things will be fine. I know that I am not alone. You do not have to come home tonight. We will be all right. Everything is fine." And even as I speak the words I know he is traveling back through time with me, back through twenty years of days and nights, and I am ten again, and he is fifteen. It is after the fire, and before Lane Dayton took Grant and me to live at Dayton School. We were staying with Michael's family. I would have bad dreams and bad days, and Michael was always the one who would reassure me, and I would always say comforting words back to him even if my heart was still broken and my thoughts were still confused.

"I'm coming home, Leah, because I want to be with you, and I need you to be with me. We can open the letter or wait, but we will be together, and that's all that matters to me. Do you understand?" His voice is like arms.

"Yes, Michael, but drive safely, take your time. Puppy is here, and we will be waiting for you." The moon must have come out from behind a cloud because everything seems a bit brighter, or perhaps Michael's words are light too. I smile to myself, still holding the phone that only waits now for its next call, and I think how John Henry would shake his head if he could hear me describe Michael's words as light or as arms. John Henry would say, 'Oh mom, you act like such a girl sometimes,' and I would have to laugh and grab him up into my arms and not mind at all being a girl again sometimes.

*   *   *   *

An hour is defined as sixty minutes or as one-twenty-fourth of a day or … but I do not classify time by minutes or hours except in my day to day routine, so I can honor my own schedule and the schedules of others. Instead, I organize my life by moments. I am a moment person, and moments are spatial not linear. Time exists within space, not the other way around, and we have only labeled time so we can communicate easily with each other, and so we can claim some sense of understanding we really do not have. May can reach her hand out to me even now, and I can look into her eyes and hear her voice, and because I exist in this time within this space she exists. She is still happening. She is present tense as I stand with my hand pressed against the smooth dark wood of the front door of my house.

Puppy makes a sound in the back of his throat, not a warning sound, but a polite reminder like a person who clears his or her throat to get another person's attention. And so we walk into the front room, and Puppy lies down in his favorite spot as I wonder if the book I am thinking of is here or at school. It is a large hardcover tome filled with black and white photos of a southwestern tribe of Native Americans. Between the pages of photos are words written by a conscientious white man who went to this group of people and wrote down their stories, personal and tribal, as they were told to him so that who these people were and are would not be lost. What I found so interesting about them was they utilized no change of tense in their language; everything for them was present tense, happening, spatial, timeless.

They recognized seasons and had a lunar based calendar, but these were only markers for them, stepping stones. They were always in the present, even when they were looking back or speaking of the future.

And now Michael will be here in less than an hour. I wonder how many moments that is? And then I wonder if I could write my life down in moments and then state quite honestly that I am four thousand six hundred and seventy-seven moments old. That would seem to be so much more meaningful than saying I am thirty years old. What does thirty years mean?

The moon's light flies in and lays itself down here and there, and depending on the surface it finds itself, it is either absorbed or curls up like Puppy and is content. I am restless and do not want to curl up in the comfort of the couch or be absorbed by arbitrary mental wonderings. I walk to the wall decorated with family photos and look into faces I know and love. Of course, there are photos here of faces I do not know. There are photos of Michael's family dating back three generations. Michael's mother's side of the family can trace itself back to the O'Briens of County Clare and to the direct line of the great king Brian Boru of the eleventh century. Michael's father's side of the family traces its roots back to the O'Connors of County Offaly in the second century and are proud of the fact their ancestors gave up all they had in the fight for independence in the 1500s against the English. Relatives from both sides of Michael's family migrated to America during the Great Famine of the 1850s.

To accompany these photos, there are letters and journals and photographs, official documents of all kinds, and more recently there are taped recordings of deeply accented voices speaking of their lives and of their memories, and all are carefully kept in a fireproof file cabinet at Michael's parents' house. I have had the pleasure of holding many of these older items in my hands and reading them. There is a comforting scent of the past, and yet they are truly timeless in their verification that human beings change, from generation to generation, very little in their motivations and desires; family and friendships, land and homes, honest labor fairly rewarded, loyalty to God and country are the subjects that fill the pages and tapes. Human emotions become the melody as the lyrics, measured in births and marriages and deaths, crescendo. Celebrations and mournings, dreams and goals connect times past, present, and future in a panoramic portrayal of the human heart.

And then, of course, there is my side of the family. There is one photo on the wall for that. Sean and May stand on the left of Papa John and my mom. Grant and I stand in front of them, centered just so. Grant and I seem so small compared to the others, and we both wear happy faces along with our Sunday best clothing. May's silver hair catches the light, and she has her head turned a bit toward Sean. Her hand is on my shoulder. Sean seems to be looking down at something, and his hair hides most of his face. Papa John and mom are looking directly into the eye of the camera, their expressions serious but open. They are almost smiling. It is as if the person taking the photo said, "I will count to three," and then took the photo on two, but it is the last photo of my family all together that was taken before the fire, and so it is cherished.

It was only after the fire that I realized that for all of May's storytelling, Grant and I know next to nothing about our family history. The only fact I really had regarding my family was that May once mentioned the name MacBride when speaking of her mother. Being a bit curious and a great deal confused after the fire took the lives of all the family I had except my brother Grant, I went to Elwood Library after school one day, a month or so after the fire, and looked up MacBride in a book on Ireland's history. On my father's mother's side 'my people' are connected to the "cult of St. Brigid." I was only ten then, so I had to look up the word 'cult,' because it only had negative connotations to me, and I could not understand how a Saint and a cult could be connected. Cult did not end up being totally negative based on its definition in the large unabridged dictionary resting on a podium of its own, as if it was going to speak on its own contents at some later time.

I walked home that day thinking more about the library's display on local marine life than I did on my ancestors or lack thereof. I can remember that clearly. The winter migration of gray whales making their way to their breeding grounds in Mexico became the topic of a report I had to write for science that was due the next week. I had focused on school work a great deal more than usual during the months after the fire, and the name MacBride and the cult of Saint Brigid seemed too distant to me. I was only ten, and the grays were right there in my own backyard, so to speak, and seemed much more relevant and thought provoking than people I did not know from a place I had never been.

But now, in this moment, with a letter from May waiting to be opened, my family's past calls to me again. I walk into the bedroom and find the book that Father Tom had given me last month. It is entitled *Celtic Christianity* and is written by a man named Timothy Joyce, a Benedictine monk of Irish descent. Father Tom had just been to hear Joyce speak at a weekend retreat and said his book would interest me, since I was always commenting on Christianity's history and trying to understand why the church stands as it does on certain issues.

I have not yet begun to read it, but I quickly checked the index pages for a reference to Saint Brigid, and there her name was, even though it was not spelled in the traditional Irish manner. Turning to page forty-three, I read,

"Saint Bridget (452–524), second only to Saint Patrick as a patron of Ireland and a personage receiving great honor and devotion. The figure of Bridget is part history, part mystery. Known as 'Mary of the Gaels,' she may be seen as one who in her very person demonstrates a definitive feature of the Celtic Christian church, that is, its ability to be thoroughly acculturated into the local scene, in this case by assimilating many of the pagan Celtic antecedents. Prior to the Christian era, there was a goddess name Bridget, a goddess of fertility, a goddess who was visaged as maiden, mother, and crone. She was connected with poetry, healing, and hearth. The stories of Saint Bridget are difficult to separate from the stories of the goddess Bridget. The Christian saint was the daughter of a Christian slave woman and a Druid master and the two strains combine in her to create her mystique."

Puppy is up and has his nose pressed against the door. I know this means Michael is home. If it was anyone other than Michael pulling up in a vehicle into our driveway at this time of night, Puppy would not be wagging his tail and making happy rumble sounds from deep in his throat. Puppy would instead be standing with his body between me and the door, and he would be making quite a different sound. I place the book on the end table next to the couch and walk to the door, not really wanting the next moment to begin, but knowing it must.

*   *   *   *

"The door is unlocked," Michael says this to me as he pats Puppy and locks the door behind him.

"You were on your way," can be my only reply as I feel his tension meet mine, but it is a gentle meeting. We are like blind people, our hands stretched out in front of us trying to sense what it is that fills the space around us, knowing we cannot see the very thing which may cause us to fall, perhaps into each other's arms or perhaps against each other.

"Lock the door from now on. I've asked you before; I don't see why it has to be an issue." He is not gentle now, but his anger is not directed toward me; something besides the unlocked door has threatened him, and he has become a protector, feet slightly spread, chest out a bit, eyes quick in their appraisal, voice hard. Under his shirt I can see the muscles of his arms and chest flex slightly; he is ready to face head-on the danger he perceives, but suddenly I know it will not be that sort of battle. I want to comfort him, but what I sense of the approaching danger will not reassure him. Protecting what he loves will demand more than male strength, and yet until seconds ago, I sensed no real danger, but now a strangeness lurks in the room and peers into the windows. There has been an intrusion. It has a presence, but it is not physical even as our physical senses respond to it.

I move toward him slowly, "Michael, I will lock the door from now on, I promise." We search each other's eyes trying to discover if the other knows what it is that is making us uncomfortable in our own home, in the company of each other. I barely whisper, "It did not feel like this until just a moment ago."

"I don't like it … it's like someone has been in here who doesn't belong. It's like the air feels strange or something." He looks around the room, "Are all the doors and windows locked?"

I am standing close to him now, and I put my hand on his arm, "I locked all the doors right after the kids and Puppy and I walked down to the lake after dinner, just like I always do, Michael. I unlocked the door when I was talking to you on the phone. I was on the deck, and then I came in here and waited for you." I move even closer to him wanting his warmth to push away the chill I feel, "Michael, I do not think this is a … physical thing, you know? I think it is more of a head or heart or spirit thing."

"I'd rather fight a damn fire, Leah, and leave the head and heart and spirit stuff to … who-ever the hell wants to deal with them. This is too strange. I'm checking on the kids, and then I'm checking the doors and windows. Someone has to have been in here. It doesn't feel right." I watch him walk into and out of Mary's room and then John Henry's room before he goes into the other rooms in the house. I hear him checking door latches and window latches and throughout his careful inspection of the house, Puppy has stayed with me, his body between me and the front door, his head tilted just a bit as if he is listening, his stance alert. And I realize that whatever Michael and I perceive Puppy is sensing also, and that only makes the apprehension more acute. I walk to the windows and begin pulling curtains across panes of glass which have seldom been covered, and even the french door I cover with its tailored shade. I have a deeply rooted desire to slide furniture across the floor and place it just so along the door and windows to barricade against whatever it is that is breathing its foul breath into my home and my heart.

Michael is walking toward me and does not stop until he has pressed his body up against mine, wrapping his arms around me and burying his face in my hair. We just stand that way for a moment, each of us holding the other. He sort of laughs uneasily, "This is weird, Leah, too damn weird. I've never felt anything like that before," and then he looks into my eyes and asks, "have you?"

I lean my forehead against his chest and speak my words into the white cotton of his shirt as if I can communicate directly with his heart and stop the progression of his questioning. "I do not think so," is all I say.

He leans back from me gently, "But you're not sure?"

"Sometimes, in dreams ... sometimes when I dream of the fire it may feel a bit like this, but never this strong and never when someone else is around." We are searching each other's eyes again; I do not want him to pull away from me, and he probably wants more of an explanation from me than I can give.

"You didn't tell me you were having the dreams again, Leah."

"I thought I mentioned it."

"Only casually."

"They seem like a casual thing to me most of the time. For twenty years they have never really stopped. For a year or two when I first went to Stanford, but even there they came back, not a lot, just sometimes."

Michael wraps his arms around me again, reassuring me as he asks, "And lately, have there been more dreams lately?"

I know I must tell him, must let the momentum of the moment have its way and allow the shadow of doubt to spread across his heart too, even though I do not want to, I do. "Yes, there have been more lately, and today when the kids and I were taking a nap together, Mary and I sort of shared the same dream."

He moves back from me now, "What does that mean?"

And suddenly I feel very alone. I feel as though I should somehow know what a shared dream means and know what May's letter will tell me, that in me somewhere are all the answers to all the questions I have, and they are just waiting for me to free them, as if they are exotic birds captured, and I have the key in my possession but do not know where the door is. And although it is the last response I want to give to him right now, my eyes fill with tears.

He moves to the couch, sits down, and leans back closing his eyes. "Okay, okay, I pulled back from you at the wrong time in the discussion, and I hurt your feelings, and this is not how I want us to be for each other right now." He pauses then opens his eyes, "I'm sorry, Leah. I'm not blaming you for anything. We'll make sense of this, and everything will be okay. I just don't want the kids involved."

I realize he is trying to be good and kind and magnanimous, but just because he would rather fight a damn fire than deal with a mystery is not my fault. I did not ask for any of this to happen. I did not—I stop myself. I cannot remove myself from this situation by building a fortress of elaborate mind-musings in which to hide. I have to stay here, so I go to the chair across from him and sit down. I cannot, of course, lean back, because there is enough energy pulsing through me to power every light in Lane. I take a deep breath, yoga style, and exhale.

Michael is waiting for me to respond, so I try not to have an attitude, "I do not even know what it is in which 'we' do not want our children involved? Do you understand that? I do not choose to have dreams; they just come. And today was the first time I had any indication that Mary might be involved in whatever is going on, and I am not sure sharing one dream makes her involved. So, maybe we should just open May's letter and see what happens."

Michael sits up straight now, "Maybe we should burn the damn letter."

I lean back now, "Maybe we should."

"I don't want to fight with you, Leah."

"We're not fighting; we're distancing ourselves from each other so we can deal with our own feelings."

Michael leans back again, "Whatever. I feel like I've fought three fires or something. I'm beyond tired."

The slight tremor in his voice indicates how truly drained he is, so I say, "Maybe we should go to bed and deal with May's letter and the dream thing tomorrow?"

"That would probably be good. A fresh start and all that."

I walk over to him and take his hands in mine, "And in the daylight would be better too."

"God, I love you, Leah, but you really are strange." I start to pull my hands away, but he quickly stands and wraps his arms around me, "Different ending, try this one, I love you, period."

We walk into the bedroom as Puppy goes to his rug that lies against the wall between the doors to John Henry's and Mary's room. In the bathroom, as we wash our faces and brush our teeth, I comment on the fact the house does not feel uncomfortable anymore.

Michael looks at me in the mirror and says quite firmly, "I don't want to talk about this anymore tonight. We'll do it your way, tomorrow in the daylight, okay? Tonight, we sleep." I, of course, find this incredibly typical of any late night differences we have ever had; he will go right to sleep, and I will think the situation and/or conversation through at least ten times trying to figure out why it turned the way it did and what brought on a change in emotions. But as I think of that I realize this is our way, and the normalcy of that is welcome, so I just smile at him, and moments later when I join him in bed, I am thankful for his presence and for who he is and for how he is.

I say my every-night-he-is-home words to him, "Goodnight, sweet dreams, God bless. I love you, husband." He sighs deeply and pats my hand that is resting on his arm. And I think to myself, men are so … interesting, but they are, after all, men, and moments are approached differently by them. I imagine that moments are oceans or deep lakes and I see men and women on the shore. The men barely linger, and instead push through the shallows diving into depths unknown as soon as they can. The females linger on the shore, and in the shallows they check for temperature and confirm footholds as they scan the sky and the horizon, realizing that the facets of the moment must be attended to in order to ensure the best possible outcome. Or perhaps, I only generalize, and it is only Michael and me on the shore confirming our own behavior patterns.

"Leah?" Michael's voice calls me back.

"Yes?"

"Go to sleep."

I know I will not right away drift off into sleep no matter how much I would like to, even if only to please Michael. My thoughts are like children who must be put to bed at the end of each day, and most often each wants his or her own goodnight-ritual. Occasionally, I have been able to tuck two or three agreeable ones in at the same time, but this does not occur often, so I put my hand on Michael's shoulder and say 'yes' as I allow my body to relax so he will feel relaxed, even as I know my goodnight moment is far from over. Sometimes my goodnight moments seem to last beyond the present, stretching out into past and future until there are silver moon and golden sun on the same horizon, dark skies with bright blinking stars and light skies with still white clouds overhead, tossing blue waves and smooth green hills just before me. A spatial kaleidoscope held within a moment devoid of minute or hourly distinctions, and thereby forever present tense.

*   *   *   *

It is only a soft call and mechanical, so the only urgency is imposed by me upon hearing it. I must come up through the deep waters of sleep, pushing off the rock-hard foundation of the last dream with my hands pressed together, fingers pointed and arms straight as I break through the surface of consciousness feeling the weight of Michael's leg across my thighs and his breath whispering against my neck and shoulder. I slide out from under him and reach for the phone on the night stand.

"Yes … hello," I say as Michael mumbles something about the 'damn phone.'

Lane Dayton's voice is calm and, as always, he wastes no time with words of apology about the hour or words of introduction to the subject at hand, "Leah, this is Lane. Teri Allenton has placed herself in a dangerous situation … life threatening. She is asking for you. Bring Michael; he may be able to help. I will fill you in on the details when you arrive. You need to get here quickly. Is that possible?"

"Of course, we will be there as soon as we can," and I disconnect and quickly dial Sarah, Michael's sister. As the ringing begins I turn to Michael, who is already sitting on the side of the bed waiting for me to explain, but first I speak into the phone having somehow heard Sarah's sleepy voice through the clamor of my own thoughts. "Sarah, I have an emergency at the school. Will you come over and stay with the kids?" We are the family members of firemen and are used to emergencies, so she quickly responds that she will come right over, and she is off the line.

I hang up the phone and turn to Michael, "It's Teri. Lane said 'life threatening' and that you should come with me. We have to hurry." And we do: clothes donned and a swift brush of teeth and hair, a splash of water on the face, and Michael in the kitchen quietly opening the fridge to take out two small bottles of juice. I am opening curtains and the shade on the french doors as the headlights on Sarah's car illume the driveway. Puppy has not moved, knowing somehow this is a situation that demands nothing from him, so his body remains still as his eyes follow our movements.

I open the door as Sarah walks up onto the deck; we hug and I only tell her I will call when I know something. Michael tells her to lock the door, and we are in my Jeep and driving through dark streets.

Michael inquires about details, and I answer, "Lane said he would fill us in when we arrive."

Michael continues to keep his eyes on the road as he asks, "Do you think I am along for moral support or something else?"

"Well, you majored in psychology and forensic pathology, and you're a fireman, so you could be along for a variety of reasons. I cannot really even theorize at this point. Teri was behaving like everything was fine on Friday during class, but there are so many triggers for victims of sexual abuse that, again, I cannot even make an intelligent guess, but Michael, I dislike it so much when these kids hurt themselves over experiences from their pasts."

Michael responds to my last statement by putting his hand on mine then comments, "She's been over to the house hasn't she?"

I answer, "Yes, last month she came over and spent the afternoon with a couple of the other kids. Teri is the one with long red hair. She is a big girl but not in a way that it keeps her from being active or even attractive for that matter. She is eighteen and supposed to graduate this year. She has already been accepted at USC, and she was excited about that."

I pause, and Michael asks, "What about her past?"

"Oh, Michael, her past so breaks my heart. Her stepfather sexually abused her for years, from the age of five until she was ten, then she was hospitalized for erratic behavior and losing consciousness repeatedly at the school she was attending. Bruises on her body discovered by the doctor who examined her led to an investigation. Her mother divorced the stepfather and pressed charges and he served time, but the harm had already been done." I allow Michael to work through that information, knowing he will not ask about how the mother could not have known or comment on the hideous crime of an adult abusing a child; he will only want information that can help in the situation we are about to face, and I am glad he is with me.

It is not the first time we have worked together in a crisis involving one of my students. His manner, in a crisis situation involving others is always calm, and the strength of who he is as a man and a person seems to be felt by the individual in crisis. His down-to-earth rationale about living honestly and well and his degree in psychology combine to form comforting arms of safety, which even my young male students sometimes seek out, wanting and needing a healthy embrace. I watch him as we turn onto Dayton Street.

When he speaks I know he has placed who Teri is and is working through the possible connections between her present circumstance and her habits and interests. "Teri is the techie, right?" I say 'yes,' and he continues, "She is into philosophy and studies religions. She doesn't read fiction at all, no stories. She is searching for explanations, truths, someway to make sense of her own life, right?"

I speak quickly trying to cover ground knowing we only have a brief moment before we will park and enter into a situation that may not allow for any exchange of information between us besides facial expressions, "Yes, and she and I talked about that; both Jan Carson, her counselor, and I have asked her to think about her motivations in her choices of reading matter, her choice of philosophical and religious doctrines, normally devoid of narrative voice. Lately, she has been a bit more social, and she has been more open with her roommate, Jacy."

We are through the gates of Dayton School and Michael parks the Jeep in between a police car and the paramedic van. That is the only sign that all is not well at the school. The grounds are quiet and dark except where illuminated globes throw small islands of light into connecting pathways of gravel. Then I notice Dale, one of our local policeman, and Jake, one of our local paramedics, standing out in front of Rose Lane Hall. Dale sees us and enters the doors of the residence hall then Lane exits the building and walks toward us.

We all stop walking when we meet half way between the parking lot and the hall. Lane shakes hands with Michael, and then he takes my hand in his and holds it. "Thank you for your quick answer to my call. Teri's mother has been notified and is making flight arrangements. Teri has refused to speak to her mother on the phone. We would be unaware of the situation had Jacy not returned from a visit home a day early. Jacy entered their room and found Teri with a jagged piece of a broken mirror in her hand. Teri has cut herself deeply and repeatedly. She now holds the piece of mirror to her neck where she has broken skin but has not punctured the jugular. That is her threat. She appears coherent and asked for you, Leah. She has stated she does not want to talk with Jan because Jan is currently separated from her husband and Teri seems upset with Jan for that. We can, of course, try to overtake her but that is not really our way here, and Jake believes she is not bleeding enough to take a chance on provoking her to harm herself more than she already has. I don't believe she is a danger to you, or I would not ask you to intervene, however I would like Michael to accompany you into the room. I have told Teri I will not allow you to enter on your own, and she has agreed to let Michael in also, but she has warned that you both must keep your distance." Lane pauses and looks up at a dimly lit window on the second floor of Rose Lane Hall, "I believe that is all I can tell you. The mother had no information about a possible cause to this event, and the stepfather's location is monitored by his parole officer and has been verified. I do not see any way that the stepfather could have made contact with her. Other than an obvious resurgence of the past, we have no explanation for what could have motivated her to do this."

We all three begin walking toward the hall, and each one of us is silent. There are nods of acknowledgment as we pass by Jake and Dale, and they open the doors for us to enter. The first floor of the hall is dimly lit and at the northwest end where the couches and chairs are arranged around a large stone fireplace, many of the young women who live in the hall and Jan, the resident counselor are talking quietly and staring into a fire that does not seem able to dispel the chill filling the usually warm and comforting atmosphere of Rose Lane Hall.

We walk up the wide stairs that connect the main floor to the second and as we reach the landing, I see Ron, Jake's partner, and Lex, Dale's partner standing by the open door of Teri's room. Michelle Payton, the third floor resident advisor and our history teacher, is standing with them. They are listening to Bradley, who has his back against the door's threshold and is sitting with one leg under him and the other bent with his arms resting on his knee, as he speaks words I cannot hear into Teri's room. At this moment, I can only hope Teri is hearing them.

✳   ✳   ✳   ✳

Ron, Jake and Michelle move back from the door as we approach, but Bradley does not take his eyes off who he is speaking so intently to within the room. When Michael and I are standing behind Bradley we hear him say, "They are here now. See, they came. Will you let them come into the room, Teri?"

There is no immediate verbal answer, but Teri's eyes and mine meet across a length of space that seems too close and too distant simultaneously; I feel too close and too far away to reach out to her. There are blood and open wounds all over her face and arms. She has used the mirror's sharp broken edge to cut herself. She is sitting on the floor with her back against the bed. She has one knee raised up and balances her arm as she holds the jagged piece of mirror against her throat. In my heart I know she is trying to cut out pieces of herself she has found she cannot live with any longer. She is desperately calm.

"Mrs. C," is all she says. Her beautiful shoulder length red hair catches the light from the candles she must have lit before beginning this tearing open of herself. There are books opened all around her, and some have blood on the pages, drops and smears, and even fingerprints from where she has turned pages during this attack on herself. Her large green eyes draw me into her, and I do not even ask to enter the room; I simply move forward slowly then sit down on the floor once I have passed by Bradley.

I reach my arm up behind me and open my hand and Michael takes it and sits down next to me. Teri watches him now, her eyes intent, searching Michael's face, and she asks him, "Do you remember who I am?"

Michael responds quietly, "Yes, Teri, you were at our house a few weeks ago, and we were on the Ropes Course with the group a month or so before that."

Her eyes are still locked on his, "Did Mrs. C tell you about me?"

Michael answers her question with a question, "Which part of you?"

Teri does not pause to think. "The ugly part." As she speaks a thin line of fresh blood seeps from where the mirror is pressed against her throat, and her eyes look into mine again. She whispers, "I have a lot of ugly parts."

As tears roll down my cheeks, my heart cries out to her in a calm and quiet voice, "When Michael and I spoke of you on the drive over here, we spoke of a young woman who is excited about college and her studies. That is what I know, and I know also that this choice you are thinking about is not a choice, it is another abuse against your body, but this time it is not another person abusing you; it is you, Teri, and you have to stop and let people who love and care about you help you."

Teri is not pushing into her skin anymore, but the mirror's edge still rests against her throat. "There are no answers in these books; I have read them and read them again, but they are just words written by old men who care more about ideas than about living or finding peace. Their gods are faceless and angry, and their ideas are convoluted and self-promoting. They make me tired. That's all they do."

Michael speaks as he rearranges his body into a new position, and I know he is trying to ease Teri into being comfortable with him moving his body as he positions himself imperceptibly closer to her. "Then rest. If your body is tired, rest. If your mind is tired, stop thinking. Stop reading. Just rest. It's okay to be tired, and we all need to stop thinking sometimes and just 'be'. Leah kept me up late into the night talking about things that are bothering her, and we finally decided, together, to just stop thinking about them and to sleep. We decided to deal with the things that are bothering us another time. It's okay to do that, you know?"

Teri sighs, "I'd like to stop thinking. Maybe more, I'd like to stop remembering. There are pictures in my head, images, that I think are gone for long periods of time, then they resurface like ... decayed bodies washed up from their graves during a flood. That happened in the south somewhere ... the ground became so saturated with water, the bodies and caskets floated up. That would be terrible to see." She pauses then speaks to both of us, acknowledging us for the first time as individuals and not just an audience to her grief, "This ... I ... this must be terrible for you to see."

Michael speaks first, "It breaks my heart, Teri, to see you so unhappy and in so much pain. You are a daughter who needs to be held by a good father, not one who will hurt you and betray your trust."

I lean toward her, "And your mom is coming. She wants to be here for you, Teri. It still is so difficult for her to forgive herself for not seeing what was going on, but she wants to be here for you now. You need to let her be here for you, let her wrap her arms around you and hold her little girl, and I know if you do, somehow you will feel better."

Teri is crying quietly, "But I'm not little anymore, and I'm fat. I don't want to look at myself anymore."

I quickly remind her, "How much weight have you lost since you have been here?"

She uses the hand that is not holding the broken piece of mirror and wipes away her tears, "Fifty pounds."

I am quick to respond again, "And what do we always talk about in family group?"

She is looking at her hand and arm now, turning it over slowly, perhaps noticing the jagged cries for help she has torn into her skin and the dried blood, or perhaps noticing her arm is thinner, but Michael and I use the distraction to rearrange our sitting positions again moving a bit closer to her, as she says, "Process ... we're in process, always ... everyone is, not just us, everyone ... working through and toward something."

Michael asks her, "Will you agree to that then? Will you agree to be in process, and let that be okay?"

Her expression turns from thoughtful to hopeless, "I'll have to go away after doing this, won't I? They won't let me stay, will they? You'll all be afraid I'll try to hurt myself again. If I don't finish what I've started, I'll get sent to some hospital mental ward somewhere to—"

Michael interrupts her, "Stop. Think about this, and I mean really think about this situation, what you've done and how you've done it. Why now? You're two months from graduation. Why in this way? Think for a moment before you answer, and then tell us what you feel, and don't go trying to make sense of any of it, and don't go beyond this moment. The people who work at Dayton and your mom will want to do what is best for you not what will make you more unhappy, but you'll have to trust that decision to them. Just think about why. Don't search for the truth, just tell us what motivated you, why now, and why in this manner."

I add, "There is no rush; take the time you need, walk through the last couple of days and share with us what Michael has asked you to think about." I can tell she wants to close her eyes, to go into her own mind with no visual stimulation to distract her, so I say, "Teri, you can close your eyes, be by yourself even with us sitting here, and we won't move at all. Do you want to do that?"

Her whole body shakes as she sobs and indicates the bloodied mirror piece, "I want to put this down away from my throat, but I'm not ready to be moved yet.

I won't hurt myself anymore; I just don't want to be moved yet. I just want to sit here and think like you asked me to but not have anything change if I close my eyes."

Michael responds first because a sob of relief has engulfed me, "We promise we will not move, just close your eyes, lean your head back and rest. But I have to ask you if you would hand me the mirror before you do that. Will you let me have it?"

She does not speak, but her hand moves away from her throat and Michael leans forward and stretches out his arm toward her and takes the piece of mirror in his hand. She watches as he returns to his sitting position then she leans her head back and closes her eyes, and the tears that flow down my cheeks are unrestrained as I lean my body into Michael's, and we sit and watch as Teri allows herself to relax, and I cannot help but wonder if perhaps she is allowing herself to be held in our arms even if we are not touching her.

*   *   *   *

We are in Lane's office. He sits behind his desk, and during the last few moments of silence he has turned his chair so he can look out the window that is centered along the back wall and reveals in the distance the stone wall that marks the perimeter of Dayton School's grounds while closer in our view is revealed the round wide trunks of towering redwoods and in the shade of one of them a birdbath and bench sit waiting for visitors of one species or another. I study Lane's profile and cannot help but compare his strong genteel features to the large oil portraits of his father and grandfather which have been placed on opposite sides of the smaller window which divides the only other wall in Lane's office that is not shelved floor to ceiling and filled with books and mementos. The wood of his desk, the floor, and the shelving is richly textured and dark but this is offset by the light sand colored fabric of the chairs and small sofa which surround three sides of his desk.

I can actually relax a bit now. John Henry and Mary are with their Aunt Sarah and probably involved in a backyard search for insects. Sarah, for reasons I cannot comprehend because I can find no relational basis with insects at all, enjoys catching insects in large or small nets and then examining them closely before she releases them back into the area in which she found them. Puppy is undoubtedly assisting in this search and seizure and release expedition. I can also relax because we have talked with Teri's mother who met us at the local medical center. The Center has a small suite of four rooms for patients who need continual care or constant watching. Teri will remain there for the rest of the day and for the night, and then be transferred to the hospital in the city if the doctor recommends that is necessary. Plastic surgery will have to come later for her, but her wounds have been cared for, and when we said our goodbyes to Teri her mother was sitting next to her bed, and they were holding hands and speaking quietly to each other. Lane requested another bed be brought in so Teri's mother can stay with her in the same room.

We have made the necessary arrangements for an all school meeting tomorrow morning, so all the questions and comments that anyone feels a need to be made can be made openly and in the large group setting. Family groups will meet after for a more intimate debriefing of the situation and its consequent emotional reactions, and then afternoon classes will resume as normal. 'Out into the light and then back into the routine' is Lane's practicum for daily life at Dayton, and it works well for both students and faculty as a means of fostering open and healthy reactions to difficult situations.

Jan, Michelle, Bradley, and Greg, the other male resident hall advisor, sit in the chairs, while Michael and I have the comfort of each other's closeness on the small sofa. After speaking with Teri's mother and discussing possible options, Lane has proposed that Terri spend another year with us before attending USC. He will call and defer her enrollment, and Teri will be involved in a full year of intense counseling sessions and also continue her studies here. Her mother will take part in several counseling sessions with her over the next six months, and then if all goes well, Teri will finish the sessions by herself and hopefully be ready and prepared to move on to the next part of her life.

Jan interrupts the silence with a personal observation, "I didn't realize how much my separation from my husband affected Teri's trust in me."

Bradley rubs his fingers across his eyes and then leans toward Jan, whose straight blonde hair is hiding most of her face as she looks down at her hands. "I don't think it's so much a matter of you separating from your husband as it is a matter of you not living with your two kids."

Lane has turned his chair back toward the group and is listening and watching now. Jan responds to Bradley after thinking about what he has said, "You're probably right. Mark and Trish spend at least three or four nights a week here with me, but it's difficult to be away from them. Maybe Teri doesn't realize how difficult it is. Maybe I should have shared more of my own feelings about my separation from Alex with the girls on my floor; I just didn't want to impose my problems on kids who already have more than their share."

Michael nods his head in agreement, "It can't be easy determining how much to share or not to share about your personal situations with these young people who are such a part of your lives, but Teri is definitely not pleased with your choice to live away from your family for a year."

Lane comments quietly, "And that year is almost over now. Have you and Alex come to any better understandings from your weekly evenings shared with each other, or perhaps you would rather not comment on that with us at this time."

Jan smiles slowly at Lane then looks at each one of us, "I am quite comfortable with each one of you, and I am happy to tell you Alex and I are planning on my returning home as soon as the spring quarter ends, and you can find a replacement for me." She pauses, but we wait for her to continue, because we can tell she is thinking about what she wants to add to the information she has already given. "It's so strange loving someone but at the same time being so unhappy with that person. We thought we could handle having a racially mixed marriage, and we can, but we just got so tired of some people's reaction to us, and we didn't talk about it with each other. I felt his family was uncomfortable with me even after nine years of marriage. That's nine Christmas celebrations and nine Thanksgiving celebrations and a few less birthday celebrations for the kids and ... well, you get what I'm saying, it started wearing on me. I took it out on Alex without meaning to. Anyway, we've met with his folks a couple of times since the separation, and they felt like I was the one who was holding back affection." She looks out the window now, "Can you believe that, I thought it was them, and they thought it was me, and I'm a psychologist and his mom and dad are both doctors, and we never talked about it. We should know better with our training, but when things get personal, it sometimes feels like we forget the very lessons we teach." She looks over at Michael and smiles as she says, "Of course, Alex is a fireman, and you know how macho and never-talk-about-your-feelings firemen can be."

We all wait for Michael's reply, which comes quickly, "Discrimination of any kind, whether occupationally or racially based, is never healthy, Jan. We firemen might surprise you. We have some real heart-to-hearts during television commercials and in between arm wrestling contests." He leans over and takes Jan's hand as he says, "Alex told me you two were working things out, and I'm truly glad. You have two wonderful kids, and you and Alex belong together. The people who know you both know that. I believe the bond you have with each other will only grow stronger, so don't question your decision to separate for a year. You made that decision, and looking back and wondering if it was the right one only robs you of the peace you've found. Sometimes creating a distance between yourself and the difficult situation really does work." Now Michael is looking at me, "Then of course, sometimes you don't even plan the diversion or the distance, but after it happens, you realize what you need to do." He smiles at me.

I study his eyes to make sure that I am reading the lightness of his mood in connection to what happened with us last night correctly, "Okay, I am assuming you have an idea about how to deal with our little issue based on what you just said, and you are obviously quite happy with yourself."

Michael stands up, reaches down and, taking my hand in his, pulls me up as he looks at Lane. "Sir, if you're done with us here, we have some unfinished business to take care of."

Lane stands up behind his desk and reaches out his hand to shake Michael's. "It is always a pleasure, Michael."

Michael winks at him and says, "Thanks, Uncle."

Michael turns to Bradley and shakes his hand as Bradley comments, "I seem to forget, more often than not, that your mother is Lane's sister."

Michael laughs, and as he shakes hands with Greg he replies, "We do live in a small town, don't we?"

Greg smiles good naturedly, "You and Leah and the kids have to come over and have dinner with Marcia and me again. I'll even barbecue some veggies for your vegetarian wife." We had seen Greg's fiancée, Marcia, earlier at the medical center. She was the scheduled physician for this weekend in case of emergencies. Our only other on-staff local doctor is a male, and Teri might not have handled that very well at this moment in her life.

Michael suggests that Greg and I talk during the week and set something up. I say my goodbyes, and we walk out of Lane's office into the reception area of the Administration Building, which is located next to Rose Lane Hall. Michael goes to the phone and dials a number. I start to ask who he is calling, but he raises his finger to his lips and smiles. Whoever he has called has answered the phone, and I listen to the one-sided conversation. Michael identifies himself then requests a dinner meeting at the Castle Rock Cafe. Two hours from now is agreed upon, and then he hangs up the phone.

He puts his arms around me and pulls me close, kissing me as if we are not standing in an office that could be entered at anytime by either people to whom we have just said goodbye or students wanting to talk with Lane, but I cannot mind his show of affection at all, even if his intensity surprises me a bit. I am in his arms, and my body is totally aware of not only his deep searching kiss but also the press of his body against mine. This is really not a normal Michael behavior.

Except for light flirtations, public displays of affection are not usually an approved of activity.

He stops kissing me and looks at me slightly amused, "Here I am offering you my love in the middle of a public place in the late afternoon and you are only half here. Your body is responding, but I could tell you were off in that head of yours playing chase with your own thoughts." He pauses as he kisses my forehead. "I'm right, aren't I?"

I put my hands on his chest so I can feel his heartbeat, "You have to admit you do not normally do things like this. I was just wondering why you did as I was enjoying it. So really I was not elsewhere at all."

He takes one of my hands in one of his, and we walk out into afternoon sunshine, "I can see your reasoning, but I still think you should have just concentrated on the kiss."

I turn quickly in front of him and stop his progress toward the Jeep, "We could try again."

He turns me around and continues walking, "Nope, you missed the opportunity, lady, better luck next time."

"You're acting strange, Michael," is all I can think to say to him.

"I have seen a light at the end of the tunnel, wife, and I'm just happy about that. And then also, we have been apart for three days and two nights, and I miss holding you in my arms, but I'm concentrating on the business at hand now, and you'll just have to hope I get in the mood again later."

He is looking at me now over the roof of the Jeep and smiling like a fool, so I look into his eyes and speak very softly to him, "You are telling me that tonight when we get home, and after I've taken a long hot bath, that you may not be in the mood when I ask you to make love to me?"

"It could happen," is his only response as he opens the car door and slides into the driver's seat.

I do the same and after I have buckled my seat belt, I look over at him, "If it does it will be the first time it has ever happened."

He starts the car and backs out of the parking space, "You shouldn't take that for granted then; there are women all over America who want what you get."

I can only laugh, "You're spending way too much time with your little male friends if you believe that."

Michael acts hurt, "My friends are bigger than your friends."

I am watching the expressions on his face change moment to moment, "We are not having this conversation. And I want you to remember your behavior when you tell me all the time that I am strange."

"But Leah, you are strange." His face is serious now. "Really you are, but I love you for it. I married an intelligent, beautiful, whacko broad and I love you, but you are as strange as they come."

I am truly not interested in the conversation anymore so I try to change the subject, "Michael, you're acting goofy because you've been through two stressful situations in the last twelve or so hours. I am trying to be patient with you because of that, but we are almost home, so please get serious, and tell me what plans you made for us."

He pats my head and smiles sarcastically, "Thanks so much for the diagnosis; I'll be serious now. We're going to ask Sarah if the kids can stay the night. You can pick them up in the morning and take them to school. I will go back to work and finish the day and be home again, probably before you considering what kind of day you're going to have tomorrow with all the debriefings Lane has planned."

"Well, that tells me about half of what I want to know. So, please continue."

"We'll go home, spend some time with the kids, shower and change, well, shower for me, bath for you, dress, get the letter, drop the kids off at Sarah's and Paul's and go meet Father Tom at Castle Rock Cafe and talk to him about what's going on. Period. End of my plan. What do you think?"

"It is a good plan, Michael. Thank you."

"I do what I can," he pauses. "I like our life together. I like every single thing about our life together." He pauses again and then adds, "Sometimes I wonder if that's normal or safe, or if something is going to happen and change it all, but that's how you usually think about things, not me, so I decide it is normal and good and okay to be happy with my life. I've worked hard, I've been honest, so why shouldn't my life be good, right? And now we have a difficult situation that has to be worked through, and I figure if we stay true to what we know, everything will be fine. Does that make sense?"

I am listening to his words and watching shadow and light dance back and forth across the road in front of us as the late afternoon sun filters through the branches and leaves of trees that have stood for hundreds of years, and once again I feel a moment's sweet blend of senses wash over me ... the strength and frailty of my husband's emotions mixing with the sun's play of light and shadow as who Michael is in his heart and mind and spirit become as timeless as the redwoods. I am thinking of my son's smile and Teri's pain and of May's letter and of running with my daughter in a dream, so all I can do is reach over and lay my hand on his arm and agree with him that within the context of the moment it all makes perfect sense.

"Leah, were you listening to me?"

"Yes. I answered, didn't I?"

He looks as if he is slightly less than pleased and comments, "I'm not tele-pathic, so, no, whatever conversation you were having with yourself I completely missed."

"If you need me to I can repeat what you said."

"I know what I said, so why would I need you to repeat it?"

"So that you know I was listening to you and focused on what you were say-ing."

"I'm sure you were."

"I really was, Michael. I was just noticing how your words and the afternoon sun sort of went together. And the trees reminded me of you, of who you are. And I thought I answered you, spoke words to you."

"I am sure that makes total sense."

"You're being a bit of a smart ass, I think."

"I thought I was being your hero just a moment ago."

"That was earlier; now you are just a smart ass with a perfect life, and I would be remiss if I did not add that from moment to moment you do have a tendency to go through these sudden transformations. Lover, clown, hero, smart ass. That is quite a bit for a girl to keep up with, you know?"

He does not say anything for a while, but then he says, "Oh, I'm sorry, were you talking to me? I was concentrating on the bird shit on your windshield which reminded me of—."

I do not let him finish. I make the loudest fake laugh I can and slug him some-what gently on the arm, as he begins a mumbled monologue regarding my need to confess to Father Tom when I see him about my poor treatment of my hus-band. I refuse to allow myself to become involved in his latest banter. I turn my head and look out the window and notice for the first time that on the edge of the pavement is the shadow of a large bird flying and keeping perfect pace with the momentum of our car, and then I wonder if I ever really awakened from my afternoon nap with John Henry and Mary.

*   *   *   *

We are home; Puppy is glad and much quicker than John Henry and Mary. He is already waiting for us when we park between Sarah's and Michael's trucks. Sarah stands on the deck smiling as John Henry and Mary run to greet us. I open the door of the Jeep and check the high branches of the trees surrounding our house for large feathered occupants, but I see no dark shapes. As we walk hand-in-hand toward the house I listen to the exchange between my husband and his sister and notice how different they are in appearance. Michael is not tall or short, not thin or stocky, but he gives the impression of being larger than he is, probably due to his wide shoulders and the firm, well toned muscles of his arms, legs and chest. His suntanned skin, sun-goldened brown hair and hazel eyes contrast Sarah's peaches and cream skin, green eyes and light auburn hair. She is petite in body and large in personality, and she is teasing Michael about taking time off last night and today to get out of the planned cleaning and maintenance day at the station house.

Michael has walked inside the house with John Henry and Mary as Sarah and I remain on the deck for a moment. I ask her about her husband and children. Paul is the principal at Lane Grammar and Middle School and Sean, their son, is completing his first year of college while April, their daughter, is a sophomore at the high school in the city. April had stopped by earlier in the day to ask Sarah if she could go to Little Bend Cove to snorkel with some friends.

Sarah shakes her head, "I think sometimes she is more like my brothers than like me or Paul or Sean. She is always outdoors doing outdoor things, and you know me, except for hunting bugs; I'd rather be inside baking or sewing. Paul and Sean enjoy the outdoors, but academics are their shared passion. We're going to have to add a room to the house to hold their books, and their computer stuff; Lord help me, they can talk that subject forever. But not April, she lettered in volleyball and softball this year, and she's only a sophomore. And those aren't even her favorites; hiking or in the water doing some activity are her favorites."

I nod in agreement with Sarah, thinking of her lovely daughter who does share physical traits and acts more like her uncles, Michael, Daniel, and Brian, than her own mother or father. Families are interesting that way, and I wonder how my sweet Mary and gentle John Henry will surprise me with their interests and their passions.

Sarah comments further, "Why if Sean had not liked to hike, he and April wouldn't even know each other. My son and his sister would have had nothing in common, but Sean can hike these mountains and shore cliffs with the best of them." She pauses for a moment, and I wait for her, "After watching my own two grow and change, I find myself wondering how your own two will surprise us." Sarah looks out over the lake as she asks, "Was it a difficult time today?"

"It could have been so terrible, but I believe the situation will only benefit the student involved now. It was a heads-up for all of us, and a clear indication for her that she has unfinished business. Past issues she thought she had dealt with overwhelmed her and ..." I pause to reflect on what could have happened instead of what did, and I turn to Sarah and look into her concerned green eyes, "It could have been tragic … but we were fortunate, and I am thankful."

"To God?"

Now her eyes are searching mine as I try to understand the intent of her question, but I only answer, "Yes, to God, and to Michael, and to Lane, and to the others."

"Lately I've had a sense that you are … searching, or at least not at peace with something in your life." She puts her hand on my arm, "I'm not trying to pry; Matilda just said we should be praying for you, but she would, of course, comment no further."

I am a bit uncomfortable with what Sarah has just told me, but I have to smile at her 'of course' and the implied reference to a Callaghan family maxim, so I intentionally try to lead the conversation in a different direction, "Ah yes, the Callaghan-way, if it is not your story do not tell it."

Sarah seems to realize what I am doing and, true to her character, allows it, "It's a good way, isn't it?"

"The best."

"Well, I will go in and say goodbye to Michael and give the kids a see-you-later and be on my way. I am looking forward to having them over; for us homemaker types the years between our own children being children and having the grandchildren over are a bit too quiet and orderly. John Henry and Mary are always welcome to come be with us."

Sarah and I walk into the house together as I say, "Thank you for your prayers and your friendship, Sarah, both are much appreciated."

I probably would have said more, but my daughter is standing in front of me with her hands on her hips and a very adult expression on her face, so I pick her up in my arms and ask, "Share your thoughts, little princess?"

She puts a small hand on each of my cheeks, "You forgot, mom."

"Forgot what?"

"We didn't do our yoga this morning together. You're going to be leaving again soon, and you and Auntie were talking a long time, and you know how you get if you don't do your yoga."

Sarah and I exchange amused glances as I hug Mary and then ask, "How do I get when I do not do my yoga?"

Mary is wiggling to get down, so I accommodate her, and the moment her feet touch the ground she begins walking around with stiff arms and legs and her neck bent at what must be an uncomfortable angle, "You know, mom. You get all tense and your body is sad."

I have a questioning look on my face as I respond, "How does my body get sad?"

Again her expression is stern, and her hands are on her hips, "Mom, emotions aren't just in your head."

"Tell me more," is all I say as I sit down on the sofa.

"Well, your body will get a headache and be sad because you have not exercised it."

"That makes perfect sense, so why don't we do our yoga before I have to get ready to leave."

"That's a good plan, mom. We will put on our yoga clothes, and I will pick the music, and you can get the mats and I'll meet you back here." She turns toward Sarah and very politely says, "Thank you for staying with us today, Auntie. I'll see you tonight," and then she runs to her bedroom after giving Sarah a hug.

"Well, obviously, my next hour has been planned and organized for me, so thanks again Sarah. We will drop the kids off in a couple of hours. Did you want them to eat here or with you?"

"We've already planned our meal for the night. I was daring and told them they could decide. We are having what the kids call 'favorites'."

"Ah, yes, it is John Henry's new idea. Each person picks a favorite item, and it does not matter if the items go together or not. According to him it only matters that they are favorites."

Sarah laughs and says, "Yes, we had to call Paul at home to ask him his favorite, and I had to choose one of April's favorites. We are having hot-dogs, ice cream, mashed potatoes, my homemade pickles, and mandarin oranges."

I can only shake my head, "Yes, that sounds like a typical 'favorites' meal, and that is why we only do it once a week."

Sarah says goodbye to me and, following their voices, goes outside to find Michael and John Henry. I walk into my bedroom to change, so I will be ready when Mary is because I do not want my body to be sad, but in my thoughts are Sarah's words from Matilda, and I wonder just how much Matilda knows about the subject of May's first letter and what insight Father Tom will have.

*   *   *   *

Mary and I have gone through all the preliminaries for our yoga time together: mat placement, candles and incense lit, music chosen. A recording of fluid keyboards, Chinese zither and vertical bamboo flute gently lead us into mind, body, and spirit relaxation. Their music is the crystal clear water of a stream I follow through shaded pools and around bends which promise no shocking surprises. I am only breath and slow movements as we reposition our bodies through the sequence of asanas known for hundreds of years as Sun Salutation, which is Mary's favorite. It is an honoring sequence of movements meant to celebrate the rising sun in all its timeless golden glory, and I am humbled by it and by the realization that the movements of Mary's body and of my body are links in an unbroken chain reaching back into human consciousness and connecting moments of time as dissimilar in the physical appearance of the participants as they are similar in the intent of the participants. I am alone now, moving into asanas my precious daughter does not attempt yet. I am wheel then crow then fish then tree. As I become eagle I allow my thoughts to surface, and I remember reading that this position called Garudasana is intended to turn my focus inward as it demands an outward practiced physical balance. The triumph of the spirit over the intellect is the eagle's symbolic meaning in this posture, and I wonder at that, place that thought in front of me in my mind where I am not entwined legs and arms and try to connect dream eagle to real eagle to yoga eagle in order to make meaning, but I cannot, and my only reaction is physical as I move into warrior pose. I picture in my mind the closing of a huge heavy door on the random hands up 'call-on-me' tendency of my thoughts, and I am again only breath and the still posture of body.

*   *   *   *

Mary and I end our yoga time together as we often do, sharing one mat and cuddling as she tells me about the thoughts she had that she saved 'special' just for me. Michael and John Henry open the front door and enter after their laughter and voices have already heralded their arrival into our quiet domain. Michael stands over us, "Well ladies, what position is that?"

Mary sits up and looks at Michael as she says, "It's our very own cuddle asana."

Michael picks her up and walks into the kitchen, "I like it. I should have known you made it up if I like it. Some of those other moves you two make remind me of a—"

John Henry interjects, "Pretzels. You look like unsalted pretzels." He sits down next to where I am now in a cross-legged sitting position, and I pull him into my lap.

I kiss the top of his head as I say, "You're just hungry, so you're thinking of food, John Henry. I know how your mind works."

"You found me out, mom, but since I'm almost always hungry, you didn't have to think very hard," he counters happily. He is letting me hold him, which is something that happens less lately than it used to happen, so I am very still as I enjoy the smell of his hair and the closeness of him. He is only six but becoming a boy-man. School and peers have broadened his horizons, and he is not often content to sit in my lap anymore.

Michael has walked back into the living room and is turning a giggling Mary upside-down and then right-side-up in his arms over and over again, "Well, wife, we better start getting ready to go. John Henry and Mary need to pack overnight bags and get their school stuff ready for tomorrow, so we all have things to do, don't we?"

Between giggles Mary asks, "I get to pack my own bag?"

Michael holds Mary still now and looks at her, "Why not? Are you going to be practical?"

Mary holds his face in her hands as she did mine earlier, "I don't think I know what 'practical' means, but it doesn't sound fun to me."

Michael laughs and responds, "Good call, Mary-Mary. You and I will pack your bag together." As he walks with Mary into her room he adds, "John Henry, I know you can be practical, right?"

John Henry bounces out of my lap and runs to his room, "No problem, dad; I know just what you mean." And as I roll up our mats and blow-out candles, I wonder if the rest of the evening will be as sweet as this part has been, and I wish we could just stay here together and not venture out and have to go separate ways. I wish we could just wrap-up in each other and watch a movie together and eat popcorn and drink hot chocolate and fall asleep in—.

Michael's voice from Mary's room interrupts my thoughts, "Leah Callaghan, stop daydreaming and go take your bath, so we won't be late." And at first I think about denying his statement, but then I do not, because my next moment is a bath moment, and I do truly love bath moments. I walk into our bedroom after I check to see how John Henry is doing. After walking into our bathroom I turn the faucet knobs to memorized location placement for water that will be almost too hot to step into initially, but after a brief getting used to will be perfect for a relaxing, if a bit hurried, soak. I add a bit of fragrance to the water, remove my clothes and put them in the hamper. I am stepping into the water as Michael enters the bathroom.

His smile is slow, sensual, "Ah, if only we had more time."

I am in the water now, so I decide to ignore his innuendo and just appreciate the heat of the water on my body as I breathe in the soft rich scent of rose. I lean back and watch him as he stands in front of the mirror rubbing his hands over his cheeks and asking himself whether he should shave or not.

He turns around and looks down at me, and suddenly I feel shy with this man whom I have lived with for at least a thousand moments. His eyes have returned to mine now, and he smiles at me, "We could save water and all that, be environmentally concerned. You could wash my back, and I could wash yours."

I sit up and return his smile, "We could do all those things, but then we would be late, which you dislike greatly." I reach my hand out touching his calf and drops of water run down to his foot. "Later you can love me, Michael."

He bends down, and we lean into each other as his lips find mine. He breathes his words into my mouth, "Will you love me back?"

"Forever" is all I can say before his kiss becomes deeper, and I think to myself how much I truly enjoy bath moments.

*   *   *   *

We are driving roads that wind around and rise and fall gradually as we make our way from Paul's and Sarah's to the Castle Rock Cafe. We are leaving the meadows and stands of Redwoods for the jagged cliffs with their Monterey Cypresses and the deep coves of Lane's shore. Castle Rock Point rises up out of sand and sea and reaches toward the now dark starred sky like an ancient hand with fingers partially closed. From its northwest side Falling Rock Waterfall plunges sixty feet into the transparent azure waters of Little Bend Cove.

The Castle Rock Cafe was originally the living quarters of the man who operated and maintained the lighthouse which stood on the point. He and his family built their home from what the land had to offer, redwood and stone. Construction on the lighthouse began in the early 1890s, and it took almost eight years to complete due to the steepness of Castle Rock Point and the difficulty in getting the construction materials up to the point's most level area. Three men and one child lost their lives during that period from construction accidents or high wind. The Intah, the Native American tribe who first lived in this area, claimed no lighthouse would ever stand long on Castle Rock Point. This proved a correct prophecy, because two years after the lighthouse was operational with its steam powered fog horn and its kerosene light that could be seen for twenty miles, it was struck by lightning and burned to the ground. The Irish immigrant who had taken care of the lighthouse for its short two year existence stayed on and became the first white settler in the area. His name was Sean McFallon and his daughter, Sarah, married Sherman Lane and they had a daughter named Rose, who married Matthew Thomas Dayton whose son, Thomas, turned the family home into Dayton School. Lane, Michael's uncle and my employer, is their son.

The child who died during the construction of the lighthouse was Sarah McFallon's brother. His body was never recovered, even though his broken-hearted mother, Kaila, stood on the sand of the cove day after day and night after night waiting for the waves to return his small body to her. Kaila walked away from the cove with empty arms, and it is said she was never quite the same after that, returning to the cove often to stand silently watching. Sometimes I believe I understand why. All she wanted was to hold her child in her arms one more time, to say goodbye to him, to wish him well in the next life, a future she would not share with him.

As Michael pulls into the cafe parking lot, my eyes turn from the point to the beautiful old building that once was the McFallon home. I wonder if Kaila McFallon, who had lost one child, had a strong enough heart to offer love and comfort to her other child, or if her mourning cast an impenetrable shadow over the family, dimming the light in even the most well lit room of their home. I believe she was able to do that, because sadness has never breathed its whispered sob into my heart when I am within the walls of their home, so she must have loved well despite her loss, only letting her sorrow take her when she stood so still on shifting sand facing the forever of the fluctuating waves. I rub my arms aware of the chilling physical sensation caused by my thoughts of her grief. I shake my head and make the transition from past to present.

The McFallon home has been remodeled only once, and that was done with great regard for maintaining the integrity of the original structure. Windows in the original house were liberally placed to capture the breathtaking views, but they were small because their glass panes had to be transported from so far away. During the remodel the windows were made larger. The living room and kitchen became the main dining area and an addition was built to house a kitchen modern in every convenience. What used to be the three bedrooms are now small private dining rooms, and I think this is one reason Michael chose the cafe for our dinner meeting. Michael's hand rests on my arm, and May's letter is in my jacket pocket. I allow myself to be comforted by both. Although the unknown content of May's letter may be unsettling, the fact that her hands held the paper I will soon hold reminds me again of the far reach of moment. Because I am alive and can still look into her eyes and hear her voice, she is alive, and we are together.

We stand, May and I, with Kaila, beyond the boundaries of past, present, and future.

*   *   *   *

Michael and I have closed the doors of the Jeep and are looking toward the ocean, watching white capped waves roll toward us as the moon's iridescent pearl light lays down what seems like a path for us across the water, as if we could go to her on that path and once in her arms look back upon the blue and green and light and dark of the earth and feel far removed from its troubles and cares. We hear our names called and see Father Tom in the distance with his hand raised in greeting, walking through wind terraced sand that surrounds and makes an island of the paved parking area on which we stand. Michael walks out to meet him, as I wait for them, enjoying the salty soft touch and taste of the ocean breeze.

I can see that Michael and Father Tom are talking as they walk, occasionally glancing at me, and I realize they are attempting to prepare for what will happen tonight. They are making plans. They are good men for trying, but I have a twenty year old letter in my pocket, and I keep a fire alive inside me that casts dark dreams. As I exchange greetings with Father Tom and Michael takes my hand, I wonder if the letter will offer me an explanation for the flames that took my family away from me. I wonder if the letter will act as lighthouse or as lightning storm.

Chapter TWO

We are in one of the small private dining rooms in Castle Rock Cafe and sit across from each other over a round table that is literally a thick slice from the trunk of a redwood tree. It has been smoothed and varnished, but the concentric circles whisper still of the tree's time on earth, of sharp winters and curving springs, of blunt summers and tapering autumns. I only imagine I can feel its pulse as I trace my finger over the stilled ripple of its once flowing veins. The scientific label for these now dry streams are medullary rays, and their purpose is the transport of food across the trunk. I remember when I was a teenager one of my science teachers explained that the center of the trunk, the heartwood, dies as the tree broadens, and it made me uncomfortable, but now the idea of life flourishing as it embraces death is less threatening, even necessary.

"Earth to Leah, earth to Leah," Michael's voice chants, and I, of course, can only smile at him and then at Father Tom. Michael is shaking his head a bit, but Father Tom only smiles back into me an approval of sorts, or at least I perceive it as such. Behind him the window frames the ocean, and I notice the moon's light softens the room, like a gentle breeze refreshes, and has breached the solid pane of glass that attempts to separate the inside world from the outside world.

"I was not being rude really; you were talking sports, so I was just doing some thinking," is my reply to Michael's summons.

Father Tom responds quickly, "Not a problem for me at all. Being a priest who must stand weekly, at the least, before different groups of people, I understand the need to allow the mind to wander here and there when the topic at hand is not pertinent," he pauses and gives me a wink before he continues. "Of late, I must also admit my own mind wanders even when it's me doing the talking, which can be a bit confusing for all involved. For that reason alone I am looking forward to my nephew Connor's arrival from Ireland next week. He will be a new and welcomed voice in the parish."

I lay my hand on his hand and notice it is like the table's top; bones and veins and skin whispering of time spent on earth. It is a strong hand that belongs to a strong man. Father Tom is in his middle sixties, and his hobbies of walking or cycling most places he needs to go, and his parental devotion to the sowing-nurturing-harvesting-process of raising flowers, fruits and vegetables have kept his body flexible and toned. Above the white collar, which claims to all his life calling, his face is tanned, and like his hands, reveals his days and years on earth. His eyes are dark brown and deep the way some people's eyes are, and his hair is short and as white as his collar.

"You do a wonderful job, Father, and we are looking forward to finally meeting Connor, but I have to tell you I enjoy your presentations of information, whether they be about spiritual matters or local history or one of your many hobby subjects, as you call them. Your mind wanders quite well, I think."

He leans toward me, "Ah, yes, daughter, but you and I are both wanderers, are we not? So it is not surprising that we enjoy what could be for others, trained and dedicated to the American way of thinking and speaking, a lot of useless digressions."

I point my finger at him as I articulate precisely, "Introduce the main idea, support it, and conclude and no digressions, to the point directly; that is the American way, and it will be followed perfectly and always, and God-forbid you are from England where they support then introduce the main idea and conclude instead of the American way, shame on them, shame on them, and forget also even mentioning other cultures' patterns of thinking and speaking; they are too far from American logic to even consider."

Michael joins in the conversation, "Humans are an interesting lot. The fact I might actually process my thoughts differently had I been raised in a different culture is a strange realization to me. For that matter, the fact that had I been raised in … let's say … France, how I hear a dog's bark would not be the same as I hear it having been raised in America. Hearing a dog's bark is a simple thing in an age when we speak of trying to achieve understanding across cultures and maybe someday even world peace."

Father Tom agrees, "World peace is an overwhelming goal when making peace with ourselves individually and even culturally has not been accomplished, but peace at every level must be the goal in these next decades, or I hate to consider the alternatives."

Michael shakes his head again, but this time as if to clear his own thoughts rather than as before when he was communicating his gentle disapproval of my daydreaming. "Stop the train; we're getting out there in hypothetical land, and that's not the purpose of us getting together tonight."

Father Tom and I look at each other and laugh as he says, "Despite this one's well documented roots and his Irish temperament, he thinks like an American."

Michael has a questioning look on his face until he realizes he has stopped the conversation in order to direct it back to our main purpose for meeting. "Okay, I get it, but we're here to discuss May's letter."

Father Tom leans toward us, "Ah, if only it was going to be that simple."

Michael's response is immediate, "What do you mean?"

Father Tom picks up his menu and indicates that we should do the same, "Let's order, and then, if you will permit me, I'll lay a bit of foundation for you before we open the letter, because, I must impress on you now, and please take what I am saying quite seriously, once opened, May's words are going to initiate a journey on a variety of levels that will be far from direct. You will be forced to wander paths that turn back on themselves over and over again and will, at moments, seem impassable, but now that you're involved in this … unfolding, there is no turning back. There can't be. Much of what you believe to be true will be proved only partially true or even proved completely false, and although you know May would do nothing to harm you or even upset your life, she's not the only one who has an interest in the matter which is the subject of the letter, or I should say, letters. Your lives will be changed, but not only your lives, how you perceive life will be altered. Change in and of itself is not necessarily bad, of course, but going though changes is seldom easy or comfortable." He looks first into Michael's eyes and into mine as he pauses then adds, "Your children's lives will be changed along with yours, and you must prepare them for that. However, to believe at this point that you still have a choice in continuing is to deceive yourselves. To believe that this very moment and the ones to follow are not meant to be a part of your lives denies the very destiny the letters will offer you, and it's a destiny worth seeking, worth the difficulties you'll encounter, of that I can promise you."

Michael and I have been looking into each other's eyes as Father Tom has spoken his strong words softly into not only the space of the room but also into our hearts and into our minds. Our bodies have tensed then tried to relax themselves as we have leaned away from and then back into each other trying to find safe ground on which we might be able to offer reassurance to self and to each other. It is one of those moments when I am viewing the scene from a far corner of the room, watching myself and the others involved, while simultaneously I am running around inside of myself checking latches on the doors and windows of all the carefully guarded perceptions I have of who I am and what my life means.

There is an added observation from somewhere deep inside me; it is as if something has flown between the moon's light and the window, and the silver glimmer radiating around us just moments before cannot penetrate this barrier; the light has been turned away, so there is no fresh breeze, real or imagined. Breath breathed out is breathed in again; a still, stale closeness presses in. And suddenly I feel as if there is a piece of broken mirror held against my throat, and I only want to close my eyes and escape.

I am pulled back. I can almost feel a hand on my shoulder drawing me away from wherever I was. As I open eyes I did not realize were closed, Michael is responding to Father Tom's suggestion of food and questioning the desirability of eating anything right at the moment. Father Tom is, however, focused only on me. Michael clears his throat and says, "Father Tom, sir, did you hear me?"

There is no verbal response to Michael. Father Tom only nods his head at me almost imperceptibly before he reaches out and places both his hands palms up on the table, one in front of Michael and one in front of me, and gestures for us to place one of our hands in his waiting ones. As we do so Michael and I also join hands, and we close our eyes as Father Tom begins to pray, "We are your children, and you are our creator, so share with us your mighty strength and your endless compassion. Protect us from that which is not of you and direct our steps. Watch over those whom you have given us to love, and bind our hearts to your heart that your purpose may be our purpose. Cause us to notice you in all the ways you reveal yourself that we might feel the breath of your spirit and the touch of your hand on our lives. Make us yours in our minds, in our bodies, and in our spirits. Today and always, your will be done."

Even after Father Tom's words have ended we remain still, the room totally quiet, hands held and holding, and I breathe in deeply the new calm I know must fill the room as completely as ocean mists cloak the shores. Even with my eyes closed, I know the moon's light also fills the room again, and then I wonder if it ever was really gone, thinking further that I could have imagined the—.

Father Tom's deep quiet voice interrupts my thoughts, "We will break bread together this evening, because it is an old way of showing our mutual agreement to join together. We will be proclaiming that no one of us is alone in this undertaking. And after tonight, we will nourish our bodies with good food, just as we will make sure to nourish our minds with healthy thoughts, just as we will nourish our spirits with times of prayer and meditation. Difficult times are not times to go without these three," he pauses, and I open my eyes to see Father Tom smiling and Michael watching him. "Unless, of course, we are called to fast. A good long fast is always a remedy for something or someone, but that's another discussion, isn't it?" Michael and I indicate our agreement with him by picking up our menus. Father Tom stands and walks to the door as he says, "Now, I'll go let Maybe know we'll be ready to order shortly and give you two a few moments alone to talk about what a crazy old priest I am behind my back. When I return we will talk of May and of times past. We will reminisce and make dinner talk."

As soon as Father Tom has shut the door, Michael is out of his chair and pacing the small room. He stops beside me and kneels down; we are face to face as I lean toward him. He holds my hands in his as he says, "I want to find words to make this better, Leah, but the only words going through my mind are … well, the only words going through my mind are 'holy shit'. I know that's sort of irreverent and totally not helpful, but holy shit are the only words in my head right now." I wrap my arms around him and whisper in his ear that I agree completely.

He pulls back but stays close, "With what? Do you agree I am being irreverent and totally not helpful? Or do you agree with 'holy shit'?"

I pull him close again, "What you are feeling is what you are feeling, and being at a loss for words and not having something helpful to offer feels like a natural response to all this. I have no words, and the 'holy shit' thing is sort of humorous."

Michael pats me reassuringly although a bit absentmindedly and stands to walk around the small room again, but he stops suddenly and turns, "You felt it didn't you?" I nod my head, and Michael says 'holy shit' again just as Father Tom opens the door. Behind him Maybe Olda Danner's facial expression clearly registers she heard Michael also.

Father Tom responds quickly, "Interesting way to greet a priest, I'll have to remember that one." Michael only shrugs his shoulders and sits down in his chair, not even attempting to explain himself. Maybe and I are both trying not to smile, but we do not succeed.

I walk around the table to greet her, and I am wrapped in warm arms as she greets me as sister in her native language. Then she continues, "It's been too long since we have walked the shore together and talked of family and the strange ways of husbands."

Michael has circled the table to greet Maybe also, and as they shake each other's hand Michael says, "Ha-ha, funny, very funny. Yeah, I really needed that, Maybe. You're a saucy wench, and I'm gonna to tell your husband on you."

Maybe shakes her finger at Michael as he sits down again, "You can try, Michael Callaghan, but he will not believe your lies. I have cast an ancient Indian charm on my white husband, and he believes everything I tell him now. So I tell him I'm the perfect wife and he believes me. Your voice will be small compared to the charm's voice which is like the wave's voice."

Michael shakes his head at her, "Good call, talking magic in front of the Father. What will he think of you?"

Maybe has her hands on her slim hips now and is nodding her head knowingly as she says, "He'll do what he always does, and ask me to write down the words of my charms. He's an Irish priest of the old ways, you know? He knows magic is from the creator. You just have to use it for good, so that it does not circle back on you like a bear and bite you on the butt or worse."

Father Tom and I are laughing, but Michael is playing along and leaning back against his chair, his arms spread at his sides and his facial expression registering utter dismay, "Blasphemy pure and simple. You're a bad Indian, Maybe Olda, and as soon as the charm wears off, I'm telling your husband. Imagine saying our good and reputable Father is an Irish priest of the old ways."

Father Tom joins in now, "Well, the noble church did excommunicate me. You have to admit that."

Michael gives him a friendly slap on the shoulder, "Ah yes, but that was only a misunderstanding, just a difference of opinion on a minor issue of doctrine, and since good ol' Uncle Lane and his father disagreed with the church's handling of the situation, they decided to keep you on despite the fact our church is no longer recognized by the great white Catholic Fathers, so you really can't complain. You're the head padre of your own little domain now." Michael pauses, and we can see he is attempting to connect thoughts which were previously scattered or housed under different categories in his head. His eyes move from one of us to the other and then back again. "Does this conversation have any relation to your earlier talk with us?"

Father Tom's smile seems to reach from ear to ear as he says, "See there now, we're already putting some of the pieces together, and we haven't even gotten started yet." He holds Michael's gaze as he hands Maybe his menu, ordering the halibut and a baked potato and requesting whatever fresh green vegetable they happen to be serving tonight. Michael simply says he'll take the same, and I order the House Caesar Salad.

Maybe slaps Michael on the back none too gently as she gathers the menus and comments, "I'd like to stay and see where this is going, but instead I have to go slave over a hot stove and cook odd and ugly white men their dinners," to which Michael pretends to be preparing to throw his thick slice of still-warm-from-the-oven homemade bread at her.

He lays the bread back down on his bread plate and looking first at me and then at Father Tom he says, "What amazes me more than the bizarre and somewhat creepy implications of what has only been hinted at so far is the fact I can joke around with a crazy Indian woman while in the midst of it. But we're like that, you know? We humans do that sort of thing, don't we? The cliché 'smiling through the tears' expresses the situation, or maybe smiling through the anger or frustration or what ever it is I'm feeling, which is probably not just one emotion."

I am reading the signs quite easily now, and Michael is definitely not the proverbial happy camper. He is, in fact, angry and wanting to as quickly as possible quell a storm he cannot quite locate that is threatening the possible well-being of his family.

The expression on Father Tom's face is thoughtful, and his hands are clasped in front of his chin. His eyes are introspective while at the same time meeting Michael's unblinking stare. "The anger will pass, Michael, as soon as you're willing to accept the helplessness it is masking."

Michael leans just a bit closer, "I've taken every damn psychology class known to man, and I think I'd prefer to diagnose my own behavior."

Father Tom agreeably responds, "Then by all means, please do so."

Michael's lips barely move, "I am."

Father Tom leans back in his chair now, "And?"

Michael does not lean back yet but replies, "The intense need I feel to punch a wall will pass as soon as I can somehow agree to allow myself to feel helpless as hell in this situation."

Father Tom nods his head, "You're not helpless in this situation, Michael. Once you understand it, you'll find the resources within yourself to deal with whatever you'll encounter."

Michael's posture is not relaxing, but he is blinking his eyes again, "I'd rather fight a fire; I know how to do that."

Father Tom is as relentless as he is gentle, "You will know how to do this also."

Michael is leaning back in his chair now, "I'm not as sure of that as you are."

Father Tom offers Michael a reassuring smile, "You'll have to trust me then."

Michael rubs his hands across his face and then back through his hair, "I always have, and I will continue until you give me a reason why I shouldn't, but I will protect my family by whatever means I need to use."

Father Tom leans forward, "I would want nothing less than that for you or from you."

Michael lets his head fall back and stretches out his arms, and then he too rests elbows on the table, "I feel as if we have agreed on something, but for the life of me, I don't know what it is."

Father Tom reaches over and pats Michael's arm. "I believe we were just letting the dust settle—" is all Father Tom has time to say before Maybe knocks on the door, and he rises to open it for her.

I can hear her voice admonishing Father Tom, "You're the guest; go sit down, old man. I only knocked to be polite, so when I opened the door I would not hear any of your talk. I am a woman and an Indian; I am a daughter and a sister; I am a wife and a mother; I have three arms, and three hands, and a mind three times as strong as yours. Do not interfere with my work." Father Tom is backing out of her way and seems to be bowing a bit.

He sits down as Maybe enters balancing three plates and smiling happily. "Men need to be reminded often of their place, little Leah, you remember that if your strange one gets out of line. I had to remind Bradley just the other day of his own foolishness. He is my husband's brother, so I must be patient with him, but it's no easy thing to be a woman among men and to be patient; they are more difficult than children to raise, I think."

She has placed our plates in front of us, and is standing with her hands on her hips again, looking at each one of us waiting for a response from Michael or Father Tom.

I reach out my hand to her, and she moves toward me to take it as I say, "I do not think they are going to take your bait this time; your food looks and smells too good to put off tasting to argue with you."

She squeezes my hand gently and shakes her head slowly, mumbling as she moves toward the door, "A sad day when men do not rise to the occasion, a sad day when men cannot...."

*   *   *   *

We each focus on the food in front of us, eating leisurely. There is no desire in me to rush to the next portion of Father Tom's serving of information, so I linger over each bite of this repast, aware of textures and seasonings. Grated parmesan, crispy croutons, delicate leaves of romaine lettuce all dressed in a creamy off-white. Food is good and can be a remedy of sorts and a reminder of the simple pleasures that are actually basic necessities. I think then of not having these necessities, of living in a place where the most basic of human needs cannot be met, and I wonder how that affects the thinking of an individual, how that affects the perspective of a family, how that affects the perspective of a whole culture. What value do children put on life when they have been denied the basic securities of living? What sort of teenagers blossom from those neglected seeds? What sort of adults loom there in the shadows of such up-bringings? Some people might only grow stronger for their hardship; some would become bitter, but whatever the consequence, it seems as if poverty should be an issue that belongs in history books not in the present. I wonder how my heart would break or at my own anger were I a mother who could not feed her children, and I stop eating for a moment and feel grateful for where I have been placed on the earth. 'Thank you, thank you' I say in my internal voice and wonder then to whom I am speaking. God? Jesus? Angel-beings? The Old Ones? Buddha? Mother Earth?

I used to be so sure. My faith was Bible based and rock solid, unshakable, impenetrable. Jesus' God was my lighthouse and from within every moment I experienced I could turn toward that beacon regardless of circumstances. But now, I question. I read and research and dialogue and quest, still praying to Abba and to Jesus. It just seems that churches and their doctrines are too small to house the God of all people, and how could the real God be less than that? I had to go out into a newly undefined world to rediscover what I thought I knew. I am still out there, symbolically climbing mountains and searching the seemingly barren surfaces of deserts, watching waves mind the moon, holding shells up to my ear, laying my head against my husband's chest to hear and feel his heartbeat, listening to the crystal clear intentions of my children's ideas and ideals, reading between the lines of the dialogue and of the writing of my students so that somehow I can remind them of who they really are without knowing who they really are as I become the blind poet of old, sure of my duties and offering words of hope and ageless wisdom even as I am unable to perceive the ever distant destination of purpose and source. And now as I am thinking of my students I think of Teri, and ask Father Tom, "Are you aware of what happened at the school last night?"

He sets his knife and fork down on his plate and responds, "I arrived just after you and Michael did. I was standing with Bradley in the doorway and praying that you and Michael would reach her, that even if she did not allow you to physically hold her, she would allow you to hold her in the spirit, to hold and protect her like elders should hold and protect the young ones." I am pulled in two directions as I hear his words. Part of me wants to comment on the fact I had seen that very same image last night in my mind, but another part of me wants to only talk of practical matters.

I choose the latter, "I was wondering if I could stop by the greenhouse in the morning before school and pick-up some flowers for Teri, so I can drop them off before the busyness of the day gets a hold of me. I am afraid I will let her slip from my mind as I focus on the other students, and I do not want to do that."

Father Tom is more than agreeable and offers to meet me at the greenhouse at whatever time best suits my schedule. That all arranged and our earlier shared silence ended, Michael looks at his watch and suggests that perhaps Father Tom should start laying his previously mentioned foundation to which Father Tom responds, "You're feeling ready and also aware of the evenings quick passing, are you?"

Michael nods and responds, "I'm aware that tomorrow will be a full day for Leah and for me and probably for you also, and that the letter is still unopened, although I don't know how ready I am for any of this." Michael pauses and looks at me as he begins speaking again, "I have a strong sense that this situation is going to involve … more than just this … reality. I'm not sure we should open the letter, and I don't understand how or why, according to you, we don't actually have a choice."

Now Michael looks at Father Tom, "I don't like feeling forced into anything. I'm uncomfortable with your implication of possible danger, and I, unlike you and Leah, am not a great seeker of spiritual truth." He folds his napkin and lays it neatly on the table next to his plate, stands and walks to the window. His back is to us, but I can see his reflection in the window's glass, and I want to go to him and smooth the lines of worry from his face, but I cannot offer what I do not have, and there is no reassurance or comfort in me; there is only a vast open darkness like a great plain stretched out in front of me, and I know, one way or another, we will have to cross it, or I will, and somehow making that journey alone seems impossible. I have no desire to separate myself from Michael, no desire at all.

So I say, "If Michael does not think we should continue in this matter, I will honor his decision. I will ask Matilda to burn the letters she still has, and I will burn the one I have, and that will be that. End of story."

Father Tom does not speak at first. He gathers up our plates and utensils and sets them on a small cart Maybe has left outside the door of our private dining room. He sits down and then slowly he begins to speak, "Not reading the letters or burning the letters will only delay the inevitable. The letters are tools, or perhaps keys, to help you. Some of the events to which the letters refer have already happened, and some of the events referred to are hypothetical in nature, some are prophetic in nature, and you can make of that what you will. There is nothing you can do to stop certain events from happening, but your involvement is certain. Only in that respect do you have no choice; only in the fact of your voluntary or involuntary participation do you have no choice. However, the choices you make in deciding how to respond to the different aspects of the situation will greatly influence the outcome. You are in a position of honor; you were chosen for this; you were destined for it."

Michael turns and asks, "Who? Both of us? Just Leah? Me because I am married to her? Who?"

Father Tom sighs, "Even before the fire you had chosen her for yourself, and you made no secret of that. Everyone knew you and Leah would marry eventually, and you made that happen. You chose her, so for both of you this is destined. You are one through marriage."

Michael replies, "Most marriages end in divorce, you know? I don't think many people see marriage as a holy union anymore."

Father Tom shakes his head sadly, "If seeing were all that was necessary to make a thing true, life would be simpler, but married in the church or married by a justice of the peace does not matter. People can divorce, but that does not wipe the so-called slate clean as if they had never been together. You've joined yourself to Leah in the spirit as well as in this reality, and believing in or not believing in is as relative as seeing or not seeing. What is … is; your ability to explain something does not justify or nullify its existence. You can deny what you don't understand, but that doesn't lessen its reality; your denial only lessens your ability to perceive that which you disbelieve."

I am swept up in the quick flow of the exchange of ideas and ideals, "Just like in a discussion of free will or fate, the discourse or personal philosophy of those involved in the discussion matters not at all. Who can know? The fact is that we cannot know, but what is the difference really between the two options? If we believe our choices are created out of free will when we are instead bound by destiny and choose because we are fated to choose this path or that, the outcome is the same. Who we are determines our choice or our lack of choice. Because of who I am, my path is set; by fate or free-will, it does not matter."

Michael is standing with his hands in his pockets, and he is looking down at the floor. "Leah and Mary shared a dream." He looks up at Father Tom, "What does that mean? Was it just part of their destiny? Did Mary choose to share a dream with her mother? What? Tell me what you know."

Father Tom is nodding his head now, "Mary sharing Leah's dream does not put Mary in danger. It was Leah's dream. Was Mary lying close to you when this happened?"

I am quick to respond, as hungry for an explanation as Michael, "Yes, John Henry and Mary and I were taking a nap. They were both with me, but I did not ask John Henry about his dreams. I would not have asked Mary but she told me."

Michael sits down as Father Tom comments further, "I'll go back a bit to bring you forward to the present, so that you can understand the shared dream and also other things perhaps." He pauses to give us a chance to ask him a question, probably about the 'other things perhaps', but we do not. We are, as they say, all ears, so he continues. "All over the world, since the beginning of recorded history, and actually even before that, people have noticed that in certain places unusual things have a tendency to happen, not necessarily bad things, just unusual things. In Ireland, the places are called Caol A'it." He takes out a small spiral notebook he always seems to have with him and writes the word down. "If you don't see the word and hear it you would never connect them. See." He shows both Michael and me what he has written and then pronounces 'keel awtch'. "If you don't know the Irish, the spelling of the words makes no sense. Translated it means 'thin places'. The people of Ireland sometimes connected these thin places to the people who lived in Ireland before the Celts from Gaul and Spain invaded, probably around 350 B.C.E. Supposedly these early people, known from the old stories as the Tuatha De Danaan, invaded Ireland and took it from the Fir Bolg. The Fir Bolg are said to have arrived in Ireland some three hundred years after the Great Flood. Another group of beings, the Fomorians, supposedly semi-divine like the Tuatha De Danaan, invaded Ireland regularly and lived on islands close by. The Fomorians were a fierce and nasty lot for the most part, but the Tuatha De Danaan defeated them finally and ruled both Ireland and the Fir Bolgs. But when the Celts arrived the Tuatha De Danaan are said to have gone underground, building mounds, some of which can still be seen today. The Tuatha De Danaan did continue to reappear and intervene in the lives of humans occasionally, and there are many stories of their exploits. The mounds may or may not signify a thin place. Thin places exist all over Ireland, all over the world really, but it's difficult to do research on such things given their supernatural and/or spiritual aspect, plus some people believe that thin places are not only geographical. Some believe that thin places connect past, present, and future. Some believe thin places are connections between this physical realm and the spiritual one. All over the world different cultures share similar beliefs, and thin places, though called by other names, are one of those shared beliefs. To refer back to my previous statement regarding thin places only being geographical, they are not. Some people have the ability to act as thin places. And to close, I will add that, surprisingly, I heard a relatively conservative preacher give an interesting sermon on thin places just last year, so the idea of such things or people who have the ability to transcend this physical realm may not be regarded as the stuff of pagan devil worship so much anymore. Many New Agers and many Native Americans find it shocking that anyone would not believe in thin places. But as we discussed earlier, believing in them or placing a value on them or not believing in them does not affect them at all. They exist and will continue to exist. May will explain about all this in her letter." Father Tom pauses to drink from his glass of water.

Michael is shrugging his shoulders and shaking his head, "And that means what to me? Tell me how to use that information. I'm at a loss here. Is my house sitting on a thin place or something?" He looks at me then, "Did you get that? Did you make a connection?"

Father Tom puts his hand on Michael's arm and continues speaking, "I need you to think about three things. One, stop qualifying existence. Stop labeling this past or that future, stop labeling this real world and that spiritual. Imagine they are all just characteristics of one thing, like the facets of a single diamond. Two, imagine for a moment that a thin place might possibly be a portal through which certain people can actually travel in what we call time. The opportunities of such a thing are limitless, and, of course, depending on the motives of the person or people involved, could be positive or negative. Three, imagine a person who has the capacity to function as a thin place. That person could be taken to a geographic thin place and upon entering the portal accomplish much more than let's say a regular person. And not all thin places are necessarily portals, so don't limit what they are or try to fit them into your thinking easily."

Michael is thinking aloud it seems, staring at the paneled wall across from him, "So it's possible that these thin places could have doors that swing both ways?"

Father Tom smiles, "Everything is possible, Michael, only our thinking makes things seem impossible."

But Michael is being practical not philosophical and persists in his train of thought, "Yes, but if something can come through these places, would we be able to see it, or would we just sense it?" I realize to what he is referring, and I understand his need for direct and clear answers to what has been happening in our lives lately, but I do not believe that is what Father Tom wants to offer us tonight.

But Father Tom surprises me when he says, "You have sensed a presence?"

Michael scoots his chair back and stands, "Oh yeah, we had a presence." He looks at me, "Wouldn't you say we had a presence, Leah?" Now he is looking at Father Tom again, "We've had a presence twice in two days, in less than two days. We had a presence at the house on Saturday night, and Leah and I felt a presence here tonight, not even an hour ago. So now tell me what that means?"

Father Tom shakes his head, "I am not here to tell you what things mean. I am here to give you background information and to let you know I will help you in every way I can, but you have to answer the questions together, you and Leah. Others will help, but each of us has only pieces of information, and in truth, you are getting ahead of yourself in this. You need to read May's letter."

Michael is leaning over the table, "I want to know what the hell that thing was I felt in my house where my kids sleep and what its intentions are?"

I stand and put my hand on Michael's back, "Michael, please sit down. Please. This is not helping. This anger is not a good thing for us. I need you to sit down, I want to ask a couple of questions, and then we will read May's letter." He is still standing. "Michael, please."

He sits down in his chair, and I do the same as I look across the table at Father Tom. Then I lean forward and look directly into his eyes and ask, "Earlier, in the spirit, you put your hand on my shoulder to bring me back. Is that true?"

"Yes," is all he says.

So I continue, "I am confirming that you can give us background information, and you can help us in the spiritual realm, and my question relates to you knowing more than you can tell us now, because Matilda told me she should not go ahead of the information in each letter. Is that true?"

Again he says, "Yes."

It makes my heart beat faster to ask my third question, "Are John Henry and Mary in danger?"

Now Father Tom reaches across the table and takes my hand, "Children are seen as innocents; they are not usually involved, and I have discovered no information regarding a child ever being hurt in connection to a thin place."

I look at Michael as he seems to breath a sigh of relief and says, "I needed to know that."

Father Tom lets go of my hand, and now Michael and I reach across the surface of the table top; we are over varnished and still streams that once carried nourishment and that circled dead heartland. It is a short distance over hundred of years, and I think to myself how everything is all so relative. "Michael, there are no guarantees. It feels good to have Father Tom reassure us, but there are no guarantees in life like that."

I pause and try to think of a way to explain what I want to express to him. "You fight fires. I am your wife, and every day you are at work I know there could be danger for you, and I become afraid sometimes for you, but I have to trust that all will be well, or I would go insane with worry, because there are no guarantees. This thing we are in cannot turn you into someone who is motivated by fear, even if it is out of love for your children, that is not who you are; it has never been; it can never be. Father Tom can tell you that our children are safe, but that is only his belief based on what he knows, and we can either have faith in that or not, but the safety of our children is our responsibility. We are their parents, just as we have always been. Father Tom says that much will change in our lives, that we will see ourselves in a new way perhaps, but who we are in our hearts must stay true. You told me that the other night, that as long as we are true to ourselves and to each other we will be all right, and I believed you then, and I believe you now, and I will believe you tomorrow and the next day, but I will not be pushed this way and that by doubt and fear. We will face this head-on if need be, but I cannot breathe right when you become angry, so you need to stop that."

He takes my face in his hands, "I forgot that, didn't I? I forgot who I was and who we are together. I won't forget again. We can see this thing through, but maybe … maybe we can get some holy water or something and sprinkle it around the house and on our clothes so that—" I can tell he is teasing because he is pressing my cheeks together as he says these last words and making me look ridiculous, so I pull his thumbs back a bit to force him to let go of my face.

He leans back in his chair and does an upper body shake like a dog does after a bath or a swim in the lake, and Father Tom looks over at him and says, "Well at least you recover quickly."

Michael smiles, "Yep, that's me. I am back to my old self: intelligent, good looking, able to leap tall buildings and even to apologize for acting like an ass." Michael extends his arm toward Father Tom, and they shake hands as Michael says again and more appropriately, "Father Tom, forgive me for losing control five or six times in the last hour."

Father Tom is smiling, but then his face changes suddenly, and he looks hurt, "I thought you were going to apologize for calling me a holy shit, but I guess that's not what you're sorry about is it?"

I interrupt them before Michael can respond, "Okay, enough is enough. We should take a bathroom break or stretch our legs break because then I am opening May's letter. It is already 10:15. Doesn't the cafe close at 9:30?"

Father Tom replies that he and Maybe already made arrangements for Father Tom to lock up when we are finished, and he adds, "She left a thermos of coffee for us too and told us to make ourselves at home."

I smile just thinking about her, "She is all heart."

Michael comes to stand beside me and says, "No, not all heart. She has a mouth on her too."

I wrap my arms around him, reminding him that he could be described in the same way, and he buries his face in my hair and tells me he has no idea what I am talking about then slaps me on the fanny as he walks away. "I dislike it greatly when you do that, Michael, and you know it."

I hear him call back to me from the direction of the bathroom, "I can't apologize anymore tonight. I can only do one a night."

"I am not talking to you anymore right now, Michael Callaghan." His only answer is the closing of the bathroom door which is fine with me, since I proclaimed quite clearly I was not speaking to him anyway. Father Tom is standing across the room looking at me and shaking his head with a smile on his face. I turn back toward the window, which is now only a dark mirror reflecting the small room, and put my hand in my pocket to hold the letter that will only be a mystery for another moment or so.

*   *   *   *

We sit around the table again and besides the fragrance of rich coffee I have no other strong sensory perceptions. The tension is gone, perhaps because Michael and I are tired or perhaps because we have prepared ourselves as well as we know how, so we are relaxed and as ready as we will ever be to begin this process that has become an unveiling of sorts, as if May's purpose fills space, has taken on a shape. I have laid the letter on the table. My hands are folded in my lap. Michael and Father Tom move only to wrap their hands around warm mugs of coffee to raise to their lips to drink. I know it is time, so I reach for the letter and, using the knife I did not use during dinner, I open the envelope, and carefully withdraw the pale rose sheets of writing paper May always used in her correspondence.

The ink is black, and her script is flowing and cursive. I do not look up to acknowledge the presence of Michael or Father Tom, for now only May and I are in the room. I read her words aloud, and even though I know it is my voice I hear, it is May's voice that fills my five senses with memories: I see her sea blue eyes, I hear her vibrant voice, I feel her hand on mine, I breath in her fragrance of soft rose, I taste the tea she made for us whenever she gathered me to her for a story or a talk. Her voice is drawing me in again.

"Child of my child, heart of my heart, my Leah, I find I must stray a bit from my purpose in writing this first of three letters, so that I can wrap my arms around you again, and give you the thousand embraces I must now owe you. I am offering you twenty years of cherishing, twenty years of celebrating your accomplishments, and twenty years of comfortings, and you must forgive me for leaving so suddenly, and for not preparing you in some manner, and perhaps I found a way to soften the leaving, but that seems far from possible, since there is no way to separate hearts gently. I have no clarity in what I see, only a strong sense that we will not be together much longer, so as much as I want to warn you in some way, I do not know how. My hands are tied a bit by an ancient purpose and a timeless commitment. This letter and the two which follow are the only pathway to you for me now, and even then I will have to wait to find my way to you.

I am stilled in realizing you will be a woman when you read this. So as I am here writing, you are there reading, and we are separated only by the arrangement of moments. Reach out to me, my Leah, find me in your dreams, so that I can again hold you in my arms. As I imagine you now, holding what I hold, our hands touching, I know the words to follow will be both gentle, like the showers of spring, but also jarring, like the crashing of waves against stone cliff. At the edge of all that you believe I will take you, and together we will stand, above a distance of future and past colliding, to make sense of your journey.

I believe as I see you reading this that you are not alone. Michael will have claimed you as his by now; he will be with you as he has always been with you. You must understand that before fate and destiny became such threats to a modern notion of free will, knowing the path that was to be taken was considered a gift. Those that could perceive the future in the present, those that could discern the particular purpose of their unique combination of heart and mind, they were the powerful ones, the strong willed ones who grabbed life up in their arms and knew that come tribulation or success their lives were their own. In Michael I saw such a man; let the strength of who he is and the depth of his love for you be both your anchor and sail.

Others, too, will provide information and support, even protection. Remember always the image I have given you; you stand on the edge; you can fall or fly, so rely on those who are sent to you, but know in your heart of hearts that you are meant to stand and to fly. Matilda is the guard at the gate; she cannot go on the journey with you, but she will stand at that place where this world and the next meet and speak words into all the times and places you will travel; trust her judgment and trust who she trusts. Father Tom can go wherever you go in the beginning; take him with you, Leah; some battles are not to be fought alone. He will have gathered others also, so trust his knowledge and also trust who he trusts. There will be individuals who cannot be involved; some will know what you are doing and others will only sense what is happening and both will want to direct you or intercept you or simply to join you; they are not to be acknowledged or invited, and I will explain more about this later.

About your mother and your father I cannot write more than this: your mother is not involved although she sacrificed much and loves you dearly; your father will be pulled in different directions and by conflicting purposes, and he cannot be allowed to sway you. I do not believe that time will have changed who they are in your journey, but I cannot know for certain. Let Father Tom and Matilda assist you in how to interact with your parents in regards to this matter. John's and Grant's destinies are not connected to yours, and I never believed Grant would remain in Lane, but if he has he can only be a loyal brother to you and nothing more. It would be dangerous for him to become involved when he is not destined to be involved. By no means allow anyone to stay with you in your home unless Father Tom and Matilda have agreed on the situation.

The only other family I can discuss with you now would be my great grandchildren. Tears come to my eyes when I think of your young ones I have not held, but at the same time I smile to imagine what you and Michael have created together. A daughter, I know, will be one of your blessings, and I cannot think that a son would not also be yours, perhaps even two sons. My sweet little Leah with little ones of her own, and Michael being a father with a firm voice and a loving heart. It would have to be a happy family that you have, and you must not let yourself worry over your young ones because of what you will be learning from me; children are cherished and not involved in these matters. Your children will be affected but should be in no danger.

I have paused here to test my own heart in what I have just written to you, because there truly are no guarantees. Those who oppose what you will be doing are not known to me except in that there has always been opposition, but in no generation has a child been endangered. I must explain to you that there has been violence and that people have died, but there are battles worth fighting and truths worth defending, and what you are being called to do must be done. You were born for this journey, so you must realize that Michael and your children are also born for this journey. Trust that and do not allow fear to dissuade you from any course of action, or you go against your own nature; fear may be a natural human emotion, but it should not be a motivation or a justification.

And now, my Leah, to the heart of the matter. Back before being human became so small, back before being human became separated from being part of the earth, a people lived and breathed and loved and fought and did all the wonderful and terrible things that humans do. These people lived wholly; they were spiritual-physical beings and the earth was their mother, and the earth was their father, and the earth was not just physical, not just mountains and meadows and oceans and deserts and vegetation and still-matter under a wide sky, but spirit too. These people were before thoughts had to be written; thoughts and the spoken word were as real as blood and bone to them. Thoughts and the spoken word were physical and spiritual. They were passed generation to generation through minds and spirits until they were part of the physical being of a person, of the people. Knowledge was the soil to wisdom's seed, and culture, the ways of a people, was the water that made lush growth flourish. These people, the Tuatha De Danaan, lived freely in the spirit and in the physical; for them what we see as two worlds was one; there was no separation.

As time passed, as we say time does, the world as we perceive it was changed by man, and the Tuatha De Danaan responded to this change by becoming more and more spiritual until their physical bodies were mere robes to be worn or not. They became legends, gods and goddesses, and were sighted now and then, spoken of by many but believed in by few, and their interactions with man in the physical world began to be seen as supernatural instead of natural. Be remembering now that just because we label something this way or that does not change what it is; it only changes how we perceive it, so when man deemed it necessary to categorize and place under his control all that lives, he lost his vision of himself as part of the whole, and the spirit became small and the realm of spirit distant. But the real oneness did not change.

All over our carefully mapped and labeled physical world the spiritual world coexists, and because the Tuatha De Danaan are human and were human, and because they did make love and war with other humans, their blood and bone and thinking mixed with the blood and bone and thinking of other humans; their spirits mixed with the spirits of other humans. So although we do not often see the old ones, they are here still and descendants of theirs exist. Their physical-spiritual hearts beat in human bodies today. And when I speak of heart, I speak of spirit because the physical heart is only the engine that pumps our blood. It was only a few hundred years ago that people believed that the stomach was the seat of the emotions instead of the heart. In truth there is only the physical and the spiritual and 'heart' is that place within who we are that is the culminating point of our physical-spiritual mix. And now, Leah, as you may have already guessed, your blood and bone and spirit, your thinking, your heart, are from the Tuatha De Danaan, and you have an obligation to fulfill. Each genera-tion's obligation is unique. My duty was to prepare you and to prepare a path for you. Your duty is to rediscover who you are, discover who the opposition is, and to walk with the Tuatha De Danaan for a brief time. More than this I cannot express until you have gone a bit of the way.

Remember, meaningful progress is a step by step process. Expectations should be based on that concept. A good parent would not take a child from kindergarten and place the child in college. Knowledge is not wisdom; wisdom is the application of knowledge, and without going through the necessary steps or stages all a person has is a collection of ideas. If Father Tom or Matilda or I were to tell you all we know, you still would not know all that you need to know. Our ideas are of our generation, and you must take what we offer you and lay it out upon a table and notice the beauty and imperfections of each concept. Then, take what you need, what is usable, what you discern to be true and of value, and go out and discover what else it is you will need to know in order to make your way on this journey that is yours. Michael will need to do the same. His path is parallel with yours, unique to him, but you will know that you are walking true to your course if Michael's course complements yours. Your children will also provide insight on your journey. They are of you and for you as you are of them and for them. They will be small but persistent voices when all other voices are silent; they will be candles lit by purposeful fingers when all else is darkness.

Nothing and no one should be disregarded. We are each and all placed just so, and when we allow the breath of life to sing through us, our music is fine and clear, har-monious. But some people are damaged by their reactions to their lives, and the music that is life is changed by greed and hate, and those people who harbor and even feed themselves on these two emotions cause pain and destruction. There will be those who oppose you for no other reason than they want to use what is yours to provide power for themselves. You must not acknowledge them or allow them to influence you in any manner. You must walk through them as if they are not actually there. Do not allow them to make you walk around them. Stay true, dear heart, to your path.

The ideas I am sharing with you should feel like reminders, like words heard once but not remembered for a long time. The truth will always be like that. It will connect to some other part of your thinking. That is only natural. You must stay true to who you are. You must allow the dream to come to you, and when you have gained strength you must go to the dream, seek it out; it is both safe harbor and gateway.

Matilda and Father Tom understand what must happen before you can receive the next letter. They will have read the letters before I seal them. If you are unable to com-plete what must be done, then you have gone as far as you can go, and you can rest from all this knowing that you did what you were supposed to do and that another will take the next step.

You and Michael must discover the truth about your father before you can read the next letter. You can begin this process by researching his military career. You must also open the metal box you asked me about so often and saw me hold in my hands more than once. Father Tom has the key. You should also ask Father Tom why he does not use his last name.

Be well, my angel, and know that more than once when I was speaking the old stories into your heart, I was speaking of our ancestors and the lessons they had to learn in life. You must go back to move forward. Be blessed and may the love that surrounds you light your way. Call to me, Leah, so I can watch over you. I am only one dream away."

✳   ✳   ✳   ✳

The silence is full. It surrounds us, fills me completely and is not uncomfortable. It is a sweater on a cool day. I pull it around me and close my eyes. Her name is playing non-stop as I call to her: May, May, May, May … only that one word repeated like a heartbeat. The silence has a heartbeat, or perhaps it is a drumbeat from the past or from the future, or perhaps it is the pulse of the earth, silent and yet beating, or it could be a bird's wings in the air, but it is there like a breeze whispering on my skin or like angel kisses perhaps, barely felt but felt. I am here, I say to myself, here. I am now. I am stretched between worlds and times. Then I think I must get new eyes to see this new world May has only sketched for me, and then I know I have new eyes, and that my heart beats everywhere at once: in Michael, in John Henry, in Mary, in May, in the wood of the tree that is a table now, in the center of the stone on which my feet rest. I am breath and breathless. I am sitting totally still, and yet somehow I am beyond where I have ever been. I am in a house in which all the doors of every room are being thrown open, and I am being invited in to each. I see light of varying hues pouring out from different doorways, and I am meant for each, to be touched by each; I am meant to cross thresholds and to stand before paintings and to touch the small and large articles sitting on tabletops and shelves. I am to fold into chairs and assume different positions on beds and couches covered in spreads and fabrics that are sunshine and night sky weavings of fabric meant to entice and welcome. I cannot see into these rooms, but I know what is in them.

I am a lady-warrior-wife-mom-sometimes-sister-person who teaches, and I am blood and bone and thought and spirit and May has called to me through a distance of time and space, and I have a journey to make. I have a box to find, a name to ask, and a father's past to discover, so I really should not be wandering around in my own head, but I am drawn to it, to this wandering, as I have always been. It is a welcomed embrace from my husband or a controlled fire beneath a sturdy hearth and contained by stone walls made to hold it. It is a good fire that draws me in and bathes me in warm light as it dances before me, and I am mesmerized and content, or perhaps I am only waiting patiently … to begin.

*   *   *   *

Michael is speaking my name, and I open my eyes, adjust my position in the chair, and shake my head a bit to restore order as if my thoughts are tiny beads in a game that when tilted resume assigned positions. I say, "Yes, yes, I am here."

I look into faces to read moods. Father Tom is relaxed but Michael is not. Michael is like he is when we are going camping. He wants a check list and all the necessary items lined up and ready for packing. I want to meet him half-way in this need he is feeling, so I ask, "Well, what do you think?"

He is running his hands through his hair as he responds, "Oh, I have to admit there is a veritable parking lot full of ideas in my head right now, and most of them are having fender-benders and some are unoccupied with motorists standing around wondering how they could have possibly locked the keys in the car." He pauses and then adds, "Yeah, I am basically clueless. Beyond the realization that I have married into a whacko family, I am pretty much out there on the lake in a boat with no frickin' paddle."

I have to stop him, so I smile and say, "Michael, I know you are only teasing me about my family, but you are mixing your metaphors a bit." He just looks at me as if I am beyond belief, so I just keep smiling.

Father Tom intervenes gently, "Perhaps we should allow ourselves some time to work through our own individual reactions before we discuss May's letter."

Michael's elbows are on the table, and he has his hands over his eyes as he responds, "Individual reactions? A time allowance? A discussion? This is just a tad more overwhelming than I thought it would be. Just a … tad. I was just a mile or so off the proverbial mark. And waiting to discuss is secondary to me wanting someone to shine a million watt light into the situation. Am I to understand my wife and I are supposed to involve ourselves in some sort of Star Trek adventure and visit other planets that aren't really planets in order to have some sort of family reunion with folks who have been dead for a billion years so that … ah yeah, here is the real clincher … May does not exactly enlighten us as to the purpose of our venture. Maybe letter two will fill in the gaping holes created by letter one." He pauses and looks at me, his hands in front of him on the table now, "So tell me, little Leah, what do you think of all this?"

I take his hands in mine and look into his eyes and say, "I love you, and I love the way you respond to things, because your reactions are always strong and clear and sometimes sort of funny and often impossible to predict. But May has laid an immense paint by the numbers canvas in front of us, and it has been a long day, and the night before was even longer, and I believe Father Tom is correct, and we should wait to discuss to allow our own personal reactions to settle."

Michael changes the positioning of our hands and holds my hands as he looks into my eyes, "Yeah, okay, good plan, but answer me first, and then we can leave. What do you think?"

"I will not explain this well, but I will do the best I can. It all makes perfect sense to me, Michael, even though I do not know what will happen next, or why any of it is happening, I am ready for it to happen. I am scared in a good way. Anticipation may be a better word, but there is a bit of fear there too, or perhaps it is only mystery, and there is actually no fear at all. Oh, I am not doing this well, but it is like … being comfortable not knowing." I stop because I know he does not understand what I am saying. I look at Father Tom and ask him to excuse the reference I am about to make, then I say, "It is like the first time we made love. I had no idea what was happening really. I had no idea how to handle the feelings I was feeling, or how I was supposed to react, but then suddenly I was not in my head anymore, and our being together was so natural, so 'the way it should be' that I was just in the moment one hundred percent. I felt like I was … home or something. And it was our first time; I had never been there before, in that place, but it was home. This feels like that to me, like I am home, like I have never been here before but somehow I will remember where everything is simply because I belong here, like I belong with you and you belong with me. That is what I think, Michael, and I do not have another way to explain it yet."

I can see he is done reacting now, has had his emotional response and is now the calm analytical Michael, the gentle almost-all-knowing-but-will-deal-with-it-husband-father-man. His voice and his eyes are gentle now, "I love you too, Leah. And your explanation makes as much sense as anything else I've heard tonight, so we'll wait and process and later we will discuss. I would, however, like to ask the good father one question." Michael turns to Father Tom and inquires, "If you are permitted, and if you know, can you tell me how much time this thing we are supposed to do will take?"

Father Tom shakes his head and replies, "Your primary involvement could take days or weeks or months."

Michael asks, "Why did you say 'primary involvement'?"

Father Tom stands and scoots his chair back as he replies, "Because, Michael, it will never really be over. Experiences are like that; they find a place in you, maintain a hold … forever."

Michael also stands and scoots his chair back as he says, "Forever?"

Father Tom smiles and nods his head, "There is no end."

Michael's eyes narrow as he ponders this, almost as if he wants to count on his fingers the incomprehensible equation he has been given, "No end?"

Father Tom puts his hand on Michael's shoulder, "Endless."

I am listening to them as I look out the window, and sitting where I am the window is no longer simply reflecting the room back into itself. There are moon and waves out there, and on the breeze an eagle floats effortlessly until it turns, and then mighty wings push against an invisible current, and the eagle cries out its song as it passes by the window over and over and over again.

✳   ✳   ✳   ✳

"Endless, the bullshit is endless, and I'm tired of it." Shay's uncharacteristic open expression of his thoughts, and more recently his anger, has added a new dimension to our family group discussions. Anytime a student's behavior changes, the group dynamic changes, which is, of course, true of any small group, be it a family or a small business. Because of Shay's change, Morgan is now the one who must attempt to moderate his own normally aggressive responses. None of us seem ready or willing to take up the glove thrown down and respond to Shay's words. Unlike Shay the rest of the group members seem to be feeling cautious and tentative.

The all school meeting was dramatic despite Lane's careful and calm relaying of some very general information regarding Teri's attempted suicide. Personal reactions varied based on what seemed to be the individual's relationship with Teri or on personal judgments about suicide. There was a definite mutual concern shared by all, and once the sea of students' raised hands calmed, Lane dismissed the all school meeting and asked that family groups meet immediately. I deem the current silence of my family group as the so called quiet before the storm, or perhaps it is more like flood waters of emotion building behind carefully constructed walls; someone's inner constraints are not going to hold. Shay is communicating his frustration; someone else's reaction will be more closely related to Teri's situation; someone else's heart will break open. I take a deep breath and try to marshal my own resources.

After my late night meeting with Michael and Father Tom, I feel rather drained emotionally. It is the type of morning in which I would have been better off doing simple tasks that did not involve other human beings, but I have no choice. Shay, believing perhaps we had not heard his comment, repeats himself, "Endless bullshit is what I am saying to you. We have to do something to stop it, now, before we all lose whatever amount of hope we have left."

I will not be the one who begins what has to happen, so I comment instead on an observation I remembered having the other day that might inadvertently connect us back to the subject that must be discussed, "Shay has said 'bullshit' a number of times. In family group I have noticed that some of you use words like that, but you never use that type of language in regular classes. Why is that?"

Shay is quick to respond, "Because cussing is an appropriate response to bullshit, and there is an endless stream of bullshit out there that we have to deal with on a continual basis."

Shay and I are looking at each other as I suggest, "You are doing it again, and you have not actually responded to my question. Perhaps someone else would like to try."

Tucker responds, "I'm thinking the cussing issue probably needs to be tabled for now, and we should maybe look at Shay's comment in response to Teri's situation."

Valerie is petting Samson's thick black and tan coat as she mentions that Jacy should probably be the one who shares first since she is Teri's roommate and also the one who discovered Teri before it was too late.

Aden comments next, "I agree with Valerie, but I also think that Mrs. C has asked us to do something, and she usually has a purpose for guiding us along in these talks we have, so I'm going to say that generally people use cuss words when situations are emotional. Of course, some people just cuss out of habit, which discounts their use as far as being meaningful."

Morgan raises his hand then looks at each of us before he says, "Shit, yeah. Out of habit, filled with emotion, or whatever, who cares? They're just words."

Angela shakes her head 'no' as she replies to Morgan's statement, "They may just be words, but they have a connotation. They have been deemed inappropriate, so some people use them simply for that reason, to be rebellious."

Charlie sighs, "Okay, so some people use them just because they're inappropriate, some people use them out of habit, some people use them when a situation is stressing them out in some way. I'm not the one who usually makes the connections in these discussions, but I think Mrs. C wants us to see choosing the types of words we use as personalized reactions. On a whole different level, suicide is a person choosing too."

Shay stands up then sits down again, "Suicide should not be a choice for anyone."

Charlie shrugs, "Yes, sir, Dictator Shay, tell us how life should be."

Shay is quick to respond, "You know I didn't say that to be a dictator. I said it because … suicide implies life is just not that damn important; it's disposable, has no value, and that's not true. Life is all important."

Angela nods in agreement, "Life is sacred, or at least it should be, but when in human history has life, all life, ever been considered sacred? Cultures create qualifications for sanctity. If a person has this color of skin or if a person believes in this type of faith or in this type of government then his or her life is sacred, but other people's lives that look differently aren't sacred. They become disposable."

Alana agrees, "Exactly, there are no absolutes in day-to-day living. There can't be. What's good for one person may not be good for another."

Aden shakes his head, "I disagree. Some things should be absolute. It is absolutely wrong to take life."

Shay laughs sarcastically, "Oh yeah, right, and what did you have for breakfast this morning? And what about war? And why are most Republicans against abortion and for the death penalty while most Democrats are against the death penalty but for abortion? The absolute sanctity of life is not even a political or cultural possibility. So if taking life is deemed appropriate by our culture, then our culture is advocating life's lack of essential value."

Jacy sighs, "And so people who try to take their own lives are just responding to their culture's overall disregard for the sanctity of life by killing themselves, admitting the hopelessness of being human. Is that what you're saying? And to what exactly did your 'bullshit' label apply? Teri's choice as an option? Teri doing what she did with no regard to how those who care about her would feel? What, Shay? What is the bullshit?"

The room is quiet. Shay and Jacy are looking into each other's eyes, and it is obvious Shay is taking time to think about his answer to Jacy's question. He begins to speak two or three different times but does not utter two or three words before he stops himself. He rubs his face with his hands and leans back as he responds, "Did she even try to talk to you about how she was feeling? Did she give any of us a chance to help her? No, she didn't. She didn't speak with Mrs. C or Mr. Danner or Mrs. Carson. She didn't, or she would have been being monitored. She just decided she was done trying. She gave up not only on herself but on all of us. Suicide is a selfish act and only a person who doesn't give a rip about anyone else could even consider it. Screw all the philosophical crap, suicide is wrong, absolutely wrong. It should never be an option. Never."

Jacy leans her head back against the couch and closes her eyes as she speaks quietly, "I've been on both sides of the suicide thing now, and I'm not pretending to know exactly how Teri was feeling or is feeling, but I know how I was feeling when I did the same thing … when I took a knife out of my mother's kitchen drawer, sat on the white couch in our living room, and cut my wrists. I remember feeling nothing at all. It was just a movie I was watching, and I didn't care how it ended. I remember what I was feeling when I decided to kill myself too. I was feeling like it didn't really matter if I lived or died, and that the people who loved me or cared about me would be better off without me. I wasn't aware of being selfish. To be selfish a person has to value who he or she is, and I placed no value on myself. Granted, I gave no one else's feelings any value either, but that wasn't out of selfishness, it was out of hopelessness, and like we've talked about before, emotions aren't controllable a lot of the time, but our reactions to them are. My reaction to my total lack of hope was to end my life, to stop it, to make not only the problems but also myself go away."

Jacy leans forward now her eyes focused on some inner horizon none of us can see, "Desperation is a powerful, consuming, obliterating emotion. I didn't know how to speak of it to others. It was too big, too overwhelming, too numbing. I can look back and see that now, but then, I couldn't see anything at all, feel anything at all except the desperate hopeless certainty that my feelings would always be more than I could possibly handle. How I made my mom and dad feel, and how I made my grandparents and my friends feel weren't considered. I had tunnel vision; I had no peripheral vision at all, and I had no words left to explain to myself or others. I didn't want to be me anymore. I cut my wrists and watched the blood flow out of me without any regard for how my dad and mom would feel when they found me. But now I know how they must have felt, because I know how I felt when I found Teri."

Tears fill Jacy's eyes as she continues, "Desperation is definitely contagious. I was overwhelmed when I saw her and what she had done, totally overwhelmed, because standing there in that doorway I knew suicide should never be an option; there is always hope, even when it seems out of reach, but I was just an observer this time, I was not Teri; I was not the desperate one this time, not the hopeless one. So maybe discussions of right or wrong aren't the discussions we should be having. Maybe we should be asking ourselves how to be better friends, more caring human beings. Maybe the only way to make suicide a non-option is on a personal level. Maybe blaming suicide on culture is just a way of distancing it from ourselves. Maybe we should, as individuals, become more accountable in our spheres of influence and not depend on governments or cultures to enforce personal morality."

The room is still and quiet, but Jacy's words and emotions echo between us. Shay is the first to speak, "I didn't know you had ... tried to do the same thing Teri did. You can see it from a perspective I don't have. I appreciate you sharing with us something so personal."

Jacy tries to smile but shakes her head instead, "Something so ugly."

I comment, "That is a word Teri used about herself, ugly."

Maddie has tears in her eyes as she comments, "I would rather people use cuss words than some of the words that are considered okay to use."

Valerie offers, "Like stupid."

Aden adds, "Sissy."

Morgan sighs, "Name calling and labeling suck."

Everyone looks at me as Morgan says his last word, because they know I dislike it greatly. I shake my head, "Words have such power. They can lift us up or demolish us, but we throw them around so carelessly. They create images in our minds, find places in our hearts, last beyond their moments. They shape us. And how 'suck' has possibly become ... fashionable for so many I will never understand, but I do not want us to become distracted."

Valerie comments, "Even calling people an appropriate label can be hurtful. I'm blind, and I know it, but the way some people say the word makes me feel like I'm of less value than someone who sees."

Charlie agrees with her, "Yeah, like why some people think that every single damn thing they notice should shoot out of their mouths with no consideration as to how the comment is going to make another person feel always gets me, but the looks people give each other can be just as bad."

Jacy stands and looks at each one of us and then says, "I feel like I have to do this now, or I'll lose my nerve. I want to do what you always tell us to do, Mrs. C; I want to put what I've done in the light and let it go completely. I want to proclaim where I've been, so I can move on." She pauses and although I am not sure what she is planning, I smile and nod to encourage her, and she continues, "My name is Jacy, and I am recovering from trying to take my own life and from an eating disorder."

As difficult as it is to do what she is doing, I need her to finish, so I ask, "And?" Jacy thinks for a moment, but is struggling, so I remind her of how she feels about how she affected her parents.

"Right, I'm going to start again." Jacy again looks at the members of the group as she states clearly and strongly, "My name is Jacy, and I am recovering from trying to take my own life and from an eating disorder and from feeling guilty about hurting my parents."

Although having students openly label themselves based upon their past mistakes is not something we advocate at Dayton School, what Jacy is doing feels right to me, and I wonder if the rest of them will let her stand there alone. It does not take long at all for Shay to stand, but after he stands he pauses, puts his hands in his pockets, takes them out again, and then he looks at each person in the group as he says, "I'm Shay. In the two years I've been here, I've gone from not letting myself feel anything to feeling very pissed off. My parents and my little brother were killed by a drunk driver, and I don't really think I've even started to recover yet." He pauses again then adds, "But I will."

Alana is next to stand, but she does not make eye contact with the group. She stares out the window as she barely whispers, "I'm me, Alana Sayles, and I … started lying to cover up my drinking, and then I … started lying about just about everything." She pauses, looks down at her hands that are clinched in front of her, then she looks into the faces of the people who surround her, "I'm still an alcoholic, but I'm not drinking today, and I don't lie anymore."

Neil rises slowly from his place on the floor. He seems to unfold gradually from his sitting position to his towering six feet-two inch height. He looks into my eyes as he quietly and carefully enunciates each syllable of each word he says, "Alcohol, drugs … using and selling, gambling, those are the things I did. I made my dad ashamed to be my dad, and I was a bad example for my little step-brothers. I said mean things to my step-mom. I used people to get what I wanted. I'm Neil Cameron, and I want to be different now; I want to be who I really am, I want to make amends or peace or something so I can go forward, start fresh."

Charlie stands next to Neil and acknowledges each member of the group with his eyes, "I am Charles Darrell Abbott. I used to describe myself as just being a drug user, but after listening to Jacy I think maybe I was using drugs like Teri used that piece of broken mirror, like Jacy used the knife. I didn't like myself, so I was just killing myself slowly. I wrecked a lot of relationships, lost friends, but my family sent me here. They didn't give up on me, so there must be something to like. I'm here to learn to care about myself, and then maybe I'll be better at caring about others. I wish I would've talked to Teri more."

Valerie stands next and Samson, who was sitting next to her, stands also. She bends down and buries her face in Samson's fur as she hugs him, and when she is standing before us again there are tears in her eyes. As she speaks one tear makes its way down her cheek, "I'm Valerie Hanlin. I'm blind because my mom hit me, and I fell ... hit my head. I need to stop hating her for that and a thousand other things she did, and sometimes I can, but I want to be able to see and do the things I used to do. I want to see the sky and the ocean and the trees. I miss seeing my own face and being able to look into the eyes of others. I can't forgive my mom for very long, but I'm trying. Not being able to see sometimes makes me feel lonely, but I am getting better at being a blind person. I guess I also have to stop asking God why this had to happen to me."

Tucker stands next. He looks at me then down at the floor again, "I'm Tucker. I don't talk much. I guess I'm shy. My dad told me it was okay not to have anything to say, but the problem is ... I do have things to say ... I have a lot of things to say, a lot of ideas about things, but I think people won't be interested." Tucker looks at Alana then back at me as he speaks, "I guess I'm afraid or something, which doesn't make any sense, but it's how I feel sometimes. So, I need to get over being afraid people won't like me and just say what's on my mind." Tucker pauses again, then a slow smile appears on his face as he adds, "I didn't want to go last, because that's a shy sort of thing to do, so I said my part now."

There are smiles of encouragement for Tucker as Maddie stands and smoothes her long black hair back from her face. "I'm Maddie Braff. I had a skiing accident, and my brain was damaged. I have a damaged brain. That's such a weird thing to say, but it's true. I can't think straight, go from one idea to another, sometimes. I forget things like where I'm going, what I've read, what someone just said. I even forget how I feel about something. I order food I don't like because I forget I don't like it. I bought the same outfit two days in a row. Sometimes my memories get all mixed up, and I don't remember what I did the day before. It made my old friends uncomfortable to be around me. That hurt, and I didn't know what to do, so my parents brought me here to see if I wanted to try something new, and also to get help with how to deal with my problem. So, here I am ... I hope I haven't forgotten anything I needed to say."

Alana reassures Maddie as Aden stands. "I'm Aden, and I was sick a lot as a kid. I missed a lot of school. I couldn't do most of the things 'normal' kids do. That's how I thought of it, I wasn't a normal kid. What made it worse was when I did go to school, some kids went out of their way to make fun of me, call me names, push me around. I was small and not strong, but I'm getting bigger and stronger now, and I am trying to trust people again. I guess that's it really; I need to learn how to trust that most people aren't total assholes." He pauses, looks down then up again and says, "Oh, and I guess there could be some anger issues I need to work on too."

Morgan stands, and looks at each one of us very intently. "I beat up a friend. I beat him up so badly he had to go to the hospital. He had to have operations. I wrecked his face, broke his ribs, there was internal damage too. I beat him up, because I felt like beating someone up, and he made a comment I didn't like, so I used it for an excuse. I hurt him bad for no good reason. I just did it 'cause I felt like it. I couldn't stop hitting him once I got started, and they had to pull me off of him once he was on the ground. Then I started hitting whoever I could. I didn't care. The cops took me to jail because I committed a violent crime, and it wasn't the first time. It was the worst I'd ever done though, and they locked me up for it." Morgan looks down now but continues speaking, "If I could go back and undo the hurt I caused I would, but I can't." Morgan looks directly into my eyes as he says, "Just like you and the other teachers tell us, Mrs. C, our response to the things we've done should be our focus. I don't ever want to hurt anyone again. My name is Morgan, and I have to let go of my guilt every single damn day."

Angela stands, starts to sit again but then stands and speaks quietly, "I am Angela Maria Pertoni. I was a model. I traveled all over: New York, Paris, London, Rome, Buenos Aires, Los Angeles. I was so busy, and I didn't want to disappoint anyone, but it got to be too much. I started so young and then worked steady until I was thirteen, and that's all I knew really. Work, always looking good, exercising, eating right, trying to study between shoots and on airplanes. Holidays were my only real family times. It was crazy. It made me crazy, I guess. The hard work and the unhealthy behavior of some of the people with whom I worked just got to me, and one day I just sort of stopped. I froze during a photo shoot, and I didn't unfreeze for almost a year. They called it a nervous breakdown. I was thirteen … it's too bizarre really. After the breakdown or whatever it was, I was different. I am different. I'm shy or something about being in front of people. Standing up like this is not comfortable, but I know I need to do it, so I am. Anyway, after the hospital, my parents asked me what I wanted to do, and at first I didn't really know, but then I remembered this place. I had been through Lane one time; we had even taken some photos here, and I'd heard about the school. I didn't really know much about the town except that I loved the way the mountains and the ocean sort of turned into each other. I loved the trees and … well, I'm not really sure, but my parents made some calls and here I am. I've been here three years now, and it's the first place that has ever really felt like home to me. There are whole parts of my life I don't remember anymore, and some people, like my parents, believe I should work to remember, but I don't want to really. I just want to be here and do well and then maybe become a veterinarian, but I don't think I should have to remember if I don't want to remember, and I guess that's it."

I stand now, and I look into each one of their young faces, and I feel so proud of who they are, so hopeful about who they are becoming, and during moments like this I fall in love over and over again with their honesty and their open hearted desire to trust despite so many reasons not to trust. I take a deep breath and speak of my own past, "I am Leah, and I lost my family, except my brother, to a fire when I was ten. Many people offered me love and support, but the world became such a dark, mysterious place to me that offering my love to someone became impossible. I just went into my own head, kept company with my own thoughts, because I believed if I loved anyone else that something bad would happen to that person too, but the people who cared about me did not give up. My brother and I were brought here, to this school, and this became our home. After a few years I began to believe I could care for someone and that person would not die or be taken away from me. So, obviously, we all have pasts, but we also all have presents and futures, and we are not alone, and that makes just about every good thing imaginable possible." I pause and smile to reassure them. "Let's sit again, and unless someone would like to add to what's been said or have some time right now to write in his or her journal, let's decide how we can best support Teri."

The group decides to journal write later, and then there are suggestions made regarding welcoming Teri home and trying to make her feel comfortable. Jacy takes notes as hospital visits are scheduled, different students volunteer to get make-up work from various teachers, and a sleepover is planned for my house when Teri feels up to it. I remind them to write in their journals, and that our family group is signed up for the ropes course on Friday. Some of them stay where they are, while others move to different places in the room for their journal writing. "Take your time; you have over an hour before classes start. If you want to go get your lunch and bring it up here you may. And thank you for being open with each other and with me today. I am proud of you." There are various responses to my comment; some are sincere and some are humorous, which is often a nice mix.

I sit down at my desk, and my eyes seek the comfort provided by the photo of my family standing with me in front of a Christmas tree adorned with our traditional ornaments plus tiny Mary made stars and careful one by one John Henry placements of tinsel. We are all smiles and arms holding, and I am in that moment again. I am drawn back and refreshed by their closeness even as we are separated from each other. I am … in my head again, and I cannot be. I need to add comments in my family group members' personal files. So I do that. I am quick and efficient and quite business like, not stopping as I usually do to wonder about this or that and then wander on from there to somewhere else. Nope, not today, today, within this moment, I am Leah, the efficient non-daydreamer. Then I realize I am daydreaming about not being a daydreamer, so I take out my lesson plan for my next class and try to focus.

Motivations of the Modern Poet is the title of the class. Its purpose is to unearth writer's purpose. We ask 'why' a lot, and then do wild uninhibited searches in the library. Some of us use the 'net' to search deep waters; some of us would rather bend down to low shelves or climb up ladders to tall stacked shelves and smell the winter closeness of old pages or the spring crispness of new pages. I am tactical in my searching; I want to bend and climb and dig through and open and close. The net is too finely woven with reliable and unreliable threads. There is no sensory draw for me on the net. It is a television with brains, and I cannot love it, and it cannot love me, but books call to me, and then I hold them like shells up to my ear, and I belong; I become a part of, I become … earth and air and water and … fire.

Chapter THREE

"There are too many things happening at once, too many lights tearing through the darkness. I am all alone, but surrounded by phantom loved ones with the features of their faces drawn down, as if they are melting in the heat, and I know I can only save them by saving me, even as the fire seeks to burn them. To me the flames reach out barely, just fingertips, blackened red nails searing quick touches. I cannot breathe. I must hold my breath, find a way out before my lungs force my lips open for air, but this air will not be welcome, will not bless but will instead destroy by degree. I can see a window across this room that is contorted and twisting in the deadly dance of flames, and outside, through the window, I can see avocado-green grass and above it an eye-blue sky with snow-white clouds floating, and I am trying to run there through leaping slashes of fire. I am moving in slow motion, but my heart is racing, and my name is being called out from a distance, but the fire is relentless and demanding and whispers into me distractions and oblivions and threatens dark recourses if I do not lay down with it and let it have its way with me. But I know I must push through and go directly toward the deep drawing of blue and the cool freshness of green. I am almost there, and I can almost sense the coolness of snow-white clouds, until a hand and an arm appear through the window. The flames are small beneath it, but intensify as the hand and arm reach farther in for me, and I can see the tiny hairs on the arm coil and melt from the heat, and then I know terror as I believe the flesh of that arm I recognize will be eaten by the always voracious flames, so I open my lips and suck the air out of the room and the fire dies instantly. As I walk the rest of the way to the window I become an eagle and fly through the window up into the sky, and beneath me I see you waving at me with your good arm while May is putting cool cloths on the arm that almost burned. John Henry and May are waving also, but then I notice May is half buried in the ground. So I circle back with wide wings to make her whole, but she disappears beneath the soil before I can reach her, and suddenly I become human again, yet I am still in the air, and now you are running to catch me, but my fall is faster than your dash to rescue, so I dive into the ground, fingers pointed and arms straight as I pass through grass and soil and even rock before I enter the basement of my family's old house, and there May sits on the edge of her hope chest that was to be mine, and in her hands is the metal box I saw often but never saw opened. As soon as my feet touch the floor, I am back up through rock and soil and grass again, and you and John Henry and Mary grab hold of me, and finally I stop moving as we lay on the grass together and stare up into a night sky full of bright stars. Staccato frog talk and the blinking stars seem timed perfectly, and you and John Henry and Mary and I cuddle up together and fall asleep."

Michael and I are almost nose to nose as we whisper talk. We are pre-dawn, and there is only a glimmer of light in the darkness. May said this barely perceivable light was the business of angels who heralded the sun's approach, and that the light was from their wings. 'They are everywhere,' she would say to me, 'everywhere and always, but our eyes aren't trained to see them, so we don't. We just get glimmers of them, like tiny breezes on our cheeks. It reminds me of fairy dust, which would make sense, since the business of angels and the business of fairies tend to overlap more often than not.' Michael's eyes draw me back, and I say to him, "What was your dream?"

"It was short, only three or four images, but over and over again. I would wake up in the night then fall back asleep and have the dream again. First there is just an eagle flying through day sky then through night sky. I must be on the ground because it flies between me and the stars and between me and the clouds, and I had to be keeping up with it, running under it or something like that because it did not turn; it just flew … through time, I guess, because the sky changed. Then the eagle would fly down to earth, to something some distance away from me and begin eating whatever was on the ground. The distance between me and the eagle lessened but very gradually, as if I was walking forward very slowly. The eagle was moving around and over the object, stretching out its wings slowly then closing them, bending its head down to tear off a portion of whatever was on the ground. I couldn't see the object clearly, and there was no blood, no ripping sounds, nothing to make me want to turn away at all. Everything about the image seemed natural, sort of like it should be. Then the eagle would turn, look into my eyes, take a few steps toward me, flap its wings once or twice and return to the air again. Then I would turn and follow it again, but only after I had turned once to look back at the object on the ground, and where it had been there was a tree instead, but not exactly like any tree I've ever seen before. It sort of reminded me of a Mountain Ash, but it was different. And the tree in my dreams would go through the seasons, changing from one to the next in a … well, heartbeat, and then I would blink or something and it would be gone, and the object was still on the ground where it had been, so I would turn and follow the eagle again. And again the same cycle would happen, except maybe the whole thing took less time as it repeated itself, or something like that, because the pace seemed like it quickened."

There is a memory in me that is stirring, but it is too vague to know yet, so I ask, "How did the tree look?"

Michael closes his eyes for a moment then says, "It was deciduous because it lost its leaves in winter. The bark of the tree was smooth and the color reddish. In late spring or maybe early summer it was beautiful with small white flower clusters, and then later it had what looked like tiny red apples on it or maybe they were berries. In fall its leaves were scarlet red and sort of a golden pink. It wasn't a big tree, and in the dream it started small and grew until it was maybe twenty to thirty feet tall. Does that sound familiar?"

I whisper, "Yes."

Michael's lips find mine in our closeness and as he barely brushes my lips with his, he says, "Tell me."

"May used to tell me about a tree called the Rowan, and we had rowan tea all the time. For the Celts, and for other cultures too, it was considered a sacred tree. Ancient burial sites and ceremonial places, circles of stone, mound hills, many of those have rowans in them or by them. I am trying to remember what she said. The Druids would use fires of rowan wood before battles, and they would also use the wood for making runes, wands, talismans, and spindles for weaving. Later, after the Christians came, crosses were made from rowan wood as a protection against all forms of witchcraft. The crosses were tied with red ribbon, if I remember correctly."

Michael's expression is thoughtful, and then he smiles, "Father Tom was right; this could be an interesting experience, and one thing is for sure," he pauses for effect then continues, "we won't have to rent movies anymore. Our dreams can be our entertainment."

"I believe the dreams are more than entertainment, Michael."

"I know they are, but it's morning, and I am trying to keep things light and positive. We can do research and have serious discussions later."

I kiss him now, just a light and positive sort of kiss, just a brush of lips against lips, nothing deep and searching, nothing hungry. We had family bed last night, so Mary sleeps next to me and John Henry sleeps next to Michael. After dinner and dinner clean up and baths and showers, all four of us climbed into pajamas and then into our big bed for talk-time and read or tell a story time and then fall asleep together time. It is one of our favorite family traditions, and one that is made more special by the sad but necessary fact it will not last forever, or even a lifetime, but instead the memories of it will be gently stored away in the memory places of our minds, like much loved old teddies and much used ABC and picture books are stored away into cedar chests and carefully taped cardboard boxes and placed in attics or basements.

I think aloud now, offer up the natural and unedited procession of my thoughts to Michael, "Perhaps our big houses and their assortment of rooms have aided the distances we have between each other as people and family members. I wonder what it would be like to live fully in one room like the people of times past, breathing into and out of each other always."

Michael rubs his nose against mine, "Well, I don't mind telling you that I wouldn't be in favor of that at all; it would play hell on the sex life."

I smile and say, "Yes, there is that to consider."

"Heck yeah, there is that to consider. Man does not live by bread alone, you know? Of course, bread is good," and now Michael smiles suggestively but not sexually at all.

"You are wanting breakfast, I believe."

"Yes, woman, breakfast, and sooner than later would be good, so jump to it. Climb over these lazy children and feed your husband."

"Vegetarian fare is all I will prepare, so if you want to consume the dead flesh of animals, you will have to come and help, husband."

"I definitely want the dead flesh stuff, and in the form of sizzling bacon, so I'll be forced to join you since you refuse to be a good wife and make me what I want."

Despite the motivated language, neither of us move. We are too comfortable, too cozy, and then John Henry's voice joins ours as he comments on our morning banter, "How is a kid supposed to get his sleep with all this talk?"

Michael rolls over and wraps his arms around John Henry and then rolls back over and deposits our sleep-mellow son between us. We both nuzzle our faces against his shoulder and neck, and John Henry, of course, does his part and starts to wiggle and shake all over as he calls out to no one in particular, "Help, help, scratchy beard and morning breath attack. Help! Help!" As I crawl out of bed, Mary giggles and rolls into my vacated spot. I slip my feet into slippers and turn to watch the mock wrestling match before I leave to begin the morning ritual of food preparation and the ushering in of our day. At the same time I send a tiny strand of thank you prayer up into the arms of a creator god who must be smiling. I think then, how could God not smile? We must look like a field of bright flowers to him ... or to her ... or ... to him and to her ... or ... I stop myself, and simply say thank you Lord, thank you.

✳   ✳   ✳   ✳

I am on a lush carpet of mint-green grass sitting beneath the wide reaching branches of a tall tree that stands beneath a deep sky of slowly drifting whiter than white clouds. I am an observer of students walking and talking and of the Dayton School hounds running and sniffing and announcing their gladness for the perfect day with a happy bark here and there to punctuate their boundless enjoyment of the simple things like breezes and vegetation bathed in sunshine and shade. Father Tom and I sit together in a comfortable silence.

He had called mid-morning to invite me to share a lunch of tomato and cucumber and lettuce on fresh brown wheat bread. He had suggested a picnic venue and a bit of talk. I agreed, and here I am. After we exchanged greetings and while we ate I described Michael's dream and my dream. Father Tom did not respond immediately, and we sit now within the secure but open embrace of the moment as I wait for him to express his thoughts.

He begins slowly and thoughtfully, "I am thinking back to pages I have turned and to my actual times spent in Ireland. I can see the tree in a variety of forms. And its relevance to different cultures is also in a variety of forms. A charmed tree, the rowan, and more than that also. A tree of power it is. And the eagle too is a powerful image. My first thoughts are not Celtic in origin but Greek. Of course, I should mention that some rather studious fellows believe the Tuatha De Danaan did indeed come to Ireland from certain Greek islands, so perhaps the distinction of origin implies less diversity than one might assume. In either case, these ancients believed an eagle fought a mighty battle against evil demons to save the elixir of life. From the eagle's blood and its feathers that fell to the ground the rowan tree was created. The rowan's feathery leaves and its berries of blood red symbolize the blood and feathers of the eagle. The Tuatha De Danaan believed the eagle was a symbol of the great cycle that is life and death, and that each is born out of the other. As the eagle eats death so life is made from death and so on. There are stories in the Irish and the Scandinavian telling of the origin of man from the Ash tree and the origin of woman from the rowan tree. The tree is also connected to the goddess Brigantia, called Brigid or Bride in Ireland."

I interrupt, "Bride like in MacBride?" Father Tom looks into my eyes and nods his head yes.

"And what do you know about the great Brigid?"

"Since I am sure you know more than I do, Father, why don't you tell me what you know about her."

"I can do that to be sure. I could write books on her, perhaps even fill a small library with what she and her descendants have accomplished, but I will only … sketch her for you now, give you a bit of insight, because you will want to be learning about her on your own soon, I think." He pauses to wave at a passing student and then continues, "Her story varies from source to source, so what I share with you is based on what I believe to be true; you and Michael may decide to make your own investigations, unearth your own truths about her. I will speak first of her father. He is Dagda, the 'Good God' and the head of the pantheon of Irish immortals. His cauldron or kettle is always full of food, and his mighty club can both destroy and restore life. I believe he epitomizes all that is truly Irish, and his daughter does the same. Dagda and Danu, the mother goddess, are the parents of Brigid, who is the patron of poets, the goddess of healing and fertility and of spinning and weaving. The spindles used for spinning were made from the rowan tree, and spinning is also symbolic of the unending tapestry of life. Interestingly, her symbol is fire. There are some who believe she has two sisters who are also called Brigid, but they are treated as one entity. For Celts all over Europe she is the goddess of the pastoral, which makes sense, because her father is seen as the guardian of nature. I should also point out that Tuatha De Danaan means people of Danu, and Danu is Brigid's mother, which implies the significance of Brigid to her people."

We are quiet again as I try to connect this new information with prior knowledge, because when I do not do this process of attaching 'new to old', I forget ideas I do not want to forget. Offspring-questions always seem to birth themselves through this combining. "So, Brigid was also called Bride by the Irish?"

"Yes, and she was called Brigindo in France. There are scholars who believe Saint Brigit never actually existed, and Celtic Christians simply turned the goddess Brigid into a saint so they would not have to lose her as the faith of the culture changed."

I am not going to be distracted from the direction I want the conversation to go, "That is understandable, but what interests me at this point is the name MacBride. It means son of or children of Bride, right?"

"Correct."

I have an inkling of sorts and decide to try to accomplish one of my to-do items from May's list so I ask, "Since we are on the subject of names and have established my connection to Brigid, if my name means anything, what is your last name, Father Tom? Why have you kept it such a secret for so long?"

He is smiling and nodding his head as he offers his hand to me in greeting, "Thomas MacBride Sullivan at your service, ma'm."

"Are we related?"

"Distantly, but, yes, we are.

"You are of the Tuatha De Danaan also?"

"I am."

"We are of Brigid?"

"We are."

"Oh, my goodness."

"Yes, goodness has much to do with it."

✳   ✳   ✳   ✳

I am at the house that is not a house anymore. John Henry and Mary are on either side of me. We are fingers through chain link fence and faces pressed up against the same, so that we look like we wear masks of diamond shaped cutouts. We are looking and waiting. Puppy is marking boundaries he has marked count-less times before but enjoying it nonetheless. At least once a month I come to this place and stand as I am standing and peer into the past and think dark and hope-ful 'what-if' thoughts. What if there had been no fire? What if there had been a fire, but they had escaped? What if Grant and I had been with them instead of sent elsewhere while they met to talk of what? What if …?

It was unusual to be sent elsewhere; children are not normally sent 'elsewhere' in this town. Children are included, talked over as if they are not there or encour-aged to join in conversations. But that night we had been sent to the Danner's house. Bradley and his older brother, Joe, and his younger brother, Calvin, ordered pizzas and Grant and I ate with them and played board games. Pastor and Mrs. Danner went to my house, and I went to theirs. I lived and they didn't. The Danner boys lost their parents, and the local nondenominational commu-nity church lost its pastor. Despite the efforts of the firemen, the house burned to the ground, and the basement almost filled itself with what fell. Only in the last few years have I allowed myself to wonder why there was no attempt to find human remains, no attempt to justify the fire at all.

I remember that two days after the destructive blaze tore my life to pieces it rained for three days straight. A week or so later a bull dozer came and scraped the ground and what little remained of the house's foundation into the gaping hole that had been the basement, scraping and filling, scraping and filling, until the lot was level. The chain link fence went up a few days after that and ever since then every month or so I would find myself where I am now, standing, fingers poked through and face pressed up against thin strands of cold metal. I stand here where so much has changed and yet within my heart so much remains the same, and I notice each time how new growth springs up here and there, but still the raw singed smell of a burning remains, or perhaps I just imagine, even after years and years, that the flames still linger, still reach out.

Shadow and light and darkness live here too. They do as they always do when someone is about, but when no one is around I know they must throw themselves down upon the earth and cry out their separate laments as I have longed to do, beating their fists against ground that only thinks of recovery, of redeeming itself. Within the well protected confines of my thoughts I have thrown myself down and beat my fists against the relentless cycling of earth and against the quick current of life and against the still silent tomb of death, but I know I cannot allow my body to depict these emotions. They are buried too deep. I would have to tear myself open to allow them to express themselves, so I do not permit my body and its emotions to become involved in the devastating fall and climb of full and uninhibited mourning. I do not—.

"Mommy, are you sad?" Mary's voice is a fresh breeze whispering me back.

I gather her up into my arms, "Being here only makes me think sad thoughts, flower, but I am not sad."

She kisses my cheek, "I'm glad, mommy, because I don't want you to be sad."

John Henry puts his hand on my arm, and I bend down to him as Mary wraps arms and legs around me securely. "Does it make you lonely, mom, being here?"

My boy-man has an old soul, I think to myself and not for the first time, as I wrap an arm around his shoulders, "A bit lonely, yes, but you make me not lonely, so it balances out, you know?"

His young eyes are searching mine, "I don't think being with one person can take the place of missing another one."

I try to stay open to his search. I try to keep my heart open to his inquiry despite a desire to back away emotionally and to break the eye contact, but I must honor his sincerity although I am unclear how to explain to him how his comments are making me feel, so I try to paint a picture for him. "This feels like ... you are a gentle healer who is touching a bruised place, trying to figure out what is wrong, trying to help the situation and maybe even helping the situation, but the place you are touching is tender and even the one who is hurt does not really know what it is exactly that is causing the pain. Does that make any sense?"

John Henry is thoughtful and does not respond immediately, so Mary fills in the silence by saying, "I don't like bruises at all."

John Henry tilts his head to one side and puts his hand on my cheek and whispers, "Bruises shouldn't last forever, mom."

I put my hand over his and move his palm to my lips and kiss it. "You are a wise old man, and I believe things will be happening that will help me feel better, maybe not right away, and maybe not easily, but down the road a bit, I will be better."

He nods his head and says, "I believe that, and I will help if I can."

"You already have, son, just by being who you are," and I pause as Mary wiggles free, and I say to her, "And you too, little miss. It is good to share your heart sometimes, so ..." and now I stand with my hands on my hips and smile as I say to them both, "thank you, thank you very much, thank you very very much, thank you very very very much...." I continue saying the phrase, adding a 'very' each time, as they put their hands over their ears and run around in circles telling me to stop repeating myself, but I do not. Puppy joins in the running in circles, and this is the scene Father Tom and Matilda and Michael see as Michael pulls my Jeep into what used to be the driveway of this house that is not a house anymore.

✳   ✳   ✳   ✳

John Henry and Mary follow Puppy to the Jeep where Michael has opened Matilda's door for her. The children wait patiently for Matilda to get both of her small feet on the ground, and then they wrap their arms around her, welcoming their great grandmother enthusiastically but gently. Father Tom has walked behind the Jeep and is throwing a stick for Puppy. While Matilda is asking John Henry and Mary about their day, Michael walks over to me, and now it is my turn to be wrapped in arms and welcomed enthusiastically but gently. We whisper into each other.

"Wife."

"Husband."

"Sometimes you take my breath away."

"I would have it no other way since sometimes you take my breath away."

"We're a perfect match."

"Yes, Michael, we are, you and I, well matched."

He bends me back as if we are dancing and then brings me up again, just as Puppy drops his somewhat slobbery stick at Michael's feet. "Others want my attention now, woman, you'll have to share me."

"It will not be easy, but I will, for the moment, share you."

Michael picks up Puppy's stick and turns to throw it as I walk over to Matilda and the kids.

Even as I must bend to kiss Matilda's soft cheek, she greets me with the same endearment she has used since she had to bend down to kiss me. "Hello, little one, I am enjoying your children."

"Yes," I respond, "I have a tendency to do the same. They are difficult to resist, but I could, of course, be biased in the matter."

"Not a bit of that now. All children should be enjoyed, but all children are not as easy to enjoy as yours, so you are not biased." She counters and then adds, "You and Michael have raised them well."

Mary and John Henry reclaim Matilda's attention. I walk toward Father Tom, who is just beyond the fence on the other side of the property. The closer I am to him the more I notice the tree that is the focus of his attention. His arm goes around me as I come to stand next to him.

I look first at the tree and then at him. He is looking at me, and there are tears in his eyes. "I planted this for you and for Grant after the fence went up when I knew its roots would be undisturbed. It is a—"

I finish his sentence for him, "… a rowan tree."

"A rowan of twenty years, and over a foot a year it's grown."

"It is beautiful, Father, thank you."

"One day, I will bring your brother here too and share it with him. For him it will be only a tree as memorial, but it's more than that for you, isn't it?"

"It is the tree of Michael's dream."

"It is more than that, child, much more, but you will come to know that, and then we will stand here again together, and share all that it is between us, and that will make this old heart glad."

I can only respond to the depth of emotion I can hear in Father Tom's words and can see on his face, since the significance of the tree is beyond me. Remembering what he shared with me earlier in the day gives my thoughts a direction in which to wonder, but I can go no farther than that. I hold Father Tom's hand in mine and thank him again for his thoughtfulness. Then I give words to a subject I have only kept to myself before this moment.

"I thought no one did anything for them."

He turns me and holds me by my shoulders, "You must remember how young you were when this happened, and you must realize how reluctant you were to speak of it in any way with anyone. Grant was always quite self-contained emotionally, so even though he was older, he too maintained a guarded silence with us. We decided then to do what needed to be done and what should be done without discussing it with either of you, since that seemed to be both of your preferences. A week or so before Grant left for college he met with Lane and with me and told us he would not be returning here except to visit occasionally. We asked him if he wanted to know more about the tragedy which had torn so many of his loved ones from him, but he said he was done with all that. He assured us that he trusted our judgment in the matter and wanted to move on in his life. We honored his choice. He signed the necessary documents regarding this property, and you are its owner. The money left to you and to Grant had been divided equally years before, and each of you had an account at the local bank. Grant closed his account years ago after transferring his funds to his own account in Seattle. Your account is still where it has always been and still untouched."

"I have an account I do not even know I have?"

"Yes."

"And when was I going to be told?"

"When you started acting like you wanted to know."

"Touché."

"There is no blame being cast here, Leah, but until you indicated to us you were interested in what happened, we had no desire to reopen areas of your life you had declared closed by your own behavior." As I am watching him, he seems to be watching Matilda. When her eyes meet his, he nods, and then he goes through the same process with Michael.

While his behavior unnerves me a bit, I do not concentrate on it. Instead, I have turned my focus inward, and I am searching my own feelings about what he has shared with me. My thoughts I do not need to search. I want to know everything. I want to know everything down to the smallest detail, but my feelings are less distinguishable. They are too numerous and are behaving like wild children. They are each demanding attention and fight for first position in a manner denying the possibility of there being a first position; they are everywhere. I am not pleased. I am ashamed. I am sad. I am betrayed. I am defensive. I am hurt. I may even be angry. I am … ten years old again, and I can see clearly what I did back then when emotions like these were overwhelming me. I opened a door, wide and tall and of dark dense wood, and when I had succeeded in rounding up my discordant and elbowing changelings, I closed the door. I can also see clearly a younger Father Tom approaching me and bending down to comfort me, offering me an opportunity to speak of my feelings and of my thoughts, but I had already marked my thoughts my own, and I had already dealt with my emotions in my own way. I can see the scenes so clearly. I may have been small, but I would not allow myself to be influenced or intimidated, and I may have been young, but I was completely determined to control my own life despite life's fiery demonstration that I had no control.

Father Tom's hands are still on my shoulders, and I have been looking down at the ground between us. It is only when I raise my eyes to his that he pulls me close and holds me. "You were, my Leah, and you are, my Leah, quite formidable in character and personality. Because you are so open and outgoing in most areas of your life, few people would suspect the breadth and depth of the areas of yourself you have closed off completely, but that is going to have to end if you plan to take this journey you have been called to take. You realize that, don't you?"

I am aware I have taken a step back from him. It is my reaction to the realization I have been observed for years, and that now I am being turned this way and that as if I am a child and adults have made plans for me, and my directions are being chosen for me. I look at the rowan tree as I respond to Father Tom's question and to the situation by simply saying, "No and yes."

Father Tom laughs gently, "Ah Leah, so seldom do you let others see the warrior side of you. Michael allows all his sides to flourish, and sometimes even more than one side at the same time, but not you. 'Yes and no' she says to me. As if there is a way to force you to open that door you locked so long ago."

Now I do look at him, "You saw what I was thinking? You saw the door."

Once again he puts his hands on my shoulders and looks directly into my eyes as he speaks, "I don't initiate anything, Leah. I can receive and respond, but I cannot initiate. This is what you will begin to realize. This is one of the ways all those years of marshaling your own thoughts and emotions and controlling what you allow others to know of you has conditioned you. You sent me the image. Just like at the restaurant the other night, you ran to me so I could pull you back. That is your power, not mine. You have no concept of what you can do yet, but you will. You have only allowed the memories of the fire to express themselves in your dreams so far. You believe the other dreams are just starting, but they have always been there waiting, only now you are allowing them to present themselves to you, and even as I am saying these words to you, I understand their meaning is unclear, but more and more the clarity will come. You'll see."

Michael is walking toward us, and Matilda and the children are behind him a short distance. Michael's eyes are searching mine; I can almost sense his desire to know what I am thinking and feeling. With his characteristic sensitivity, he stops a few feet away from us, and I am certain he is deciding how best to respond to what he is sensing. His thoughtful expression changes to match the lightheartedness of his words, "Well, Father Tom, you've definitely said something to shake-up my unshakable wife, and that is no easy feat, so now all I have to do—." His words stop then start again as he notices the tree, "It's from my dream … I saw that tree in my dream."

Before there is any response to that, Matilda and the children walk by us and go directly to the tree. John Henry and Mary lean their heads back to look up into its branches, which have begun to dress themselves in their feathery-leafed foliage. Matilda lays her hand against the smooth trunk and closes her eyes for a moment, as John Henry does the same. Mary moves closer to it and wraps her arms around it, hugging it wholeheartedly.

Matilda opens her eyes and looks into mine, "They are here, little one, right here."

I am only one word, "Who?"

Matilda responds easily, "May is here and your dear mother and step-father."

I ask the obvious, "Where are Sean and the Danners?"

"The Danners are buried in the cemetery. As to the whereabouts of Sean, we are not sure. He may have been the one who could not be identified, but we doubt it, and seeing the expression on your face I should add that May asked you to begin to discover the whereabouts of Sean in her first letter to you."

I am quick to clarify, "She asked me to look into his military career."

Father Tom interjects, "She asked you to discover the truth about your father; those were her words. You have to remember May's letters were written before the fire. In her first letter she explains she cannot see what will happen, so she had no way of knowing she would die along with your mother and step-father and, perhaps, Sean."

"My father may not be dead?" No one answers me, so I continue, "Then who was the sixth one to die here?"

Michael comes and stands next to me, but only his eyes reach out to me, because he can easily read how I am feeling, "Matilda brought you a file containing the official reports and other papers. It's in the Jeep."

I only say, "How kind."

"Mommy?" Mary's voice is uncertain and small and seems to come from much farther away than from the few feet which separate us.

I walk to her and rest one hand on her shoulder to comfort her. I look into John Henry's eyes and reassure him with a small nod of my head as I reach out my hand and lay it against the smooth bark of a tree with roots that have thrust slowly through or wrapped around the fired blood and burnt flesh and scorched bone of my family.

I feel no fairness in me. The gratitude I feel for what has been done out of love for me is minimized by the quickly shifting shadows of uncertainty which cloud my outward vision almost completely and only act incendiary to the, as of yet, scattered rage inside of me. If I open my mouth to speak I am afraid what shape my emotions will give my words. If I allow my eyes to meet those of Father Tom's or Matilda's or even Michael's I know there will be no need for words to be spoken.

The ramifications of this situation have become larger than I am, and once again I am backed against a wall of circumstance by a pushing wind of other people's motives. I am seething. I am myself becoming a fire which is just beyond the perceptions of those who stand in its quick consuming path, and I have no desire to be a fire. There are children present, I remind myself. My children. And they are watching me. I hold out one of my hands to each of them, and they respond quickly. I allow my eyes to meet the watching eyes of Michael, Matilda, and Father Tom.

I choose my words carefully. "I am grateful for all you have done, although I am completely unsure how to respond emotionally at this time. I suggest Michael drive you to wherever it is you need to be taken, and John Henry and Mary and Puppy and I will walk to our house now." I do not wait for acknowledgment or approval. I call to Puppy who joins John Henry and Mary and I as we begin our walk through tall trees and along paths that will allow us to avoid the main road except to cross it twice. I do not look back. I make small talk with my children and remind Puppy to stay close when he ventures off drawn by a scent on the late afternoon breeze. John Henry and Mary make small talk back to me.

We pass houses, and we wave hands as we pass people in their yards who wave at us. When we reach the lake we walk along its shore, and I tell myself I do not care about the eagle flying above us, but I do. I tell myself I do not care that so much of what I thought was true is not, but I do. I tell myself I do not mind that out of love or compassion elders, whom I trust, chose to allow me to live with half truths and lies, but I do mind. I am before a door I closed years and years earlier, and I can hear the pounding of fists against that door, or perhaps it is only my own heartbeat echoing in my ears, only my own pulse signaling the ongoing current of bloodstream surging through me, reminding me that beneath a tree buried bodies call to me to dig up old ground and to uncover old secrets even though no matter how deeply I dig, I cannot recover the ones I love. So, I think, to what purpose do I bend if I cannot have them back, what need for me to be swept up in the drama of an old priest or by the concealing rather than revealing written words of an old storyteller?

I notice the breeze is gaining strength and becoming wind. It ruffles the lake's surface and pulls my hair back from my face. We push against it as we walk onto ground we call our own. This is my yard and my house. These are my children and my Puppy. This is my time and my life. Then I look up into the sky and wonder if I can claim the eagle circling above us. My eagle, I think, and as I do it sweeps down toward me as if to confirm the thought. I decide this situation is not bigger than I am, and in my head I pound my fist against the door I have closed, demanding silence, and there is silence. I decide to make dinner and to be mom and to be wife and to let the other 'things' wait till tomorrow ... or perhaps the next day, or even the day after that. There is no rush, after all.

What is going on has been going on for twenty years, or according to Father Tom, it has been going on for even longer, in which case there is definitely no need to rush. So that is that, I think, and I feel momentarily content before the image of a fire flares in my mind as an eagle's cry cuts through the doors and windows and walls of my house, and then both arrange themselves in my head, just to the right and left of the door. I shake my head and pretend again I am one of those games that when tilted a bit all the pieces go back to where they belong, but my brain does not work like that, and I know Father Tom's words from the restaurant are true. My only freedom in this situation is the choices I make; my involvement was decided long ago.

✳   ✳   ✳   ✳

We are in the kitchen, each of us stepping over Puppy as we go from stove to fridge to sink to pantry and back again. This is how Michael finds us. He stands in the doorway of the kitchen, and in his hand there is a large file.

Without looking up I say, "We did not hear you come in."

He says, "You didn't lock the door again."

I answer, "You were arriving right after us."

He responds, "Not a good reason."

John Henry and Mary stand in between us waiting, so I do look into his face, which is not set in any expression at all, and his eyes tell me nothing. Puppy's tail hitting the floor in happy staccato and the kids wanting to run to greet their father soften my response, "I am sorry I did not lock the door, Michael."

He nods and greets the kids, and then they return to their tasks. Mary is standing on her stool in front of the sink washing vegetables for the salad, and John Henry is carefully slicing whatever veggie Mary hands to him. Michael has walked around the corner and is sitting on one of the barstools watching us. "Salad and what, may I ask?"

John Henry winks at me as he replies, "Fettuccine and white sauce."

"I believe I am not being given the whole story. What may I ask is marinating in that glass dish on the counter?"

Mary giggles, "It's a surprise for Puppy."

Michael leans over to reach for a carrot as he sighs deeply, "For Puppy? What about for daddy? I'm thinking you're teasing me. I'm thinking I will be asked in the next two and half minutes to become," he pauses for effect, jumps up from his seat, dashes into the living room, and yells, "barbecue-man!"

My helpers and Puppy are gone in an instant. Michael is doing super hero poses, flexing his muscles, picking up one child and then the other, lifting them up toward the ceiling and then laying them down on the sofa. He is yelling 'barbecue-man' over and over. Puppy is barking and running back and forth between the kitchen and the living room. Michael finally tires himself out and falls into one of the big overstuffed chairs, and then he is buried under two children and a large dog for a moment.

I hear John Henry ask to watch TV as I turn from watching them to get the fresh parmesan from the fridge for grating, and when I turn back Michael is right in front of me. He steps closer until there is no space between us. He barely touches his lips to mine as he says, "You made meat for me."

"I have been known to do such things, yes."

"Are you all right?"

"I am fine."

He is speaking softly into my ear as his arms press me even closer to him, "I can't believe you used the f-word."

"Very funny."

He is speaking softly into the other ear now, having kissed my forehead and lips and eyes on his way across my face, "You're the one who often comments on how generic 'fine' is, aren't you?"

I sigh, "Yes."

He has returned to my lips. The kisses are deeper now, and he speaks between them. "So … (kiss) … now I'll ask again." Kiss. "Are you all right?"

I lay the block of cheese on the counter and put both my hands on the back of his neck and gently direct his lips down to mine. Now I give him my undivided attention, and we forget about words. We forget about everything except the feel and taste of each other, and I know dinner will be just a bit later than planned.

*   *   *   *

Stories were read in the living room, so we could cuddle together on the sofa, and now John Henry and Mary are in bed. Michael and I stand on the deck watching Puppy run from tree trunk to tree trunk marking his area. I notice, as I often do, how the moonlight softens the dark shapes of the night. I sigh deeply.

Michael takes my hand in his, "I wanted to talk with you about an idea. I wanted to ask you first, but … well, I discussed it with Father Tom and Matilda as I drove them to … wherever they wanted to go, and they thought it was a good idea. I really want to do it, but I won't if you don't want it to happen."

I sigh again, "Please share your idea with me, Michael."

He steps in front of me and looks into my eyes, "I want to take off work for a while, and do the excavating to find May's metal box. Actually, I want to be around … to be close … for more than just that reason. We can afford it for a month or so at least, if it's okay with you."

"Did Father Tom talk to you about my account?"

"What account?"

"I have a savings account that was opened after the fire."

"Did Father Tom talk to you about this today?"

"Oh yes, that and other things. But the point is, we have more money than we thought we did, so affording time off may not be an issue at all."

"Okay, but money is not the only issue here. Do you want me to be around and help out more with … this situation?"

I lay my head against his chest, "Yes, I want that."

He holds me close, "Father Tom and Matilda wanted me to tell you they understand this is not easy for you, and they only want to help you … help us. I only want to help you, to be with you in this. You have to call the shots, but, Leah, you have to let me … maybe even them … know how you're feeling and what you're thinking. You can't pull back from me or them. We have to be together and honest with each other."

"I am not the one who has not been honest, Michael."

"You think they should have told you more and told you sooner?"

"I want to say yes, but I am not sure. Perhaps they handled it perfectly, but it is just so ... unnerving to hear all this now, years later. It is strange to think there are people who have just been sitting around waiting for me to ... grow up or wake up or something. It is uncomfortable. I felt ... angry. I just had to leave when I did, or I was afraid I would say things I did not mean, because all I wanted to do was ... vent, to express the incredible anger I felt, but that is not what I wanted to do either; it just felt like I did."

Michael gives me a hug then steps back from me, "Most people just vent, Leah."

"I have never vented really, have I?"

"You are not a venter, no."

"It scared me, Michael, how I felt. I cannot imagine feeling that way and opening my mouth. No wonder people get into fights."

"Yeah, that's true, but people have to have some healthy way to express how they are feeling, or they do end up fighting. What do you do when you are angry?"

"I just think about the situation, and the anger usually goes away after I have looked at all the circumstances and after I have distanced myself from what is happening."

"But you can't depersonalize and distance everything, can you?"

"Why not?"

"Some things that happen are personal."

"Of course they are, but just because something is personal to me does not mean that it is not also personal to the other person or people involved. Not taking something personally or giving a situation a distance does not mean I do not care about it or do not care about how the situation is resolved."

Now Michael sighs, "It's always been a mystery to me. I'm a venter though, so it's difficult for me to relate to the thinking of a non-venter."

"I think we've made-up a new word."

"Venter?"

"Yes."

"It can be our v-word."

"Cute, Michael."

"I thought it worked rather well."

Puppy finally joins us, and we walk into the house. Michael locks the door, and we talk about our plans for the next day. He asks me what I am doing at school.

"We're doing the ropes course after morning classes are over."

"I want to come; I like the rope's course."

"You do not have to work?"

"No. I just have to call dad and let him know my leave of absence starts tomorrow."

"You already talked to Hank about this?"

"Yes. I didn't want to suggest it to you then not be able to do it, so I talked with him this morning. He is all for it, by the way."

"How much does he know?"

"We didn't exactly speak of it. We just alluded to it, so I don't really know what he knows."

"That is exactly what bothers me. I do not know who knows about this thing, and if I do know they know, I do not know how much they know."

"Just be like you normally are and ask."

We walk into the bedroom after checking on the kids. "I guess I will start doing that. It will make me feel better."

Michael laughs softly, "Ah yes, everything in the light, right?"

"Yes, everything in the light."

"What about all those thoughts and feelings you keep inside that you don't share?"

"Well, there is an inner light and an outer light, and some things I only share with myself in the inner light."

"I'd ask you to explain that, Leah, but it doesn't sound like a just before bed kind of topic."

"I agree."

We are in the bathroom preparing for bed. He stops putting toothpaste on his toothbrush and looks at me in the mirror, "That's unusual. Normally you want to finish every conversation no matter what time it is." I am washing my face and do not stop or respond to his comment, so he continues, "If we'd been talking about something other than you sharing all those feelings you don't share you wouldn't have agreed. You only agreed because you knew if we kept talking I would've called you on that inner light/outer light bullshit."

I am patting my face dry, "Bullshit?"

Michael is brushing his teeth but it does not stop him, "If your students tried to pull the same thing, you'd call it bullshit." He is literally foaming at the mouth and enjoying his reflection in the mirror.

I shake my head, "I cannot imagine myself referencing bullshit for any reason."

He rinses his toothbrush then rinses his mouth by catching water in his cupped palm even though a small glass sits next to the faucet to serve that very purpose, "You're playing games, Leah."

I walk to the bathroom door, turning to face him again as I reach it, "I thought you did not want to talk, Michael."

He joins me at the door, but when I turn to walk into the adjoining bedroom, his arm blocks me, "Not about inner/outer lights."

I lean back against the doorframe and look up at him, "So, then tell me, what would you like to talk about, husband?"

He rubs his face in my hair, "Maybe talking wouldn't be the best use of our time, wife."

I smile and say only what I had said earlier, "I agree."

✳   ✳   ✳   ✳

I am aware of the hum and the whiteness. I am within the walls of Lane Medical Center. I have greeted nurses and now stand before the door of Teri's room. She is being released and will return to Dayton School and to her room in Rose Lane Hall. Jacy worked with some of the other girls, and the room has been cleaned and remodeled. Lane was going to have it done professionally, but Jacy wanted to do the work herself. She became cleaning-and-painting-woman-slash-interior-decorator.

I knock on the door and Teri's voice invites me to enter. She is sitting on the edge of her bed. Beside her a small travel bag is packed. On her lap are three books. Our eyes meet as we greet each other. I go to her and take her hand, "Are you ready for this next step?"

"Yes."

"And when does your plastic surgery begin?"

"Next week, so I'll only be staying at the school until then. Mom will fly here, and then we will rent a car and drive to Los Angeles together. I'll be there a month, and mom will return every weekend to stay with me."

"Greg told me Marcia talked with your surgeon, and he felt very confident about the results."

"Yes, there will be no scars on the outside at least."

"And the ones on the inside, what about those?"

"Those will take longer, but I have already met with Mrs. Carson once and with Mr. Danner once," she pauses and smiles. "Mr. D says they are double teaming me."

"They are good people to have on your side."

"I know. Mr. D is good at mixing humor into our sessions; he does a great impersonation of Freud. Mrs. Carson is going back to her family, which is good, I think."

"Would your meetings with her be less effective if she was not going back to her family?"

"No, not really, but I just think families should stay together. I mean if she is going to counsel people, shouldn't her own life be … right?"

"Ouch," is all I say.

"You know what I mean."

"Well, Mr. Danner is gay. Some people think that makes him inappropriate to be a counselor."

"That's just sexual bias."

"Then your thinking about Mrs. Carson is … relational bias." Teri's expression is thoughtful, and I give her a hug as I say, "Be so careful 'how' you think. Judgment is usually a double edged sword. You are judging Mrs. Carson for one reason. There are some who judge Mrs. Carson because she married a black man. Others judge Mr. Danner. Some people judge people because of how they look. Some people judge people based on what beliefs are held. For me, one of the most destructive actions we, as people, do is to believe we have the right to judge at all. More than anyone else, Teri, you judged yourself, and one judgment seems to lead to other judgments; they are prolific. One day a person only judges this or that; the next day that same person adds another human characteristic or even an attribute to the first this or that, and pretty soon there is a list, and all kinds of people are not okay anymore. Once I was so proud to say I was only prejudiced against prejudice people, that everyone else was okay, but I later realized I was being prejudiced against prejudice and even that is a judgment."

Teri repeats 'prejudice against prejudice' then says, "That's interesting. I never thought of it that way before, but I will think on what you've said. I'll have lots of time to think about things, that's for sure."

"And to read."

She nods her head then indicates the books her in lap. "Father Tom brought me a book of Irish legends. Dr. Brightstar brought me a historical romance about an Indian woman and a white man, and Jacy brought me her favorite story from when she was a little girl. It's entitled *The Littlest Angel*; I've read it three or four times already, and the drawings are beautiful. It's about a little angel who just can't seem to fit in or do anything right. It turns out she judges herself more harshly than anyone else."

"So, do you feel ready to go?"

"Yes, Dr. Brightstar came by earlier, and I have said goodbye and thanked my nurses already. The flowers you and others gave me I asked the nurses to put in other patients' rooms, since some of them haven't received any."

I tell her that was a thoughtful thing to do then say, "Off we go then, little angel," and we both smile.

As we walk down halls and through doors and finally out into the soft light of a misty morning, Teri wonders if she made the right decision to come back to school, "I'm afraid my face will scare people."

I ask her, "Are you aware of the cuts all the time?"

She thinks for a moment before she responds, "I haven't thought of it in that way; it would seem like I should, because they still hurt a bit, and it's difficult to forget what I did, but I'm really not aware of them all the time. I do forget about them."

"I have been talking with you and looking at you for the last five or ten minutes, and I became unaware of them also, so that's what I think will happen. Of course, there are some rather rude people out there in the world, and even in our school, unfortunately, who will stare and perhaps even ask unnecessary questions. There are also those people who have to give their opinions even when no one has asked for them, and for some reason, their mouths fly open and out comes proof of their own self-absorption. You will have to deal with them just like all the rest of us do, but you cannot let them bother you, or you allow them to steal your peace of mind or contentment with the moment." I pause thinking about the ideas I have just expressed. "That's it really. Being in a moment with someone or a group of people and not allowing the kind or the unkind to instigate a riot inside your own head or your own heart."

I realize I am standing by the door of my Jeep and Teri is standing by the passenger door on the other side waiting for me to unlock them so we can be on our way. "Oops, was I off in lala land again?"

Teri smiles, "I don't think you ever go to lala land based on the ideas you share, Mrs. C, but you do have a tendency to get into your own head and forget where you are sometimes."

I push the unlock button, "Sorry about that."

"I don't really mind. The other kids and I, we sort of find it interesting actually because you usually share parts of your musings with us when you get done."

We buckle up as I start the car, "I suppose there are worse things to be than interesting."

Teri laughs, "Definitely there are. You could be boring or grouchy or stuck-up or mean. And anyway, you're a teacher, so you should be interesting."

We are driving toward the campus as I say, "Well I do so like to be what I am supposed to be especially when it does not interfere with who I am."

Teri laughs again, "See there, that's interesting. I mean at first it may seem like it doesn't make sense, but if I think about it, it makes sense."

I say aloud without meaning to that 'I'd rather make dollars,' and Teri asks what I said, but I just wave my hand in the air as if I can erase the words, and I change the subject back to school and her plans for the next week. The sun is in and out of clouds as I drive down streets, and I am making strong attempts to stay within the parameters of the present moment, even as I am feeling strongly drawn to wander around inside my own head where shadow and light and dark are produced by an inner arrangement of organizational ordinances, and the sun and clouds occasionally dance in warm rain together on a shifting plain of color without causing disaster or confusion in the abstract-art-organizational-realm of my thinking. And I am glad I am a teacher who is interesting and not boring or grouchy or stuck-up or mean.

*   *   *   *

Morning classes are over. I traveled through them easily, journeying through the thought-continents of American Literature to Beginning Composition and Speech to Advanced Syntax and Semantics without unnecessary delays or distractions. I am preparing mentally for the Ropes Course as I organize assignments and handouts for Monday classes.

As much as I truly believe in the philosophy that is the foundation of Outward Bound Education and its offspring, the Ropes Course, I am not always emotionally ready for the mind-body-spirit-earth-team correlation essential to its process. I have to prepare myself for the adventure. Michael, on the other hand, is always ready to balance on thin beams and be the definitive team player. He is probably standing on the deck right now peering down the driveway watching for me as he does knee bends and leg stretches. I whisper to him in my thoughts that I am not late and to relax, but inside my head he ignores me, his hand to his forehead shielding his eyes to block sunlight keeping him from seeing my approach.

As I gather my various necessary and unnecessary-but-I-want-them-with-me-anyway items to take home I think about fathers who are not dead, and metal boxes buried deep, and fat files filled with facts and unknowns, and a goddess-slash-woman name Brigid whose blood pumps my heart, but then I stop myself, because there is no way I can venture into those domains currently without causing schedule delays. My day is planned. The next three days are planned: ropes course with family group and Michael, pick up John Henry from music lesson and Mary from daycare, then home for dinner and bedtime rituals, then breakfast and packing for our picnic at Little Bend Cove and for our stay at the cabin for family fun and relaxation, then mass and welcome party for Father Tom's nephew, Connor. A full three days to be sure, but a good full, not an I-am-making-myself-crazy-full. I turn at the door of my classroom and double check I have left it in neat order, and then I am down the hall, down the stairs, out the door, and across a newly mowed lawn that smells inviting and just like late spring should smell. The sun is alone in the sky and the breeze, sent from the ocean, reminds me of sand and shells and waves, and I realize it has been too long since I have been to the shore, so I look forward to that as I once again find myself loitering beside my own car door, daydreaming instead of making speedy progress toward home, toward Michael, and toward the next moment.

*   *   *   *

Michael and I drive up Lake Road to Forest Road, the western boundary of Dayton Forest, which surrounds the town of Lane on three sides. The forest is privately owned by the Daytons. A bridge over Castle Rock River and five small very rustic cabins spaced about a quarter mile apart and a little over two hundred feet from Forest Road and the Ropes Course elements are the only signs of humans existing within the forest. Four of the cabins are leased. The cabin south of Castle Rock River is leased by the school and is adjacent to the land donated to the school for the Ropes Course. The other three cabins are across the river to the north. The cabin closest to the river is owned by the Dayton family. The next cabin to the north is leased by Michael's family; the next cabin is leased by Castle Rock Resort, and the last cabin is leased by Father Tom and the church. The forest is a sanctuary for all living within its boundaries. Hunting, fishing, and motorized vehicles are not allowed. It is pristine, a haven for wild flowers and natural grasses and shrubs, magnificent trees of three or four different varieties, small and large creatures, and man, if he can behave himself. Steep fines are imposed for breaking of the rules, and the Dayton family keeps four to six conservationists employed full-time to monitor the forest and its creatures, from insects to brown bears. Private security guards are hired for three seasons of the year to enforce proper behavior by humans at all times, and more than one story is told of tourists being escorted out of town for neglecting to follow the rules protecting Dayton Forest. The Dayton men, who have overseen the town of Lane and its shoreline and forest for over three generations are known for their kindness, generosity, and compassion, but a sure way to incur their infrequent but formidable disdain is to harm the land or the creatures these men feel destined to protect.

Michael's voice accompanies the pat of his hand on my leg, "Okay, where are you?"

"I was just thinking about the forest and how the Daytons have cared for it all these years."

"They take that responsibility quite seriously. Imagine what America would be like, even our large cities, if all of our leaders in politics and in industry had the same dedication to protecting our natural resources."

I shake my head sadly, "Yes, but so many people would not go along with that. Interest in making money and an almost addiction like need to have fun, no matter the consequences, seem to continually override what common sense tells us will happen if we do not stop polluting the earth. A few days ago, during family group, Shay was commenting on how each generation tends to dig the hole deeper rather than make the changes necessary to ensure healthy modifications in our behavior and thinking. He was quite upset about it actually, but lately he has been more emotional."

Michael is turning into one of the four parking areas that precede footpath entrances into the forest. "Wasn't Shay the quiet one?"

"Not anymore. I suppose this is his delayed reaction to the death of his family. His anger does seem to be more philosophically based than a physical outlet, but we are watching to see where it takes him or where he allows it to take him."

We are parked now, and Michael has turned off the engine. It is suddenly very quiet. We are both gazing into the rampart-like wall of trees before us, and I am again amazed at the grandeur of tree after tree with trunks too large to put my arms around and be able to touch fingers. Between the trees, shade fills space with such a depth the shade becomes as solid as the trees themselves.

Michael whispers, "I feel like a little kid again."

I whisper back to him, "It is impressive, isn't it?"

Michael leans over to me still talking quietly but exaggerating the movement of his lips and says, "It must be intimidating too, or why else would we be whispering?"

We both jump suddenly as someone taps on the window, then we are laughing at our own reactions. I look out to see my family group members looking in at us, deciding I do not even want to know what they are thinking about our behavior.

I open the door and step out into air scented and cooled by trees. My students stand in a half circle around me as Michael walks up to Teri and gives her a hug. Her expression is tentative but open.

Michael greets each one of them then adds, "Are you ready to get your butts kicked?"

I grab his arm and pull him back so he is standing behind me as I say, "Forgive him, he is just a little competitive."

Michael is quick to respond, "I was only kidding. I am completely aware of the non-competitive nature of the Ropes Course. Unlike its parent, Outward Bound Education, the Ropes Course is a challenge by choice, and, like its parent, it promotes team effort, not …" he pauses and then yells, "individual glory."

The kids are smiling or laughing as I begin to walk away, "Okay, we need to just leave him here. Please, just ignore him completely. He will come to his senses." My students know us well enough to play along, and they follow me.

Michael is standing still, "Oh, nice way to make the non-family-member-guy feel like a part of the team. Nice, Leah." I am diligent in my ignoring of him, so Michael continues, "I'm beginning to feel abandoned, and I think someone should apologize and invite me to join the group. Maybe the decrepit-over-the-hill-thirty-year-old should do it since she started the ugliness."

I do not stop walking, but I do respond, "Please, please, Michael, join us."

I am beginning to enter the trees as Michael calls out, "I didn't hear an apology." If he said more after this I do not hear his words; the dense vegetation muffles sound. Once inside the tree line, even the sound of passing cars on Forest Road is not heard. I can, however, hear Michael excusing himself as he passes this student then the next until he walks next to me. "Were you just going to leave me there?"

I look at him but keep walking, "Would you have stayed there?"

"No, but that wasn't my question."

"If you had not joined us in mere minutes, I would have returned to your last known destination to search for you."

He puts his arm around my shoulders and says, "Are you in your teacher mode?"

I push his arm off my shoulder, "Michael, you are not behaving well."

He puts his arm back on my shoulder, "I'm sure you're right, but I can't quite stop myself. You're so official in your manner, but then your ponytail is doing this back-and-forth-sort-of-happy-swing-thing which totally negates the official-thing all together."

I step up the pace of our walk, realizing the only way his mood is going to change is when his mind is focused on something else. The cabin where we will meet Cami and Tom before we go to the course is just around the next turn in the path, and I am determined to get there as quickly as possible.

As I speed up, Michael slows down, and when Shay and Morgan catch up with him they begin talking. Entering the cleared area, which surrounds the cabin, I notice the bicycles of Tom and Cami Hayes leaning against the porch. Tom and Cami are standing a short distance from the cabin with their backs to me and do not hear my approach. Cami is Dayton School's Health and Yoga teacher. Tom is the Fitness and Swimming Coach. They are also our Ropes Course instructors which allows them to have personal contact with the entire student population and every staff member at the school since everyone, from student to chef to maintenance man to Dean of Admissions, is required to be on the Ropes Course at least once a month. This gives the Hayes a unique advantage in offering insights into individual situations and on group dynamics. Also, after any self-destructive behavior by a student, the family group involved must be on the Ropes Course as soon as possible, so even if we had not been scheduled to be here, we would have been here.

I stop at the cabin, not wanting to interfere in Tom's and Cami's conversation. My husband and students are not as quiet as I am, and Tom and Cami turn and wave. They take a moment to finish their discussion then join us at the cabin. After a short greeting, Tom asks us to stand in a circle, "I am here by choice. I choose to be a member of this group. I choose to behave in a manner that will not endanger myself or others. I choose to listen and to hear. I choose to look and to see. I choose to become a part of a whole and to remain whole in the process. I acknowledge three responsibilities: to trust in myself and in others, to honor the physical place in which I am, to leave here what is said here unless I am released by the group to do otherwise." He pauses then continues, "Normally, I would begin our time together by asking each of you if you can agree with the statements I have just made, but because we are in an emergency situation, we'll talk first. After we have a better understanding of this emergency, then we can see if each of you will agree to the statements, and if so, then we will do ropes. Now, we'll have a moment of silence, a time to breathe deeply, to really get a sense of where we are, and to quiet our own thoughts so we can hear what will be said."

I bow my head during moments of silence, because moments of silence seem to require a humble spirit, and a bowed head is a physical expression of that for me. I even still my thoughts by focusing on my breathing and looking into the shifting darkness of my closed eyelids. After a few minutes, Cami invites us to join her at the Circle of Talk and Listen, which is actually a circle of relatively flat-topped boulders set in a circle a short distance from the cabin. We walk there quietly and choose a place to sit. Shay and Teri seem to have difficulty making up their minds where to sit, but since there is no hurry here we are patient, and they do find a place for themselves in the circle.

Tom begins speaking, "We were here together in this circle just a little over a month ago. We sat on these stone seats. We listened to each other. We were under this same sky. The trees surrounded us just like now. Are we the same?"

Teri responds quickly as if she wants to get through what she knows will have to be discussed with as few delays as possible, "No, we're not the same, because I ... did a bad thing."

Cami questions, "A bad thing?"

Jacy's voice is strong, "I don't think she has to say things that aren't comfortable for her."

Tom nods his head, "Okay, you're being protective and that is a natural reaction for you to have to the situation, but my question is still, are we the same? Teri says she is not, are any of us?"

Shay is shaking his head, "Are we the same what? The same people? Yes. In the same headspace? No."

Cami questions, "Last month when we were here together, did you feel like you belonged to a group strong in its parts and in its wholeness?"

Alana starts to stand then sits back down, "I'd like to ask Teri a question." Teri nods her head it is okay for Alana to ask after Tom says it is Teri's choice. Alana's expression is thoughtful, "Last month when we were here together, were you thinking about doing what you did?"

Cami interrupts, "We need to get real here, ladies and gentlemen. Teri's behavior will not go away or become less than simply by avoiding referring to it by its actual name. From this point on attempted suicide will be how we refer to what Teri did. Any concerns over that?" There is no disagreement, so Cami asks Teri if she will answer Alana's question.

Teri stares into her hands which are cupped in front of her. She brings them up to her face as if they hold cool refreshing water or refreshingly simple answers. "Yes. No. I've thought about ... suicide ... before, but I don't think I was thinking about it on that day. I usually only think about it when I'm alone."

Maddie asks Teri, "Is there no one here you could talk to about thinking about suicide? There is no one you trust enough?"

Teri thinks for a moment before she responds, "When I'm here with all of you or in my classes, I feel pretty good about things, about life, but at night if I can't sleep or on days when I choose to just be alone, thoughts about how ... tired I am of ... the memories ... or what I look like ... or just negative thoughts ... get too big. They ... fill my brain with images and ... I really don't think about being a part of a group, this one or any other. I didn't get a gun and start shooting other people. I just wanted the memories to stop."

Tom as straight forward as always comments, "So, since you didn't do your attempted suicide to me or for me or against me, what kind of feelings would you like me to have about your attempted suicide? How would you like me to react to your attempted suicide?"

Teri looks directly into his eyes, "I would like you to realize I made a mistake, a bad choice, and I'm so sorry I did it, but it's over, and I do want to live my life."

Tom rises from his sitting position and walks over to Teri, "I can do that. I can say to you, you made a bad choice, knowing as I say it I have made my own bad choices. I can say to you, I will trust you again to care about yourself as much as I believe you care about us ... if you tell me I should."

Teri looks down then up again, "You should."

Tom responds, "Then I will." He returns to his seat and continues, "Now, I will ask my question again. Are we the same? Would we be the same if Teri had not attempted suicide? In the days and nights since we last met, have any of us gone through experiences or had thoughts that have made us different than we were? And if we have, have those experiences changed us so much we can no longer be members of this group? Or, have the experiences we have had only deepened our understanding of who we are as individuals and as a group? Are we changed but not changed?"

Morgan responds tentatively, "This is going to sound sort of strange coming from me, but it's like we all might feel more ... fragile ... than we did, like we need to be more aware of each other, but that doesn't mean we're different people."

Valerie's face is turned toward the sun as she strokes Samson's thick coat, "We change or maybe we become more. We're more than we were, but who we are is the same."

Shay is nodding his head, "Yeah, it's like that bumper sticker 'shit happens'. Shit does happen, and we deal with it and go on."

Tucker laughs, "Every farmer will tell you that without some manure mixed in, crops aren't as strong."

Teri is looking around the circle, "But what I did was wrong. I could have died and none of you would have been able to ask me why. I created doubts in you. What I did was so wrong."

Cami agrees with her, "In my eyes, in my heart, totally and one hundred percent wrong choice, but you survived it. Now, make a life built on what you learned from it, and when you're strong enough figure out a way to share what you know with others."

Charlie looks at me, "It's like you tell us, Mrs. C. There's a ton of information out there, but we have to learn it to make it knowledge, and we have to apply it to our lives so it can become wisdom, right?" I nod at him and smile, but I do not comment, because I do not want to sidetrack Tom's and Cami's focus.

Tom claps his hands and rubs them together, "Okay. So, is Teri the only one here who made a bad choice in the last month?" He is answered with a chorus of negative responses. "Okay. Groups don't have to fall apart because of a member's bad choice, but groups can fall apart because of the group's reactions to a member's bad choice. Judgment, unforgiveness, lack of compassion, selfishness, apathy: these reactions by individuals destroy group trust. If everyone here can still trust Teri to be a member of the group and if she will agree to trust us, then we can make an agreement right here and now to trust and honor each other by sharing not only our words but also our intentions and our troubles with each other. But, I want a sincere effort made by each person here to listen a little closer and be a little more attentive to how a group member is doing. We each have to make the time and then take the time to be actively involved in the relationships in which we have made commitments. Teri's process of recovery is just beginning, and we may only play a small part, but I, for one, am not going to be small in my effort even if my responsibility is small." He pauses and looks around the circle before he continues, "If you can agree right now then stand. If you feel you need more time to think about your commitment based on the state of your own thoughts and feelings then please stay seated. There is no 'should' in what I am asking you to do; we just need to be honest with ourselves and others."

Shay, Morgan, Neil, Tucker, Alana, Maddie, Jacy, Aden, and Charlie stand after only a minute or two of thought. Then Teri stands. Angela and Valerie stand almost at the same time a minute or two after Teri. Michael and I stand as Cami and Tom stand. Cami asks the group to join hands and we each step closer to the center of the circle to accomplish that. Cami speaks quietly, "Not just words thrown out there or this means nothing. Just a game played. People with judgment and unforgiveness in their hearts stand in circles and hold hands and throw out words all the time. If you're standing here, you've made a commitment to other human beings to care, even when you're tired or just don't feel like it. If you're not sure, sit back down, please. Better to admit you're not sure you're ready than to say you are and not be."

I notice Shay, Morgan, and Tucker all firm their stance a bit by repositioning their feet on the ground. Maddie and Alana raise their joined hands toward the sky. Valerie gets a headrub from Samson, and somewhere near by a bird chirps approval. Teri and a few of the others are looking down at the ground, and there are tears rolling down cheeks. It is a moment that has breathed in so deeply of itself that both the joy and sorrow of life and of living are exhaled into the waiting hearts of the humans who are present and are willing to accept the sweet tearing paradoxes of being.

*   *   *   *

Tom is leading us to our first activity as Cami and Teri walk together at the end of the group. Ropes courses can be set up in small areas and function quite well, but ours covers almost an acre of land. Walks to and from activity sites allow for reflection, so we walk a great deal. Talking is usually not recommended; pre-activity conversations and post-activity debriefings are the time for sharing. Of course, different Ropes Course facilitators lead their groups in a variety of ways, but Tom and Cami feel strongly that personal reflection is paramount to the process, so we walk together in shared silence. And I do try to reflect, but the beauty of my surroundings calls to me. Breezes brush against my face. Small animals on different paths than mine make themselves known intentionally or unintentionally. Sunlight and shadow claim distinctive spots as their own, as craggy boulders, some the size of large houses, seem to spring up from either sandy soil or moss covered ground. I forget to reflect on feelings as I am drawn into the sensing of tree texture and wildflower hues. I become mesmerized by all that is; I become aware of my own skin and the placement of first one foot then the next. I am aware of my arms' natural swing as they balance the movement of my body. My breathing is deep but relaxed. I am conscious of all this as I walk, while at the same time, I am not looking out of myself into the world around me as much as I am aware of my place in the world and the manner in which I fit so perfectly. I like that thought, so I let it repeat itself over and over again; it becomes my mantra … I fit so perfectly, I fit so perfectly, or, within this moment I am fit so perfectly. I sigh and smile and breathe deeply and place my feet just so and somewhere up above me one of the forest's birds chirps its approval at my perfect fit within the moment, and I am sure the ancient rock beside me is smiling too.

*   *   *   *

I realize there is no one in front of me anymore, so I stop my perfect placement of feet and the perfect swinging of my arms, and turn around, knowing
what I am almost certain I will find. Michael is standing in the path about twenty
feet from me. His arms are crossed over his chest. His lips are pursed and one eyebrow is raised just a bit higher than the other. One foot is positioned out just a
bit farther than the other. Mary does the exact same pose. I smile thinking of
that, and he uncrosses his arms and lets them fall to his sides.

Michael talks to me as we walk toward each other, "You are so wonderfully
and irritatingly beyond me. You turned and saw me, joined me in this reality for
maybe a heartbeat, then wham, within a second you were right back out there or
in there or wherever it is you go. That amazes me, and I can tell by your eyes if
you're there or here, so you can't fool me, wife."

He has wrapped arms around me. "I was not trying to fool you." He kisses my
cheek, turns me around, and pats me on the behind. "Why do you do that when
you know I do not like it?"

He does one of those snort-laughs signifying derision, "I could ask the same
question of you?"

I snort-laugh back, "Oh, right, daydreaming is comparable to smacking someone's butt?"

He passes me on the path and simply says 'yes'. I tell him I disagree, and he
raises and lowers his shoulders stating we will have to agree to disagree, saving the
discussion for later, because the group is just around the curve in the path. I pass
him and say, "That's just f-word with me, honey."

He would probably have had a comment for me, but I am welcomed back
from my detour with applause from my students. I bow graciously, refusing to
feel self-conscious.

Tom is smiling at me, "Thanks, Leah, for scouting the trail for us. Things
look okay in that direction?"

I smile, "Why yes, as a matter of fact, I found Michael wandering around lost,
and I am returning him to you."

Michael has resumed the same position he was in when I turned and saw him
on the trail. I smile my least endearing smile and slap him on the behind as I walk
by him. His response is quick, "Hey, Leah, now who's not behaving well?" I
make a special point of allowing my ponytail to swing back and forth as I walk
away from him. Morgan and Shay are both smiling and shaking their heads at

me, so I grab Teri's and Jacy's arms as I walk by them, and we continue up the path together. I can hear Cami teasing Michael that he got just what he deserved and him denying any culpability, and then we are all quiet again, alone in the forest together, reflecting.

*   *   *   *

Rope Courses are comprised of both low-ropes and high-ropes activities. Our course is interspersed with both instead of a low-course area leading to a high-course area. We stand now in front of a four foot high wooden platform made of two-by-sixes for its frame and a two-by-ten inch piece of treated lumber for its top. Construction of course elements is prescribed and half inch stove bolts and aircraft nuts and bolts are used to secure the platform. The area around the platform is clear of any rocks and has been leveled.

Tom begins the activity in the traditional manner, "I am here by choice. I choose to be a member of this group. I choose to behave in a manner that will not endanger myself or others. I choose to listen and to hear. I choose to look and to see. I choose to become a part of a whole and to remain whole in the process. I acknowledge three responsibilities: to trust in myself and in others, to honor the physical place in which I am, to leave here what is said here unless I am released by the group to do otherwise." He then looks at Aden who is standing next to him.

Aden responds, "I am here by choice, and I accept my responsibilities to myself and to my group." Tom's eyes move to the next person as soon as Aden is done speaking. With small differences in word choice each individual responds. Cami has positioned herself last, and after she responds, she reminds us of this element's challenges.

"You have all experienced this before, so I will be brief. This element is called the Trust Fall. The person falling and the people catching must be willing to trust each other. The person falling climbs onto the platform, faces away from the catchers, stands with his or her heels lined up with the edge of the platform and waits until the catchers ask if the person falling is ready. The catchers will line up on the ground behind the person falling, four on a side, about one foot from the platform, with arms in L-position and legs apart, knees bent and heads back. Communication between the person falling and the people catching and communication between the catchers must be clearly established. We are in no rush. If we accomplish nothing today but this element, we have accomplished all we need to accomplish. This, like all the other elements, is a challenge by choice. Is there anyone here who would rather not be involved in this activity?" No one speaks.

Cami looks at Teri, "Are you agreeing to take part in this challenge?"

Teri looks around at the group before she answers, "Yes."

Cami obviously wants more information, "That's good, and I'm glad, but I need to know why you're agreeing to this challenge when you have repeatedly refused the challenge in the past."

Teri takes a deep breath, "I'm … overweight."

Cami responds gently but firmly, "You're not the thinnest person I know, Teri. I'm not the thinnest person I know either, but light as a feather or heavy as a rock is not the issue. Why are you accepting the challenge today?"

Teri closes her eyes and then opens them, "I'm accepting this challenge today because I think the group will not let me fall even if I'm fat." Teri pauses and then continues, "Also, I think before I didn't want to be a burden, and I didn't trust my friends to … catch me when I needed to be caught, not just in this, but in other ways too. Mr. Danner and I are talking about that. He says everyone has a part of his- or herself that can be perceived as a burden, but we have to trust our friends to accept those burdens and live with those burdens just like we live with them." She pauses and looks around at her friends. "Today, I am accepting the challenge so you can catch me. And I'm sort of afraid you might drop me, but if you do, I know it won't be on purpose. I'm giving you a chance to try and catch me at least."

Cami and Tom exchange nods, and then Cami asks for the first volunteer. Teri steps forward, and without meaning to or even thinking about others' responses, all the group members, including Michael, cheer. I, of course, have tears in my eyes and feel like I could clap my hands together and cheer for the rest of the day.

Tom's voice silences the applause as he asks for catchers. Every member of the group steps forward, including Valerie with her Samson, and my heart feels like it is undergoing a tender but thorough spring cleaning by a diligent joy that believes all else can be cast out but hope and love.

*   *   *   *

We are walking toward our next challenge, but I am still back at the last one. Teri volunteered to fall twice. Each group member, plus Michael and I had the opportunity to be a catcher for her. And as always when possible, Tom and Cami, taking all the precautions necessary, gave Valerie the chance to participate also. Her desire to be a catcher for Teri was made possible through teamwork. Tom and Cami positioned Neil and Tucker, the two strongest family group members on either side of Valerie. Tom stood behind her, his arms under hers but not touching hers for support unless it became necessary, which it did not. The catchers had to pick one person to speak in order to keep Valerie informed of what was happening, and the rest of us had to stay totally quiet after the required questions regarding readiness were made between faller and catchers. Valerie told Samson to stay with me, and he did, but I could tell he wanted to be with his charge, sensing her excitement. After Teri fell backward into the waiting arms of her friends, the catchers slowly stood her up and kept their arms around her, cradling her longer than may have been physically necessary, but emotionally the timing felt perfect, just perfect.

✳ ✳ ✳ ✳

Low-course activities almost always require teamwork. High-course activities can require teamwork, but more often than not, high-course challenges are focused on the individual. Group support can often motivate a person to overcome a moment of fear or doubt, but it is the individual's determination that is put to the test. I know where Tom is leading us, and this new activity will complement the last.

We walk out of the trees and off the narrow path which we were following into a clearing about forty feet in diameter. In the center of the clearing is a twelve inch wide pole cut to a height of approximately twelve feet. Half inch thick galvanized metal rods have been bent into 'u' shapes and placed around the pole to function as climbing steps. Lined up and at equal distances of around fifteen feet from the pole, two large redwoods are connected by two paralleled three-eighth inch galvanized aircraft cables. A belay cable is attached to the top cable, and a trapeze is attached to the lower of the two cables. This element is called the Eagle Perch.

Tom is unlocking the metal bin which holds the harnesses and other equipment necessary for this challenge. Tom and Cami check equipment and prepare the activity, while I pass out bottled water also stored in the large metal bin. Michael is debagging the small shovel and environmentally-safe-quickly-dissolving-toilet-paper and asks if there are any 'takers' before he sets them beside the bin.

Tom and Cami ask us to gather at a Talk and Listen Circle identical to the one at the cabin except the boulders are smaller. Tom drinks from a water bottle then hands it to Cami. He looks up at the sky, and I notice just a touch of gray in his hair. Both he and Cami are in extremely good physical condition; both have dark hair and intense brown eyes. Cami's hair is only slightly longer than Tom's, and they are about the same height. Cami likes to say they are 'evenly matched almost', and Tom does not seem to mind the healthy competition to be the best they both can be. The most significant difference in their appearance, beyond the fact that Tom is male and heavier built while Cami is female and lighter in build, is Tom's mustache. Tom's mustache is larger than life. Cami says they do not need a dog or cat because they have Tom's 'stache'. He is running his hand over it right now, smoothing it as he thinks. Cami clears her throat to get his attention.

Tom smiles at her and says to Michael, "My wife is sending me a signal."

Michael comments as he looks at me, "Yeah, they do that sometimes."

Cami and I just shake our heads and take our places in the circle. Tom is standing between Shay and Charlie and has a hand on each shoulder. "Last challenge, team effort. This one, you self-challenge. Sure, you depend on your belayer, but you climb the pole yourself, you stand on top of it, your two feet in a twelve inch area, you balance; you think, maybe you experience a bit of what-the-heck-am-I-doing-up-here? You make your statement of faith to yourself or aloud, you jump, you catch the trapeze, and you hang there feeling pretty good about things, or you miss the trapeze and you hang from the belay cable, and wish you hadn't closed your eyes when you jumped. There are about ten challenges involved. What's the main challenge in this activity? Is there only 'a' main challenge? Or, does the main challenge change with the jumper?"

Tom takes a seat in the circle as he finishes speaking. Alana raises her hand. Tom nods his head at her to share her idea. She gazes into the distance before she speaks, and I notice how her blue eyes seem even more blue as they reflect the sky, and I like the softness of her face without the eyebrow and nose rings. But even as I think that thought I shake myself a bit, not wanting to be judgmental, then her words help me to regain my focus. "The main challenge has to be jumper-based, because some people are afraid of heights and some aren't. It's like a mathematical equation, and the height factor is the determining aspect of the problem."

Three or four hands are raised and Tom points to Tucker, "Height is an issue, but it seems to me the main challenge is the jump through the air. Even though you know you're connected to a belay, you're still jumping. You still have to motivate yourself to take the leap."

Tom signals Shay next, "I'm thinking back to our de-briefing after the last challenge. You asked us what was easier: to be the person falling back and trusting to be caught, or to be one of the catchers who has the responsibility of catching the faller. Most of us said we thought it was easier being the faller, because then we were only responsible for ourselves. But really both situations are an equal risk because a person could fail at either one. At least, that's what some of us thought. This activity is really no different. The main challenge is deciding to risk failing."

Most of us are nodding our heads in agreement, but there are a couple who are not. Valerie is one of those. She raises her hand, and Tom calls her name. "Everyday I wake up and the world is just an empty black canvas for me, even though I know there is a chair beside my desk and a bookcase next to the chair and Samson sleeps on the rug by my bed. I know they are there, but I can't guarantee it without getting out of bed and touching them. I cannot be one hundred percent certain without doing that. I've caught the trapeze twice before and missed it twice before, and all four times Tom or Cami were directing me, and I knew absolutely that the trapeze was where they said it was, but I didn't catch it all four times. The only difference in the situations was my level of certainty that I could do it. When I had doubts, I missed; when I didn't have doubts, I didn't miss. The main challenge is to believe that you can no matter what the situation is. It's a faith thing; that's the main challenge. When I get out of bed every morning, I get around by believing in one thing and one thing only, that I can. When I start having doubts, I run into things."

Aden is chosen to share next, "I understand what's been said so far, and I even agree with the ideas to a point, but for me it's more than faith, and it's more than risking failure. It's more than being off the ground or jumping. When I was sick all the time and smaller and weaker than everyone else, it didn't matter how hard I tried or how much faith I had, my life sucked. It wasn't about failing or succeeding or trusting or not trusting; it was about just getting through each damn day no matter what the day looked like. The main challenge is just doing what needs to be done, because it needs to be done. Not for glory or feeling better about yourself, but just because getting through the day is what we are supposed to do. In this challenge, you climb and balance and jump and catch. You just do what needs to be done in a situation. You accept the situation and deal with it."

Everyone is quiet. I watch Tom and Cami to see where they will lead the conversation next, and after a moment, Tom nods at Cami, and she begins talking quietly. "Figuring it out, figuring it out, that's what we do. We seem to always try to find a way to make it work, to not run into things, to make it through the day. And just like we often take things apart to understand how they work, we have to get to know people to appreciate the validity of their opinions. I don't want to have to build a fort or something around my idea to defend it from you or you or you. No way, I want you to come visit my idea, and I'll come visit yours. Some-times it takes a whole lot of perspectives to see one thing well. My idea may need yours." She looks at Tom as she finishes speaking.

He smiles at her as he begins, "I am here by choice. I choose to be a member of this group. I choose to behave in a manner that will not endanger others or myself. I choose to listen and to hear. I choose to look and to see. I choose to become a part of a whole and to remain whole in the process. I acknowledge three responsibilities...."

✳   ✳   ✳   ✳

We have said goodbye to family group and to Tom and Cami. We stand together by the Jeep and watch my students begin their walk back to the school, as Tom and Cami don their cycling gear to begin a ride to the shore and then to their home. When we are inside the car Michael does not start the engine right away, but sits looking into the trees, and I am reminded that this is the way our afternoon together began, but now we have more to be hushed by than natural beauty.

Michael's voice is quiet as he says, "I like the way Tom and Cami repeat the commitment pledge so often, and that each person involved also says the same words or a rendition of the words. I like that a lot."

I agree with him, "I appreciate it also. I like words that promise."

He reaches out to me and takes my hand, "Remember our vows to each other?"

I smile as I close my eyes and let my head rest against the seat, "Wasn't it only yesterday?"

Michael's voice describes the ceremony as I see the images in my mind, "Father Tom took our hands in his, and he said something like, 'Michael and Leah, you have come here today to ... pledge your love before God, before fam-ily, before friends. You have come here to say you will love each other forever and a day.' I liked that he said it that way. Can you remember the rest?"

I begin where he left off, "He said, 'You have come here to offer yourselves to each other in honesty and in devotion.' Then remember he said something like we had to promise to laugh together and cry together, to rest together and to work together forever and a day."

My eyes are open now, and Michael has leaned over close to me. We are just inches apart as he says, "Then we spoke our vows to each other at the same time." He begins, and I join him, "We take each other as husband and wife, as man and woman, and we promise to love each other truly, for better, for worse, for richer, for poorer, in sickness and in health, for all the days of our lives."

He likes to breathe his love words into me, and so he does, "Forever and a day, wife?"

I breathe back into him, "Forever and a day, husband."

As he starts the car he says, "And I want the day after that too."

Chapter FOUR

There are one thousand colors here. Then the light changes; the sun blossoms out of cloud and sky, and cliff walls beige-blue become white-golden. Sand shimmers under sun's touch, and ocean deepens as it lightens to reveal purple-green strands twisting and flowing beneath its lavender surface. Wildflowers with tiny-sun-centers beckon bees as rose and apricot shells once so still walk away to find new shade. The other senses are drawn from here too. The sounds are deep and wild and too transparent to fathom. The language of sea otters and shorebirds accent the lull and crash of waves pulled in then pushed back. Even the cypresses balancing on the high cliff above the cove are played by fingers of air strumming-through. My skin is warmed by sun then cooled by breeze. Beneath my feet sand supports then gives way. I reach out and touch timeless rock shaped smooth or sharp, and once again the contrasts become only circumstantial; everything makes sense because without the contortion of human desire, the moment is always true to itself. I am just breath and skin....

Mary is tugging on the back of my shirt, "Mom, Elwood forgot his clothes again."

John Henry stands between Mary and her view of Elwood, "It's impolite to notice things like that."

I glance down the beach a short distance, and sure enough, Elwood is definitely naked. "Well, John Henry, it really is not impolite to notice things about people's appearance or behavior, but it is impolite to stare or make unnecessary comments. And anyway, Elwood is not completely naked."

John Henry sits down in the sand, "Right, mom."

Mary sits down next to him, "He still has his necklace on, mom. I can see it shining."

I join them on the sand, "He got that when he was a soldier in WWII."

Mary nods her head, "Daddy said he was a hero."

I agree with her, "Yes, he is a hero."

John Henry says, "It must have been hard for Great Grandpa Thomas to have his brother come back from the war and not be the same as when he left."

I take John Henry's hand in mine, "I am not sure people come back from wars the same as they were when they left."

John Henry looks out at the ocean and then back at me, "But most people don't come back as … different as Elwood, do they?"

Mary climbs into my lap as I answer, "Different people are affected by situations in different ways. Elwood saw too many terrible sights, felt too much pain. Grandpa Hank told me Elwood was in the top of his class at Harvard and did equally well at medical school where he trained to become a doctor. He volunteered to be a soldier as soon as he graduated. I cannot imagine what it must have been like for him. He wanted to be a healer, and he went to war. Then when he got back from the war, he worked part-time at the medical clinic. He had good days and bad days. He met his wife there. She was a nurse, and they fell in love, and then he had months and months of good days. They got married, and they were so happy. They had a baby, a little boy, but then one night during a sudden rainstorm, his wife and son were in the car coming home from a visit to the city, and something happened. She lost control of the car on Ocean View Bridge, and the car went over the guard rails and into the ocean. And Elwood's heart was broken for the second time."

John Henry tilts his head questioningly and says, "But, mom, people don't think with their hearts; they think with their minds."

Mary comments, "Even I know that, mom."

I hug Mary and smile at John Henry, "I am not so sure about all that. The heart is just an organ in the body that pumps blood, but we say heart when we talk about our emotions, so what does that mean?"

John Henry pushes the sand around with his hands for a moment then says, "Maybe my heart or where my emotions come from is inside my head with my thoughts. But if that's true, why don't they get along better or go together better? I mean, sometimes what I think and how I feel are from two different planets or something."

Mary turns in my lap and puts her hands on my face to make sure I am look-ing at her as she whispers, "John Henry doesn't want his heart to be in his head, mom. I don't think he should have to have that, if he doesn't want it."

I whisper back to her, "We're just sharing ideas with each other, little blossom; John Henry can think about thinking however he wants as long as it does not hurt him or anyone else."

John Henry pats Mary's shoulder, "I'm not upset, Mary. But I am getting hungry. Hasn't dad been gone a long time just to go to the car to get the picnic basket?"

I have been keeping track of Elwood while we have been talking, and before that we were walking the shoreline and climbing rocks to investigate tide pools, so I really have no sense of how long Michael has been gone. I look at my wrist even though I do not wear a watch. I have tried to wear watches, but they stop working a few days after I put them on my wrist. I have met other people who affect watches the same way I do, but Michael says it is because the watches some-how sense my preference for moments versus minutes, then he whistles the theme song from that old TV show, The Outer Limits.

I stand and make a suggestion to take John Henry's mind off of his tummy, "Maybe I should get our blanket, and we should go see if Elwood will wrap it around himself until we can find his clothes. That's it; that is our plan. That is what we will do until your da returns."

Mary hugs my legs, "I like it when you call daddy 'da'. Is that what you called your dad?"

We all three hold hands as we begin walking toward Elwood, "I called Sean ... Sean, and I called John ... Papa John. My mom called Sean and John 'da' when she was talking to us about them, and May did the same thing too. So, it is a fam-ily tradition, I guess. When I talk to you about your daddy, I call him 'da'."

Mary laughs then exchanges the hand I am holding with her other one and begins walking backwards, "I don't want to embarrass Elwood, so I'll walk this way."

I agree with her idea but suggest she and John Henry see if they can find Elwood's clothes, "Maybe he left them on the benches at the edge of the sand. I will still be able to see you both if you go check for me and that will give me a moment to get Elwood in the blanket."

As we walk by where we left our blanket and our beach bag full of what Michael calls our fun-equipment, I pick up the blanket. John Henry comments, "Maybe Puppy and dad got sidetracked by something."

Mary suggests, "Maybe Puppy ran after a good smell, and daddy is chasing after him."

I throw the blanket over my shoulder and put my hands on my hips, "Well, let's take care of Elwood, then we will go find da and Puppy."

John Henry takes Mary's hand in his and says, "It's a deal, mom." Mary says 'bye' to me three or four times, and I say 'bye' back to her each time as I walk toward Elwood, who has not moved since we first noticed him.

Elwood is a tall, thin man. From photos taken of him earlier in his life I know he once had dark wavy hair he liked to wear a bit longer than men of his generation normally wore their hair, but now at the age of seventy-five his hair is gray, and he keeps it cut short. He looks so very lonely standing there so still for so long, his face turned toward the sun, his arms at his side.

I check on the kids and see that Mary is walking along the benches as John Henry holds her hand. Except for Elwood, there is no one else on the beach but us, probably because it is so early, but I like to be at the beach for sunrise. It is my favorite time of day, and my family is sweet enough to travel in the dark to get here, so we can watch the golden orange glow stretch itself out over horizon and sea when the morning mist allows us to do so.

I call Elwood's name out softly, not wanting to startle him, and he turns his head toward me but keeps his body still. I look into his eyes to see if he is present in this moment or somewhere else, and I can tell he recognizes me.

I hold out the blanket to him, "I thought you might be getting chilly in the breeze."

He takes the blanket and wraps it around himself, then says in his deep resonant voice, "You are being kind, little Leah." And it is a voice from my past wrapping around me reminding me of the many times I went to visit him at the library. After his wife and infant son died he had the house remodeled. The first and second floors became the town library, and Elwood made the third floor his home. I remember walking up the staircases to knock on his door. I remember putting my hand on the gargoyle knocker and always being startled by the coldness of the metal in my hand.

"You are thinking back, aren't you?" Elwood's question startles me. I shake my head and feel shy again like I used to feel when I went to visit him. I smile and take the hand he offers me, "I was remembering walking those wide carpeted stairs up to your third floor apartment, so you could show me your newest wood-carving or tell me about the book you were reading."

He winks at me, "You did some sharing too if you remember. I became quite intrigued by your devotion to the mystery novel, although I never found the same enjoyment in the stories when I tried to read them myself. You made them more interesting by your telling of them."

I am watching John Henry and Mary, as we walk toward them. They are looking up toward Castle Rock Point, so I turn to see what is capturing their interest, and I see my husband and Puppy, miniaturized by the distance, standing at the summit waving at us. I wave back and think, oh well, so much for food anytime soon, and return my focus to the conversation.

"I did love a good mystery, didn't I?"

Elwood squeezes my hand, "You liked stories in which clues were given and solutions revealed themselves, stories that had definite beginnings and middles and ends, and stories in which, most of the time, no innocents died."

His reasoning is clear to me, but I have never thought of my youthful dedication to the genre in that way before, "Do you think that is why I read them so much?"

He is smiling as he watches John Henry and Mary playing leap-frog, "That and just enjoying the puzzle a good mystery provides."

I stop walking, and he turns to face me, and as I search his eyes I say humbly, "I have not been to see you much lately."

Elwood shakes his head as if to put my mind at ease, and pats my shoulder with the hand not holding mine but which was holding his blanket, and it almost falls. He manages to grab hold of it, and we both smile at each other. "Look what I have become, little Leah. Look what sorrow does to a man."

I lean my head against his shoulder, "You are the most gentle soul I know."

He pats my head absentmindedly, "I lose myself in it. I forget where I am. No, that's not right. I forget when I am. I go back and save a thousand lives I couldn't save. I go back and hold my wife and son again. I go back before the war ... to med school ... I can feel the way I felt then, so confident, so sure. Now I am this ... the crazy old man who lives on the third floor of the library and forgets the present to remember the past. Maybe it would be easier just to be ... absent all the time, instead of going away and returning to find myself standing here in less than proper attire for the situation."

My mind is already questing for possible solutions, "You only do this out of clothes experience at the shore. Do you remember walking here?"

Elwood shakes his head, "No, no, little Leah, I cannot be your mystery. From what I understand, you have your own mystery to unravel."

"You know too?"

"I know what I know. Matilda and Lane know what they know. Hank knows a bit, and Katy knows her part. Patrick and Katherine know what they know.

Father Tom knows most of what we know and some that we don't. And there are others, who know what we don't know, and someday there will be you and your Michael, and you'll know your part of it, and then the rest of us can be done with our parts of your mystery. Anyway, I belong to the third letter, so you'll have to wait to hear my part of your story. Hank is the one you'll want to speak with for the first letter."

He has listed all of the elders in Michael's family: Katy, Michael's mother; Matilda, Katy's mother; Lane Dayton; Hank, Michael's father; Patrick, Hank's father and his wife, Katherine. Then I think of May, and of Sean and of Papa John and of my mother, Colleen, and there is such a desire in my heart to hear their names spoken, to hear them referred to in the present tense. I want to hear my mother's voice again, watch her laugh, listen to her 'push buttons' just for the sake of a good discussion, and to feel her arms around me again. I say 'mom' inside my head just to hear my voice say that word again.

Two voices sing out, "Mom!"

John Henry and Mary are running toward us with Elwood's clothes. When they reach us, Elwood's smile of thanks is genuine as my son and daughter hand him his clothes. "I bet you're thinking I'm a crazy old man to be going naked on the beach."

Mary replies quickly, "Heroes can do whatever they want, and it's nobody's business if your heart and your mind are fighting."

Elwood has a puzzled expression on his face, but he smiles at Mary, "Let me get these clothes on so I don't paint quite so pretty a picture, and then you can explain your ideas to me. And let me assure you, just to put your minds at ease, that your mom, when she was only a little older than you, used to share some very interesting thoughts with me. Some of them I still haven't figured out yet." He winks at Mary and John Henry, and requests I hold the blanket as he dresses. I do, and John Henry and Mary start talking about which of their ideas they should share first. My senses, instead of being drawn in by this moment's contrasting and blending of colors and textures, are drawn back, and I am being held in the strong but gentle arms of Papa John where, for a daughter, there is no safer place. I call his name as the image fades, running through rooms of memories until I find the scene I want, and then, once again, the past wraps its arms around me, and I am home.

*   *   *   *

We have made sand castles and tossed frisbees into the air. Michael returned with our small cooler and large picnic basket after three or four of John Henry's and Mary's ideas had been presented to Elwood and thoroughly discussed. Michael's trek up and down the steep path of Castle Rock Point only invigorated him. We had food then fun, and now Elwood and I sit and watch Michael and the kids chase waves only to turn and run from them. It is a good game and full of laughter.

Elwood turns to me and asks, "If you would permit, I would share a concern with you, but I do not want to steal you away from the joy of watching your family enjoying the shore and its waves."

I turn toward him, "Yes, you may, and also, that is an interesting way to see the waves."

The expression on his face tells me that he is thinking back over his own words, "That they belong to the shore?" I say yes, and he smiles as he comments, "It is a mighty love affair. They come from across the world to sojourn here on this shore."

We are playing an old game with each other, so I ask, "How long do they stay?"

He winks conspiratorially, "Forever and a day, of course."

I nod and look back at the waves and at my own loves, and say, "Of course." Father Tom believes in 'forever and a day' and uses the phrase in conversations, sermons, and ceremonies. He says the phrase captures how people should and could be: one hundred percent aware of the depth and breadth of the present moment and also one hundred percent aware that the next moment derives its form based on the handling of its predecessor.

Elwood lays his hand on top of mine, "As for my concern, I would start by saying good people do not expect ... no, it's more than that; good people have no idea of the terrible destructive power inside a person who is primarily motivated by hate or fear or greed. No comprehension at all. I saw that in Germany at Dachau. I was sent there as part of a medical team. It was 1945. The camp had been established in 1933. Twelve years. Seventy thousand people murdered by vile acts or cold-blooded neglect. I remember walking through the gate, and it felt like the air changed, the texture of it. There was the smell of death, but it was more than that. It was a presence, almost as if so much hate, pain, and fear concentrated for all those years had become tangible. It was like an unpleasant exhalation pressed up against all those who walked into the place, and there was no breeze that day, because I remember thinking perhaps that was what I sensed. But it was totally still. I had experienced death on the battlefield, and it can be excessive and demoralizing, even desensitizing, but not necessarily evil, or not viewed as such by society because it involves soldiers facing soldiers on a field of battle. But this ... this thing I felt ... was evil. I laid my hands on human beings whose skin hung on their bones, who looked dead except when I looked into their eyes; there was hope there. They had somehow managed to keep death on the outside of themselves, and it had depleted them, but their eyes reflected their hearts, which had not been invaded by hate. Those with whom I spoke did not speak of hate or revenge. They had seen too much of hate to want to embrace it in order to return it."

He pauses looking into my eyes, "Leah, the people here, the ones who plan to help you, perhaps protect you, they are all good people. I do not believe most of them have had any real experience with ... malevolent people: people who are motivated by greed to the extent it consumes every human and non human resource coming within its reach, or people who are so self-involved it suffocates any good intention they might have as it blinds them to the good and to the worthwhile in others ... and my God, the depravity of hate or its not quite mature cousin, indifference. Some guards from that place went home and sat down to dinner with their children, thinking they were only doing their jobs, as if morals can be put on and taken off like a uniform." He pauses again and looks at Michael and the children, perhaps at the waves which have traveled from across the world to be here. "This situation is bigger than you think. The implications ... the mystery deeper and wider than you could ever imagine. And I must tell you hate and greed and desire for power are involved. No matter what you have been told, there is danger involved. I believe you and Michael can resist and even overcome the evil that will present itself to you, but the price may be so very great. Father Tom and I, even May and I, disagreed on the extent of the danger involved, but I had to tell you how I perceive the situation before you go any farther. I felt like you should know. I am in no way trying to influence you, and my opinion is discounted by many due to my moments of ... extravagant sadness, but I know what I felt in Germany in 1945, and I know what I have felt here in this town at certain times, and lately I have felt it more often, and it felt, if this makes any sense, closer."

I take my hand out from under his and lay it on top of his, "I will always ... always take you and your words seriously."

Michael and the children are running toward us. They are covered in sand, and smiles express their carefree joy. Puppy is racing between them, almost causing them to fall but only causing giggles. Elwood says, "We can talk more of this later, if you wish."

I only say, "Yes, later," as I think to myself, 'in the next moment, or even the one after that'.

*　　*　　*　　*

We are driving home after dropping Elwood off with sincere promises to visit his third floor sanctuary soon. Michael is speaking of the lighthouse foundation and of the cypress trees bent by wind. John Henry and Mary are playing an association word game; Puppy is panting contentedly. I am everywhere at once. I am listening and hearing, and I am here, but I am at the edge of a dream too. I do not recognize it, but it is familiar nonetheless.

I probably interrupt Michael, but he paused so I take the opportunity, "When we stop at the house before we go to the cabin, maybe we should get the file and read it after the kids are sleeping."

Michael glances over at me then back at the road, "Okay, we can do that." He is waiting for me to elaborate, but I cannot. The dream is unfolding in front of me. The car is gone and the road too. I am on the edge of something. Before me are a pair of eyes, opaque yet deep in their drawing, human yet unusually shaped. Behind me, formless but exerting a pressure that is felt, is—.

Michael has his hand on my shoulder and is gently shaking me as he repeats my name. I see the road again. I turn to look at Michael, but he does not have the amused-but-a-tiny-bit-annoyed expression on his face he usually wears when he is calling me back from one of my wanderings. Instead, there is concern in his eyes.

His voice is soft so as not to concern the children, "That felt differently than it usually does, Leah. You really weren't here, were you?"

I answer, "No, not here."

Michael's hand is still on my shoulder, and he is watching the road again as he speaks, "I don't like how that felt."

I can only whisper his name as the dream fills my vision once again.

*　　*　　*　　*

Before me is a wall of stones worn by wind, and rain, and time. I want to press my hands against it, because it seems to call to me to do so, but it is beyond my reach. I am aware I stand on the edge of another stone wall, but this one is only five or six feet high and not quite a foot wide. The other wall towers over me, and trees have grown tall beside it. In places tree and stone touch. The trees' limbs have shaped themselves based on this closeness, some of the branches forming themselves into almost ninety degree angles. In a heartbeat my mind has registered all this. In another heartbeat I perceive what is behind me, and from the two realizations I know I stand on the edge of the world as I know it. Behind me are towns with streets and houses with rooms; there are moments of months and of days and of hours: all through which I have walked. I would rather focus on the wall, but the seemingly still images behind me are gathering themselves up as if they are water and have come up against a barrier. I know I must jump down from the wall on which I stand or be pushed off, so I jump, but the five or six feet estimate I made alters, and I am falling too quickly within what appears to be a tunnel through solid rock. I notice there are small groupings of vertical and horizontal lines arrayed at varying intervals, but I fall too quickly to make sense of them, and when I look up the images I saw behind me previously are hurling themselves over the upper opening of the tunnel. Then instead of falling I feel as if I am being pushed or thrown down. I reach my arms out to try to stop or at least slow my descent, but there is too much force; I only feel the stone scraping against the skin of my hands. I feel panic invade my mind and heart. I start to cry out, but I am suddenly still and hovering above the strongly muscled outstretched arms of a man whose eyes I recognize from before. I am in the air inches from the safety I feel he wants to offer me, but then the force that was throwing me down reverses itself, and I am being drawn up into the vertical flood of images still hurling themselves over the opening of the tunnel. An instant before I enter that torrent I am seeing the road again, and Michael is asking me 'what?'.

I am dazed but respond, "What do you mean 'what'?"

Michael shakes his head, "You called my name; I said 'what'. You're going to have to tell me 'what'."

I am baffled now instead of dazed, "I just said your name?"

Michael nods, "You said my name; I said 'what', and now we're having this conversation about it. I'm not quite clear about the mystery over the last few seconds' chronology, so are you going to tell me what we're talking about, or perhaps you'd rather tell me how you hurt your hands? Did you fall when you and the kids were climbing the shore rocks?"

I look down at my hands. Tiny beads of blood dot the dashes of the scrapes on my palms and fingertips which makes me think of Morse Code which makes me wonder if the vertical and horizontal lines on the tunnel's wall are more than decoration. Perhaps they are written language in a form I do not know.

"Leah?"

"Yes, Michael."

"Did you just experience something and I missed it? How did you hurt your hands? Answer my questions, please."

"I can't now. We will talk at the cabin after the kids go to sleep, okay?"

Michael looks at the road then back at me, "Do they hurt?"

I smile to reassure him. It is sweet of him to be concerned even though I am perplexing him, but I want him to stop asking me questions. I want to remember the man with the eyes that feel as if they want to draw me into them. When I notice the eagle flying through the trees next to us I am not distracted, because the eagle and the man seem to belong together.

*   *   *   *

Once again, I am amazed by human behavior. I think of a soldier on a battlefield, or perhaps a mother who rushes home to care for and offer normalcy to one child while her other child fights for his or her life in a hospital room. We humans are built to weather shocking circumstance as we nurture circumstances unchanged. The man on the battlefield speaks of sports' scores and laughs at jokes moments after and moments before facing death. The mother prepares a meal or helps with homework or just embraces the child at home having only moments before held the hand of the child who is slipping away from her despite her unparalleled desire to keep the child with her. We behave normally in order to maintain a balance or to fool ourselves into believing we can compartmentalize our lives.

I behave normally and yet my life and its moments no longer fit the definitions of my carefully created labels for the variety of areas, distinguished by time and purpose, in which I live. I live between and within a perceived and a previously unknown world, and yet I am simply me as I have always been, both spectator to and participant in moments colored and textured in the wondrously wrought momentum of still-lifes created just so. Beyond the visualized canvas, the moment preceding it and the moment to follow can only be suggested based on perspective, which is only an arrangement of light and shadow, a relational balance within the accepted paradigm of the reasonable and the hoped for. Concrete sensory perceptions are abstracted almost leisurely by circumstance, and what was considered paranormal yesterday becomes normal today. We humans are waves at the mercy of a moon we cannot find on any chart, and yet ... I stop myself, thinking I should perhaps leave a bread crumb trail if I plan to go this far out into my own thoughts again. I shake my head and stretch my arms over my head.

We are at the cabin. We have prepared and eaten the evening meal, played a board game chosen by John Henry and Mary, held flashlights in our hands to follow Puppy on a zigzagging course through tree and rock, and read stories. John Henry's and Mary's even sleep breathing has lulled Puppy to forget to listen to the unfamiliar sounds of forest life, and he too sleeps. Michael and I sit at the large round wooden table that is between small kitchen and small living room with an empty file folder between us, its contents gone through and organized into neat stacks. We are quiet, but if the traveling of thoughts created sounds like cars moving, this small room would be filled with noise: the whoosh of passing, of breaks squealing, of horns honking at illegal u-turns, of slamming doors at rest stops.

Michael's sigh draws my eyes to him as he asks, "Why is it all these papers with their ... well-documented but tragic facts are less disturbing to me than a warning from an old man and the dreams of my wife?" He pauses then continues, "Granted, I know what fire can do, but some of what is said here does not make sense, yet the investigators' findings make sense. The incendiary device, the chain securing the front door ... don't add up when the point is made no one was supposed to be home that night. You were all supposed to be at my folks' house. I remember half the town was probably at our house that night, which accounts for the slow response time to the fire. The coroner's reports on cause of death support the device being in the upstairs room over the living room and the ceiling or floor, depending on the perspective taken, falling on the people gathered in the living room. The unidentified man died in the basement where the breakers for the house's power were. No gun or weapon was found, yet the front door was secured so that exit through it was impossible for the ones inside. The thoroughness of the investigation is unquestionable, but I cannot conceive of a motive. Why kill John? He was a history teacher. Your mother was a part-time nurse. May could have been involved in some secret organization for Irish grandmothers, but where was Sean? He was supposed to be there too. And the Danners called the meeting according to two different sources, so in what naughty business could a community pastor be involved? Or his wife who was a Sunday school teacher? We're missing something."

I lean back in my chair, "Remember Elwood said I needed to talk with your dad. Perhaps he will shed light into the shadows."

Michael leans his elbows on the table, "There are more than shadows here, Leah. Damn it, these people were murdered. You were hurt in a dream while you were sitting right beside me in our car. An eagle is tailing us. Monday we start digging for May's metal box, but we have no idea what will be inside the box. I remember you said you saw May with the box in the basement when we were telling each other our dreams a few days ago. If it's still there, we're not going to find it until we've excavated the debris from the fire and a whole lot of dirt."

I interrupt him, "What do you mean 'if' we find it?"

"Well, think about it. The unidentified guy is in the basement when he dies. Maybe he was looking for May's box. Someone else, maybe Sean, maybe not Sean, stops him and takes the box."

The thought numbs me, "So my dead father who is not dead may also be a murderer?"

Michael rubs his face with his hands, "If he is alive, why did he disappear? What keeps him away from you or his son? If Sean had contacted Grant, Grant would have told you. So, what motivates a person to stay away from his own children, and his old friends, for all these years?"

I put my hand on his arm, "Michael you are 'supposing' too much. We need more information about Sean, or at least I do, before we label him a murderer."

Michael agrees with me, "I know, I know. I'm just messin' around my own head and then thinking out loud. I'm sorry, baby, I didn't mean to upset you. We'll see dad tomorrow at mass and the welcome party for Connor, and I want to talk with Father Tom about you hurting yourself. I can't even 'suppose' about that. How can a person get physically hurt in a dream, or a vision, or whatever the hell they are?"

I stand up and start putting the papers back in the file as I ask, "I wonder how the man and the eagle are connected? In some way I cannot explain, they feel connected. And the lines in the tunnel … I know I have read about them somewhere. They have to be a language of some kind, but more than anything else, the man intrigues me. I want to talk with him, I think. His eyes … are … human, but not. I know he would have caught me too. It is strange, but I trust him."

I finish putting the papers in the file and notice Michael is looking at me, so I look back at him. He pulls me close to him and whispers into me, "Permission denied, wife. If these dream/visions you're having are real in the physical sense, you're not hanging out with this guy until we understand his purpose. Understood?"

I whisper-kiss back, "I am not sure if our wishes or your husbandly-permissions are taken into consideration, Michael, but my interest in him is not ... physical in that sense." I pull back from him a bit, "I cannot even believe you are acting jealous of a man from a dream."

Michael pulls me back into his arms, and his kisses are no longer lips just barely touching my lips and skin. His mood has changed completely. He grabs the blanket off the back of the couch and leads me out of the cabin and into the night, and I know he is claiming me as his own in a ritual both romantic and primal. I do not mind the mix.

✳   ✳   ✳   ✳

My eyes are closed, but I know what surrounds me: four foot thick walls connected to each other by foot thick, overhead beams; the walls' glossy white surfaces islanded by stained glass windows deep in their predominant hues of blood red, sky-blue, and emerald green. Imaged in the windows on the side walls are the tree of life, the dove flying up from the cross of resurrection, Mary holding her god-child, and the god-child, grown to man, praying. The window which faces the congregation portrays the lion and the lamb, and all who enter the church walk under a window with an image of an eagle flying with wide wings across a sky of blue and white. The statues of Mary and Joseph stand on either side of the altar and shallow enclaves on the far sides of each statue are home to one hundred small glassed candles in escalating rows of ten. Floors of stone are softened by the patterned placement of thick rugs. On each side of the large wooden doors a fireplace, six feet wide, fills the corner. The center aisle passes between rows of pews of rich dark redwood, and the scent of incense has permeated wood, wall, stone, and rug so that even when incense is not actually lit, its fragrance whispers of its own history here. Its own history ... adobe walls made of earth and straw and sun reaching down like roots; bricks formed by human hands ... Indian, Mexican, Irish, English ... heritages mixed like the bricks themselves. This sanctuary was built on the site of another only after asking permission; it was chosen by one culture to honor the holy place of another.

I have been here forever it seems, serenaded by Irish flute, Indian drum, and Gregorian chant; this designated increment of time before the service, called simply the music hour, stretches itself out beyond me and becomes for me a horizon. I wander toward it, passing through all the days I have had between this music hour and the last, and as I make my way each burden, each blessing falls away from me until who I am is revealed. I am separated from and joined to by heart-beat and breath only. I am free.

I am free as defined prior to the seventeenth century, not freedom based on autonomy but instead freedom through my human heritage of integrity and mag-nanimity; freedom through a nobility that has nothing to do with birthright but instead draws on a compassion which connects human to human. I whisper the name of my culture's holy one; I whisper 'God' as I look into the light show pre-sented on my closed eyelids, and that is all I see: falling stars, and shooting stars, and plains of light turning into darkness, and plains of darkness turning into light, and snow flakes zooming toward me and past me. I seek an image. 'In his image' the Bible claims, but that tells me little really, and so much is lost in trans-lation. Does 'his' mean he or is 'his' representational? Was 'he' black, white, red, brown, blue? I more than seek, I crave an image: a round, full breasted female fig-ure, or an omniscient grandfather, and either one with battalions of warrior angels as helpers, because we need helpers, intercessors, winged-ones who can fly between worlds and act as buffer to the righteous rightness of a god of creation, a god of all people, because we are, after all, only human, and we do have a ten-dency to create conflict and trauma and despair just as easily and naturally as we create harmony and reliance and trust.

A whisper in my ear startles me, "I can tell you stopped being peaceful about two or three minutes ago, and now you're just zooming on the Leah-thought-express going God knows where."

I smile as I lean my shoulder against Bradley's shoulder, "Know-it-all."

He arches an eyebrow and asks, "Did your family abandon you?"

I suggest, "We should go outside if we are going to talk."

Bradley grabs my hand, and we move from pew to aisle to door to portico. Then I answer him, "Michael and the kids sometimes come to music hour, but usually they like to go exploring to use up some of their energy before their move-ments are confined to sitting, standing, kneeling, and so-on. But I am glad you decided to be here."

"Well, even though we homosexuals are defined based on one aspect of our lives, which just happens to be physical, that does not mean we aren't spiritual. And recently I've been thinking about something that would illustrate this point perfectly: what if everyone was described by his or her sexual preference? Can you imagine? Job applications would be titillating. We'd have position-people; we'd have lights-on/lights-off people; we'd have extensive-foreplay people; we'd have wham-bam-thank-you-ma'm people—" I punch his shoulder gently and pull him away from the door where people are beginning to gather. He looks at me like I have lost my mind. "What? I am not saying anything … naughty, and I wasn't nearly done with my list, and it only gets more interesting, I swear."

I put my fingers to my lips to shush him, "Okay, okay, something is bothering you I can tell, or you would have chosen a more appropriate time and place to discuss this with me. Tell me what, so I can comfort you."

He shakes his head, "No, I am not ready to be comforted."

I compromise, "Then tell me what anyway, and I promise not to comfort you until you are ready."

We are walking slowly around the church, following the tiled walkway, "The elders at my brother's church finally found it necessary to openly condemn gays. Unless I want to 'change' I am no longer welcomed there."

I am stopped by his words, so Bradley stops also, "But Joe is your brother, and he's the pastor. Surely he can reason with them."

Bradley looks at me and steps closer, "Joe and Rachel came to my house last night. They sat together on my couch, and it felt like Rachel had come along to comfort her husband instead of to offer her condolences to me for being condemned. Joe said it was difficult for him to persuade others on a subject which he is also … let me see, his exact word was … uncomfortable." Bradley pauses, closing his eyes, then speaks softly, "I make my own brother uncomfortable. Yes, the subject of me is uncomfortable for my brother and his lovely wife. They explained that I was, of course, still welcome in their home, but the church has to honor the Word of God on the matter."

I ask, "Would a hug be okay at this point?"

He looks at me, "I'm not at all sure I'm ready for a hug. I wasn't even going to bring up the incident, but … well, for some reason, despite the integrity with which I have lived my life, I now feel … unclean. And that's insane, because I don't believe it for a minute, but I have been feeling it since last night."

I ask Bradley if Calvin and Maybe know. Calvin Danner is Bradley's and Joe's younger brother, and he owns and runs Big Bend Marina. All three of the Danner men are dedicated and intelligent human beings, and simultaneously as different as brothers can be in other ways, obviously. Bradley shakes his head, "That's the second part of the story. Joe, wanting to be on the up-and-up as he put it, called Calvin prior to our meeting, and told him what the church had decided." Bradley pauses to watch my expression.

I am not even blinking, "Did he want Cal to be a distraction or something? Joe could not have, even for a moment, believed Cal was going to be polite about the situation."

Bradley begins walking again, and I follow, "As I've mentioned before, I do not try to understand how some people choose to think; I do not want to know. In any case, Calvin and Maybe arrived shortly after Joe and Rachel made their announcement. Calvin told them to get out of my house, that judgmental, small-minded, religious-not-spiritual fascists were not allowed in my house or his. Maybe didn't need to say anything, because she has that ability to communicate so well her utter disdain for what she labels the tininess of some of our white-ways without uttering a word. I tried to calm Calvin, because I was thinking suddenly of Joe's and Rachel's kids, and of Calvin's and Maybe's kids, my nieces and nephews. I was thinking about a thousand great memories of my brothers and me both before and after our parents died, and I was also thinking of who I am as a person, that my being gay is only a part of who I am. Yet somehow because my sexual preference is an issue for some people; my sexual preference becomes all I am to them. Calvin was yelling, and Joe had his head down and was praying or avoiding eye contact with Calvin or something. That's when Maybe picked up one of my favorite framed photos of Calvin and Joe and me as boys and threw it on the floor. It worked. Joe looked up and Calvin shut-up. Maybe walked across the room and hugged me, walked over to Cal, took his hand in hers, and as they were walking out of the room, she said very quietly, "You're focusing on the wrong part of that book of yours, Joe."

We had stopped walking half-way through Bradley's explanation. Now he is staring out into the beauty of the day but not seeing it. I ask my next question because I do not want Bradley to go inside his own head and heart and be by himself right now, "Does Lane know what the church is doing?"

"I doubt it. What do you think he'll do?"

I look out across the peaceful grounds of the church: a statue of Saint Francis, surrounded by flowers, holding out his hands, beyond that Father Tom's greenhouse, and beyond the greenhouse, the orchard. So peaceful. I look back at Bradley, "If I know Lane, he will ask the church to reconsider, and if they refuse, he will cancel their lease. It is that simple, and it has been that simple since the Daytons have been the overseers of the town of Lane and its surrounding acreage. Prejudice of any kind is not permitted. If a person wants to be prejudiced, that person needs to do it somewhere else. All the land is owned by the Daytons, so we all live here on leases, for better or for worse, and that is the way it is."

Bradley shoves his hands in his pockets, "This is going to get ugly isn't it?"

I put my hand on his arm, "If it does, it is for a good reason. If Joe's church had decided to strike out at divorced people, or people from different cultures, or people who wear black clothing, or people who pierce or tattoo their bodies you would be outraged, but because these people are striking out at you, you feel a bit angry and a lot hurt. Admit it, Bradley. You know why Lane will be firm in this matter; throughout history when a society has allowed one group to be demeaned, it was only a matter of time until more groups joined the condemned list. Prejudice spreads and can be deadly. It's like cancer, and no one says, 'Oh, it's just a little cancer, nothing to worry about.' Cancer is cancer. Prejudice is prejudice. You are a wonderful, caring human being, and what you do or do not do in or out of bed is no one's damn business as long as you are not hurting yourself or others." I am talking with my hands now, maybe even my arms are involved. "The issue for us will be to fight prejudice without becoming prejudiced; that is where well intentioned people usually lose the battle. Think about it; what would Jesus say about people, who have named themselves after him, who harm or kill other people over land or beliefs or skin color. The Bible is powerful, but parts of the old testament seem more a reflection of a specific people rendering God in their own image than the testimony of a righteous God, and parts of the new testament seem more devoted to proclaiming the holiness of Jesus' followers than a precise rendering of a God-man, whose primary desire was to exemplify, through word and deed, a new way of following ten relatively simple and very livable commandments: acknowledge and honor there is a higher reality than man's wisdom, which continually changes; do not bow down before what has been made by man; do not call holy what is not holy; on a given day honor all creation, setting aside worldly pursuits and respecting all living creatures; honor family; do not destroy; do not be unfaithful to your heart, or mind, or to promises made in the use of your body; do not take what does not belong to you; do not gossip; do not be greedy." I am smiling as I finish, because Bradley is smiling.

He hugs me, "If you don't mind me asking, from what translation did you get that wording?"

I lean back and look up at him, "When I was ten or so and asking way too many questions way too often about God and all the rules and regulations of the church, May and Father Tom suggested I make the commandments mine by writing them in words that made sense to me. This did not save them from questions, but my questions became more specific and not quite so metaphysical in content. I remember mom helped me. We would sit on my bed and discuss, and she never tired of it or lost her patience with me. She helped me find words to express my ideas and made me so aware of the importance of choosing and using words." I smile again after the memory fades like the image on an old tv set slowly disappearing into its own center. "Anyway, I memorized my translation way back then, and I still remember."

Bradley sighs and is about to say something, but we hear someone else sigh. We both turn toward the bench behind us to discover it is very much occupied. The man is not at all embarrassed we have caught him listening to our conversation. He is smiling, looking at us through bright blue eyes as he pushes shoulder length blonde hair back behind his ears. His grin is wide, his skin fair. He stands slowly. He is about the same height as Bradley but even thinner. I want to be annoyed, but his manner makes it difficult.

His Irish accent confirms his identity, "It's glad I am you both just happened on my little corner of the churchyard to have your conversation, for it was an insightful introduction to my new home." He enthusiastically shakes both of our hands.

I say, "Connor."

He says, "Leah, I'd have known you anywhere." Then he quickly turns toward Bradley before I can ask why, "And sir, I'd be believing your sex life is of less interest to Almighty God than the state of your heart, mind, and soul, but God's word, represented by scripture, must be honored, even though religious wars and witch hunts are too often the consequence."

Bradley nods his head and comments, "You are definitely your uncle's nephew."

Connor is quick to respond, "I'll be taking that as a compliment, to be sure, and now little Leah, ask me your question before you grab me by my poor old collar and beat me for teasing you so."

So I ask, "Why did you say you would know me anywhere?"

Connor puts his arms around both Bradley's shoulders and mine and begins walking back toward the entrance of the church, "Your story is not made in America, cailín; it's from Ireland, and I am from Ireland, from the same line of MacBrides you are. I claim Saint Brigid as ancestor. I shouldn't have to be saying more than that. I could ask though if you are onto the second letter yet?"

I ask 'what?' and Bradley asks 'what letter?'; Connor just laughs in response to both of us then walks into the church before we even realize he is ending the conversation. He turns just before he joins a small group of people who seem to be waiting for him, "We've all the time in the world, now don't we, Leah? All the time in the world."

*   *   *   *

Father Tom stands before us. Michael, John Henry, Mary, Bradley and I sit half way back on the left side. We are surrounded by family, friends, and acquaintances. Scattered here and there are the faces of a few unknown, and they are most likely visitors from other places who are lodging at Castle Rock Resort, which is across the lake from our house. The front pews of the church are occupied by Lane, his wife Lilly, Matilda, Michael's parents and grandparents, and other elders of the town. Many of my family group members and students are also present. I notice Connor and another man sit in two of the high backed, ornately carved chairs that grace the walls on either side of the altar. Father Tom stands on the second stair leading to the altar. His head is bowed. We are all quiet and waiting. Even the youngest of our congregation are within the moment. Because Father Tom believes in the old adage 'raise a child up in the way he should go', there is no childcare or nursery here. Given the repeated opportunity, children learn to behave appropriately; they learn to read the situational signs and markers we, as a culture, post so clearly on both conscious and subconscious levels.

Father Tom looks up and takes a moment to allow his eyes to welcome those who have gathered before him. Then he repeats one word over and over. His voice, when he speaks, and the silence he allows to linger after each utterance are like a wave drawing us forward, holding us there, then pushing us back. "Holy … holy … holy …" whispered, then called out, then spoken lovingly, then spoken with no inflection of tone at all. When he begins in earnest to draw us to him, his words maintain the same wave like momentum. "I call this place that … holy. This is a holy … place. I prepare myself to enter here…. I bathe my body…. I clear from my mind … thoughts unrelated…. I put matters and concerns about next week … or about tomorrow … or about yesterday … away … out of my reach … so I cannot and do not … grab them back and in doing so distract myself … from what is here for me now … in this moment." Our eyes follow his gestures, "I come to this place to honor that which is beyond me always and yet … is as much a part of who I am as … this hand … this heart … these eyes. I am a spiritual and … physical being. I live in two worlds … or one world with two aspects … perhaps not unlike the moon in its phases…. Depending on the moment then … do I appear whole or half or … just a sliver of myself …? Where is my spirit part?"

He pauses then walks down the center aisle, no longer a wave but a waterfall, "What do you see when you look at me? Am I whole? Am I half? What do you see? Only a man? Just a body with a heart pumping blood and a mind manufacturing thoughts? Where is the spirit part of me? And what of the moment? What of time? Is moment made up of parts also? Are moments physical and spiritual, clothed in one or the other, or are moments instead the two intertwined, and if so, is that me also? The physical and spiritual parts of me intertwined? And then I am the moon, whole always, but seen by others based on perspectives which are based on position in time and place. And then I am also the moon, whole always, but stratified by self so I forget … the blend."

He pauses as he walks back to the altar, "How far, in my discussion, have I wondered? What do holy and being physical and spiritual have to do with each other? Why is this place holy? Can the forest be holy? Can the waves crashing on the shore be holy? Is the moon holy? Is their a place in your home where you go to pray, to meditate, to nurture that which is in you that is not fed by food or rested by sleep? Can that place be holy?"

He whispers, "What is holy?" He speaks more loudly, "What is my definition? My perspective? My 'take' on holy? Holy is…. Holy is…." He reaches out to us with his eyes; we are quiet as we attempt to complete his statement, and I do. Then I look over and can tell from the expressions on John Henry's and Mary's faces they are both involved in Father Tom's request. Michael's eyes meet mine over the heads of our children, and our smiles join there also. Then I look around at the faces I can see. Some heads are bowed with eyes closed and some heads are titled back with eyes open, and I appreciate we are all searching in our own ways. And I appreciate that Father Tom allows the silence to fill itself completely before he allows his own words to reflect what we may have claimed as being holy.

His voice is soft and yet it fills the room as completely as the silence did, "Holy is … sunrise. Holy is … the face of a loved one. Holy is … a child's innocence. Holy is … the love between two people which has stretched over decades. Holy is … the dark, rich soil of earth. Holy is … God's creation. Holy is God." He pauses, raises his hands, "And holy is … within you. Holy can come from within you and it can bathe others in compassion. Holy is an expectation, an aspiration, a desire so pure, so sweet, and so completing it can become a way of life. Holy is God's choice for us. Holy is captivating and startling and soothing and warm and fresh and as ancient as the earth on which we live. Holy is an awareness that each moment has been deemed sacred in its creation by God, and that each moment is to be lived through with an honoring dedication to achieve, within that moment's span, communion not only with God but also communion with others through God. Holy is the meeting place of the physical and the spiritual; it is where I express who God is through who I am, through my thoughts, my words, and my actions with no influence inferred by circumstance. Holy is the understanding I should be a reflection of my God, make the difficult journey to where he is, not take his name and attach it to my own perspective, to my own desired outcomes. That behavior denies God's power, and I will remind you that God … is God, and he is holy in his righteousness. He is both the gentle light of dawn and the crushing weight of the tidal wave. God is … holy, and I reflect his holiness by being constant in devotion to all that is good and kind and honoring to self and to others. Holy is without compromise. Holy is relentless and undefeatable; it is timeless and can no more be regulated to that which is only spiritual anymore than God can be regulated to that which is only spiritual. God lives and breathes, and when he sighs the whole world quiets, pauses, looks up, closes eyes, reaches out without knowing why, cries out, smiles. God is there—" Father Tom points to the back right corner of the church, and we turn in unison.

Smiles and soft laughter are seen and heard as we turn again to face this physical-spiritual man who leads us so gently. "Quest peacefully for him, and wherever you look, he will be. Quest internally for him, and within you he will be. He is above all things, beyond all things, before all things. He is the holy of holies … go to him, think of him … search for him in the face and heart of another human being. See him as the morning sun reaches out light hands and draws back the thick velvet curtain of darkness, which God also fashioned, and know within your heart-mind, within your physical-spiritual being you are a child of God, as all people are; you are made by God … to reflect him. Go to him now, in this place, in this moment, and make your peace, sing your song, cry your tears, be thankful for the blessings in your life. Go now, in silence and totally still, dance before him, dance before the holy of holies, raise your arms to his sky. Praise and glory to him! As it was in the beginning, is now and ever shall be … glory … glory to him … glory to his anointed son … glory to his holy spirit." Father Tom begins singing in Latin a simple melody and chant he uses when he wants us to look within ourselves for a moment before he gives his final blessing, and before we once again allow thoughts and matters and concerns about next week or about tomorrow or about yesterday to resurface and put themselves very much within our reach.

I whisper-sigh 'yes' and smile as I let my head tilt back and close my eyes. In my thoughts I say, "Thank you, Lord-God, for my life, and for my loved ones, and for all your people and for all your creation, and for this moment, and for the next, and for the moments before this one, even for the ones that were difficult.

Your plan is so much bigger than I am. I pray I could honor you with my thoughts, my words, and my deeds. I pray you would watch over me and mine, and protect us and guide us. Thank you, God, thank you."

* * * *

We have walked, Michael, John Henry, Mary and I, to the fountain centered between the church and the meeting hall. We stand together watching water fly and fall. The fountain is round and wide and from the center a bird rises, wings spread, with only its tail feathers joined to the fountain's base and under the water's surface. All around the giant bird, water rains up instead of down as tiny jets propel, at varying intervals, a transparent barrier that could symbolize the permanence and solidity of our own self-made and self-imposed partitions. Like a child on the shore making walls of sand, or as I mark off this part of my life from that part of my life, and then a wave comes....

Michael sits on the side of the fountain and asks John Henry and Mary how they completed Father Tom's statement. Mary is quick to respond, "I know this isn't the best answer, but I think holy is ... well, it's when I put my toys away before you or mom ask me, and then ... neither of you notice I did it before I start playing again, and it's a mess again, but I don't say anything. Holy is doing what's right when no one knows it and not telling about it, just doing it because it's right." She pauses but we can tell she is not done speaking, "That's how I can be holy, but I don't know yet what God's kind of holy is. I know it's got to be much bigger than my holy."

I reach down and pick her up, "I like your answer very much."

Mary laughs and pats my cheeks, "You're my mommy, so I knew you would." Now her eyes search the area and she whispers, "But God is listening too, and he has lots of other kids besides me, so he may only think my answer is okay."

Michael responds, "Well, I'm the dad, you know, and I say that God being who God is, he can probably believe all our answers are the best answer because of how big his heart is." Michael looks at John Henry, "What do you think, son?"

John Henry nods his head, "I think holy is, like Mary said, our kind of holy and then there's God's kind of holy. I guess it's like my holy is 'trying to' and God's holy 'is'. Does that make sense?"

Michael gets up and stands behind John Henry, putting his hands on John Henry's shoulders, "Yes, your answer makes good sense, and I'm proud of both of you."

John Henry asks Michael and I to share how we completed Father Tom's statement, and Michael begins to answer, but a voice calls out our names. We turn to see Cal waving at us as he walks toward us with Maybe, and their two children, Hope and Rocky. Bradley is with them. Cal's booming voice and waving arm cause the birds at a nearby feeder to take flight. Maybe is trying to 'shush' him, but it does no good as he seems dedicated to conversing with us from across the large expanse of lawn. "Hello Callaghans, hello … good to see you. What a day … a short sermon followed by a large meal. Can't beat that, can you? I should let Maybe drag me here more often."

Mary runs to Hope, Cal's and Maybe's eleven year old daughter and Hope picks up Mary and swings her around carefully but exuberantly. Rocky is a couple of years older than John Henry but both boys enjoy each other's company, and they stand together talking quietly. Cal's handshake is as energetic as his greeting, and Maybe only shakes her head at him as Michael and Bradley shake hands more calmly.

Maybe is looking into my eyes as she speaks, "Well now that the men have completed their ritual of greeting, and my Cal has scared away any birds for miles and any visitors new to Lane, I say quietly to you, good morning, little sister."

I smile and respond, "Good morning, big sister."

Maybe is done with her greeting, but not done with her husband, "And as for you, Calvin Danner, I did not drag you here. You said you wanted to come to be with your brother and to welcome Father Tom's nephew. So, don't be painting a harsh picture of your sweet wife."

Cal reaches for her, pulls her to him, and wraps his arms around her, "This is how I keep her quiet, physical attention. She craves physical closeness with her man." Cal looks down at his small wife who is standing perfectly still, and I can tell by his expression and the set of his arms he was sure she would struggle a bit to get out of his arms, so he asks "What are you doing?"

Maybe makes no reply and stays totally still until finally he releases her. As his arms drop to his sides, Maybe steps back. She looks up at him, "My heartbeat is slower than yours; I compared them, and thank you for my morning hug, oh-wise-husband, but you should admit you came here of your own free will and honor the emotions that influenced you to do so."

Cal looks at each one of us then back at Maybe, "I could be fishing, and I could still do that, so don't try to move me this way and that. Brad knows why I'm here. Men don't have to explain everything to each other like women do." Maybe raises her eyebrows in response as he continues, "But enough chit-chat, let's go see what we came to see and do what we came to do before the nephew realizes he should have stayed in Ireland because we are a heathen lot and ... before the food is gone."

∗   ∗   ∗   ∗

Long tables with centers lined with bowls and trays of hot and cold food offerings array themselves between rows of seated people. And once again Father Tom stands before us, but this time a young man stands on each side of him. Father Tom raises his hands and slowly the muted but loud noise of a hundred different conversations is silenced. "We are gathered here to honor the arrival of my nephew Connor Sullivan Maguire and his friend and co-worker, Malick O'Brien." We applaud and there are words of welcome called out, then we are quiet again as Father Tom continues, "I have asked Connor to give the blessing."

Father Tom steps back and Connor steps forward. Father Tom bows his head as does Malick. Connor's voice is strong and his accent adds to the flow of his words, "It is grateful I am to be here. It is grateful I am, God of my fathers and God of my mothers, to be of service to you. May I also be of service to those gathered here. I ask simply that we, each one of us, are thankful for the bountiful fare laid out before us, and I ask that you would, dear God, bless the hands that prepared this meal. 'May the words of our mouths and the meditations of our hearts be a blessing to you, O God.' Amen."

Once again words of greeting are called out to Connor and Malick as they and Father Tom take their seats at the end of one of the tables in the front of the room. The noise level rises as conversations are renewed. I feel so glad to be here as I look around at those seated around me and my family at this long table made by the joining of at least four rectangular tables together: Bradley and his brother and his family, the elders of Michael's family, including Elwood; Michael's older sister, Sarah, her husband, Paul, and their children, Sean and April; Michael's brother, Daniel, his wife, Sharon, and their children, HJ, Nathan, and Laura; Brian; Alex and Jan Carson, and their children Mark and Trisha; and Duke Brightstar, assistant fire chief under Michael's father, his wife, Dawn, who owns and manages Nature's Way Health Food Store, and their sons, Catcher and Cruz.

Duke is Marcia Brightstar's older brother, and since I do not see Marcia and Greg Holcomb, her fiancé, I wait until he looks my way then ask him where they are. Seated half way down the table from me, he raises his hand to his ear, so I join others in speaking more loudly than is normally considered appropriate when inside, but Duke still cannot make out my words. At this point, Cal decides to lend me assistance; he yells my question so not only Duke can hear it but also half the room. Conversations stop in our area, Cal shrugs then many of us laugh. I move my chair back and walk over to Duke who is still smiling at Cal.

I greet Dawn and Catcher and Cruz as I ask Duke if he heard Cal or if I need to repeat my question. Duke shakes his head, "No, no, I definitely heard the question. Marcia had the weekend off so she and Greg went to the city to be alone, which is sort of interesting if you think about it. If I wanted to be alone with my woman, I wouldn't go to a crowded city."

Dawn laughs and pats his shoulder, "So true. He would take me to the shore or to the forest and we would camp out, and that would be his idea of a romantic weekend." Duke and Dawn are full-blooded Native American and the beauty of their features, hair so black it reflects every light and golden brown eyes just a bit darker than their skin color, is also visible in their sons. As I tell them to enjoy their meal and walk back to my seat, I look at Maybe, whose mother is full-blooded Intah and father is European-American, and I also appreciate the mixing of races that is so apparent in her. Her eyes are the blue of the ocean and of her father while her hair and skin are from her mother. Before I sit down again I hear my name called, and when I turn I see Father Tom is using hand movements to request I join him.

As I walk toward him I notice the two men on either side of him. Connor's fairness is contrasted by Malick's dark hair and skin color. Both of their eyes are blue, but Connor's are the blue of a summer sky while Malick's are so dark blue they are almost purple. Father Tom smiles at me as he introduces Connor and Malick to me. I smile at Connor as he explains to Father Tom we have already had the pleasure of meeting, but my eyes are held by Malick's gaze. His hand takes the place of Connor's holding mine, and he does not release it as he speaks, "Leah May MacBride Callaghan, it is a pleasure to finally meet you in the flesh."

My expression must indicate the unease his words cause, but that does not seem to bother him at all. It is Father Tom's hand on his shoulder that finally causes him to release my hand. Father Tom's words do not make me forget the uncomfortable sensation caused by Malick's words or his touch and seem to be meant as much as a gentle reprimand to Malick as they are meant to comfort me. "You must forgive Malick. He takes an inordinate pleasure in wording his statements in such a way one is not totally clear of his motivation or purpose." Malick does not apologize or correct Father Tom, but simply nods his head at me and resumes his seat. Connor watches us, seems to remember to smile and tells me he is looking forward to meeting my family as I walk away from them. Angela and Teri call out my name as I walk by them, and I put my hand on Valerie's shoulder to let her know I am standing next to her, as I ask them how they are doing. Samson is on the left of Valerie, and I pat his head as I walk away from them after we have discussed the girls' plans to go to the shore when they leave here.

Michael is watching me as I resume my seat. John Henry and Mary sit between us, so I only suggest that Michael make sure and meet both Connor and Malick before we leave. He nods, then I notice Bradley and Maybe are watching me, and I somehow know they were, as Michael was, watching me when I met Malick. I have no doubts at all that, not only Michael, but also Bradley and Maybe, will be seeking out the person of Malick to discover what caused not only my facial expression to change during my introduction to him, but also has caused a change in how safe I feel in the room. I put up my guard, realizing I am no more protected by my defensive measure than the bird of the fountain is protected by the fountain's gossamer cascade of water. In this place surrounded by family and friends I should sense no barely perceived murmur of trepidation; I should sense no barely perceived whisper of danger, but I do.

*   *   *   *

The opportunity for Michael and Bradley and Maybe to meet with Connor and Malick occurred quite easily due to the fact Connor and Malick joined us at our table as soon as children and elders and a few others left with Father Tom at Father Tom's open invitation to all those gathered to walk with him through the orchard. Seats were abandoned by their occupants and Father Tom had no more than exited the room when Connor and Malick took the seats across from Michael and me.

Bradley and Maybe moved from their seats and took the empty seats next to Michael as I felt a hand on my shoulder, and turning watched Elwood sit down next to me. We exchange smiles, and for a heartbeat or two no one speaks at all. Maybe and Connor begin to speak at the same time, then each stop, and again it is quiet.

Michael reaches across the table and offers his hand to Connor, who takes it, and then Michael offers his hand to Malick. As Michael and Malick are shaking hands Michael introduces himself, "I am Michael Callaghan. Leah is my wife." Michael then introduces the others, beginning with Elwood followed by Maybe and Bradley. Connor and Malick shake hands with each of them, and after that pleasantries are exchanged regarding the journey from Ireland.

Malick responds quietly, his accent less pronounced than Connor's, "Actually my trip was shorter than Connor's; I was in the states already."

Michael asks, "Where?"

Malick who has been looking around the room or down at his hands before Michael's question, looks first into Michael's eyes then into mine as he answers, "Oh, here and there mostly."

Connor laughs, "Malick makes friends easily. I'm of the idea it's because he is so forthright in the giving of information." Connor pauses as he waits for Michael to shift his gaze from Malick to himself before he continues, "To be sure, we all have our strengths and weaknesses, now don't we? Malick here …" Connor puts his hand on Malick's shoulder, "is one of those lads who could go a month of Sundays without the company of another human being and not be minding that lack of camaraderie at all. But he is the best at what he does."

Bradley leans forward and asks, "And what is that, if you don't mind me asking?"

Connor leans forward also and looks directly into Bradley's eyes as he responds, "Why he was one of the Church's finest investigators of paranormal activity. I say 'was' instead of 'is' only because he left the Church over a bit of a difference of opinion on the handling of a certain matter a couple of years ago, not so unlike my uncle did years before that. Not a big deal really, if you believe that … God is … God, and church is only a way of responding to him. We can all have our opinions and a thousand little churches with their own ways of responding without getting all war-like and defensive now can't we?"

Michael puts his arm around my shoulder, "Somehow the feeling I get from the way you make that point and the feeling I get from the way Father Tom makes that point are different."

Connor nods his head, "And here I've come to learn, don't you know? I'm sure after a month or two, or maybe a year or two, since I am a slow learner if the truth be told, I'll be sounding just like the good father himself."

Michael only says, "Anything is possible."

Connor slaps the table with his hand, "And isn't that the truth, and so we're agreed on that. And let me say even though I am feeling some tension here, like maybe we got off on the wrong foot with you and yours, first impressions aren't always the most reliable."

Malick speaks to me, "I meant no offense, and what I said may make more sense as time goes on and after we get to know each other, so I apologize for any difficulty I caused. I meant no harm."

I am perplexed by this man and his ways of being. He feels honest and dangerous at the same time, but I only say 'thank you' to him. Then Connor begins asking Maybe about her family and the conversation becomes lighter. When the conversation turns to local Indian customs, Malick joins in to make comparisons between some of the old Irish beliefs with some of the beliefs Maybe has shared. Elwood invites both young men to the library to see a model he just completed of a typical coastal Intah village.

Then John Henry and Mary join us. John Henry stands between Michael and me, as Mary climbs into my lap. Michael introduces the children to Connor and Malick. After Connor asks how they enjoyed the orchard and both children respond, Connor and Malick decide to go see for themselves if the children's detailed and almost wondrous description of the one hundred year old orchard is true. Maybe and Bradley join them.

Mary turns in my lap, her little legs managing to fold and unfold themselves without causing me too much damage, and again she holds my face in her hands, "I don't want to clean up really. I know I should, but I don't."

John Henry replies before I can, "Sometimes it's not about wanting to, Mary; it's about supposed to. What if the people who signed up to bring food had decided they didn't feel like doing their job?"

Mary snuggles even closer but turns her face toward her brother, "We'd have hungry tummies, but there wouldn't be any dirty dishes to wash. And anyway ... you're not my dad; you can't tell me what to do."

John Henry looks at Michael and me then shakes his head. "She's being silly again. I wasn't telling her what to do." And then my very intelligent and articulate children forget their verbal acuity and involve themselves in that age old recital of 'were too' and 'was not' over and over again. Michael and I can only smile as we look into each other's eyes, then Hank's voice from across the room interrupts my children's volley, which would not have ended until Michael or I had asked them to stop, because for reasons quite clear to me the son and daughter of Michael and Leah are just a bit persistent in their verbal exchanges.

We all turn toward Hank. He is holding the door open, which leads into the large kitchen behind him. "Well this is a fine how-do-you-do. Here we are, the old folks, all gloved up and ready to wash, but the young ones have brought us no dishes."

Mary is out of my lap and runs to catch up with John Henry as he walks quickly to their grandpa. All three of them disappear into the kitchen as Michael and I make our way through the long rows of tables to join them. When we walk through the door we are greeted by the voices of the Callaghan elders. Matilda and Katherine are cleaning counters while Katy and Sarah are putting away an assortment of items used during the preparation of the meal. Michael's grandfather, Patrick, now in his eighties, stands with Paul, and both hold drying cloths in their hands. The kitchen is a visual blend of old and new. The large stainless steel oven and stove, sinks, and refrigerator contrast the roughly hewn ten foot long redwood table with its benches and the six foot wide fireplace still equipped with cast-iron hooks and hanging rods once used for cooking. My children standing in the midst of their grandparents and great-grandparents accentuate this pleasant mixing nicely.

Hank and Michael open wide wooden shutters that will allow us to directly pass to them trays of dishes, utensils, glasses, serving platters and bowls after we have gathered them. I look from face to face, first Patrick's, then Hank's, then Michael's and lastly John Henry's and cannot help but notice the Callaghan features so obviously shared by each. I realize simultaneously these shared traits go deeper than coloration of skin and eyes and hair and shape of bone; Callaghan men laugh easily and often but are relentless in their dedication to family and friends; they are strong willed and persistent in all matters in which they involve themselves; even hobbies and fun times are done well, with care given to process and/or product.

As I begin to notice the features of the women these men have chosen for themselves, I am grabbed from behind and swung around and around in strong arms.

His laughter gives him away even though I still cannot see his face, "Brian, you brat, put me down." As my vision is circling the room, I notice Daniel and Sharon and their children must have entered with Brian, and they stand, at a safe distance from my swinging feet, smiling at Brian's enjoyment of my predicament. I try to reason with Brian again, "If you do not put me down now, my lunch will be coming up faster than you can say—" My threat works, and I am released before I can finish my statement. And even though I am now stationary, the room is still circling in my head.

Brian laughs as he comments, "No way am I going to be responsible for causing more clean up work. You may not lose your lunch, do you hear me?"

I am still unsteady on my feet but reply, "You are a nasty boy with fiendish ways, and you should think about your actions and their consequences before you do them, not after."

Daniel walks over to me and gives me a hug then slugs his brother good naturedly on the arm. "You need to get married, brother, so you can learn how to treat women correctly. They're not toys, you know?" Daniel walks over to Sharon, his wife, and puts his arm around her. Sharon and I exchange knowing smiles, because both Michael and Daniel, despite Daniel's words, do on occasions take great pleasure in treating their women like toys: picking us up when we do not want to be picked up, holding us down and tickling us when we would prefer not to be tickled or held down, and the occasional and gentle, but nevertheless ill timed by our thinking, toss in the lake during picnics when we are fully clothed.

Sharon responds, "Daniel, think about that statement you just made, then think about modeling by example instead of by do-as-I-say, not-as-I-do. You remember the last family picnic at Michael's and Leah's, don't you?"

Now Michael and Daniel look at each other, and both shrug their shoulders as Daniel asks, "You mean when you fell in the lake, and I had to save you?"

Sharon just shakes her head as Hank Jr., called HJ and so like his father in appearance he appears to be just a smaller model of Daniel, slaps his hands together and says, "Right dad, you're telling a whopper and your dad is standing in the same room. If I did that, what would happen? House arrest until the moon changes. Not fair. Do something, grandpa; your son is lying like a rug."

Katy responds before Hank can, "Go gently now, Hank, or I will have to share some of your behaviors."

Hank shakes his head, "Not me, I'm not getting involved in this."

Patrick's voice is clear and strong, "Well I will get involved but only to say there's far too much talk going on and too little work. There's a pre-season baseball game set to start in an hour, and I plan to be watching it from the first pitch thrown to the last, so get a move on. Callaghan clean up starts now, or we'll be here until dinner."

The patriarch has spoken, and we all oblige him. The children, John Henry, Mary, HJ, his younger brother and sister, Nathan and Laura, all grab plastic bins to pick-up silverware or napkins from the tables. Michael, Daniel, Brian, Sarah, Sharon and I are handed large metal trays by Katherine so we can gather dishes and serving platters and bowls from the tables. Callaghan clean up has begun, and soon cheerful voices accompany the clamor of dishes stacked and water running and silverware clinking.

When the opportunity avails itself I ask Hank if Michael and I can talk with him about May's first letter. Hank's eyes meet mine after my question is asked.

"I've been wondering when you would come to me." He pauses as he sets the plate down he just finished. "All these years I've had this information. I knew someday I would have to share the words with you, and part of me is ready and wants to be done being their safekeeper, but part of me wants to take them with me to my grave and not make you have to deal with them. But the choice was never really ours was it?"

I put my hand on his arm, "No, I do not believe so. I really have no idea what you will tell me, but I do know Michael and I have something to do. I have to believe we will be all right, that we will be able to handle whatever it is we are being called to do. Perhaps that is just me being me and being hopeful and optimistic, but the assurance I feel comes from somewhere ... beyond who I am, if that makes any sense. It is like I am walking a path I know but do not know at all at the same time."

Hank wraps his arms around me, and I remember him doing this same thing in the past, using the comfort of his fatherly arms, when words of encouragement have seemed too fleeting a solace to offer. I thank him as he steps away from me, and he nods his head telling me six-thirty tonight will be a good time to meet. When I am half-way across the kitchen from him, he calls out to me that Katy can watch John Henry and Mary as he and Michael and I talk. I smile in reply and return to work, as I think many-hands-make-light-work is not only applicable to physical tasks but also to peace of mind. Michael and I are not facing our unknown task alone; his family stands with us.

*   *   *   *

We are turning into our driveway when I notice Bradley's black BMW parked next to Michael's truck. Then I see a Frisbee sail through the air and Puppy chasing after it. Bradley walks from the side of the house into our view as we park. Puppy, with the bright yellow Frisbee in his mouth, is running circles around Bradley as he makes his way to us.

Michael takes the Frisbee from Puppy's mouth and throws it for him again as he says to Bradley, "You just can't get enough of our good company today?"

Bradley smiles in response to Michael's question, "Your dog is wearing me out. He never tires of his games does he?"

Michael is again throwing the Frisbee for Puppy, "Too true, I'm afraid. He can do this for hours."

John Henry and Mary greet Bradley then go into the house. Michael and I are walking toward Bradley, but Michael stops. "The kids just walked in the house."

I turn to him, "And?"

He looks into my eyes, "The door wasn't locked. I locked the door when we left."

Bradley is closer to the house than we are and upon hearing Michael's words he runs to the front door, opens it and enters. We are right behind him. John Henry and Mary are standing totally still three feet from the door. Sofa cushions and drawers are not as we left them, and two framed photos on the wall are hanging at an angle.

Michael's voice is barely above a whisper, but his words are in the form of a command, "Leah, take the kids and go wait on the deck. Call Puppy to be with you. Bradley if you wouldn't mind, stay with them."

Bradley and the kids and I move to do as Michael has requested. On the deck we stand. Puppy has dropped the frisbee at my feet but having sensed the discomfort of the children, the protectiveness of Bradley, and my fear he is no longer interested in playing. Puppy stands with his head raised, smelling the air. I try to do the same, but I only smell the scent of trees on the light breeze. John Henry and Mary are on either side of me, and I have a hand resting on each one of them. Bradley moves around us, first in front of us then behind. None of us speak; we only listen to the out of door's silence that is not silent at all; sounds are everywhere: the water of the lake lapping at its shore; bird song from a distance, a car passing on the road, frog-talk, a man's and woman's voices from across the lake.

Michael stands in the door. He nods for us to come in, and after we do, we sit on the sofa and chairs and wait for him to speak.

Michael sits down in one of the big overstuffed chairs and opens his arms to John Henry and Mary; they run from me to him. Once they are comfortable, and he has kissed the top of each one of their heads, he speaks, "Bradley, you must have arrived and surprised whoever it was in here. The screen is off the back window in our bedroom, and the latch on the screen door on the patio is broken. It would seem if you had not forced his quick exit, we might not have known anyone had been here. I can tell drawers have been searched, but he was careful. The mattress on our bed is not quite centered. Books and things are moved on shelves but only barely. John Henry's and Mary's rooms do not seem to have been searched at all. There is only one set of footprints leading away from the house out back. My guess is he entered through the front door and was planning on leaving the same way. What I don't understand is why our dog let someone enter our house. He's friendly, but I've seen him protect this place from trespassers on more than one occasion, and one time he backed a friend of mine right back to his car because Puppy didn't know him. I'm going to check with the neighbors to see if Puppy was off visiting again and also find out if anyone saw or heard anything. The only thing I can tell is missing at this point is the file. We put it in the drawer of the desk, but it's not there now."

Bradley comments, "Puppy wasn't here when I first arrived, which was probably a half hour to forty-five minutes ago. He came running up about two or three minutes after I turned off the engine of my car. I, of course, didn't even try the front door. I thought I'd just wait for a while; if you didn't show up, I'd leave a note for Leah to give me a call."

I ask, "How did the person get in the door without a key?"

Bradley rises and checks the lock on the outside of the door, "There are no scratch marks or indications it's been jimmied or messed with in any manner."

I repeat my concern, "So, how then?"

Michael leans his head back against the chair, "Good question. We can call Lane Security, but I've done everything they will do except dust for fingerprints and cast the footprint out back, but I have no doubt the guy wore gloves; he was too careful in every other way, until Bradley startled him. I really don't think anything the security guys will do will tell us what we really want to know or give us additional information in regards to what we already know, do you?"

Bradley prompts, "Meaning?"

Michael opens his eyes, looks at Bradley then at me, "Whoever was here wanted the file. There's cash lying on my bedside table; your jewelry is still in your jewelry box. Professionals know how to get through a lock without leaving any marks to indicate they have done so. Or there is the possibility whoever entered used a key. That option would concern me more than the other." Michael pauses and rubs his face with his hands. "We already know what the person was after, but I believe learning 'who' is going to remain a mystery for the time being."

I look at each of my children's faces to try to sense what they are feeling, but they both have their eyes closed and appear to be resting. Since I know Michael will not stay stationary long, I call their names, "John Henry, Mary, how are you feeling about all this?"

Mary presses her face into her father's chest then covers her head with her arms. John Henry sits up, looks down at his folded hands then up into my eyes, "I'm not scared, but I'm not happy either." He pauses then asks the question which I am sure is also on Bradley's mind, "What was in the file, mom?"

My eyes go to Michael's face, and he nods his head. "Well, your da and I are involved in …" I pause and look at Bradley, then I continue, "… in discovering what may have happened the night my parents, Grandma May, and Bradley's parents died. There's more to what we are doing than that, but for now, that's all I can share with you. The file had information from investigators and police reports, transcripts of interviews, and other paper work like that."

There is a look of amazement on Bradley's face, but I want to stay focused on the children for now, so I look back at John Henry and at Mary, who is now watching me out of the corner of her eye. John Henry asks, "Wasn't the fire an accident?"

I answer slowly, "We are not sure the fire was an accident, but we do not believe it was anyone's intention to hurt Bradley's parents or my family. From what we have discovered so far, it may have been two individuals were involved but not working together, and they may have struggled and something went wrong. No one was supposed to be home that night, so the deaths could not have been part of the plan. We are very much in the beginning stages of understanding anything, so I am not sure if what I have said has made any sense."

John Henry turns to look into his father's face, "Is what you're doing dangerous?"

Michael puts his arms around John Henry's shoulders, "We won't let anything happen to you or your sister, son."

John Henry lays his hand on his father's chest, "Okay, but who's not going to let anything happen to you and mom?"

Michael smiles at John Henry reassuringly then looks at me, "Mom and I are going to take care of each other."

John Henry's voice is soft but firm, "Promise me that, because I know if you say you promise it will happen, because you always do what you say you will."

Michael looks into his son's eyes and says, "I promise we will do our very best to take care of each other."

Mary's voice is muffled but insistent, "Promise me too, da."

Michael's hand smoothes her hair as he says, "I promise you too, honey."

Bradley has a somewhat skeptical expression on his face, "Well now that we are all wondrously reassured, I am going to leave you to your Sunday evening, but I would like you to," he pauses for emphasis, "promise me you and/or Leah will agree to clarify this situation for me at your earliest convenience."

Michael and I nod our heads in agreement. Bradley leaves after he has said goodbye to each one of us and to Puppy who is lying at my feet. Michael suggests he and John Henry and Mary come cuddle on the couch where I am. As they are moving to do so the phone rings. Michael indicates he wants to answer it so I hand the phone to him. He says 'Callaghan residence' then listens for a second or two, hands the phone back to me, and I set it back in its stand.

As soon as I am done, Michael reaches down and takes hold of my hands and pulls me up to him. "I'm stealing your mom for a minute because I need a hug, okay? If you two want to get a snack you can, and you should probably check Puppy's water and food bowls." John Henry and Mary and then Puppy, as soon as the pantry door is opened, are in the kitchen as Michael whispers in my ear, "A man's voice said, and I quote, 'No harm was intended.' And that was it, except for one thing."

I whisper back, "What?"

Michael leans back so he can look into my face as he replies, "The man on the phone had an Irish accent."

Chapter FIVE

We drive down the hill on Vista Way to Hank's and Katy's home. Like almost every street in Lane, houses are on half acre lots, so stands of trees with flickering views of seascape fill the windows during our short journey. Hank's and Katy's house is close to Dayton School, and Patrick and Katherine live in the house closest to them. I can see Matilda sitting in one of the cushioned rattan chairs on the covered front porch of Hank's and Katy's log home as we drive to the edge of the lawn and park. Ever since her husband, Thomas, the founder of Dayton School, died, Matilda has lived with her daughter, Katy and son-in-law, Hank. And according to Hank, Matilda's quiet ways make it impossible for him to tell mother-in-law jokes and have anyone believe him, "Just like Thomas used to say, 'She's too good to be true.'" Depending on whether or not Hank is attempting to amuse himself at Katy's expense, he will add either "Too bad the daughter didn't inherit the mother's gentle ways" or "My wife's a chip off the old block." Katy just smiles which ever one he says; having lived more than three quarters of her life with this man, whose constant love and frequent humor have been the bedrock of their time together, she has no doubts in her mind or heart about the esteem she holds in his mind and heart.

I watch John Henry and Mary run up the stairs, kiss Matilda, then go into the house. My thoughts of a long life lived with the one who fills my heart and mind so much of the time prompts me to reach out and take Michael's hand as we walk across a perfect lawn, the fruit of one of Hank's favorite hobbies. I give words to the gesture, "I love you, Michael Callaghan."

He squints his eyes at me, "Don't try to get on my good side, woman."

I laugh at him, "You're not still complaining about dinner are you?"

He squints at me again, "Eating healthy all the time is boring, and I like real food, meat food."

I squint back at him now, "You do not eat healthy all the time, and I serve you meat often enough. No more meat talk, Michael, or I may lose the sweet, healthy dinner I made for us."

Now he smiles, "Then I am truly satisfied. You're going to throw up on my dad's lawn, and I'm going to faint from starvation walking up his front steps; so we're equal. Yeah, me."

I stop walking and remove my hand from his, "Maybe you can get your mommy to make you a second dinner."

Michael steps so close to me we are touching but just barely, "She would if I asked, but I won't because suddenly I don't want food anymore." He leans into me and whispers in my ear, "Now I'm hungry for sustenance of a different sort."

I push him away, "You are a sick man, Michael Callaghan. Arguing with me should not be considered foreplay."

Michael grabs my hand and raises it to his lips then turns it at the last moment, kissing my palm, "Everything can be foreplay, Leah."

Matilda calls from the porch, "I can't decide if you two are courting or arguing." Michael and I both laugh and walk toward her. Her smile and the tilt of her head to receive our kisses is the last thing I see before the vision overtakes me ... or outruns me to be more exact, because I am running, running hard, and the place I am is the landscape for the presence from which I run. I know all this in a heartbeat. I turn to see it, and in a heartbeat I am overtaken. I am drowning in a flood of emotion that at first twirls around me, then bumps against me, grinds against me, jars my very soul. I can only see colors and sense sensations like numbing fear, stabbing pain, a gagging rage; I can no longer breathe. Then there is a hand on my shoulder, and I am aware of myself lying on the smooth painted wood planks of the covered porch where I first saw Matilda.

I am looking into eyes I recognize. I am looking into Malick's eyes. Michael is beside him. I try to focus on Michael instead of on Malick, but my focus is pulled back to Malick as he says, "Just breathe and relax. Close your eyes if you feel the need, but you need to relax; your pulse is racing."

I reply quite naturally, although there is nothing natural about it, "I was running."

Malick's reply does not have a calming affect on me, "At least in the beginning you were, but like Lot's wife, you had to turn and look back didn't you?"

His eyes are mesmerizing, but I find the words flickering on and off again in my mind, "How do you know I turned?"

Malick replies quickly, "Matilda cried out when she thought you had fainted. Michael caught you in his arms. I was talking with Hank; we ran out here together after Matilda cried out. We saw Michael lay you down gently exactly where you are now. You were just at the beginning then; you were running, so I thought you'd be fine, but then you stopped and turned, and it had you."

I ask again, "How do you know all this? You cannot be inside my head."

Malick looks away from me, but I tighten my grip on his hand and only then realize I am holding his hand, "You're not inside your own head, Leah; you're going to another place. I thought you knew all this; I thought it had been explained to you."

Michael's words come faster than mine, "A thin place?"

Malick's words are filled with frustration, "She doesn't have to go to a thin place. Almighty God! Neither of you understand what you need to know to make it through this. You have not been prepared. Blood of Christ! She is a thin place."

I let go of Malick's hand, "Move away from me." Neither Michael nor Malick move, so I throw out each word at them with an intensity I have never felt before, "I said move away from me now." But they do not move back, they are thrown back, Michael against the rattan chair and Malick against Hank's legs, which causes Hank to hit the hard wood of the door.

The moment stills itself. Expressions on the three faces I see range from Michael's shock to Hank's utter disbelief to Malick's respectful awe, but I cannot reassure or question, because I am gone again, but this time I run only to gain a distance between me and the thing following I know now is more than just an image within a dream. I am running in a landscape foreign to me, but I am no longer fearful. When I have gained the distance I require, I turn purposefully and tell what I can only describe as a twirling mist of emotions 'no', and it stops, shudders, then dissipates. Then I say Michael's name, and I am lying on boards of painted wood again, and the three men have not moved.

Malick is the first to move. He stands, reaches down, and helps me to my feet. He looks into my eyes, then walks down the stairs to the grass where he turns and says simply, "May was wrong; she had no idea of where you are in the cycle. And Connor is wrong; you don't have all the time in the world, but at least you learn quickly. You just might survive this." He takes two steps toward us then stops again and looks at me, "You'd better learn very quickly or—" he looks at Michael and says so softly that only I can hear, "he won't." Then Malick walks away from us, across the perfect lawn and down the winding driveway and out of our sight.

I close my eyes, and try to make sense of what has happened, but I do not know how to do that. I turn and look at Michael and Hank, "I am so sorry. I have no idea how that happened. Are either of you hurt?"

Michael stands and walks to me. Hank stays leaning against the door but indicates he is not hurt. For the first time in my life, Michael's eyes are guarded as he looks at me, and that frightens me more than what I have just experienced, and so my eyes fill with tears my heart has manufactured out of a hundred different emotions all bred by fear and uncertainty. I reach out to him, and after only one beat of my heart, he takes me in his arms and holds me, and I know then that as wrong as Malick believes May and Connor to be is as wrong as I believe Malick is. I know Michael will survive simply because I would not want to survive without him.

*   *   *   *

We enter the house together and hear the laughter of John Henry and Mary coming from the kitchen. Hank, Michael, and I enter the kitchen together and find the air filled and the counters covered with flour dust.

Katy's hair and eyelashes are white with it, "We had a bit of an explosion, you see. I thought my hold was firm, but it was not, and down from the high shelf the bag of flour came. I almost caught it in midair, but instead I tore the sack and now you see the outcome."

Mary is enjoying herself immensely, "We're making cookies, mom. Want to help?"

Matilda rises from the chair where she was sitting and comes to Mary, "Now, now, too many hands do not make a good cookie, and besides, your grandpa and parents need to have a talk. We'll clean-up, make cookies, and have them out of the oven in time for milk and cookies before you and your parents have to return home. Go get the broom and dust pan for me, please. John Henry, please help your sister." Matilda pauses as the kids go into the large pantry to retrieve the items she has requested. "The children did not hear anything. Are you all right now?"

I hug her and answer, "Yes." Then I look at Katy, "I could help clean up before we go talk."

Katy shakes her head in response, "No, no, we're fine, truly. We'll have this mess cleaned up and be making cookies in no time at all. You three go make yourselves comfortable in Hank's den. Did you want something to drink before you get started?"

Hank and Michael look at each other, "What Michael and I want to drink is in the den already. Leah can join us or get something else here."

I walk over to the cabinet and remove a glass, "Water will be fine, and I can get that myself."

We walk through the house that is decorated in warm earth tones and accented in the fragrance and shine of antique furniture waxed weekly for as long as it has been in Katy's possession. Hank's den is cozy in a masculine manner; dark leather chairs and a couch are centered in a room that is shelved from floor to half way up three of the four walls. Large framed black and white photographs of the local landscape or of groups of men standing proudly in front of fire trucks or of individual firemen involved in various aspects of the trade are hung above the shelves, and testify to another of Hank's hobbies. Hank's desk is neatly organized, which is the way he likes his life to be, but I can tell this room and its contents are cared for by Katy's loving hands. The early evening light gleams on the waxed surfaces of wood and the dust free surfaces of trophies and photographs taken and framed by Hank.

Hank walks to a small refrigerator sitting in one corner of the room. On its top are glasses and two or three bottles of liquor all light golden or dark amber in color. Hank pours a whiskey for both himself and Michael. We sit down, Michael and I on the couch and Hank in 'his' chair. He leans back, and it reclines. He raises his glass to each of us, then takes a long slow drink and sighs.

Michael is about to take his first drink when his hand stops midway to his mouth. I follow his stare and see the file which was taken from our house lying on Hank's desk. Michael looks at his father.

Hank looks at both of us and takes another drink before he says, "It just keeps getting more interesting, doesn't it?"

Michael takes a drink then comments, "I'm not quite sure if 'interesting' is the first word that comes to my mind, dad." Michael takes another drink, this one longer than the last and looks at Hank, "What do you think, dear? Does interesting describe the last couple of hours for you?"

I look at Hank instead of Michael, "He only calls me 'dear' when he is being facetious or getting cranky."

Hank takes another drink then sets his glass down on the small table by his chair. He folds his arms across his chest, "Well Michael, are you being facetious with your wife?"

Michael looks at his father, takes another drink, sets his glass down on the rectangular coffee table centered between the two chairs and the couch and replies, "It's possible, dad, that I'm being somewhat facetious. Pardon me, please." Then he turns to me, "Leah, sweetness, pardon me, please. It must be so inconceivable I would be having a somewhat less than pleasant emotional response to the events which have transpired. Pardon me, pardon me, pardon me."

Hank laughs, "He's always done this. This is what he does. Something happens, Michael runs through anywhere from five to six emotions right in a row. Did it as a kid, still does it now." Hank picks up his glass and again raises it to Michael, "You're a pain in the ass, kid, but you're always entertaining."

Now I laugh as Michael looks from one of us to the other, "You can't get away with it in front of your dad, can you?"

Michael picks up his glass and before he takes another drink he replies in a tone of utter disdain, "I have no idea what either of you are talking about." Hank laughs again, and soon Michael is smiling and nodding his head, "Okay, okay, so this is what I do. No big deal, except you cut my process short by two or three emotions, so I'm not sure and can't be held responsible for how I will react to all the info you are undoubtedly going to share with us any moment now."

Hank's facial expression is serious now, "Unfortunately, what I have to tell you is pretty much unavoidable, and it will be startling, but first I have to ask Leah what happened to her out there on my porch in broad daylight. Is what Malick said true? Are you a thin place? I didn't think a person could be a thin place; I thought a thin place was a place."

I shake my head, "Michael and I are sort of learning all this as we go, so I cannot actually explain more than Malick explained. But I would like to know why Malick was here, and how the file came to be in your possession."

Hank rubs his hands across his face just as Michael runs his fingers through his hair pushing it back from his face, "I'm trying to figure out if I should start in the present and work back, or start with the information from the past and work forward to the present. It's going to be overwhelming no matter which course I choose, so I will try to give some background information first, lay a foundation, so to speak, but even that may be difficult. It's important to me that you understand why something like the fire could happen, because sometimes our own lives and perspectives make it almost impossible for us to relate to the motivations of others. I'm not trying to excuse anyone's behavior, but it's too easy to look at something and not see it for what it really is just because of personal ideology. Plus, I'm aware I'll be giving you information I have gathered over the years from books and personal experience that may be much different than someone else's information on the same subject. So remember that, please, not only when you're listening to my words, but also when others speak to you. I can only tell you what

I know to be true, and truth isn't often one sided." Hank hands his glass to Michael, "Pour me another drink, son, and yourself one if you're ready. Leah are you sure you don't want anything stronger than what you're drinking?"

I decline his offer and make myself more comfortable on the couch while Michael pours their drinks then gives his father his glass before sitting down again. Michael and I look at Hank, and Hank clears his throat, reclines back a little farther in his chair, crosses his legs at the ankle, and focuses his eyes on the ceiling. His first words are slow and paused between, but then he is caught up in his own story and almost indiscernibly his voice takes the cadence of the Irish lilt.

"Sean and I were boyhood friends. You probably didn't know that, but we were. In ways that will be made clear, he became as close to me as a brother. We followed Father Tom's predecessor, Father Seamus, around asking him questions, doing errands for him, eavesdropping on conversations when we could get away with it, and just generally making ourselves a nuisance. But he loved us, and we loved him, and he taught us to love Ireland and all her ways. Back then Father Seamus taught a class on Irish history, and Sean and I were there for every class. Ireland's fierce struggle for independence became our struggle, but the history class was not just about battles fought over land and the struggle between the rich and the poor; it was also the battles fought over the ways of the Church ... the Romanization of Ireland's faith. Obedience to the old ways or obedience to the new ways ... was the inner struggle for Sean and for me. That was and is Father Tom's and Father Seamus' struggle also. Their love of God and of Jesus and their dedication to ways older than most of the events portrayed in the Old Testament were too intertwined to be cast aside in order to serve a church they also loved, and they were not alone. Irish-Catholic meant something different to them, to us, and also to others who shared our same beliefs. We became ... passionate about everything Irish, and we were at an age when 'a cause' could become all-consuming."

Hank takes the chair out of its reclining position, sits up straight setting the glass of whiskey on the end table beside his chair, "Father Seamus left the Holy Catholic Church in 1956 and returned to Ireland; Sean and I went with him, and we saw Ireland in what Father Seamus called the old way because we walked its paths from north to south, from east to west, step by step. We learned its history by listening to the voices of its people, fireside gatherings in small rooms in small towns after working side by side with the people in their daily labors. Although we pretty much covered the whole of Eire, we stayed mainly in the Republic because that's where our hearts were; we wanted no connection to the British Commonwealth."

Hank leans back rubbing his face with his hands again, "Eamon de Valera was still alive. He was born in New York in 1882, but at three his mother sent him to Ireland to live with her mother. He became an Irish Nationalist out of a true love for all that is Irish. He led the Sinn Fein, the Irish provisional government, the anti-treaty forces, and then the Fianna Fail. He was prime minister then president. He retired at the age of ninety-one and died two years later in 1975, but the powerful patriotism which filled his life denies the silence of death; his voice is still strong in the Republic, still strong in every country and group of people that are fighting for their own right to their own destiny. We heard him speak, but even more than that we heard his voice in the voice of his people, the ones he served loyally even when it meant going against the opinion of countries he respected. During what the Irish call the Emergency and the rest of the world calls WWII, he stood firm and stayed neutral to prove the Republic controlled its own destiny and was no longer a part of the British Empire. The Irish people would not be forced to fight another country's war. Granted, the Irish supported the Allies in many ways that are well documented, and thousands of Irish volunteered to fight and to willingly sacrifice their lives in Allied armies, but officially the Republic remained neutral. You can imagine how difficult taking such a position must have been, but de Velera remained true to his purpose; the world would see the Republic of Ireland as an independent country."

Hank no longer looks at us as he speaks, and his voice softens with sadness as he continues to speak, "The Republic was poorer than poor. De Valera believed, as others did, they were in no position to make war anyway. The Republic was one of the poorest countries in Europe, with an army of less than seven thousand. Also the country had still not recovered from the Gorta Mor, the Great Hunger, of the late 1840s. The destruction of the potato crop in 1845, by what we now know was a fungus which originated in the Americas and was inadvertently transported to Europe in cargo ships, eventually led to the deaths of over one million people. They died from starvation and disease; one million men, women, and children died because their stomachs were empty. Two million Irish people emigrated, left their homeland. Most of the victims of the Great Hunger were Irish Catholic, who at that time comprised eighty percent of the population. They were the poor and the illiterate. Because most of Ireland's rural population depended on the potato as their staple food, and even the pigs, chickens and cows ate potatoes, the failure of the potato crop over the next three years devastated a culture already torn by a ruthless landlord/tenant system."

Hank's words are no longer softened by sorrow. Anger punctuates them, "This system made it necessary for the Irish farmer to use most of his land and spend most of his time growing a cash crop to pay rent instead of growing food for his own family. Back in 1695 the Penal Laws had outlawed everything Catholic. Irish Catholics were denied the right to make a will, the right to vote, to purchase land from Protestants, to worship God in their own way, and to bear arms for almost two centuries. Those types of restraints tear into the flesh and spirit of a people in ways that are passed from generation to generation even after the restraints are removed."

Hank pauses and rises up in his chair, reaches for his glass then takes a drink, "Do you need a break yet?"

Michael and I look at each other, and I know we are of like minds, so I answer, "No, we want to hear what you have to say."

Hank nods, sets his glass down and continues, "After the Emergency came the times called the Troubles in Northern Ireland, where the Catholic minority was denied social and economic equality through a sub-system so buried in the larger system of the culture that the discrimination in education, housing, and employment were nearly impossible to identify, but the products of that discrimination were evident in the lives of the people it held down and refused to let up. Also realize the split between Northern Ireland and the Republic has its roots in the years between 1169 and 1530 when England repeatedly tried to conquer Ireland, and more specifically in 1535 when Henry VIII broke with the Catholic Church. Perhaps the most obvious cause of internal Irish conflict is rooted in the early 1600s when King James I of England decided to create the Ulster Plantation to rid the land of the Catholics he referred to as 'savages' by settling English and Scottish Protestants there. So three hundred years later the struggle between the Unionists, who want Northern Ireland to remain loyal to the United Kingdom, and the Republicans, who believe Ireland is one country, is not just a difference of politics; most Unionists are Protestants and most Republicans are Catholics."

Hank pauses, apparently thinking about either the words he has spoken or what he will tell us next, "Protestants and Catholics.... Father Tom pointed out today what is spiritual in man can't be separated from what is physical; they coexist in us and outside of us, so I have to take you back even farther. Ireland's spiritual struggle began when Saint Patrick arrived in the four hundreds. That's when the division began that truly separated the Irish people from their spiritual roots."

Hank scratches his head, "Now despite my original plan to be chronological, which I've already messed up, I have to go back even farther. I have to at least touch on information already shared with you in May's first letter. I have to go back to the beginning of what we know as the real beginning of that which would later blossom and became Irish spiritualism. I believe May's first letter described the arrival of the Tuatha de Danaan. The Fir Bolg, who some researchers believe were of late Neanderthal stock, based on their physical descriptions, had faith leaders they called druids. The Tuatha de Danaan defeated the Fir Bolg in battle, but the two people co-existed in some degree after that. The Fir Bolg maintained their faith beliefs, and within a few generations the faiths of the two cultures intertwined."

Hank reclines back in his chair reminding us that Father Tom and May tell the story of the Tuatha de Danaan differently, and Michael and I aren't here to memorize details but to gain a sense of Irish history. Then he continues, "The Tuatha de Danaan ruled Ireland until the Milesians invaded anywhere from as early as 3,500 to as late as 300 B.C.E. depending on whose research you're reading. The Milesians were the sons of Mil, often called Gaels, who came from what is now northern Spain or southern France. A huge battle was fought between the Tuatha de Danaan and the Milesians. The Tuatha de Danaan were defeated, but the faith beliefs of the Tuatha de Danaan lived on even after they reportedly departed from this physical reality to live in another. Their visits to and intercessions in our … reality are evidenced in not only the stories of old, but also, as you are discovering, in the here and now, and their places of entry are referred to as 'thin places'."

Hank pauses to take a drink from his glass, "Background information given, I will return to the part of my story where Sean and I are in Ireland, and share with you that we met people active in a faith which combines the old ways of the Fir Bolg and the Tuatha de Danaan with Saint Patrick's gentle rendition of Christianity. Remember in cultures which have been invaded and subjected the historical documentation is normally based on the perspective of the dominating culture's belief. Although the Irish language is said to be at least three thousand years old, the old ways were recorded by Patrick's Irish monks and Christianized to a great degree. Not to take any glory from that accomplishment. Few realize the importance of Ireland's place in history; without the written documentation of the Irish monks much of what we know today about early Western thought would have been lost during that dark time of Europe before the advent of the Middle Ages."

Hank shakes his head, "We must be thankful, no matter our faith belief, but we should also not fail to see the irony in the fact that Patrick was taken prisoner during an Irish raid on Britain and worked as a slave for six years before making his escape, only to return to the Emerald Isle as a missionary years later. The early Irish Church was more an embodiment of rural Irish ways than of its mother church in Rome. Without large urban centers, the organization of the Irish church was more relational and community-based than hierarchical. Power was not the goal of the Irish priest or his church. Women still held places of honor within the organization of the church just as they were treated with respect and equality in the culture. Only later after Romanization of the church began did Irish women suffer the fate of women the world over at the powerful hands of corrupt church leaders. Also, celibacy among the priests of the early Irish church was not mandatory or even esteemed; individuals were given the right to choose their style of living, and married or single, this choice in no way lessened or raised them in the eyes of God. Earth and all God's creation were celebrated, and, again, the hierarchical placement of man over creation was deemed an honorary positioning by God to protect and serve all that God had made. It was not a release by God to subject creation to man's abusive, shortsighted, self-serving greed. The earth was alive with God's spirit, as was all of creation, the physical and spiritual in harmony."

Hank returns the chair to its upright position and stands. He walks to the window facing the backyard as he speaks, "Sean and I, well ... we were in heaven, if I may use that expression, and we wanted heaven on earth, as they say, and so we joined a group of individuals working to restore the balance between the physical and the spiritual here on earth. We were idealistic, and to make a long and not unique story short, after a year or so of working with this group, I came to believe that not all involved were motivated by the ideal of harmony between the physical and the spiritual; some were there to gain power, to achieve certain political goals, to acquire money, and some were working to manipulate the old sacred ways to achieve their own goals.

Sean and I began to see things differently. For him, the means justified the end; he wanted a strong and united Ireland at whatever cost was necessary. There was a splinter group off the original that was solely political in its aims, and he made a place for himself within that group. Father Seamus became recognized as a leader in the primary group of which I was a member; he believed Sean would recognize the dangers of his involvement in the fringe-faction to which he belonged, but I had no such faith. I came home. Sean returned a few years later, married your mother and seemed to settle into life in Lane. Even though his love for your mother was genuine everything else about him was a front. He never went to Vietnam or even served in the armed forces, but he served on many other fronts, and he was a soldier though he wore no uniform. May and Colleen both knew what Sean was doing. May tried to keep the peace between your mother and Sean, and to be fair to May she loved Colleen and did see her side in her problems with Sean, but, truth be told, May had allegiances of her own to a group as dedicated to its spiritual goals as Sean's group was and is dedicated to its political goals. As Sean's wife, Colleen was of importance to both groups' goals. So May was caught between loyalties to her group and to Colleen and to loyalties to her son."

Hank pauses, and as the silence lengthens I ask, "What's wrong? Why have you stopped?"

Hank still does not respond for a moment, but then he says, "I am seeing the times I am describing to you, and reminding myself of what I can tell you and what I can't tell you."

Michael asks, "Why is there information we can't know? Don't we need to know everything?"

Hank nods, "No one knows everything, but some of the information I do know belongs to the second and third letters. That information is not mine to tell."

Michael responds, "But why? This makes no sense. We should have all the information. May can't know—"

Hank interrupts him, "May did know, and she did leave careful instructions that we are all—"

Michael interrupts again, "Obviously May didn't know everything she needed to know or she and John and Colleen and the Danners would not have died in a fire."

Hank is not defensive, but he is firm in the position he takes, "As cold as this may sound, the deaths caused by the fire have no bearing on what you have to do, Leah. The deaths don't change what May wrote in her letters or my responsibility to the process."

Michael is defensive, "This whole … process … is out of control, but this Malick, who came from 'here and there', seems concerned about our lack of knowledge."

Hank's eyes are focused on Michael's intently, "So far, son, I've given you only a thin slice of historical perspective, and so far you've lived through a few out of the ordinary experiences, but your very limited perspective on the situation doesn't give you any right to an opinion. You need to be quiet and listen and hopefully learn what you need to know. Once you've read all the letters, then talk to me about how all this makes or doesn't make sense." Hank pauses, "Now, shall I continue or would you prefer to meet at another time?"

Michael leans back and looking only at the wall opposite him replies in a manner I have never heard him take with his father, "Continue." His father does not move to do so, and eventually Michael has to look at him. Their gazes lock, then Michael looks away, "Please continue, father."

I try not to smile, but Hank is smiling and it must be contagious. After he takes a drink from his glass, he comments to me, "He only calls me father when he is being facetious or beginning to get cranky."

Michael's only response is to be totally unamused. Hank shrugs, leans back in his chair and begins speaking again, "After Grant was born, Sean tried to stay home more, but he had risen to a place of power in the group, and he had responsibilities. I believe someone else in Lane was involved with Sean, or at least it seemed like it from some of the references he made, but I never learned who that person was. After your birth, Leah, Sean left less but he was gone for longer periods of time. Your mother tried to be patient, but his main loyalty was centered somewhere else, so they agreed to separate and later to divorce. Father Tom left the church over it actually; he would not excommunicate Colleen. The Daytons supported the Father in the matter, and our Catholic Church became The Church. Sean's visits became less frequent, then after the fire I only saw him one more time—"

I interrupt Hank, "You saw Sean after the fire?"

Hank answers, "Yes, but you need to let me explain in the order the events happened. You have to trust me here. Let me tell the story without being asked questions, or I will leave something out, and I don't want to do that."

I nod my head, and Hank continues, "We had a get-together that night here. Basically we had invited just about everyone we knew. A couple of fellas were playing the pipes, people were talking and laughing. Colleen had called about an hour before the party started and explained they would be late, because the Danners had called and asked to meet with them. I remember Colleen said the Danners seemed upset about something, but they would not even tell her what it was about over the phone. I asked about coming to get your brother and you, Leah, but she said the Danners had already sent Joe over to pick up you and Grant for pizza. She said they would stop by the Danner's to get you and come to the party as soon as the meeting was over." Hank pauses. He sets in his chair, his elbows on his knees. He lays his head in his hands. When he looks up there are tears in his eyes, "I'm not sure if there was an actual explosion, like a bomb, or if the device found at the house after the fire simply ignited. No one heard an explosion, but someone, I can't remember who now, saw the lighted sky over the fire and pointed it out. Katy called the local sub-fire station then the county station. Every fireman in the place ran to the cars. We went directly to the fire knowing the equipment and the truck would be coming, but it didn't matter; it was too late by the time any of us got there." Hank pauses again and looks at me, "I've never seen a house burn like that. When we got there, we ran around the entire parameter, trying to find a way in, but flames were shooting out of the windows. Maybe the most frightening sight for us, because we were firemen used to seeing houses burn, was that damn chain around the handle of the front door and looped around the base of the stair rail. You and your brother and the Danner boys arrived soon after we did. You stood on the lawn, Leah, watching. When Kate and some of the other women arrived they took you back to our house, but we were there all night. We thought at the time the people we knew who were inside had tried to get out and found the door chained, but if that had been so, John or Pastor Danner could have broken the front windows. After the investigation we knew no one had time to even try to escape because the ceiling had fallen on them."

Hank leans back in his chair now, "Sean came to see me, a day or so later. His hair, eyebrows, and eye lashes were singed. He wore gloves on his hands, but I could see gauze coming out at the wrists. He had a cut over his left eye on which he had used a butterfly bandage, but it was obvious it needed stitches. Of course, he wouldn't even discuss his injuries with me. There were no feelings expressed in his eyes at all. His voice was flat; he made no attempt at eye contact. I had come in to my den after dinner as I often do, and he was sitting in the dark in the chair. He told me to lock the door, and I did. I turned on the light; we talked, or really he talked, and I listened. When he was done, he went out the same window through which he must have entered. I still don't know how he got it open without leaving any tell-tale signs."

Hank pauses again, "I know you want to hear the conversation we had, and I will tell you, but first you have to understand something. Sean was not a bad man, and sitting here looking at him that night, I knew that, just like May knew that. He had become so wrapped up in his cause he'd lost himself to it. He was just a soldier for his cause, just a warrior doing what he was told, yet I knew his heart had to be broken over the deaths of his loved ones, but he showed me none of that. He told me he had come out of respect for an old friendship, that he wanted me to know he had not known his group was sending someone to take care of something he had been supposed to do years ago but had lied about it. The group had found out about the lie, and Sean had been reprimanded. As soon as he found out about the man being sent Sean returned to Lane. Sean said he got to the house as soon as he could. He saw a van parked across the road from the house he recognized as belonging to the group. He'd even used the van before on group business. He saw the chain on the door, and through the windows he saw the Danners talking to May and John and Colleen. He said he circled the house to determine where the man the group had sent was when he heard a noise in the basement. He discovered the outside basement door was not locked. He entered, made his way down the stairs, saw the man rigging the breaker box. He also saw May's cedar chest open and the contents thrown about all around it. Sean said he grabbed the guy from behind, threw him down, pressed his knee against the man's back and bent his arm back until he almost broke it. Sean spoke to the man and only then did the man realize who Sean was. He told Sean to let him up, but Sean wouldn't. Sean wanted some questions answered first. Sean wanted to know why the front door was chained, and why he was rigging the breaker box. The man answered Sean without hesitation. No one was supposed to be home, but they were, so he had chained the front door to slow down any chase in case he was discovered before he'd either found the box or set the fire to start after the people in the house had left. He'd heard the people talking say they would be leaving the house to attend some party within the hour. He hadn't been able to locate May's metal box, and his orders were to either find it or destroy it, so he had rigged a device in an upstairs bedroom that would cause the house to burn in such a manner the floors would fall one on top of the other, burning hot enough to melt even metal. No one was supposed to die."

Hank shakes his head, "But you see, Sean knew May's metal box was not kept in the cedar chest, but beneath it, in a fireproof safe kept in a secret compartment within the basement's floor. Then Sean said he must have heard something, because he allowed himself to be distracted. The man he was holding to the floor moved in such a way Sean lost his balance and his hold. The two fought each other, Sean says more to control the situation than to hurt each other, because they were brothers in the cause, but Sean delivered a blow to the man's face and he fell backward, hit his head against the breaker box, then fell forward hitting his head on the basement floor, and after that he lay totally still. Sean says everything happened at once. The man's head had hit the breaker box in such a way the device upstairs was signaled, since the timer had not been set yet. Screams and the first floor ceiling falling froze Sean, then he bent quickly to the man on the floor, but he had no pulse. Sean says he ran up the stairs to try and help the people in the house, but the fire was already burning out of control. He burned his hand trying to open the backdoor. Windowpanes were exploding and shooting shards of glass into him. He claims his training must have taken over, because he doesn't remember walking away from the burning house to the van, or finding the hidden key or driving away, but he says he must have done all those things, because the next thing he remembers is looking through the windshield of the van, realizing he was parked at the entrance to the path to the cabin where he stayed when in town. He didn't have much to say to me after that. Once or twice he said he was sorry. Then he'd say there was nothing he could do. We sat in silence for a while, and then he looked at me for the first time really and said he wouldn't be back. He asked me to look after you, Leah, and Grant, to set things up with the Daytons, to make things right if I could for his children and the Danner boys. Then he stood and walked across this room, opened the window and left. I haven't seen or heard from his since. And that's all I know."

I am numb and do not speak, but Michael fires quick questions all in a row, "What are the names of these groups? Who was the man in the basement? Why was Colleen important to May's group? What did the Danners want to talk about with May and the others?"

Hank sighs then speaks, "My part of the information you were to be told basically involved Sean and his involvement in the group, his love of Ireland. I think May wanted you to understand in some manner the passion that can motivate a man to lose sight of who he is if he isn't careful to maintain his personal values and morals, his faith, his love of family. It's a sad tale, and Sean is not the first to fall to it, but too often the idealist becomes blinded by his own perspective, then any sense of compassion is lost, and the idealist becomes a fanatic. For those types of people the end can justify the means, I suppose." Hank pauses, takes a deep breath then continues, "The rest, the fire and Sean's explanation, about those May could have, of course, not known. You need to understand the group to which Sean belongs is still active, still has the same goals, and your awareness of that can help determine some of the choices you make."

Michael asks again, "What is the name of the group?"

Hank replies, "The name of such groups is insignificant to all but those who belong to them. They are not 'known' and do not claim their deeds. Sean's group is connected to other groups all over the world. The only criterion for making a connection seems to be the desire to overcome what they label an oppressive regime."

Michael moves on to his other question, "Who was the man in the basement with Sean?"

Hank looks at the file and then at us, "Malick's father."

Michael repeats Hank's words in the form of a question, "Malick's father was the man in the basement?"

Hank simply nods his head, so I ask, "Is that why Malick broke into our house and took the file?"

Hank shakes his head, "Malick is not the one who broke into your house and took the file."

Michael asks the most obvious question before I can, "Who then?"

Hank rubs his face again, "According to Malick, he found it in the room he is sharing with Connor."

Again Michael summarizes the information given in the form of a question, "Connor broke into our house and took the file?"

Then I ask, "But why would he? What would be his motivation?"

Michael stands and speaks quickly, "Unless Connor is involved in one of these groups too."

Hank again shakes his head, "You're jumping to conclusions, son. You can't do that in this. Malick seems to trust Connor and thinks the file was planted. I know for a fact Malick has no connection at all to his father's old group. In fact, he—" Hank does not finish his statement, but instead says, "Well, that is Malick's story to tell, not mine. But I've known Malick for years, and I don't believe he would cause you or anyone else harm or steal or break into your home. His focus is more in line with May's."

I ask the next question in Michael's previous list, "How was my mother involved?"

Hank reaches out and takes my hand, "Her importance in this is based totally on her being Sean's wife and the mother of his children. You'll understand that better after you read the third letter."

Michael is pacing now, "I say we just get both of the next two letters, open them, read them, get all those involved together and take care of all this at one time."

Hank very quietly says, "That could be dangerous for you and for Leah. Trust me. Trust May. There is a reason for the process May prescribed."

Michael sits down on the couch again, "Okay, fine. But why did the Danners call the meeting? Can you answer that?"

Hank shrugs, "May's ways could have been upsetting them." I ask why and he responds quickly, "Mary and Joseph! Which of May's ways would not have bothered the Danners? She did things like you did out on the front porch today. Not quite that aggressive, but just things that aren't considered ordinary, and the older she got, the more she liked to entertain the young ones, and either someone saw or one of the young ones was very convincing, and the Danners could have come to speak of that. I can't be sure why they called the meeting, and at this point, neither can you. Needless to say, May was a true follower of Brigid, and—" Hank stops himself and stands up. "But that's not my story to tell. No more talk for now."

He moves toward the door. "I believe we should join the others for milk and cookies now." And he does. He is out the door and down the hall, and we can hear him calling out to his wife it is milk and cookies time. The abruptness of Hank's departure offers me no closure or transition.

Michael and I only look at each other then he stands, moves in front of me, offers me his hands, and pulls me up when I put my hands in his. We both shake our heads and share tired smiles with each other.

His voice is soft when he speaks, "We never did get to tell each other how we defined 'holy' at church today."

I am again wondering at the lack of transition, so I ask, "What made you think of that now?"

Michael shrugs his shoulders and answers at the same time, "Maybe our definitions for things are going to change, and that worries me some, because I've always liked our definitions."

I put my arms around him and pull him close to me, "Are you worried we will lose our way like Sean did?"

Michael rubs his forehead against my shoulder, "No, I don't think so."

I step back from him a little and gently hold his face in my hands as I look into this eyes, "I believe the territory of the heart should be sacred ground, a holy place where love reigns supreme and is unchanged by momentary circumstance. I agree with the kids there is our kind of holy and there is God's kind of holy. I cannot come close to his holiness, but in my heart I can make a sacred place where all that is precious to him is precious to me, where I honor all he has created." I pause and close my eyes as if I might possibly find words to illustrate what my heart knows, "Perhaps holy is compassion completely expressed, or maybe holy is being wholly aware of him and allowing myself to be changed by that awareness. What would the world be like if every single creation of his became precious in our sight? Wouldn't that be something?"

Michael holds my face in his hands now, "What about flies? Are flies 'precious'?" He moves my head, negating that option, "No, I don't think so. I can buy the compassion part, and I like the idea of the heart being unchanged by circumstance, but dog crap is not precious. Bird shit, buggers, maggots—"

I interrupt him, "Okay, okay, you have made your point."

Michael runs his hands through his hair then looks at me, "It's a valid point, and I'm going to give you until maybe next week or something and then I want a definition that can be stated in less than five billion words." He has my hand, and we are walking out of the room, down the hall and toward the kitchen as he continues, "I think maybe you should make a goal of ten words. Yeah, ten words would be good. Can you do that for me?"

I only say I will try, and he tells me he will tell me his when I can tell him mine in ten words or less. So I say I will, and he laughs saying, "There is no way. You're not a ten words or less kind of gal, wife."

We are in the doorway of the kitchen. The kids and their grandparents and Matilda are sitting at the table, but I stop Michael and pull his head down close to mine, "I can be any kind of gal I want to be, husband."

And he says, "We'll see."

And I say, "You'll see."

And he says, "We'll see."

And I say, "You'll see."

And then Matilda says, "I can never tell if they're arguing or courting." Michael and I smile at each other, then at her, then we join our family for milk and cookies as I, once again, usher troubling thoughts through a door which I firmly close.

✻   ✻   ✻   ✻

I have served morning to my family. Awakened them with kisses, motivated them to climb out from under warm covers, orchestrated the breaking of our nightly fast with fresh squeezed orange juice, scrambled eggs, biscuits, and started Michael's coffee and bacon so their scent will greet him even before I do. I am on the deck now watching Puppy in a now-I-see-him-now-I-don't experience, because heaven and earth are one. The mist and cloud of sea and sky are laying heavy on the ground, just barely moved by a breeze not truly dedicated in its bound by duty stirring of them, so Puppy becomes a phantom appearing and disappearing as even the trees seem to take slow tiny sidesteps this way then that way. My students will be subdued by this weather, so I am preparing myself to be more ardent than the breeze in causing them to become involved in the lesson.

The door opens behind me. Michael is pajama bottomed and slipperless, his hair flamboyant. His hands are curled around his large coffee mug. His toes curl up from the cold wet deck. I mention a fact of which we both are aware, "You have slippers, you know."

He replies quickly, "Fetch them for me, woman."

I shake my head, "I cannot."

He takes a sip of coffee, "Why not?"

I look at him now with a very solemn expression on my face, "That sort of behavior would spoil you, and what kind of wife would I be if my behavior influenced your behavior in a negative manner?"

He takes another sip of coffee, this one a bit bigger than the last, "Why don't you just will them to fly out here then."

Now I turn and face him, "I am totally serious, Michael Callaghan. Stop making jokes. Last night you wanted me to levitate you. I have no idea how what happened on the porch happened, but I am certain I do not want to play around with it whatever it is. I do not even want to talk about it, and I told you that last night. I do not want to talk about what your dad told us either. I need time to think. Additionally, and I should not even have to make you aware of the fact, I made you bacon, and you are still being a brat."

Michael whistles for Puppy, "I am not a brat, and as to the other matter, I just think we should experiment a little and test your abilities. But fine, just damn fine, I won't bring it up again. I'll be silent." Michael and Puppy walk through the door, and Michael never stops talking, "I won't say another word except mum is the word. I will be speechless. I will …" his voice fades away as he walks farther into the living room, and I can only shake my head again. I look around the yard one more time, wondering why the eagle is not around anymore. It has been two days since I have seen him, and as strange as it may sound, I miss his presence. Perhaps he is hidden by the fog. Perhaps I will see him later.

I walk into the house to find John Henry and Mary clearing the table as Michael stands at the sink, squirting dishwashing soap into the running water with one hand and eating bacon with the other. He interrupts his own humming to tell me, "What good children you have. What a good husband you have. We will do the clean up and make lunches, and you may do all those things you do in the morning."

I lean over the counter that separates kitchen and living room, "You are trying to make-up with me, aren't you?"

Michael raises his right eyebrow, "I haven't done anything to make-up for; the children and I are simply doing our part."

I say 'fine' to him, and he says 'fine' to me. I remind John Henry and Mary the morning could bring rain and to choose clothing wisely then Michael informs me he is keeping the kids with him today.

I turn and ask, "What?"

He replies, "I'm taking them with me today to your old house. They can bring books and read, and they can ride with me in the back hoe. Of course, if you object—"

Mary interrupts, "Don't object, mommy, please, we want to ride in the back hoe. Please, please, please!"

I look at John Henry, but he says nothing, however I can tell he feels the same way Mary does.

I look down for a moment then up into Michael's eyes, "I am not against the idea, but usually we discuss things like this."

Michael turns off the water and dries his hands on the cup towel, "You're right. I apologize for not talking with you about it first. Brian and Alex are coming to help me, and Alex said he is going to bring Mark and Trisha, so I just thought I'd bring John Henry and Mary. I should have talked to you about it."

I can see he is sincere, "Thank you. You and Brian and Alex will not be too busy to watch the kids?"

Michael walks from the kitchen into the living room and stands in front of me, "All we're doing today is replacing one of the sections of the fence with two gates and having the back hoe delivered. We might get a little digging done, but mainly we're just getting organized today. Father Tom is going to be there too. He's bringing over the church's motor home to park on the lot, so we can have all the comforts of home while we're doing the job." Michael pauses then continues, "In fact, Father Tom said he might just stay there nights to make sure nothing happens."

My eyes are searching his, "What does Father Tom think could happen?"

Michael pats me on the shoulder and walks back into the kitchen, "Oh, you know, once we start excavating some of the more adventurous town kids might want to explore the hole."

I have a thousand thoughts running through my head, but I choose none of them and say instead, "Right, Michael, and I was born yesterday."

Mary is trying to balance a glass on a plate as she also holds a fork and knife, but she pauses and looks back at me, "It wasn't your birthday, yesterday, mom."

John Henry begins explaining the meaning of the phrase to her as I look at Michael one more time before I turn and leave the room.

I hear Michael turn off the water again, "Oh, great look, Leah. Even your looks are more than ten words, did you know that?"

He has followed me into the bedroom. I turn to face him, then walk around him and stand in the doorway facing the living room, "John Henry and Mary, we are not fighting, so don't worry, okay?"

John Henry gives me the thumbs-up gesture, "We know, mom. You're just discussing."

I say 'right' to him, then turn and face Michael, "You are acting strange. You are not treating me like you normally do. Why is that?"

Michael sits down on the edge of the bed and thinks for a moment before he responds, "I guess I'm not, but I'm not trying to be different. Everything just feels sort of strange to me right now." He looks up and meets my eyes with his and in a soft voice asks, "Can you understand that?"

I walk over to him and he leans into me. I let him rest his head against me as I whisper into him, "I understand, my love."

He is rubbing his face into me and whispers, "I'm the one who said we just had to stay 'us' and everything would be okay, but I'm having trouble adjusting, I guess. I feel a little out of sorts toward you, but I know none of this is your fault. Does that make any sense at all?"

I run my hands through his hair and make him look at me, "It makes perfect sense, Michael."

His closes his eyes and rests his head again me again, "I am the husband. You are the wife. I am supposed to protect you. How am I supposed to do that when things are happening that are way of out my control? It's going to get more complicated than I thought. I'm not even sure if I'll know how to protect you."

I only tell him, "Protection is not just one thing."

He asks, "What do you mean?"

I lower myself to my knees so I am looking up into his eyes, "I mean you protect me by loving me the way you do. And God forbid, but if I do need physical protection, you are more than capable, but more often than not it is the emotional protection you give me, have always given me, that keeps me safe, makes me strong ... sustains me."

He bends down gently kissing my lips, "I sustain you?"

I kiss him back, "You sustain me, husband."

He smiles, "Then I'll remember that, and handle all this better. I promise." I smile in reply, stand again, and turn to walk away, but he grabs my hand, "I love you, Leah."

I sigh as I say, "I love you too, Michael Callaghan. I love you too." And I make myself believe our love will be enough, as banished thoughts beat small, clenched fists against the door of my defenses.

✳   ✳   ✳   ✳

I stand behind my desk and look out past tables and chairs through windows where heavy mist laden clouds push up against the panes. Students will be here soon, and some of them will not appreciate the shades of shimmering opaque gray that are the windows' witness to the morning. I decide to make the most of the moment's mood instead of trying to circumvent. I will even invite the mist into the room; I will let our shared view set the scene, or perhaps we will venture out into it, but which ever we choose, I will tell an old story.

True to form, the ones who I know will be downcast are. Jacy and Charlie and Neil walk into the room clutching coffees and mumbling about the cold, and it being May, and what's up with the weather, then drop book bags and slump into the couches. Valerie's Samson seems pleased with the day's beginning, and once Valerie has found her seat she releases him, and his wet nose is investigating students' shoes and bookbags and the room's window ledges. Tucker is smiling and asking Valerie if the morning's gloom is giving her ideas for her short stories which are usually, from first word to last, gripping in their all-senses-involved horror.

Valerie smiles responding, "I like this kind of weather, because I can feel it even if I can't see it. The air brushes up against me. It's great."

Jacy comments, "It's eerie."

Valerie's replies with a Count Dracula accent, "Yes, yes. More, more."

As soon as the other students have entered and taken their seats I walk to the front of the room, and the conversations quickly stop. "Welcome. The morning is providing the perfect venue for what I have planned for us today. And after the pre-write, the first activity is anticipatory in nature. All you will have to do is listen closely and allow the story to get you into the right mind set and mood for the real assignment."

Shay raises his hand, "Is the real assignment a secret?"

I smile and nod my head 'yes'. There are a few exaggerated moans, but students are already pulling their journals out of their book bags for the pre-write they know they will be doing as soon as I give them their quotation for the day. I wait until they are each ready to begin, then I say, "'In nature there are neither rewards nor punishments. There are consequences.' Write your personal reaction to the quotation as you explain what it means." Then I repeat the quote slowly so they can write it down, "'In nature … there are neither … rewards nor punishments. There are consequences.'" When I see all my young ones are writing I turn and walk to the windows forming the corner of the room which overlooks the fountain and parking area of the campus. Today, however, nature has fitted her own curtains for these windows; I see nothing beyond their billowing curves and folds, but I know what is beyond what I can see. There are trees and the patioed roof of Lane Medical Center, and beyond that there are sand and waves and the high peak of Castle Rock Point. And like a child raising shell to ear, I let my imagination bend itself around me, then the tide's incantation whispers to me, and I am suddenly roomless and free, beyond walls, beyond the clock's pounding pulse, beyond—.

"Mrs. C," Shay speaks my name.

I say 'yes' and turn to face them.

Alana announces the obvious politely, "We're ready."

I smile and shrug my shoulders, "Thank you." I reestablish my stance on the shifting plain of this moment, gathering my thoughts like a good shepherd. "I would like to give a bit of background information on Robert Green Ingersoll, the gentleman responsible for the statement." I pause and spell the last name for them. "Jot down any part of what I share that you believe could be relevant to understanding Mr. Ingersoll's perspective." I try to pace the facts I share, but my students are used to the quick speed of my delivery. Their pens and pencils have been trained to fly across paper. "Ingersoll lived from 1833 to 1899. He was the son of a Congregational minister.... He became a lawyer and after serving in the Union Army during the Civil War changed his political affiliation from the Democratic Party to the Republican Party.... He later served as the Attorney General of Illinois but only for one term ... due to the fact he voiced publicly and often his anti-religious beliefs. He came to be known as 'the Great Agnostic'. His verbal eloquence was highly praised, and his lectures were printed and much read by his generation."

When everyone is done writing, I ask, "Which fact do you believe is the most relevant to gaining a perspective regarding Ingersoll's motivations?"

Aden's hand is raised first, so I nod at him, and he comments, "Clearly it's the fact the man's father was a minister."

Shay's hand shoots up as soon as Aden is done speaking, and Shay barely waits for me to indicate he can share next, "That's only true if we're aware Ingersoll later became an agnostic. If he hadn't become an agnostic, his father being a minister would not be as relevant." Alana asks 'why' and Shay responds, "Becoming an agnostic could just be a ... path taken instead of a reaction to or against something."

Valerie's raises her hand; I call her name to let her know she can speak, "Ingersoll's reaction to his service in the Union Army during the Civil War was to change political parties, so his motivations may not be entirely religious or anti-religious."

Jacy's hand is in the air next, "Just a point of interest, but agnosticism is the belief human beings are not capable of understanding the essential cause or nature of things, so isn't it interesting we're trying to understand a quote by an agnostic?"

Shay responds immediately, "Yes, interesting, but agnosticism also means God is unknown and unknowable by humans in their present state, and that point would bring us back to religion."

Neil's hand is raised tentatively, and I can tell my American history connoisseur is mentally paging through internal text, "But the political info on Ingersoll is just as much an issue. And if we're discussing Ingersoll's change in politics then we need to at least take a look at the two political parties mentioned. Ingersoll went from Democrat to Republican. The Democratic Party began in 1792. Supporters of Thomas Jefferson created the Democratic—Republican Party, promoting states' rights and a limited centralized government. Jeffersonian Democracy, as it came to be called, advocated a society based on faith in the virtues and abilities of the common man. There was a connection formed between Southern agrarians and Northern city dwellers which made the party strong and dominant until it was divided by the issues of slavery and states' rights. In the 1830s the party's name was changed to the Democratic Party. In 1860, within a year of the Civil War starting, the party split. In contrast, the Republican Party wasn't formed until 1854. The slavery issue was its main focus, but national interests versus states' rights became almost as important in the party's development and expansion. So, if we put the issues into modern terms, a belief in the sanctity of human rights and a desire to be involved in the world-community split the Democratic Party, and when that split occurred, Ingersoll joined a lot of other Northern Democrats and became a Republican. I doubt seriously, however, if Ingersoll was alive today, if he would still involve himself with the ideologically-conservative-class-system-maintenance and money-is-my-motivation-and-damn-the-environment-rationale of the Republicans, but I could be wrong since I don't really know much about the guy."

Tucker's hand moves slowly into the air, and I indicate that he may comment next, "You went from historical fact to opinion pretty darn fast there. For me Republicans represent the idea that government should be involved in citizens' lives as little as possible, but that's not what I wanted to say, and maybe it's just my country-boy upbringing, but I didn't think of any of those things about Ingersoll. I just thought this Mr. Ingersoll had this nice life as a preacher's son, went to school to become a lawyer because he believed in the law, in right and wrong; the war broke out; he joined because he probably believed it was the right thing to do, but what he saw changed him. He came back from the war, changed his politics and his religion because none of what he'd been taught to believe could stand up against what he had experienced, so he sort of 'threw the baby out with the bath water' just because he was trying to make things make sense."

Morgan responds after he looks around the room to see if anyone else has raised a hand, "Yeah, Tucker, I like the way your brain works, boy. It feels 'American' to me; it's straight-forward, simple but covers all the bases."

I lean back against the board and smile, my officiating officially over for the moment. The game has begun, and as long as the players volley nicely, I will stay the observer. As long as they continue to let each other finish speaking, then look to see if someone else is also raising a hand before speaking, I can just enjoy the intricacies of a group well practiced in healthy discussion.

Alana asks, "And you define 'American' as …?"

Morgan nods his head as we can see him putting his thoughts in order, "I define 'American' as … well, like I just said, straightforward, but into progress, into trying to figure things out, but always trying to do what's right."

Shay reaches out and puts his hand on Morgan's shoulder, "I respect your opinion, Morgan, and I'd like to agree with you, but I can't. I can't." He pauses as he leans back in his chair and spreads his arms wide, "I mean, look at us, we're the most powerful nation in the world right now, and I should emphasize 'right now', and we do some real arrogant things as a nation. So obviously and unfortunately, powerful and intelligent don't necessarily develop simultaneously with each other. We tell other countries their ways of thinking and believing are not as good as our ways. We assume our form of government, our level of technological dependency, our materialism, are all better ways of being. We preach to other countries they aren't treating their people right, but we let people die here, people like little kids and old folks, for no other reason than they can't afford health insurance or doctors' fees or heating oil. We burden the middle class with medical costs and taxes that grind them down until paying debts and being able to afford the property taxes on their homes when they retire become their central motivations instead of maintaining a meaningful and change provoking voice in the running of their country. And forget being able to put their kids through college easily; higher education is no longer part of the American Dream, unless tens of thousands of dollars in debt upon graduating is okay. The credit system has the young professional in its sights before the kid can even pick up his diploma. The American Dream? The American Spirit? What about American common sense? Give me a break. We're the only developed Western nation that still has the death penalty. Don't get me wrong though, I'd like nothing better than for America to be like a good ol' John Wayne movie where justice is always served despite the overwhelming stereotypes, but it's just not so. The stereotypes aren't okay, and every time we say they are, our sense of justice gets a little more out of whack."

Before hands can be raised in response, I interject, "Good. All your comments are insightful, and Shay just happened to mention the word which is to be our next focus. Please write down your definition of the word 'justice'." Students either begin writing immediately, or I can see they are thinking about writing, so I open the dictionary I have placed on the podium. When everyone is done, I give my next instructions, "I'm going to read the definitions of 'justice' according to Webster's Unabridged. While I am doing that, you need to listen carefully and decide if your definition corresponds with one or more of the definitions I read, because somehow I would like us to agree on one definition before we move on to the next part of our activity." Again I try to pace my delivery, knowing as I do I will gain momentum as I progress. "Number one: justice is the quality of being righteous; it is honesty.... Number two: justice is impartiality; it is a fair representation of the facts.... Number three: justice is the quality of being correct or right.... Number four: justice is retribution by either reward or punishment. Number five: justice is sound reason or validity. And number six: justice is the use of authority and power to uphold what is right, just, or lawful."

My students are finishing writing or looking at their own definition or definitions, so I give them a moment before I continue. "Any questions or comments before we begin?"

Neil raises his hand, "I guess my problem with what you say we're going to try to do is I would need to understand the scope or ... the why of our definition. History has to be considered. And even Shay's comment makes it pretty clear a great deal of what a person believes is based on culture, on day-to-day circumstance. So are we defining justice just for this discussion, or are we really trying to define justice as a universal?"

I say 'exactly' and smile, and Charlie comments, "Okay, okay, she did it again, guys; she's leading us around, and we don't even know it. Maybe we should just skip discussions, and Mrs. C can tell us where we're going to end up."

I am shaking my head now, "No way, Mr. Abbot, no way. I never know where we are going to end up exactly, and I would not want to know, but I can usually surmise what key concepts will arise from the discussions, and from those 'directions' I can set a course. That we will veer to the right or to the left, I do not mind at all, and sometimes my destination does change, but usually, because we have learned to be logical in our thinking patterns and because we are human and because we know each other, I can pretty much rely on the fact we will at least stay on my map. And … I do not think that should bother you, but if it does I am sorry, but that how I teach."

Charlie laughs, "I don't mind the way you teach at all, Mrs. C, but sometimes it feels like that adult-kid thing where the adult knows what the kid is going to do, and, of course, no kid really likes that."

I look around the room, "I do understand, but I never want you to believe I am manipulating how you think. I am just orchestrating a learning experience. I never want you to do the old thing where I speak, you take it in without considering it, then regurgitate it back at me. That is not learning to me, and I do so enjoy the process or journey of learning. But anyway … if anyone else has a concern about this, please comment now or talk with me later, because I really would like to ask my next question and hear your responses." Everyone nods their approval or gives an indication of agreement, and I continue, "So Neil is suggesting that justice is, perhaps like every other value we hold dear, culture- or, at least, perspective based. In other words, what we, as a group of people, may take as a universal truth may not actually be a universal truth. Does anyone disagree?"

Angela raises her hand, "I'm not disagreeing as much as I'm just pointing out it's very difficult for me to believe God is not a universal even for people who don't believe he exists. But I'm just pointing that out, we don't have to discuss it."

I ask, "Would anyone like to discuss Angela's idea?"

Morgan comments, "If we do, we'll be here for hours."

I agree but add, "Being here for hours may happen anyway, but that's not the issue. Do we need to discuss God as a universal truth?"

No one speaks, so I continue, "Ingersoll's quote states in nature there are only consequences, not rewards or punishments but only consequences. I am going to ask some questions which I want you to think about but not answer out loud.… Is man part of that nature of which Ingersoll speaks? Does human law, as culture based as it may be, reflect the laws of nature, or does human law, as culture based as it is, reflect the culture's own sense of justice? Think about how you respond when you read or hear the news and discover a teenage boy or girl has saved a younger child from drowning but ends up dying in the process. Think about how you feel when you find out a perfectly nice person is dying of cancer while some cancer free pedophile, who has repeatedly abused young children, is living next to an elementary school and being allowed to do so because of our culture's laws which define the protection of personal freedoms. And lastly, how do you respond to that over asked question, why do bad things happen to good people?" I pause and allow the reaction process to take place. "In nature there are only consequences. What does that mean to you? Look back at your first written response to the quote and decide if you still agree with what you wrote or if you have modified your thinking in any way."

Again, I allow them time to do what I have asked, and then I explain the next step in my plan, "I am going to share a story with you which was told to me by my grandmother, May. It is a story from before Ireland was Ireland, and it has the three elements of ancient literature which we have discussed in the last few weeks. Can anyone tell me the three elements?"

Maddie raises her hand, "Well, I don't usually try to do the memory-based questions, but here goes. In most stories from ancient times the number three is significant; the stories have supernatural elements, and the stories have some kind of bargain or negotiation that takes place."

I smile and say, "Perfect. Thank you. I thought this story would be good for today because of the weather and because of its content, so we can stay in here or we can grab some blankets and go over to the gazebo, and I will tell you a story as relevant today as it was when it happened."

Jacy asks, "This story really happened?" I do not respond, wanting a student to respond instead.

And Alana does, "I believe all stories have some truth in them. Some aspect of all stories was real once-upon-a-time. Even the most outrageous mathematical formula started out from someone counting on his or her fingers or from some-one noting the pattern of snowflakes."

Jacy laughs, "I think I get what you're saying. You're referring to the place where all humans, despite culture or perspective, can and do connect, maybe like Jung's belief in the collective unconscious or something."

Valerie adds, "Even most horror stories have a basis in reality and certain motifs are shared across cultures. The idea of vampires originated in a spiritual or at least non-physical context actually, people stealing other people's energy or life force. It was only later that vampires became drinkers of blood."

I allow the mini discussions erupting all over the room to run their course, then suggest moving to the next step in our process by offering them a choice of staying inside or going outside. "Raise your hands if you want to stay inside." Not a single person raises a hand. "Excellent! We're going to have an adventure. Let's meet in fifteen minutes at the gazebo. You can get something warm to drink and grab whatever type of outerwear and/or blankets you may want. You don't need to bring anything else; just come ready to listen."

*   *   *   *

We have gathered together and arranged ourselves over and under blankets. We are in a cathedral of mist, and words shared are softened by it. No ornate carving or massive walls or majestic stained-glass windows inspire this awe. We are in a moment fashioned by nature which inspires awe. I close my eyes for a moment and listen. The quiet of the dense, moisture filled fog reminds me of the quiet of snow falling; its sound whisper soft, hushed but audible, like the young voices in conversations around me sharing insights and struggles and ideals, which I realize are the very fabric of 'story'.

I recognize Alana's voice as she asks, "Are you sleeping, Mrs. C?"

I answer, "Only listening."

Tucker replies, "I thought that was our job."

I open my eyes and smile as I look at them, "Are you ready to listen?" Their responses vary and indicate their readiness, but I am not convinced.

I lean into the circle which we form, "Are you really ready? Have you put away your worries? Have you turned your to-do list face down? Have you taken your mood by the hand and reminded it to sit quietly beside you without interfering? Because we live in an age of entertainment, we are not practiced at the art of listening, at really hearing. I will offer no commercial breaks to benefit short attention spans. Will you sit till I am done, doing nothing but hearing and doing that thing which is inspired by hearing, seeing? And then if hearing and seeing are occurring as they should, will you let yourself feel what you are seeing and hearing? Will the words spoken move you through the story as you do nothing except hear and see and feel? Can we go back together to times of old when story was teacher, historian, and prophet?" I pause and look into each set of eyes looking into mine, "Are you really ready?" I have reached out to them, and they have heard my words, so they do not speak their responses, but their facial expressions and the language of their bodies answer me instead, and that was the response I wanted. They are ready to hear words which have been handed down for a hundred generations, so I take a deep breath and begin.

"It was a day like this, in a place of hills and lakes, in a land of emerald green laid down just so between a gray sea and a blue ocean. It was morning, but the golden sun did not reveal itself except to shine translucent in a mist so thick and wet it seemed alive. This particular piece of the island was ruled by a gentle but strong king named Lir. It was his wedding day. He was a wise man, who loved his family and his people and the land which provided for them. His life and his fort and his heart were full, but for so long he had been lonely for that which a wife brings to a man's life, because his wife had died when his sons, Aed, Conn, and Fiacra, were very young, and so his eldest child, his daughter, Fionnuala, had cared for them and managed his home well, and he had taken no new wife. He could not imagine doing such a thing, even though custom suggested it. Even his father-in-law, Bodb Dearg, the great over-king of the Tuatha De Danaan, suggested Lir remarry, but three years passed, and he took no new wife, and his loneliness deepened. Then one evening, a Druid who lived in the south and was on a pilgrimage took refuge at Lir's fort, and the Druid had his daughter, Aoife, with him.

"Aoife was beautiful and young but not a strong woman, and she was tired of all the walking; she felt worn thin with the hearing of all her father's well intentioned words of wisdom, so when she met Lir and saw he was a good and gentle man as well as a mighty warrior and respected king, she felt drawn to him, and she let him know how she felt. There was a reluctance in Lir regarding Aoife's youth and her indifference toward his children, but he wanted a wife by his side, and he reasoned a natural, deep affection would grow in Aoife for Fionnuala and Aed and Conn and Fiacra out of the love she claimed for him, so he ignored the voice in his head and warning from his heart that whispered 'no' to the 'yes' of his loneliness. And now that Aoife's father was preparing to leave to continue his pilgrimage, a wedding was being held, and Lir realized not only had he obtained for himself a wife, but he had found a mother for his children, and he felt as if he could once again reclaim the sweetness of his life with his first wife.

"But that was not to be. Aoife was an only child and much attention had she received in her own home due to her father's great abilities and her own beauty. Days became weeks, and Aoife's resentment of the love and time Lir gave to his children, and her jealousy, well fed as it was by her own selfish nature, grew to hate. Soon she could not bear to look upon the children any longer, and so she made a plan and hid it in the brooding shadowlands of a heart, which served only itself, until the time became right for her to act.

"That day came when Lir, busy with his men, agreed to Aoife's request to take the children to their grandfather, the great king Bodb Dearg. The younger boys were delighted, but Fionnuala asked her father if they could wait to go until he could join them, but Lir knew he and his men would be involved in their matters of soldiering for at least a few more days, so he told Fionnuala she should go, and he would join them as soon as he could.

"Aoife and Lir's children reached Lake Derravaragh and being halfway to their destination, Aoife suggested the children swim in the lake. The three boys, delighted with the idea, ran into the lake and shouted to each other and splashed each other, but Fionnuala stayed on the shore, because she knew in her heart Aoife meant them harm. Aoife yelled harshly at Fionnuala to join her brothers, and knowing she must obey her step-mother, Fionnuala walked slowly into the lake's cool, clear water.

"Her brothers swam from the deeper water to join their sister in the shallows begging her to join them in their fun, and no sooner were they together than Aoife removed a druid's wand from the deep folds of her cloak, and pointing the wand at the children, she chanted her spell: 'Children of Lir, no longer shall I share what is mine! Most beautiful of children in your father's eyes no more, your only family to call your own the waterfowl will be. Let your cries be mingled with the cries of the birds.'

"Within the space of a heartbeat, the beautiful Fionnuala and the handsome Aed, Conn, and Fiacra were transformed. No longer were there children wading in the waters of Lake Derravaragh but instead, on its surface, four beautiful white swans. The three smaller swans cried out to Aoife, but she turned from them and began to walk away from the lake. The larger swan of the four took flight and flew to just two or three feet from Aoife, lowered her long thin neck humbly and begged her stepmother to release them from the spell, 'Stepmother, stepmother, do not make us keep these shapes forever, put a limit on this deed you have done that we might one day have back our true forms. Do not, stepmother, condemn us forever.'

"Aoife turned toward Fionnuala, and the darkness that had filled her heart, the jealousy which had blinded her toward her husband's children, released its hold on her, and she realized what she had done. Aoife held the wand in her hand again and spoke, 'You will not be swans forever. For three hundred years you shall live here on Lake Derravaragh, and for three hundred more years you shall just barely survive on the Sea of Moyle, and for the last three hundred years you shall know some small bit of peace on Inish Glora. And then when a king from the north marries a queen from the south, and when you hear the bells of a new faith ringing out, then you will know your exile is over. But until then, your appearance will be that of swans, even though you will keep your own minds, your own hearts, your own voices.' Aoife paused then added, "Your song, your voices, will be so sweet that all who hear will be comforted. Now I must go. Do not call to me again." Aoife ran from them. She ran from the lake to her chariot then ran the horses all the way to Bodb's fort so horrified she was by her deed.

"When she arrived she told the great king his grandchildren had stayed with Lir, because Lir was jealous of the children's love for their grandfather. Anger at the words spoken was Bodb's first response, but that lasted only the smallest part of a moment, because he knew his son-in-law, knew his heart and knew his mind. He knew his dear daughter had chosen well her husband and knew her husband had mourned her passing for three long years before he had taken this new wife. Bodb realized also Lir's visits to this very fort had been numerous, and Bodb had never seen in his son-in-law the emotion Lir's new wife attributed to him, so the great king sent a message to Lir and requested he and his children come to Bodb's fort.

"Upon receiving the message, Lir felt as if a dark hand had grasped his heart, and suddenly he feared for his children. Lir set out immediately in the company of his best men. When they reached Lake Derravaragh four beautiful swans flew from the center of the lake to its shore, and from these swans came the voices of his children. At first he did not understand how swans could have stolen his children's voices, but then the hand that had held his heart earlier, grabbed it in a vise-like hold, and Lir fell to his knees there on the shore of Lake Derravaragh. His swan children saw the despair on their father's face, and Fionnuala began singing to him, remembering the words Aoife had said, and true they turned out to be, for instantly Lir's expression changed, and soon he and all his men laid down by the water's edge and watching the swans and hearing Fionnuala and her brothers sing, the men's eyes closed and they slept deeply.

"In the morning, Lir asked his children what he could do for them, and for the third time his heart was gripped by despair as Fionnuala told him he could do nothing against the spell of the druid wand. Lir left his men to watch over his children, and he rode to Bodb's fort to expose his wife's treachery and to reveal the fate of his children. The great king rose up in a fury and pointing a druid's wand at Aoife he spoke her fate into her. A cold wind born out of nowhere swept her up and slowly turned her over and over until she lost all form and became the very wind that held her. She became a captive of the air, and it is said on stormy nights in lonely places her moaning can still be heard as she is carried here and there, never to know rest or peace.

"Lir and Bodb rode to Lake Derravaragh, and there they stayed as days became weeks, as weeks became months, as months became years, and as years became decades. Decades became centuries, but Lir and Bodb and their households remained there on the shore, until one evening Fionnuala told her father and grandfather that she and her brothers would have to leave at daybreak. One last time Aed, Conn, Fiacra, and Fionnuala offered their love and sang the despair from their father's and grandfather's hearts.

"As the sun's first rays were just barely breaking over the hilltops, the swans spread their wings and rose into the air. They circled over their father and grandfather and the people of these two noble households then turned east and flew toward the Sea of Moyle. Lir and Bodb watched the swans until the length of sky and curve of earth swallowed them.

"The swans did not sing to each other on their way to the Sea of Moyle. They knew what lay ahead for them. The dark, storming skies and thrashing waters of the Sea of Moyle would change only from bad to worse with the seasons, only change from gales to ice and hale then back again. The swans knew they would need each other and every ounce of faith, hope, and love each other had in order to survive this angry place that would be their home. They also knew this second three hundred years would have none of the sad sweetness of the first. No longer would they raise their voices and bring joy to those whom they loved. Only jagged hateful fingers of cold, black rock pushed up out of the water, and only vengeful, grasping waves would be the swans' company in this gloomy place.

"Upon their arrival, and bleak day after bleak day, their worst fears were realized. Even when they called out to each other to offer solace, the bitter wind tried to steal their voices from them. There were times when Fionnuala thought she had lost one of her brothers to a ranting storm or to a pounding wave, but each time when her last hope was all that sustained her, she would search the sky and there the almost lost brother would be, his wings brittle with frost but beating like a heart refusing to offer up its last breath. On the day before they were to finally leave this place of sorrows, her brothers flew to her against a harsh wind and were almost swept away from her by waves leaping from their depths to steal away her only joys. But the brothers made their way to her, and she covered them with her wings and when the night sky began to pale, Fionnuala and Aed and Conn and Fiacra rose up into the sky and flew west to a quiet inlet bordered by the island's coast and the gentle shore of a smaller island called Inish Glora.

"On their way across this land they had once known, they decided to fly over their home to see their father and grandfather. The hills and lake of their childhood greeted them, but no voices called out their names. Only grassy mounds filled the places where Lir's and Bodb's forts once stood. The swans circled lower and lower and came to rest in the field where their father had run his horses, but there were no horses running now. Fionnuala gathered her brothers to her and comforted them even though her own grief threatened to overwhelm her. She stretched out her long white neck and sang her father's favorite song and on the last note held, she pushed up from the ground and let the strength of her wings pumping the air fill the vein of faith inside of her that had almost been bled dry.

Her brothers followed her into the sky, and they made their last long journey together.

"Aoife's promise of some small peace during their last three hundred years of exile proved true. And their hope, though strained by harsh circumstance, was rekindled like a small banked fire with the knowledge they neared the end of their ordeal; they had survived together, and so they spent their days singing together and riding gentle waves together and during the nights they sheltered together on the small island.

"Then one day, over the loud beckoning of wave to wave and over the persistent baptizing by breeze of leaf and branch, they heard their names being called, and they rose into the air and searched the island to find the caller. The swans saw a man standing before a small building, and as they did, so he saw them. He ran into the small building and rang a bell over and over and over. When the bell stopped ringing, the man ran out of the building, and he called their names again, and the swans landed before him. As he said each name, the swan-child of that name, spread its wings and stretched out its long thin neck. The man fell to his knees and cried for them.

"When he had dried his tears, Fionnuala asked how he knew them. The man explained he was Mochaomhog, and the fate of Lir's children was legend. Mochaomhog explained what the swans already knew: the Tuatha De Danaan no longer lived on earth, and while some said they had gone underground, others said they had gone somewhere far enough away to be too distant a journey for humans to make unassisted. Mochaomhog explained there was a new god, a Christian God, and Mochaomhog had built the church and now rang the bell for that God, but he also knew the truth doesn't change because the times do, and the old ways don't become untrue; they only allow themselves to become foundation for new ways.

"'It is like,' he said, 'the layers within a stone or the layers made visible in the side of a hill cut-away; the old layer is still there even though it may not be seen.' He paused, looked at the swan-children and smiled, 'But old or new, you are here, and I have come to help you during these last years.'" Then for the first time in over five hundred years, human arms wrapped around the swan-children and offered them love. The swans offered their love in return and sang out a song of such sad sweetness Mochaomhog cried again, then he assured them the worst part of their struggle was over, and they never had to fear losing each other again.

"The days passed evenly for the swans and Mochaomhog, then one morning, a morning like this one, a morning veiled by mist, a knock sounded against the door of the church. Mochaomhog and the swans were startled, but he quieted them as best he could then went to find out who was at the door. Fionnuala warned him not to answer the door, but her warning once again had gone unheeded.

"She called out to her brothers to gather closer around her, wanting to prepare them for what she felt in her heart was going to happen, but the booted steps of the visitor approached their small alcove in the church before she could do more than remind them of her enduring love for them.

"The man who stood before them was tall and dressed in fine clothing, but he seemed unsure of how to speak to swans. He waited for Mochaomhog to enter the alcove with him, then he spoke, 'I am Lairgren, king of a northern province, and my new wife, a queen from the south, believes our marriage is the one spoken of by Aoife, and wants you to be my wedding present to her. So I have come to take you with me.'

"Mochaomhog argued with the king, but the king was not one with whom arguing was done, so the king reached toward the swans looping a golden chain loosely around each of the swan's necks and began to drag them from the building. At first there was only the sound of flapping wings behind the king, but then the chain in his hand pulled against nothing, so he turned and what he saw silenced and stilled him just as it silenced and stilled Mochaomhog. The swans became almost transparent, and then four very frail, very old people stood huddled together for the briefest of moments before they fell to the ground.

"Expressions flew across the king's face like shadows: horror, compassion, fear. He backed out of the room, his steps growing fainter as he ran from the church. Mochaomhog rushed over to the ones he had cared for and loved and tried to comfort them, but Fionnuala, her sweet young voice now replaced by a gentle old one, told him her brothers' and her time had come. She asked Mochaomhog to bury them in this place where they had known peace in one grave together, that as they had lived so they might face eternity. Mochaomhog put his face in his hands and cried for them just as he had done on the first day he had met them, but then and for the last time, Fionnuala's words filled his heart so completely there was no room for tears, 'Dear friend, we thank you, but do not cry for us, for we have lived and now die with the only three things which can never be taken by force but only relinquished willingly, and we never relinquished them or each other.'

"The four old people held each other's hands, and as their final breath whispered out of them Mochaomhog heard their last three shared words. And then he could only smile at the grace of who they were and at the privilege of having served them. He buried them as Fionnuala had asked and raised a stone over their grave and carved the three words they had spoken, and then some say he simply left the island, but others say on his way to somewhere else, an old king stopped him in his path and spoke with him, then led him away into an eternal mist that has hung forever and still hangs to this day, like a gossamer veil, between this world and the next."

We share the silence together, my students and I; emotions, as solid as the mist, cast from eyes into the center of us become a bonfire of feelings. I almost stretch out my hands to it, knowing I would be warmed by hospitable flames of empathy and compassion, but I do not. I sit still and watch and wait. Soon eyes will meet mine again, and I will be released to move, to send out words in order to gather responses, and then to shepherd us back to where we started, but now Lir's children, Aoife, Lir himself, Bodb Dearg, and Mochaomhog will be joining us and adding their perspectives to ours, and then justice and laws may seem less important than personal character and grace.

*   *   *   *

I am driving up the hill to 'the excavation'. That is the label I have given it. The excavation. It is not my old house anymore. My old house is gone; it has been buried under a file full of facts and lengthy explanatory conversations and wild dreams and a letter from a woman I thought I knew. I am driving up the hill on a road shadowed by trees almost hidden in a mist determined to drape itself over rocks and soil and surf all day. The sun had the day off. The mist may be softer voiced than the sun, but when she decides to do something, the sun does not even attempt to dissuade her; they have been together long enough to know when and where to take their stands. It seems a fair arrangement. I am driving up the hill to children and husband. And then I wonder if Puppy was invited, if the eagle has visited, if the bodies beneath the ground mind terribly the reverberations of hard steel powered by large engine tearing through their eternal encampment.

I stop the Jeep behind Michael's truck and look out to see a motor home with awning out and table underneath. I see the backhoe being climbed on like a jungle gym by John Henry and Mary and Mark and Trisha ... and Connor, which is somehow not surprising. Michael, Brian, and Alex have beers in their hands and were talking but are now watching me. So I open the car door and step out. Puppy greets me by rubbing a very dirt encrusted mini football against my leg.

I am then greeted verbally with an assortment of 'moms' and 'heys' and 'hi-Leahs'. I walk to where Michael and Brain and Alex stand and say, "This is very festive."

Michael smiles, "Well you know, we're a festive bunch."

Father Tom steps out of the motor home and joins us. He and I hug, then we all watch Connor and the kids climbing on the backhoe as I comment, "Connor seems to be enjoying himself."

Father Tom replies, "Connor enjoys himself very easily."

I turn to Michael, "Have you had a good day?"

Michael nods, "We took a whole section of fence out and then got the gates in. Then I nearly tore another whole section of fence out getting used to driving the backhoe, but I think I've got it now. You should see Brian on that thing. He'll be doing wheelies in no time."

Brian takes a drink from his beer, looks at me, belches, then smiles as he says, "It's a gift I have, not to brag, of course, but me and machinery like each other. We get along. We have a copasetic relationship. If I could find a woman who had an engine and controls, I'd be—"

I interrupt him by hitting him on the shoulder, "Shame on you. I was almost impressed when you used the word copasetic, then you had to ruin it all by being … well, you."

Brian lays his head against my shoulder, "Ah, sis, don't you love me still?"

I pat his head, "Poor baby, a sexist and delusional. I have never loved you. You are not lovable."

He staggers back from me as if he has been mortally wounded and looks at Michael, "Control your wench, brother; she's drawing blood here."

Michael just shakes his head, "I think you'll survive. Of course, I could call Cal and have him send Maybe over, then Leah and Maybe could team-up and—"

Brian interrupts Michael, "Stop. Stop right there. I'm leaving. Don't even try to thank me for giving up my day off to come do labor for you." He is yelling over his shoulder now as he walks to his truck, "Just wait till I tell dad on you. Then you'll both be begging for my forgiveness."

Michael yells back at him, even though there is really no reason to be yelling at all, "Hey Brian, thanks for your help, brother. And thanks for eating more food than Alex and I put together."

Brian has the door to his truck open, "I may not be back. I can't take all this abuse."

Michael waves at him, "See you, tomorrow."

Brian climbs into his rig and rolls down the window, "Yeah, tomorrow. Hey Leah, promise to stop by after work again, it was just too fun."

I hold out my arms to him, "Do you need a hug, little brother? You know I was only kidding with you."

Brian smiles, "If you weren't my sister-in-law I'd get back out of my truck and walk all the way over there for a hug, but you are my sister-in-law, and that means I'd be putting out a whole lot of effort for little to no return." He starts his car, backs it up and drives off with a smile on his face.

Alex slaps Michael on the back, "Well I'm guessing the entertainment is over, so I think I'll take my kids home and see what the wife is cooking us for dinner, or maybe it's my night to cook dinner." Michael and Alex shake hands and Michael thanks him for helping out today. Alex turns to me and says, "Jan says things are going well at school lately."

I walk with him over to the jungle gym-backhoe, "They are. The students seem content and inspired, and if the students are content and inspired, the staff is usually content and inspired. Of course, I suppose it could work the other way just as well. Anyway, it is good of you to come and help out here."

Alex looks at me, "When Jan and I were going through our troubles, you and Michael were always there for us. You'd have us over, Jan and the kids or me and the kids, and you always called to see if I needed any help. All the ladies in your family kept my freezer full of meals. Jan would come over on Sundays to help with the house chores and to cook meals for the week to help me out, but she'd open the freezer, and it would be full. The Callaghans to the rescue. So, since I've always been a believer in one-good-turn-deserving-another, here I am. But I'd probably be here anyway, you know how we fire-boys like to work together all week then do weekend work together as well."

I agree with him, "That is so true. I've often thought it has something to do with how intense your job can sometimes be. Even though I can try to relate, I cannot really know what it would be like to realize on a regular basis my life depended on the choices someone else makes." I shake my head, "It's a bit mystifying ... like you are soldiers facing an enemy together."

Alex comments, "It really is like that sometimes too, or at least it feels like the fire is an enemy, an intelligent enemy, but I guess it's really just fire being a fire and doing what fires do."

I am thinking back as I respond, "My students and I were discussing something along those lines today. We were talking about nature and how it does not reward or punish; there is simply cause and effect."

Connor has jumped down from the backhoe and is helping the kids climb down. All five of their faces are smudged with dirt and their clothes bear the same marks. Connor looks at himself and then at Alex, "Doesn't that just prove it to ya, now? Poor me, arriving only after the work had stopped, so I joined the young ones in play, and judging by Alex's appearance and my own, I had the more difficult task."

Alex is smiling but asks, "And what was proved exactly?"

Connor nods his head, "I sort of left ya hanging there, didn't I? It's a bad Irish habit of mine to be sure. My point is that in seminary when I was reading a book or two on sociology, one of the authors wrote for young ones play is work, demanding effort and creativity and wit." He pauses looking down at his hands and clothes again, "And obviously, dirt. For sure dirt must be a necessary ingredient. It's the proof of a day's hard labor."

Michael has joined us. John Henry and Mary are leaning against me, and I hold one of their hands in one of mine. Connor looks at Michael, "I'll be sleeping here tonight according to Father Tom, so I'll give ya a full day tomorrow. I didn't mean to be so late today, but I'm still on Irish time it seems."

I look at Michael then at Connor, "I still do not see the need for that, especially since there is not even a hole to fall into yet."

Connor seems unsure of how to answer at first then he responds, "Well, I'm simply honoring a request, so if its explanations you're wanting, you'll have to ask Father Tom or maybe Michael here."

I look expectantly at Michael, but Alex chooses that very moment to say his goodbyes, and Michael decides to walk Alex and his children to the car. Connor laughs, "Can't timing just be everything, and don't you think Alex read it all quite well?"

John Henry and Mary run to say goodbye to Father Tom, who is standing next to his bicycle, binding pant legs and securing his water bottle by a strap to the handlebars. So I look at Connor, "Meaning?"

Connor steps just a bit closer to me, "I wouldn't be believing for a moment you believed in coincidence, so you'd have to be seeing the sweet escape by your own dear husband as assisted by his workmate and friend."

I step back, "Perhaps."

Connor stretches out his arms, then steps just a bit closer to me again, "You're not comfortable with me, are you?"

I choose not to step back this time, "Did you enjoy reading the file?"

Connor seems unsure of how to respond, "What file?"

I reply quickly, "The one Malick found in your room. The one you took from our house."

Connor looks toward Father Tom and seems as if he wants to call him over, but that could be me just reading something into the situation that is not there, because he does not call to Father Tom. His eyes look into mine as he states, "Leah, I've never been to your house, and I don't know what file you'd be talking about."

There does not appear to be any defensiveness motivating in his words, so I try a different approach, "Then you are implying Malick is lying."

His response is not rushed but the intensity of it does make me step back, "No, I didn't say that. I wouldn't say that, because Malick does not lie."

I can only ask, "Then how did the file get into your room?"

Connor's eyes have not left mine, "I share the room with Malick, but I have no idea how or why or who." He seems to have regained control of his composure as he responds, "But, Leah, if this is only the beginning, think how interesting it may all become."

I have no response; I simply nod my head at him, turn, and walk away. Michael and Puppy are in the truck and the kids are in the backseat of my Jeep. Father Tom is standing with his bike and talking with Michael as I walk to the Jeep and open the door.

Father Tom smiles at me, "Here we are both leaving, little Leah, and I haven't even asked you how your day was."

I look at Connor, who has walked over to Father Tom, and say, "It has been … interesting. I hope you have a good evening, Father." John Henry and Mary call out their goodbyes to Father Tom as I shut the car door but fumble with the key because my hand is suddenly shaking. Finally I manage to start the car and back up out of Michael's way so he can turn his truck and take the lead. I try to keep my thoughts focused on my driving and on John Henry's and Mary's happy chatter about their day, but a shadow falls across my heart, and I cannot make it go away.

∗   ∗   ∗   ∗

Baths and dinner and bedtime stories are over. Our children are sleeping. Michael and I lay in our bed. I am listening to our quiet house. Moonlight shines through our bedroom window, and I think the moon has done what the sun could not. The misty fog has finally gone. Michael sighs.

I say, "Tell me."

He says, "It was just a sigh."

I ask, "So you enjoyed your day?"

He rolls over on his side as I do, so we face each other, "It was a good day. How was yours?"

I reach over and put my hand on his chest to feel the even beating of his heart, "Good, too, mostly. I told family group the story of Lir's children. We sat in the gazebo, surrounded by mist. We had blankets so we were warm, and the conversation afterward was insightful. I have good students."

Michael touches my cheek, "They have a good teacher."

I whisper, "Thank you."

We just look into each other's eyes for a moment, then he moves closer to me and asks, "Are you ever going to tell me how you feel about all the information dad gave us?"

I respond without really knowing what I am going to say, "About most of it I am not thinking at all. I am not thinking about Sean, but I think about that night. That night, the night of the fire, has been playing over and over again in my mind for so many years ... Hank just put words to the images. Every time I think I have some sort of vague idea about all that is happening, something new occurs, and everything changes.... I am just ... holding on for now, trying to respond when I need to respond, trying to listen when I need to listen, being a wife, being a mom, being a teacher ... then, just being ... me, the way I am." I think of my conversation with Alex, about fires just being fires. I think about the sun and the moon and the mist. Then I think about Aoife and about Fionnuala, about May and Sean and about Connor and Malick. Then I am looking into Michael's eyes again. "It was a good day to tell the story."

He lays back and raises his arm, so I can put my head on his chest, and he can put his arm around me, "It's always been your favorite, hasn't it?

I say, "Yes."

I can feel him shake his head, "It's too sad to be my favorite."

I whisper-talk now because my eyelids are getting heavy and my body feels totally relaxed ... totally safe because of my closeness to Michael, "But beyond the sadness, you have to look beyond the sadness."

Michael kisses the top of my head, "Faith, hope, and love, right, wife?"

I am almost asleep, but I let the words breathe out of me just like Fionnuala and Aed and Conn and Fiacra did during their last moment. I breathe them out into my home and into the hearts of my family, "Faith, hope, and love, husband. Faith, hope, and love."

Chapter SIX

"Super human strength, genius like intelligence, and dashing good looks," Brian pauses to smile, "that's all it takes, babe."

Brian is looking up at me waiting for a response, but I do not make one. I am standing on the edge of the gaping hole Michael and the others have dug, first with the back hoe then with shovels over the last few days. I am watching Michael and Connor sweeping away the dark earth from what used to be the basement's concrete floor. The soil attaches itself like lichens on the rocks of shore and forest creating a patternless pattern. Michael looks up at me between the smooth forward-back movements of his arms. He and Connor are sweeping the moist and clinging soil into the center of a room that is no longer a room.

It is a grave, I think to myself, or a tomb. Perhaps, since it has held so dearly and deeply that which May saved for me, it is a sepulcher offering its relics even as it guards them. Then I wonder if I am truly ready to hold in my hands this buried box for which a man died, for which a father left. I shake my head and let my head fall back and open my eyes to sky and cloud and tree tops. Then I see it, almost hidden in the cover of branch and leaf, looking down at me. And looking up at it I say to Michael, "The eagle is back."

Michael's responds, "Perfect timing."

I look down and see the cleaned concrete has relinquished its secret. Michael stands over a rectangular shape made by the dark earth still clinging to parameter indentations of the safe's cover. So aware are we of the crescendo of moment and the culmination of quest we do not move. We are only eyes focused and breath as the breeze whispers of other opportunities, brushing against the skin of our cheeks and hands and against the back of our necks. But we are not distracted, and I believe our stillness has sent tremors of intent out from itself because Father Tom comes out of the motor home and stands next to me. Then I think perhaps it is more than just breeze brushing against us and more than just the voice of breeze that seeks to distract us.

Connor's voice from directly beneath where I stand interrupts my thoughts, "There's no time like the present, I'm thinkin'."

I look at Michael. He is looking at me then we are both looking up because the shadow of the eagle has crossed between us. Father Tom already walks around the excavation to the other side where an earthen ramp created and used by the back hoe allows wide access in and out.

I move also, walk slowly toward the future and the past, but think no relevant thoughts; I am only a camera taking in visual perceptions: boot prints pressed into soil, meadow grass and small wildflowers bent down or crushed under the heavy intent of humans blinded to vegetation's' plight by the urgency of task. I think perhaps I should tiptoe through to avoid further destruction, but instead I allow my feet to make their own decisions, and they seem content or even possibly determined to do nothing more or less than follow Father Tom's feet. Then feet become herd animals in my mind, eared and tailed, short and long coated.... I shake my head like an etch-a-sketch to erase that image, looking into Michael's eyes when my feet find themselves on concrete. He holds out his hand to me; his expression offers comfort while Father Tom's and Connor's and Brian's faces are tense with a Christmas or birthday anticipation. I do not look at them, but instead I join Michael, my hand in his, and he pulls me close and whispers, "It will all be okay, Leah; it will all be okay."

My forehead is pressed against his chest as I speak my words, "It will be whatever it will be, and you and I, together ... we will make it okay."

He wraps his arms around me and says, "Yes." And that word repeats in my mind over and over until, with a gentle tightening of his arms around me, he releases me, and I turn, fold down, like clothes worn emptied of body suddenly. I am on my knees, and again the eagle's shadow slides across the cement floor, but I do not look up. Michael slides a pry bar beneath one of the edges. Brian reaches down to remove the lid once Michael has angled it up enough for fingers to grab hold.

I am holding my breath. I am ... thrown back against the wall of the excavation. It is as if hands are pressed against my shoulders. I can feel the dirt of the wall crumbling against the back of my head. I can see Michael and Father Tom and Brian and Connor trying to move toward me, but they are in slow motion, so I close my eyes seeking the other reality instead, that place where I am being held against my will, and it is like before … the slashing, unilluminated colors … my senses are overwhelmed by the crushing onslaught of dark emotions … pain, fear, rage. I raise my hands against it to push it away, but nothing changes in its relentless attack then I remember. I let my hands fall to my sides. I send it away with my mind, and it is gone.

My knees bend. I let my back slide down against the wall of earth. Michael is at my side at once, saying my name, touching my face with his hands, but I am still in the other place too, one visual perception shifting quickly into the other: first here looking into Michael's eyes then there standing before a wall of stones towering over me. As I lay my head against Michael's chest I am also laying my head against an ancient depth of stone that is cool and silent compared to the quick beat of Michael's heart and the warmth of his body.

Then it is a fire's warmth and fluctuating flame drawing me in. I am before the fire, and beyond it is the man from the other experiences. He sits on a stone layered with the light catching and varied furs of animal skins. His robe is cobalt blue in color and within the tight weave crimson red strands seem to dance around him like the flames of the fire. Beside him on a metal stand of bronze an eagle rests so still I initially believe I am looking upon a sculpture, but its eyes search mine. My gaze returns to the man. He is ageless. His skin is alabaster white, but I can sense its warmth and smoothness as it reflects the fire's light like a pearl. The color of his eyes match the deep drawing blue of his robe. His feet are sandaled in dark leather.

I am aware we are not alone. Beyond the man there is a woman in white, but I can see her barely. She is like a whisper, her eyes and the jewelry she wears around her neck and on her hand the only aspects of her the fire's light reveals. Between the man and me, around the fire's circle of light, others sit on large stones also. Despite their closeness to me, they are even less distinct than the woman. I can sense them more than see them; they are bright shadows only, almost transparent, but I do not mind this for I sense it is the man I have come to meet, not the woman or the others; it is the man who compels me, elicits my attention without movement or word. So I let my eyes meet his again, and I become, like the eagle, sculpture-still. The man, and I believe that is what he is, is letting me acclimate, get my bearing, find handholds within this moment … within this place. I become aware of my own breathing then, and the thought comes upon me that my breath fans the fire and with an almost imperceptible nod the man agrees with me as his voice crosses the distance like a wave far off; it is soft, but I can feel its power, sense his 'yes' even though his lips do not move. Then I wonder about the others, who are almost but not quite out of my range of sight—I stop myself, because I know it is more than range of sight … they are almost beyond the domains of this moment … this place in time. Then because my eyes still focus on the man's I see him barely nod again, and again his word of agreement is in my mind. Instantly he stands before me, the fire's light behind him; he holds out his hand to me, palm up. I lay my hand palm down upon his upturned hand then I am everywhere at once.

Panoramic visions, torrential in their flow, flood over me. I feel as if I am flying over geoscape after geoscape until I recognize an unchanged arrangement of massive black and gray cliff-like stones and a grove of trees set like emeralds amongst them. I realize I am seeing only one place and with that realization the flood of images stop, and the man's eyes hold my focus. His whisper soft voice resonates around me, seems to enter me through my skin, finds my center; sensations like floating or peaceful falling detain me from reaching for the meaning of his words; meanings become simply ornate renderings, abstract forms, or like the flight of birds perceived from a distance, intricate patterned lines on the horizon, and I am too content to reach far or to decipher, but the pressure of his palm under mine strengthens, causing his words to land solidly within me, "I am Shal," and turning his head to indicate the eagle he continues, "You already know Malick."

I am … thunderstruck … being held in arms and against a body demanding response. My name is being called. Even though I thought my eyes were already open, I open them. Michael's kisses on my cheeks and lips and forehead are his response along with "Where did you go? Don't do that again. Why didn't you answer me?"

I raise my hand to Michael's face, touch his cheek, and then let my fingers touch his lips to still them. I close my eyes again to see if that place where I was is still visible, but it is not, and I sigh as I again look into the concerned eyes of my husband. I make a small smile in my heart and send it out to him, and then I look around reassuring each one of them: Father Tom, Brian, Connor, Malick.

I sit up quickly, "What are you doing here?"

Michael and the others look at Malick. He shrugs his shoulders as if to dismiss the intensity of my question as his words do nothing but intensify it, "I was here with you. I left with you. I came back with you. It's as simple as that really."

Michael, sensing my fear, stands suddenly in a quick gesture of very male protectiveness not thinking about the fact I am leaning against him and so sudden is his movement that I, unprepared for it, fall back upon the concrete floor. So now I am looking up into the blue of sky, and there is within my view the half circle of men standing over me, who are in turn encircled by the trees. We are all momentarily still, but the tension which had threatened us earlier has flown. I smile.

Michael throws up his arms as he looks down at me, "Only you would smile at a moment like this, only you." Father Tom helps me stand. I brush off the soil, which managed to escape the men's sweeping that my sweater and jeans collected quite easily.

I turn to Michael, touch his face again, "I am smiling because your quick desire to protect me caught me by surprise, and I fell. I undoubtedly looked silly laying there with my legs going this way and my arms going that way. Then too I was looking up into the sky and there was this circle of faces over me, and around them was this circle of trees, and well … we have May's box … and Malick is part-time eagle, part-time man, and I was in a strange place … and then again, I wasn't because I was here too … not to mention, we have accomplished our tasks from letter one and now get to read letter two, wherein there will undoubtedly be more tasks, more mysteries, more … well, damn strangeness … and, so yes, I smiled even though running for my life makes more sense or having a mental meltdown makes more sense, but … well, damn, damn, damn, I am wife, mom, and teacher, and people depend on me, so I cannot have a meltdown or even scream for the rest of my life … so I smiled." I pause to catch my breath then continue, "Now please get the box. We will all go to our house, open it and … who can possibly guess what will happen after that." I pause again, "I am walking home, by the way. I will see you all when I get there. And another by the way, someone should call Matilda; she should be there when we open the box … and maybe call Hank too. And my goodness, if Hank and Matilda are coming we might as well invite Katy, who is, at present, watching over my children." I am walking up the ramp away from them, but I keep talking, "And then again there is Maybe; she'd get a kick out of all this I am sure … and why not—" but I stop at the sight of the rowan tree. I take a deep breath, think about touching it; I am leaning toward its smooth trunk to do just that, but I shake my head instead. 'Enough for one day,' I say to myself, 'enough.' I walk by it and into the trees wanting my house, the feel of its walls around me, noticing, as I realize I am feeling a bit drained of intellect and emotion, the shadow of an eagle flies over me.

*   *   *   *

We are many; we are one. We are one set of eyes with bodies filling chairs and couches or with bodies folded and sitting on the floor. We are looking into the metal box, its lid laid beside it. There is the pale yellow tint of stilled time in the air as if the box breathed finally when its lid was removed after over two decades of holding its breath, stilling its heart. I think if I were to take Michael's hands in my own and look closely at them, his fingertips would tell of his involvement; as when touching a butterfly's wings, his fingertips would be covered with a pale dust of faded lemon yellow.

I lean back in my chair. I am glad Katie decided to stay at her house with John Henry and Mary. This is no place for children. This is a place of dark winding passages and catacombs, of spaces within spaces dug out of the earth by hands with a purpose now unknown. What place could children have here within this moment of the past raising its dark hooded head and gazing forthright into the present, reaching out its long arms into the present and perhaps even into the future? What place? I sigh and notice the eyes of others go from me to the box. I realize they are waiting for me to … reach into and pull out first the ring, then the feather, then the necklace, then the stone with its ancient leaf imprint, then the tiny metal box clasped tightly shut to hold dark soil deepened in its hue even darker by the blood that once saturated it. I sit up suddenly shocked by my own thoughts.

Michael notices and asks, "What is it, Leah?"

I say simply, "I know what is in the box."

Michael tilts his head, "But the contents are still covered by the cloth."

And they are; he is right. We have removed the lid of the box, but the contents are still shrouded in an ancient but still vibrant blue velvet, embroidered with scarlet red orbs and emerald green diving arcs lanced through by dark golden arrow-straight lines of varying lengths. How could I know?

I do not look at any other face but Michael's as I respond, "I know what is in the box, even though I cannot see the items themselves; I know the list of contents, that's all."

Michael asks, "But how?"

I ask back, "But how any of this, Michael?"

He only nods, and knowing what must be done next, checks for and gets my approval. He folds back the cloth serving as both bed and canopy and the light of the room touches a ring with a pearl setting, a long feather with its dark colors paling into the whitest of whites at its tip, a necklace of delicate chain and a finely sculpted heart, a smooth gray stone with a dark imprint or impression of a rowan leaf, and a tiny bronze box inlaid with an ivory and amber outline of an eagle.

I lean forward and carefully pick up the box moving it to rest in my lap. I breathe its scent into me as I hold the ring between my finger and thumb for all to see before I slip it on the middle finger of my right hand. The ring fits perfectly, as I sensed it would, its muted golden brown metal somehow warm as it embraces my finger, its pearl setting glistening with the powdery soft shadows of lilac-rose and silver-blue. I gently move the feather from where it was covering part of the necklace's heart to discover the dainty chain of the necklace passes through the tiny eye of a clasp holding not a whole heart but half a heart. I hold the necklace up for the group to see then clasp it easily around my throat where the small half heart rests in the shallow concave hollow at the base of my throat as I realize the necklace too is not cold but warm or at least body temperature. I lay the stone in my palm. I am reminded of Shal's palm touching mine, and even though I know the stone sits still where I have placed it, there is a sensation of movement or pulse. Then I am reminded of those two sweeter than sweet times when my children's bodies were within my own and even before I could sense their pulse or feel the movement of their arms and legs, there was inside me a sense of life within me. The stone in my palm feels the same. I allow the others to look at it, or to be more precise into its imprint, each of the tiny chiseled or chipped indentations darkened with a dye so darkly crimson it appears to be black. I return the stone to the box and remove the smaller box which is no more than an inch in parameter. As I turn the box so the others can see it, I realize the ivory and amber silhouette of an eagle has been crafted so that viewed from one perspective it is an eagle's shape but viewed from the opposite perspective the silhouette becomes that of a human being. When I look up from the box my eyes meet Malick's. He smiles knowing I have seen what had been made to be hidden. But I am not ready to smile with him yet; there are questions he needs to answer before we can be in any type of agreement, so I only acknowledge his smile with a nod as I return the box to its place within the larger box.

Michael's voice stops me as I reach for the feather, "Aren't you going to open it?"

I answer him gently, "There is soil inside of it, soil soaked in human blood, and please do not ask me more than that about it, because I know nothing more. I do not know how I know; I do not know whose blood soaked the soil; I only know what I have told you."

Michael's words are gentle, "That's all right; we will figure everything out later. Maybe the second letter will tell us something about it."

I smile to hear the hopefulness embedded in each of his words, "Yes, that will probably be so, Michael." Then I turn my attention to the feather, but as I raise it out of the box I am stilled by an impression I do not recall actually registering as an impression when it was occurring. The woman I barely saw behind Shal held a feather in one of her hands while the fingers of her other hand seemed to start at the base of the feather and work their way up the plume reaching its tip only to return to the base and begin the whole process over again. How can I remember that when I could barely see her? But I do remember it, and I remember it clearly. I look at the feather I hold in my hand. I place the fingers of my other hand at its base and let them follow the change of color, dark to light, to the tip. As I repeat the movement I faintly perceive something so tenuous flutter within me ... or perhaps within who I am, because I cannot label the sensation as physical although I can sense it like an internal breeze or a whisper or the softest of lover's touches.

I shake my head and glancing around the room see everyone watches me, simultaneously realizing I have no idea how long I have been in my ... reverie. I shake my head again and look for Michael. I need him ... to anchor me somehow. He has moved over to the windows across the room, but he still watches me.

"Why did you move away from me?" My voice sounds like a petulant child's, which I do not like.

Michael runs his fingers through his hair as he walks back over to me, "I'm right here, Leah."

I lay the feather back in the box then take Michael's hand in mine, "I'm sorry; that was silly of me." He kneels down next to me and his closeness is so welcomed, as if I can breathe normally again, not realizing before that I was not. "I guess I just like having you close, husband."

He gently reassures me with his eyes before his eyebrows raise and lower and the smile on his face prepares me for his next comment, which he whispers into my ear, "I will, of course, be as close to you as you want me to be and as often as you want me to be, wife, but with that closeness there comes a certain obligation to—"

I interrupt him, "You are being a brat, husband; you know what I meant."

He does not answer me, but he does keep smiling and looking so deeply into my eyes I am a bit embarrassed by his intent when others are so close, so I glance up at them as I run my fingers uncharacteristically through my hair, "Well, shall we discuss the items or read May's second letter?"

Father Tom raises his hand, then realizing that he does not need to raise his hand, he stands, "The significance of the items may be touched upon in May's second letter, so instead of guessing, although that might be interesting, we should hear May's letter and save discussion for afterward."

Connor rubs his hands together and agrees with Father Tom, "Let's be about it then."

Hank stands and walks over to Michael and me, "Are you sure you want all of us here for that? Perhaps it should be as it was for the first letter: just you two and Father Tom."

I put my hand on Hank's arm, "You are thoughtful to think of that, Hank. You and your Kate are well matched, but if it is okay with Michael that Connor and Malick and you and Matilda are here, it is okay with me."

Michael nods his approval, "It would seem all those involved should be present." He turns and looks at Malick, "You're not going to need to have a wee break to go out and stretch your legs or … wings or anything are you?"

Michael's question is met with silence, and the tension which threatened to overtake us back when we found the box seems to threaten us again, but Father Tom moves to Malick and puts his arms around Malick's shoulders, "A little shape-shifting is not a huge concern now is it, Michael?"

Michael shrugs his shoulders, "Two weeks ago my answer might have been different, but now, even though I don't have any idea what is involved in shape-shifting, as you refer to it, I suppose, like everything else, we're learning and will come to understand that too, at least enough so it won't seem like something from a damn horror movie or a nightmare."

Connor moves so he stands on the other side of Malick and looks directly into Michael's eyes, "Shakespeare's Hamlet said it best now don't you agree? 'There are more things in heaven and earth, Horatio, than are dreamt of in your philosophy.' I'd be of a mind, Michael, to think you'd be wanting to thank my good brother Malick here for watching over you and your family rather than poking fun at him. Of course, that's my thinking; you may be of a mindset completely different than mine."

As Connor finishes speaking, I watch Michael's face and sense the emotion in him that could so easily send him across the room to place himself directly in front of Connor, even as I know it is not so much Connor's words but the tone in which they were stated and the look on Connor's face, which I will not classify as being cunning, but I cannot classify as purely good natured either. Father Tom is quick to respond, and with his usual honesty, "And what is it you're doing now, Connor? Peace keeping? Defending a friend? There's an intent, something behind your words, I am not able to discern, nor have I seen it in you before, nephew. Michael's comment may have been … impolite, but he has more at stake here than you do, and his emotions may be overriding his better judgment." Father Tom pauses and looks at Michael then back at Connor before he continues, "Am I correct in stating, Connor, Michael may have a great deal at stake here?"

Connor tries to smile but cannot quite make it happen so what appears for the briefest of moments on his normally handsome face is a grimace, but his eyes cause me to catch my breath, to pull Michael closer to me. Connor's response does nothing to alleviate the growing sense of unease, "I may have been out of line, but calling a man something from a freak show doesn't seem right to me."

Malick turns his back to Michael and Hank and me to respond to Connor, so I cannot see his face as he speaks, "Watch yourself, Connor. Michael said nightmare and horror movie. Freak show came out of your mouth. And just for the record, Connor, we are not brothers; we've been friends, even comrades in a cause or two, but we've never been brothers. I was always part of an order in the church that made you uncomfortable, and you have to admit we disagree more than we agree on most matters concerning the church and what it is supposed to represent and to protect. You've never done anything more than tolerate my beliefs and actions ever since I left the church, so I think I'd rather you did not try to defend me now."

Connor's face is expressionless, and it is easy to see he is struggling to maintain control. "My mistake, Malick. And Michael, if I have offended I offer my apology." His expression does not change when he turns to Father Tom except the look in his eyes softens, "You're my uncle; if I've disappointed you, it's more than sorry I am." He pauses and looks around the room, "Perhaps it would be better if I left; it seems I've overreacted." Connor moves toward the door, but Father Tom looks at Michael apparently asking Michael with his eyes to stop Connor from leaving.

I can see Michael is reluctant, but he speaks anyway, "Connor, stay if you'd like."

Connor looks at Malick, but before Malick turns to Connor to speak, Malick looks at Michael with what appears to be a disappointed or frustrated look on his face, "Do as you please, Connor; you and I ... we've had worse disagreements than this before."

Connor raises his hands and smiles a big Connor smile, "And isn't that just like the Irish souls that we are to be so ever lovin' forgiving. So, let's settle down here and discover what May will be teaching us next, shall we?" And even though there is an obvious desire by all in the room to forget the discomfort of the previous moment and move on, a shadow of doubt remains on the faces of my family regarding the two strangers in our midst.

*   *   *   *

Finding myself the center of attention again, I remember that I almost did not become a teacher because being the center of attention interests me so very little. But I am here, May's second letter in my hands, watched and waited for. I remember too what I felt just before I read the first letter, but the sweetness of the first time is marred by the unfolding of events since then, and that brings tears to my eyes. That I would distance myself from May emotionally feels so wrong, but I know that is what I am doing, no matter how wrong it seems. Feelings and emotions may be herded and held captive behind doors of persistent restraint and self control; they can be quieted by a firm and reasonable voice, but they cannot be altered by a desire to have them transformed. I can almost see them calling out into the space May filled, 'traitor', 'liar'. Though I am shocked by those words and try ever so briefly to be reasonable, I do feel betrayed by May, by her secrecy, by the overwhelming cost of her secrecy. I lay the letter on the table before me and look at my now empty hands as I say, "I am not at all sure I am ready to read this letter."

I look up to witness reactions even though the reactions do not actually inter-est me. I am too far away to care, so I look down again and close my eyes. I become … small again … I am the child I was, but because of the passage of time, of my passage through time, I am not only distanced from those currently around me, I am distanced from the child I was, so she is even smaller, and no matter how I try, no matter what attempt I make … to be reasonable … to be proper within this moment … I will not move beyond where I am. I will not read the words meant for me. I will not satisfy others' curiosity out of a sense of obli-gation. I will not.…

Michael's hands surround mine, but I do not look up to see the disappoint-ment in his eyes. He has a plan for me, however, other than my own, "Leah, look at me." Then we are just eyes looking into eyes and hands touching, and I find no disappointment in those eyes, no tension in those hands. I find only love.

His voice, low and soft, says 'wife', and there is no question attached to it. I say 'husband' back to him and look around the room. We are alone.

I ask, "They are outside?"

He brings my hands to his lips before he answers, "They went home. We will read the letter another time, just you and me and Father Tom. I believe that will be better for you."

I whisper, "Better for me?"

He whispers back, "Yes, Leah, better for you, and better for you is better for me, and besides May would want you to read the letter when you are ready, and not feeling ... feeling unsure of yourself or her."

I tilt my head and look at this man who is mine, "How do you know what I was thinking about?"

He stands and pulls me up to stand with him, so we are almost too close for words to fly between, but he manages to place words and light kisses just right, "You are like a deep lake ... inviting and on the surface so beautiful and clear, but what you hide from view ... that has taken me so long to see." He pauses and leans back to look into my eyes. "Sometimes I misread, but sometimes I don't, Leah. You are human, wife, and some of what I know is based on just being human. You were in overload. You were wondering how May could not be honest with you all those years ago when she held you close, but now ... after a lot of pain, she wants to tell you all, wants you to help her. That has to be difficult to take in and make sense of. Don't you think?"

I smile at him, "Yes, I think. I think of how good you are to me and for me. I think about how much your love means to me." My smile fades as other thoughts enter my mind.

Michael's words come quickly, "Don't stop, Leah. Tell me what thoughts just made you so sad. Don't shut me out. Trust me. I'll never do anything to hurt you. You know that."

I shake my head slowly, "No ... and yes. I know you would never intentionally hurt me, but I also know ... knew May would not either, but what happened because of her hurt me. Because of her my mom and Papa John are dead. The Danners are dead. Malick's father is dead. Sean left." I pause and look around this home that is ours that has always felt like a safe shelter, a place filled with the laughter of our children. "Do you realize how totally strange our lives have become because of May?"

Michael pulls me close, his words barely more than breath in my hair, "Leah, listen to yourself. Because of May this, because of May that. Do you really believe what you are saying? Or are you just tired of being brave? Tired of going back and forth between two worlds ... or wherever it is that you go? Tired of not knowing? Do you really blame May for all this?"

I let my head fall back and close my eyes. Michael's arms are all that keep me from falling as I ask myself his questions. I let moments filled with fast darting thoughts pass before I answer, and even then I do not move to stand on my own. Finally, when the thoughts have slowed and become repetitious I open my eyes, "I believe we each and all walk a course set but unknown to us. A destiny of free will. I believe May walked her course, and now I walk mine. I guess I believe it was my parents' time. But no matter what I believe, Michael, I resent … I regret not having them, all of them in my life for longer. To have been able to watch them hold our children, to have felt their arms around me for longer … for May to have shown me her real self in real life instead of through words on paper, and perhaps … to have had my prayer answered … to have seen them saved somehow…." I pause as I look into Michael's eyes, "For this moment, for right now, I know exactly what I want. I want to be … as tired as I am. I just want to lay down with you and sleep … a deep sleep, and in the morning to wake up, for us to make love, then while you drive over and get the kids Puppy and I will make breakfast. That is what I want, Michael Patrick Callaghan; for the moment that is all I want."

I am swept up into strong arms and carried into our bedroom. After being set gently down upon the bed Michael asks me if I want bed or bath. I say bed. I say thank you. We smile.

Michael goes to the phone and calls Katy and Hank to ask if John Henry and Mary can stay the night at their house. Of course, of course they will say, of course, of course. Good to have family like them, I think to myself as I undress and crawl into bed, amazed I am not washing my face and hands, not brushing my teeth, not putting clothes where they belong. There have been only one or two times in my adult life I have not felt compelled to complete the nightly rituals, but tonight I do not care. Tonight, I am only for sleep.

Puppy comes to the edge of the bed to say goodnight. I pat his head and say goodnight. I hear Michael locking doors and moving through the rooms of our house, turning off lights, closing windows. I hear the wind rushing through the waiting branches of tall trees. I feel the mattress move as Michael lies down, and then I feel Michael's body press up against mine, his heartbeat against my back, his breath in my hair as sleep starts from an ember deep inside me and spreads.

My goodnights are silent but sent out nonetheless. Goodnight husband, goodnight John Henry, goodnight Mary … goodnight Shal, and I am so tired I do not even mind when his voice answers mine 'goodnight'.

*   *   *   *

A week of days has passed, moments filled with times and places. I have been wife, mom, teacher, and except for the rearrangement of our home, tiny items moved barely and the contents of drawers slightly askew, the days have been normal. The days have almost been normal. There is a sense in me of being watched, of phone calls being made, of quick question filled conversations motivated by the proverbial touching of bases: has she? is she? when will she?

I have decided not to mind anything except the anonymous visitations to our home, which are undoubtedly inspired by a desire to see, touch, hold, read, and/ or take the letter or the box. Whoever is questing will have to search Michael to find the box and the first letter or search me to find May's second letter. The letter is either in a pocket or purse or between the pages of whatever book I am reading or it is in my hand. I am making friends with it. It has become alive in my thinking. We watch each other. It is like a cat sitting statue still just watching or when being held is equally content and still. I have decided to be as patient as it is. When Michael and I talk of reading the letter he smiles, because he knows I am taking control over the larger than life situation in the only manner afforded me, and for some reason he is enjoying the process, but I know he is not as relaxed as he acts.

There are a multitude of undercurrents in the stream of our existence now. Michael drives John Henry and Mary to and from school or preschool; he drives them to and from lessons; he visits me at school at different times of the day; he searches the soil and low growing vegetation around our home for unfamiliar tracks or imprints. At night he glances out windows often, and for the first time since the children became old enough to wander on their own there is a loaded rifle hidden somewhere and moved often to a new somewhere. When I question him regarding this he tells me I should respect the choices he is making just like he is respecting the choices I am making. His answer quiets me but does not remove my concern.

I have visited the church twice. Each time Father Tom and I have spoken of all matter of things, but we have never spoken of the letter. Connor waves but comes no closer, and Malick, in either of his forms, I have not seen at all. I go to the church to peak under pews to try to find God. I know he is in there somewhere, because I have sensed him there before, felt his presence, and I want to feel his presence again, to breathe in his closeness. I have gone to the shore to watch the waves also, because there too I have sensed him, felt his presence, but other than the sheer shimmering of anticipation that makes even the breeze suspect and causes me to turn quickly first this way and then that way, I cannot get close to him; he must be hanging out in heaven, because it is by faith alone I am existing lately. Perhaps my journeys into that other place have cut me off from him, but I cannot believe that. I cannot imagine being able to travel anywhere he is not. He is God, after all … creator, ultimate father, rock. I thought about maybe asking

Shal where God is, but changed my mind; I do not want to talk with Shal again yet. I am being normal, and there is no Shal in normal.

The quiet of my reverie is interrupted by a tapping, back of the hand or knuckle against the glass of my car window. I turn and see Bradley. I open my car door as Bradley shakes his head at me, "If everyone could focus like you do we would most assuredly have the cure for cancer and the common cold. On the other hand, someone could most likely also steal your hubcaps, which are actually quite nice, and you wouldn't even notice."

I point my finger at him, "Hello to you too, Bradley Danner. Hello. Say hello to a person before you begin sermonizing."

Bradley responds, "I truly believe my comments and tone were more anecdotal than sermony."

Adjusting the strap of my purse on my shoulder and removing my keys from the ignition I get out of the car and remind him, "There is no way 'sermony' is a word. If Mary was here you would be in for quite the discussion."

As he steps back to let me close the door, he looks up at the sky, "I would be so much happier if it was Mary with whom I was about to have a discussion, I can assure you. I'm not looking forward to this … discussion, for lack of a better word, at all, but I do thank you for agreeing to accompany me."

I put my hand on his cheek, "I am honored to stand with you and beside you and for you, Bradley, but I am not sure why I am the one you chose to represent you."

He puts his hand over mine, "Who better than you? We are friends. You have known me forever. We work together. You are a part of both my social and work worlds. And, last but most assuredly not least, you know my heart and what is important to me. Who better to speak for me against the goblin-men we go to face than you, the voice of fairness and balance? At meetings you are most often the one to smooth out differences in order to show the actual similarities. You were and are my first and only choice. So again, thank you for being here with me, even though I know your life is full right now with … obstacles of your own, and despite the blaring fact you have not shared with me any real information regarding the situation in which you find yourself, I am trusting you will. I trust that you will, at some point, at least share with me the information regarding my parents. At the very least I am expecting that, but I want to know it all."

I use my other hand and squeeze both his cheeks giving him a most uncomplimentary 'fish face', "Shush, shush. We can only deal with one issue at a time. First, we face the elders of your brother's church; second, we deal with the strangeness of my life in regards to your parents' involvement."

Bradley pulls my hands from his face, "Qualifier. I distinctly heard a qualifier. I think I am, as one of your dearest friends and just possibly your only gay friend, completely entitled to hear all the details. You know how my kind likes to hear all the details."

I turn and walk toward the Administration Building, "You need to focus on the task at hand, sir, and since the meeting begins in five minutes I do believe we should be about our current business, don't you?"

Bradley catches up with me, "Evasive. Now, you're being evasive."

I do not take the bait, "Bradley, be serious. I have to get my thoughts going in the right direction, and you are not helping me."

He stops me by grabbing my arm, and then goes down on one knee, "I am at your service. I will be quiet as a mouse so you can gather your thoughts. Silent, I will be totally silent, like a mouse."

I look into his eyes, "Oh Bradley, I know this must be beyond terrible for you. I do know that, and I know you are being this way to make the situation lighter than it is so you can … bear it. I understand, but the moment is here and prepared for it or not, we must face it. And I am here for you, thinking of nothing else but this, so … trust me, trust yourself to handle it well, whatever comes, whatever is said … be you, the sincere, intelligent, and caring man you are."

There are tears in Bradley's eyes, but as he stands I know they are more of frustration than any other emotion. I know even though he is about to face a direct attack on who he is as a person he will face the accusations with the honor and the strength of character that are his to claim. After we hug each other, we are quiet as we walk to the building then through its doors. I ask my seemingly distant God to be close and trust that, regardless of my perceptions, he is.

✳   ✳   ✳   ✳

Five men, from late thirties to mid seventies, surround Bradley and me, as they sit to both our left and right. Lane, in his chair behind his desk, is directly in front of us. Joe sits next to Bradley, and I appreciate the fact that Joe chose that particular place when he and his church elders came into the room after Bradley and I were already seated, our positioning Lane's idea: in his words, an attempt to circumvent the obvious 'us and them' nature of the meeting, to perhaps allow for individual thoughtfulness instead of a group mentality regarding the issue to be discussed.

Lane's hands have been in his lap as he seems to be focused on thoughts of his own, but as he begins speaking he places them on the desk, fingers intertwined as he establishes eye contact with each individual in the room, "Dealing with unpleasant circumstances is never enjoyable or easy, but that is our task here today. We are here to decide the future of your church, gentlemen. I state that quite clearly. Bradley Danner is not on trial here. His humanity, his worthiness, his validity are not in question." Lane pauses to allow his statements to be comprehended completely, and there is some shifting in seats, a throat cleared as if someone is preparing to speak, but Lane continues before that can happen, "Your church's future, gentlemen, not Bradley's morality, is what we will discuss. If each of you is willing to honor that, then we will continue. However, and I reiterate, Bradley's sexual preference is not the issue here. The issue here is if I, as the sole administrative agent of all that occurs on Dayton land will agree to continue your lease of a portion of that land or decide to cancel your lease. Having set the parameters of our discussion, I will now explain the basis on which my decision will be made. What I must decide is if I can, as the sole responsibility holder, allow prejudice to not only occur within the area of my responsibility but allow it to be sanctioned by one group against another or against an individual. This, and this alone, is my duty: to decide if, by my own definition of morality, you and your church have become unacceptably immoral by your display of prejudice."

The room is so still and quiet our breathing seems loud. Joe has leaned over in his chair resting his arms on his knees. His head is down; his eyes are closed. Stan Laughton, the eldest of the elders, stands and moves to the window, his back to us. Larry Holden, Stan's son-in-law joins him, but they do not speak. They are both tall men, broad shouldered and thin. After a moment, Larry raises his arm and puts it around Stan's shoulders. Joe has not moved. Murphy Black, a normally jovial man in his late fifties, adjusts the glasses on his nose and opens his bible, quickly finding the words he is seeking. Adam Crane, a retired fireman and good friend of Hank's, has simply closed his eyes and remained in the same position he first took upon sitting down. Lane allows the men to think about his statements as each one of us must be fully realizing, some of us, perhaps, for the first time, the sad consequences of this meeting.

Bradley and I exchange glances, but we both give no expression to what has to be our mutual surprise at the manner in which Lane began the meeting. In no way are we unprepared for the firm stance he takes, the unrelenting determination to quickly set parameters for the discussion. That is his style at such meetings where emotions and ideals are so juxtaposed on the surface, but he also knows he is dealing with fair minded people. It is the stance he has taken, the refusal to allow any discussion at all of sexual preference, but to instead focus entirely on the underlying factor of prejudice that has caught us off guard. He normally allows guided discussion to bring all those gathered to the same playing field before he illuminates what he considers the hidden error in a certain type of thinking.

Stan speaks, his back still to us, "Didn't I go to Germany to fight against the idea that one group of people was less worthy than another?" He pauses and turns to face us, but not before he puts his arms around Larry's shoulders and then releases him to return to his seat, "I did. I went there, a young man full of ideas and ideals to fight against hate and prejudice. And the only thing that got me through the horrors of that war, perhaps the same horrors experienced in any war, was my faith in God's plan for his children. And now I stand here with men I am proud to stand with to defend God's truth as it is represented through his word, the Bible. And yet, an old friend has reminded me that … that just maybe I have … somehow become the very thing I fought against all those years ago." He pauses and looks at Bradley, "I have judged you, but you'll find no hate in me for you." He pauses again and looks at Lane, "I hear your words, old friend, but try as I may, realizing I've made judgment against another human being, I still can't ignore what God's word says to me. You say the issue isn't what I think it is. I've known Bradley since he was a baby, how do I not fight the good fight to help him be … right in the eyes of the Father? You're a wise man, Lane, but this is not as simple as you suggest." Stan shrugs his shoulders after looking at each of us, and then he turns back to the window.

Adam sighs heavily before he speaks, "God's reasoning; man's reasoning. Lane makes sense, but human sensibility doesn't equal God's clear direction. What you call prejudice … our immorality, I call obedience to God. The world and its devotees may not agree, but God's word is clear. How can you ask us to waver from that?"

Lane shrugs sadly, "How can I not?"

Larry stands and looks to each of the other elders, "Isn't it out of love for Bradley, out of concern for Bradley we take our stand? I will not apologize for that. I want Bradley in heaven with me. That is why we stick to what we believe, so younger men, even children, don't look at Bradley's lifestyle as even an option anymore. Prejudice is motivated by hate and fear. I'm motivated by love and obedience. How can that be wrong?"

The room is quiet again. Then Joe leans back in his chair, looks at Bradley then at me, "You are here for a reason, Leah. Some might think because Bradley asked you; others, like me, who believe in God's eternal plan, would hear what you have to say about all this, because as it stands now we have no recourse but to leave this place our church has called its home since before I was born, because

Larry is right; we are here out of love and obedience. I want my brother in heaven with me. If that means upsetting him and questioning his ideas and rejecting certain of his behaviors in this world, I can't back down. I believe God speaks through the word, through the text of the Bible, and I can't choose the parts I like or the parts that are easy and leave out the difficult parts. We are at an impasse, I believe, and I guess what I'm feeling is ... torn, pulled apart, but unable to alter my course."

I see myself standing on the edge of my perceptions, of my ideals, of what I call truth, and across a chasm Joe stands on the edge of his perceptions, of his ideals, of what he calls truth, and I can find no bridge by which we might move closer to each other. I look at Lane and wonder what he will think of what I am going to say, but like him and these men around me, I must speak what I believe to be true, "I believe judgment against another human being or group of human beings is wrong, but, to reference Stan's example, we as a culture judged the Nazis as wrong. We judged them and found their behavior immoral. We as a culture defended the rights of those who the Nazis would have exterminated, but it took Pearl Harbor to push us into action. Most Americans did not want to fight another war so soon after the last to defend the rights of people or fight for the lives of people on foreign soil. Too many believed it was not our problem. What does that say about human beings? What does it mean? And on what moral ground do we find ourselves as a culture if we couple our fight against Nazism with our dropping of the bombs on Hiroshima and Nagasaki?" I pause and refocus, "From out of his long life full of experiences, why did Stan respond to Lane's opening comments by choosing his fight against Nazism as a comparison to the decision you have made as a group against Bradley? Why? You need to wonder about that, and find an answer from inside your own heads and hearts."

I pause to allow my question to find a place in them to settle then I continue, "To this discussion I add the following for consideration. I love God, but I am not as certain of his plan as you are, and I can no longer claim I believe his heart and his truth, as revealed in the Bible, are not veiled to some extent by time and translation and cultural values. But if we are truly guided by Lane's parameters, none of that even matters." I look at Lane before I begin speaking, "I believe if Lane asks you to leave this place he is judging you just as you have judged Bradley, and no one in this room believes two wrongs make a right. But if Lane is America defending Bradley, who is the Jews, against prejudice and judgment, then the decision you are making as a church is Hitler. And I believe America was morally correct in defending the Jewish people against Hitler. Beyond that I only know real love is healing not destructive. You say you are motivated out of love for Bradley, but it states quite clearly in the Bible people can know their motivations by the fruit of their actions. What is your decision producing? I have never seen condemnation be healing. So, somehow you must undertake a new search of your hearts and your minds and decide if you are being contradictory, truly ask yourselves if you are not being motivated out of fear. The motivating love of which you speak cannot live in a fearful heart. I believe you must also realize if you followed every statement made in the Bible, as you state is your way, you would stone your children for disobedience so their behavior did not incite other young people. Your women would sit in the back of the church, if they were allowed in at all, and they would not be allowed to speak. You say you are not choosing which parts of the Bible to follow but in truth you are. With some you mix the quotient of time, allow for differences in cultural mores, while in others you do not. Banishment of Bradley from your church; banishment from your church from our town—are those really our only choices? Do we have to drop the bomb of banishment or is that just the quick fix?"

And once again the room is quiet. The clock on Lane's desk ticks to remind us of the passing of time, yet it does not matter because we are each and all faced with the frailty of human reasoning, the bindings of personal perspective, the sometimes shattering ramifications of a faith belief.

But my own introspection is stopped as Lane stands, "A desire for truth, a desire to do what is right is in all of us. I don't deny that. I don't deny the motivation of love in this room, but I can't be other than I am any more than anyone of you can, and Leah is correct, my judgment will be as your judgment is … out of a sense of morality. Out of obligation to the ideals held by myself and my father and my grandfather, out of my own sense of what is right and good, I must ask you to withdraw your sanction against Bradley or any other homosexual person or I will suspend your lease. I will be prejudiced against your prejudice, right or wrong; I can make no other decision. I will give you two weeks to make your decision. Should you decide to maintain your present position I will have to ask you to cease meeting as a congregation within thirty days. You may maintain your offices until you can relocate, but as a church your beliefs make you unwelcome in the town of Lane."

Joe nods his head at Lane to indicate his understanding then puts his hand on Bradley's shoulder, "Don't you wonder how dad would have handled this? I think about that all the time; I ask myself, what would dad have done? And sometimes I believe I really know, but in this I don't."

Bradley covers Joe's hand with his own, "I wonder what he would think about a lot of things, and I understand you believe you are doing the right thing, Joe. I really do understand that. Neither of us can make this easier for each other with-out a change of mind and heart, and you have to know this, Joe, I am being true to my mind and heart. I am not being defiant or reactionary. I am not … a bad man. I am not a bad man in any way, and I sometimes imagine dad would have understood, but like you I can't know for sure what he would do or say to all this. Maybe I just don't want to face the truth about how he would feel about who I am."

Lane stands behind his desk and looks at Joe, "Your father would have done exactly as you are doing, Joe. He would have followed the Bible's direction and listened to his elders even if it broke his heart, but you aren't your father; you're who you are, and you must make this difficult decision based on what you believe and know to be true. You're the head of your church as I am the head of Dayton Land Management; we are the ones who are accountable, so please take the two weeks, pray and meditate and seek out the counsel of those you hold in esteem then let me know what you have decided."

Murphy stands slowly, his normally happy face almost unfamiliar in its present despair. He readjusts his glasses on his nose and speaks for the first time, "This is one of those times I would like, more than anything else, to have Jesus right here, but obviously that's not going to happen, because-" he looks around the room as a smile almost appears on his face, "well, because Jesus would have already been here, right on time. He's not the sort who would be late." He opens his Bible after his gentle smile is returned to him seven times, "In Jeremiah the Lord says 'Stand at the crossroads and look; ask for the ancient paths, ask where the good way is, and walk in it, and you will find rest for your souls.' I pray that for each one of us right now: Almighty and loving father, help us to see. Make the light of your truth shine before us that we may know the way you want us to go. We ask for your wisdom and understanding, Lord. In the righteous name of Jesus Christ we pray." Murphy sits down when he finishes and again the room is quiet.

Joe stands, "Thank you, Murphy." Joe looks at the rest of us, "More words of discussion will not change anything. Ending in prayer seems a good way to close. I want to thank Lane and Leah for being here with us. I don't know what to say to you, Bradley, except I'm sorry for the pain we have caused you. I have always loved you, and I always will, but as Stan commented this is no simple matter; I am the pastor of my church, that is my main responsibility, and these are my brothers in Christ. Our hearts are joined in our desire and dedication to serve him who is the righteous one. I will never regret that fact. I will take the two weeks as Lane has asked, but I don't see what difference it will make. What could possibly change that much in two weeks?"

＊   ＊   ＊   ＊

"And so the meeting ended with a question?" I nod my head to answer Michael's question, because I am holding Mary's hat between my teeth while I attempt to pull her sweater down over her bobbing head and wiggling arms. We are in the canoe on the lake, our house becoming smaller and Puppy running back and forth along the shore. John Henry and Michael man the oars. We decided to make a quick trip around the lake after I returned home from the meeting before the sun pulls the covers of night over itself and us. There is a scent of wildflowers carried by the wind from the shore, and Puppy's happy but insistent barking serenades us. Now that Mary is as settled as Mary is going to be in the midst of our water adventure, I watch John Henry intently watching Michael, who sits behind Mary and me in the steering position, because John Henry wants to do his task well, moving his oar in perfect rhythm with his father's. I appreciate the sweetness of his desire to please a parent and wonder what it must be like when unhealthy parents make unhealthy demands of their young ones, how contorted and damaged the thinking of those young ones must become. But I shake my head and clear it of sad thoughts. Not today, I say to them, enough sad thoughts for one day.

I ask John Henry to tell me about his day and he does so, but maintains his visual focus on his father, "Teacher made us stand up in the front of the class to share our homework." I ask what his homework was, and he responds, "We were supposed to write a paragraph about our family using descriptive words. Our words were supposed to paint a picture."

Before I can comment, Mary asks, "Am I in your paragraph?"

John Henry answers her question with a question, "Are you in my family?"

Mary laughs, "You know I'm in your family." Then seeing the expression on her brother's face she continues, "Oh I get what you're doing. You think my question wasn't nuhsarry."

John Henry corrects her, "Necessary, Mary, is the right word."

Mary laughs again, "It rhymes, it rhymes. Mary, Mary, necessary or necessary Mary. No, I like the first one better. Mary, Mary, necessary. You made a rhyme, John Henry."

John Henry disagrees with her gently, "No, I didn't, you did."

Mary leans forward intently, "No, you did."

John Henry shakes his head and smiles, "I think you do these things on purpose just so you can get me in a yes-no back and forth argument."

Mary turns and shows me her smile before she gives it to John Henry along with, "No, I don't. You do."

John Henry moves his oar to the other side of the canoe without missing a beat, "No, you do."

I turn to exchange a parental 'oh aren't our children too precious' smile with Michael, but instead I yell for him to duck as I see a large gray and black bird, its wings wide, its sharp talons at the same level as Michael's head. I push Mary down and stand to reach for John Henry to....

∗   ∗   ∗   ∗

There is only music here in this darkness, an arrangement of flute and violin calling out to cello and clarinet who answer back from a great distance. As the cello's call becomes closer and more insistent, the violin's wings beat faster until they are both stopped by a sheer foreboding cliff of oboes and trombones and deep drums. Then violin and cello soar quickly over the top as the darkness I am peering into flutters as if fanned by the music's diminishing undulations.

In the new silence I raise my hands to touch my eyes and feel eyelids beneath fingertips. My thinking plods along, a moo cow on a steep path up from somewhere already forgotten. I suggest to myself that I open my eyes. Roll up those eyelids, lady, I say to myself. Then I think, what would Michael say if he could hear me? But I need to focus on the matter at hand, so I put all my effort into the simple task of raising my own shades to let light into me as if I am a room in a house with windows. I see a window now. Within its frame I see a blue sky and white clouds. I see the tops of trees and wonder where I am.

So I ask, but words do not come easily. My throat and lips are dry so I only make a croaking whisper sound. Feeling movement, I move my eyes from the window and see Michael's head resting on his arms as they lay folded on the bed. It is not my bed. It is not my comforter of deep green and deeper red. This spread is thin and of the palest rose. I look around to get my bearings before I attempt to wake Michael. I am in a hospital room. Then I wonder if this was Teri's room, but I reason that it cannot be, because she was on the ground floor, and I have treetops in my window.

I moisten my lips and swallow to make clear words, "Michael, Michael" as I lay my hand on his head noticing at the same time the hospital identification on my wrist.

He sits up quickly and startles me. I begin to sit up quickly too in response, but I am instantly stilled by a lightening strike of pain beginning just above my right eye then racing around my head, zigzagging with jagged claws through my brain. I look into Michael's eyes remembering the talons racing toward his head.

I ask, "Are the kids okay?"

Michael moves slowly now, speaks gently, "We were not hurt, only you. You were hurt … are hurt."

I try to remember more details, "I was reaching for John Henry to get him out of the way. I had pushed Mary down. That is all I remember. What happened after that?"

"You fell forward and hit your head, there above your eye, on the side of the canoe. You almost went over the side, but John Henry and I grabbed hold of you. Mary put her arms around your legs. We steadied the canoe, tried to stop the bleeding, tried to get our oars back, which were floating away. Puppy was going crazy on the shore. I was afraid he was going to jump in and try to swim to us. Mary and John Henry were calm but more out of fear than really feeling calm. You know how head wounds are. There was a lot of blood. Puppy's frantic barking brought out Gladys and Harry next door, and they called 911, then got in their canoe and came and helped us. You were out cold, Leah. I've seen others unconscious from trauma but seeing you that way … it scared the hell out of me."

After a moment of shuffling through the images he has described, I ask, "What happened to the bird?"

Michael's expression is guarded, "What bird are you talking about, Leah?"

I speak my words calmly even though there is nothing calm about the way I am feeling, "The hawk. There was a hawk flying right for you. It was huge. It would have struck you with its talons if I had not warned you."

Michael looks down and then back up and straight into my eyes, "There was no bird, Leah."

I am still calm, but I will not be doubted; I know what I saw, "There was a hawk, Michael. I saw it. It was not an imaginary hawk, not a spirit hawk, it was a real hawk. It was not a figment of my imagination. Its eyes were black; its beak was parted. Its wingspan was at least five feet."

Michael sits back down and pulls his chair closer to the bed and to me, "I've never heard of a hawk with that kind of wingspan." He pauses and then asks, "Are you sure it wasn't an eagle?"

I am sure and say so, but I am not sure Michael is convinced, "It was not Malick if that is what you are implying."

Michael smiles but not pleasantly, "Oh yeah, and you're an expert on Malick's eagle shapes. Who knows? Maybe he can … shape shift into a variety of forms.

We really can't be too certain about shape shifting at this point can we? And, not to beat the point to death, but … what happened to the bird? None of us saw a bird of any kind."

I will not back down, "I believe that none of you saw a bird, but I also know that I did."

Michael stretches his arms out and lets his head fall back then moves it from side to side before he looks at me again, "Okay so this bird or whatever it was appeared and disappeared … maybe through a thin place … maybe … damn, who knows? We don't know about this kind of shit, Leah. I'm a fireman. You're a teacher. What do we know about this kind of other-world crap?"

I look around the room noticing the box and May's second letter sitting on the top of the small dresser across from the bed. There is a vase filled with many of Father Tom's favorite flowers from his greenhouse. There is a homemade card on either side of the vase, one from John Henry and one from Mary; I can tell because I know the way they each draw their people. Behind the vase, the portable CD player from my classroom sits now silent. I close my eyes and ask, "How long have I been here?"

Michael's voice sounds tired as he replies, "Two days. And next you're going to ask me where the kids are; the kids are with my parents. Brian is staying at our house to keep an eye on things and to keep Puppy busy. That dog was going crazy on the shore, and he didn't stop, not even when we got you to the shore, and I let him give you a once over so that maybe he would calm down. He checked you out pretty thoroughly, but then he returned to the shore and would not stop barking no matter what any of us did."

I open my eyes and look at Michael, "Maybe Puppy saw what I did, and maybe even after we were out of the canoe and on the shore, maybe Puppy still saw what I saw. Did you ever think of that, Michael?"

Michael stands and goes to the window, "No, Leah, and why would I? Why would I ever want to think about something like that? I didn't know until now what happened, what caused you to jump up like that."

I sigh, "Well, now you know. Now it all makes sense, right? Ha!"

Michael walks back to the bed and takes my hand in his, "Ha! Ha! All I know is we don't know enough; that's all I know. We're going to have to read that letter and hope we get some insight. And maybe you need to invite this Shal guy over for dinner, so we can have a little talk, him and me, man to man, ya know? Get some things straight. And maybe we should invite ol' Malick too and ask him about his bird tricks. Offer him some damn bird seed." Michael pauses to catch his breath and I know I should not be smiling at his verbal antics, but as he has been speaking he has adopted an accent combining a Midwest drawl with an Australian intonation and it is a difficult combination to not find amusing, but before my smile is even more than an almost smile, both of us are stopped in whatever it is we are contemplating saying or doing next.

Malick's voice stops us, "I'm not really into bird seed, but a steak would be great."

Malick walks across the room and extends his hand toward Michael. Michael pauses, then shakes Malick's hand as he says, "I'm going to have to trust you aren't I?"

Malick tilts his head at me instead of offering his hand then answers Michael, "It would be to your advantage to trust me. Trusting me is going to make the next few days or weeks a great deal more bearable, because things are going to start happening that will take all of us working together to overcome."

Michael asks, "Things like this bird Leah saw but none of us did?"

Malick nods his head, "That's the tip of the iceberg, Michael, only the very tip."

*   *   *   *

Home is good; the best medicine is what I told Dr. Brightstar. She laughs when I call her that instead of Marcia, but when she is being healer to me or my family I call her by her title. She did not try to keep me, probably because of the looks on John Henry's and Mary's faces as they lay next to me on the narrow hospital bed. So, I am home, and now I not only share my bed with my two children but also Puppy. He lays at our feet content but watchful, his head raising at any new sound from another room or from outside. Since I arrived home yesterday, he follows me everywhere, and if I even try to close the door to the bathroom he begins pacing and howling, so we are inseparable.

John Henry and Mary are asleep. Their deep and rhythmic breathing almost puts me to sleep, but I cannot allow that to happen. Father Tom and Malick wait with Michael for me in the living room, so although the calmness I feel is good, I cannot allow my thoughts or my energy to become slow and thick like golden honey, the hue of that peaceful presleep place I go just before the deep amber shadows of real sleep slide over me like covers pulled up. I test moving my arms to see if I will hear a mumbled protest to remain, but my children are beyond the golden honey stage; they are in sleep's amber shadowlands.

Disengaging myself from their closeness without disturbing them or moving my own head, which disturbs me, is time consuming. Puppy watches my maneuvering and begins to rise up from his position on the bed, so I shush him, and he too moves slowly. Despite his size, the mattress barely moves as he jumps down to the floor. I turn at the door to look upon the faces of my children and think again that there is so much more at stake than I thought originally. My fall in the canoe could have turned it over, and even though the children wore lifejackets … I stop myself from thinking of 'could have beens' as Puppy takes the opportunity to rub his head against my leg. I pat his head and rub his ears.

As I enter the living room the men's quiet talking stops. I mention that Puppy probably needs to go out for his 'nightly'. Michael stands and moves toward the door commenting, "I'm not sure he'll go if you don't, but you aren't, so let's see what happens."

Puppy goes to the door as Michael opens it but looks back at me and then up at Michael, so Michael rubs his head, "Go ahead, boy, I can take this watch; I'll keep her safe for you." Puppy goes out and Michael stays at the door looking out, "I say that … but," he pauses and looks first at me then at Malick, "we know that's not true. I couldn't keep her from getting hurt on the lake."

Although I believe each of us in the room would like to reassure him, we cannot. Father Tom sighs, "There is so much more happening than May or I believed." He looks at Malick, "Your warnings to me about the cycle, Leah's place in it, must be correct." Malick does not comment but only nods his head accepting Father Tom's acknowledgment. My understanding is Malick is here to remedy that, but I still have reservations about his motivations, and Connor's motivations, in this whole matter.

I take my seat in my big overstuffed chair, curling my legs up under me and leaning my head back carefully. My hand, in the pocket of my robe, holds May's two letters, the opened one and the one to be opened. I close my eyes remembering certain words and passages from the first: child of her heart, she called me … that others would help me … that I would stand on the edge of all that I know … that there has been violence involved, but my children would be safe … that I was born for this journey, as she called it … that back before humans became small, back before humans separated themselves from the earth, people lived wholly as spiritual-physical beings, and that words were the same, physical and spiritual … and then later after a superficial but lasting disjoining occurred connections were made only through certain individuals or special places … that our labels for what 'is' are only labels … that her words would feel like reminders, be familiar even in their newness … that I was to walk through those who oppose me … that I need only go as far as I can and then my part would be over.… Those were her words.

I take the opened letter out of my pocket and read her last words: Call to me … so I can watch over you … I am only one dream away. I lay my head back against the soft cushion again and close my eyes realizing I have not called to her; I have not stood on the edge of what I know. I open my eyes and look at Michael as he lets Puppy back in the room, "Michael, I have not stood on the edge."

He turns after he has locked the door and walks over to me taking my hand as I hold it out to him, "What do you mean?"

I choose my words carefully wanting to be clear, "May comments over and over in her first letter about the symbiotic relationship between the physical and spiritual worlds, and that I am to stand on the edge. I believe I have definitely been on the edge of what I know in terms of belief based on what I know of my physical world, but I have not stood on the edge physically, and I have not called to her. She said she was only one dream away, and that I should call to her. I have not done those two things yet, Michael. I must do those two things. I must stand on the edge and call out to her. This feels so right to me … no, it is more than that, it feels as though it is something I know how to do or even something I have done."

Michael bends down next to me, "Okay, but what edge?"

I smile at him, "You know the edge on which I must stand. You even suggested it to me."

He stands, "Of course, we were at the beach. I went to get the picnic basket. I knew you and the kids would be waiting for me, but I felt so drawn by Castle Rock Point; I had to go, and I stood on the edge. So what I was feeling was correct; I was just supposed to take you with me. Could that be right?"

Father Tom and Malick are watching us but make no attempt to comment. Michael returns to his earlier position by my chair, "Leah, even the word you chose to illustrate the connection between the physical and spiritual … that word was not in May's letter, but it expresses even better than May expressed the unimaginable necessity of the balance between the two realms … or states of being. Symbiotic. I'm going to look it up. I want to see the definition. I feel like I have something … an idea or something right on the tip of my tongue, as they say, but I can't put words to it."

I laugh gently and somehow remember not to shake my head, "I love this. You are looking up a word." Michael is in the den getting the huge unabridged dictionary from the shelves and cannot even hear me. I look at Father Tom and Malick and realize they do not know why I am so amused by the present situation, "I should share with you I am a compulsive dictionary user; it drives my sweet family crazy. We can be watching a movie or reading a story together, and I will stop the movie or stop the reading to go look up a word if I am not sure what it means, or if I want more clarification based on the context in which the word is being used. And now Michael is looking up a word." Both men smile at me good naturedly, their patience evident as they trust that Michael and I are on the right track in our dealing with information from the first letter before reading the second.

Michael returns to us, "' … the intimate living together of two dissimilar organisms in a mutually beneficial relationship … symbiosis.' Mutually beneficial … and how long have most humans and their cultures disconnected the physical and the spiritual in the real sense of symbiosis. The idea that each might need the other … poverty, war, hate, violence, fear … all so prevalent in our physical world because, possibly, the symbiotic relationship between the physical and spiritual has been denied. The Native American tribes speak of their mother the earth and their father the sky and of their own requisite connection to the earth; the Irish who held on to their belief that all matter had spirit even when the old ways were replaced with Christian dogma. The 'old ways' that we, as a culture, historically condemn as being simplistic, archaic. Remember, Leah, that night with Father Tom when we read the first letter and a couple of days later you shared with me what you had been thinking at the time about the table at the cafe. Tell Father Tom and Malick about it."

Again I choose my words carefully realizing Malick may not have been to the Castle Rock Cafe, and I want him to see the image clearly, "We met Father Tom at the cafe to read May's first letter. The cafe has small private dining rooms. The tables in those rooms are these magnificent thick slices from the trunk of a redwood. Sitting there I noticed the rings, the concentric circles, which tell the tree's age in death but in life allow the transport of food across the trunk. The center of the tree dies as the tree broadens and the heartwood, as it is called, is less permeable and more durable than the surrounding sapwood. I was struck, at the time, by the idea of life surrounding death, of life needing death, of death as an actual measurable space. We take this idea for granted in nature, out of death and decay comes new life, but we do not necessarily apply the concept to ourselves, to our humanity. We do not give credence to the idea that death fills space just as life does. At the time, in my thoughts, I used the words life embracing death, and later when talking with Michael I wondered, if I may generalize, at our whole western-Christian attitude toward nature. We allow it no spirit; we make it dead, perhaps because we took ourselves out of nature so long ago it had to be made 'different than' so we could be above it or better than; only humans get to have spirit. Then we took the breath of God out of our religion by scripting it and removing if from all that is earthly. We defined the spiritual in physical terms but gave it no physical domain. The spiritual world became a reflection of what we know about the physical world instead of allowing the spiritual to be and have a reality of its own with parameters and logistics incredibly different than our physical world. What we cannot decipher we deny." I pause, and then ask, "Am I making any sense to you? Can you see the relevance of what I am saying as it relates to May's directions in the first letter? Or perhaps I should ask Michael if I even went in the direction he thought I would?"

Malick leans forward, "In no way do I want to interfere, but if I might just ask you, Leah, to continue with your discussion a bit more before Michael adds to it or amends it. I would ask you to put your ... visits to ... that other place into words based on what you have just stated. Will you do that?"

I wonder aloud, "Can I do that?" I pause and think about what I know about where I have been. Michael is encouraging me with his eyes, and so I make an attempt to verbalize for the first time my experience in that other place, "It is another place, not a dream world; it is a world with physical properties similar to ours but different. In the place where I was with Shal my breath or heartbeat fed the fire. Shal told me I was right in thinking that. But what does that mean exactly? In that world, which is our world too, all elements are connected. All elements breathe into all other elements." I pause and look at Malick, "I could have put that fire out by simply thinking about it, and its energy would have become ... what? Mine? Free to assume another identity? No, I am not sure about that. I did not control the fire as much as I knew I controlled how I perceived the fire ... is that it? Perhaps thin places are spatial in that 'being' as in filling a place in space replaces linear time as the controlling domain." I stop and look into Malick's eyes, "Shape shifting fits in here somewhere, doesn't it? And ... God? And this whole universe ... the moon ... Mars ... even the sun ... are places of 'being' aren't they?"

Malick crosses the short distance between the couch he shares with Father Tom to come to my chair, to kneel down so he can look directly into my eyes and match Michael's position to say to me, "Little one, I am only here to assist, to offer ... a wing ... a sharp eye ... an arm's strength. You and your Michael have to find the way, but I will say 'yes' to your wonderings, that I will say. I will say ... continue on ... fully open ... to where you are being led. And know this, Shal is only the first of those you will meet who are part of this cycle of revelation. Trust him and trust the one who stands behind him."

Michael leans his head against my shoulder and says, "Holy shit." I laugh remembering the last time he said this particular phrase, and I am glad the tone he uses is much lighter than before.

Father Tom must also remember, "There he goes again." Father Tom looks at Malick who cannot know what Father Tom and I find so amusing, "You'll have to watch out for Michael. He's a bit of a name caller."

Michael just shakes his head and walks to the kitchen asking if anyone would like something to drink, commenting next that we will have to wait to read May's second letter until I feel up to the steep climb necessary to reach Castle Rock Point, then asks, "Do you both think you should be there?"

Malick is quick to respond, "It might be good if I was there."

Michael returns to the living room and asks Malick, "Why good?"

Malick shrugs his shoulders and states simply, "Well, she is going to be standing on the edge of a cliff and … I can … fly, you know? It may be helpful."

Michael looks at me, "We have the oddest conversations now, don't we?"

I answer, "Yes, dear."

Michael looks at Father Tom expectantly, and Father Tom responds, "I would like to be there … to see what happens, but it is your decision to make. I will cover you in prayer whether I am there or not, of that you can be sure."

Michael looks at me, "Doc Brightstar said five to seven days and that she wanted to see you again before you resumed your normal activities, but I really don't believe she has any idea what your normal activities have been like lately, do you?"

I smile instead of answer. Part of me wants to rush my recovery and race to Cattle Rock Point, but there is a part of me that wants to use every moment between now and that seventh day to think deeply about the ideas expressed tonight, because there is still an aspect of the relationship … of our discussion about the symbiotic nature of the natural world and that other world I cannot yet give words to but that stands, as ideas sometimes do, just beyond me, and I have to figure out what 'it' is, then lay all the ideas and pieces of ideas down before me, place my hands on them and make them something whole and holdable. I want also to prepare myself to see May. If that is what is going to happen, I want to face her humbly and not in a defensive manner over the thoughts I held against her. I have to meet with Bradley about my classes he is covering while I am out 'sick'. I need to love on my children, share moments with my husband, pat my dog, and also allow my thoughts to have their way with me, stop resisting … trust. I take a deep breath as I notice Michael is watching me with that look he has that makes me feel as if we are touching even when we are not, and despite the fact we are not alone, I open my heart and accept his invitation for intimacy.

He says, "For five more days you're mine to boss around and take care of."

I respond quickly, "No, no, five days could never be enough."

I know he has not moved but he feels closer as he replies, "The day after … forever then?"

I smile, "At the very least, husband."

His words embrace me, "At the very, very least, wife."

✳   ✳   ✳   ✳

I am hiding out … but just for a moment. I have run away without traveling anywhere. Puppy and I are in the bathroom. I am sitting on the edge of the bathtub; he is at my feet, and even though no one is in my bedroom, which adjoins this bathroom, voices have pulled me from my solitary dance with my own thoughts. Voices have run or walked slowly from their places of origin in the living room or the kitchen or on the deck and found me. I smile as I identify the ones separating themselves from the others by their loudness or by their high or deep pitch: Brian, Cal, Bradley, Alana, Mary…. Somehow my house has become full, even overflowing. Spontaneous and expected, they came 'just to say hello' … 'just to see how you're doing' … or, as Mary commented earlier, 'just to see your face, mom, because sometimes just seeing someone's face makes a person know the other person is really okay'. I reach down and pat Puppy's head, "Okay, we have had our breather; it is time we rejoin family and friends, old dog. You can play with Samson again but not in the house this time." Puppy is already standing at the door waiting for me to open it. I look into the mirror to check my appearance and the reflection draws me. I step closer even as I distance myself, observing the deep hued bruise that seems to be trying to get out from under the bandage which covers the stitches sewn so carefully by Dr. Brightstar just days before. I think quickly about current healing and about future edges then Michael's voice raises itself above all the others. He is calling my name. I open the door just as he knocks upon it.

He smiles as he looks into my eyes to access mood, "Did you fall in, sweetie? No one has seen you for a while."

I lay my hand against his chest and tilt my head up toward him, "Are you really expecting an answer to that or was it simply rhetorical in nature, an ice-breaker, a checker of moods?"

He gathers me into his arms, "All of the above, I guess. An answer to a question is always … nice, and I am wondering how you are handling all your visitors?"

I reassure him, "You are the social one, husband, the one who thrives on communal gatherings, not me, but in truth, it is good to have so many of our friends and family, and my students, who I have not seen in over a week, all together."

He steps back from me to watch my expression, "And you're not tired out by it all? It's not too much too soon?"

I reassure him again, "Michael, don't worry; I am fine. I am feeling good, and my head does not hurt when I move it, and the sun is shining and people are laughing and talking and—"

He interrupts me, "Well, the sun is no longer shining actually. That's why I was looking for you."

I am not clear on what he is saying, "You were trying to find me because the sun is no longer shining?"

He takes my hand and begins walking toward the bedroom door, "Come see for yourself."

As we enter the living room I discover it is empty of people, but I can see its previous occupants standing on the deck or in the yard, and they are all looking up into the sky. Michael and I walk out to join them. And once we join the others, I know why Michael was looking for me and what he wanted me to see.

Above the spiraling tops of the trees and through the clearing of trees over the lake the sky is moving. I watch as obese gray and black curling and uncurling swells throw themselves out over the placid baby-blue and white of a sky still attempting to cover us. I watch as beads of sweat from the angry darkness above blend with tears of regret from the blue's broken heart and begin to fall upon me. I watch as anger wins out over sorrow, and as the humans around me run for the real cover of our house and for the emotional comfort of a home.

Michael has to take my hand and lead me in because I am captivated by the display. Inside, my vision is still skybound just like when a photo is taken and the flash's flare remains, pulsing, denying sight. I am spellbound and return to the window as soon as Michael releases my hand and sight returns.

I watch the light die. Water pools on the deck while flowers and other plants bow their heads under the onslaught of torrential rain. I cannot even see the lake. I raise my hand to touch the window as the silent sharp toothed scream of lightning rips through the wet air slamming itself against the earth just beyond the deck. Thunder's answering roar is shattering; sound waves shake us. Samson and Puppy respond. From deep inside them their response begins then pushes out of their bodies through their throats and mouths and their bays haunt the already shredded air and intensify a tangible uneasiness. The storm feels ... unnatural ... too driven. Our human response is stillness; we are only breath and heartbeat until the second streak of jagged white light cuts down through the already torn surface flesh striking deeply to hit the bone of our yard, digging in almost in the same place as the last. My home shudders once and then again when thunder throws itself against the panes of glass and walls of wood ... wanting in, wanting to touch us with its thick, throbbing hands.

Mary presses against me, and I become mom again. I turn my back on the monsters outside, denying their power, to offer solace to my daughter; her closeness, as I hold her in my arms, a mutual comfort. My eyes find Michael's intuitively. He holds John Henry.

Bradley is holding the phone in one hand and pressing numbered buttons with the other. Cal and Maybe stand together with Brian. Tucker stands close to Alana who has an arm around Maddie. Aden, Charlie, Shay, Neil, and Morgan stand near the windows looking out into a rain so heavy and thick it denies them vision. Jacy and Valerie sit on the couch, their hands in Samson's fur, his body pressed against their legs. Father Tom has his arm around Angela's shoulders. Except for the boys who are looking out the window, we all are looking at each other, eyes moving from one set of eyes to the other offering comfort and/or confirmation of feelings as yet unspoken.

Cal turns to Maybe, "All right, woman, 'fess up. Have you and your weird women friends been rain dancin' again?"

Maybe does not even look at him, so Brian decides to add his insights to Cal's remark, "It's true, you know? Women and nature need to be kept apart. When women start messin' around with their connections to old mother earth, all kinds of weird shit starts to happen."

Maybe walks away from the two men to join me near the windows, "Their kind really should not be allowed to speak. Their kind function well in only two places: in the bedroom and at the woodpile; for all else they are hopeless."

Father Tom sides with Cal and Brian, "Well, Maybe, it is true that you have been known to rain dance on occasion, and isn't their a legend about a group of your female ancestors inciting a bit of trouble by taking part in a dance to celebrate mother earth's power?"

Maybe glares at Father Tom, "Legend? Legend, my—" she pauses to look at my students and then continues, "legend, my foot! I'm more than tired out by people labeling our 'history' legend. I am more than tired out by it. You know why? Because it's thievery, plain and simple, if the truth were told, which it rarely is. You steal a people's history, and what do they have left? Ass ... imilation. Mutilation. Which ever you choose, old man, but that story is no legend. It happened. It still happens."

Cal shakes his head at Father Tom, "Now you've done it. Now she's gonna want to tell one of great-great-great-great-grandmother Hitaw's stories."

My students' voices encourage Maybe to tell her story. I watch Cal smile and nod his head at his wife. Brain slaps Cal on the back, "You wanted a story the whole time. I bet you always get your way, don't you?"

Cal's face takes on a sad expression even as his eyes deny it, "No, no. She has me whipped for certain, but I love her, so what can I do?"

Maybe has her hands on her hips, "Fetch your woman a glass of water, so she can teach these young ones some history, if you would, please."

Brain laughs, "She even said please."

Cal walks into the kitchen, "I can't hardly stand it when she sweet talks me like that."

I am aware Bradley is talking with someone on the phone, so I delay the beginning of Maybe's story until we can all give her our attention, "If we're going to have a story, let's get ... comfy. We can get blankets and pillows from the den, and—"

I am interrupted by Shay, "Excuse me, I know I'm cutting you off, but before we get ... comfy and have story time I just want to say that—" he pauses and turns toward the windows and then back again, "that did not feel ... like any storm I've ever felt before. It felt like ... it made me feel like I feel when I'm watching a horror flick or like when I was little and I'd get scared at night. Am I imagining it, or did anyone else feel strange?"

My students are tentative in their responses to Shay's question, but each one of them indicates by verbal agreement or gesture they concur with Shay's appraisal of the situation. Michael speaks quietly, reaching out to rest his hand on John Henry's who is now standing next to him, "It did feel strange ... unusual ... not normal. I think it's fair to say you speak for all of us, Shay, but Bradley is on the phone to my dad right now, and if I'm overhearing correctly he is getting some information on the storm, so maybe we're going to get some clarification or explanation, or maybe we won't. Which ever happens, and based on my experiences over the last few weeks, dwelling on it isn't going to help or make anyone feel better. So let's get some food and some hot coffee or tea or some cocoa, get some blankets and pillows, like Leah said, and hear a story." Looking at Maybe, he shakes his head, "Of course, how comforting Maybe's kind of story is going to be is a mystery to me."

Maybe just raises her eyebrows and crosses her arms in front of her, "As even your own people's history shows, one person's comfort is usually at the cost of another person's comfort, so I will tell the story, and then you can tell me if I comforted you."

Michael says 'deal' and motions for John Henry and my students to follow him. Mary wiggles to get down and calls out, "Wait for me, daddy."

I watch as Michael suggests tasks to be completed: cocoa, tea, and coffee preparation, popcorn popping, crackers deboxed and cheese sliced, grapes rinsed, and the gathering of pillows and cushions from the den couch and blankets from the den closet. I turn back to the windows stroking Puppy's head as he wags his tail wanting to follow the movements of the others but steadfast in his dedication to remain by my side. I say, "You can go, Puppy." But he remains.

Valerie calls my name, and I turn to her. She is sitting on the couch, Samson still pressed against her legs, his eyes alert. "Shay is right. This storm does not feel right, Mrs. C."

I go to her and sit next to her, "Yes, it is intimidating, isn't it?"

She shakes her head, "No, it's more than that, and I sense you know that too. But I sense something else. I didn't want to say it in front of the others, but I need to say it to you. Is there anyone else around?" I tell her 'no' and she continues. "Mrs. C, I've talked with you before about what I see even though I can't see. And maybe what I say I see is not really seeing in terms of how other people see, but the images, abstract as they are, still make sense to me. And what I see is a connection between you and this storm."

I look into her beautiful eyes that cannot look back into mine and take her hand in both of mine, "Yes, I know."

She waits for me to continue but I don't, so she asks, "Is that all you're going to tell me?"

I reply quietly to her, "I am not trying to be rude, but I cannot really say more at this time."

Valerie takes her hand from mine then lays her hand on top of mine, "There is real danger here for you. I am certain. And it's huge, Mrs. C, it's huge."

I try to comfort her, "I understand you are worried, so am I. So is Michael, but we are going through something we cannot control or stop. We are just doing the best we can. Beyond that, I cannot elaborate. I am sorry, Valerie. I am so sorry you are feeling threatened or in danger."

Valerie shakes her head, "No, no, it's not that. I don't feel danger or even threatened for myself. What I sense is a power ... it has dressed itself in this storm, and it isn't out to hurt anyone ... but you. If anyone else is hurt by it, that's unintentional, but my sense of it is it wouldn't care one way or another. It's so dark, Mrs. C. It's the darkest thing I've ever felt and, you know, I'm blind so I'm used to darkness, but this thing is so different. It's like a thing but it's not anything, so it wants you to fill itself with." She pauses and then continues, "That's it; the storm is just camouflage or a way to make its presence known, but 'it' is not the storm itself." She pauses again but quickly adds, "This is how you hurt your head, isn't it? It has tried to get you before."

I begin to say her name, but Father Tom comes around from behind me and speaks first, "Valerie, I overheard your conversation, and I need to tell you Leah is not alone in this, and as strange as it all sounds, it's—"

Valerie interrupts Father Tom, "Father Tom, I write and read about the supernatural. What's happening is strange, but I've read and written about much stranger, so you don't have to reassure me. I just wanted Mrs. C to know what I was feeling, to know I will help her if I can. All of us, all of her students, know strange things have been going on with her for quite a while, and we talk about helping her if we can. We're not afraid." She pauses and talks to me now. "Some of us get a bit freaked out when you start talking in a language none of us can recognize during a lecture but you don't seem to notice you're even doing it, or when you are looking out the window and we can see another sort of ghost-face looking in right back at you and you don't seem to see it at all, and there have been other things we've noticed, but we didn't want you to lose your job or anything, so we didn't say anything to anyone, but we have been trying to watch out for you. You mean a lot to us, Mrs. C. You've helped each one of us in some way, and we don't want anything to happen to you."

I can only repeat, "You and the others have been watching out for me? I speak in a different language? There are ghosts outside my window?"

Valerie smiles and nods her head, "Yes, but when those things happen they never feel bad or strange, if that makes sense. We've been watching out for you ever since the man came to each one of us and asked us to."

Father Tom asks, "What man? When?"

Valerie looks reluctant to answer at first but she says, "It was right after Teri … tried to hurt herself. He spoke with each one of us at different times, and he said he would watch out for us now, but he couldn't protect you, Mrs. C. He said we just needed to watch out for you, and to sort of pray or just imagine you in our minds as protected, so that's what we've been doing."

Father Tom asks Valerie what the man looked like and she laughs and reminds him she is not really the one to ask that particular question, but I do not need her to tell me what the man looks like, because I know exactly who he is. I know exactly what he looks like, because he has just whispered words into me from across a space of time I am only beginning to comprehend.

Chapter SEVEN

"Grandma Hitaw told her daughter who told her daughter who told her daughter and so it went being passed down generation to generation to the present when my mother told me," Maybe pauses and smiles, "that this man who tried to steal her from her people and their ways was a big man yet fast, or he would have never been able to catch her. She said that because everyone knew Hitaw could run like the wind, but still the big man, whose arms were as strong as a bear's, caught her and held onto her until she agreed to stop struggling against him. He assured her he just wanted to talk with her, but she knew his words might be as changing as the seasons, so even as she stilled herself, she did not let her guard down." Maybe pauses to take a drink of water from the glass sitting next to her, and perhaps also to look out the window where the storm seems to have somehow intensified. Jacy apologizes but asks if Maybe will wait for her to make a quick trip to the bathroom, commenting she has had two cups of tea. Maybe reassures her such things are natural and not to be embarrassed. As Maybe and Cal exchange humorous but barbed comments regarding other natural behaviors I allow my thoughts to wander.

The lights have flickered on and off a couple of times, but we still have power. I am again thankful all power lines are underground in Lane, or by now we would be candlelit and building fires to keep warm, which really does not sound like too bad of an idea, except then Michael would have to get up, and I am too comfortable sitting next to him with his arm around me to want him to move. I notice John Henry is enjoying leaning against one of the couches like the older boys, even though it took a couple of extra pillows to position him so his head rests, as theirs do, against the top edge of the couch's cushions. Maddie is holding Mary and smiles at me as we both notice Mary's eyes are closed. She is resting peacefully despite the storm's unsettling relentlessness.

Bradley told all of us what Hank had shared with him regarding the storm. A freak occurrence … sprang up out of nowhere and though intense and causing problems on the roads and bridges, the storm is centered right over Lane and not moving. Weather bureaus are at a loss to explain the storm. Having learned what I did from Valerie about my students' awareness of my strange situation, and having talked with Bradley two days prior about the same situation with its tie-in to his parents' death, except for Maybe and Cal and Brian, everyone else just looked at me briefly, reasoning it was just another weird Leah thing, because few if any questions were asked. Father Tom seems ill at ease despite my reassurance to him and will not tell me what thoughts keep him glancing at his watch, so I decide not to worry about what I can do nothing about.

I smile on the inside as I think that thought then wonder if my habit of pushing away from me troubling situations will have consequences beyond the obvious. For the briefest of moments I consider the consequence thing, but as my eyes wander around the room I notice Aden yawning, and because yawns are contagious, I yawn too. Just as I begin to wonder about yawns being contagious, Jacy returns, Maybe quiets Cal, and our late afternoon story time continues.

Maybe's eyes search the eyes of all those watching her and when she seems satisfied with our attentiveness, she raises her hand to her throat to touch the small, perfectly round, white stone of the necklace I have never seen her without as her words somehow easily carry themselves out over the beating drum of the storm, "This man was a polite man, as men go, and knew the correct ways of being, so once he saw Hitaw was going to cooperate and not struggle against him anymore, he stopped restraining her and introduced himself, which is what civilized people do upon meeting each other. He said, 'I am Shadowmaker, son of Springmoon and Mountainbear. My people once lived in these woods and stood on the cliffs overlooking the Big Water, but we left the land to follow the path the moon makes on the water and much happened after that which I cannot tell you. Now we can only walk on the land for short periods of time. On my last three visits here I have watched you, and I want to take you with me when I leave.'

"Hitaw had a big laugh; some say she used it to scare the pine nuts from the trees during harvesting but that could only be an exaggeration because she never admitted it was true, however she used her laugh now and even let it roll around in her belly to gain strength before she let it fly from her mouth and hit this big man named Shadowmaker. Shadowmaker only smiled and told her that her laugh felt like the waves of the Big Water washing over him. He asked her to laugh again, but she would not, of course, because pleasing him was not her intent.

"Hitaw realized she would have to use powers other than her own to convince this man she was not for him and to do that she would need to go to a place of power. She suggested they should walk as they talk about this plan of his to take her from her people, but he should know her heart was set against him.

"As they stood to begin their walk, Shadowmaker asked, 'What can change your heart?'

"He was so tall Hitaw had to lean her head back to see his face as she replied, 'My mind.'

"Now Shadowmaker laughed, amused at her answer, but his laugh was so strong it pushed Hitaw backwards. She fell, hitting her head on a rock on the ground. Hitaw says she had no voice anymore and could not push breath through her body. Hitaw said the rest of the story she saw from a close-distance, as if she could reach out and touch Shadowmaker easily but it would have taken a lifetime, by her earth way of marking time, to accomplish.

"She saw Shadowmaker kneel beside her and seeing no breath moved in her, he picked her up in his big arms and went to talk with his mother, Springmoon, who is a weaver of dreams and only available to talk with him during her daily journey back across the silver path her people had taken on that first journey too many years ago to give numbers to. He walked from the forest to the edge of the Big Water and waited for his mother to appear.

"He stood holding Hitaw in his arms, waiting for day to turn to night, but he did not allow himself to tire. His eyes went from Hitaw's face to the edge of the Big Water where his mother would appear, just as her mother before her had appeared, generation after generation, since before time became known as a thin line stretching between now and then and what's to come.

"Shadowmaker stood very still but inside him his thoughts accused him; he should not have let his laughter out that way, should never have let his heart's eyes choose one not of his kind. His laughter was too big for this place, too big for these people still bound to the earth; he should have remembered, but the joy Hitaw brought him had made him forget, and now his love lay breathless in his arms, and he wondered again if his mother would know how to help him. He wondered if perhaps he should have gone to his father instead, but that was a difficult task even if he had not been carrying Hitaw. His father, Mountainbear, lived deep within the earth in a cave where it was his duty, as it had been his father's and his father's father before him, generation after generation, to keep the fire burning that keeps most of the earth from freezing year around. Shadow-maker knew his father was wise, but in ways of love he had always sought his mother's guidance, so he continued to stand, still as a rock, holding his love in his arms.

"So focused was Shadowmaker's attention on Hitaw he did not notice his mother approaching until she called out his name. From a still great distance she called out to him, 'Shadowmaker, my son, what are you holding in your arms?'

"Shadowmaker raised his eyes to his mother and replied, 'It is my love, Springmoon, my mother.'

"Springmoon, still not close enough to see Hitaw's body in her son's arms, questioned Shadowmaker, 'Son of my husband's and my own heart, why does love lay so still in your arms? Love is a bird that flies or a fire that dances.'

"Shadowmaker let the tears fall from his eyes that had been hiding in his heart, 'My love is a woman of the earth, and I have taken the breath from her body.'

"Springmoon was now close enough to reach out and touch her son, and she does this, her fingertips on his cheek. She caught three of his tears and let them slide down her fingers into her palm where they gathered in a tiny pool. 'Why did you take breath from her?'

"'I did not mean to, but she amused me and I laughed. She fell and the breath left her,' was his quick reply.

"Springmoon looked into her son's eyes, 'How did she amuse you?'

"Shadowmaker looked down onto Hitaw's face, 'She said her heart was set against me, and I asked her what could change her heart. She replied that only her mind could change her heart.'

"Springmoon smiled sadly, 'Did she agree to speak with you about this matter, or did you have to chase her until you caught her then subdue her until she stilled?'

"Shadowmaker sighed, 'It was as you say.'

"Springmoon moved closer and looked upon Hitaw's face along with her son, 'So her response to your unreturned desire has cost her dearly.'

"Shadowmaker hung his head in shame, 'It is as you say, mother, but I want to make things right with her. Will you give her breath again?'

"Springmoon shook her head sadly, 'Am I the one who gives such gifts? I am a weaver of dreams, not the giver of breath.'

"Shadowmaker asked, 'Then what can I do?'

"His mother's eyes now held tears of their own, 'You know the answer even as you ask it. Do not ask me to say the words.'

"Shadowmaker looked up into the starred sky, 'Ah, but I don't want to join my ancestors yet; I am too young.'

"Springmoon countered gently, 'And how old is she?'

"Shadowmaker looked into his mother's eyes, 'What makes me more sad than losing my Hitaw before I even was able to make her my wife, is losing you who I have known and loved all my life. The sadness I feel is too big for my body to hold.' And it was true, because Shadowmaker's body was growing steadily larger. He looked down from his increasing height upon his mother's sad face, 'Take Hitaw in your arms, my mother, and lay her down there in the sand where she will wake and think all this only a dream.'

"Emotions pushed words out of Springmoon's heart, so she only nodded her head agreeing to do as he asked, but first she closed her hand around his tears pooled in her palm. When she opened her hand again, there was a smooth, white stone which she placed in the leather pouch hanging from Hitaw's beaded belt. Then taking Hitaw in her arms she laid her in the sand as Shadowmaker asked. Returning to him, she raised her arms to him, and so large had he became he lifted her easily in his arms. Finding her words scattered amid her shattered emotions, she reminded him where he was going she would soon join him, that all life leads to the same place. Shadowmaker looked upon his mother's face one more time then once more he looked upon Hitaw, 'I would have made her happy,' he says.

"Springmoon shook her head, 'We do not make happiness; it bubbles out of us like an underground spring. My heart breaks to say goodbye, but you must make your peace with Earth Mother and Sky Father. Perhaps they will offer a way we may still see each other from time to time, my son.'

"Shadowmaker closed his eyes, but his heart knew his mother had turned and was walking away from him. His sorrow deepened and grew until Shadowmaker stood like a mountain on the shore. Hitaw also cried as she prayed that somehow this mother and son would be allowed to visit one another from time to time, that out of the shared heart of Earth Mother and Sky Father a way would be made for Shadowmaker and Springmoon.

"Shadowmaker lifted up his hands and offered his own breath to take the place of Hitaw's breath that she might once more walk the paths destined for her to walk. Sky Father and Earth Mother heard the cries of Springmoon and of Hitaw as they heard Shadowmaker's prayer to restore to Hitaw that which had been taken, and suddenly Hitaw felt breath move through her and felt the sand beneath her. She looked quickly to find Shadowmaker, but even as she longed to call out to him he was already kneeling down to accept the Earth Mother's embrace. Hitaw watched as he was transformed, as arms of rock and soil encircled flesh and blood until where Shadowmaker had knelt a great cliff now rose out of sand. She noticed Earth Mother did not transform his tears, for from the uppermost peak a waterfall rushed down the stone face.

"Hitaw, turning to leave this sad place, noticed the moon, now at its highest point, had laid its silver path out across the water and its light touched the base of the cliff. Suddenly Hitaw's sorrow turned to joy, and she danced knowing mother and son would once again meet each other along the moon's path. For many nights after that, she danced there in the moonlit sand. During the day she slept in the hard arms of a spirit-man who had become the largest shadow maker on the edge of the Big Water.

"Hitaw climbed the cliff almost everyday of her life to thank Shadowmaker for honoring the balance that makes life possible. When Hitaw became an old woman and her legs would not take her up the steep path anymore, her daughter's son would lift her in his arms and carry her to the very steepest point of the cliff so she could wait for the moon's silver path to touch the cliff. On many of her last visits to the cliff, when Hitaw's age had made her flesh so weak she was more of the spirit than of the earth, she told of hearing a deep rumbling of laughter that was always answered by a lighter but similar rejoicing. Although Hitaw lived to tell her story not only to her children's children but also to her children's children's children, she never changed her story, so it is told even now so all those with ears able to hear the truth will know that breath is sacred and that everything breathes."

And with a perhaps imagined sigh, the power in our house seems to sputter then die as lights flicker and the low electric hum of appliances are silenced. The slate gray gleam of the storm's dusk light streams in through the windows and bathes us in itself.

Valerie is first to comment, "Something has changed, hasn't it?"

Shay responds, "Oh, yeah, most definitely, and with such …" he pauses and looks at John Henry who is also looking at him, "frigging uncanny timing that—"

Jacy interrupts Shay, "The power's out, Val, that's all."

Shay counters, "I was going to explain that."

Charlie changes the subject as he looks at Maybe, "My question is if you and Mrs. C know any happy stories? The last one Mrs. C told had all the girls crying. I think Shay may have even shed a tear or two."

Shay shakes his head, "Yeah, right. Everyone knows Morgan's the sensitive one."

Angela uses a family group warning, saying 'ouch', as Morgan remains seated but is no longer relaxing against the couch. He turns to face Shay, "Screw you." Then 'ouch' is said by three or four of the other students as Michael and Bradley stand and approach Shay and Morgan.

Father Tom's voice stops them, "Sit down, please. And everyone be quiet." He stands as Michael and Bradley sit down again. "I was afraid of this very thing. This is why May, in her first letter, wrote you were not to have others over to your house. I wanted to believe that perhaps it would be safe as long as they didn't spend the night here, but I should have known it couldn't be, not under these circumstances." He pauses and walks to the windows, "Listen very carefully to me now. Some of you know more than others about what is going on with Leah, and further explanation isn't going to happen, because if we don't quickly get our thoughts in control, if each one of us doesn't do that, events could happen here far beyond losing power or Shay's and Morgan's verbal exchange. This storm … the fact that night is approaching … that we are unable to safely move these students who are in Bradley's care from here back to the school … some of their unresolved personal issues … some of our own unresolved issues … this storm feeds off of itself and off other emotions within its perimeters. We must control our thoughts and emotions. We must be serious in that endeavor or—"

A knock at the door interrupts Father Tom.

Michael, Bradley, Cal, and Brian all move toward the door as the knocking repeats. Then a hooded face appears at the window, followed by a body as the person moves from behind the door with its shade down to stand before one of the windows. It is Connor, waving hello with one hand while the other hand holds a large black bag filled with objects with corners pushing against and even threatening to tear through the bag's plastic fiber.

And then I know, so I say, "Michael, let Connor in, please; I believe he has brought pizza and wants to join us." The word pizza mobilizes all except Father Tom who sits down on the now vacated couch, his head in his hands. I stand and walk over to him, place my hands over his, and reassure him, "It will be all right, Father. Please try not to worry. Food will take their minds off of their emotions. It is perfect timing."

Father Tom looks into my eyes, "Or not. If Connor made it over here, maybe we can get the students back to the dorms, but if we cannot then his arrival only adds fuel to the fire."

For the first time today, Father Tom's uneasiness fosters an uneasiness in me, "Fuel to the fire?"

Father Tom now holds my hands in his, "Yes, fuel, Leah, our thoughts, all of our thoughts, our emotions, are fuel for this ... thing that is acting like a storm. Malick explained more to me about the manifestations you've encountered, unseen to this point except for the bird when you were in the canoe, but there is no time to go into that now, and I can't imagine why Malick is not—"

I stop his words by saying, "No." I pause to make sure he is listening to me. I lean closer to him, making sure he can hear me over the talking and preparations occurring for a candlelit dinner of pizza and salad. "No more words right now. Eat pizza, Father Tom, and pray. There are too many people here for us to try to have meaningful conversations and explanations. If my students are being pro-tected like Valerie said then they are only dangerous, not in danger. We cannot be overwhelmed by this or it will win. You know that. I know that. It knows that. May says I can push through ... whatever that means, but I am focused now; I was being lazy before I guess; I was relaxing, listening to story, being held by my husband; that is obviously over now, and I am supposed to climb into some sort of save-the-day type of thinking at which point I am sure what I am supposed to do will become crystal clear to me, but I'd like to also know where Malick—"

The word to follow and every other sound being made in the room is instantly unmade, sucked into a void created by a wood splintering blast against the front door that seems to collapse the moment in on itself. The structure of the house breathes in, shudders, and breathes out. I am pulled forward and then back by the momentum. It is as if we are underwater; the air is liquid. We are moving in slow motion. I look to Michael, and it is as if he can read my thoughts. He picks up the children in his arms and nods his head to me, both of us dreading and knowing what I must do. Then thoughts become instinctual, cyclical, flat. I must think to move; I am aware of taking breath and releasing it. The door continues to be just beyond my reach. It takes too long for me to lay my hand against it. Opening it I am struck by time righting itself and by an exhalation of rancid breath from the thing clothing itself in storm.

I focus, build a barrier right before me then move it back until what I have constructed parallels the edge of the deck. I maintain the barrier by willing it to stay, and I look down to see the bird from the canoe, but it is larger than before; its wings, spread out to the left and right of its body, are at least twenty feet from tip to tip. It draws breath, is only battered and stunned by the impact from its crash into the door, but there are other marks on its body its impact with the door could not have caused.

Then I hear the movement of wings through air. I raise my eyes to see, coming straight toward me, the eagle, and like the other bird it is three or four times larger than the other times it has appeared. It battles now against the momentum of the storm, which appears to be holding the eagle in its place despite its attempt to reach me. I can see this great bird has also sustained wounds. But my attention is drawn back to the bird on the deck, which is attempting to move its wings. The eagle cries out. As I look into the eyes of the bird on the deck, the barrier I have set up against the storm's fury weakens. I feel myself being consumed by a flood of base emotions that spiral around me and loosen my hold on maintaining the barrier even more. I hear the eagle's cry, but it comes to me from a great distance. Equally distanced are Michael's voice calling my name and the cries of my children, but these incense me. I know what I must do.

I shake off the dark emotions seeking to hold me. I walk over the bird, a hawk of some sort, feeling my feet pass through it, but I do not stop. I walk into the storm toward the eagle. Around me the storm's howling beats at me relentlessly, but I am untouched, aware only of a pressure being exerted. The eagle is closer now and appears to also be overcoming the storm's strength. Horrifying images are presented to me by the gnawing emotions of the storm: Michael and John Henry and Mary cast into flames, burning alive, my worst fear visualized and drawing me just as the flames of the house drew me, wanted me, so many years ago, but I say 'no' and the images disappear. I say 'no' to the storm's rage, 'no' to the storm's fear, 'no' to the storm's crushing sorrow, and suddenly there is only silence around me. Malick stands before me, his clothing torn, bleeding from several wounds, but we stand before each other under a night sky with air sweet-scented and fresh from the rain. Malick looks into my eyes as Shal's voice whispers through me, "Yes, little one, yes, make this first battle ours."

I think I have misheard because I believe the battle is over, but behind me movement on the deck turns me around. The man is attempting to stand but through the torn fabric of his pants I can see a bone is protruding through a jagged tear in his flesh. Blood belches out with each heartbeat, each attempted movement. His face is contorted with pain as he looks up at me, his voice more like a growl than human, "This is not over, bitch." Then he is gone.

I turn to Malick whose own facial expression indicates he is fighting to remain composed in response to his own suffering, even though his wounds appear less threatening than the other's leg wound. I go to him, and put my arm around him, "I will help you."

His body stiffens at my touch, "No need. I can walk."

I let my arm fall and move away from him as Michael rushes out the door, John Henry and Mary still in his arms. I take them in my arms and watch as Malick allows Michael to help him into the house. I focus primarily on comforting my children, but in the back of my mind I wonder at Malick's response to me. His reaction to my arm around him is in such contrast with my own dawning awareness that at some point in time, in some different place, I had reached out to this man before, and he had not been negative in his response. But when could that have been, and why?

I shake my head at the new mystery as I walk to the deck and sit down, allowing John Henry to sit beside me while I keep Mary wrapped in my arms. I sigh, "Well, I know one thing for certain." John Henry takes the bait and asks 'what?' so I put my arm around him and reply, "I thought my back was going to break holding both of you. You are getting too big for me to carry around, son."

John Henry leans his head against me, "Mom, of all the things that just happened, I don't think me growing should be what you're thinking about."

I kiss the top of Mary's head, "It makes total sense really, because there is no way I can think about any of those other things that happened right now and not want to get in our car and drive far away from here."

Mary looks up for the first time, "We could go to Disneyland, mom."

I have to laugh, but John Henry is not amused, "We're not going to go to Disneyland, Mary."

Mary responds, "But we could."

John Henry counters, "But we're not." And they are off in their verbal volley, which is good because it distracts them from the shock they must be feeling having gone through what they just experienced. It gives me time to try to figure out how to explain to them and to my students in some reasonable fashion what has occurred. But I do not think about reasonable explanations. Instead, I lose myself in the closeness of my children and make my mind focus only on what they are saying, and wonder a bit if getting in the car and driving far, far away is even an option or if what is happening would follow me to the ends of the earth.

Shal's voice whispers through me, "Farther than that, Leah ... to the ends of time and from there back again. Stay in the moment, Leah; stay in the moment."

Bradley's voice beckons me, "Okay, I don't think ignoring me is polite at all."

I apologize for not hearing what he said as Bradley sits down next to John Henry, "I'm new to all this, of course, having only just been introduced to the concept of this strange encounter in which you are presently involved, so I have not had time to acclimate, so to speak, but that is the singularly most bizarre and frightening experience I have ever had, and I was inside looking out through a window. Perhaps you should consider posting warning signs so innocent well-wishers or just common everyday visitors don't enter your property without some inkling of what could possibly occur."

Before I can respond, Mary asks, "What's an inkling?" And before I can respond to that John Henry takes Mary's hand and tells her to come inside with him so Bradley and I can talk.

But now I do respond, "Now wait just a darn minute. You and Mary and how you are feeling about all this is most important right now, so if you want to stay with me, you can."

John Henry reaches out his hand and pats my shoulder, "It's all right, mom. We'll just go in and eat some pizza then you can explain everything to us later." He smiles, but a look of doubt replaces the smile. All I want to do is hold him and somehow offer him an assurance I do not really have.

Mary imitates her brother and pats my shoulder too, then turns with her brother and walks into the house where I can see my students are eating pizza. I cannot even imagine eating anything right now, but I am obviously in the minority.

I call after John Henry and Mary, "Well, at least have some salad too."

Bradley shakes his head, "Yes dears, eat some salad before the bad storm comes back and—"

I interrupt him, "Who is tending to Malick?"

Bradley looks out across the lake as he replies, "Michael and Brian with Maybe's help. Although the ways of firemen-paramedics and the ways of Maybe aren't proving to be incredibly congruous, so I left to find you. Cal is eating pizza with your students, but how anyone could eat right now is beyond me. Of course, this entire episode is beyond me. Truly, it's too strange. I can understand why my parents, if they knew anything about May's involvement in such matters, would have wanted a meeting to clarify. But this sort of thing, with this magnitude, wasn't going on back then was it?"

I sigh, "My understanding is we are in a different place in the cycle, so events are more extreme."

Bradley asks, "Could this cycle tie-in with the new millennium?"

I look at him, "Probably, but I really do not know."

Bradley looks at me, "My God, Leah, do some research or something and get a handle on this. Are you just letting these events, as you call them, happen to you? Read a book, make the proverbial phone call, but get some help. Let me help. I will do whatever research you need."

I let him know Malick is helping me, along with others like Father Tom and Matilda. What Bradley would have said next I cannot guess, because Connor sits down next to me.

He quickly acknowledges Bradley before he looks at me and says, "Interesting, Leah-lass, to say the least. It's a shame I missed the initial happenings, but I'm a bit out of the loop now, aren't I?"

I look away from him and focus on the moon's and stars' light reflected on the lake, "Meaning what, Connor?"

His attitude is not unpleasant, but there is an edginess to him that makes me uncomfortable even before he begins his statement, "You don't trust me, and so I'm not invited to take part in discussions or planning. I want to tell you I can be trusted, and I want to help you in any way I can."

I look at him now, "Planning? You make it sound like we know what we are doing. We do not, and as far as trusting you, it is less that than just not knowing you, Connor. We just met you a couple of weeks ago."

Connor's response is quick, "You only met Malick a couple of weeks ago also."

I stand up and turn to face him, "Okay, are you an eagle too?" Connor shakes his head no, and I continue, "Well, it is not so much Malick has been invited as it is he flies around and lands when I least expect it. He goes pretty much wherever he wants to go." I pause and realize I am suddenly very tired, "Look Connor, Father Tom believes you are trustworthy and he knows you. That should mean more to you than what I am or am not feeling. Father Tom can tell you whatever he wants. We are not keeping secrets from anyone really, but at the same time we are not telling everyone everything either. I do not know what I can say to you to make you feel better, and right now I just want to go inside and—"

But that is not to be, for I can feel myself being drawn toward another moment, or another place in this moment, and I surrender to it, knowing whether I want to go or not does not matter because I am already there.

*   *   *   *

I have stood here before, upon this ancient wall of stone. I have stood here and looked onto the stones of another wall, taller than the one on which I stand, but made with the same type of stones. I turn to see if the tree is still here also. It is, so I walk along the wall to the tree, and notice once again how the branches on one side have grown to facilitate its closeness to the higher wall. As I get close enough to observe the tree I can see lines have been carved into its bark, and these lines remind me of the ones I saw when I was falling—.

I am falling again, but I do not put out my hands to stop myself this time, instead I imagine sitting across from Shal with the fire between us—. I am there.

Shal is standing rather than sitting. I look beyond him into the darker corner of the cave; she is here also. Head bent, her long white hair falling over her shoulders and reaching past her waist. As I am looking at her, she looks up at me. Her eyes are midnight blue and her eye lashes are long and as white as her hair. Her skin, like Shal's, is alabaster and captures the fire's light like a pearl. She is smiling, and her lips, like her cheeks, are a pale rose in hue. I am captivated by her and notice she still holds the feather, running her fingers over it, from bottom darkest color to the tip's whiteness.

When I refocus on Shal he is smiling, so I smile back. He gestures with a tilt of his head to indicate the woman who stands behind him, "She is beautiful is she not? Others before you have appreciated her appearance, and all who have had the pleasure of getting to know her, come to appreciate who she is as much as how she looks. This is not always so, as I am sure you are aware. Many times beauty houses its opposite, but she has simply grown more beautiful over time because of the grace residing within her heart and spirit, because of the control she has over those emotions, which bend minds this way and that into ugly unnatural contortions, and even though many would attribute such emotions to an intrinsic nature, it is not so. She would tell you the same, if she spoke, but she has not done that in a very long time."

I look back and forth between them, "Are you related to each other?"

Shal laughs. It is so mesmerizing I almost forget the question I asked, but Shal does not, "She is my sister."

I ask her name, and Shal turns toward his sister and with his hand outstretched invites her to join us. As she joins him I can see she is even more beautiful than I perceived from a distance. Shal and his sister look at me as Shal's words pour over me and fill my mind completely, "Your friend Bradley is not far from the truth. You must seek truth and guidance from the letters, and you must stop waiting or the manifestation you experienced today will by comparison be innocuous compared to what can transpire if you do not proceed quickly. You must wake up to the urgency of your calling, Leah. Stand on the edge; call out to May. Read the second letter where May will introduce you to my sister ... Brigid."

Then suddenly Connor and Bradley are staring at me, and Connor comments, "Will you look at that, Leah, one minute empty handed and now with a feather you are."

I choose to ignore Connor for the moment and ask instead, "How long was I gone?"

Bradley comments gently, "Leah, you just said something about wanting to go inside, then all of a sudden you had a feather in your hand."

Connor stands and walks toward me, "And where might you have been now?"

I answer his question with a question of my own, "I was in a place where an ancient stone wall about six feet tall and a foot wide stands next to another stone wall that is much, much taller—"

Connor interrupts me, "You were there? Just now? In twenty seconds you were in Ireland and back again?"

I am not sure how to answer, "Perhaps it is not Ireland, but it feels like Ireland."

Connor is watching me closely and asks, "Might there be trees between the short and tall walls spaced every twenty feet or so?"

My response to his question is quick because I am interested in what he might be able to tell me, "I saw only one, but the place where I have been both times is on a curve as if the walls are concentric. Does that sound familiar to you?"

Connor responds to my question with a question of his own, "Does Malick know about this place?"

I fold my arms and look at him, "That is not an answer to my question."

Connor laughs, "True, and I could be about apologizing, but I'm a competitive sort of fellow."

I keep my facial expression stern, "You are a priest."

He smiles, "So, I'm a priest who's competitive; there are worst ways a priest can be, you can be more than sure." I start to walk into the house and he yells 'stop' good naturedly then adds, "I'll tell you. I'll tell you what you want to know, just stop."

I look at Bradley, "Should I believe him, or do you think he is going to distract me again?"

Bradley looks at Connor, who tries to look sincere but can't help smiling, and then back at me, "I believe he understands what is required and will do as you ask."

I look from Bradley to Connor as I say, "Thank you, Bradley. Tell me, Connor."

Connor almost succeeds in looking tortured, "You just cannot be expectin' me to tell ya' this tale quickly now, can you? Surely not. We should be going inside and getting comfortable. We should probably wait until your students have taken their leave, since Father Tom has a strong feeling that's important, and Malick and Father Tom could be adding information to what I will be offering you, for you can be certain those of us who know Ireland and her history, for those of us who have walked the paths that are Ireland's history, especially the way Father Tom and Malick know her history, the place you've been is legendary."

Bradley sighs, "I can see I must honor my first obligation and take the young ones home, but you have to promise to recount Connor's tale for me Monday, Leah, at school, because you are returning Monday, aren't you?"

I respond in sequence, "Yes and yes and yes. And thank you for all you have done for me; I appreciate it so much. I have to admit, however, I could easily take another day or two." Bradley begins to react, so I quickly add, "But I will not, of course."

Bradley relaxes, "Then I will go and gather my borrowed flock, so to speak. They are going to want to stay up all night and talk about Leah's storm, and all I want to do is go to sleep."

I give him a hug, "Tell them you are exhausted, and ask them nicely to respect the fact you are old and need your rest."

He steps back from me, "And that is your idea of being helpful, to remind me of my age then suggest I throw myself on the mercy of youth? I think not!"

Connor is trying to be patient but not succeeding, so Bradley and I curtail our banter and walk inside to gather the students who still stand around the empty pizza boxes, looking a bit dazed but still talking. I notice Shay and Morgan are standing next to each other, so I assume they have come to terms with their earlier discord, but the situation will have to be dealt with on Monday either way.

John Henry and Mary are sitting on either side of Father Tom and he is telling them a story. Maybe, Cal, and Brian are listening also. Michael and Malick are not in the living room. I walk to the den and look in to find Malick lying on the couch and Michael reclining back in 'his chair'; both sleep. As much as I want to hear Connor's information, the idea of sleep appeals to me, and I wonder if I can get him to wait until morning when my body and brain will have more energy and be more receptive. Perhaps sleep, like yawns are contagious too, because I was not thinking about sleeping until I saw Michael and Malick doing so. I hear my students and Bradley saying their goodbyes to the others, so I close the door to the den and join them.

After 'goodbyes' and 'see you Mondays' I notice the lights have come back on, so I begin to blow out candles. Maybe is stacking pizza boxes back in the sack in which they were brought. I gather a stray glass or two from table tops and take them into the kitchen, noticing, happily, dishes have been done and counters cleared of the various snacks offered earlier.

Standing in my kitchen, I cannot tell there was a storm, or a power outage, or even that almost twenty people spent the last few hours here. Connor is sitting in a chair across from Cal and Maybe. John Henry and Mary both look like they are struggling to keep their eyes open but do not want to admit they are tired.

Connor stands and holds out his hand to me, "If you wouldn't mind, and I don't believe you will, perhaps Father Tom and I can return after mass tomorrow, and we can talk then."

I place my hand in his and look up into his eyes. I am uncertain but hopeful about his motives, "Are you sure?"

Connor shakes his head, "No, but I think I've learned from my past mistakes enough to know you don't like to feel pushed or be rushed."

I want to trust him, to believe he is not here to act against me and what I am to accomplish, and since there is really no way for me to know one way or the other, I decide to lay aside previous feelings of uneasiness and trust this man to whom I am, like Father Tom, related. "Thank you, Connor. I will look forward to you and Father Tom being here tomorrow after mass. We can barbecue or something like that." I pause remembering who is sleeping in the den with Michael, "Perhaps we should just let Malick stay the night, since he is sleeping and comfortable."

Connor nods, "Probably a good idea, but we can ask Father Tom to be sure. The overnight thing seemed to worry him earlier. I believe the story he is telling your children is one I was told as a boy and is nearing its end."

I notice Maybe walking out the door to put the pizza boxes in the trash cans outside. I ask Connor to excuse me and follow Maybe so I can talk with her, since I have had no opportunity to do so all evening.

The air is cool and fresh. The silver light of moon and stars fill the darkness with shadows. Owls, from the branches of trees, and frogs, from the shallows of the lake, fill the night with sound. Ten or so feet away, Maybe stands, one arm raised to the moon, the other at her throat, her fingers touching the white stone of her necklace. She is captured in moonlight, stilled. Her eyes are closed and from her parted lips come a low chant. I am mesmerized, stilled by her stillness. I sink to my knees, knowing I am witnessing a ritual of faith and wanting to honor her and the moment she has carved out of black night to embody her hope and her gratitude, her awareness of a being or beings bold enough to have created all we know and yet gentle enough to breathe into our mouths life. I bow my head and join her, raising up my own silent prayer as her chant carries my words up into the night like sparks transported on the breath of fire.

✳   ✳   ✳   ✳

We sit together, Maybe and I, on the deck. We are face to face, leaning into each other, our voices softened by prayer and its solace. She reaches out and takes my hand, "Any moment the men will come, mine to take me home, Father Tom and Connor to return to their home, so I'll speak quickly and perhaps comment on what isn't my business, but it's what I feel I should do." She pauses; I only nod my head, and she continues, "The story was for you, Leah. For so many more nights then I can count, I've seen you standing on Shadowmaker, where Hitaw stood, and I know you're called to do so. We go there often, the people I pray and worship with, and it is a place where this world and the one we call the 'other' touch. You need to know that time and its moments narrow and widen like a strong river rushing then slow moving toward … well, toward big water, toward that place where all life flows to and from. I sense such a narrowing coming. I think for what you're called to do, which I can't know in my mind but I know in my heart, that you must move now." She pauses again then continues, "Little sister, be wise, which to my people means be aware of your place in the harmony of life; do not wrestle with your own purpose or need to hold it in your hand to understand it. Understanding is like the happiness Springmoon spoke of: we do not make it; it bubbles out of us. It births itself out of the mixing of who we are and who we are to be. Trust the path laid out before you; trust its blind bends and midnight shadows as much as its straightaways and gentle morning sun. You're going to have to get wet and ride the wave of this thing you're doing and stop standing on the shore waiting for the canoe to come; there's no canoe for this journey you're taking, no canoe at all. Do you understand what I am saying?"

I nod my head and whisper the word 'yes'. And since we both know there is nothing more that needs to be said, we stand together and hold hands, which makes me feel like a little girl again, but also makes me so aware that this woman, whose people are not mine, is my sister nonetheless. We enter the living room and find it quiet, no story words or conversation. My children's heads rest against Father Tom's chest, one of his arms around each of them. Connor and Cal sit in two chairs facing each other, all three men sharing comfortably the silence that opens itself to those who seek it like a much appreciated sanctuary.

*   *   *   *

I stand at the door and watch Puppy taking care of his nightly blessing of numerous trees as Cal's and Maybe's crew cab truck backs out of the driveway, Father Tom and Connor in its backseat. I have opened the door to the den. I have carried my sleeping children into my bedroom and placed them on either side of the bed, so once nightly rituals are complete I can easily climb in between them. After removing shoes and socks and covering them with sheet and comforter without waking them and the whole time only wanting to join them, I am being patient with Puppy. He seems more than determined to stop and visit every tree edging our yard even as he keeps his eyes focused on me. I whisper his name into the darkness to remind him I am waiting. Movement behind me causes me to turn quickly.

Malick's arms are around me. His lips touch my neck. He calls out the name 'Aidrea' and says something in Irish as I push him away. His look of shock must mirror my own. He raises his hand to reassure me, but I move away instinctively. His words are rushed, "It wasn't you … I wasn't … I was half asleep, Leah. It was dark in the room and the moon's light coming in through the door and the windows … I thought you were someone else."

I whisper the name I heard him say, "Aidrea?"

The look in his eyes softens for the briefest of seconds as he must be seeing her in his mind, then he focuses on me again, "Yes, Aidrea."

Any danger I felt is gone, and I am only curious now, "It is an unusual name, but somehow familiar to me. Is she someone connected to all this?"

He covers his face with his hands, "I cannot begin to—" he stops himself and looks into my eyes with such an intensity I step back from him, "You must move more quickly. You must. You have no idea … and I cannot explain what you want to know, because you are not where you must be for me to tell you. And I am not the one who will … introduce the idea to you. May, in her third letter, will tell you of … Aidrea." Her name changes him in some small way each time he says it.

I smile, "You must love her very much."

Malick's smile is gentle, and his words make me know he has found in his Aidrea what I have found in my Michael, "She is … I am … she is everything to me."

I lay my hand on his shoulder, and he does not pull away from my touch, "I am happy for you, Malick."

He has already become the Malick who is distant and a bit stern, "Then be quick for me, Leah, so we can both be happy."

I ignore his comment and ask, "But why does her name mean something to me if I do not know her. Why is that? Surely you can at least tell me who she is."

He steps closer to me, "I can tell you nothing more than what I have already said. I must go." I tell him about Father Tom and Connor returning tomorrow after mass and what we plan to discuss. I can almost see the frustration and anger rise in him, "Leah, you're wasting time. And Connor is wasting your time and knows it. What does it matter the name of a place you've already been and will return to? Do not be sidetracked. Stand on the edge. Call out May's name."

Malick's comment about Connor makes me ask, "Why did you say that about Connor? Is he against what I am supposed to do?"

Malick seems to be searching for the words he wants to say to me, "Connor is moved by motivations that aren't in keeping with yours, but he isn't against you. He is … unaware to the point of disbelieving so many aspects of this … endeavor that in that sense and in that sense alone he could be dangerous to you. Personally, he means you no harm, but there are forces that could use his … self defined good intentions to work against you and what you must accomplish. It was better when he was keeping his distance from you. Now he will have to be dealt with so that he can't unknowingly—"

I interrupt him, "What do you mean dealt with?"

Michael's voice from the den calling my name makes us both turn, and I also notice Puppy is standing at the door. I reassure Michael I am coming as I let Puppy inside. I almost close the door on Malick as he is attempting to leave without answering my question.

We are inches from each other and both of us clearly not pleased but probably for different reasons. I whisper, "You are not leaving before you—"

He interrupts me, "I am leaving, Leah. I'm leaving right now. And if you're concerned about all the people who are becoming involved in this, you might want to consider the longer you take the more dangerous things become for anyone not an innocent or under some other type of protection." I recognize the change in his eyes as he leans closer to me. I recognize the change because I have seen it in Michael when we are having a heated discussion and his desire for me is somehow awakened. When Michael changes like this, it is odd to me, some sort of male-thing, but I do not mind the maleness of it from him, but this change in Malick is more than disconcerting. His words are low and his lips too close, "You are so much like her, I could close my eyes and almost imagine holding you would be holding her, so don't stand so damn close to me, Leah, and don't push me. Your inattentiveness to what you need to be doing is keeping me from her. And that makes me lonely for her in a multitude of ways. You could push me too far and—"

Michael's voice is much closer now, and we both turn to see him standing in the doorway of the den, "What in the hell is going on?"

Malick looks from Michael to me and replies, "Explain it to him, Leah." As I begin to close the door behind him and turn toward Michael I hear wings pushing into and against dark night air made heavy with moisture, and I wonder if Malick flies to his Aidrea or to Shal.

✳   ✳   ✳   ✳

Our sleeping children force our strong words to soften themselves before exiting our lips to be pushed out into each other. Michael is insistent, "You're being ridiculous, no, insane; you're being insane. There is absolutely no damn way you're going up there tonight."

I lay my hand on his folded arms he has either consciously or subconsciously placed across his chest to make me keep my distance. I cannot press up against him and gentle him, even if that was my desire, which it is most definitely not, but I do not want him angry, because the momentum of that tide is too much for me to push through, and the moon is nearing the apex of its climb and I want to be on Shadowmaker when that happens. I want to stand where Hitaw stood and call out to May. I want to do that tonight. I want to leave now, so I try to convey the depth of the need I feel, "I am not fighting against your logic, Michael, because what you are saying is logical, but I must go. I must go now, while Malick is gone and Connor sleeps and before that thing we bested today returns. I must go now before another person gets pulled into this or hurt. Shal, Maybe, and Malick told me I must stop procrastinating," I pause and offer him a small smile, "so I do not want to procrastinate about not procrastinating."

He uncrosses his arms and puts them around me where they always feel like they belong, "But why can't I go with you? I can't even believe you want to go out there alone. Shouldn't I be with you?"

I have laid my head against his chest, and I am lulled by his heartbeat, and the warmth of his body, and his arms around me. Why do I want to go tonight? Why not go tomorrow night? What is one more day in the—. I stop myself, because I know. I know this is a moment in time, and it calls out to be filled, not with me laying next to my husband and letting sleep wrap us in its arms, but instead the moment wants to be filled with what I feel called to do. I tell myself I must listen, not to the voice of my body, which is calling out Michael's name, but instead to the voice that is mine but not mine, which is calling me to walk the path destined for me to walk, and to trust as I move forward who I am and who I will be will dance together and understanding will birth itself out of that union.

Michael whispers into me, "Leah, are you asleep or are you having one of your one-sided conversations again?"

I look up into his eyes, "Oh Michael, I so much want to do as you ask, to not worry you anymore, but I cannot. I have to go."

"Without me?" he asks.

I answer him, "You are always with me."

He is not being insistent any longer, but he is not done with the discussion, "Without me in the physical sense though, of me being at your side, helping you if you need my help?"

I close my eyes. I am again the little girl in front of a burning house. Then, in my mind, I race through my years observing myself, watching as I seem to be moving, but I am only standing still really … standing in front of a burning house, changing from small girl to woman, but never really moving out of that moment. What all that means is just beyond me, and I cannot give words to it, so I say to this man I love, "You are going to have to trust me in this matter, husband."

Michael steps back and puts his hand under my chin, his lips almost touching mine as he sighs into me, "I trust you with my life, because that's what you are to me, life. I don't really know if I could even breathe. No, I know that's true." His lips are touching my eyes, my lips, my neck as he continues, "I would not breathe at all, because you are my air; that's the sense of you I have, that's what you are to me, air; your heart beats my heart. I would not want to live without you, Leah; so every time you breathe, you're pushing breath through me too." His hands are in my hair as his mouth finds mine and we breathe into each other, deep breaths back and forth, over and over, until the kiss becomes all that we are, all that is.

＊   ＊   ＊   ＊

From the beginning of the beginning, back and forth, over and over, waves push, rippling reflections. Moon and stars watch. I watch. I stand in sand. I listen. Night sounds, ocean sounds, an awareness of my own breathing draws me out then into myself, back and forth, over and over. Castle Rock Point is a shadow maker even in night's cover of darkness. The space the crag fills reaches out, looms over, darkens and deepens beyond itself; the sand and rocks at its base somehow dimmed by its presence. I take a breath to still the whining of my nerves and walk into it, into this deeper darkness.

I walk a path walked so often and for so long the way is clear, feet aware when eyes are not. The moon's light does not touch the path; Shadowmaker takes that light for himself, holds it in stone arms and stone hands, dips it into the waves then raises it to his sad stone face only to release it again to catch it up to himself again perhaps wanting to wash away his own tears, but the tears fall despite the desire to make tears stop. I think of Brigid, and I know why she has not spoken for hundreds of years. She and Shadowmaker share a destiny of such steep sorrow they are stilled by it. I am stilled by it and have to force myself to continue walking, have to be strong with legs and feet and force them to move, speaking to them over the other voice in me that only wants to turn back, turn and return to Michael's arms again, but I remind myself May is waiting and I must go to her. My thoughts simplify, abridge, and repeat themselves. May is waiting. I must go to her. Go to her. Waiting. May. Go to her....

*   *   *   *

On the edge I am moonlit and starred. Beneath my feet Shadowmaker breathes deeply, or perhaps it is just waves crashing against stone almost one hundred feet below me. Perhaps it is both, or perhaps it does not really matter how I seek to define or describe. Perhaps what I feel, this movement beneath my feet, is the whole earth breathing in, breathing out, and in my busyness I have just failed to ever notice. Or perhaps because the earth breathing has never really been a real option for me, it has always been so, but it could not be so for me, unawareness limiting the possibilities. Every religion, every political philosophy, every belief, even my very own feelings all and only sensations, only perceptions experienced through the filter of who I am, perspective limiting discernment. Even love is filtered through a variety of moments and situations, so then everywhere—filters. Water through sand, breeze through curtains, sunlight through wave. Images through sight. A still breeze reminds me I am standing on an edge. Does the universe end somewhere and if so why? Does life end somewhere and if so why? Why do I bother asking? Why do I let uncertainty drag me around like wounded prey? There is no peace to be found in this search; there are no answers offering sense. Save me from this, I think. I think, save me from this, please. I am standing on an edge for what reason, for what purpose? Then I try to get a handhold on the moment and think, at least I am still standing. I have not thrown myself down on hard stone and beat my fists against the senselessness of it all, against the arbitrary fluctuations of existing and not existing. I am here now. I am fine. I am all right. I am just here standing on the edge of a high cliff. I am being normal, even if the world is not. I almost smile but do not because the stars are not doing what they are supposed to at all. They are not stationary and twinkling. They move in closer to me then back again. The moon magnifies itself then shrinks back again. The waves are driven and do not roll toward the shore; they roll toward me. The breeze bellows. I am being pushed from behind.

Is this real, I wonder or is it only perspective? I cannot know. I am being pushed from behind off the edge of this cliff, so I call out her name, "May." Then the moon and stars and waves are righted or my senses are, and she is before me, unchanged. I do not think about the fact she stands in mid air. I just say her name again, "May."

She responds, "Leah." Her saying of my name resonates. My eyes take her in. She is the same small person with the same blue eyes. Just as she did on the night of the fire, she wears her favorite dress and around her shoulders her favorite shawl. Her hair is the color of moonlight. My heart breaks.

My heart breaks seeing her again. I call out without words. I send out emotions. I sob. Silently she watches me as tears run down her cheeks. I hold out my hand. The air ripples as if it is water, but her image remains constant. "Are you real?" I ask.

She offers words to me, "Define real, my love." She opens her arms; her eyes draw me.

Without hesitation I take that first step … across time, through space, by way of night air perhaps I move toward her, or perhaps I do not move at all. Perhaps I am only moving through my own mind, but I am in her arms and we are suddenly … no where I know, and that is all right, because May is holding me. I breathe in her scent of rose; I feel her breath against my hair. "You are real," I say to her. I pull back from her so I can look into her eyes and see her face, "Why did you have to go away, May? Why couldn't you have stayed?"

Her gentle laughter precedes her reply, "Why anything, Leah? I can give you one thousand answers and would not be giving you anything at all. Is this how you want to fill this moment we share?"

I lay my head against her shoulder again, wanting only her closeness, "What do you mean?"

She wraps her arm around me, "What have you learned, heart of my heart? What have you learned? Isn't that such a much better question than asking why about anything? Why-questions demand explanations, a sifting through, a going back then returning again. What I have learned about explanations is that we paint our own pictures, sketch out our own maps, create our own horizons. The stage is pretty much empty, sweetheart, but the emotions … ah, the emotions and the moments they fill, they connect us. So, you and I, we are here together; let that be enough."

I am not understanding and tell her so. Her response is quick, "And don't you know from Maybe's story understanding comes from the balance made between the continuum of who you are and of allowing yourself to be complete within a certain context."

I feel like the little girl again, "Context meaning moment of time?"

May gently responds, "Context meaning awareness of one moment's wholeness within the wholeness that is."

I am still the little girl, "I understand your words, but their meaning is beyond me."

May replies, "Then you'll have to wait. You'll have to walk a little, or a lot, farther down the path for the meaning to find its place in you."

I smile, "I do not even care right now, because I am here with you." I pause and look around, "Where is here?"

May brushes my hair back from my face with her hand, "A place I like filled with a thousand times I like. A place you've been."

Then I know we are sitting within a meadowed circle made by the tall stone wall even though I do not see it. "Where is the wall?"

May smiles now, "Where it has always been. Where it will always be."

I shake my head at her, "Am I to get no straight answers from you at all?"

May shakes her head back at me, "Well, if it is straight answers you are wanting then don't sit in the center of a circle. Go stand, instead, on a line of explanations, then you can be right and all will be well ... or not, but you won't care because you won't wonder. You will have your answer."

I take her hand in mine, "Okay, all right, I give up."

May raises my hand to her lips and kisses it, "If you were prone to that then you'd never have been chosen, Leah."

I attempt another question, "Was I chosen or destined?"

May answers this question with one of her own, "Is there a difference?"

I look away from her now to see what is around me. I sit on green grass. There are trees, oaks and rowans, and bushes growing around rock clusters. Above me the sky moves, white clouds across blue space. Birds sing and somewhere not too distant, water rushes. I look back into her eyes, "I have said the same, asked myself the same question and believed I knew what I believed. I have said it makes no difference if we are destined or have freewill, because we cannot know our destinies. So when I ask you if I am chosen or destined, what am I really wanting to know? Chosen means selected because of who I am. Destined means I walk a certain path, but is that not also based on who I am?" I pause to draw breath, to take the sweet meadow scent of this place into me, "Then there is also the circle and straight line. Is that a reference to how people think, or how people choose to think, or how people have been taught to think? Christianity and Judaism and Islam seem linear while Native American and certain Eastern religions seem more circular. Is the circle representative of reincarnation or the constancy of energy even in its transformations? Where is God? Why do so many seek to know him? Why does God pour himself out into our hearts and minds in such different ways? Or is it that he is constant and because of who we are we see and hear him differently, and does that mean we are all correct in our renditions of him? Is there more to life than just trying to live well and honorably and then dying? There must be; you are here. I am with you. I want my life to make sense. I want the world to make sense. I want my place in it to make sense, yet now my own existence makes even less sense. Strange things happen to me. Malick flies. How did I get here? And that … that thing without physical form in and of itself but feels like every negative emotion … and that other man … the hawk that fought with Malick? And Shal and Brigid who look so young, did they die young so they look young even after centuries? Or maybe they never died being second generation Tuatha de Danaan; maybe they just chose to be beyond this … realm. And the others who were there around the fire but were so faint, who are they?"

May pats my hand, "My, my, such a list we have, but really not such a list, because all you really want is reconciliation between what is and your own understanding. All you really want is to see your stepfather and your mother and me walk out of that house that burned so long ago, but, Leah that cannot happen. You are so close to letting go of so much that holds you back from seeing what is valid and timelessly real, but you resist. You want to understand what is too simple to make sense to you yet; you believe life has to be complicated; you want to fix what cannot be fixed, make the difficult situations and circumstances go away, but they are only manifestations or reflections of human emotions expressing themselves in physical actions. In every culture values and concepts are scattered like seeds on the ground and what grows is what is nurtured; truth becomes a secondary or even non issue. In the Bible there is a verse in Matthew, chapter eighteen I think, in which Jesus says what we bind and what we loose on earth will be bound and loosed in heaven. Now whatever your persuasion, I'm of a mind, those words make sense. Let heaven be all of life, all of creation, that is beyond this physical world we have classified and diagrammed, then accept the idea that what we do here affects there, and imagine the emotions released, imagine the oblivious and driven momentum we have created not only in our own time and place but also in our own understanding, then imagine all those emotions released, filling not only space but also perceived by hearts and minds and spirits. Remember, too, Maybe's story."

Her words have held me; I will myself to hold them, so later I can review, seek an unfolding of meaning, but I ask, "What part of Maybe's story?"

May's eyes reflect the sky; I watch clouds pass, "Which part would you be wanting to hold onto more than any other?"

I look around me and say, "The earth breathes. Everything breathes. Everything is connected."

May smiles, "Not a new revelation, but what should be grasped here is it's really true, and it's true on every level of being: mental, physical, spiritual. Then let me add the ones around the fire, who are there but ever so barely are the ancient ones. Even when they choose to take physical form they are so much spirit now, one can barely perceive them. Think on that, but more than anything, Leah, more than anything be the child you were before the fire and the woman you were and are after the fire then be the fire itself and let the moment itself fly through you. Let it fly through you completely, let it pass and belong to that space which it filled. Breathe in that moment one more time, breathe it in then breathe it out. Continue to care about your time and place in this world and its inhabitants but move, Leah, and be moved by more than circumstance. Offer yourself up, lay on life's altar, be taken, stop resisting. Fly, little bird, fly."

And I am. I am winged and moving through air and space. I am moving and moved. My eyes see differently what I know; how I perceive is transformed. There is a depth to sky that is new and everywhere shadows that are not shadows. They are like faded colors misted and sprayed out. They move too, slowly or quickly. And I see the ancient ones, sometimes just a face, sometimes just a hand, sometimes whole, sometimes stilled or in slow motion or sometimes faster than my wings carry me. The air is full of life, full of living. The air is prismed and shimmers in the sun's light, realities are glimpsed then replaced by other existences. Even sounds are layered. I am within an unfolding of being cascading only to cascade again only to again cascade. And beneath and above and within all I perceive, there is a single heartbeat that prevails, sustains itself and perhaps all else too, but I cannot know more than I sense, and I do not mind. I am in flight. I am a bird woman, a woman unbound by intent and purpose; I am only flying and aware, a perceiver. I am—. The sky changes; the air becomes just air again and toward me flies a bird I recognize, but it is not Malick; it is not the eagle. It is the hawk, and it heads straight for me.

My breathing changes. I do not know how, but I have intent now; I have purpose. I will do as I have been told. I will take May's words from the first letter and use them. From someplace inside of me that is beyond me too the drum of that one heartbeat intensifies, propels me, and somehow overshadows my intent with its own purpose.

Vicious eyes capture my gaze, but I do not care because I know what I am to do. I will fly through … and I do. At the point where impact is certain there is a spatial undulation; the hawk is gone and I am unwinged suddenly. I am only a woman falling, waving my arms as if they are still wings, feeling silly for that and thankful my earlier flight was close enough to earth, close enough to the wave I am falling into that water is only too cold and too sharp as I hit and pass through, feel myself slowed slowly, then allowing the water to float me, I linger and want to laugh, but remember where I am and kick my feet as I seek a rippled surface. As my head breaks water I remember Maybe told me I would have to get wet, and I have.

$$* \qquad * \qquad * \qquad *$$

Elwood stands on the shore taking the blanket from around his own shoulders to wrap around mine, the expression on his face a blend of amazement and acceptance. I stand before him wrapped in his blanket and remember back into a time when I was smaller and he was younger, and we had stood just so. He had taken Grant and me to swim. It was before the fire.

His words replace my memory with another, "The world turns, does it not? Did you not offer me your blanket not so very long ago, and now here I am able to offer you mine?"

I smile up into his face, "And I am grateful, my uncle."

His smile is offered to me, but his eyes move from mine to the shore to the horizon, "Ah, no, it is I who is most thankful. Almost every night now I find myself here. Morning comes, and I am still here. Nothing rational about it, of course, but somehow I feel closer to them here. Sometimes I believe I can almost see them. Her voice is stronger here, my son's face clearer. On this beach I can believe they are still coming home, just a little late, so I wait for them as I always do." His eyes fill with tears, "God, why? God, why?" He closes his eyes, "Tonight you gave me hope. That sight of the two birds in the air, then the collision, then you falling and for the briefest of moments the air was different, had filled itself with … images and sounds." He opens his eyes and looks into mine, "I gather hope from what I saw. They are out there, my wife, my son; I am not just a crazy old man who watches the shore, searches the horizon; they are out there … waiting for me."

I raise my hand and touch his cheek. Teardrops wet my fingers. I step closer to him and lay my head against his chest. I stop being Leah. I lose myself in his need. I become the wife and son he longs to hold, and again the air changes as time bends down and offers itself to life, and the moment fills itself slowly, allowing an old man a sense of the forever in which he wants to believe.

*   *   *   *

Michael and Puppy sit on the edge of the deck as I park the jeep next to his truck. Michael walks toward me searching me with his eyes. Puppy just smells my shoes and pant legs and after an ear scratch goes to explore the yard.

Michael speaks first, "You're wet."

I say, "Yes."

Then he asks, "Are you going to tell me?"

Again I say, "Yes."

He asks 'when' and I answer 'after a bath'.

He nods his head, "I can wait that long." I begin to walk past him, but he grabs my arm and pulls me to him. I remind him that my clothes are wet. He rubs his hands over my back and then lets them venture a bit lower, "Wet or dry, Leah, I don't mind. I'm reclaiming what's mine."

I look up into his eyes, "It really can last forever, you know?"

The tone of his words is softer, "What can?"

I touch his lips with my fingertips, "What we have. What we feel for each other. It really does not have to ever end."

Michael smiles, "I was counting on that."

I pull his head down to me and breathe words into him like he always does to me, "But, Michael, it really, really can … we can … love each other forever … the emotions do not end."

I kiss his mouth before he can say anything. Then he picks me up in his arms and carries me inside, being very quiet, not wanting to wake sleeping children, and I know my bath will be later, that this moment wants to fill itself in an entirely different manner. I surrender to the moment's momentum as, over and over, waves of emotion move us back and forth, closer and then closer to that shore where lovers rest, restored.

✳   ✳   ✳   ✳

"I want to fly, too," Michael sighs. We are in the living room. We have break-fasted and now watch the kids playing on the deck. I have shared my experiences with him, and his wanting to fly is his first verbalized reaction. I allow him a bit of time to make another comment as the 'I wanna-I wanna-boy-expression' fades slowly from his face. He is tapping on the chair's arm with his fingers, an identifi-able sign that he is organizing his thoughts. I wait, but still he says nothing. I clear my throat and reposition myself in my chair.

Michael looks at me, "What?"

I ask him, "Are you going to tell me what you think?"

He leans back in his chair and rests his head against its high back, "I think for all that we're going through, we're not really getting anywhere. We're idling. We're in neutral. We need a chase scene or a villain that isn't a damn storm, doesn't have wings, and is smaller than the house. I want to sword fight and leap from tall buildings."

I shake my head at him, "You are not being helpful."

He leans forward now and looks at me, "You want me to comment on the philosophical aspects of your conversation with May and your experiences; I understand that, but I'm still mulling it all over. I have nothing intelligent to add to what you shared. Personally, I'd like to know where the wall is. I wouldn't mind if Connor shared with us what he knows. A place name, a little historical background would be good. After all this is over, we can go visit, get postcards and stuff. Family vacation in old Ireland, family vacation in really, really, really old Ireland, but watch out for time shifts and little things like that."

I stand, "Okay, I can see we are done here, so I will just let you know Father Tom and Connor are coming over after mass, and I am going to read May's sec-ond letter. I am just letting you know so you can be here if you want. No pressure though, just a friendly heads-up. Additionally, I will try to arrange a chase scene at some point for your enjoyment, because, after all, your enjoyment is para-mount."

Michael is smiling, "Okay, okay. Calm down, sunshine. You're reminding me of what that bad guy called you before he vaporized?"

My hands are on my hips, "That is not funny, Michael. He said it very ... it was just so ... so cold, like he wished I was dead or something, like I had no value. I do not like name-calling, and I do not like being called that name even jokingly." I pause and take a deep breath then continue, "And, lastly, I do not even know what happened to him. Is he gone for good? I became me again, but he was nowhere around, so where is he?"

Michael stands too, "Just another mystery to add to all the others."

I am thinking aloud, "Maybe Malick will know."

Michael walks to the windows to look outside and waves as the kids notice him standing there, "I'm not sure about those guys. One minute I think Malick is okay then I decide he's not. Same with Connor. I can't get a handle on them. I don't want you to depend on either one of them until we know for sure what their motivations are, but given the way things have gone so far, I'm not sure what kind of clarity we're ever going to have. I think you're just supposed to realize life is ambiguous and unknowable and go for it anyway."

My hands are again on my hips, "I disagree."

Michael turns from the window, "You may."

I cannot decide if he is just trying to antagonize me so we can play verbal games, or if he is being sincere but irritating me anyway, "I was not asking nor do I need your permission."

I know if he was being sincere at some point, he is no longer when he says, "Don't get your panties all in a bunch, babe."

I counter, "Oh, good boy, to at least attempt to glamour up that tacky expression with a bit of alliteration. And in case you have any doubts, my panties are no longer any of your concern and will not be until I forgive you for being such a twit."

Michael is moving toward me, so I move around to the back of the chair putting it is between us, "A twit?"

I can see he is strategizing his next move, "If you even touch me I'll scream."

Michael laughs, "Oh sure, all satisfied after my good loving and now cold as ice."

I smile at him, "Your love making was adequate and in this conversation you ceased to amuse me eons ago."

Michael puts his arms on the chairs arms and leans toward me, "You lie, woman. The love-stuff was great, and I always amuse you."

I shake my head, "You are a boy-man and so terribly self-deluded I will not even attempt to correct your tragic misconceptions."

Michael leans closer, "You're not getting out of here without paying for that, you know?"

I ask, "Really?"

He answers, "Really."

I call out to John Henry and Mary to come inside, and Michael stops leaning toward me, stands and turns toward the door now being opened but not without commenting, "You're a chicken, Leah."

Mary asks, "Why is mom a chicken, da?"

Michael gathers her up in his arms, "She's not; I was just teasing her."

Mary pats his cheeks, "Bad daddy, teasing is not nice."

Michael hangs his head, "You're right, and I will apologize to mommy any minute now."

Mary is still cheek patting and says, "Good daddy."

John Henry smiles knowingly as he closes the door after Puppy comes in and suggests, "Sometimes I think you two play more games than Mary and I do."

Michael grins, "And I, son, am man enough to admit it."

I ignore the numerous comments I could make in response to Michael's statement even though he is looking at me, wanting me to reply. In the momentary silence John Henry asks, "Are we going to church?"

I respond, "I was hoping we could visit the other church today."

Mary combines questions and statements in response, "Can we do yoga before we go? I like that church 'cause they let people dance around in the back and wave flags, but Pastor Danner talks more than Father Tom. Can we do yoga now, or do you and dad have to make-up? Why is Pastor Danner's church so different than Father Tom's? I bet God likes them both, don't you?" Michael sets Mary down; she comes and takes my hand then leads me into her room to change her clothes as she continues her comments, "How can God be everywhere at the same time? Maybe he uses angels to help him. Maybe we should have a snack after yoga and before church 'cause I think I might be getting hungry. I want to wear my blue yoga pants and my white sea horse shirt. I want—"

I listen to the rest of her words; they dance around me like butterflies gone a bit wild, while in my mind I see myself listing thoughts and asking questions of May; May's words, Mary's words, and my own words, perhaps too solid to be butterflies, are only syllabled emotions, inflected I-wants, prefixed there-ares, rooted-questions, coined-certainties.

I am on an edge again standing in Mary's room watching thoughts suddenly shadowed by firelight and somehow brighter for it. I see myself standing in front of a burning house, behind me a little-boy-Grant, but I am not a little girl; the Leah there is me now, but I am really not there at all, or here, for that matter. Instead I am on a shore standing with Elwood, our eyes focused on a horizon that is never present tense. I gasp as anguish uses sharp claws to work its way through me. Then I am falling through a darkness I know. It is tunneled this darkness; it ends in fire.

*   *   *   *

Shal sits. Brigid stands. The bird that was a man that stood on my deck and as a bird again tried to fly into me, tried to crash against me, lies on the cold stone floor. I can see his leg is bandaged through the tear in his pants. His ankle is encircled by a metal band connected by a thick chain to its mount on the wall. His eyes, reflecting the fire's flames, glare into mine. His lips, set in a grim line, move only to sneer as he rises up on one elbow; the movement causing him pain barely changes his expression. This man with fire in his eyes is both hotter than the fire and colder than the stone. Shal's voice whispers 'yes' in my mind. I turn to look into his eyes.

I use my words instead of my thoughts to communicate with him, "You are taking prisoners, now?"

Shal still does not speak but answers me by sending his words into my own thoughts, "He is your prisoner, Leah, not mine. I simply hold him for you until you tell me what you want done with him."

I ask, "How can you hold him? Can he not just fly away if he chooses?"

Before Shal can answer me, the man with the dark hair and darker eyes, speaks, "One cloaked in ignorance has been chosen to fight for you this time, Shal. The course may not be as set as you would like to believe."

Shal's facial expression mirrors the man's. They look upon each other with such animosity I step back, "I believe in only one thing, Bantok; you more than anyone should know that. And I would add, brother, she overcame you easily enough."

Bantok's words are whispered in a room well heated by the fire in its center, but they chill me nonetheless, "This battle will intensify; she is weak and slow to act and filled with doubts. The fire calls to her now more than ever. She will fail; we will have her. Your reign will be over; my time will come."

Shal's one word response flames the fire, "Never."

Bantok looks at me and speaks, but his words never reach me. Shal has raised his hand and although Bantok's lips move and I know he is speaking, silence conceals them. He glares again at Shal then lays back down, closing his eyes.

I look at Shal and Brigid. She appears smaller as he somehow seems larger to me, like a flame fanned. His exchange with Bantok has—.

"I can fill this room, Leah. I can stand taller than the tallest oak. Space defines me no longer. Time and its moments are all that can contain me, and even then my thoughts prevail against those constraints. My thoughts reach out to you in your time, do they not?"

I ask him, "And to my students? They think they saw you as you spoke, but I believe it was only your thoughts sent out. May came to me in her form but cannot send her thoughts to me while you can send thoughts but not come to me in your form. May died. I am assuming you did not. Why is what you and May can do different?"

Shal no longer speaks to me from across the room but stands before me, "Why anything, Leah? Ask a different question."

I look over at Bantok, for no other reason that to escape the intensity of Shal's eyes so focused on my own, "Why did you—." I stop myself and reword my question, "Is he really your brother?"

Shal does not answer me until I look back into his eyes, "We share father and mother, and a now silent sister, but he is my enemy more than he is anything else."

The instant I stop fighting against the drawing intensity of Shal's eyes I am overwhelmed; images choke me; conflicting emotions flood me, scents overpower me. A heartbeat prevails over all. Another heartbeat, closer than the other, beats out of time with my own, and I cannot breathe. I gasp for air as Shal pulls me against his chest and breathes into my ear, "Behind that door where you have placed your own memories I have placed mine; we will be of one mind, one purpose. My life is yours in images; my purpose will be yours as well … the momentum builds, turns in on itself and out again, each time it breathes deeper, from a deeper place; the present is attempting to spread itself out to cover the past; move, Leah. Time will narrow itself until its edges cut and life bleeds out. Move, Leah. Take to be taken. Go to the altar before it's too late."

There is no gentle release from him; he pushes me back, and I think I will fall, but I do not. I am locked in stillness, inside me images from a past I do not know whisper to be let out as my eyes refocus; Michael's eyes look into mine. I look to see where I am. I stand in Mary's room as I did before, but she is not here.

Michael does not reach out to touch me. He is quiet. I ask, "What's wrong? Was something different this time? Where is Mary?"

Michael replies slowly, "You left, Leah; you were gone this time. Mary said you were standing here then you weren't."

I start to walk around Michael, "Where is she? I want to explain, let her know I am okay."

Michael's hand stops me, "Father Tom is talking with her and with John Henry. He is explaining. Father Tom sent Connor to go for a walk."

I look at the wall where Mary's clock hangs. It is two in the afternoon. It was eight in the morning when Mary and I came in to change her clothes. "This makes no sense. The times before I did not leave ... I mean I did, but ... and they lasted only seconds or minutes at the most. It did not feel like that much happened to take that long. I am not understanding."

Michael leans into me, "Are you supposed to? Are you supposed to understand all this, Leah? Or do you have to just move, go for it? Read the letters and do whatever it is you're supposed to do. Get done with this."

I am stilled by his words. His words are like Maybe's and May's and Shal's. Move. They keep telling me to move, but I do not know where or how. They tell me to forget the why, but I still do not know the where or the how. And inside my head, Shal's memories fight for space with my own. I stand before that door I know. I reach my hand out to it, but I do not want to open the door ... see his images, feel his emotions. Would I learn his purpose even if I did? Should I open the door? I do not want life too bleed out or time to get more sharp, more cutting, than it already is.

Michael shakes me gently and whispers, "No way, not now, you're not going to get lost in your own thoughts. Do you hear me?"

I focus again, my eyes on his, "I am not deaf."

Michael runs his hands through his hair, "Look, I'm sorry, but disappearing in front of Mary, that's too much."

Tears fill my eyes, "I frightened my own daughter."

Michael reassures me, "You know Mary, and she's young enough to just sort of take it all in and not make too much of it. She was pretty matter-of-fact about it actually."

Worry has a hold of me, "And John Henry, what about him?"

Michael smiles, but it is a sad smile, "He just looked to me, waited to see how I was going to respond. I was calm ... on the outside. We just sat on the couch and waited. Puppy laid on my feet. The house was so quiet. We were all so still. It was sort of comforting or maybe the not knowing was just numbing. We sat there like that until Father Tom and Connor showed up. I explained. Father Tom told me he knew how to handle the situation. I let him. You came back. We're standing here talking. End of story."

I sigh and wish it were the end of the story, "I need to read May's letter, but I do not want to send the kids away."

Michael shakes his head, "Oh yeah, let's keep them here with us where they're safe and nothing strange happens. I don't think so, Leah. I already called my mom; she and dad are on their way. Matilda is coming with them, but she is staying with us to hear the letter. Father Tom says she may have information he doesn't."

I reach out and put my hand on his chest, "You feel far away from me."

Michael closes his eyes and then opens them, and I think perhaps my tears from earlier that did not fall are in his eyes now, but he only says, "I'm sorry."

I ask, "You cannot move closer to me?"

One tear escapes and falls; he raises his hand to wipe it away, but I stop him. I raise my hand and touch his cheek and then my fingertips are wet again, but unlike Springmoon I have no white stone to offer in return, to make the moment somehow softer than it is, to mark the sorrow and turn it into something else. So as I did with Elwood I move closer to Michael and lay my head against his chest. I put my arms around him. I stop being Leah. I become only comfort to his need, and the air changes as time bends down offering itself to life, and the moment fills itself slowly; time widens if only for an instant; the present covers the past easily, my heartbeat in time with Michael's heartbeat, in time with that other heartbeat coming from far off and from within, and we are moved in our stillness to deeper stillness. We are only a whisper apart again. He calls my name, but I cannot respond to it.

Shal's voice has opened the door, and I am flooded with images. Too fast they pass until, as if chosen, one lingers, lays itself down, pressing itself into my perception: green hills darkened by dusk's light, a golden altar, Brigid stands before me, I see her tears. There is blood on her lips and blood on her hands. There is blood on the flowing white gown she wears, blood darkening the ends of her hair. I hear her sorrow sent out from deep within her, and the sound she makes is … shattering.

Michael's voice refocuses my vision; I can see him again. I say, "Yes?"

His voice is soft and close, "Your arms around me felt different somehow. Did you feel the difference?"

We step back from each other to look into eyes, and I say, "Perhaps we have never had to come together from that far before."

He apologizes again, "I'm sorry. I don't know why, but I couldn't help what I was feeling; the emotions were not mine, but they were. Loving you did not feel like an option or a choice I had. You weren't mine anymore. It doesn't make sense, I know, but that's the best I can explain it, and I don't want to ever feel that way again."

I want to reassure him, but I can't. I am looking down at my hands. There is blood on them.

✳   ✳   ✳   ✳

I am hoping Michael did not see the blood. I am hoping I turned quickly enough. I ran to the bathroom, turned on the faucet and quickly put my hands under water warming as seconds speed toward the next moment. The harsh deep red of blood mixes with water and turns a softer pink as it disappears down the drain. I cup water in my hands and pour it over the faucet where my crimson fingerprints threaten to give me away. I pull tissues from their box and wipe the sink's edges as Michael walks into the bathroom.

He apologizes again, and after I dry my hands he holds me in his arms. I want to tell him everything, but I do not; my heart will not let me take the chance of him moving away from me again. Keeping secrets from him seems so wrong, but the situation is … insane, and I have made my choice, thinking perhaps later I will tell him, perhaps later, but then the image of Brigid returns and the sensation of the blood on my own hands returns, and I wonder if the ending of this may be more than I can bear. I wonder if standing, year after year, before my house as it burns with the bodies of my family captured in the fire's flames, feeling my heart break again and again, may seem … the less difficult of the two. I begin to think about May telling me to go through that moment completely so it can truly become only a memory in relation to Bantok telling Shal the fire calls to me—.

I hear a car in the driveway. Michael sighs, "You should come and tell the kids goodbye, so they can see you are okay."

I say 'yes' and move toward the door, but Michael stops me, "I love you, Leah."

I say I love him too then walk into the living room as John Henry and Mary walk through the door. I sit down on the couch, and they come to me. There is nothing held back in the way they throw their arms around me and press their little bodies up against mine. There is nothing held back in my response to them.

John Henry is the first to speak, "Don't worry about us, mom. You just take care of what you need to do. We'll be fine." He pauses and then adds, "So will you, mom. You'll be fine too." I agree with him.

Mary stands in front of me and rests her hand on my shoulder, "We'll do yoga tomorrow, mommy." I say yes to her. Hank and Katy wave from the door. I wave back. Father Tom and Connor stand on the edge of the deck. Michael walks his father and the kids to Hank's truck. Puppy whines a bit as he watches Michael lift

John Henry and Mary into their seats and fasten their seatbelts. I go to the window and wave to them. They wave back, and then they are gone. I watch as Father Tom goes to Michael and speaks to him as Connor and Matilda remain on the deck.

Malick entering the yard from the path by the lake does not even surprise me, and I think to myself perhaps I am getting used to walking through darkness up steep paths to stand on sheer edges, or perhaps I am just too tired to be surprised by life and her timing. Or perhaps I want only to be like Springmoon and lay in strong unchangeable arms and know I am safe, or perhaps I want to know from sorrow comes joy, that it has always and will always be that way. Yes, that is it, that is what I want to know as I look at May's second letter on the table waiting for me, that out of the ashes of sorrow, love, faith, and hope blossom into forever. I hold on to that thought even as Brigid's ancient blood covered lips cry out into the present, denying it.

Chapter EIGHT

"I'm not denying it, but I won't justify it either." Malick's words fill the room even though they are quietly said.

Michael's words crash against them, "We don't merit an explanation?"

Malick responds, "That's not what I said. I said I wouldn't explain where I go, because my whereabouts are none of your business. As long as I'm here when I am needed, I won't explain or justify my absences. That's what I said."

Michael persists, "And if we wanted to contact you, if Leah needed you or if Father Tom needed you, then what?"

Malick looks at me, "Leah knows how to reach me, because she knows Shal can always reach me." He looks at Father Tom, "I don't believe Father Tom knows where Connor is every minute of the day, and Father Tom has managed to exist without us for a number of years," Malick pauses and looks at Michael again, "so again, I'm unsure of the soundness of your reasoning. Maybe you're just tired of following your wife around and having little to no control. Maybe you just want or need to be aggravated at someone, and since you don't really know me, but I do play a part, which means my choices affect you and yours whether you like it or not, I am, to you, an annoyance." As Malick has been speaking his tone has softened, "To be honest, and I am, even when it serves no purpose but its own, I can relate to how you're feeling. I wouldn't like what you're feeling either, but there's little to nothing about this to like, so we're sort of stuck with each other until it's over."

Michael's expression has become more thoughtful. He shrugs his shoulders, runs his hands through his hair, and almost smiles as he says, "You could be right about some of that, or maybe even all of it. I was out of line." Malick seems to accept Michael's implied apology.

Connor comments, "And isn't that just like the good men that you both are not to have to dive into each other with fists but instead to work through the emotions all nice and peaceful like."

Father Tom sighs, "I'm wondering if we shouldn't get started. Leah seems ready to read, and although I read the letters before they were sealed, I have to admit some of May's insights have become vague in my memory."

Matilda smiles and agrees, "I find myself having the same thought, Father. I find myself wondering what my mind has created to replace what I've forgotten so I can link the lines and phrases I do remember. The letters have become shorter and shorter over time."

I smile when Matilda's eyes find mine, but I am not focusing on anyone's words but May's. They are calling to me; I am tired of waiting and want to do as I have been told; I want to … move and be moved through the moments with purpose and intent and with full acceptance my only certainty is a fluctuating faith in the belief all will be well. I sit in my chair and Michael takes the chair across from me. Father Tom and Matilda and Connor share the couch. Malick is the last to take a seat and chooses to sit on the raised hearth of the fireplace. I think for a moment about asking him if he will be comfortable there, but decide against it, realizing I really do not care and would only be inquiring to be polite, to play hostess, and I do not feel like being polite or playing at anything.

I want to press my face against the pages, rub them against my skin, inhale their fragrance but I do not do either; I just begin reading, my words floating out into this moment, her words stretched out from a thousand moments ago.…

"My Leah, so many thoughts wander through my mind. How much time did you take between this letter and the last? How much of the child I knew is in the woman who reads these words of mine? You may not remember her as well as I do, so I will take a few lines, one small part of the moment to remind you of her. I will remind you when you were eight your good mother and kind step-father were becoming concerned about your handling of what they liked to call, and you learned to call, life matters, the making of decisions that had lasting or at least lingering consequences. You would not be rushed. When asked you would say quite strongly you would not pull or push against the moment. You said instead you would wait and watch for signs and then, and only then, would you know what you were supposed to do. You said doing so gave God a chance to have his way in your life. Do you remember feeling that way, little one? Is there still a bit of that child in the woman you have become or have the days

and months and years changed your heart and mind about life matters and about God? Do you still stand on the shore, your arms stretched out like the wings of a bird, and let the breeze move you? Are you still watching and waiting for signs? How I wish I could hold you again. Perhaps I have, but I cannot know that now, so I will turn from these matters of my heart to the matter at hand, which is of course a matter of heart also, and a life matter, to be sure. To that I will go, but once more I remind you of how much love surrounded you, and pray the same still holds true for you. Love, Leah, regardless of situation and circumstance, in that never allow yourself to be moved; be steadfast, for in the fabric of life, love is the strongest thread. Let life and the thousand altars it constructs in our lives to honor love be served by you, my Leah, sweet heart of my heart, dear blood of my blood.

And blood began it all really. Blood of birth, blood of growing, blood of love, blood of deceit, blood of death. So red the first and last images, so torn the hearts involved, but I must take you to the beginning of the beginning or my words will confuse you. Remember in the space and time of one lifetime there are many beginnings, but the beginning of the beginning is the process of physical birth, from conception to first breath, and through all the blood of life flows. And although the Tuatha De Danaan were very spiritual beings, they conceived and birthed in the same way as we do, and Brigid and her twin sister Taen lived quite peacefully with each other within the tiny womb-room offered by their mother. Now immortals, as I believe Brigid's father and mother were, put a great store in little room womb behavior, especially with twins. I don't need to be reminding you of other stories from a variety of cultures documenting twins struggling against each other before birth, but Brigid and Taen knew no such conflict; they were at peace in their cocoon of flesh and blood and spirit. They were born under a clear night sky lit by dancing stars, a moon at its fullest, and a woven spread, crimson red, so no one would know which babe arrived first. Know that not a sound did either make until both lay, cords still joining them to Danu, their mother, side by side, and then, and only then, did they sing out their loud birth cry in perfect unison. At their harmonious beckon the spread was lifted, and all those there to witness watched as Dagda, their proud father, cut the cords simultaneously. And so they were not first and second born but sisters of equal standing, and so they were raised, and so they grew. There are those that say there were three birthed and not two; for the Tuatha De Danaan twins are three because of the special bond of relationship existing between them, that bond considered an entity in and of itself, a thing to be nurtured and raised up and maintained.

So they lived as they were born, abiding sisters, equally adept and well trained in all the arts and skills considered essential to the immortals who walked the Emerald Isle in harmony and peace. Of course, their lives on the island were not always peace-

ful; humans, 'invaders' if you will, arrived and were defeated countless times, and sometimes not easily, but among the sisters there was no strife or jealousy or any of the arrogance that births those small, clenching emotions which push humans, and immortals, to brutal acts of selfishness. For so many years this was true. And so it was and so it would have been except as the Tuatha De Danaan became more and more spiritual, matters of the earth became more and more distant, until one day a new people arrived on the shores of the island, and when the Tuatha De Danaan walked down from the high places to observe them, most of the new arrivals did not see them, and those who did covered their faces and prayed or ran screaming of ghosts.

Not wanting to forsake through their own disuse all that made the island such a good home, the Tuatha De Danaan allowed the new ones to make the island their own, but not the whole island because there were special places where the Tuatha De Danaan still walked and celebrated, and those places they would not give up. These new people to the island, the Celts, quickly learned where they could and could not go, because when one of them ventured into a place the Tuatha De Danaan had deemed their own, strange and unexplainable things would happen, and so the word spread about these places and the boundaries became known and accepted.

But don't you know there will always be a few in every population group who want to understand what others are quite content to let be a mystery, and so it was that among the Tuatha De Danaan and among the Irish Celts there were accidental and then planned meetings between individuals of the two groups. And because of this it was discovered if a Tuatha De Danaan stayed in the physical realm for a prolonged period of time his or her physical form became more distinct, more knowable by mortals.

And all this would have been fine, but among the Tuatha De Danaan and among the mortal humans attractions occurred and children were born, mortal immortals, who understood both realms, both ways of being, but were always either less than or more than depending on the environment in which they found themselves. Most accepted their bittersweet fate, the eternal sweep of their awareness coupled with the limits of their abilities, but some did not. And because these dissatisfied creatures had access to both worlds neither world was safe from them. These few dissatisfied creatures created such dissension and parented such hatred and distrust that between Brigid and Taen they drove a stake so deeply into the hearts of each that life was sacrificed upon its own altar, and the very fabric of time was torn.

The fact of this would be known to all except in the fifth century Christians brought their beliefs to the island. It was not difficult for the Irish to understand how Adam's and Eve's one choice could cast its shadow over all time. Easy to understand how forward into the future that choice spread easily, but also know because our minds decipher for us, that choice cast its shadow back into time also; we perceive the reality of the past through the present's filter. Also because the writing of the Tuatha de Danaan was Ogham and considered sacred, its use bound in ritual, the history most read of those times was recorded by Christian scribes who consciously and subconsciously altered history through their choice of words on a page. Adam and Eve are known, but Brigid and Taen and their people became mere legends, characters in fairy tales, images reflected in dreamscapes, but think now how real dreamscapes can be when one is in them, and know that reality is not a windowpane to see through or a chalk line to mark evidence—it is! It is prismed, multifaceted, and the validity of dreamstate is as real as the validity of the accepted tangible state labeled 'reality'. Limits and understandings become self-defined based on cultural mores and values, and most will accept those confines, but there are always a few who fly against the accepted, as I wrote earlier; there are always a few. And within those few some will work for the good of all and some will work for self gain. Shal and Bantok personify this choice.

Remember too how true the adage, 'power corrupts and absolute power corrupts absolutely.' The old ways were changing. Immortals moving through the prism of realities freely became less acceptable. What was deemed to be good became based on this people's or that people's theocracy: one chosen people choosing one god or a set of gods; one place of reward or punishment or a stratum of such places; one birth and one death or a series of births and deaths; one prophet-teacher's words invalidating all other prophet-teachers' words. Human awareness of truth splintered, became one room in the great palace of life and its various entries heavily guarded by this faction or that faction. Life's altars were torn down if they did not honor this belief or that belief; the God of Creation marginalized to fit within the pages of this people's holy book or that people's holy book. This is the reason the Tuatha de Danaan did not allow the physical manifestation of their thoughts and beliefs to be written carelessly. As action is born out of thought and emotion and becomes a physical reality, so written words are born and become a physical reality. Words become foundations, sails, ramparts. Written words were called 'shapers', because words can either be tools or weapons, depending on how they are used and dependent on the motivations of whose hands hold them. Once again, Shal and Bantok are examples.

Shapers in the hands of the unscrupulous destroy perceived truth as effectively as a blade or a gun destroys human life. Recorded history has been shaped, is shaped, to meet desired ends. What is read as fact is only shaped perceptions. But Leah, what is, is. Life will not be shaped. It may allow itself to be handled, may allow itself to be pliable, but it will not allow permanent alteration; life is alive, not a state of being, and the God of Life is God and will not be formed by human perceptions, emotions, desires, or words. See all the religions and all the philosophies as rivers and streams, and then see God of Life as ocean and write that down, choose words to describe the mystery of 'all' as a knowable 'it'. Realize that what can't be done is attempted none-theless, and so the pieces or stands perceived have been deemed 'all'. From this realiza-tion I offer you freedom comes, winged and wild yet harmonious in its rightful place within a moment of being, just as when the water of the river finds the water of the ocean and is within the ocean but is still the water of the river.

Look always for the blade of grass that has found its way through the seemingly impenetrable mass of manmade concrete. Look always for the space created in stone by wind and water. Truth is equally found in the discernment of the tangible blade of grass and in the intangible space. God of Life breathes, has heartbeat, flourishes, and human words cannot equal that, cannot define that, cannot decipher that. Knowing is spiritual, beyond words. Knowing is diving through or flying through past motiva-tions, memories, or desires, beyond the edges of moment into the heart of the God of Life. You will never understand why you are until you understand who you are. You will never understand life's purpose without honoring the sanctity of living. The river is not the ocean, but the river lives within the ocean without boundaries; you cannot be the omniscient God, but you can live within God's omniscience without bound-aries, time and space merely markers, road signs.

Look to see and in seeing know, without documentation or filtration; breathe life in, breathe life out; let God of Life move through you like water and wind through stone; a space will be made in you, I promise, but you must open yourself to the process, willing to have preconceptions ripped away; take the unknown path to be taken up into the arms of life. Take to be taken. Take Brigid's hand; find your way through her silence, her unworded renderings of what was. Look to see. See to know. Be taken. Offer blood for blood, Leah. Trust me. My love wraps itself around you, gives you wings. And although I know I shouldn't, I must ask you to remind your father of who he is and could be and that new choices can change old choices. Save him, for me, if you can. You will know how, Leah; trust the moment to show you, and when the moment appears to deny you, read between the lines, angel.

Always and forever, your May"

* * * *

Michael whispers, "Blood for blood?" I have no response for him.

Connor is shaking his head, "Jesus is the Son of God, the Christ, our Savior. He is more than prophet-teacher." I have no response for him.

Father Tom takes Matilda's hand, "New choices transmuting old choices, I had forgotten that somehow. That is offering more than forgiveness. What a rich hope."

Matilda sighs, "And somehow I've made life smaller than it is without meaning to. Without meaning to I've stopped being amazed. How did I slip so easily into the ritual of the daily and forget the ritual of always?" She pauses, closing her eyes as she whispers, "Thank you, May, for reminding me."

Michael repeats himself, "Blood for blood?"

Malick stands, "Don't get hung up on the details, Michael; there has already been blood and she survived. Trust the process. That goes for you too, Connor, don't act shocked; you knew what was coming; you knew what you'd hear. You chose to be a part of this knowing how the people believed with whom you'd be involved, so no righteous indignation now. You're here to assist Father Tom at the church; do that, so he can do what he needs to do. All any of us can do is stay in the moment and do what needs to be done. We have to get through this; we have to help Leah. We have to be aware of any change even if it's a small one; we have to respond, have to move or pray or just carry on." He pauses and looks at me, "What are you feeling right now?"

I look from Malick to Michael as I speak, "I have seen her, seen Brigid, at the altar, or more accurately I have seen her walking away from the altar. She has blood on her hands, her face, her clothing, even the ends of her hair."

Michael asks, "What was on the altar?"

I share what I know, "My focus was on Brigid only, so I cannot tell you more than that about her except even though I did not recognize the place I know where the place is."

Michael nods his head, "Within the circle of the stone wall?"

I say, "Yes." I turn to Connor, "You said you wanted to tell us about that place. Will you do that now?" I look at Malick, "I know you said the information would only be a distraction, but I want to know its history. I do not really care about its exact location. Obviously it is in Ireland. I would guess it is one of those places the Tuatha De Danaan claimed as their own, a thin place. I can surmise all that, but what I want to know is what happened there in the past and if Connor's telling will be different than yours or Father Tom's?" I look at Matilda, "Do you know its history too?"

Matilda looks away from me, glancing first at Connor then at Malick, "I believe Connor should start the telling and then the rest of us can add information Connor may not be willing to share."

A look of sadness changes Connor's expression, "I can tell what you will tell. I can tell the history according to the old ones unaltered by the written record made by Christian scribes." He looks from Matilda to Malick, "And in my telling I mean no disrespect or denial of who Jesus is."

Malick nods at him, "Then tell it, Connor; perhaps the history of the place and the ones who made it theirs will provide Leah with something she will need."

Connor leans back and closes his eyes as his voice draws us in, "The beginning of beginnings is creation: the emptiness of space filled, breath of God breathed out into to make earth and sky, vegetation and animals, man and woman. Cultural renderings do not change the essence of that, even scientists raise their hands in dismay, bow their heads to the miracle of life. It says in the Word man was created in God's likeness, and the first ones, the first humans, lived long lives. The Bible gives them no godlike characteristics other than long lives, but the old ones, the old storytellers of Ireland, speak of the beginning differently. They tell that the God of Life breathed out and gave his consciousness form; that those who first appeared were godlike, were immortals; they walked and talked, communed, with the God of Life; they had children who had children who had children and none died, but it was realized that the children of the children of the children were more earth-bound than their parents or grandparents, and they aged. They aged very slowly, still living hundreds of years, but the third generation was not immortals in the same sense as the first two generations, and so it went until the seventh generation when the first death occurred. Blood ran, and for the briefest of moments God's breath, which is life, stopped, and time, which is God's awareness of life, paused. You can imagine, I'm sure, the effect. It was like the proverbial stone thrown into still water … there were ripples … but if the water is God's omnipresent awareness, which has no boundaries, then it must be realized the ripple ripples on … forever, and because the world is a spiritual-physical place a cycle began wherein that which we call time flows freely but narrows markedly as the ripple's circle widens. The paradox of the widening leading always to a narrowing never made sense to me, but I know Leah has already experienced the cardinal response given to 'why' questions, and because I don't need to understand to tell the story, I will just continue. The generations which followed became more physical and less spiritual until the spiritual became unknowable and only a yearning for something not remembered but missed. And so it was according to the old ones who were … are the immortals, who become more and more of the spirit with the passage of time, many of whom are beyond recognition to those of us who are still earth-bound. The place where the first death occurred is where the altar stands, where they say the God of Life … paused within the context of one moment, which somehow denied the next, and stopped time. Another paradox, to be sure, and as beyond me as the first mentioned. The place resonates with a power that fills human hearts with itself and, dependent on the person filled, motivates thoughts and behaviors. In this place, at the altar, the first murder occurred, and since then countless murders. So it was then, so it is now, life calling out to life, blood calling out to blood."

Connor only briefly pauses, but Michael seizes the silence, his voice loud, "She's not a sacrifice."

Father Tom holds up his hand, "Stop. Right there, stop. You're jumping to conclusions, Michael. There is more to the story."

Michael does not back down, "Yeah, well, skip to the part where it says she does not have to make a sacrifice."

Malick comments patiently, "There's a difference between her sacrificing herself and her making a sacrifice."

Michael shakes his head, "Not enough. And the continual reference to blood is ... making me crazy."

Malick responds, "Blood is blood, of course, but blood can also be symbolic. Blood is life, so blood could refer to the honoring or dishonoring of life. You don't know enough to understand."

I ask, "Will we ever know enough to understand?"

Malick answers my question with a question, "What did May write about understanding and about knowledge?"

I remember her words easily and repeat them, "Knowing is spiritual."

Malick prompts, "And so what does that mean?"

I look at Michael and can see that he wants to respond to Malick's question, so I say, "Tell us, husband."

Michael runs his hands through his hair then says, "It means Leah will know what to do without having any precognition. She will know because of who she is. She won't necessarily know why, but she will know how."

Malick wants more from Michael than a statement of comprehension, "And does realizing that calm you at all regarding what Leah is called to do?"

Michael looks at me, "Calm me? No. The only thing making this whole thing doable for me is the fact we have no choice, so moving forward gets us closer to it being over. The most difficult part for me is Leah could be in real danger. If it was me instead of her, the whole thing would be easier, but it's not, and she is my wife."

Matilda gracefully, but slowly, rises from the sofa. She walks over to Michael and even more slowly lowers herself to her knees. She takes his large hand in her two small ones and looks into his eyes. Then she raises his hand to her lips and kisses it, "I honor the sacrifice you make in this. I am thankful for your strength and faith in life; many husbands have not been willing to walk through this with their wives, but you are willing, and I am grateful."

Michael takes his hand from her and touches her cheek, grandmother and grandson looking into each other's eyes needing no words. Then Michael leans his forehead against hers for a moment before he helps her up and Matilda returns to her seat as Michael asks, "You said husbands willing to walk with their wives. Does that mean women are the ones always called to do whatever it is Leah has been called to do? And are they always wives?"

Matilda nods, "Always the chosen is a wife."

Michael asks what I have learned not to ask, "Why?"

Matilda looks at me and smiles, but does not refuse him, "The story will tell you, so I could answer your question for you, but the answer by itself is less compelling than when it takes its shape within a context, so I will let Connor continue."

Connor clears his throat dramatically, crosses and uncrosses his legs comically, and then pretends to fall asleep, snoring briefly before opening one eye to look around at each one of us as he says, "Oh, yes, of course, the story." He pauses and looks a bit disgruntled, "A bit of a wee reaction would have been good by my way of thinking, a tiny ha-ha or something of that nature would have warmed my heart. But no matter, I'll be straight to draggin' the story out of old Ireland's cellar to plop it down here on this nice table before you without another word."

I say, "Yes, please, and thank you."

Connor nods and begins, "Brigid and Taen, Shal and Bantok were second generation immortals. Together they built the altar to honor life, to celebrate the All. The construction of the altar marked the passing of leadership from Danae and Dagda, who, along with other first generation immortals the All had placed at different locations around the earth, were taking less and less interest in the physical world. This change in leadership for the Tuatha occurred during the seventh generation, so be remembering by this generation most of the Tuatha were totally mortal. Among these mortals the two sets of twins were deemed gods. Among the immortals the two sets of twins were greatly esteemed and had precedence over other second generation immortals because they were the children of the first male and female, Dagda and Danu, who had the All to themselves in a way no other immortal had experienced. But I need to go back further than that if what happens later is to make sense to you, so I'm just going to spit it out," Connor pauses and looks at Malick before he continues, "the All made Danu first, not Dagda, and here it gets real interesting, sort of a twist on one of my favorite stories: through Danu Dagda was conceived. That, of course, makes Danu both mother and wife. According to the old ones, she is the most revered among the immortals. Dagda, her son-husband, stands beside her, but among the first generation immortals Danu is second only to the All. Now remember how Brigid and Taen were born and raised, side by side as equals, and then realize the same was planned for the birth of Danu's second set of twins, but something happened, something as small as a breeze changed reality forever."

Connor pauses and looks around, but none of us speak, so he comments, "I'm of a mind that storytelling should not be a dry adventure, that a bit of the brew would be—"

Malick interrupts him, "Tell the story, Connor, or I will."

It is obvious Connor wants to respond, but Father Tom lays his hand on Connor's hand and Connor's storytelling begins again, "Danu gave birth in the same place she had given birth before, in the same place where the All had breathed her into being, in the same place where Dagda was birthed. She lay there, family and friends gathered around her, under oak and rowan trees that shaded her from the bright midday sun, the birthing spread of crimson red over her lower body. With Dagda sitting next to her and holding her hand and with Brigid and Taen sitting next to her on the other side doing the same, Danu birthed the first child and just as the second was being born a breeze lifted the spread and Dagda, Brigid, and Taen saw the light blond hair of the first child born, and so the dark haired child born second would always be second. In matters of love and nurturing treatment offered to the twin sons was no different, but birth rights are birth rights, and Shal would always be first son-third child and Bantok would always be second son-fourth child.

"The immortals had no preconceived notions of male-female-based characteristics; sons and daughters were given access to training in all aspects of their culture: weaving, storytelling, gathering and preparation of food, carpentry, masonry, jewelry making, warrior training, to name only a few. I should tell you also animals were not killed for food for at least another four generations. Even the harvesting of plants and of fruits and vegetables was not undertaken callously. The old ones make it very clear every aspect of creation is God breathed, so everything is part of the All and to be honored; there was no hierarchy of being established in the hearts and minds of humans until perceptions of the spiritual realm became separate from the physical one. The circle of life had not been broken and stretched out into a chain. So with that bit of explanation given, I will return to Shal and Bantok. The boys were inseparable and like their sisters excelled in every undertaking. It is noted by the old ones, however, that Bantok resented his older brother for his birthright and Brigid for being the favored of Danu. It's also noted Brigid was favored because of her fair mindedness in all situations."

Connor pauses and shakes his head, "Ironic, isn't it, that because Brigid was most fair in her thinking she was most favored by some but resented by others? After Brigid was chosen by Danu to be queen of the Tuatha, Bantok's resentment birthed itself in Taen. Brigid tried to remedy the situation by dividing the leadership responsibility between her sister and brothers, but Bantok and Taen only took advantage of Brigid's kindness by creating dissension among the people. Shal tried also to speak peace into the situation, but peace was not what Bantok and Taen sought. Danu and Dagda intervened, but the ways of the world had become so almost foreign to them by then they chose or were only able to delay the inevitable. The mother-wife and her son-husband couldn't make half of their progeny behave, and of course the female Brigid was chosen over the male Shal to lead the Tuatha, because she was wombed, a carrier of life, and the All's first creation."

Connor pauses and is about to continue when Malick stands, shoves his hands in the pockets of his pants and says, "Your tone has an edge I don't like."

Connor stands and begins to stretch his arms, but it is only a gesture, his eyes never leave Malick's eyes, "Really? Does it seem just a bit unnatural?"

Malick responds quietly but firmly, "No more or less than an all powerful father-god sacrificing his virgin-born-son when the all powerful father-god could have taken care of business in a thousand other ways."

Michael and I look at each other, but Father Tom stands and speaks before either of us can intervene, "Are we to have another religious war right here right now?" He is looking first at one of them then at the other, "You embarrass me in front of Matilda and Leah and Michael. You shame me. That you would allow your own opinions to override the purpose of this moment; that the rivalry you have fed and fed upon since you were boys would be allowed to exert itself over your purpose for being here now shames me. I am the one who thought you should come here to help us—"

Malick interrupts him, "Do you honestly believe your request was the only reason we came here, or that either of us would not have come anyway, requested by others? Old man, think about what is at stake here, and realize we are each and all only pawns. Our parts are smaller, but we are being used as much as Leah or Michael in all this. You have to realize that. And all the storytelling and opinions and assistance in the world are not going to change or make easier what will happen one way or another now or in the next cycle, through Leah or through the next chosen. Bantok will die; his influence removed from this realm forever. The old ways, the new ways, Danu, Jesus, Buddha, or World War Three are not going to change that. I'm more a soldier than a peacekeeper, and I'm most definitely not a nanny for the inept, no matter who asks me to be one." Malick looks at Connor, "Tell your story, boy, mark it, like a dog in a neighbor's yard, with your sarcasm and innuendoes. I'm leaving."

And he does. He walks across the room without a backward glance at anyone and out the door. Connor remains standing. Father Tom and Matilda both have their eyes closed. Michael and I look at each other again, and I feel like I should raise my arms to fan the tension filled air out of my way, but I do not. I am trying to get Connor's words from the story and Malick's words from his last statements to behave, to peacefully sort themselves out, to settle down and line up meaningfully so I can look at them, search them for intent and examine them for background information. I will ask each: did you come alone or do you have attachments I cannot see? are you good witches or bad witches? are you clothed in good intentions or are your obvious intentions secondary to your hidden ones? But they will not cooperate, will not settle down and behave, so I open the door to my present thinking and grab a broom that just happens to materialize and sweep and push and tap none too gently until each is in and the door closed. Of course, there is a continual tapping at my conscious to be let back in to take their place in my mind, but I am ignoring them for the moment. I lean against the door to catch my breath and say to them, you should have come in twos and threes, because coming in mass as you did has overwhelmed me; coming disguised as a history lesson and as front guard for an old argument between boy-men is your downfall.

I realize I am looking into Michael's eyes and smile at him sitting in his chair across the room from me. Connor is still standing; Father Tom and Matilda still sit with their eyes closed, and I have not traveled to distant places. I have only done what I always used to do and wandered around in my own head. That makes me happy for some reason, and I decide I want to see my kids and make dinner with them. I want to watch a movie in our den wrapped in blankets and cuddling until we fall asleep. I do not feel guilty about this at all, because Malick did say there is an inevitability that will fulfill itself, so why should I worry about or be dragged around by ghosts and old letters. I realize Shal's words are coming to me, but I say 'no' to them before they can reach me. I send words back: 'I have to go to work tomorrow; I want to make dinner like a good wife-mother; Leah, the chosen, is closing down for the evening … see you later'.

*   *   *   *

And that's what we did. Michael and I made my plan happen. We drove Father Tom and Matilda to their homes. Connor refused a ride saying he preferred to walk. We picked up the kids. We made dinner together. We talked to and listened to each other. We laughed. We took Puppy out for an evening walk. We washed faces and brushed teeth, and we clothed ourselves in pajamas and wrapped ourselves in blankets and watched an old movie, a family favorite, then we fell asleep together in our den in our house just like we have always done. And it was good.

The morning revealed itself gently, light through windows, and we rose to greet the day in our traditional way: Puppy nuzzling and the scent and sound of Michael's automatically timed coffeemaker pulling us from sleep; more cuddling; baths and showers and breakfast; Michael driving us to the places where we begin our days.

And here I stand in my room in Dayton Hall ready to be teacher to my students, who will come wanting me to be here standing at the window looking out when they arrive. They will arrive knowing inside my head a clear plan waits for them, and I will be focused in my own way. I take a deep breath, tell Shal's words 'no, not now' and send them back to him with a postscript: 'after school and before dinner I will meet you there by the fire; tell Brigid I am coming.'

Their urgency denied, the words and the place they are trying to fill in me empties so my thoughts are again on what my eyes see and on the plans I have made for the morning. The sky is a brilliant blue but hides itself behind thick massive stone-gray clouds. I watch the clouds move, pushing against each other, across the sky. A movement at the base of the trees standing guard with the stone wall surrounding the campus draws my gaze down from blue and gray into green and brown. I press my palms against the cool transparency of window glass. The man knows I see him, has made sure I have seen him, and only turns to climb easily back over the stone wall after his eyes have bored into mine with cold drilling calculation. He has thrown me off my own inner guarding and Shal's words from earlier, only ignored impressions now, somehow still manage to blare in my mind. 'Others are coming, others are coming, others are coming' repeating over and over again as my palms pressed against the window turn into fists softly drumming the repetitious rhythm of the phrase until my answering thought spoken into the quiet room stills Shal's words, "Let them come then, let them come."

I turn as I hear the turning of the doorknob, then sigh as Morgan and Shay walk into the room together smiling and welcoming me back. I respond appropriately, commenting it is good to be back while on the inside I am locking doors and pulling curtains on thoughts unrelated to my teaching. I am determined to be teacher Leah today and refuse to be called away. I will not be distracted.

Morgan and Shay stand before me, look at each other then back at me as Shay says, "We wanted to apologize for mouthing off to each other the other day after Maybe told the story. We were out of line."

Morgan comments, "We're sort of figuring things out as we go now."

I ask for more information, "Because?"

Again they look at each other, Morgan shrugs then nods his head at Shay who finds his words slowly, "You know … because I used to be the one who sort of calmed things down when Morgan would get mad about everything and nothing, but now, well, I seem to be the one whose got these … I don't know … these feelings that just freak on me." He pauses, looks down then right back into my eyes, "I used social commentary, nonpersonal issues, bullshit words before to keep myself in control. I piled them up, created this huge mother of a mound of pretense and propaganda or something, thinking I could bury the hurt, the anger over losing my family for no damn good reason, but lately it's like the words just aren't solid enough to hold down what I tried to bury, what I feel, and, I've got to tell you, I've got some super-size, kick my ass every time, phantoms running around in my head, and in my heart too, I guess. It's like the things I was feeling, the things I buried, that I thought were too big for me to handle in any other way are even bigger now. They're not staying buried, hell no, they're camped out, cheering each other on, building each other up." Shay shakes his head and body like a dog shaking off water, "Anyway, Morgan is putting up with it, and I'm seeing Mr. Danner about it, three times a damn week, and I'm running again or swimming laps before and after classes to try to use up some of the energy I would rather use to kick someone's … really just about anyone's ass." Shay smiles at me then looks at Morgan, "I guess it's good the school gave me a roommate that's twice as big as me, so even when I feel like taking a swing, Morgan just stands there and gives me this bring it on expression, and although I may be angry I'm not stupid enough to really push him too far. So yeah, you know, I'm dealing with it, but I'm sorry, and we didn't come early so we wouldn't have to apologize in front of the others; we just wanted to let you know we weren't trying to add to the … strangeness that's already going on in your life."

Morgan nods his head in agreement, "Exactly, Mrs. C. You've got enough on your plate, but Shay did want to ask you something, and he asked me to make sure he did even if he tried to weasel out of it, which is exactly what he seems to be trying to do."

I have a sense of what Shay's question will be, and I am aware of the fact I will have trouble answering it, if I can respond to it at all, but I encourage him to ask anyway, "Now is good, Shay. Ask me."

Shay's eyes search mine almost as if he is trying to see into my thoughts and find the answer to his question without having to say the words. I want to tell him no answer is in me and not to waste his time, but he may have discovered that on his own. "You lost your family to a fire. I lost mine to a car accident. How did you deal with that?"

I can visualize a list of appropriate responses, and I would like to be a good model for him, but I will not dishonor his honesty by mouthing words that are not true, "I am so sorry, Shay, to disappoint you, but I do not believe I really ever dealt with the deaths of my mother and stepfather and grandmother. I have never really walked away from the fire. I have lived my life, but I made their deaths and that night into some kind of altar and I return to it, too often, and kneel down before it offering bits and pieces of the present so that somehow, someone, or something will whisper the why of it all into me, so I can understand and move on. I cannot seem to stop myself from going there no matter how sweet the present moment. There is a part of me, a place in me, I keep to myself, and over the years it has grown darker and deeper and at the same time also easier to access. I go there more often; it seeks me out wanting its offering of the present to the past." I pause, look down at my hands, then I allow myself to once again look into Shay's eyes, "So do not wait to make things right, do not cut yourself off from Morgan or from Mr. Danner; allow them to help you. Bury the dead and clean up the scene of the accident so you cannot go back and walk through the broken glass and blood. Stop looking for them; stop trying to find them; they are not there anymore."

We stand for a moment without speaking, then the Shay who doesn't like to be touched wraps his arms around me and holds me, "Thank you for being honest with me. You could have done that adult thing and made yourself look good, like you had it all together, and I would have bought into that because you seem like you have it all pretty much together, like you know how to deal with your feelings, and maybe you do despite what you just said. None of us are perfect, right? So, I will try for both of us, Mrs. C, and I will find my way."

We step back from each other smiling as Alana and Maddie rush into the room. Alana stops suddenly dropping her backpack full of books on the floor, "Okay, Okay, what did we miss? I can tell something is happening." She puts one finger in her mouth, and then holds it up as if testing for breeze, "Oh yeah, it's tangible; I can feel it, so tell me, tell me."

Maddie picks up Alana's bag from the floor, "Too much coffee this morning, Mrs. C. She's all wound up."

Alana shakes her head, denying Maddie's words, "Nope, that is definitely not it. I just have this truck load full of intuitive sensibility and I can feel … stuff."

I act shocked as I say, "Stuff? One of my students using a generic like 'stuff'; I am shocked, Alana, truly."

Alana shakes her head again, "No you're not; you're attempting to distract me, but it won't work."

I look around and notice all my young ones are here, present, waiting, and safe, so I simplify the situation, "I have to make a quick phone call, then we'll get started. While I'm making the call why don't we write Teri letters … but not just normal, everyday kind of letters. We're going to write Teri letters based on what I am sure we all agree is my amusing way of reinforcing the need for transition by not allowing you any. Remember? We did it just last month. You write for two minutes then when your time is up, you may only write one word on the next line. Next you fold the paper so only the one word on the last line is visible and you pass it to the next person who also only has two minutes to write with just that one single word to inspire, and the process continues. Teri should have fun reading them, yes?" Papers are already being taken out of notebooks, and Tucker has volunteered to keep track of the time. I walk to the phone and dial Lane's private number as my students begin writing.

Lane answers the phone after the second ring, "Good morning, Leah."

I return his greeting then tell him about the man I saw climbing over the wall. He asks me to describe the man and I tell him what I noticed, "He had a dark green baseball cap; there was no insignia of any kind I could see. He wore a windbreaker and gloves. I believe those were both black. He had on jeans and boots or high top running shoes; the shoes were also black. I could not really see his face, but somehow we looked into each other's eyes, if that makes any sense to you. My feeling was he wanted me to see him."

Lane's first question shreds the pretense I had been holding around me like a cloak, "This just occurred?"

I respond knowing he will not be pleased with my answer, "Probably not more than fifteen minutes ago."

Lane's next question is rhetorical, "You waited fifteen minutes to call me?" He barely pauses then tells me to stay on the line as I am put on hold. After a minute or two he is back on the phone with me, "You have made it virtually impossible for us to easily or quickly find this man. Why do you think you did that, Leah?" I do not respond immediately, so Lane asks another question, "I can only assume you have a reasonable basis for your choice in this matter. I cannot imagine you would knowingly put yourself or our students in danger." He pauses and again I offer no explanation, so he adds, "Leah, did you recognize the man?"

I answer him without thinking, "I did not really see him; I told you that."

Lane counters, "But you did say that you looked into his eyes."

I only add, "There was a distance separating us, so I cannot be sure."

Lane's voice is gentle but demanding, "Leah, who do you think you may have seen?"

I speak carefully as if the words are glass and could break and draw blood, "It has been years, Lane, but it may have been Sean."

Lane is quiet for a moment then asks, "Your father, Sean?"

I nod my head, and then remember I am on the phone and say 'yes'.

Lane's voice is stronger now, "You will remain in your room with your students; I don't care what plans you had; you are not to leave the room. I will call Michael. I have notified security and the local police already. Do you understand what I am saying to you, Leah? Are you paying attention?"

I am thinking about my plans for the day, to be teacher Leah and not be distracted. I am thinking about the last time I saw Sean. I am listening to the laughter of my students. Then suddenly I think about the fact Mary is at daycare just down the street from where the man … I still cannot allow him to be my father … climbed over the fence. I say her name into the phone.

Lane responds immediately, the gentleness gone from his voice, "Crystal has been notified, and so has Paul at John Henry's school. Nathan is at home, at the Center, with Crystal and has been for the last week. Paul added security at the middle school last week when I increased our own here at Dayton. We have taken precautions, Leah. Why Michael chose not to inform you of that is between you and him; for the moment, however, be content in the knowledge your children are safe."

I am not content; I am numb, "Yes, Lane, thank you."

Lane's voice is again gentle, "Are you able to continue with your lesson for a little longer, or should I send someone to you immediately?" My thoughts are scattered, so I do not reply before Lane repeats the question, "Are you able to continue with your lesson or not? Please answer me."

I answer him, "I will continue with my lesson."

Lane attempts to be reassuring, "Michael will be there in less than an hour, and I will have Bradley there by that time or shortly thereafter. Security is already in the building."

I do not know how they got there, but there are tears in my eyes, "I am sorry about this, Lane."

Lane's voice embraces me, "Leah, dear child, you must realize no one expects you to continue teaching at this time. We are prepared for you to take the necessary time off to do what needs to be done. Even your students understand that. We have only been waiting for you to suggest it. Michael believed it would be better for you to suggest a short leave of absence than anyone else suggesting it to you. I believe the current situation makes any choice or preference you had quite moot."

I only say, "Yes, of course. Thank you. I have an hour with my students, and then I should not plan on seeing them for a while. That is what you are telling me?"

Lane replies, "Yes, that is what I am telling you, Leah, for the sake of the task to which you are called and also to ensure the safety of our students."

The tears are gone from my eyes as I say thank you and hang up the phone. I lean into the wall, my forehead pressing into the cool comforting darkness of wood paneling as I realize my attempt to believe I have any control over the flow of my days, the filling of my moments, is just one more pretension. I stand before a fire vented by past and future watching the present burn, and wonder why I still continue to resist the drawing whisper of the flames.

*   *   *   *

I hear voices, but they do not belong to the images I see. The name is mine but does not turn the head of the young girl who stands before the cruel dark mouth of the fire and its hungry flames. Then I remember where I am, who I have become; the name reminds me. I am Mrs. C for at least another hour. I can be her for at least an hour, which is only a moment or two, maybe three, then again maybe only one long drawn out moment. I breathe deeply and turn toward my students and say, "I am here. Are you done already?"

Jacy smiles, "She is going to love these, Mrs. C. They are too funny."

I smile back and say, "I am glad then."

Aden asks, "Would you like to hear them?"

I answer, "Yes, I would, but I am afraid we do not really have time now."

Jacy nods and looks down at the papers she has gathered from the other students, "I will mail them to her."

I thank her as I move slowly to the front of the room, returning to the podium. I place my hands on both sides of it, holding on, attempting to regain my sense of place within the context of the moment. "We have an hour actually before I have to leave." My comment is not met with any looks of surprise, so I continue, "I had this idea for our next few days based on the reading you did last week. Mr. Danner will want to take you through it in his own way, but for now, I will just share the passages that inspired the idea for the lesson, and we will see what we can do with it in the time we have."

Aden comments when I pause, "We'll have more time together later, Mrs. C."

I nod and say, "Of course, I guess I just dislike sharing you, not being the one to hear your ideas and the discussions or read your writing."

Morgan agrees, "Yeah, we know, and you should know it's mutual, the sharing part, I mean. So get done with whatever it is you have to do, so you can come back."

Other students smile at me and nod their heads or voice their agreement with Morgan's statement. I take another deep breath and decide not to allow my emotions to waste anymore of the time we have left, "So, without further ado ... last week you read Gretel Ehrlich's The Solace of Open Spaces. She comments, 'everything in nature invites us to be who we are.' She also states, 'space has a spiritual equivalent and can heal what is divided and burdensome in us.' Additionally, she suggests 'we might learn how to carry space inside ourselves in the effortless way we carry our skins.' The first statement I shared with you is rather straightforward. Nature, more than just inspiration, calls to us, even demands from us an honesty, perhaps a relevancy, possibly lacking in the many social contexts in which we find ourselves. With that said and allowing it to function as a foundation, what do the second and third statements by Ehrlich suggest we, as humans, should do?"

Tucker sighs, "Do you have the whole book memorized?"

I shake my head, "I wish, but no, only parts." I allow them a moment to think about my question then add, "We are just brainstorming here; feel free to verbalize considerations, please."

Valerie is first to respond, "I like the idea of carrying space inside of me, and also Ehrlich's reference to carrying our skins. That would support her statement about space being a spiritual experience."

Shay comments next, "Ehrlich gives credence to the coexistence of the physical and spiritual. And I agree with Val; the image of carrying my skin is cool. It adds a new twist to the religious precept of the bodies we wear, but wearing and carrying are different actions. Carrying is more of a conscious choice than wearing or having been fitted with something and just hanging out in it for a lifetime."

The room is quiet, so I add another ingredient to what I am offering them, "T.S. Eliot, in his poem "The Dry Salvages", writes,

> 'For most of us there is only the unattended
> moment, the moment in and out of time,
> the distraction fit, lost in a shaft of sunlight,
> the wild thyme unseen, or the winter lightning
> or the waterfall, or music heard so deeply
> that it is not heard at all, but you are the music
> while the music lasts. These are only hints and guesses,
> hints followed by guesses; and the rest
> is prayer, observance, discipline, thought, and action.'"

I pause before I repeat Eliot's lines one more time for them, then I allow the room to fill with a silence as deeply hued as dark velvet as they think about Eliot's meaning.

Tucker raises his hand and asks, "This may seem like too simple of a question, but what are dry salvages?"

I smile at Tucker, "It's a fine question, do not sound apologetic for asking it. Eliot offers a notation, which prefaces his poem, that states, 'The Dry Salvages ... is a small group of rocks, with a beacon, off the N.E. coast of Cape Ann, Massachusetts.'"

Tucker nods, but I can tell by the look on his face he is not satisfied. He holds out his hands, palms up, to me as he asks with a bit of an English accent added to his Texas drawl, "'Please, sir, may I have some more', or are you saving the rest of the poem for a different course, 'cause I have to tell you I'm feeling like I need something I can get my teeth on and chew before I can deal with this fancy fare you're serving me."

Charlie slaps Tucker on the back good naturedly, "I'm with you, brother. I like the whole food comparison thing too." Charlie pauses and looks at me, "I'm with him, Mrs. C, we want steak."

I cannot help smiling at their comments, "Okay, point taken. I can provide a solid reference, a tangible visual, if you will, that not only relates to the poem's title but also to Ehrlich's comments.

Charlie grins, "Go for it, Mrs. C. We're ready."

I have to run through the poem in my mind before I can begin, "This passage is from earlier in the poem, whereas the first passage I shared with you is very nearly his closing lines." I close my eyes to see more clearly the lines as they lay upon the page then I give voice to Eliot's words:

> "The sea has many voices,
>
> many gods and many voices.
>
> The salt is on the briar rose,
>
> the fog is in the fir trees.
>
> The sea howl
>
> and the sea yelp, are different voices
>
> often together heard: the whine in the rigging,
>
> the menace and caress of wave that breaks on water,
>
> the distant rote in the granite teeth,
>
> and the wailing warning from the approaching headland
>
> are all sea voices, and the heaving groaner
>
> rounded homewards, and the seagull:
>
> and under the oppression of the silent fog
>
> the tolling bell
>
> measures time not our time, rung by the unhurried
>
> ground swell, a time
>
> older than the time of chronometers, older
>
> than time counted by anxious worried women
>
> lying awake, calculating the future,
>
> trying to unweave, unwind, unravel
>
> and piece together the past and the future,
>
> between midnight and dawn, when the past is all deception,
>
> the future futureless, before the morning watch
>
> when time stops and time is never ending;
>
> and the ground swell, that is and was from the beginning,

clangs

the bell.'"

I pause for a moment then suggest, "I will recite it one more time for you, but first ask me any questions you might have regarding word meaning and the like."

Val asks, "The line about 'distant rote', what is rote?"

I ask if anyone knows and when no one offers a definition I supply one, "Rote is the sound of waves or surf upon the shore."

Val's expression is one of thoughtfulness as she speaks, "I see—" she pauses and smiles, "I always amuse myself when I say that." Then she pauses again, "Well, it's not always amusing. If I'm down it makes me more sad, or sometimes more angry or frustrated, but today I can smile about it. But anyway, I do see the image now, 'the distant rote in the granite teeth' is waves crashing against the massive rocks of a shore; no soft sand to lie upon there, I would guess."

Tucker comments, "The reference to a chronometer is interesting. Chronometry is the science of measuring time, and a chronometer is a time piece used to measure time with great accuracy. Eliot's tolling bell must be a buoy with a bell, so the time kept would not be based on the passing of minutes or hours." Tucker shakes his head, "Whoa, that was kind of deep wasn't it?"

Jacy raises her hand after other students have made agreeable comments to Tucker and says, "I'm just brainstorming here, but for me Ehrlich's awareness of space and its qualities is comparable to Eliot's portrayal of time. Like … both space and time are more than we often allow them to be. His description of the sea, its voices, the salt on the rose, the fog in the fir tree, create a feeling of the sea's presence permeating the shore, and his references to people may be vague for a purpose, only speaking of worried women and the hearing of the rigging's whine alluding to sailors. Perhaps the sea is time, and the ship on its surface and the women waiting on the shore are indicative of how humans live their lives: surface perceptions and worrying about the unknowable."

Shay adds, "That, or at least some of it, would fit with the first lines Mrs. C shared. Eliot writes about the unattended moment that is in and out of time."

Aden then suggests, "Yeah, plus in those earlier lines he writes something about music heard so deeply we become the music while the music lasts. Because we concentrate so much on a single internal or external visual focal point, like the music or the winter lightning or the waterfall, it becomes a 'fit distraction'."

Maddie, "That makes sense to me, and although everyone knows memory stuff is not my strong suit, what about the idea in the last lines of the second reading: 'time stops and time is never ending', then he writes about the ground swell 'that is and was from the beginning, clangs the bell'. So isn't that mixing time and space because the wave fills space and the wave is, according to his words, from the beginning and marks time?"

Tucker shakes his head, "Now I'm hungry and drowning."

Alana leans toward him and suggests, "Shame on you, Tucker, you understand more than you let on, at least that's what I think." Tucker only smiles in reply.

The room becomes quiet, so I make a suggestion and offer them a choice, "The decision you make has to be unanimous, and what you have to decide is—" I pause for effect, remove a stack of papers from the podium and then continue, "whether you want to see Eliot's words or just have me repeat the two excerpts again."

Charlie and Tucker are pounding on the table and saying, "Paper, paper, we want paper."

Shay raises his hand, and I call out his name over the drumming which quickly stops, "Normally, I'd be up for continuing to work the poem without seeing it, but, and isn't it interesting time would be an issue for us, since you're going to have to leave soon, maybe we should move things along. So I'll go along with Charlie and Tucker."

Charlie laughs a big fake laugh, "See there, I always knew you were one of us at heart. Meat and potatoes and paper, that's what life is all about, boy."

Angela, in her quiet voice asks, "Are you giving us the whole poem, or are we working out of context first, as you like us to do?"

Charlie shakes his head, "She wouldn't do that to us again. We don't need that lesson again. We all understand anything taken out of context can be misinterpreted." He looks at me and continues, "You wouldn't do that to us and then leave."

I smile mischievously, "I would, and I am, and it is not just an exercise in the importance of context relevance; I do it also because sometimes, especially with poetry, a piece, like a moment within a moment, can stand on its own and be valid and somehow maintain its validity even when its scope and sequence are altered by its relationship to the whole."

Shay stands up suddenly, "Damn, that's right, and it works on so many levels and in so may different situations. I'm me. I'm me when I'm alone; I'm me when I'm with others; I'm me five years ago, and even right now I'm me tomorrow. I'm who I am, the places I've been, the people I've spent time with, the circumstances I've experienced, but there's more to me than those, because … well, there's a non tangible part, a non experiential part, maybe like Ehrlich's space idea … I have space within me that is just mine; no one else can go there. I'm rambling now, but there's something to this, and I will get it." He pauses then looks at me, "I read the assigned book last week, <u>The Solace of Open Spaces</u>; I read the whole thing, and I liked it, the writing, what Ehrlich shared, but I didn't focus in. Maybe I did what Eliot refers to when he writes about the unattended moment and the fit of the distraction. You gave me three little pieces out of her whole book and my focus changes, Mrs. C. Then you offer a piece or two of Eliot's work and wham, right between the eyes, more focus. Yeah, I'm up for this. What do we do next?"

Shay sits down and after a moment of silence when all of us are obviously attempting to make our own sense of Shay's comments Tucker shrugs and says, "Well, put that way, I guess I shouldn't mind these little appetizers you give us."

I have to ask him, "Are you hungry, Tucker? You are making continual references to food."

Tucker and the rest of my family group look at each other before he continues, "It's like this, Mrs. C. I am hungry; I'm almost always hungry, but that isn't it. What it has to do with is how you teach. I'm not even sure how it got started, but when we get together we talk about our times with you like … well, meals. We walk in here, and we don't know how hungry we are, or a lot of times we even think we're full, but then you do one of your lesson-activity-things and we all realize we're hungry. Sometimes we're starving and didn't even know it. You're teaching us there's more to life than fast food, or just getting a grade, or just passing a test, or filling in the blanks with what we think you want us to think. Your tests are never fill in the blank, and neither are our discussions. You're more interested in how we get to an answer than the answer itself. And the way you make everything seem important; that surprised me at first, sort of set me back. It felt like too much; how can everything be important? But you showed us everything is important, and that is true in reading poetry and in our lives. You somehow made us understand you can't go through life skipping over the words you don't understand. And the way you do it is not pushy or oh-look-how-brilliant-I-am-so-do-what-I-do. You set things up like a meal. You serve appetizers and all these courses, and the dessert at the end is usually something unique for each one of us, something we actually made from ingredients you set out or let us go out and find ourselves. Questions get answered about life-things that I didn't even know I was wondering about, that don't even seem like part of the lesson, but I walk away knowing more about myself and how to live than I did before. You fill us up, Mrs. C, so thanks, and I can't believe I talked for that long."

The students clap their hands and nod their heads, and I am so amazed at the sweetness, the momentary completeness, of how Tucker's words make me feel I do not even realize I am looking into Michael's eyes and smiling. He is standing in the doorway, and from his expression I realize he must have heard most of Tucker's comments, because he is smiling with me and sharing what I feel in the way only family and close, long time friends can feel each other's joy. Michael puts his finger to his lips and motions for me to continue, and I realize he does not want to distract from what is going on.

I bow to make the clapping stop, "Thank you so very much. I was not looking forward to leaving you, and I am still not, but now I can at least go knowing you have appreciated what we have accomplished together. So, again, thank you all, and thank you, Tucker, for sharing with me." I begin handing out the copies of the poem excerpts, "Your progress through Ehrlich's and Eliot's ideas should be like … mountain climbing. Handholds up steep rock faces then choosing paths when the cliff becomes more level but you enter dense forest. Remember, speed is not the goal, stop and rest even on the cliff, even in the darkest part of the forest. Journal all your thoughts and ideas. As usual, no cross-outs; you may rethink and adjust ideas continually, but I want to be able to see your process clearly. Your product or destination, depending on how you want to look at the experience, will be a persuasive essay and a tangible project of your own choosing but it must be a visual expression of your culminating realizations regarding Eliot's purpose: the essay should deal with his choice of imagery to express his premise, and your visual should illustrate your perspective regarding the relevancy of the poem on your own life or on human life in general. Use Ehrlich for support and for extension. Mr. Danner will set due dates. Questions?"

Shay raises his hand, "It's not a question really, but I want you to remember we may be young and your students, but you can count on us if you need us. We're here, and we'll be here when you come back."

There are, of course, tears in my eyes, and though no more words are spoken I am hugged goodbye by each of my students. Bradley stands with Michael at the door, and as I make my way to them I force myself to breathe deeply thinking if the movement of air can wear down rock perhaps I can, at least, dilute the emotions within me with air to keep them from overtaking me. I have to give instructions to Bradley; I cannot be overwhelmed. At my desk I open my lesson plan book and turn to Bradley, who knows me well enough to know I am wanting and not wanting to cry.

He is at my side immediately, "We can go over your plans later, Leah. There is no rush. I'll give you a call after classes are over today. I was going to find you today anyway, because there is something I must talk with you about before tonight when I have a meeting with Lane and my brother."

I look into his eyes to try to read how he feels about this meeting, but his eyes are only filled with compassion for me, so I make a suggestion instead, "We should talk now, Bradley."

Bradley shakes his head, "Now does not seem like—"

I interrupt him, "Bradley, I have no idea what is going to happen next in my day or in my life, so we should talk now." I look at my students, my family group, and they are all working quietly, highlighting and making notations on the poem. "We can take a moment to talk now."

He agrees, and I pick up my purse, turning back to make sure my desk is in order, and to look at my room and the young people who have shared its comforts with me. Each one of them looks up at me and nods or smiles or waves, so I answer them with all three; I smile and nod and wave, then I am in the hallway with Michael and Bradley, and the door is closed, and I am just Leah, the wife-mother-sometime sister-friend, not Leah, the daughter-wife-mother-sometime sister-friend-teacher. I feel suddenly resigned to the loss somehow and sense the emotions threatening to overwhelm me just moments earlier are distant now; I stand on a plain and see the dust cloud of their departure.

Michael lays his hand on my shoulder. I look at him then at Bradley, "You did fine last week with my lesson plans, so we won't worry about that now. Tell us about your meeting."

Bradley looks down at his hands then up at us, "I don't want my brother to lose his church. I don't want all those people to be, in essence, thrown out of town because of me. I don't want Lane to be put in a position where he has to do something like cancel the church's lease. It feels so wrong."

I lay my hand on his arm, "Bradley, what's happening is wrong, but Lane's decision is not something that will be changed easily. I had heard your brother found a place just south of here, did that plan fall through?"

Bradley shakes his head, "That's not the point, Leah."

Michael comments, "The point is Joe and his elders, in doing what they believe is right, ostracized you and anyone who is like you, and Lane cannot stand by and allow that to happen. Did you ever wonder what would have happened if Hitler had been stopped early on?"

Bradley shakes his head again, "My brother and the elders of the church are not Hitler, or anything like him, Michael."

Michael looks at me and then at Bradley again, "Prejudice is prejudice. Judgment is judgment. Prejudice and judgment were Hitler's foundational motivations. Look where they led him."

Bradley's expression has changed. His words are hard and thrown at us, "Yeah right, and do you want John Henry to grow up and be gay? Are you going to present him or Mary with options when you give them the bird-and-bee talk?"

Michael takes a step back, "Left field, man."

Bradley's words are less forceful when he replies, "I'm not mad at you, and your answer is none of my business really, but damn it, neither of you can stand back from this. You have to go sit in their church and be in their heads. They believe allowing my attendance there sanctions homosexuality. So, left field or not, you can't handle this like a politically correct discussion; you've got to be these Christian parents sitting with their little Christian kids when I sit down in the pew next to them."

I step closer to him. I look up into his eyes and say words from my heart, "I love you. You are one of my closest friends. If my son is gay I will support him one hundred percent, but that is not what you asked. You asked if I would offer choices to my children when we have our sex talk, but, Bradley, what about the talks before that one? What about the questions children ask about people having different colored skin, or speaking different languages, or having different faith beliefs; those conversations should come first and should set the foundation for talks about friendship and companionship and trust and respect and honoring. Sex should be more than just intercourse and the positions involved. Before your partner, Daniel, died there were at least two years where he was bedridden and too sick to have sex, but you two loved each other through all those moments. You were intimate without intercourse. You held him in your arms when he breathed his last breath, and he holds a place in your heart to this day. I will teach my children that. I will try to teach my children to have compassion and to love well; those are my first responsibilities. I will admit I would like it if my children were like me in their sexuality, just like I enjoy seeing other aspects of Michael and myself in them, but if they choose another way, I will not be disappointed. What would disappoint me is if they became prejudiced and fearful in their thinking; then and only then would I question how I raised them; then and only then would I question my parenting. Gay or straight, does not the person make. Lane has to be strong in this, and you cannot feel guilty about it, or you can 'feel' guilty, but you must 'know' you are not guilty. Joe and his church are doing what they believe is right; Lane is doing what he believes is right. Do you believe being gay is wrong?"

Bradley shakes his head, "I cannot believe my love for Daniel was wrong, so I cannot believe being gay is wrong."

Michael reaches out and takes Bradley's hand in his, "You can sit in my church with me and my kids any damn day of the week, and isn't that the way churches should be: different people coming together to celebrate life and the God who gave it to them? Have your meeting, express your sorrow, but don't ask Lane to alter his thinking or his stance in the matter, or next month or next year another group of people will be found unacceptable. This isn't just about you, Bradley; you've got to realize that."

Bradley sighs, "Thank you both for being the friends you are. Somehow I just have to allow the process that must occur, but it was my father's church before it became my brother's, and I guess I have to accept my dad wouldn't have allowed me in his church either. If he hadn't died I would have had to face him with who I am, and it probably would have broken his heart."

I offer a possibility to him, "How can you know? Yes, it would have been difficult for your father, but we can only guess how he would have responded, and guessing—". I pause remembering Eliot's words, "In class today we were talking about one of T.S. Eliot's poems, and there is a reference to guessing. He is referring to our perceptions of our moments and he writes, 'These are only hints and guesses, hints followed by guesses; and the rest is prayer, observance, discipline, thought, and action.' Bradley, do not fight phantom battles when there are so many real ones. There is so much more to life than making our own hints and guesses 'right' for others. You could guess about so many things and have nothing but doubts and shadows to show for all the time spent. Pray, observe, be disciplined, be thoughtful, take action, but don't guess about your dad and your mom … let them be, remember them the way they were and remember how they loved you. Anything else you can't know."

Bradley and Michael are both looking at me with expressions on their faces that clearly indicate mixed reactions. I take a deep breath before I continue, "All right, I know why you're both looking at me that way. I stand before my own past often, reaching out to it, wanting answers, guessing based on hints, wanting more than the past can ever offer to the present. I realize I am being one of those people who ask others to 'do what I say, not what I do', but … well, yes, do that: do what I say, not what I do. I have nothing else to offer you for now except that."

Michael puts his arms around me as Bradley says, "Fair enough, Leah, for now, fair enough."

*   *   *   *

Michael is driving. I am making attempts to attend to the moment. I am aware of the tenacious fingers of the sun trying to find weaknesses in the tightly woven fabric of the fog, and once that is achieved, once treetops have been grasped, trying to work themselves down through branches, holding tightly, barely moving but seeking to touch down on soil and rock. The fog is, however, equally determined. I am aware also within my mind one of Bradley's words plays over and over again: fair ... fair ... fair. Then another word is added: fair enough ... fair enough ... fair enough. I wonder how fairness can be metered; fair is fair. Fair is not a matter of degrees; not fair is not fair. Life is not fair; life is life. I measure it, at times, by its fairness or lack thereof, but my measurements are not what life is; my measurements are only my perceptions. I shake my head, my thoughts creating their own fog, and see we are nearing the church where we hope to find Father Tom, where we will talk about the man who appeared only to disappear, who could possibly be and could never be my father. I sigh.

Michael takes my hand in his, "The kids are safe. My dad and Brian will not let anything happen to them, and for that matter," he pauses then smiles as he continues, "with mom and Sarah there too, I am not sure if they wouldn't be the most unrestrained if anyone tried to mess with our kids."

I lean my head back against the seat, "I hold on to the assurances given us our children will not be involved. I have to."

Michael turns into the church parking lot, "This fog is more like winter fog than summer fog." He looks at me, "This is just normal fog, right?"

I look at him, "I sense nothing else, but the storm felt like just a storm when it first started."

Michael has stopped the car and has the keys in his hands as he leans over to me, "Get in the game, babe. Let's go after this, be offensive instead of just waiting for things to happen to us and then reacting."

I lean closer to him, "I just love it when you talk sports talk, 'babe'."

He rests his forehead against mine, "Okay, so I won't call you babe anymore, but I thought the sports analogy worked."

I am enjoying the feel of his breath and the closeness of his lips, "Are we ready to take the offensive?"

His lips touch mine, "Do we have a choice, Leah?"

I lean back from him, touch his face with my fingertips, "No more choices, just 'prayer and observance, discipline and thought, and action'. Lots of action, just for you."

He stills my fingers with his own and presses mine against his lips, "Are Eliot's words going to become your mainstay for the day?"

I only say, "Possibly."

Then only his fingers and mine connect us as we hold each other's hand. We look at each other for a moment, and somehow within that moment a hundred other moments offer themselves up to us. We are connected by what I sense we are both experiencing: walks taken, the first time Michael's lips touched mine, the first time our eyes revealed to each other how we felt but had not yet given the shared emotion words, sharing music that moved our bodies closer to each other, the vows we exchanged, the first time our bodies expressed the closeness we desired and a thousand other times when we have talked and touched, the births of our children, the arguments and making-up after, children's first words and first steps, family dinners, family laughter, shared tears ... and then the moment is over, and both of us realize it.

I whisper, "Are we drowning?"

He gently squeezes my hand, "No, no, never ... just pre-game hall of fame stuff, getting us pumped up and focused, making us sure about what we are fighting for ... that's all," he pauses as he turns away to open his door, then looks back adding, "babe" as he steps out.

I smile but not in a friendly way, "Ooh, Coach Michael, thank you so much. I am definitely all pumped up for the big game now." I close the door noticing the fog seems to be moving in slow thick waves as I wish I knew what the rules of the game are and who my team members are, and who is opposing me. Then I shake my head and try to stop myself from talking in sports talk by turning through the volumes in the library in my head to find a literary reference to better suit, but then the fog becomes so dense I wonder if I can even breathe it in. Then flames replace veils of mist, and Shal's voice surrounds me.

✳   ✳   ✳   ✳

His words are low and push against me, "Never deny me again. Never."

His eyes reflect the fire's flames that reach up and are between us. They fill my vision completely. I am incensed and instantly stand in front of him, the fire behind me. I mentally push back against him, and he is moved physically, falling into the chair behind him. The flames flare and Brigid moves from the shadowed corner and lays her hand on his shoulder. From the other side of the room, Bantok's words challenge Shal further, "Losing your hold on your chosen one once again, Shal?"

I ignore him. Shal looks at Brigid, lays his hand on hers then looks back at me, "Testing your wings, little bird? Do it carefully. Remember more often than not, the chosen one, the one honored for his or her gifts is also used for his or her gifts. You may not be as special as you would like to believe. You may be no more than a resource to me."

I counter, "And you, what are you then to me? What is your cause that I should care or want to be used for it? And if I choose to test my wings, if I choose to test my strength, how will yours match up? Who will win? What will happen to your cause if you and I fight against each other? What will be lost? Who will care more, you or me?"

Only the dance and the whisper of flame fill the room. The anger flung out of Shal and of me, almost visible in its intensity, dissipates. I do not want to be distracted by my reaction to Shal's emotions. I look at Brigid, "I want your memories in my head, not his. I want to see through your eyes what happened." I look at Shal, "Take your memories back from me. Please. I know your perspective is not the one I need. I knew it before I came here this time. I was planning to make the request before we argued. I am not asking out of anger; I am asking because I know I have to see the altar for the first time through Brigid's eyes."

Except for the somewhat unsettling rattle of metal chains as Bantok changes positions, again there is only the dance and whisper of the flames in the room. Brigid looks from me to Shal, holds out her hand toward me, and I feel Shal's memories leaving me. Extending her other arm toward me, she offers me what I have requested, her hand palm up, her expression one of deep sorrow and resignation. I realize she will not send her memories to me as Shal did: I must make a place for them, because she will not bombard me. I extend my arm toward her, lay my palm on hers. I look into her eyes, "I must see what you saw, feel what you felt, and know what you knew at the moment in time without your knowledge of the moments that followed, without my knowledge of what has happened since then. I must live through it as you did. Please, show me. Give me your memories." And she does. Her memories come like butterflies and broken glass, some soft and some too sharp, too cut by sorrow, made too jagged by terror, to find a place within me without causing pain. I am shattered. I fall.

✳   ✳   ✳   ✳

Michael's arms hold me as I lay on the gravel of the church's parking area. His words are gently said but urgent as they call my name and then God's, "Leah, Leah, oh God, God. Leah, can you hear me? Leah?"

I open my eyes as I taste blood, feel it in my mouth, "I am here, Michael."

His lips kiss my forehead and cheeks, "What happened? Why are you bleeding? You were standing so still when I came around the car, then you seemed to faint. Now there's blood on your lips."

I close my eyes and open them again as I raise my hand to my lips and remove it, feeling the wetness and seeing the red on my fingertips. I swallow the wetness tasting the redness, then hold up my hand to Michael as I sit up, "I need to wipe my hand off."

He offers his pant leg, but I shake my head. He walks to the car, keeping his eyes on me, opens the door and removes a tissue from the small package of tissues I keep in the door pocket. After he returns to me I clean my hand off and wipe my lips, "I am fine now."

I stand and move into his arms as he asks, "But what happened?"

I recount the experience to him, his arms tightening around me at different times, then when I complete the telling he steps back from me still holding my arms, "Holy shit, Leah, do you think pissing off Shal is the correct move right now? Don't we want him on our side?"

I look up into Michael's eyes, "Our side is his side, but I somehow know how I allow myself to be treated must be established. Also, it's Brigid who is at the center of this, not Shal. Shal and Bantok surround her, struggle against each other, and one or both may have caused what happened, but Brigid holds the key to whatever it is I am supposed to do. That much I know, and I know it as well as I know anything."

We are quiet and still until through the fog that diminishes our vision the muted sound of a man's voice, chanting slowly and melodically words foreign to our ears, comes from within the church. We walk to the wide doors of the church and Michael opens one of them slowly. We enter but stop half way up the center aisle.

Candlelight from the altar and alcoves along the side walls barely illuminate the interior. The day's dim light through the stained glass windows does little more to brighten the interior; the windows become incandescent paintings only. The man's voice, like the candles and the windows, is not light fighting against the darkness, not pleading in its tone, perhaps because the darkness is comforting in its depth and softness. There is a drawing acceptance to the darkness' allowance, a spaciousness permitting uncertainty and certainty to lay next to each other, to perhaps gaze into each other to celebrate the other's fathomable soundness, as if the qualities of knowing and not knowing that are so often represented by lightness and darkness coexist here, rely on each other in a timeless embrace of faith barely stilled in its forever flow. Acceptance breathed out and partaken of wholly, a spatial continuance and consummation of moment embraced and embracing.

My eyes are drawn to the man who, on his knees with his head bent, is robed and reverent. Only when he raises his head to gaze upon the altar do I recognize Connor by the cut and color of his hair. His words, on completion of his song, are now spoken without melody to accompany them, "Father in Heaven, Christ Jesus, Holy Spirit, guide me. Show me the way. Make my will yours. Make my thoughts your thoughts. Build my faith in you upon even my own weakness, my own uncertainty. Let me do nothing to dishonor you. Make me yours in thought, emotion, word, and deed. Make me worthy that your name might be praised, your heart revealed, your righteousness known. Fill me with your purpose, Holy Spirit of God, that I may please my father. I ask in your name, Christ Jesus, my savior, my shepherd, my king."

He stands, turning slightly and sees us in his peripheral vision. As he turns to face us, Michael says, "We didn't mean to interrupt. We came to see Father Tom."

Connor acknowledges us sadly, "Better it would seem had you come to see God, to call out to his son knowing he will answer you."

Michael responds gently, "It's good your faith is so strong. I'm sort of used to just looking for him in the circumstances of my day and trying to respond accordingly."

Connor nods his head then looks at me, "And you, little bird, what about you?"

I am unsettled hearing him refer to me in the same way Shal had only moments earlier, "More than anything I suppose I am wondering how Jesus and what I have learned in the church fits in with what I am experiencing, wondering if one contradicts the other or if they are connected in ways I cannot know or understand."

Connor again nods his head, "I'd be leanin' toward the unknowable connection rather than the contradiction, but I'm a priest of the Catholic Church, on sabbatical here to help my old uncle during a time of need, and on Church business too because the Church is not unaware of what is going on or unaware it has a stake in the outcome."

Michael asks, "Meaning?"

Connor walks closer to us then stops and turns toward the altar, "There is only one true altar. How it's perceived, how it's approached, how it's served may vary, and humans may build altars of their own, but the true altar, the altar that stands at the center of life, that is life, overshadows all others. It always has; it always will. Wording and scope may differ, but the acknowledgment of good and evil is foundational in most every human culture and religion. To deny the existence of evil is to contradict the very essence of life. To deny the existence of evil denies every other parallelism of the universe. Good and evil exist; the struggle continues."

I ask, "How can you reconcile Jesus and Brigid and that storm at our house so easily?"

Connor's certainty is felt as he speaks his words, "I'll not even try to reconcile what you are experiencing to God because you, like every other person, who has walked this earth, must choose faith over understanding to find the true altar of life."

Connor pauses, closes his eyes and tilts his head as if he listens to a voice Michael and I cannot hear, then speaks words to me that make me want to both laugh and cry at the same time, "Leah, you must stop trying to guess at your own purpose. You must pray, observe, discipline yourself, think, then act. You must not be distracted, tryin' to piece together the past and the future. You must attend to the moment, Leah." He pauses again, looks at me, or into me the way some people can do, and then asks, "Would those words be makin' sense to you?"

I say 'yes' as I look at Michael, who I know must be wanting to hum the theme song to the Twilight Zone.

Connor seems to want more from me though, "The words have special meaning to you?"

I clear my throat to speak, wishing I could as easily clear my thoughts, "They are words from a poem I introduced to my students today in class. How did you know?"

Connor smiles, "I didn't. I'm just the messenger."

Michael is not amused, "Messengers don't always fare well in your business, you know?"

Connor turns to walk away but then stops and comments, "Faring well is not always, or even often, a main concern in matters such as these. You hold on too tightly to that and to those who are not really yours to hold, which can keep you from seein' what's truly holdable. Enjoy what you have while you have it, Michael. Physical life has no guarantees. You must be realizin' that, despite the reassurances of an old priest."

Connor does not wait for a reply and makes his way out of the church through a side door. Michael is looking at me when I turn to face him and speaks quietly, "So much for leaving on a good damn note."

I rest my head on his shoulder as I say, "Perhaps that is just how he is: agreeable in a sort of carefree way and then almost always unsettling. I do not believe he means us any harm though, and that is good to know."

Michael wraps his arms around me, "To know? I'm not sure if we know that or not, Leah."

I pull his face down to me and kiss his lips quickly, "Connor says it is a faith thing, remember? And May wrote the same. I think we know enough to know we don't really know."

Michael takes my hand as we start walking to the door, "Yeah, please remind me to write that little pearl of wisdom down somewhere."

I am about to respond to him when both of us become completely still. In front of us, standing in the doorway, is Sean.

Chapter NINE

Motionless, we are just heartbeat and breath. In fact, Sean seems to be having difficulty catching his. Michael and I are as still as stone sculptures. We are only eyes looking into eyes. I watch as Sean's face changes from surprise to wonder then to hope. I can almost feel his eyes touch the necklace at my throat, and as I reach to cover the half-heart, which always somehow feels warm against my skin, his eyes move to the pearl ring on my finger. He begins to raise his hand but then shakes his head; his hand falls and the hopefulness in his eyes darkens into sadness, then anger, then he is gone. Michael and I do not move even after Sean turns in the doorway and steps back into the mist hanging like a shroud blocking any view of what lies just beyond the door.

I realize I am calling out my father's name as motionlessness is replaced by sudden movement, and I am out the door, but just as suddenly the heavy mist presses against me. It is as if I am pushing through sand. I turn to watch Michael, hearing him call my name, but he is being dragged down, crushed from all sides. I want to scream out my frustration, but the fog holds me, denying breath and mobility; its swirling emotions flooding over me. In my mind I imagine it rising up off the ground, dissipating. It presses against me relentlessly as I maintain the image of it weakened and lifting. I am aware that Michael, on his knees, gasps for breath, and my resolve strengthens. I become what I know, that which I have honored and feared all my life. I become fire. The fog rolls back from us lifting slowly, retreating as if being pulled away, wet gray fingers digging into soil to try to save itself, but phantom flames deny its grasping hold. My determination burns.

I hear Michael cough and breathe in deeply as I watch Connor, still robed, run from the rectory, next to the church, across the wide green lawn and disappear into the orchard as if he is following the now retreating shroud of mist being pushed further and further back from us. I inhale and exhale deeply; the image of the fire flames then dissolves. Sunlight bathes us; one small song bird calls out to another and is answered; a breeze moves through chimes. I hear my name, somehow no more than a whisper but cried out from a distance, and it pulls me from my own stillness.

Michael, now standing by my side, follows me as I run toward the rectory. As we near its door I almost hesitate, almost slow my pace, but I do not allow myself to do that; I have hesitated enough; I will face what is there within the walls of Father Tom's living quarters and answer the whispered call cried out. I will no longer believe that around every corner flames wait to eat up what I love, what I hold dear. Fire will be no altar on which I sacrifice who I am anymore. I will not draw out my moments behind me or lose myself in them as if they are billowing fabric forever being torn away from me; I will tailor them instead, wear them, walk around in them. I promise myself, and I will remember my promise; I will live by it.

Live, be alive ... those words play over and over in my head as Michael and I fall on our knees beside Father Tom. Blood runs from a deep laceration just above his forehead. We call his name then Michael grabs the phone from the desk to call for help. Father Tom's eyelids flutter. I bend down to him, believing he will speak if he can when his eyes open and he sees me, but instead his eyes indicate his left hand. When I look there his fingers are barely moving, but I can see the key and know he wants me to take it. I realize the effort he is making to give it to me taxes his waning strength.

I reassure him, "We are here, Father, we are here. I am holding your hand. Stay here with us, please. I have the key now. I will do what has to be done. Do not leave us. Do not waste your strength."

Michael has made the call and has taken a blanket off Father Tom's bed and covers him. I do not take my eyes off Father Tom's face as I ask, "What can we do, Michael? What can we do for him?"

Michael hands me a towel he has found somewhere and tells me to hold it firmly against the bleeding wound on Father Tom's head. Michael checks his pulse. Father Tom's lips open again. His voice is almost too soft to hear, "Behind the altar ... beneath the third stone ... the last ... last letter."

I try to comfort him, "Yes, yes, we will take care of it, but you must only concentrate on staying with us now."

Michael leans closer to him, "Who did this to you, Father?"

Father Tom's eyes open again. He begins to speak as Connor rushes into the room, but his eyelids flutter then close as he applies a bit of pressure to my hand, whispering, "Not what … seems."

Then his head rolls to the side and Michael's hand is on Father Tom's throat checking for a pulse. Michael becomes fireman-paramedic telling me to keep pressure on the cloth on Father Tom's head as he administers CPR. Beneath my legs Father Tom's blood soaks my pants, and I become only a voice calling out to him, "Live … live … live …" as a siren wails in the distance.

※   ※   ※   ※

Jake and Ron have taken Father Tom to the hospital. Connor, Michael, and I stand with Dale and Lex. Michael and I have explained how we found Father Tom and Lex is turning to Connor as Dale adds, "Well, Michael, you kept him alive from what Jake and Ron said. You can feel good about that. Sometimes when something like this happens it's good to hold on to the idea you did all you could do, no matter how it turns out."

Lex shakes his head, "You're sort of preaching to the choir there aren't you, partner? Michael is a paramedic, you know?"

Michael puts his arm around me and responds before Dale can, "I am, but situations change when someone is personally involved, and I'm very involved in this one. So, thanks for reminding me, Dale."

Lex is looking at a small notebook where he has written down the information Michael and I shared with him and with Dale. He looks up from it and addresses Connor, "Your name is Connor Sullivan McGuire, correct?"

Connor nods his head, "Yes. I'm Father Tom's nephew."

Lex continues his questioning, "My understanding is you're here on a visit, working at the church, and you live on the premises."

Connor points to the opposite side of the church, "I'm livin' in the guest cottage just over there."

Lex looks at Dale and then back at Connor, "According to Leah, you ran from the rectory and into the orchard after she heard Father Tom call her name. Why were you running?"

Connor's eyes briefly meet mine then he looks at Lex again, "I'd been about my duties in the sanctuary. After that, Michael, Leah, and I had talked a bit, but I left them because I was supposed to be meetin' with Father Tom after my prayers. On my way there I saw someone run from the rectory. I went in to find

Father Tom. He was standing next to his desk, his hand on his chest, his face pale. I wanted to be stayin' with him, but he told me to go after the person who had just left. I tried to take the same path as the person runnin' had taken through the orchard, but the fog made followin' difficult to be sure. I even wondered at one point if the person had doubled back and was behind me, but I'm believin' it was only the mist playing its games with my mind. When I arrived at the opposite side of the orchard I knew there was no sense to me runnin' around unable to see, so I rushed back to be with Father Tom. I found Michael giving him CPR, and Leah sitting next to him holdin' a cloth to his head. You and the paramedics arrived shortly after that."

Lex looks doubtful, "Did Father Tom say a name?"

Connor explains, "Father Tom seemed to be havin' trouble breathing. He was holdin' his chest as I said before. If he said a name I don't remember now. I wouldn't have even left Father Tom, but he's my uncle, and I did what he asked me to do."

Lex looks at Dale and then back to Connor, "You are careful to say 'person' instead of 'man'. Do you believe the person you were chasing could have been a woman?"

Connor thinks for a moment before he answers, "I can't be sayin' why I'm not sure it was a man. The fog was thick. It was lifting a bit but still next to impossible to see anything clearly. For some reason I remember thinking the person I was chasing could be a female, but I can't tell you why now. Man or woman, I can't say. Maybe it was just an impression, or maybe I just don't want to be misleading."

Lex jots down a few notes, "Well, thank you for not wanting to be misleading. Maybe since you want to be so helpful you could comment on the robe Leah mentioned you were wearing. When and where did you take that off?"

Connor answers quickly, "I took it off as I was running."

Lex looks at Dale, "Officer Stuart will go with you to retrieve it."

Connor nods his head, "I'll be appreciatin' the assistance no doubt seein' as I'm not sure where I was in the orchard when I took it off. As I said before it was foggy."

Lex reassures Connor, "I can promise you, Father McGuire, if it's there we'll find it. If we have to bring in the other team of officers to do it, we will. And you should understand finding the robe is going to prove what you're telling us is what really happened. No robe and we're going to have some trouble believing you, and if Father Tom doesn't make it, you could be facing a murder charge."

Connor looks at each one of us, "I would never hurt my uncle."

Dale nods, "And the robe will help prove that. So, let's you and I go find it."

Connor does not turn to go with Dale but instead looks at me, "I saw someone run from the rectory. Are you sure you or Michael didn't see anyone else but me while you were here?"

I begin to mention Sean, but Michael puts his hand on my arm, "They'll find your robe, Connor; that will clear you of any wrong doing."

Although Michael answered Connor and not me, Connor's eyes have not left mine, "What if the robe is not to be found?"

I try to reassure him, "Why would someone take your robe, Connor?"

Connor begins to step toward me but Michael, Dale, and Lex stop him. He holds up his hands, "I wasn't going to harm her, but I'm thinking she may know more than she's tellin'. And the answer to your question, Leah, seems more than a bit obvious. No robe and I look guilty of hurting my own uncle."

Dale puts his hand on Connor's arm, "Or killing him."

Connor shakes his head as he turns to go with Dale, "He won't die."

I ask, "How can you be so sure?"

Connor looks back at me, "I have faith he'll recover."

I remind him, "You will find the robe, Connor."

Connor stops and turns, "To be sure, Leah, and the same people who start fires can take robes. Remember that."

Lex asks, "What fire?"

Michael holds up his hand, "There's no fire. We need to concentrate on what's happening here and not get sidetracked."

I look into Michael's eyes to try to stay focused and to help me remember the promise I made to myself just moments earlier, but I cannot help but wonder why neither Michael nor I have spoken of Sean, who, as easily as Connor, could have been in the rectory with Father Tom. Surely we are not protecting Sean. Why would we?

Looking into Michael's eyes I realize the answer: we are trying to keep the past separate from the present, but I cannot help but wonder if that is ever really possible. The present is born out of the past as surely as the future is born out of the present. By knowingly omitting information we should have shared how have we influenced what will happen next? Perhaps my promise to myself will be more difficult to keep than I even imagined. But I will not think of that now. I close my eyes and send a prayer to the God of whom Connor is so sure, 'Let Father Tom live, please; let Father Tom live.'

*   *   *   *

Michael and I are driving to the cabin where Sean used to stay. Hank and Katy and Brian are staying at their house with John Henry and Mary, but Patrick and Katherine and Matilda are going to the hospital to be there for Father Tom and to pray and to call us the moment they know anything. I look over at Michael, "It must be like you thought. Father Tom must have been having a heart attack when Connor came into the room, then he fell and hit his head. I don't want to believe that anyone—"

Michael interrupts me, "Wanting to believe or not, Leah, we don't have the facts yet. Until the forensic team has evidence all we know is the room was torn apart, Father Tom has a deep head wound, and he has had a heart attack. Whether or not someone was in the room other than Connor, or whether or not someone ran from the room, we don't know, and if you put your wishes in one hand and a pile of—"

I interrupt Michael now, "Enough. I get the point without the illustration you were going to make. We have to talk about why neither of us told Dale and Lex about Sean."

Michael keeps his eyes on the road, "Well, why didn't you?"

I look at the road too before I answer him, "You stopped me."

Michael counters, "I stopped you when they were questioning Connor. That was after we told what happened originally."

I do not say anything, and the silence we share is not comfortable, so I try again, "I really am not playing games with you. I am unsure why I left out the information regarding seeing Sean. I thought maybe if you knew why you did not mention him, then that would help me figure out why I did the same."

Michael takes one hand off the wheel and runs it through his hair, "I didn't not tell them, if that makes sense. I mean ... it seemed like it would only complicate things, so I just left it out. For the people in this town, Sean died along with Colleen and John and May and the Danners over twenty years ago. But the more I think about it, the more I realize I was wrong. I do need to tell them. We have to, and we will as soon as we check out the cabin. If Sean is there then he wants to talk to us, because he knows that's where we would go to find him, which would mean he probably didn't do anything to hurt Father Tom. If he isn't at the cabin, then he's hiding somewhere else, and we have to assume he did the deed, and we have to tell Dale and Lex immediately. We're assuming he's innocent ... for the moment."

I sigh, "Except for two or three huge assumptions, your reasoning is good."

Michael sighs too, "A handful of assumptions is about as meaningful as a handful of—"

I interrupt him, "Wishes."

Michael shakes his head, "Not what I was going to say, but I'll let it go."

I turn the key over in my hand. We stopped by the house to change our clothes and clean-up. Father Tom's blood no longer covers the key or my hands, but the memory of it is strong. Michael notices me looking at the key, "I still think you should have left that there, and the box and the letters too. They were safe. No one was going to find them where I had them hidden."

I shook my head, "No, they are only safe with us now and maybe not even then."

Michael reaches over and places his hand on my shoulder, "Puppy and the kids are with dad and mom and Brian, and the box and letters are with us. So if someone does break into our house no one or nothing can be taken from us that can't be replaced."

I say 'yes' to him then add, "I have to make time to talk with Brigid. I want to know the significance of the necklace and ring and feather. I want to know whose blood is mixed with the soil. I have to go to the altar with her and see what she saw."

Michael comments, "Yeah, plus May wrote you had to talk with Sean and remind him of who he is and that new choices can change old ones."

I lean my head back against the headrest, "Is it not strange she wrote these letters, then the fire happened, and now all of this is happening, and Sean has been alive all these years, and I did not even know."

We are turning into the parking area. Three small wooden signs mark three trails, each leading to one of the cabins. All are marked private property. The most remote cabin is leased by Father Tom and before Father Tom took over the church it was leased by his predecessor. It is there Sean stayed all those years ago. It is there we hope to find him now, although I cannot imagine what I will say to my father, who was not the father of my childhood. Papa John was that man: kind and strong, humorous and loving, a practical, hard working man but also playful. I remind myself too it is because Sean's blood flows in me I am involved with Shal and Brigid. Then I remember it is also May's blood, and that connection is sweet to recall, and I cannot regret my tie to her. Next my mother's laughter whispers to me from the past. I see her so clearly that I almost reach out to her, but then I see flames, so I stop looking through the memory book in my head. I open the car door and let the cool air breathed out by a thousand trees clear my thoughts. The next moment is here.

✱   ✱   ✱   ✱

Sean sits on the small covered porch of the cabin. A rifle sits next to him. As we approach he stands, and we stop. Time has not changed him much: the same unruly auburn hair, the same distant gray eyes, the same unsmiling lips. He even stands as I remember him standing: more weight on one foot, one hand in his pocket, the other at his side tapping his leg slowly, his head tilted just slightly to the right.

The silence lays solid between us, even the birds and breeze are stilled it seems. I look at Michael and begin walking again, slowly, with my eyes looking into Sean's eyes, and he speaks, his heavily accented voice, missed for so long, stops me and my eyes fill with tears but his words deny my emotions, "If it's taking me back you've come to do, turn around now, for I won't be going."

I ask the question most current, "Did you harm Father Tom?"

He answers me with a question of his own, "How can you even be asking me that, little Leah?"

I feel little even though I deny it, "I am not little anymore."

Sean closes his eyes for a moment, then opens them as he says, "To me you will always be little Leah." He looks at Michael, "I thank you for the love and care you've given my daughter, and for the young ones, John Henry and Mary; they appear to be fine and good."

Michael nods his head once acknowledging and accepting what Sean has said but returns the conversation to my question, "We have to know if you are in any way responsible for what happened to Father Tom."

Sean leans toward us, putting his hands on the railing of the porch, "I am as responsible for Father Tom's condition as I am for the fire that took my mother, my Colleen, John, and the poor Danners, who had just come to preach and burned for it."

Michael pushes for a clearer answer, "My father explained your part in that, but I would like a simple yes or no regarding the Father."

Sean turns now and leans against the railing, his eyes never leaving us, "And by now, as many years as you've had, you're still not convinced that simple yes and no answers seldom offer a proper fit."

Michael walks close enough to me to pull me back to stand beside him, "We have to know before we can continue talking with you. By now, as many years as you've had and as much sorrow as you've caused, I would think you could understand that."

Sean disagrees, his eyes bright with emotion, "Sorrow is; what causes it isn't always as obvious as it may seem. I was in Father Tom's room, but I heard someone walking to the door. I was certain I had heard Father Tom in the sanctuary, so I reasoned whoever was coming was not him. Not a social person by nature, and even less so in this town than in others, I was not wanting to make introductions. I left through the back, made my way around the church and thought to wait in the sanctuary until Father Tom was alone, so I could speak with him about matters you can probably guess the nature of, but I found you there instead. Two surprises in such a short bit of time made me think it would be asking for trouble to wait for the third, so I came here ... to wait for you. That's as simple as I can make it. Does it suit?"

Michael asks, "But you somehow knew Father Tom was hurt because you weren't surprised when we asked you if you were involved."

Sean sits in the chair again, "True. With the ceo sith so heavy I thought to be staying a bit to make sure Leah found her way through it. I was closer than you might believe and watched her out fairy the fairy mist. Then I was off, as I told you before, to come here to wait for my long lost daughter to come to her old athair. And here she is fine as fine can be and lovely like my sweet Colleen, with the same gentleness until you rile her a bit and then the Irish wildness overtakes her and she rides her anger like a priestess warrior wanting blood."

I am not amused with him, "I want no blood, Sean."

Sean whistles before he responds, "Ah cailin, if only wanting were all that was measured, we'd all be singing like larks."

I ask him another question, "Why are you here?"

Sean smiles, but only his lips move, his eyes stay dark like the gray clouds over a storming sea, "To see you with my own eyes ... to help you if I can. To see what you find on your journey. To take back what is mine from those who took it from me."

Michael asks, "What was yours that was taken?"

Sean stands, stretches, and then reaches down for the rifle. Michael holds my hand and starts walking backward as Sean cradles the rifle against his chest folding his arms, "What was taken you ask? The right to be father to my own children. The right to be a part of the journey one of those children must take. A chance perhaps to find a treasure, buried in time, and to make sure that golden treasure ends up blessing the people it should. For those reasons I am here. For those reasons I will stay."

Michael and I have both stopped walking, and I am looking at Sean not believing what he has said could possibly be true, "You are here for gold?"

Sean nods, "Among the other things I listed, I am."

I begin to walk toward him again, but Michael grabs my arm, "My mother, my step-father, my grandmother, the Danners, Malick's father, they all died because the crazy group to which you belong wants gold?"

Sean is watching me closely, "You speak of things you don't really know." He pauses then adds, "I knew you had anger in you and all that talk about what a calm cailin you are was just talk. You're a MacBride after all and my very own daughter."

I can almost feel the anger to which he refers. It is building in me, and his words are like breath on an ember, "And the journey I am on, as you call it, what is your interest in that?"

Sean offers me nothing, "If you're asking you're not far enough along for me to say."

I say 'fine' to him. He says it back to me. Then I add, "In May's second letter, she asked me to remind you of who you are and to tell you old choices can be changed by new ones."

Finally something we have said seems to cause him to pause in his free flowing banter. We look at each other for a moment, and I think there is a chance he will set the rifle down and we will talk sincerely about what has happened, but I am misled if only for the moment. His words burn me, "I am who I have become."

I ask, "Then you don't believe in where I've been?"

He responds quickly, "I believe I am in this world, and I do here what is my duty here. The next world I will wait to know and make my decisions for it when I am there, but as for your question, I have no doubts at all about where you've been."

I offer him one more chance to show some interest in May's request of him, "Then the power that is of that other world does not interest you."

He gestures toward his rifle, "I have all the power I need to do what I am called to do here."

I look back at Michael, and he lets his hand drop from my arm, "I do not think that is true, Sean. There is no wall separating one world from the other, and I believe you know that and are just playing some game with me. However, if you truly believe your rifle is sufficient you should learn now how terribly wrong you are, and you should do what May asks you to do and reconsider past choices. You should do what I am asking you to do now and lay down that gun."

Sean stands taller, but there is an expression on his face that touches my heart, "I could, you know, but I won't, daughter, and be remembering you know nothing of my life now. But more than anything know this: not you or anyone is going to make me do anything I don't want to do."

I see my home burning as the rifle is pulled from his arms then, as if thrown, sails into the air, crashing against the massive trunk of a tree. Sean's eyes widen for an instant then he is over the rail and running through the forest. His speed and agility surprise me, and I wonder sadly if he did not outrun Connor through the orchard.

Michael whistles, "Nice one, honey, a little dramatic, but I think he got the message. Or maybe he was just pushing you to see what you could do."

I lean my head against his chest, "It does not matter; he is gone again. There is no point in trying to go after him either. He knows these woods better than anyone probably, but we will see him again. I have no doubt of that. I just wish I knew in what context our next meeting will be."

Michael kisses the top of my head, "Not quite the reunion I was hoping you'd have, but I'm not completely hopeless about him. It felt like the way he was acting was a front more than anything else, like a cop who takes on the role of tough guy to intimidate and to control the situation. Did you feel that? And I believe what he said about not hurting Father Tom."

I breathe in and out and close my eyes, comfortable in Michael's arms, surrounded by the same trees I ran through so often as a girl, "Perhaps May's words will cause him to question his choices." I pause and lean back, look up into my husband's eyes, "But whatever he chooses, he has been told. I did what I was supposed to do. I am ready for May's last letter ... and a bath. No, I am ready to find out how Father Tom is, then stop and see the kids, then a bath, then May's letter." I pause remembering the shape my day has taken, "Of course, things could happen totally contrary to what I would like and I know it, but it is nice to have a plan, even if it is just window-dressing."

Michael keeps an arm around my shoulders as we walk back down the path to our car, "And Brigid ... when will you see Brigid?"

I sigh, "After May's letter."

Michael reminds me, "Didn't Elwood say he was involved with the third letter?"

I nod, "Yes, he did. Should we call him to see if he wants to be there for the reading?"

Michael agrees and checks his pager, which he had on silent mode, "Patrick paged me. Maybe we will have good news about Father Tom."

I try to smile, "It has to be."

Michael asks, "Has to be … why has to be?"

I stop walking and put my arms around Michael, "Because like Connor said, there is a God in heaven, and people are praying, and because I want so very much for Father Tom to be okay."

Michael kisses my lips gently, "Prayers don't always heal the sick or injured, Leah. Plus, what you think you need may not even be an factor in the bigger plan. You should know that better than anyone because of what happened to your family."

I shake my head, close my eyes, and lean back against his arms, trusting him to hold me, "Have faith, Michael. We have to believe he will be okay."

Michael pulls me close to him, "I'll do that, wife, but I just don't want you to—"

I interrupt him, "Do not say it, husband. Just believe. Be fearless."

He propels me down the path again, his arm still around my shoulders, "Fearless and full of faith. I hope to all that's holy that isn't the same as a handful of wishes and another one full of—"

I pull his head down to me and kiss his lips to stop him. I whisper 'faith' against his lips; he whispers 'yes, wife' against mine. In my mind, like a heartbeat, the word 'live' drums. I offer it to God as my prayer and send it to him in faith, understanding even as I do my faith must remain strong no matter what happens.

✳   ✳   ✳   ✳

What is it about the faces of my children that can make me forget all else going on in my life? How deep their eyes must be that they can draw me in so, how sweet their hearts, how inspiring their love, unravaged by disappointment or betrayal. They, in their smallness, in their innocence, become sanctuary for me. I rest in them feeling safe, protected, and somehow protecting.

John Henry, Mary, and I lay next to each other on the floor in Hank's and Katy's front room with Puppy as our pillow. His breathing moves our heads up and down, and Mary is beginning to giggle, but John Henry rises up on one elbow, his face serious, "What's a coma, mom? I've heard the word before, but what does it mean exactly?"

Mary puts her hand over my mouth before I can respond and whispers to her brother, who is on the other side of me, "Father Tom's in one, and I don't want momma's eyes to get sad again, so you can wait and ask grandpa later. So, shhh." She takes her hand off my mouth, pats my cheek, and begins speaking in her normal voice, "I was just about to giggle 'cause Puppy's breathing is making my head go up and down."

John Henry shakes his head, bends down and kisses my cheek before he stands, "I'm going to find dad." He looks at Mary, "So you can giggle all you want, and don't 'shhh' me; I'm your big brother."

Mary crawls on top of me, and we are nose to nose as she says, "Well that's a fine how-do-you-do."

I have to laugh and bury my face in her soft hair, tickling her neck with my breath and lips. "You have been hanging out with your grandma for certain, young lady. That is one of her favorite sayings."

Mary puts her hands on my face, "I'm adopting it."

I sit up and pull her into my lap as we both rub Puppy's tummy, "And that is a new word too, is it not?"

She nods her head, "Yep. Grandpa and I were watching this serious channel on TV, and there was a story about this momma cat that adopted a puppy because the puppy's mom got killed and the two families who owned them thought it might work, but they weren't sure, but they tried anyway. And since the momma cat's babies had just died and the puppy was only two days old it worked. And grandpa said it was a bigger story than just the puppy getting a new mom, 'cause the two families had not gotten along for a really long time, but the puppy and the momma cat brought them together. So everyone lived happily ever after. The end."

As she says her last words she throws herself across Puppy and hugs him then turns to me again, "Father Tom will live happy ever after too, mom. Grandma said so, and I believe her. The end." And she is definitely done with the conversation, because she begins dancing like a ballerina, standing on her tiptoes, then lifting and lowering her leg very slowly before leaping into the air. "Watch me dance, mom." I lean back against Puppy again and do what my daughter says, wanting the moment to last longer than I know it can.

✳   ✳   ✳   ✳

Elwood Library is surrounded by stone fountains of diverse proportions and distinctions set in islands of lush grass. Paths are everywhere. Elwood likes paths, and the proof is evidenced by their number. They crisscross and circle back only to suddenly end in a foliage covered gazebo or a chair swing. Some paths just end. When I was John Henry's age, Elwood and I would walk the paths, and he would tell me the why of them. The paths ending abruptly and without apparent reason he explained as vista points, places to stop and to see. I would ask him, I remember, what I was supposed to see, and he would repeatedly tell me I was to see whatever I happened to be viewing. I would say to him, 'There's just grass.' He would reply, 'Ah, yes, but if you stay for an hour it will have changed; there may be a shadow cast by tree and sun working together just so, or a squirrel could be resting, or perhaps there will be a white glove or a blue comb left behind by someone you can then begin to imagine as looking this way or that: young or old, male or female, laughing or quiet.' He would remind me there was no end to the possibilities of such vistas.

I realize Michael is watching me and probably waiting too. I walk to him, and we climb the wide steps together. I cannot count the number of times I have been here, but I realize in the last five years or so I have come here much less. Sadness accompanies the realization, because Elwood always made time for me when heartbreak was my most steady companion. I am disappointed in myself for not offering him the same sweet solace in return.

Michael pulls me close to him, "I know what you're thinking. I can tell by the expression on your face." I only press my face into his chest, so he continues, "You're feeling badly because you don't visit Elwood as much as you think you should."

I say, "It is true" without changing position.

He pushes me back from him gently, "It is, but he understands the same way you will when your kids are grown and busy with lives of their own."

I look at him questioningly, "Is that supposed to make me feel better?"

He draws me into his arms again, "Sometimes, Leah, feeling better isn't an option."

I shake my head at him, "My goodness, but your comforting is not comforting."

He strikes a ponderous pose, his hand rubbing his chin, his other hand on the small of his back, one foot turned sideways, as he speaks in a sort of Transylvanian-Freud like voice, "Ah, yes, the uncomforting comfort dilemma."

I hit his shoulder somewhat gently, "You are being strange again."

He remains in his original position, "Ah, yes, the being strange-again-dilemma."

We just stand there for a moment, trying to out wait each other, until he hikes-up his pants and begins scratching himself in various areas, while making strange sounding words like 'guhday-guhdee' over and over again. I am trying not to laugh when I notice Elwood is standing at the bottom of the stairs looking up at us with an amused expression on his face. Michael looks at me to see my response to him then follows the direction of my eyes and is suddenly stopped in his bizarre gyrations as he realizes he is performing for someone besides me. Then I do laugh and so does Elwood.

Michael bows solemnly and explains, "She made me do that. Don't ask me why; she is just a bit off that way."

Elwood nods his head in agreement, "That was, of course, my first guess. Having been married myself to a wondrous creature with similar fancies, I am not at all surprised."

Michael joins Elwood at the bottom of the stairs then they both look up at me as Michael says, "Exactly."

I put my hands on my hips and shake my head at them, "You are both, my husband and my uncle, too weird for words. I will not even try to respond; it would be senseless and pointless, I am sure. It would be, at this moment in time, like speaking into a void, a vacuum, and perhaps even like pissing into the wind, if you will be so kind as to excuse the vernacular."

Michael looks at Elwood, "Thank God she decided not to respond or we might've been here for hours."

Elwood nods, "My thoughts exactly, Michael."

I say to them both as I walk down the stairs and past them, "Exactly nothing; there is not exactly anything happening here at all; it is all peanuts and poppycock."

Elwood looks at Michael, "Peanuts and poppycock? I'm unclear on what meaning to attach to peanuts and poppycock, Michael. I'm at a loss."

Michael whispers loudly, "Ignore her; it's the only way. Just smile at her and pretend everything she says makes sense, or we will be here for hours and tragically miss dinner, which I know she must be planning diligently in the quarreling corners of her fevered little brain, because she knows her man needs food soon, and that is, of course, a prime and essential concern of hers, being she is my wife and is duty bound to feed me."

I pretend to lift long skirts and walk away from them, "You shall starve and rightly so for your poor manners and odd ways. I am done with you and your friend. I shall forsooth and soothfor go forward without you."

Michael and Elwood laugh together then rush after me as Michael says, "Forsooth and soothfor? You're definitely making up words now. You must be tired." He picks me up in his arms, "I will carry you, so you can marshal your energy to prepare dinner for your menfolk."

I cross my arms and shake my head as he carries me, "I am menfolkless and not hungry, which makes you terribly out of luck where food preparation is concerned."

We are almost to our car and Michael throws me over his shoulder as he counters, "You don't believe in luck, and I should add, just in case someone is keeping track of points here, it's horribly sad I even have to remind you of that. Additionally, you will make my dinner as soon as we arrive at the castle, wench, or be cast out into the gloomy forest to fend for yourself."

He sets me down none too gently, and I respond haughtily, "You are a heartless brute, and I am quite sure Elwood will take my side in this at any moment."

Elwood shakes his head slowly from side to side, "I must disappoint you, little Leah, for I find myself in much the same state as your good husband here; my hunger is overriding by huge leaps and bounds any motivations being promoted by my compassion; my only hope being you will indeed, and with more than feigned decorum, feed us."

I look at Elwood with a disappointed expression on my face, "You would truly rather be fed than honor my feelings?"

Elwood looks down at his feet, whether to play along or to hide a smile I cannot know, "It's true, my niece."

I open the car door with one hand, as I pretend to wipe tears away with the other, "Then I shall do as you request."

Michael yells 'victory' as both he and Elwood climb quickly into the jeep, but before he turns the key in the ignition, he rests his forehead against the steering wheel and asks, "If Brian were acting like I've been acting I'd tell him he was a total jackass. It must be stress induced." He looks over at me, and then into the backseat at Elwood, "Don't you agree?"

Elwood agrees with Michael, but I shake my head indicating disagreement with him and add, "I could buy into that if I had not seen you behave as strangely on countless other occasions when the situation was stressful."

Michael starts the car, "No shit, Sherlock, but the point I was making was 'this time' the strangeness was just a release or something. And don't argue with me just to argue, because suddenly I'm tired in every way."

I lay my hand on his shoulder as we pull up to a stop sign, "I am sorry you are tired. Perhaps the food you have requested will refresh you."

Elwood leans forward, resting his elbows on his knees, "Actually exhaustion would seem a natural state after the previous behavior. Also, remembering what we face, you two more than I, it would seem the jocularity was a momentary escape with, I might add, no ill effect. As a previous occupant of many a dank and depressing foxhole, I recall quite well the humorous or at least silly behaviors preceding the worst or most feared battles. Long waits too were dreaded, the long hours of not knowing when the silence would end. And the darkness, which seemed more than just a matter of light or lack of it, weighed down on us even more. Perhaps the not knowing was the worst. As a medic, my fears may have taken different shapes than the soldiers because the enemies were not just those wearing a different uniform or personal doubts; my enemy was also death's accomplices that came dressed in lack of equipment to heal, lack of hope to heal, lack of time to heal." Elwood pauses and leans back before he continues, "Then, of course, there are aspects of life, of living, sometimes worse than death."

I look at Michael then back at Elwood, "Losing your wife and son?"

Elwood agrees, "Losing my heart."

He takes my hand when I reach back to him, "But, Elwood, you didn't lose your heart, because if you had lost your heart you would not feel so strongly their loss. You would not celebrate the sweetness of them each and every day in the sad and lonely way you do if you had lost your heart."

Elwood speaks softly, "I sometimes wonder, although I don't believe there was choice in the matter because of who I am, if I could have somehow let them go, buried the missing of them in the empty caskets we placed under soil. I can't forget those horrid boxes, the one so small, can't forget the distance they created in me that was all around me and still is. I can't forget the words that were said, but the ocean's waves crashing against sand and stone seem like the more appropriate epitaph for the infant son and wife-mother stolen away from me by wind and sea. How could I, a doctor having served in peace and war, not be able to accept that even a just and merciful God takes from us based on an eternal plan regardless of our ability to understand or the depth of our self proclaimed need." He leans forward again, "I often think of Jesus on his knees in Gethsemane when he looked up and spoke to the Father, asking, even as he knew there could be no other way, if just perhaps he could pass the chalice. He had to ask and accept God's answer because we ask and are supposed to accept God's answer."

Elwood sighs, "I think often of Jesus, knowing my pain is softened by his mercy and love for me. I say his name often, even when my anger denies prayer, and his name comforts me always."

We are parked in our driveway, but none of us move even as Elwood's words are followed by silence. Michael and I turn to Elwood, and there is a peace in his expression that does not contradict his tears.

I ask him the question his words have created in me, "Meaning no disrespect and please do not answer if my question seems inappropriate to you, but if you feel this comfort from Jesus, from just saying his name, then why do you end up on the beach without clothes and lost to reason?"

He wipes the tears from his face as he leans forward, placing one of his hands on Michael's shoulder and the other on the back of my head, "Leah, sometimes I don't want to remember to say his name. To be honest, sometimes I want the loneliness to take me. I want to be lost in my own despair to the extent I become numb to it, lost in a fantasy or even a nightmare, lost to everything of this world. I choose, dear niece, to deny his comfort. I make the cross I bear larger than the one he bore. I deny the hope he offers, because I do not like the way he painted my life. I want to destroy the canvas, rip it to shreds, tell him in strong willful words I had a better plan." Elwood sighs deeply, "I choose to forget him and what he did, so I can resent him, be mad at the way the colors and lines of my life have been arranged. My anguish, a madness of sorts, even in tiny increments becomes so convoluting I can't always find my way back from it. I should have died so many times in those moments, but some part of me always remembers at the last possible moment his name, and then I am always rescued somehow … by women and small children on beaches or by other means; my purpose, his plan for me not completed yet, so I linger, remembering how much heavier his burden was than mine, and humility becomes my door to his peace." Elwood breathes in and out deeply, "You find yourself in a place that seems beyond Christian parameters, but you'll find before the end of your journey that God and his power know no parameters. Perhaps all this talk of mine was for no other reason than that one last sentiment, or, if you will, that one last truth: God, before the beginning and after the end, boundless in his infinite grace."

Inside of me, in a deep place beyond the carefully constructed inner doors and pathways I have created for myself, a child's hands fold into each other and a small head is bowed. I remember the trust and the peace, the sweet solace of a faith upon which I once sailed, my God's breath my breeze. I remember. I remember. I remember even as I pull the rope taut on the motor of the craft upon which I now make my own way. I remember, but I still do not say his name. Not yet and maybe never, but I cannot help but remember.

Nor can I help but wander back into my classroom and to the words I shared with my students from Eliot. From the first part of the poem the words I shared come floating up, white script etched upon the darkness: "These are only hints and guesses, hints followed by guesses; and the rest is prayer, observance, discipline, thought, and action." But those words disappear as quickly as they appeared, no pier and rope to hold my attention. Then the lines "The sea has many voices, many gods and many voices" appear, but they too pass quickly. I rub my hands over my face as new words appear amid the tiny silver stars blasting against the black of my eyelids: faith, hope, and love ... faith, hope, and love. These linger and taste sweet on my tongue; they fill me up, so I decide to let them come like waves upon the still shore of the moment. Then I decide to let them be my anchor as my hands make dinner for these men who sit in the car waiting for me to speak or to move. Faith, hope, and love, I should tell them is what will see us through this time confronting us like a building storm, but I realize I cannot speak words I cannot yet find foundation for beyond the scope of myself, and for this moment, the God to whom I pray and who should be the foundation of my hope, faith, and love is as incomprehensible to me as the mist that filled my morning. He is too distant, too deep; he is too much like the ocean with all its unchanging transformations.

I decide to move instead of to speak. I do not want to be misleading or misled, but still 'faith, hope, and love' whisper inside of me, and the little girl who is and is not me anymore bows her head.

✳   ✳   ✳   ✳

Malick stands with his back to us then turns slowly as we exit the car. Somehow I believe he has not only heard Elwood's words but my own thoughts as well. The look in his eyes tells me that. The look on his face tells me nothing. I do not even greet him, and he returns the courtesy, but our eyes lock, as a struggle ensues, beyond me in its scope and sequence. I hold on to what I cannot see to keep him from invading my thoughts even more.

The nonphysical hold Malick and I have on each other is broken as Michael unceremoniously declares, "Stop looking into my wife's eyes that way, or I'll kick your ass from here to next week, you piece of shit."

Malick studies Michael's face then laughs, "Interesting."

Michael just shakes his head, "I don't feel interesting. I don't know why you're here, or I do and don't know how you knew we'd be here. Why aren't you at the hospital praying for Father Tom?"

Elwood and Malick shake hands without exchanging words as Malick answers Michael, "I can pray for Father Tom anywhere."

Michael steps closer to Malick, "Do you pray?"

Malick does not step back or step forward, "Do you?"

Michael lets his head fall back and looks up into the sky, "I like you as an eagle better."

Malick laughs again, "You're feeling a little ruffled again and want to rid your angst on me?"

Michael shakes his head, "No, I don't think that's it. I just genuinely don't like you. Just looking at you pisses me off."

Malick shrugs, "And if I cared that would undoubtedly create some sort of response in me, but I don't. I'm here to help Leah. When that reason is gone, I'm gone. It's that simple. So let's get to the third letter then Leah can go see Brigid since she obviously has some sort of problem with Shal now."

All eyes are on me again as Elwood asks who Shal is, but I do not respond except to say, "I am making dinner."

Malick smiles but not happily, "Thanks, I'd love to break bread with you."

I want to tell him I am not serving bread, but I realize how trite that would sound. It could also possibly bring about a whole new conversation with him, which is definitely not a goal. Michael and I walk to the door of our home as Malick and Elwood follow us and begin talking about the weather. Our realization the door is no longer locked as we left it does not even surprise us, but Michael still puts his hand up and motions for me to wait. Elwood comes and stands at my side as Malick follows Michael into the living room. Elwood and I turn and look at each other as the aroma of corned beef and cabbage wafts from the interior of the house. I shake my head as Elwood smiles, realizing he must truly be hungry if a smile is his first response to some uninvited person breaking into my house and cooking a meal in my kitchen.

*   *   *   *

Michael comes to the door, leans close to me, kissing my cheek as he says, "Your daddy left you a note and a meal."

Malick comments from inside the house, "Old Sean even set the table for you."

Michael does not move to let me in, so I look at him, "Is there more, or is there some other reason you are not allowing me into my own home?"

He pulls me into his arms and whispers in my ear, "There's more, Leah. Prepare yourself."

Michael takes hold of my hand as we walk into the house together. My eyes take in what I see, but thoughts do not come. Every drawer is opened and its contents on the floor. Sofa and chair cushions are ripped open and their inside stuffing is strewn here and there. I walk from room to room and find each the same, except for John Henry's and Mary's rooms; they have not been touched. I remember what I was told: the innocents are not involved then wonder of what I am guilty. My eyes return to their task, but still my thoughts are far behind. I am monosyllabic in my thoughts. I can only think, 'oh' or 'no' or 'why'. I stop the tears building one by one into a tidal wave that will surely sweep away my hold on the moment. I try to grab on to something, and then remember Michael saying to me everything that could not be replaced had been removed from these rooms, but we were wrong to believe that.

We were so wrong. The sadness in me is overwhelming, and I could easily replace it with anger, but that has never been my way, and I will not walk that path now. This was done out of anger to cause anger and fear; I will not be led so easily. The men are watching me. I look at each one of them. I take a deep breath as I pick up a small framed photo; its shattered glass distorts a photo of me sitting with Michael, who is holding our son for the first time. I want to scream, but I choose to remain silent. I set the frame on the small table next to the sofa. I look around the room then into Michael's eyes, "Perhaps I should read Sean's note."

Malick removes it from the table. A single sheet of computer paper has been folded in half, my name printed boldly and underneath a large, circled 'S'. I unfold then read the note aloud: "'*Leah, I did not think to find such easy entry or that your housekeeping skills would be so very remiss. Michael is more than a saint to put up with you in that, but I am amusing myself at your expense again, and you, no doubt, have had enough of my humorous ways, so I will be brief in what follows. I did not touch anything or move anything in case you were thinking of calling in the authorities, but I can mention to you doing so will only be a waste of your time and theirs. Whoever did this deed left no signature on his work. Anything in the kitchen I touched has been wiped clean. I set your table wearing plastic gloves, so if you do decide to call the coppers, your old man will not be blamed. I mention that only in case it was a concern you might have. In regards to whoever was in your house before me, I would take caution. Violence is violence whether it's against sofas and dresser drawers or people. Old lines drawn on what is or is not permissible fade as one deed bleeds into another; the years wear away at distinctions like reality wears away at idealism. Whoever did this to your home was doing nothing more than sending you a message and a warning. Take the warning and know the message: what you're doing involves others whose motivations, like mine, you do not agree with, but they, unlike me, are not concerned with your preferences. Take care of you and yours, daughter. I will be watching. I only hope that will be a comfort and not a sad reminder. Yours, S'.*" I pause before I read the postscript, "'*I hope the fixins are to your liking; they were your mother's favorite.*'"

* * * * *

How odd, how strange, to be sitting at a table set by my father who cooked my mother's favorite meal, a detail which I had somehow forgotten: corned beef and cabbage with potatoes and carrots on the side. How odd to be sitting at my dining room table surrounded by cushion stuffing and the scattered innards of drawers and the contents of shelves. I turn my head when out of the corner of my eye I notice the pale lavender of one of my camisoles laying beneath one of Michael's *Sports Illustrated* magazines. Each item having come from a different room leaves me wondering if this person who violated our home and our personal life carried things in his hands as he pondered what vile deed to do next. He had touched my underclothes, my unmentionables, some of them slightly sexy silk purchases made by Michael for Valentine's Day or anniversary presents and in stark contrast to the simple black or white cotton items I purchase for myself. A tiny flame becomes the central image in my mind. It grows bigger, consuming my attention.

Suddenly Michael leaps from his chair yelling, "Holy shit, Leah, stop it." I realize the pale lavender camisole is now burning along with Michael's Sports Illustrated. I say 'oops' in my mind, but I feel no remorse really. Life has become too strange. Nothing makes sense anymore. Then I change my mind as I think of moments earlier when we talked with John Henry and Mary. That made sense. Michael had called to let his father know what happened at our house. Lane was also called. Extra security is being brought in I was told, but I am not reassured.

Michael's voice interrupts my thoughts again, "Gees, Leah, when did you learn how to do that?" He is walking back to the kitchen after dumping water on the burning magazine and camisole.

I look at him as I respond, "This is not exactly like a traditional sort of learning experience, Michael. I am not learning anything. Things just happen then I realize I can do something. It is sort of ironic and too sad really to realize fire has become my friend?"

Michael is about to run his hands through his hair as I say this, but he stops in mid-motion, "Oh yeah, get dark now; go for it. This is not a damn gothic novel in one of your literature classes. This is our life. Don't go melodramatic on me." He lets his hands finish their activity, walks back into the dining room and sits down in the chair next to me, "I'm a fireman remember. Fire is not our friend. You're my wife. This is all strange and weird, but we're okay. Granted, you're acquiring some new talents, but skills do not change who we are. Right?"

I lean toward him and kiss his lips, "Right. It was just a momentary lapse into lala land. Fire is not our friend. We need to read May's last letter. I need to see Brigid. I will clean up dinner, and then we can get to those undertakings before some other distraction diverts us."

Michael leans back in his chair, "Dishes before letter? Where are your priorities?"

I stand and begin gathering dishes and silverware as Malick and Elwood do the same, "My priorities are obviously where they should be. Clean up one mess before possibly making a new one."

Michael sighs and stands, gathers his own dishes and silverware and follows Elwood, Malick and me into the kitchen commenting, "So you think May's third letter could be messy?"

I look at Elwood as I say, "You should ask him. He knows what is in the letter."

Michael turns, takes Elwood's dishes from him and hands them to me, "Is May's third letter going to be messy?"

Elwood's eyes look beyond Michael and into my eyes, "You should be prepared to hear news more unsettling than anything you have heard previously."

Malick looks down at the floor so I ask him, "You also know?"

Malick looks up and nods, his expression sincere, "You should prepare yourself for quite a shock, Leah."

I look at Michael then begin rinsing dishes and placing them in the dishwasher, "Well then, first things first. I will do the dishes. You men clean up the area by the fireplace, so we have someplace to sit."

Elwood puts his hand on my shoulder, "If you would allow me to suggest an alternative I would like to invite you all back to my home where we can read May's letter. It will also provide a safe base for you as you go to Brigid. After that, there are beds for you and Michael and for Malick, too, if he believes he should stay close based on what has happened here in your home and what happened earlier to Father Tom." Michael agrees, and Malick agrees to stay as long as Michael wants him to stay. I say 'yes' to them all then allow myself to think of nothing but the comforting task of rinsing dishes and placing them just so in the racks of the dishwasher, this mundane activity making my life seem momentarily normal again.

When I am done, Michael and I gather up a few necessities from here and there and everywhere. Outside, as we walk to the jeep, the light offered by moon and stars changes. The night deepens. The darkness seems to breathe against me, inhaling and exhaling deeply. I tell it 'no', but it does not respond appropriately;

like the mist of the morning, it wants to have its way with me. Inside the Jeep I sense it clawing somehow fingerlessly at the windows. I tell it 'no' again, but it does not listen. Michael looks at me, his expression reflecting my own concern, as I notice how his hands grip the wheel, realizing even though tree branches and bushes are not moved at all, the Jeep is being pushed first one way then another.

Malick leans forward, "Leah, you need to make it stop. You need to show your power clearly here or it will only become more sure of itself, which only makes it stronger and more difficult to control later."

I close my eyes when his words end. I breathe as deeply as it does. I see myself standing before it, this thing that has no shape to provide boundaries for its heart of emotions and only wears the mist and the darkness like capes. I take breath from this moment, from this center of forever, and like an archer I focus and aim as I exhale, sending all I am into a shapeless center. I say 'no' to its 'yes'. My arrow hits its mark. I open my eyes and watch as Michael's hands relax, but I am also seeing its retreat and although I cannot be sure, for one moment it seemed to wear a face contorted by raging mouth and violent violet eyes. Wild hair streamed behind it. Gnarled fingers clutched at a throat stretched taut. My hand goes to the necklace I wear, and then I know without having seen clearly that the ancient hand was grabbing the chain of a necklace the complement to my own, and I cannot stop myself from turning to look at Malick.

Almost gently, his gaze holds mine, "Don't jump to conclusions. Just remember the impression, forget nothing, but don't attempt to guess at this; you must feel certain. Then when you draw back to marshal your strength in order to move forward, your focus will be as it was just now. That is the only way you will be effective. You must be dead center every time or you'll be overwhelmed and unable to regain position. You can give no ground, Leah; you can offer no compassion."

I ask incredulously, "How could I possibly feel compassion toward it?"

Malick shakes his head, "It's no longer faceless is it?"

Again I ask, "How can you know what I saw? How do you do that?"

He sighs, "The gifts vary, Leah. What you have, what I have, what Father Tom has, what Michael and Elwood have, what Brigid has, what Shal has, what Taen and Bantok have. The gifts vary and so the outcome of each cycle varies based on the players, on those involved. Take nothing for granted, because, as you've discovered, the gifts not only vary, they spawn in the stream of the individual's personal experiences. To know what you're facing at any given moment demands acute awareness."

I lean my head back against the seat, "You answer without answering, Malick. And although it is probably useless I have to ask why in your list are Michael and Elwood and then Taen and Bantok placed together? Do they share their gift or gifts?"

Malick's voice is soothing but offers me little more than new aspects of the same mystery, "My response cannot answer your question any more than a response from you could answer one of my questions. The real questions, the ones that matter, the ones that go deeper than what to place on daily itineraries, are not empty blanks to be filled in by rote or even reasonable responses. Only the one who asks the question can formulate the answer. In the place where this struggle will reveal itself fully, perspective will overshadow reality. The strongest perception becomes the reality. Just as you overcame the wind that was darkness earlier and was mist this morning, so you must overcome it when it wears a face that will have eyes that will try to sway you. It will offer you fresh tears and old blood. It will offer you gold, ageless wisdom, health for your loved ones, perhaps even a future in the past or a future with no past. It will create what it sees you want, so show it nothing of your heart, Leah. Don't let it into your mind. Close those doors for which you are so well known. Wear a mask of indifference to all but what you know to be unchanging truth despite perspective or placement in time. Give it no quarter; give it no pause. Relinquish nothing." He pauses as he looks at Michael then back at me, "Blaze against it, Leah, burn it up, once and for all and forever. Be the one to end this. Be the one who is three."

Michael turns off the ignition as Malick is saying his last words. No words are spoken because Malick's words seem to have filled themselves with space and to have grown wings; they fly around me. Inside my head they take on different shapes, more stationary than beating wings and wild hearts, they become as solid as walls. I make doors in them with keys only I can hold. I wonder about becoming a 'one who is three', but the movement of the curtain covering the large window I know is Elwood's living room on the third story of the library distracts me from the picture show in my head. I feel like someone who has been the victim of a cold water dousing more than once; I am startled and shocked but almost accustomed to the sensation. I ask calmly, "Did anyone else see the curtain move up there on the big window in the center of the third floor?"

Elwood does not answer me but comments, "That's my living room window."

Michael and I say 'yes' at the same time. Both Elwood and Malick are bent down and leaning forward to try and look up into the window being discussed. Elwood sighs, "I was sure my home would be safe for you."

Malick reassures him, "Perhaps it is. Perhaps whoever is up there is a friend ensuring our privacy and safety."

Michael suggests, "Like a friend who cooks corned beef and cabbage maybe?"

Malick laughs but not happily, "I hate to even acknowledge we think alike, but in this instance we are."

I look at Michael, "Why would it be more likely to be a friend than a foe based on what has transpired today?"

Michael looks at Malick then at me, "Sean has been one step ahead of us all day if you think about it. It makes sense it would be him. I suppose we won't really know until we get in there, but I don't feel like I did when we discovered the door of the house was unlocked. This feels okay to me."

Elwood sighs, "I can't imagine anyone being able to gain entry without setting off the alarm. It's a state of the art system and was just installed a few months ago on Lane's recommendation. I suppose Sean is more than adept at breaking and entering, but truly if you understood the dynamics of the system itself, you'd understand my dismay."

Malick asks the most obvious question, "Who has knowledge of and access to the system controls?"

Elwood sighs again, "Only Lane and myself, as far as I know, and the gentlemen who did the installation, but they can't know the numeric password."

Michael wonders aloud, "Wouldn't Lane let us know if he were going to be here? He wouldn't want to startle us. It doesn't make sense it's Lane up there. He would have waved instead of moving back from the window the way he did. Sean, however, likes to appear and disappear, and he did say he would be watching out for Leah."

I open the car door, "Why are we sitting here speculating when we will never know unless we go in and find out for ourselves?"

Malick has opened his eyes after having them closed, "I sense no danger, no element out of place, but if there is an unknown entity it could be shielding itself from me."

Michael whistles softly, "An unknown entity, huh? That puts a different slant on walking in there now doesn't it?"

I push my door open, "Not really, Michael. We have to go in at some point don't we? Now is as good as later."

Michael also gets out of the car, asking Malick a reasonable but silly sounding question, "So are we dealing with the supernatural or bad guys with guns or both?"

Malick closes his door before he replies, "I believe we could experience both of those possibilities before the night is over."

Michael swears under his breath, "Damn!" He walks to the back of the Jeep and lifts the tailgate. I join him as he removes our small duffle of clothing and other necessities, which he hands to me, and then he slips the backpack on that holds the items we have kept with us over the last few days. Next he surprises me by taking his handgun from beneath the spare tire and slipping it into the pocket of his jacket.

The possibility of Michael having to shoot a gun at someone settles on me heavily. I reach out to him, "I am not terribly fond of the idea of you carrying that around or of you using it."

Michael looks at me as if I have made an irrational statement, "Oh gee whiz, Leah. I'm so surprised by that. You set your underwear and a perfectly good issue of *Sports Illustrated* on fire, but you have qualms about me carrying a gun?"

Malick closes the tailgate, "Can we not get into one of your feisty little discussions that ends in adorable hugs and kisses? Can you two just move into the next moment without turning every single situation into some mild to medium-hot form of foreplay?"

Michael and I look at each other as he counters, "Although I'm not totally in favor of your slant on some of our behavior patterns, I do have to admit that somehow making every single situation, no exaggeration there, into some mild to medium-hot form of foreplay, actually sounds good to me." He pauses and pulls me close to him but looks at Malick and comments, "And not because you asked, but only because of our timetable, I'll make the moment to moment transitional foreplay brief." Michael bends down to me and kisses my mouth, but I am more than aware of his awareness of Malick watching him kiss me, and I am in no mood to be used in his game, so I push against him to make him stop, which he does, smiling at me and then at Malick and then at Elwood. "That should hold me," is his last remark before he grabs my hand, and we walk up the stairs to the wide double doors of the library's main entrance.

I hear Elwood commenting on how interesting family is, and for the briefest of moments I long wholeheartedly to be anywhere but here. I long for Michael and I to be with John Henry and Mary and Puppy, all curled up together in a presleep cuddle, but breaking glass causes us all to pause then rush forward. We wait as Elwood enters a numeric code, however the door is opened slowly before he can finish. Sean stands before us, blood dripping down the side of his face from a jagged cut almost hidden by his hair.

He smiles at our shocked expressions and asks us how dinner was as a gun shot's crack causes us to throw ourselves on the ground. As the bullet buries itself in the door frame only an inch or two from where Sean's head had been seconds before, I cannot help but notice that now Sean's expression mirrors our own. As we scurry on all fours into the dark interior of the library's main room, I cannot help but wonder if Sean's assailant waits in the dark for us, but when the second bullet crashes through the window and its shutter to the right of the door the library's dark stillness becomes the safer of the two possible dangers. I stop my mind from its noticing and wondering and become sense driven; I become vision and hearing and touch. I breathe and hear Michael's intake of breath next to me. Barely a whisper, Sean's voice beckons us to follow him as he reminds us to stay in our crawling positions. Across the hardwood floors of the library we crawl as quietly as possible. Michael's bag being dragged sounds eerie, like someone dragging a body. We wait for the next bullet to rip through the darkness as we continue our shuffle. My mind asserts itself, flashing images of a younger me playing games with my brother and friends on these same polished boards as my hands press against something wet and warm, and I realize Sean's blood is tattooing my palms.

*   *   *   *

We have pressed our backs up against a wall separating the main room from a smaller room that is home to the library's local history collection. Sirens come to us through a distance; we anticipate their increasing volume. As we wait we are still but not. Michael taps his hand against the gun. Elwood holds a cloth, probably one of his white cotton handkerchiefs, to Sean's head. I press my palms together, too aware of the cause of their stickiness as I run through my own brain checking locks on doors I know must remain shut if I am to make it through this night. Inside my head I talk to myself, offering generic words of comfort I make louder as other words try to steal the peace I hold on to like a tired swimmer holds on to a raft.

Elwood interrupts my one-sided conversation suggesting he should turn on the lights. Sean tells him to wait until security arrives. Michael says nothing. I say nothing. The sirens with their cars have arrived. In a movie the music would change, or, if there had been no music, music would start. Big men casting larger than life shadows would burst through the doors; their cars' headlights streaming into the room illuminating the smears of blood marking our small journey from door to wall. Nothing like that happens. The sirens stop and moments pass. The silence stretches out, becomes transparent, inverts itself until its noisy insides press up against us. Now every sound is magnified. We breathe like asthma victims. The clock on a far wall drums the passing of seconds. Even the shelves, holding their books, seem to be attempting to barely shift their burdens. And then it is as if we are thrown back against the wall by a tidal wave of light. I gasp at the suddenness of it. I wonder if these men I am with have their eyes closed also, but I refuse to check for confirmation. Instead, I wade into the light as if it is the first swim of the season. I am squinting and breathless.

✳   ✳   ✳   ✳

Lane's voice booms through some sort of magnifying device, "Leah, all floors within the building and also the surrounding area have been secured. You and those with you are safe. I am entering through the front doors." As soon as he does, other men appear in doorways on all floors of the building. They are dressed in black and have various items strapped to their legs, backs, waists, and wrists, plus spy-movie type headgear. I turn my attention to Lane who is walking toward us. Lane's eyes stay on Sean once he has assured himself the rest of us are unhurt.

Lane looks to his left and nods his head. A man is at Sean's side in seconds. No one speaks as the man cleans then butterfly bandages Sean's wound after he has taken Sean's pulse and checked his pupils for telltale signs of concussion. The man's eyes take in the smeared trail of blood as he stands. He nods his head at Lane, turns to Sean, salutes, then leaves the room.

Although we must all be wondering I am the first to speak, "Why did he do that?"

Sean shrugs as he slowly rises to his feet, "Probably for no other reason than he could tell I was an old soldier, and this wasn't first blood."

I look at Lane as I stand; my eyes tell him that Sean's answer will not suffice. Lane looks out the doors, still open to the night, and then back at me then at Sean, "We all know this will be a night of Leah discovering truths. We might as well start with you and with me in that process, Sean." As we all begin to talk at once, Lane holds up his hand, "However, we will move to a more comfortable and private place for that. Sean's assailant left the building before we arrived. I can assure you from human opposition we are safe here. From the other forces opposing us, we can only try to be prepared; I can, unfortunately, offer no guarantees." He walks toward the stairs then turns indicating we should follow him, and we do, silently; if Michael and Malick and Elwood are like me, each of us are prisoners to our own jostling thoughts, our own shoving and tumbling questions.

*   *   *   *

A dominating square redwood coffee table sits in the center of three high-backed sofas and a rustic stone fireplace. Lane stands with his back to us looking into the flames of the fire Elwood has just started. Malick and Elwood sit on each end of one sofa. Michael and I sit on the sofa across from them, but we sit close together, Michael's body leaning against mine, his arm across my legs and his eyes drawn by the same flames holding Lane's gaze.

Sean enters the room with two of Lane's men who carry a glass pitcher of ice water, a carafe of steaming coffee, glasses, and cups. These are set on the coffee table next to the items Michael and I have kept safe for what seems like much longer than a few days. May's letters, the feather, the small metal box, and the stone draw Lane's eyes finally. He walks over to the table, leans down toward them, but makes no attempt to reach for them. Instead he looks at Sean and indicates Sean should take a seat, but Sean only looks away setting his feet a bit further apart then crossing his arms over his chest. The two men still stand at the door. Lane nods his head, and they leave but only after acknowledging Sean by nodding their heads.

This exchange between Sean and the men is noticed by Lane who lowers himself slowly onto the couch directly across from the fire. He seems to relax, which contrasts greatly with Sean's stance and attitude. Lane closes his eyes for a moment as if searching for words then he opens them as he begins to speak, "There are usually a variety of ways to begin telling a long concealed truth, and often much thought is given to such a task. I have had years to prepare my words for you, Leah, but never has such careful preparation fallen short of its task. Motivations are normally—"

Lane is interrupted by Sean, "If you think I'm going to stand and listen to another one of your speeches you should reconsid—"

Lane interrupts Sean, "Then by all means, have a seat, Sean. I believe I suggested the option to you earlier." The two men look at each other, but their expressions give no emotional context for their words.

Sean responds evenly, "I'll sit when I'm ready and where I choose."

Lane looks away from Sean and straight into my eyes, "Up until the death of your mother and John and May and the Danners, Leah, and of your father, Malick, Sean's … activities were undertaken on my command. Except for the lie he told me about May's box, and until the night of the fire, he never gave me a reason to question his dedication ... or his loyalty."

Sean interjects, "That's an oversimplified explanation for a night of complications, Lane, but a parlor general has little to no way of understanding that."

Doors are ripped open in my head, and as fast as I can run to close them, others open wide allowing the past in all its varied images and contexts to bleed out onto the present; fresh blood pouring from old wounds. I say 'no' then realize I have said the word aloud. Then except for the fire the room stretches out in the silence.

I look at Sean, but it is not enough, so I go to him across rug and boards and around a table where I colored inside and outside of the lines so many years ago. I stand close. We are almost touching. I lay my palm against his chest; his heartbeat drums against my hand. I breathe him in through my eyes and fingertips. I realize blood and heritage have a scent. I see the pattern of us unfolding, and I am with him. I am with him.

I am with him as he runs from window to window, their shattering glass denying him. I am with him when he grabs the handle of the door; I feel his flesh sear as the metal of the handle seems to breathe, its heated expansion an inhalation. I am with him as he runs, the flames and the dead left behind him. I feel the coolness of his tears against the fire scorched skin of his cheeks. I watch as his terror rises up before him like a tidal wave, but then he brings us back to the present by placing his hand over my hand. The scar on his palm presses against my skin. I lay my forehead against his chest. He kisses the top of my head. For a moment we are just father and daughter, but only for a moment.

I turn around and look at Lane, who is watching me closely. I keep myself between them, so I can feel that thing they have created between each other. Their relationship takes shape before me. It is rope of light and dark twining, forgiveness woven with bitterness, strength knotted by pride. I reach out in my mind, put my hand on the rope and realize how terribly tight it is stretched, feeling future breaking points now only frayed but too numerous. I shake my head to clear the image as I walk to Lane.

He is not mine to touch. His blood connection to me is only through marriage to Michael, so I sit down next to him and lean into the space around him to draw him into my mind. His breathing changes. Within the space and time of my thoughts, of my senses, he will have no control, and we both know that. I want to giggle like a little girl, and he wants to scold me, but neither of us do either. We are in a place with walls. His shadow walks ahead of him, but I do not know what that means, so I let it have its way, but I am watchful of it. Lane stops at one of the doors along the winding hallway in which we walk, but these are my doors; he has no power here. His shadow tries to force me through the door, but I change the light, and then the shadow follows Lane. We walk further down the hall before stopping in front of an oil painting of a robed and hooded man whose face is hidden. There is a key in one of the man's hands, and in the great distance captured by the painting there is a small shining splash of gold drawing my gaze. Lane touches this place of illumination in the painting. When he removes his hand the shining gold light has gone. In my mind we look into each other just as we looked into the painting, and I know then what I wanted to discover. So we return to the fire lit room and to waiting men, our eyes still locked; we are guarded with and yet seeking of each other, but he is clear to me now, both him and his shadow. They are transparent. I could if I chose, and as May suggested I might need to do, walk through him. He is only a man with soldiers and money who owns a small town. His spirit is locked in his body; he has no special gifts to use for or against me. I am saddened knowing he is willing to do either one with the resources he does have in order to achieve his goal, and I realize goals can make very unethical gods.

I sigh as I stand and walk to Michael. I sit down next to him curling up beside him as my knees become a pillow for my head and his arm a shawl around me. Because I do not want Michael to move, I ask Elwood to hand Michael May's last letter. I ask Michael to read it to me. Then I relax into the sinewy tension emanating out of the men around me. I watch from the safe distance I have created for myself; I take what they fill the air with and breathe it in, turning it into a sweet mixture of my own making: just a bit of spring light interlaced with my children's laughter. Then Michael begins to read, but May enters the room, soft and constant as an ocean breeze, and takes back her words from him, whispering them into my ear and heart and soul. I sense her arms joining Michael's to hold me. I become still while at the same time I dive beneath the surface of my life as May leads me deeper and deeper away from what I know. I am not falling. I am in control. I dive. I dive beyond myself only to find I face my own reflection.

*   *   *   *

May's words have stopped. Elwood speaks now from across the dark surface of a table that once was a tree that once was ... but the image in my mind does not illustrate his words. I am letting them collect, letting them fall like raindrops into a metal pail I have placed just far enough away that I can observe the process but not involve myself in it. I will push my hands into them later. I will gather them, bring them up to my lips, taste each one, but for now I am on a playground instead, hanging by one hand and reaching for the next swinging circle of sun warmed metal, so I can plant my feet on the top step of the three rung ladder that encourages young ones to attempt to stretch themselves out and reach far for the next handhold. It is a game I am in, I know, and it is a childhood game I am creating to make participation in the other game possible. I keep the image clear in my mind anyway so that if, just by chance, or by fate, I do miss the next handhold I will only fall into sand not more than a foot or so beneath my swinging feet.

I will stay here for as long as I want, I say to myself, but even as I think that, above Elwood's words the name, the new name, flies like a bird, back and forth, back and forth wanting my attention, so I let my feet hit the sand and sit with Michael on the sofa again. I look at Elwood as I say, "Start again, please. I was not listening well enough, but I will now. Start with the birth, please."

Elwood smiles gently for me and begins softly as if he is speaking only to me, "I add little to what May's words already described. Your dear mother chose a home birth out of necessity more than anything else. Records at a hospital would have complicated things. When labor began I was called and your brother was taken to the Callaghan house where your own children wait for you now. Sean and I and May and Matilda sat with Colleen as the labor pains progressed. Sean can tell you himself not a sound did she make. Her eyes would widen, her lips would part. Perhaps she held his hand a bit tighter, but only he can tell you of that. Matilda prayed, as Matilda does, hour after hour. The light of day wore itself out waiting, you might say. Night came and with it a cool breeze in through the open windows of the room, but there were beads of perspiration on Colleen's forehead. Finally she spoke and only then to let me know that she had a desire to push. She said it was the strongest desire she had ever felt in her life. She said it came from beyond her, that it was foreign and too strong, too pure in its intent to be human. I checked her progress, and she was indeed ready to begin that last aspect of the process she had both longed for and dreaded.

"And as May described in her second letter you were born like Brigid and Taen were born: under a woven spread of crimson red in the time of a full moon. You and your sister, Aidrea, were born just like Brigid and Taen were born, no one knowing who was birthed first, who was birthed second. When the second cry joined the first, May lifted the spread, and Sean cut the cords of life connecting you both to your mother. It was a simple action in and of itself, but all in the room knew its significance, knew the cut he made cut relationships in half, separated lives, perhaps forever, that in every sense but one belonged together.

"May and Matilda and I wiped your skin and your sister's clean and handed each of you to Colleen. She held you both in her arms, kissed your faces over and over, and would not allow us to take you from her until she had fed each of you at her breasts, both of you for the first time, one of you for the last. Then with tears streaming down her face, she handed her daughters to May and Matilda, and you and your sister were taken from the room. Moments later May returned with you in her arms. Sean said goodbye to May and to you, then sitting next to your mother, he let his tears join hers as they said their goodbyes to each other. When he finally stood to leave, he looked at May in such a way I was sure he wanted her to tell him what was about to happen could happen in another way, but May could not offer him that hope he longed for so dearly, so without looking back he walked from the room, knowing that even when he did return, nothing between him and his Colleen or him and you could be as he would have chosen for it to be. Your destiny and your sister's were too strong for him to change their course." Elwood sighs and smiles for me again, but I know the tears in his eyes are of sadness, and I let my own sorrow join his, then we both put our heads in our hands and cry for what had been lost all those years ago, but even as my loss billows out like a sail I know it is filled with more than just one emotion.

*   *   *   *

I dry my tears and breathe air in deeply, then I look at Malick, "You said her name to me once before. I remember that now. You know her."

Malick looks at Sean then back to me, "She's my wife."

I repeat his words trying to make them feel real to me, "My sister is your wife ...?"

Malick nods, "As May's letter explained, Aidrea was raised in Ireland by May's sister, Megan. We grew up together, much like you and Michael from what I've been told. Of course, because I was certain I would be a priest our relationship was different. She was my dearest friend. When I left the church our relationship changed." Malick's expression is gentled and full of awe, "She said she always knew we would be together as man and woman, but I had to get some of the church's bizarre traditions out of my head first." He pauses smiling at me, "When you get to know her you'll understand why that makes sense, but I can say now I appreciate her perspective: to Aidrea her ways are normal, of the earth and of the spirit, but the church's laws and parameters are strange and barbaric."

I quickly ask, "She has ... gifts?"

Malick leans back against the couch, "She does and always has. Unlike you she was raised knowing who and what she is, but only one of you can be the one chosen, and unfortunately for both of you, it's not her."

Michael leans forward, "What do you mean by that?"

Malick closes his eyes, "What is an intrusion for you and Leah would be for Aidrea a culmination. May and her sister disagreed on very little, and no one knew for sure which of you was the chosen one, but May believed the one chosen should be an innocent facing a practiced evil. Megan believed the one chosen should be trained and disciplined in the gifts. Aidrea was raised knowing, and you were not. No one could be sure of who was the chosen until the cycle opened itself. Until Shal called your name we couldn't know."

I try to sort through all the information, "But why is Aidrea not here too?"

Malick looks at Michael as he says, "There is a danger, but to understand that you will have to go to Shal or Brigid. You have to learn the past to know the way into the future."

I am unbelieving, "So I cannot meet her?"

Malick explains, "Until you have done or attempted to do what is required it would be dangerous for you, perhaps for both of you, to be together for two reasons. First, she is tested and proven in her abilities to overcome opposition from the 'other side'; second, she has known she has a sister since she was old enough to understand the concept. She has loved and missed you all these years; she would be quick in her response to protect you, and that could alter your choices."

Sean comes over to me taking my hands in his, "When you do meet each other, you will feel as if you've loved and known her forever. I promise you that, Leah. And when you stand face to face for the first time you will be amazed. It will be like looking into a mirror."

I am not satisfied, "Was it the same for May and Megan? Did May and Megan grow up together? Were they twins?"

Sean responds quickly, "They are twins, but being in a different place in the cycle they were called to prepare, not 'to do' as you have been."

Michael asks, "This cycle thing confuses the hell out of me. Why now?"

Sean shakes his head, "For that type of information, Leah has to find her own way."

Michael falls back against the sofa, "Ah, we're back to that again."

Malick responds quickly, "And again and again until Leah decides to do what she's been called to do."

Malick's words turn all eyes to me, and I know Malick is right. I know I must go to Brigid, but I have one more question for Malick and one more question for Sean, "Malick, what is my sister doing right now? Where is she?"

Malick looks at Sean, but he only shrugs, "She is not far. She is closer than she has ever been before. And she is waiting as all of us are."

I look at Michael and he comforts me with his eyes. I look at Sean and ask, "When you were gone from us were you with her?"

Sean's eyes find Lane's before he answers me, "Sometimes I was with her; sometimes I was doing other things that needed doing."

I take Michael's hand in mine and raise it to my lips. I breathe 'I love you' against his skin, then he does the same to me. I stand and look at Elwood, "Thank you for being such a good friend to me for so long. Thank you for carrying around the sadness of that day for all these years until you could share it with me. I hope your heart will be lighter now."

Elwood begins to respond, but I cannot hear him. My heart is beating too slowly; I cannot breathe, cannot take enough air into my lungs. The room appears to be struggling against itself like an image captured by its own distorted reflection in a fractured mirror. I hear only a heartbeat echoing my own, so sauntering in its pace it is taunting and lulling simultaneously. Suffocatingly, the burdensome weight of the lack of momentum drags me down. Then suddenly I am tossed about; Michael is shaking me, his hands on my shoulders, his breath on my face as he calls my name over and over. My heartbeat resumes its regular pattern; my lungs welcome the air, as I become aware of the other heartbeat distancing itself from me, its sound diminishing, as dread's clutching fingers scratch against the uneven surface of the moment. I stand and almost fall as dizziness attempts to overwhelm me. I push it away as I say, "We must go. Father Tom is dying. We must go."

I repeat the words again. Time turns back on itself. Just as Michael and I stood in the church this morning, we stand motionless again, just heartbeat and breath, staring into the eyes of Sean. We are as still as stone in our panic. We are only eyes looking into eyes looking into eyes. I watch as the expression on Sean's face changes from despair to hope then back to despair again; there can be no mixture of the morning's surprise or wonder. Tonight offers no reunion. Tonight it is not a fluctuating mist hanging like a shroud blocking any view we might have of what lies just beyond the moment. Tonight it is death, embalming and too potent, that saturates a spiraling collection of shared memories and tentatively planned tomorrows. Silently I call out to Father Tom as Lane's voice suggests departure, but I cannot respond. I hear only Father Tom's voice now. Fragments of our shared conversations create a mosaic of sound in my mind, so Michael takes my hand and leads me out of the room, down the stairs and into the night. Sean walks on the other side of me. They want to keep me safe, so I do not tell them I see flames everywhere. I do not want to worry them, especially when I know, with a stark certainty, they cannot save me anyway, but I cannot think other thoughts now. I have to hold on to Father Tom's voice, so he cannot leave until I lay my head upon his barely moving chest to listen to the slow song of his dying heart, so I can remember the gentle power of his love over the years we shared together.

One more time I will hold his hand. I will remember the solace of his presence when he held mine. One more time I will be death's witness, but this time I will not let the flames cheat me out of my goodbyes. This time I will prepare a place inside of me just so, and once the memories have been sorted and the missing softened enough to fold and place on a waiting shelf, I will simply close the door knowing it will open easily and only when I want it to because goodbyes were said. I call out to him again without speaking, 'I will beat the flames this time, Father Tom. I will.' To myself I reassure: I am not a little girl anymore; this time I will not just stand and watch.

Chapter TEN

I call out to him, whisper his name, hold his hand in my own, but I have come too late. He has slipped away, given up his consciousness for another awareness. I can only stand and watch again. I want to close my eyes and listen in the other way I have now, but I worry when my eyes are closed his will open, and I will miss my last chance to know him. The doctor does not believe Father Tom will open his eyes again; the doctor believes Father Tom's failing heart weakens with each shallow breath taken.

I call out to him. I whisper his name. I try to breathe the scent of him into me, but even that barely lingers. I lay my hand upon his chest craving the expected life-dance of heart. The faintness of his heartbeat draws me closer to him, and I wonder if he is not far away already. Already—but instead of finishing the thought I close my eyes and listen in my new way; I seek him out, but there is no sense of him there either. I think to myself, perhaps he is between worlds and unreachable. I lay my head down on the bed, lay my arm across his legs to anchor him to my here and now, and let my sorrow find expression in my tears.

I say goodbye to him aloud, "Goodbye, Father Tom. Goodbye. My days will not be the same without you. I will miss the sound of your voice and the certainty of your love. I will miss sitting together and watching my children play while we exchange ideas back and forth, as if they are items of clothing, interchangeable despite our obvious differences. I will miss doing that with you. I will miss your wisdom and your sense of humor and your deep faith. Thank you for loving me and for being a part of my life."

My brain must have a scratch for the needle of my perception plays that word over and over again: life ... life ... life.... Life? What is that word; what does it mean, this word I throw around and sometimes do not catch, this word I gobble up and sometimes spit out, this word on which I create dreams and sometimes on which I pound my fists, this word I cherish reverently and sometimes dismiss carelessly, this word I celebrate and mourn selectively as if I am its only witness. Within its parameters I give and take, I acquire and relinquish. I breathe it in and send it out. I love and fail to love within its perspective bound borders. I hold it to me like a favorite childhood toy, sometimes ignoring the warning label burying it as if it is a treasure I can unbury at a later time believing it will still have value. I make it a physical entity, but I know instinctively it is so much more than that. I pretend it is mine to manage, but I know my control is a grand illusion because life happens, has its own agenda, or has no agenda which is even more difficult to weigh on scales that only register self-contexts. Life is like the weather; I can plan for it, grab my umbrella before I leave the house, wear the appropriate shoes, but that is the extent of my control.

And I am not alone in these endeavors. I am not alone. People from everywhere and from anywhere join me. We play scientist and dissect, and label, and argue over life, but all our sharp and shiny ideas are only based on personal experience, learned or experiential. Without carefully acknowledging it, we translate life into our own inner language, but we are each and all blind to its real dimensions or lack thereof. We only touch singular and collective moments with our fingertips to make meaning, to give definition. So life is made small by me and by the man in Africa forced to bury himself in the earth to dig for the diamond a sixteen year old pregnant girl will wear at her wedding in a small town in Southern Texas, but only after the diamond has been sold by a French business man who owns the mine but has never seen it and does not know the name of the poor miner or the bride to be. The business man does not even care about their names. He is a man who has made life into a dollar sign. The miner has touched life and found it darker and more limiting than even the mine in which he is forced to work, and the young pregnant girl just wishes life offered do-overs, but she is willing to have 'the kid'; she doesn't want to kill 'it'; she believes 'it' should get to have a life too; she just hopes 'it' won't change 'her life' much.

Each person, in his or her own way, is like that girl. Each person, in his or her own way, is like the man forced to spend his days working to make ends meet that will never meet. Each person, in his or her own way, is like the business man whose self worth is shaped by external reward. Each person, in his or her own way, is just a small child trying to force too many items into a perceived safe space. We try to make life fit within the confines of living; we try to make life living's cocoon, but life will have none of that. It cannot be contained, and it will never be a butterfly. It just is.

Life is, for lack of an appropriate label, an entity, a breath, a single forever moment, a timeless action; it is the self-aware forever-child of the relationship between time and space. Illustrated or dissected or anthropomorphized, life is. And perhaps like Father Tom and others believe, it is the breath of a creator God who cares. Or perhaps, like some believe, it is nothing more than the esoteric spasm of an ever-changing universe.

Why does it matter to me how life is defined? Perhaps it is only because I want to climb life like a mountain; I want to know life's structure so I can identify proper and appropriate placement of hands and feet, so I will not fall. Or maybe I want to pin life down to a styrofoam board and study it closely, which means I will have to kill it to do so, and by no stretch of my imagination can I rationalize that, so if I must choose I will be climber instead of scientist. Or maybe it is much more simple than that, and I just want to know which damn fork to use at dinner. Maybe my desire to know is based on nothing other than just wanting to do life right. I want to follow the rules, prove myself honorable, get my reward, and feel good about my efforts. But there is the so-called rub; I cannot find definitive rules anywhere.

The rules and rewards are changed by time, by culture, by faith belief or lack thereof, by individual preference, by mass indifference. So this entire thought process has only brought me back to where I am and who I am and what I am trying to do at this moment, which is to keep Father Tom from leaving. I am still holding on to his legs as if, like a bird, his flight to elsewhere can be delayed.

I realize it is a silly thought, but it is comforting to believe I can delay him until I am ready for him to leave. I open my eyes to look upon his face. I place my hand on his chest again and again feel the whisper-soft, exhausted panting of his heart. And then I do not see him laying on the bed; I see him walking through a meadow toward a forest that surrounds and makes its way up a mountain with a summit bathed in sunlight and softened by clouds.

His words feel like a breeze when they reach me, "Leah, be well, be true, and know I will also miss our talks."

I see myself running to catch up with him, and when I do I say, "I wanted to say goodbye to you. I wanted to make you stay."

He looks away from me and listens as if he is hearing another voice not audible to me, then responds, "You can't have it both ways, a goodbye and a stay."

Hope flashes in my heart, "Then I can help you to stay?"

Father Tom seems distracted, "No, but if those were the desires of your heart for me, they were divided, and you can't be divided in what you'll soon face."

Disappointment invades, "I do not want to think about that now, Father Tom."

His eyes look into mine, his voice pushes against me, no longer like a gentle breeze, "You still play at this as if it's a game and you have choices, Leah, but there is no game. Make your stand. Be in the moment. Be who you are, and stop wrestling with your thoughts and your philosophies. You don't need to have a label for what I call God; you don't need to search for handholds or foot placement within a given moment; just be who you are and live the moment, Leah. Stop trying to figure 'it' out and move instinctively and intuitively, letting your spirit and your heart and your mind be one. That is when life will lift you up like the wind offers flight to the wings of a bird. Catch the wind, Leah, ride the breath of God."

He turns away from me, but I reach out to stop him. I touch his arm, and the consequence is sudden. Time and space ripple like the once still surface of a pond now disturbed, and the fabric of his shirt beneath my fingertips becomes the fabric of the sheet on the hospital bed. The movement takes my breath away. I reach out and press my palm against Father Tom's chest, but his heart beats no more. I call out 'no' then seek him where I saw him last, but no voice answers mine, no image fills my mind. I am just a woman sitting in a hospital room holding the lifeless hand of a man she loved and will miss and could not save ... could not save, so I do not mind when the flames begin to dance around me; I do not mind at all.

✳   ✳   ✳   ✳

"I do not mind being here with him. I want to go to Brigid now. I do not want to get back in a car and drive to the library and walk up stairs and get situated all over again." I say this to my husband and to my father and to Lane and to Malick.

Lane acts slightly offended, "Father Tom's body needs to be taken to the mortuary. Connor is here to make the arrangements. Why would you want to sit in this room with his dead body?"

I look away from Lane. I look upon Father Tom's face as I touch his hand again. His skin is still warm. He looks only like he is sleeping, except his body seems weighted down somehow, as if the leaving of his spirit has made him heavier instead of lighter. I look away from Father Tom and into Michael's eyes, but he is not sharing what he is thinking with me.

I look to Sean, and he comes to me. He lays his hand on mine that still rests on Father Tom's. Sean's voice is a whisper, "Daughter, let him go. There are so many waiting to pay their respects to him. Let Connor take Father Tom's body to the mortuary, come back to the library, or we can go to the cabin. You may choose where but leave from here."

I nod to him and look at Michael again as I ask, "Library or cabin, Michael? And please decide, because I do not care."

Michael turns to Lane, "We will return to the library for now. Your men are there still, right?"

Lane looks at Sean as he replies, "My men are everywhere."

Sean turns his back to Lane and takes my hand in his, and we leave the room. At the door I stop to look back, but Michael is close behind me and touches my cheek with his hand, "The next moment is waiting for you, Leah. Father Tom is not here anymore. You said your goodbyes; let others do the same." And so we walk slowly down hallways and through doors and into the night. We climb into Lane's large black SUV that is parked close to a door of the hospital normally used only by the doctors. Few other cars are parked in this lot; the shadows of men, still and moving, are more numerous. As we drive around the side of the hospital I am once again comforted to see how many cars fill the main parking lot; Father Tom did not die alone; so many came to see him off. When the car stops and Lane rolls down the window to speak with one of his men, I can hear voices singing Father Tom's favorite hymn. Michael squeezes my hand gently. I lean my head against his shoulder and close my eyes, realizing as I do I did not need to worry about where I should be when I went to meet with Brigid, because she is right in front of me. I reach out to her through time and space, and she takes my hand.

＊　　　＊　　　＊　　　＊

We are in the meadow where May and I sat and talked together. Colors and sounds shimmer. Even the air is sweet and tangible as I take it into me. Through the leaf and branch of trees and bushes I can see the stones of the wall. The vibrato of waterfall and chorus of birdsong serenade. Islands of vibrant wild flowers bloom in the sea of meadow grass moved by breeze. Above me the cerulean blue sky stretches deep and clear. Brigid stands beside me. I turn to greet her, as Shal appears, suddenly filling space.

He smiles easily, and I am drawn to him as I was when we first met. He speaks quietly, "I knew you'd choose to be with her on your journey. I knew you wouldn't simply open that door in your mind where you've held her memories. I respect the wisdom of your choice in choosing to see through her eyes instead of mine. The ones who came before you never chose that for themselves."

I search his face for intention. I sense nothing but openness, so I say to him, "This is the first time I have seen you in daylight."

Shal steps around me to take Brigid's hand, "We walk here often together."

I look around me again, "It feels good here."

Shal sighs, "It can."

I ask, "But not always?"

Shal comments, "The meadow is a space filled with time in the landscape of always, which is nothing more or less than life's awareness of itself. It is the breath and heartbeat of what you call God. God is. Life is. Your honoring or dishonoring of life, of always, is the choice you have within the moment. This moment in the meadow is and always will be this moment in the meadow."

Brigid takes a step away from Shal, smiles at him but holds her hand out to me. I step toward her, but turn back to say 'thank you' to Shal only to find Brigid and I are once again alone in the meadow. In the same instant his words surround us, "Be strong for each other." Brigid and I look into each other's eyes, agreeing with Shal's words, then she turns and I follow her, her hand still holding mine. I am noticing all that is around me, but as we proceed deeper and deeper into the branch canopy of rowan and oak trees surrounding the meadow by far the most interesting aspect of our walk together is the fact that with each step Brigid becomes more and more transparent, her physical form diminishing as I sense her spiritual essence intensifying. Her hand, holding mine, is visible, but I can see my hand quite clearly through it.

I begin to comment on this to her, but an eagle flying over us demands silence, its piercing cry shredding quickly my fabric-thin sense of comfort and ease. I remember then I am on no picnic; this is no holiday. The image of Brigid bloody and in despair fills my mind, then her memories spread out before me, panoramic and sweeping but without detail, and I know what I must do. I must seek the place that is both beginning and end. I must narrow my focus, allow the faces to draw me so deeply into the moment that Brigid's heart will beat mine, her tears will fall from my eyes, the blood that covers her must cover me. I will go to the altar, but before I can do that, I must sacrifice … me, so I can be … Brigid, daughter of Danu and Dagda, sister to Taen and to Shal and to Bantok.

Even as I realize what I must do, I realize the danger; for the first time I understand shadow aspects of the task chosen for me unseen before due to the blinding impact of the obvious ones. Can I deny my own awareness then somehow remember who I am and find my way back to myself again? Can I close and open doors that well? Won't I only be doing what I do when I am watching a movie or reading a book? I will suspend my disbelief, cease to be Leah, become the character. Surely it is more than that, but if I think of it in that way, perhaps I can accomplish what I have been called to do. The ability must be mine if I have been chosen for this. Just as quickly doubt has its way with me, holds me down, rips away at my cover of good intentions, until I realize Brigid still holds my hand. Then I know … she is my way back; as long as she holds my hand I will be safe; I will know to return. I can close doors never closed before, so I can open new ones.

Just before I close the last door, Michael's voice comes from too far away, and then it becomes only a voice no longer remembered.

*   *   *   *

Floating then in flight, a deep silence surrounds me until voices swell up like a wave, falling upon me as if I am their shore, then only silence again, until a heartbeat drums barely into my ears as if from a great distance. I cannot tell if my eyes are open or not; there is only darkness starred or cut through with slashes of white-silver until flashes of color come slowly shaping themselves into recognizable but unknown forms. When the wind comes it is wild and demanding, pushing away the images and pushing me this way then that way, but since I am nowhere I have ever been I do not care, reasoning one place is as good as another until water rushes against me and I breathe it in, choking … choking then I am grabbed up and pulled through air. I can breathe again, and my breath, loud in my ears, beats in rhythm to a heartbeat somehow close in its distance until lips touch mine and hands press gently against my back. I am in a kiss. I want to surrender to it, the longing as golden and warm as the sunlight of summer until hard hands beat against me as I try to shelter a child in my arms, then I am running and free until a screaming voice beats against me as crushingly as fists. Then I am only falling and twisting, turning to save myself from a danger I cannot see or know or even imagine. Then there are only flames, a dusk sky, and a quiet voice calling me back from where I have been.

Brigid sits next to me, her deep violet eyes comfort me, draw me in, "Too quickly, Leah, you must ... control the experiences ... or they will have their way with you ... instead of you with them."

I am lying by a fire; we are in the meadow again, but it is Brigid's voice that holds my attention, "You are talking to me."

She puts her fingers to her lips and smiles behind them, "It seemed necessary. You needed help. You almost let go of my hand."

I sit up and ask, "Where was I?"

She touches her own forehead, "Here" then spreads her arms wide "and everywhere."

I shake my head, "I love that you are talking to me. It has been centuries since you have spoken."

She only responds, "Yes, centuries."

We look into each other's eyes then I ask her, "Who was kissing you?"

Her eyes close and I sense she is seeing that moment for herself. When she speaks her words come slowly, "Jhace, my husband, on the night before we were to be acknowledged as King and Queen of the Tuatha."

I ask another question, "And the water.... did you almost drown?"

Again her eyes close before she responds, "I sought that solace but couldn't dishonor life by relinquishing life to my own sorrow."

I lay my hand on hers and offer comfort before I ask my next question, "The child I had in my arms while I was running?"

She does not close her eyes to answer, "My daughter."

My next question makes her smile again, "The heartbeat I hear and feel, whose is it?"

Her answer confirms my own thinking, "You are sensing the All's presence." Then she looks at the necklace I wear and asks my permission with her eyes before she touches it. "This was mine then my daughter's. It's come to you through the generations." I hold out my hand so she can see the pearl ring hoping she will explain its significance, "The pearl was given to Danu by Dagda; it was his first gift to her. When Jhace was chosen to be my husband, it was given to him to give to me. He had the metal workers create a setting for the pearl. Like the necklace, it has come to you through the generations. There are symbols on the inside you may want to decipher at some point in the future, after all this is completed and before you give it to your daughter." She pauses then touches my cheek, "There is no time now for all the explanations you seek, Leah. You must move in faith."

I sigh, "Then I will have to be satisfied, but will you take me to the altar? I believe I need to see it before I try again to see your life."

She stands and holds out her hand to me, "I'll take you there. It's not far from here. Come."

I put my hand in hers and stand noticing my surroundings, "This is not the same meadow."

Brigid smiles, "It is the same place in a different time, Leah." I ask 'what time?', but she only shakes her head, and as she replies I can tell she does not find the words easily, "Does it matter? If I tell you a specific time, give you a year, number a century for you, will it matter, change anything or make anything more clear for you?" We begin to walk as I say 'no', and she comments further, "We are in forever. Think of time that way, as always happening, never stopping, one experience lasting forever, just as the next experience lasts forever. Layers of being, strands of experience, that's what time is. It fills space. It's what you were falling through before, just as when you came to meet with Shal you went through time. Falling or flying or floating will be your choice once you understand what you're doing." She pauses then smiles as she finds the words she wants, "Time is a meal we dine on until food no longer interests us, and then time becomes nothing more or less than communion."

Her words linger between us as we walk into another meadow. In its center the sun's light is captured and then sent out brighter. I blink my eyes against the brilliance of the gold and the gems. The air becomes sweeter, more tangible. I feel the All's heartbeat pulsing around me, and I can see almost transparent beings everywhere. When they walk through me I feel pleasantly chilled … whispered into gently. Brigid and I both stop a few feet from the altar and fall to our knees, awed by its splendor, humbled by its magnificence.

When I begin to let go of Brigid's hand, she holds mine tighter and without words indicates I should look around me. As I do I notice the meadow's parameters are shadowed but not because the sun has changed position. As I watch the shadow becomes fog and within seconds the trees surrounding the meadow are hidden. The air I breathe is still sweet, and I still sense the gentle presence of the beings I experienced earlier, but some force pushes against me. The beings begin to move. Standing shoulder to shoulder now, less transparent than before, they surround Brigid and me and the altar. Before I can look at Brigid to see her reaction so I can gauge my own, the fog takes the shape of a serpent, its body wrapping around the meadow as its head raises up. The serpent's eyes glare down at us; its posture indicating it is ready to strike, but before it can every other being in the circle arches his or her back and floats up from the ground creating a protective covering over us.

Brigid and I sit on the soft carpet of thick emerald green grass before the golden altar under a canopy and within a wall of bodies almost transparent yet somehow iridescent. We sit with our knees bent under us holding hands. I want to laugh with joy and cry out in amazement at what I am seeing. I try to look everywhere at once, but return constantly to the serpent of fog and shadow. Its eyes are dark, its flicking tongue a smaller rendition of the serpent itself. It begins to move around the circle holding its position but gaining speed with each rotation. Taloned wings, smokey then flaming, burst from its sides as it raises up from the ground, screeching its outrage. Up from the soul of earth, out of the heart of the All, a pulse beats faintly then stronger as the beings on the ground and in the air begin to move to its rhythm, their mouths open and voices, so pristine, filling the air.

I look at Brigid and tears are running down her cheeks. Her neck and back are arched, her face turned up toward the sky and her eyes closed as her voice joins the others' voices. I close my eyes and let the moment wash over me; I let it fill me. I surrender to it, and it takes me up into it as the heartbeat becomes more distinct than the singing. I feel cupped in the palm of a mighty hand. Breath like a gentle wind bathes me as words spoken in a voice deeper than I can comprehend resonates around me, then the singing becomes louder, the heartbeat diminishes, and I am once again sitting with Brigid before the altar in a meadow lit by a round, full moon and a starred sky. I look around and sense we are alone.

Brigid smiles and leans toward me, "Don't let yourself try to make sense of it. Just know it happened and remember it. Let it be a moment you return to often for solace and for strength and to give you hope." She pauses, closes her eyes then whispers, "Even now she gathers her strength to come against us again."

I want to ask who the 'she' is, but Brigid's need to move into the next moment causes me to look at the altar. We stand together, my hand in hers. The altar appears to be solid gold. It is rectangular in shape, waist high, each of the four legs cast or deeply carved to look like a variety of vines intertwining. Within the voids of these swirling raised and incised impressions are human faces or masks shaped like leaves or buds. The rim of the somewhat concave top surface appears to be three to four inches deep; its almost six foot length divided into three panels based on the type of design. The middle panel has a smooth surface except for small straight lines arranged in obviously meaningful patterns. I recognize these patterns as being identical to the carvings in the tree by the wall surrounding the meadow. I believe they must be a type of written language, similar to Ogham perhaps. The panels to the left and right of the middle panel are deeply inlaid with ivory, amber, and mother of pearl to create images of animal figures bordered by snail shell spirals and raised roundels of silver. What appear to be sparkling sapphires and shimmering diamonds act as the eyes of the carved creatures on the panels and of the human faces and masks appearing on the legs of the altar.

Brigid breaks our silence by saying, "You must allow yourself to see what happened, but you must control the images … you can slow them down or make them pass quickly, but you must look to see and in the seeing know. The answer is here."

I can only whisper, "But I do not even know the question, Brigid."

She only whispers to me 'go', and I am suddenly taken up into a downward flowing stream of images. So fast they fly by me I cannot catch my breath. I cannot breathe, but I do not allow fear to overwhelm me. I seek to control the images. Initially the only change is I am stilled and no longer being propelled upward. The images still stream past me. I concentrate, and they begin to move more slowly. I choose one on which to focus, and then I am drawn into it. I am drawn into Brigid.

I am at the altar under a full moon and a sky filled with stars. I am in the presence of others. Danu and Dagda stand on the other side of the altar from me. Beside me Jhace stands. I hold our daughter in my arms. On both sides of the altar an elder stands, robed and chanting. In the center of the altar, lay an eagle feather and an intricately carved gold handled knife, its long, sharp blade reflecting the moon's light. Danu and Dagda simultaneously reach up to remove their golden neckrings, the symbol of their leadership of the Tuatha, and lay one on each side of the knife. Danu reaches for the knife, places the tip of the blade into her palm, then looking into my eyes she cuts herself. Her blood drips from the small incision onto the altar. She hands the blade to Dagda who does the same as he looks into the eyes of Jhace. The blade is taken by an elder as Dagda's blood joins Danu's, then they take white strips of cloth and wrap them around their palms, binding the wounds. Jhace picks up the eagle feather and dips it into Danu's and Dagda's blood, anointing the center of my forehead. Then using the other hand he dips three fingers into the blood and touches the place just above my heart. I then anoint him in the same way. An elder comes and leads Jhace away in one direction as another elder leads me away in the opposite direction. We are being taken to small shelters deep within the surrounding forest where we are to remain alone and in prayer until the next night when we will be reunited in the ceremony of acceptance, the ceremony in which our people acknowledge the passing of leadership from Danu to me.

I feel joy in my heart as I am being led away. My daughter must also for she makes the sweet gurgling sounds of a babe contented. I feel ready to take my mother's place in the leading of our people. I am confident Jhace will make as good a king as he has been a husband and father to me and our child. I begin to sing as I walk, a song from my childhood my mother sang to me that I sing to my daughter. I stop and close my eyes to give praise for life's sweetness, but before I can finish my prayer I feel the point of a knife against the small of my back. I realize suddenly I have let my joy blind me to the danger that must have been stealing its way closer to me with each of my steps. The elder who walked in front of me is lying on the ground, a gag in his mouth, his hands and feet tied. When I am turned around and can see into the eyes of the one who threatens me, I look into the eyes of my brother, Bantok.

We do not bother with words. We struggle against each other in the spirit. I will the knife to drop from his hands; he wills his hands to hold tightly. I know without clear understanding he only wishes to hold me here, struggling against him, to detain me, or he would have cut and weakened me already. His will battles mine as I seek to connect with the spirits of my parents and Shal, or with any of the first and second generations who are strong enough in the spirit to hear me in the spirit. I think of Jhace, who is of the fourth generation, and I know he cannot help me, and then suddenly I realize I'm not the one in real danger; it is Jhace, my chosen, my king, who will not see morning's light unless I can find a way to save him. Bantok sees all this in me and steps closer, but my spirit is enraged.

I move in the spirit more quickly than Bantok. Simultaneously I cry out in the spirit to all those who can hear me as Bantok is hurled against the tree behind him, falling to the ground unconscious. I untie the elder but do not wait to see if he can raise himself or walk. I turn and run back through the trees to the altar, to where I know whatever has been planned will take place. I run. I cry out in the spirit. I scream the war cry of the Tuatha. I alert my people to the threat, to the danger, but when the ground beneath my feet and my very essence are shaken, as if the air spasms, I know I am too late. Upon entering the meadow I know I am too late. Over the heads of people standing between me and the altar I see Taen standing atop the altar, the bloody gold handled knife in one hand, her robe splattered with blood. I must walk through people I thought I knew but can no longer recognize, their faces distorted by hate; hands reach out to push and hit me as I shield my daughter. I am stunned, but I will a path through them cleared and bodies fly backward. I walk, making myself proceed slowly, even though my desire is to run. I make my way around the altar to join Danu, Dagda, Shal, and others of our generations, who stand together. Behind us those loyal to us from later generations stand, their weapons in their hands, ready to defend us. I notice on the other side of the altar few immortals but at least twice as many mortal Tuatha stand ready to fight against us.

Hate is birthed in me full grown. I look into Taen's eyes and know that is what she wants. She feeds on the fear of others, breathes in bitterness and breathes out unforgiveness; she breeds hate, nurtures it in herself and others. Ever since I was chosen over her to be queen she has separated herself from us. She wanted Jhace for herself, but that could never be; his heart was mine from the beginning. Even now as she raises his heart in her hand, his love still beats in my heart, will always have a place in me. Even now as she wears the bloodied neck-ring, I know she will never lead our people; she has struck out against me by killing my husband, the man chosen to be my king and in doing so has positioned herself against the sanctity of life.

I place my daughter in the arms of my mother. I look into Taen's eyes and deny the hate I feel for her. I offer her pity instead, and she shrieks and flies at me from where she stands over Jhace's body on the altar. I knock the knife from her hand and grab her by the throat while she is still in the air, throwing her to the ground. Shal and others assist me in holding her down. I do not release her throat and her eyes begin to bulge. In the spirit I tell her to open her hand and release Jhace's heart. She resists me until Shal tells her he will cut through her wrist if she doesn't open her fingers, so she does.

I remove my hand from her throat. When she begins to scream, Dagda stuffs her hair into her mouth to silence her then covers her lips with his hand. I gather Jhace's heart into my hands. Around me, those loyal to me who have gathered with us, except the ones holding Taen, fall to their knees. I walk through them, Jhace's blood dripping though my fingers, his heart still warm in my hands. I notice none of those loyal to Taen remain in the meadow. I know they will hide in the forests and vow each will be found.

Upon the altar is my Jhace, his eyes still open, his mouth gaping, his tongue cut out, his chest ripped open. I kiss Jhace's heart before I return it to his body. I pick up his tongue and place it back in his mouth. I close his lips then his eyes. I climb up onto the altar and lay my body over his. I seek my Jhace in the spirit, but I can't find him there, it's too soon, so I return to find his body as cool beneath me as the rain beginning to fall on my back. I move my body away from his, for the last time, and stand by the altar, by his side, for the last time.

I notice the neckring worn by the king of the Tuatha around his throat and seek to know how it came to be there. My mother stands next to me, tears joining the rain drops on her cheeks. She holds my daughter in one arm as she offers me her hand. I take it as she says, "I will help you see what you seek to know, daughter." I am in darkness until a light grows at its center, fanning out into an image. I see Taen straddling Jhace, his arms held by four hooded figures. I see her placing the neckring on Jhace's neck. I hear her telling him to join her or die, and I hear him choose death over her. I hear him proclaiming his love for me, and then I see her cut out his tongue for saying so. I watch her dig into Jhace's chest with the knife. I watch her tear out his heart then I can watch no more. I let go of my mother's hand and look upon the face of my love as I call to my people to bring to me the ceremonial oil.

When they do I pour oil over Jhace's body then reach for the flaming torch offered to me. I touch the torch's flame to Jhace's body then I stand and watch my husband-king burn in a rain that continues to fall as my people sing the song of journey. As the flames reach higher, defying the rain, the first words of our joining ceremony repeat in my mind: 'Hearts joined never distant. Spirits joined ever close. Flesh joined forever faithful. Love and honor betrothed.'

I can contain my despair no longer. I run to the altar to grasp the hand of Jhace that hangs over the side of the altar still untouched by flames, but Shal stops me. With his arm around me, holding my arms to my side, he walks me close to the altar. He reaches out and gently places Jhace's hand upon the altar. We back away from the altar as Shal whispers to me, "Let him go, sister. Let your king go. Let him go that you may find him. You are Queen of the Tuatha; be strong for your people."

But I don't want to be strong. I want to throw myself into the flames and be joined with my love. Dagda comes to stand on the other side of me, as Danu comes and places my daughter in my arms, then Danu kneels before me. After a moment she raises her eyes to mine and says, "Offer your daughter and your people your love, Brigid. Offer them the love given to you by Jhace. But also offer blood for blood, my daughter and queen, or this rain may never end. The All's heart breaks along with your own for this treachery. The All's tears will wash away the tears from our faces, but you, as queen must seek and find justice. Offer blood for blood."

I look down into the eyes of my daughter then turn my face up to the dark sky. I stand with my brother, with my parents, with my people until the flames of sorrow are put out by the rain's relentless downpour. I realize I, too, feel as if my heart has been ripped out, my body burned, my ashes washed away, and then I fear for my people, fear they have an empty queen to lead them.

*   *   *   *

Empty … no air here for breath … no darkness, no light … just falling … but not falling, but not floating … no air to fall through … sightless … only sorrow, unbreathable sorrow, suffocating sorrow … numbing, soundless … an airless void without heartbeat or pulse … nothing to grab hold of … then sounds fly against me … far away somehow … breath or a breeze … touched … called to …'Leah, Leah, I'm sorry, Leah, come back … come back' … air pushed in, pulled out … lips moving on mine … then from another direction jerked up, thrown sideways, pushed down … scratching hands pulling me down … then again the lips on mine as words become constant … my name called pulling me up, my name, my name … Leah, I am Leah … other names come … fill the external void, the internal emptiness, then I know who I am … Leah … I am Leah … I fight against phantom hands trying to drag me back into the nothingness … I struggle against them as the other names … Michael, John Henry, Mary become handholds … become breath, and gasping but breathing again sights and sounds surround me.

I am looking up into eyes looking down into mine. Malick's lips almost touching mine, I breathe his breath in. He moves back from me. There is morning sky around him. Brigid's face replaces his. Her tears fall on me, "I let go of your hand. I'm so sorry. I was with you there in that moment and the sorrow took me again, wrapped me in its dark coils, dragged me down, so tight I couldn't breathe. I forgot about you. It was only the smallest of moments. I let go of your hand." She pauses to kiss my cheek and to smooth my damp hair, "We almost lost you. I almost lost you."

I think about sitting up but decide against it. I feel … spent. I decide to remain still. I look around me. The sky and trees, Brigid and Malick. Malick? I ask, "Why … why are you here?"

He almost smiles, "I was sent." I ask by whom, and he answers, "By your sister."

I ask, "How did she know what was happening?"

Malick shakes his head, "How could she not, Leah? She's watching. She's with you in this even if she can't stand by your side. She can even feel what you feel when she lets herself. When Brigid let go of your hand, I was sent to help you."

I notice Shal standing a short distance away. He walks over and kneels down by Brigid, "I was not sent, of course, but I came when I realized what Taen was trying to do." He reaches down with three fingers and touches the fabric over my heart and then my forehead. As I look down to see where he has touched I notice the marks of blood on my shirt. Now I do sit up and everything circles around me wildly.

I put my hand on my forehead and feel the dried blood there. When the world is still again, I look into Brigid's eyes, and I ask, "So that is what I was called to do?"

Brigid shakes her head 'no' and looks at Shal, so he answers my question, "No, little one, it isn't as simple as that. You've brought my sister out of her silence, but what you've been called to do is … a different task to be accomplished not in this realm but in your own. You had to understand all this to do what needs to be done next." Shal pauses and takes my hand in his, "Brigid needs to tell you what happened after that night, then you can return to your world, to your Michael, to your children, but once there your destiny will unfold around you. Choices will be made." Shal stands me up as he rises then kneels back down again before me, "Thank you for what you have done. You have accomplished more than any of the others before you dared to accomplish. You allowed yourself to be taken. Your heart, the way you offer love, has opened my sister's heart, which also offered love. I humbly thank you, Leah. I pray to the All your way in this will be guided and your mind, body, and spirit protected."

Malick adds, "My prayer and blessing for you are the same. You have gone through Brigid's silence; may the rest of your journey go as well. Remember May's letters, Leah. There are keys in her words to doors you will need to open."

I nod my head at Shal and Malick but turn to Brigid, "Can we begin now then, so I can return to my family?" Brigid reaches out to me to take my hand as Shal and Malick disappear suddenly. Just as suddenly two eagles appear overhead, circle the meadow three times then fly into the horizon. I look at the altar then at Brigid, "There is more for me to do here, isn't there?"

Brigid sighs, "This is your journey now, not mine. What assistance I can give you I will, but you must be both blind and seeing to find your way." I repeat 'blind and seeing' as a question and Brigid replies, "You must look to see, but remember that knowing is spiritual, so what you see when you look with your eyes may not be all that is necessary. You have a sense there is more for you to do here, so you're sensing more than can be seen. Can you understand?"

Now I sigh then say, "I hope that is a rhetorical question, because little of this actually makes sense to me, and you did tell me not to try to figure everything out … to let the experiences be … beacons more or less for the moments to come. So, I will take your advice and mention instead that some of your words are like some of those in May's letters: look to see, knowing is spiritual. I remember those. She also said I must take to be taken and I must offer blood for blood." I pause and look again at the altar as I suggest, "Perhaps you can tell me the rest of what happened as I go to the altar. I feel such a need to lay my hands on it, even though, given what I have seen, I have no desire to do so."

Brigid lets go of my hand and indicates I should do what I need to do. She stands still and begins speaking, "To me it fell to decide Taen's and Bantok's and their followers' justice ... to me, but I didn't care what happened to them. For days and nights all I did was walk the shore and stand before this altar. Even my daughter's care was seen to my by mother. My father or Shal would find me and return me to my shelter, place food and drink before me I refused to touch. As my mother said it would, the rain fell. Day after day, night after night without stopping. My parents and brother, some of the elders, would sit around me and speak words of healing into me, but I made their words mean nothing.

"Taen and Bantok were bound by chains and gagged with the cloths used to clean the blood and ash from the altar and knife. They were placed on a large flat boulder at the foot of the mountain at the edge of the forest. They remained there without food, only receiving water through the rags, wet from the rain that gagged them. They remained there until the water from the sky, combined with the water from the sea, began to wash over them. Mother brought me to see them, also reminding me that my people needed me. Just days before we had been forced to remove our belongings from our shelters due to the flooding of our village and move into the caves high in the mountain, but still I let my sorrow numb me into inaction. My mother had Taen and Bantok moved into one of the smaller caves higher up the mountain, but I could make no decision regarding their fate."

She pauses as she notices I am running my hands over the middle panel of the altar's top rim, the panel with the arrangement of connected and unconnected straight lines of varying lengths carved into the gold. An image comes to me, and I fall to the ground beneath the panel to dig into the soft earth with my hands. Brigid moves closer to observe what I am doing. Just inches below the ground's surface my fingertips touch a metal surface. I dig around the circular shape and bring into the light of day the two neckrings. Then I notice something else has been buried beneath the neckrings. With a bit more digging I unearth a metal box. Brigid comes to my side, sits down across from me, reaches her hand out toward the neckrings but then lets her hand fall into her lap again.

I wipe the soil off of them and the box as best I can and set them on the ground between us as Brigid explains, "These were stolen in the days after Jhace's murder." She pauses and shakes her head, "I cannot blame my mother or father or any of the elders for not seeing what Taen and Bantok had been doing. I was chosen for queen over Taen and served my apprenticeship, which by your standards of time lasted a lifetime. During my training we all noticed Taen was bitter with jealousy, but none of us could have ever imagined the terrible deeds she was planning. How could we? How can those unplagued by hatred perceive the twisted minds of those who allow themselves to be hatred's servant?"

Brigid shakes her head, "After I was chosen to be queen, Jhace was chosen to be my king. We had always favored each other so there was great joy and little surprise in the choice. Jhace was respected and well liked by mortal and immortal. He fought beside Shal bravely in battle, and he was considered one of the best weavers. He was beautiful in that way men can be, and so strong in mind and body he could be gentle in mind and body."

She closes her eyes before she continues, and I imagine her seeking the image of his face again to replace the image of him we had just experienced. She takes a deep breath before she continues, "I chose Shal to be over the council of elders. My choices infuriated Bantok and those who had presumed to lead with him when he was chosen by my sister when she was made queen. We were so blind to behaviors that should have forewarned us, but now I understand in the light of true innocence the darkness of evil casts no shadow. We could not recognize betrayal having never experienced it. If Taen had been honest with herself she would have realized she had chosen her life and made mother's and father's and the elders' choice for them; her lack of compassion for those who willingly served us, her lack of dedication to the daily work of our village, her unrestrained seeking of the satisfaction of her physical senses … all these behaviors made her unacceptable to lead the Tuatha, but looking back offers insights a present view can't offer. We were all and each blinded by our own perspectives."

With her eyes she asks permission to open the metal box. I pick it up and offer it to her. She lays it down and removes the fitted lid. Inside lying next to each other are a feather and a stone similar to the one in May's box. The imprint on the stone appears to be different though. As she touches each one she explains, "The feather of anointing and Jhace's seal."

Then she reaches out and touches the neck rings as she continues, "Evil had been loosed upon us, and justice was sought. Those mortals who had taken part in the conspiracy were rounded up from all over the island, and those who would not take an oath of allegiance to me were banished, put on rafts and set out to sea. Shal and the council of elders decided on their fate and the fate of the five immortals loyal to Taen and Bantok. The immortals were bound and gagged and buried alive in the earth which is one way to mute the power of the spirit while an immortal's physical body is still alive. Once an immortal's body dies in such a way the spirit is unable to move on to the next realm. Even to this day humans can feel the dark power in those places where the immortals were buried and died, their spirits unable to depart."

Brigid leans back allowing her arms to support her as she closes her eyes, "I often wonder what our time on earth would have been like if Taen and Bantok had chosen differently." Brigid shakes her head and almost smiles, "Ah, but Taen was always headstrong and so full of her own desires. Waiting for anything was difficult for her, and behaviors amusingly accepted in her as a child and tolerated in her as a young woman made her unacceptable for queen to our parents and the elders as a mature woman. It was the same with Bantok. They sought continually that which was not theirs to have believing they deserved more than they ever tried to earn. They felt entitled. They were never satisfied, never content to live in harmony. I didn't understand then how dangerously contagious attitudes can be or how deceptions planted carefully can grow so quickly."

Brigid sighs and leans forward, "But you want the story not my lessons learned too late. Shal and I, alike in our choices of behaviors and beliefs, were chosen over them. What is that saying you have in your time: Taen and Bantok made their beds; let them lie in them? Father and mother, the elders only followed the ways of our people; it was Taen and Bantok who chose their destinies, their fates. But understanding does not change what happened."

I put my hand on hers, and she returns to the story, "I can't tell you how many days and nights had passed, but after the rain had forced us to seek the high caves of the mountain and while I was still watched to ensure my safety I slipped away without my guard knowing it. I went to the cave separate from ours where Taen and Bantok were being held. Shal and the council would not take action against them; they waited for me to make a decision. There was no need for guards to be present to guard Taen and Bantok; elders were keeping them bound in the spirit, and their physical constraints offered them no escape in the physical realm. I stood over Taen and looked into her eyes, but I could find nothing of my sister, only madness beat her heart and filled her mind. I knew if I went to her in the spirit the elders would sense my presence, so I could not seek her there. I stood looking at her wondering how I was to offer blood for blood. I could feel Bantok watching me, so I turned from Taen and looked into his eyes. What I saw there seemed worse than what I had found in Taen; Bantok was quite sane and seething with anger. I felt it made Bantok more dangerous somehow. Taen was controlled by hatred while Bantok controlled the hatred he felt, kept it alive within him and was aware of doing so."

Brigid pauses again and looks into my eyes, "I was at such a loss, Leah, and that is when I let the sorrow take me. I walked from the cave, down the path, into the turbulent water that had swallowed up the lower part of the mountain. The water picked me up and spun me around, tossing me against the side of the mountain as it took me deeper. In my mind, as my last breath left my body and I sucked water into my lungs, my last desperate thought was I was giving away what had been taken from my Jhace; I was dishonoring life. I had a daughter to love and raise-up. I could not dishonor her or life or the All to allow myself to join Jhace in the next realm. I could not. So, in the spirit as I was quickly losing consciousness I called out to my mother and father and to Shal to help me, and suddenly I was pulled up with such force that I was thrown into the air above the water then gently grasped by the talons of Dagda as eagle." She pauses and almost smiles, "I knew the eagle was Dagda, because I could feel the presence of my father quite clearly. When I awoke sometime later one eagle feather had been placed next to me. My father told me, before he left with the Danu for the next realm of being, he wanted me to have the feather to remember the moment in which I had chosen honor and life over self-pity and death. I gave it to my daughter during her ceremony of joining. The feather in the box May gave you was Dagda's gift to me." She pauses then takes my hand in hers, "You can't know how I long to be with them."

I ask 'why she can't, and she answers, "Both Dagda and my mother are in the other realm now … I can sense them, like I can see Jhace, but they are beyond my reach … completely out of the physical realm. Until I am with them there I can't know them in the way the physical realm allows us to know each other. I miss knowing them, but I'm not released to go to them, so here I remain, with Shal; besides Bantok and Taen we are the last of our people with connections to this realm."

She looks down at the neckrings, "We can't know their significance yet. That you had to find them tells us they will have a purpose, but what that purpose will be, you'll have to discover. Our time together nears its end, Leah."

I am surprised by her abruptness, "But you said I would find the answer here. Then I told you I did not even know the question, and I still do not know them, the question or the answer. And where is the gold handled knife? You have to tell me before I leave, don't you?"

Brigid stands and hands me the neckrings, kisses each of my cheeks, touches the fingerprints of blood on my shirt and forehead and smiles as she says, "The knife is beyond my knowing. The question and its answer you have experienced and will recognize them as the question and its answer when you need them, or you may not. Stay in the moment, Leah."

I am insistent, "But you did not tell me what happened to Taen and Bantok."

Brigid's violet eyes darken, "Taen waits as I do. She remains chained and gagged in the cave, dead in her body, her spirit trapped in this realm in which you live with its mix of physical and spiritual. Her spirit is bound in fog and smoke. Bantok did escape as he was being brought to the council for judgment, but Shal holds him prisoner, and Shal will decide his fate; Bantok will not escape again. You know your enemy now, Leah, and she will destroy you if she can, but I don't believe she will. She grows as weak in her powers as I do, but you must feel no compassion for her. There is no goodness in her. Offer blood for blood, Leah, to stop her, end this for all of us."

✳   ✳   ✳   ✳

I do not open my eyes immediately, do not want the physical sensations of being inside my own body again and looking out into wherever I am to bombard me, to come flying into me too quickly. I let my spirit stretch out and adjust itself as if I have just climbed into bed, beneath covers, and am adapting myself to new but known surroundings. I listen; I sense my surroundings without seeing them.

I hear the quiet musings of a controlled fire; I hear branches moved by breeze gently rubbing against the glass of windows. My body rests on a sofa, and I am covered by a light blanket. My shoes are off so I wiggle my toes as I lift up my arms and let my hands touch my own face confirming for myself I am truly back. I notice a weight on my stomach and realize the neckrings lay there under cover of the blanket covering me. I hear Michael call my name and smile as I open my eyes and say 'yes' to him.

He is kneeling beside me, his face close to mine. We look into each other's eyes, and then he lays his head on my shoulder and whispers against my neck, "I missed you."

I whisper back, "I love you, Michael Callaghan," as I realize we are in Sean's cabin.

Michael again looks into my eyes, "You were gone for almost twenty-four hours this time."

I sigh and say 'a lot happened' as I touch his lips with my fingertips, willing them closer. He understands and kisses me, just lips barely brushing against lips and cheeks until our missing of each other expresses its deeper longing. He begins to move his body onto the sofa when I hear someone pretend to cough.

Our kiss ends as Michael says, "I forgot we aren't alone." I sit up, so he can have a place next to me but keep the neckrings under the blanket. My father leans against the opposite wall, his face turned away from us as if he is somehow looking out the curtained window. Michael comments, "I was just making sure she was okay, that nothing was broken, that sort of thing."

Sean's eyes find mine, "And how is she?"

I answer, "She is fine."

Sean sits in one of the two chairs across from us, "I'm more than glad then. Why don't I make us some food while you tell us what happened?"

I put my hands on my stomach, "I am hungry." Then I move the neckrings beside me, keeping them under the blanket as I ask, "Was I really gone for a whole day?" Sean replies 'more or less' as he walks into the adjoining kitchen. I ask Michael how John Henry and Mary are. He tells me they are safe and that his parents, and other family members, are keeping them entertained so our children do not have time to worry.

I ask Michael if we can see them soon, but Sean interrupts, "Your sister dropped by."

I look at Michael then at Sean, "What do you mean my sister 'dropped by'?"

Michael leans back looking at Sean, indicating he plans to let Sean provide me with an answer, which Sean does, in his own fashion, as he moves around the small kitchen, taking items from refrigerator and cupboard to place on the counter, "Dropped by is pretty clear, but I'm supposing you're wanting to know why."

He does not continue to speak, so I prompt him, "And?"

Sean stops his food preparation, turns and gives me his biggest smile, "And it did my father's heart good to at last have both my girls together in the same room." He pauses as his expression changes from smile to mock concern, "Of course, there wasn't much conversation. She just walked in, looked at Michael and me, walked over to the sofa, knelt down and watched you. You were just laying there not doing a damn thing I could see, but Aidrea was sensing more than I could. I'm sure of that, because her expression would change then she'd stand and look into the fire or close her eyes, then she'd sit again on the floor next to you. One time she reached out and held your hand in hers. After a couple of hours she turned and finally acknowledged our presence. What was it she said to you, Michael?"

Michael is resting his head against the back of the sofa. His eyes are closed as he responds, "She said, 'I look forward to getting to know you and my sister.'

Then she walked over and said something to you, Sean, that I couldn't hear. Then she left."

I ask Sean what Aidrea said to him, but he tells me it was just small talk. I do not believe him, but I know him well enough in my not knowing of him to understand if he chooses not to share information with us he will not, so I do not push, do not waste my breath or my words. There are too many other matters with which to concern myself, so I promise not to let my thoughts wonder about Aidrea's words to my father. I take Michael's hand in mine and move closer to him; his closeness a comfort I find myself hungrier for than food.

✳   ✳   ✳   ✳

We sit at the kitchen table, our plates pushed away from us, so we can rest our elbows on the table and lean into each other, moments of shared silence feeling as meaningful as the moments filled with descriptions of my experiences with Brigid. Sean rubs his face with his hands and leans back as he asks, "You say you brought the neckrings with you, but they're not here, so what happened to them?"

I try to keep any expression from my eyes and face as I ask, "Do you think the neckrings are important?"

Sean looks at Michael, pushes his chair back, stands and walks over to the counter and opens a drawer. He indicates I should quietly join him. When I do I find myself looking at what I can only guess are bugs, the mechanical type used for invading the privacy of others. Next to the bugs another small device plays barely audible music. I turn and look at Michael, who indicates I should take my seat again. I do, and Sean closes the drawer then takes his own seat. Sean nods his head at Michael and Michael explains, "Sean debugged the place while you were in never-never land. He says Lane is responsible."

My question is based on hope, "To protect us?"

Michael replies, "Not entirely according to Sean. Lane doesn't want us hurt, but he does have another agenda. Sean also says Lane believes, has always believed, the end justifies the means. He'll do anything to accomplish that end. The bugs are in the drawer because Sean says whoever is listening will be able to hear the soft music and maybe us talking, but won't be able to make out what we're saying. Who ever is listening won't know we know about the bugs."

I close my eyes so just perhaps my father will not see the doubt reflected in them, as my hand, laying on the table, is covered by another, and I know it is not Michael's. I open my eyes. Sean's eyes search mine. When he speaks his words are gentle, "I've given you little reason to trust me, Leah. I know that with as much certainty as I know anything, but I tell you this now, and can only hope you believe me, I'm not here on business any longer. I'm here for you, to help you in any way I can. If that means going against ... what I've fought for almost all my life ... I'll do just that. I'm your father, and I'll help protect you like a father should. I was too late to help Colleen and my mother and the others; I won't let that happen again."

Initially my response to Sean's words is only the awareness he carries the same burden as I do. We were too late, but then a door opens in my mind.... memories from my childhood present themselves to me; they preen, turning this way and that as if I am their mirror. Sean is in very few of them, but despite his apparent absence I have such a sense of his presence, his closeness somehow mixed with my missing of him. I do not try to make myself understand that strange combination, instead I take a deep breath and shepherd the memories back into that place in me where memories are kept. Then I look into the eyes of this man, who is asking for the opportunity to make amends, to take his rightful place as my father, and I realize for him to do so I must allow myself to trust him. Then I wonder if trusting my father means I cannot trust Lane, a man who offered my brother and me a place to live after our family was taken from us and who has been friend and mentor to me.

Sean's words comment on the same theme, "Lane isn't your enemy. It's just his main motivation is remaining loyal to his father's and grandfather's goal. Lane inherited his responsibilities from them. He is a man, a powerful man, with a mission, and neither of you can possibly imagine the power and responsibilities he has."

Sean says no more, but Michael is not satisfied, "Then why don't you explain Lane's power and responsibilities to us, so we can understand."

Sean seems uncertain for a moment then replies, "Explain Lane and his motivations? I'm not sure I'm up for that and doing the dishes."

Michael stands, "Screw the dishes, Sean. I'll throw the dishes in the trash; I'll do the damn dishes later ... whatever. Just explain. I'm more than done with Leah and I not getting straight answers from anyone. Let's change that here and now. Tell us about Lane."

Sean leans back in his chair and looks at Michael before he looks at me, "Seems like your boy has a bit of the old Irish temper in him."

Michael remains standing staring at Sean, so I make a suggestion, "You ask us to trust you then withhold information from us. I believe this could be your opportunity to show us you mean what you say about helping us ... father."

Sean looks at Michael then me, "Well ... daughter, I suppose I could do as you ask, but I won't be doing it to prove anything to you. You either trust me or you don't. Telling you a story isn't going to change that."

I shake my head, "First, stories can change how people think about situations and even other people, and, second, I had no intention of blackmailing you into telling us about Lane."

Sean's mood changes quickly, "Of course not, not Saint Leah. You're one of those people who is so sure what the right thing is, who always seems to do the proper thing in every situation, and you're not judgmental about people doing things you disagree with, oh no, not you. You're a bit of a daydreamer, but other than that no one has any complaints. Except for being way too quiet according to some, your childhood behavior was praised. You didn't even try pot in college or make a fool of yourself on booze in high school. Comments regarding that range from you being just a good young woman who follows the rules to you being afraid to lose control of yourself. You married your first boyfriend and have been true to him. You studied hard and work hard, always giving a hundred percent. You're a good mom, a good wife, a good teacher. Hell, you don't even cuss when you're mad. Hell, you don't even get mad. You donate your time to help out in the community. You pay your taxes and never fake even a single receipt. You vote in every election. You're a good citizen. You sign petitions and write letters about social concerns. You don't believe the end justifies the means. You go to church even when you're questioning the basis of your faith. You always have time to help out a friend or even a stranger. Your file is about the most ... you've kept your life orderly and neat like you keep your house and your car and your class-room; everything in its place; everything has a home, a correct place to be, according to you. How can you never get mad, never go a little crazy over the injustices of living in this world? Even your mother, God rest her soul, got angry now and again. Your sister sure as hell does. Do you even know who you really are inside? Does that girl ever get to come out and see the light of day? Doesn't anything piss you off enough to make you lose control?"

Michael's expression reflects the dismay I am feeling inside. I take his hand in mine then look at my father, "I am not hiding who I am. This is who I am. I am like everyone else; I am really nothing more or less than my response to what I have experienced in my life. And yes, I want to believe everything has a place, a home. I watched flames destroy my family until my family and my home were gone. I was ten, in case you have forgotten. I stood on our lawn and watched everyone who mattered the most to me be taken from me. I lost what was sweet-est to me. I felt ... anger, despair, betrayal. I felt them so strongly I could not eat;

it was difficult to even breathe. I hated so much I was afraid I would hurt someone, anyone, the next person who offered me a kind word, a gentle touch. I
wanted to scream until my voice gave out. At the same time, I never wanted to
speak another word again. I imagined taking a knife and ending my own life. I
imagined walking into the ocean and allowing the water to fill my lungs. I imagined a God who would let something so horrible happen, and I hated that God. I
was very quiet on the outside, but inside … I was on fire." I pause because I cannot find the words I want, but then an image fills my mind, and I continue, "I
held on to my hate so tightly it became like a small smooth stone in my hand. I
controlled it. I made it small. I could carry it around and no one could tell I held
onto it. I still hold onto it. I will always hold onto it, because if I let it go it would
fill me so completely you'd feel my anger even standing across the room from me.
It would come out of my eyes, my mouth, my heart; it would suffocate you, it is
so strong. I hold on to it, keep it small because I am not the fire, not its hot
uncaring flames, not its destroying touch. I am the little girl on the lawn instead.
I made a choice in the months after that fire to be what the fire was not. I chose
faith and hope and love. I am so incredibly sorry if my boring niceness bothers
you, father, but that is who I am, who I choose to be, because I know, more than
most, even though I may have no choice in what happens to me I have a choice in
how I respond. I am the little girl, not the fire. I will always be that little girl. I
will always believe mom and Grandma May, Papa John, and the Danners will
walk out of the fire, and one day in another place in time they will, and everyone
will be saved and safe and okay. If I stopped believing that, stop being the little
girl who believes that, the vile sucking noxious crap that people allow to motivate
them and spew all over others would … make me like Taen, self-serving and
blindly-hating. I will not apologize to you, or to anyone, for who I am. I will hold
on to my hope, ridiculous as it seems to you, forever, because it is what I want my
children to take from me, and I'll keep my hate small and controlled and hidden,
because it is not what I want for them … for anyone, for you, even for Taen. I
will not offer hate and despair into a world already so filled with it. I will not."

Sean's eyes have tears in them. I notice that as Michael puts his arm around
my shoulders, and then we stand together, still and silent waiting for Sean to
respond, to turn away and walk out the door or to be open with us. I make my
heart firm in its resolve. I will accept no half measures from him.

After a moment he speaks quietly to us, "I'm sorry. Maybe your choices made
my choices look bad, and I needed to defend my life to you. You're a good
woman, and I'm proud of you. I shouldn't have said those things to you. Now

you'll have to forgive me for something else, and after I just asked you to trust me. Go figure."

I let his words find a place in me where I can run my hands over them, check them for sincerity, but then I stop, suddenly too tired to care. I only want sleep. My body and mind are done; my heart feels too full. I lean into Michael, and he wraps his other arm around me. I look at Sean again and tell him I accept his apology, tell him I am too tired for any more words.

Michael is not done though, "What file?" Sean's expression indicates he is unclear as to Michael's meaning, so Michael clarifies, "You said something about a file on Leah. What file?"

Sean sort of lets his body fall into his chair, "Leah was closely watched even before the fire, since birth actually, as was Aidrea. No one could know which one would be chosen. After the fire, Leah has had body guards around the clock. Pretty much every move she's made for her entire life is documented."

Michael asks, "Lane?" Sean nods and Michael continues, "So if Leah is being guarded then someone probably knows who broke into our house both times and someone probably knows who Father Tom surprised in his room that led to him having a heart attack and to his death."

Sean nods his head again then sighs, "My bet is you're going to definitely want to hear about Lane now even if Leah's only wanting to sleep."

Michael replies, "You've got it, Sean. Leah can sleep. You can talk. I'll listen, and just in case you're thinking about going domestic on me, the dishes can wait."

*   *   *   *

Morning light sneaks into the room around the edges of the window's curtain, but that is not what awakened me. Weight on the mattress brought me out of dreamless sleep. I turn to find Michael, dressed in Levi's and a t-shirt, lying on his side, facing me. He leans over and kisses my forehead then comments, "We've had multiple visitors, and it's only eight in the morning."

I move closer to him and say, "Tell me about the visitors and also what Sean told you about Lane last night."

Michael says, "Yes, ma'm."

So I amend my previous request, "Please tell me about the visitors and also what Sean told you about Lane last night."

Michael says, "It would be my pleasure." He rolls over on his back, and we adjust ourselves, my head resting on his chest, his arm around me. "I'll tell you about Lane and then the visitors, but then I have some questions for you about your time with Brigid. Sean does, too."

I sit up, suddenly remembering the neckrings. Michael does not move as he speaks to reassure me, "I'm guessing you just remembered your souvenirs." I nod and he continues, "We found them last night after I carried you in here and put you to bed. Sean picked up the blanket on the couch." He pauses again and pulls me down next to him before he continues, "They're safe, Leah. Sean didn't even touch them until I handed him one to hold. They're impressive and heavy and worth a small fortune, and they're safe. You can trust Sean. After you hear about Lane you'll understand why I'm so sure of that."

I ask, "Where are they?"

Michael smiles, "I knew you'd ask that. They're between the mattress and the box spring at the foot of the bed. They're safe at least for now, so are you going to listen and focus on what I'm going to tell you, or do you want to hide them someplace else?" I just pat his cheek and tell him to tell me, adding I am content, for now, with the whereabouts of the neckrings. I close my eyes and let his words fill my mind. I focus and make myself a good listener.

*   *   *   *

Again the shifting of the mattress wakes me. I sit up and find Michael standing beside the bed. His expression is amused but he comments, "I can't believe you fell asleep."

I cannot help myself and yawn, covering my mouth with my hand and apologizing when my yawn is done. Michael shakes his head. I smile, "I did not plan to fall asleep, and I am sure, based on what I heard, you were almost done."

Michael folds his arms over his chest, "What's the last thing I said that you remember?"

I prop the pillows behind me and lean back against the headboard, "The last thing I remember? The last thing? I cannot do it that way; I am a chronological kind of gal. In the beginning you told me about Lane's grandfather, Matthew Thomas Dayton, coming here from Ireland, not the typical poor Irish immigrant but a rich man with connections in America and in Europe. He married Sarah McFallon, the daughter of the man who was to be the lighthouse keeper. Sarah's father, Seamus, also an immigrant from Ireland, and Matthew knew each other from the old country, as you called it, and despite the destruction of the lighthouse, Matthew and Seamus purchased the land that is now the property of Dayton Land Management, a company begun by Matthew, and a responsibility he passed on to his son, Thomas, who passed it on to his son, your uncle and my employer, Lane." I pause as Michael sits down on the bed, "Then you talked about how Matthew and Seamus undertook a variety of money-making ventures. Next you told me about Thomas incorporating the land and protecting the forest under some of the first environmental legislation to be created in the U.S.; you described how he set up the township and attracted the people and businesses he wanted using monetary incentives in regards to the fifty year renewable-option leases."

I take a deep breath and ask Michael how I am doing so far. He calls me a sho-woff and tells me to continue, so I do. "Thomas built the medical center, which included what was called at the time a Restorative Center. He brought in the best physicians and staff, catering to the rich. Hollywood was just beginning to blossom—my word not yours—and the studios availed themselves of the center for a variety of purposes, ranging from just giving their stars a healthy holiday to getting the stars cleaned up and off alcohol or drugs. Much of the money made was sent back to Ireland to finance a much longed for home-rule and a strong Ireland. Thomas also began funding what he called freedom crusades in other countries. Thomas began hiring professional soldiers, and here you commented 'professional soldiers' was just a nice way of describing mercenaries. You also commented on the fact Thomas was gifted in maintaining a low profile even when powerful politicians started making use of the clinic and restorative center, but at the end of Thomas' reign, your word, it was deemed necessary to move the focus off of the town of Lane and begin diversifying investments. The clinic remained, but the center was moved to the Los Angeles area, and is now one of the prominent reconstructive surgery facilities in the world. When Lane took over leadership he made timely investments in a variety of new technologies, getting in on the ground floor, as it were, of the computer and software industries. And that, husband, is the last piece of information I remember hearing, so now please tell me anything else I need to know, and I promise I will not fall asleep again."

Michael runs his hands though his hair, squints his eyes, then lays back on the bed as he begins, "I'm giving you highlights here. The issue of greatest concern for Sean is Lane's freedom crusaders don't always seem to be fighting on the side of the oppressed people in a given area. Sean says sometimes they fight for the side that can pay the most. A few years ago, Lane and your dad had a discussion that ended in Sean refusing to work for Lane anymore. Sean could no longer support Lane's belief that certain countries aren't ready for democracy and supporting one less-than-perfect regime over another, as Lane expresses it, is more beneficial for the people than doing nothing. A few of the soldiers went with

Sean, but the rest continue to give their loyalty to Lane. Sean says when the loyalty switched from an ideal to a man, his exact words were 'a paycheck' then what men were willing to do changed also. Sean said he never considered himself a mercenary, but that's what they had become. So Sean and about ten others went back to Ireland and worked with a group already established there. This group has ties to Lane's group, but only to the extent that Lane provides them with money on a somewhat regular basis. The focus of the group is more uniting the Irish people to give them strength than advocating or perpetuating the violence. Your dad sort of smiled at that point saying there was no chance of greed being a factor, because the group operated on next to nothing, using most of the money donated by Lane and others to rebuild areas destroyed by bombing or just run-down due to poverty."

Michael sits up and looks at me, "Your dad is carrying a hammer around more than he's carrying a gun. This group he works with has him training inner-city kids in basic construction skills. Don't misunderstand, he isn't totally out of the business, as he refers to it, but he is the first to admit that maybe the old ways aren't the best ways to bring about lasting social change." Michael pulls me into his lap, rests his chin on the top of my head for a moment, and then rearranges me a bit so he can speak without tapping my head with his chin as he is speaking, but his handling of me is aggravating.

I wiggle around in his lap using my elbows more than is necessary, "Are you done arranging me like I am a doll?"

Michael pats my arm, "Don't get all fussy and feministic on me. There's something else I need to tell you." I fold my arms and make no comment, so he continues, "According to Sean, Aidrea is not just into spiritual matters. Or she is, but the spiritual goals are achieved using very physical means, if you get my drift. She doesn't work for Lane, but she is definitely involved in some … projects … that aren't quite legal. Sean says Malick works with the same group, and also that we should see Connor as a soldier willing to do just about anything to protect his faith, and that he is connected to a group of like-minded individuals. Sean's not sure but he doesn't believe Connor is the only one here from that group. Last but not least, and before I tell you about who has come to see you, I need to tell you that the weather outside is far from typical."

I am processing slowly, or perhaps I am processing quickly, but there are so many connections and overlaps in the information I have just received I am on overload. Also, I cannot help but wonder how long it will be until I can be with John Henry and Mary again. I miss Puppy and my house and my bathtub. I shake my head and accidentally smack Michael's jaw. I roll out of his lap in a most undignified manner then stand up in the middle of the bed looking down at my husband as he rubs his jaw.

I say, "Oops. Sorry about that." I look around the room, hoping I have other clothes to wear, but do not see the backpack Michael and I packed when we left our house to go to Elwood's. I voice my concerns, "I need to clean up and have fresh clothes. Then I will hear about my visitors, answer your questions and Sean's about Brigid, then I guess I will have to decide how I want to handle Taen, if I can actually make a plan regarding Taen at all. Maybe I am just going to continue to react, and she is going to continue to initiate our interactions, but that does not feel right to me." I shake my head, "But I cannot think about that now."

Michael stops rubbing his jaw and points at the closet, "The backpack is in there."

I climb down off the bed, retrieve the backpack and let him know I am going to 'freshen up a bit'. He says something like 'good' or 'go for it' as I open the bedroom door, walk past Sean sitting on the couch and make my way into the small bathroom that barely allows for me with the backpack to stand between the toilet and sink and the curtained shower stall. As I am turning on the hot water, I turn off my concerns about Lane and Sean and their motivations. I will not let my thoughts run around like crazy people inside my head. As I am washing my hair and body I will get organized and perhaps, if I can be very, very good, all the new pieces of information will have homes before I am through.

✳   ✳   ✳   ✳

I am just walking out of the bathroom and saying good morning to Sean when the cabin's walls and floor begin shuddering violently. I watch as Sean and Michael try to stand and turn toward me at the same time. I stand with my feet apart, trying to maintain my balance as if I am in a boat pulled and pushed by angry waves, then as suddenly as the movement began it stops. We do not move; we are waiting. I have a sense of air being pushed into the room, but there is no sound or perception of the air moving.

Michael and Sean both reach over the couch, grab my arms, and pull me to them and then down onto the floor. We lay on our sides. They drag the large square coffee table over us as a low rumble begins, but the floor does not move; it is only a sound and an awareness of the air becoming difficult to breathe, as if it is too dense to take into our lungs. Suddenly the low rumble becomes a high shrieking and the glass of the windows shatters as the walls and floor begin heaving. Michael and Sean, on either side of me, are holding onto the table to keep our covering over us. The sounds of wood splintering and objects falling are barely heard through the shrill piercing shriek rising and falling with the movement of the cabin.

It takes me a moment to realize I must do something. As soon as I close my eyes to marshal my strength before facing Taen, she is there, seemingly only inches from my face, the distance between us lessening as she expands. Her face of smoke and fog contorts itself and a dark cavity where her mouth should be opens wider and wider. She is going to swallow me, take me into her. I hold up my hands against her and say 'no'. I yell it into the darkness beginning to surround me. I will her to be gone, and she pulls back from me, her shape changing as she rises above me, but she does not leave. She is serpent again and flames shoot down from her mouth toward me. I do not change my tactics, "Be gone, Taen. Be gone." I can feel the heat from the flames as they near me, and I question if I am really feeling heat or if because they appear to be flames I am imagining the heat. I put my hands down by my side and imagine rain falling. I imagine the rain and it surrounds me just before the flames touch my skin. I say to Taen, "Be gone. Be gone."

The serpent form changes as it shrinks, then I am facing a woman who resembles Brigid in her features, but stands before me, a fog of gray and black smoke. We stand on the ground in the clearing surrounding the cabin. The raindrops fall through her. She steps closer to me, opens her dark lips to speak, but raises a gold handled knife instead. I grab her arm as I step to the side, but my hands travel through her, so I grab the handle of the knife through her hands. She shrieks as we struggle. The noise she makes is painful. I will myself not to hear her and suddenly her twitching lips are the only indication I have she is shrieking. In the new silence I try to focus my thoughts and will her to let go of the knife. I realize we are flying through the walls of the cabin, out into the forest then back through the cabin again. Our feet do not touch the floor or ground at all anymore. Her face keeps changing, the fog and smoke twisting into different stages of Taen's physical decomposing, but her hold on the knife does not alter. She is distracting me with her manifestations. I close my eyes and say, "The knife is not yours to hold, Taen, let go of it then be gone." A burst of turbulent air explodes against me. I am pushed down until my back hits against a hard surface.

I open my eyes. Sean and Michael are leaning over me. I am on the ground in front of the cabin. I can see their mouths moving, but their voices are too soft for me to hear. I realize I can hear nothing but a soft distant drumming. I realize I am holding the gold handled knife in my hands over my head. I let go of it and bring my hands to my ears. My fingertips feel wet, and I think it is from the rain

I was in because my clothes and skin are wet, but when I bring my hands forward in front of my eyes my fingers are red with blood. I look into Michael's eyes and there is fear in them. I look into Sean's eyes and there is anger in them. I close my eyes again. The physical danger threatening me becomes real to me as the fear and anger reflected in Michael's and Sean's eyes try to find a place in me. I say Shal's name and go to him. I take the knife with me.

✳   ✳   ✳   ✳

Shal and Brigid stand before me. We are in the Meadow of Gathering. We stand before the altar. Brigid reaches out and places her hand over my heart. Shal takes the knife from my hands. I say their names in greeting but do not hear my words even though I sent my voice out.

Shal answers me without moving his lips. His words come to me in my mind, "She can harm you, Leah; you've learned that already, now you understand it more fully. More than that I can't tell you, and you must realize we can't protect you. We can try to shield the innocent and the uninvolved, but you must defeat her on your own as the one chosen. Even our guidance is limited. Her body remains in the physical world and though dust is all that remains, the dust being there in your realm gives her a power Brigid and I can't duplicate. Brigid and I are immortal, not limited by time, but we are of this place. Bantok lived in both realms, creating havoc in each, so he could take form in your world; Brigid and I can't, but Bantok will never bother you or anyone else again, of that you can be certain. We can see what is happening to you, but we can't intercede for you except perhaps to speak into the minds of others. We can offer you sanctuary here, but we can't protect you in your own world." Shal hands the knife back to me. I hold it in my hands and wonder what to do with it instead of allowing myself to think of what awaits me.

Brigid's voice interrupts my thoughts, "Take it with you, Leah. It no longer serves a purpose here and can only be a sad reminder." Shal disappears then returns, hands me a scabbard for the knife that is also gold and has inlays of amber and ivory and pearl. The scabbard has a sturdy chain of gold attached to it with a clasp at one end. I do not try to figure out how to wear it but instead wrap the chain around the scabbard and hold it in my hand. Brigid's words come to me again, "I will lay my hands on your ears and speak words of healing into you, and I will pray that your greatest strength be your constant shield, Leah." She lays her palms against my ears and bends to touch her forehead to mine then steps back from me.

Shal's eyes look into mine. He sends no words to me. He bows his head slightly, and then he and Brigid are gone. I stand alone at the altar with my knife in my hands and become aware of birds singing from a great distance. I look around me to find them and see them not more than six feet away, but I decide to smile anyway; some hearing is better than no hearing at all. I take a deep breath and let my head fall back, looking up into the sky. I exhale as I bend my knees and kneel before the altar. I say words I can barely hear, but I know they are heard by the one to whom I speak, "I am just a woman who is a daughter and a wife and a mom, a sometime sister, and a friend and a teacher, God. Is that your name or should I call you the All? It does not matter, does it? You are so much more than a name. You are everlasting and always present, and I have had such a sense of you in my life. Thank you for that. Be with me now, please. Help me. Show me what my greatest strength is, so it can be my constant shield. Protect my family and let my choices and actions honor you and honor life." I breathe the moment in, stand, then close my eyes as I return to the cabin and to my father and husband and to an opponent I have no idea how to defeat.

✳   ✳   ✳   ✳

I return and find myself in Michael's arms. Sean sits next to us. They are look-ing at the cabin, and I notice its walls no longer stand straight and the roof is askew. I wonder if I can go in and retrieve the neckrings. I move a bit in Michael's arms to let him know I have returned. He looks down into my eyes and says something to me but his voice is too soft for me to hear.

I touch his cheek with my hand then reach out and take my father's hand, "I can hear a little but you will have to speak up for me to understand your words." Michael looks away, so I cannot see the emotion filling his eyes. I stand, noticing Sean's eyes are on the scabbard and knife. I begin to walk toward the cabin, but Michael and Sean are quickly behind me holding my arms to stop me.

I explain, trying to keep from yelling to hear my own voice, "I have to get the neckrings." Sean shakes his head and points to himself indicating he will get the neckrings. Michael and I watch as he carefully walks across the porch to the door, which is open a foot or so, and enters the cabin. The porch roof balances on the door and one remaining deck post. I look at Michael, who has just taken my hand in his, and from his nod I gather he is telling me Sean will be okay.

Michael holds out his hand and glances at the scabbard and knife. I hand them to him. He unwinds the chain, removes the knife from the scabbard. We both watch as the long sharp blade captures the sun's light, reflecting its warm brightness onto our faces, but then the light is gone and the metal of the blade is only cold and gray. We look up and watch fast moving dark clouds fill the sky. I take the scabbard from Michael's hand, wrap the chain around my hips twice then secure the clasp into one of the chain links. Michael slides the knife into the scabbard, wraps his arms around me and holds me close before he steps back from me.

I can tell he is almost yelling as he speaks to me, "Do you know what we should do next?"

I shake my head to signify a negative answer then we both turn to watch for Sean. He reappears carrying the neckrings and a rifle. A pistol of some sort hangs from a leather holster draped across his shoulder. As he approaches us his eyes remain on the scabbard and knife I now wear.

He hands the pistol and holster to Michael and the neckrings to me. I put my arm through them and slide them up my arm so they hang from my shoulder. Sean begins speaking in a normal voice, then looks at me and begins speaking more loudly, "Asking questions seems like a waste of time now, and I don't like talking loud enough for the whole world to hear what we're saying. Lane said when he came by this morning he would return with his men. I'm more than sure some of them are already here. What do you want us to do?"

Michael has the shoulder holster on and the pistol in his hand. He waves the gun back and forth as he asks, speaking loudly enough for me to hear, "Is shooting the Taen-bitch going to accomplish anything or are we just going to piss her off?"

I put my hand on his to make him stop waving the gun around, "As I have seen her she has force but no substance, and I cannot believe shooting her is why I was chosen. I hope this is not about me answering violence with violence, but I am wearing the knife because Brigid told me to bring it with me."

Sean looks into my eyes and asks, "If you have to could you use the knife?"

I do not look away from him as I answer, "I cannot answer that now. I will have to respond to each moment, trusting myself to do what I must do, but I know that if this forest fills up with men with guns the situation will only become more dangerous. Remember Taen feeds off of negative emotions. Anger and fear have to be her favorite meal. Lane's men should not be here at all."

Michael's and Sean's eyes are no longer looking into mine. They are watching movement behind me. When I turn, not knowing what to expect at all, I find Lane standing at the edge of the clearing. I think to myself it could have been Taen instead and feel some relief, but then I wonder if I should feel any relief at all as I look upon at least twenty men entering the clearing, each with some type of weapon. They stand behind and around Lane, who is speaking words I cannot hear.

I turn my back on Lane and his soldiers. They are only complicating the situation for me. I choose to ignore them. I look into Michael's eyes then into my father's as I reach out and take each of their hands. I am about to tell them I have to fight this battle alone when Michael's face pales as his eyes darken with anger. I turn quickly and see a woman I know must be Aidrea and Malick holding John Henry's and Mary's hands. Puppy is on a leash held by one of a new group of five or six of Lane's men, who are acting as escorts or guards or captors. My eyes go to Lane's. He is moving his hands and lips, but I am beyond listening even if I could hear. He has brought my children into a situation dangerous beyond anything he can imagine.

My sense of betrayal turns to a burning hate I am unsure I can control. It is seductive in its desire to grow inside me, but I have seen what hate produces and want no part of it. I make it small again like a stone I can hold in my hand then I hold it so tightly it becomes nothing but a dust the breeze blows off my palm and fingers when I open my hand. As I begin to walk toward Lane I allow myself to feel nothing for him at all but instead allow the love I feel for my family to fill me. I let that be my motivation; I let that become my shield. I shake my head to clear my thoughts and take a deep breath to steady myself.

I am ready to face this ... new fire; I am ready. I tell myself this time I will not be late, then I focus on the situation before me as Michael and Sean walk close behind me. I can see John Henry's and Mary's faces. I remember the blood that has dried in my hair, and on my neck and shirt, and I know my children must be my first concern, so I turn toward them as I hold my hand up to Lane, indicating he should remain still and stop talking. He seems shocked I am giving him a command, but I do not allow myself to be concerned with his reactions or disapproval.

Two of his men begin to step in between my children and me, but I do not even slow down. I do as May foretold; I walk through them. Since I cannot really hear and do not choose to turn around, I do not know the reaction I caused or if Michael and Sean still follow me as closely. I am only aware of my children's faces before me. I am on my knees in front of them, remembering to speak quietly to them. I want to hold them in my arms, but their eyes are on the dried blood, so I only take their hands in mine, "I have missed you so much, so much. I know I look scary but do not be afraid for me. I will be fine. I promise you that. We will all be fine. I am not sure how, but I have faith we will. Do you trust me?"

They nod their heads. I tell them I love them then turn to Michael and Sean, "I cannot be who you protect now. You cannot protect me anyway. I am trusting you, both of you, to take John Henry and Mary away from here and to keep them safe for however long this takes. I am trusting you to do whatever you have to do to ensure their safety." I bend down and rub Puppy's head and tell him he is a good boy. He is sensing the danger and sitting quite still, but then he stands and rubs his head against me.

I stand and touch both my children's hair, then put my hands on their shoulders and guide them to Michael and Sean. Malick and Aidrea move to stand with them. Lane's men are moving to form a circle around us, but I ignore them. I try to take the lead from the man's hand who is holding Puppy, but he is looking at Lane, so I look at Lane also. I put my hand on the knife's handle as a gesture to emphasize my words, "You will let my children and Puppy go with Michael and Sean and Malick and Aidrea out of this forest before I will listen to anything you have to say, Lane."

He has made sense of the dried blood around my ears and speaks loudly, "I brought them here, so we could protect them for you." His eyes go to the man holding Puppy's leash indicating Puppy should be released, and he is.

I shake my head and hold my hand up again, "Until my family is safe and gone from here we have nothing to say to each other."

I turn my gaze from his and look at Aidrea. She reaches out her hand to me, and we move closer to each other. I think for a moment I am looking into a mirror and seeing my own reflection, our hair styles the only noticeable difference. She places her hand over my heart, leans toward me and lays her forehead against mine, then whispers something I cannot hear.

I want to ask her to repeat what she said, but Lane interrupts, speaking loudly enough for me to hear, "I'm not the enemy in this, Leah, so of course, if you don't want your family protected by my men then your family is free to go, but I can't be responsible for what happens to them once they leave."

I turn my head but not my body, "You cannot protect my family, Lane. Keep your men away from my family. With your men will be the most dangerous place to be once Taen reappears, and she will, and then we will see how much good your men and their weapons are."

I turn and face Michael and Sean, wanting to reassure them, but I cannot think of a way to actually do that. I smile at my father and say thank you to him then look at Michael and say, "I 'will' see you later, husband."

There are so many emotions being expressed in his eyes, but he only reaches out to me and touches my cheek as he says, "I'll see you later, wife, and John

Henry and Mary will see you later too. Hell, as soon as you get home we'll have a barbecue, invite the whole damn family over, and introduce them to Aidrea." He tries to smile but cannot quite manage it, so he just repeats, "We'll see you later." He shakes his head and takes a step closer to me, "I can't leave you like this, Leah; it's insane. I have to be with you."

I reach up and place my hand on his cheek, "You have to take care of our children, Michael. I have to know you will do that so I can do what I have to do. And you have to know you are with me … you are always with me … you will always be with me, no matter where we are or how far apart we are. I am never without you, Michael Callaghan. Now take care of our children, and my dad, and my sister, and her strange husband, and Puppy. Do that for me and go now before Taen comes back. Go now." I touch John Henry's and Mary's shoulders one more time then turn and walk toward Lane without watching my family leave, but I can hear Puppy barking as if they have made their way farther down the path already than they possible could have, then remember my hearing is impaired. I walk slowly toward Lane as I run through my mind, closing every door but one.

$$* \qquad * \qquad * \qquad *$$

I stand before Lane; his men circle around us, but I do not look at them at all. I look only at Lane. My eyes do not even blink, and the silence surrounding and filling me strengthens my resolve, but he is not looking into my eyes. He is only looking at the knife in its scabbard and at the neckrings.

I move the neckrings off my shoulder and down my arm and hold them out to him, "Are these … things … the reason you are endangering people's lives? These things, Lane? For gold?"

Lane ignores the meaning behind my questions when he responds remembering to speak loudly, "No one else has been able to bring back anything. None who have gone before you came back knowing much more than they knew before they went." He pauses, and I realize I do not know this man I thought I knew so well then he continues, "Can you understand what this means? What we can accomplish?"

I stress my first word, "We will not be accomplishing anything together, Lane."

He steps closer to me, and I have to resist stepping back from him, "You have been to the altar. Describe it to me. I have the information from my grandfather's diary based on the recollection of the one chosen of his generation who got that far, but she wasn't able to handle the experience as well as you have. It was difficult for anyone to know how reliable her descriptions were. The adventure sent her over the edge, I'm afraid, but none of that matters now, does it? Tell me about the altar, Leah. Is it truly solid gold?"

I do not answer him. I do not try to make him understand that everything, every moment, every intention, every action, matters so much more than gold. Instead I lay the neckrings at his feet as I say, "Take them and leave with your men. You will only make the situation worse by being here. The scabbard and knife I cannot give you, and you should not attempt to take them from me."

Lane speaks too softly for me to hear, so I ask him to repeat his words, which he does as he picks up the neckrings at his feet, "But this is only the beginning. You can go there and come back. 'You' are a thin place, so you can not only carry items through time and space, you can also take others with you, Leah. Imagine the opportunity we have. Imagine it. And not just for the gold either; think of the information. There is power in information. We could change the way people think about life, Leah."

I say 'no' to him, and his expression changes; he is no longer trying to sell his idea to me but stands like a general with his small army surrounding him. He begins to speak but is silenced when he looks over my head and beyond me. His eyes reflect shocked disbelief. I turn around and see Taen in the shape of the serpent above the tops of the trees and know now that her flames are real, because Lane's forest, the one Lane and his father and his grandfather have protected for so long, is burning. Taen flies back and forth fanning the flames with the movement of her wings.

Smoke from the fire is being blown into our faces, but my concern is no longer for myself. Michael running with Mary in his arms, and Sean and Malick running with John Henry between them, and Aidrea running with Puppy come from the path's entrance into the meadow through the billowing smoke; Taen's fire has blocked their escape. Without stopping to think I will myself off the ground. As I fly up through the air to meet Taen I imagine rain falling and it does, but just as quickly she is pushing me back down into the same clearing where my family has run to take cover.

I am aware of what is happening on the ground and in the air and I realize the confusion and fear being felt on the ground is giving strength to Taen. I watch as she flies around the cabin clearing, igniting tree after tree, creating a circle of fire and blocking any escape for the people trapped in the clearing. I watch and do not know what to do. I do not know what to do. I go through the one door I left open in my mind and see myself standing before the flames of another fire, and then I do know what to do. I walk into the burning house in my memory as I fly into the flaming serpent-mouth of Taen, and then she and I are both falling. I slow my descent, landing on my feet, but lose sight of Taen.

Lane's men, not trained to deal with flame spewing serpents of fog and smoke, are taking positions behind anything they can find as Michael and Sean, and Malick and Aidrea try to form a human shield around and over John Henry and Mary. Puppy is running around them, stopping to bark when one of Lane's men passes by too closely. Then I see Taen moving toward Lane, tiny flames darting from her mouth, her body of smoke and fog difficult to distinguish from the fire's smoke billowing around us. Lane appears unable to move as Taen moves closer and closer to him. One of Lane's men runs up behind Lane, kneels down beside him, raises an automatic weapon and begins shooting into Taen's form. The gun makes only a repetitive tap-tap sound for me and has no effect on Taen, her dark lips sneering as she moves steadily closer to Lane. The man, who is shooting the weapon, stops, pushes against Lane and attempts to grab the neckrings from him. Lane begins to struggle with him half-heartedly, unable to take his eyes off of Taen.

Suddenly I am aware of a tap-tap sound from a different direction. Lane's men are divided by loyalty to the man, who I believed at first was protecting Lane but who only wanted the gold, and a group of men who are actually trying to protect Lane by shooting the first man, who now has the neckrings in his possession and is moving away from Lane. I have stopped thinking and observing. I am only running now. The man trying to steal the gold has been shot and Lane is using his body to hide behind while the tap-tapping has increased to a steady rhythm with occasional bursts. I am running because my family is in the middle of the two groups of men. I am running because Taen is growing more distinct; I can no longer see through her, and she has changed direction and is moving toward my family.

Sean is moving to intercept her as Michael and Malick and Aidrea are shielding John Henry and Mary. Puppy is at Sean's side then jerked sideways as a bullet hits him, but I cannot stop for him; I can only keep running. I see one of Lane's men move from behind the cover of a small shed. He has raised a rifle to his shoulder and is aiming at Sean's back.

I run between Sean and the man aiming at Sean's back and a bullet rips into me. The impact flips me around. I fall to my knees but stand quickly and push Sean out of the way just before Taen reaches him. Her hands reach for my throat as I pull the knife from the scabbard and plunge it into her chest. We fall to the ground, my hands wrapped tightly around the knife's handle, her hands wrapped around my throat. I cannot breathe. My eyes cannot seem to focus; shifting planes of light and dark deny me sight. In slow motion my thoughts dart about; I cannot grab even one to hold onto to help me stay in the moment, to help me maintain my hold on the knife in Taen's body. As my strength fades and her body continues to thrash against me, her hands tighten around my throat. Blood from my shoulder drips down onto Taen and then suddenly blood seeps from the gaping wound around the knife where no blood flowed earlier. I use the last of my strength to raise my eyes to her face. She has become flesh and blood. Her hands loosen from around my neck as blood gushes from between her lips. Then I am only laying on ancient bones that support my weight for the briefest of moments before I find myself laying upon a white dust my blood dyes a crimson red, then the light is gone and only darkness surrounds me and even the darkness disappears and then there is only a heartbeat not mine.

Conclusions

Morning sun glides through the curtainless window and falls upon me as I try to hold on to the dreamscape as if I can, like an almost napping fisherman, remember to keep a tight grip on the pole which is connected to deep water by a thin line of consciousness, but physical sensations demand I open my eyes, let go of fanciful images pulling and pushing against me like waves, to clarify why my right arm is tingling and numb and why my left shoulder is stiff and painful. Breath against my cheek that cannot be Michael's or John Henry's or Mary's makes me open my eyes in wary caution, and when I do a tidal wave of memory overwhelms me almost making me close my eyes again. Puppy's large brown eyes look into mine; his head lies on my arm. I can see Puppy's side where his hair has been shaved and bandaged. I gently move my arm out from under his head and feel my own shoulder. It is also bandaged. I touch my ears but realize even before I do so that I can hear again, because I can hear Puppy breathing and beyond the door of my bedroom I can hear voices speaking.

I do not try to identify them. I roll over on my side gently and lay my hand on Puppy's head then rub behind his ear. I offer him baby talk and very slowly he rolls over onto his back, so I can rub his tummy. Movement of my hand and arm quickens the pulse of the throbbing pain in my shoulder, but the pain is bearable, so I continue to soothe Puppy as I wonder how many hours or days have passed since I lay on the ground in the forest holding a knife in my hands. No sense of time answers me, but the door being opened slowly and quietly focuses both Puppy's and my attention.

An eye peers in at us, and then the door is closed again. I hear voices, excited but shushing each other, as the door is opened wide. Mary stands in front of John Henry, who stands in front of Michael, and they are each smiling and holding a long stemmed red rose. I can see the difficulty John Henry and Mary are having in moving slowly to my bed instead of running and jumping to join me, but they manage and stand next to me, hand me their roses then bend to kiss my cheek, John Henry whispering 'Mom' and Mary whispering 'Momma'. I touch each of their faces as I tell them they do not need to whisper.

John Henry continues to whisper anyway, "Dad said to."

Mary adds, "And we aren't supposed to climb on the bed either."

I look at Michael, "Good morning, husband."

He walks across the room and hands me his rose, smiling as he whispers, "Good morning, wife."

I thank them for the beautiful roses then ask Michael, "Do you think it would be okay if Puppy and I could have cuddles and normal voices?"

John Henry and Mary look up at his face, and he winks at them, "That would be my first choice." Before he can finish reminding them to take off their shoes, John Henry's and Mary's shoes are off their feet, and they are crawling carefully onto the bed. Michael takes the roses from me and places their long stems in a half filled water glass sitting on the nightstand. Puppy's tail is thumping the mattress as Michael joins us, and then we lay together in a silence interrupted only by contented sighs.

✳   ✳   ✳   ✳

I shake my head and find myself standing in front of the window of my bedroom, daydreaming again, going back in time. I hear Papa John and my mom laughing. I see May's face animated by a story she is telling. I see Sean and Grant cooking in the kitchen of the cabin. I see Father Tom and feel my hand in his. I hear Brigid's and Shal's words and see them standing side by side before the altar. I see Aidrea and Malick together, sitting in my living room, and feel a sense of wonder at the closeness Aidrea and I have already found with each other.

I raise my arm slowly, stretching it above my head, aware of a dull ache but thankful a bandage is no longer necessary and then remember how I came to be standing here. I was walking from bedroom to bathroom to prepare for my day when a bird's song drew me to the window. Looking through the window, out into the yard, Puppy's slow but happy movement from tree to tree, to reclaim his area, had made me pause and led me to wander around a bit in my close and distant past.

After a week of bed rest Puppy and I have both begun a gradual resuming of our normal activities. I had been in the hospital for a week, in and out of consciousness while Puppy had been at the local vet's clinic fighting for his life.

Michael had brought us home on the same day, late in the afternoon, so we could be at home and sleep the sleep that can only be had at home. The very next morning both Puppy and I had been ready for family cuddle time, and within two days brief visits from extended family members and close friends began. Then just yesterday Bradley and my student-family group came to see me, and I knew it was time to return to Dayton School and to my students. Conversations with John Henry and Mary confirmed what Michael had told me about their acceptance of what had happened; John Henry commenting to me, and Mary agreeing with him, that 'sometimes life really is like a crazy story no one would ever believe is true.' After Maybe heard a brief version of my experiences, her comment to me was that just like Hitaw's experience with Shadowmaker, my experiences with May, Shal, Brigid, and Taen will, over time, become less and less believable to others, and a generation or two later it will only be a story crazy grandma tells. I told Maybe I cannot imagine ever doubting what happened or making it less than it was, but she only said to me, "And don't you think Hitaw thought the exact same thing? Don't you wonder why she went as often as she could up that winding path to sit with Shadowmaker?" I wonder as I walk into the bathroom to turn on water for my bath if there really are any completely fictional accounts or if every story has its foundation in actual human experience. Then I wonder if the routine and ritual of the day-to-day will have its way with my memory of the experience just as the rain, year after year, has its way with the rock of Shadowmaker.

✳   ✳   ✳   ✳

John Henry has been dropped off at Lane Grammar and Middle School, and Mary and I are driving toward Dayton School. We are on a street lined with trees that have reached their height and now sweep out toward each other, their branches layered upon each other so only tiny bits of sunlight are scattered on the street below. Mary holds out her hands to catch the rays of golden light. After driving through the massive gates of the school, I cannot help but look over at the Administration Building, across from the small graveled parking lot where I am parking, and think of Lane. Because this is my first day back, I have not been into Lane's old office that is now his son's new office, but I do not let my thoughts focus on Lane or his decision to not only leave the school but also 'his' town. Mary is humming and kicking her feet against the seat happily, and I decide to share the moment with my daughter instead of letting myself wander around inside my head.

As I turn off the ignition, Mary leans back and looks at me, her forehead wrinkled by some serious consideration. I ask her what she is thinking about.

Mary replies quickly, "I am hoping you won't take forever getting out of the car, mom. I want to go to the fountain."

I pretend to be shocked by her words, "I cannot believe you are asking me to hurry."

Mary's expression is quite serious, "Well, I am. I really, really am."

I sigh, "But what about all my things?"

Mary leans toward me as far as her car seat allows, "Leave them. Just take what you need for right now."

I lean my head back against the seat and turn my head to look at her as I say, "I can do that for you but only today. Tomorrow I get to take my time. Is that agreeable to you?"

Mary imitates me, leaning back and turning her head to look at me, "Da would have said 'is that a deal?' instead of 'is that agreeable to you?'"

I am enjoying just looking at her and listening to her speak, so I do not rush our conversation, "And why is that interesting to you?"

Mary shrugs her shoulders, "Maybe because words are fun to listen to most of the time, and maybe because people use them in different ways. I've been noticing that some." She pauses and turns her body toward me, patting her own cheeks as she says, "Words are pretty important, ya know?" I tell her I agree then ask her why she is patting her own cheeks. She wiggles in her seat, "Because I can't reach yours, 'cause I'm trapped in this seat." She stops wiggling and asks very politely, "Could I, do you think, just this once, undo my own seat buckle?"

I shake my head 'no', and she asks why not. As I undo my seatbelt and move closer to her, ignoring the fact I am crushing the bags lying on the seat between us, I whisper to her, "Because I feel like tickling you right now, and that will be easier if you are buckled into your seat." I begin tickling, and she begins giggling, and it feels like a good start to my first day back.

We are taking turns tickling each other, but she is making much more noise than I am when we are interrupted by Bradley tapping on Mary's window and telling me I should stop abusing my child. Mary begins yelling 'help me, help me, I can't get out.' I only smile at both of them, push the button unlocking the doors and indicate Bradley may rescue my poor, mistreated daughter. I tell them I will meet them at the fountain, so they do not have to wait for me and then take my time gathering small items like keys and pens and photos in small plastic accordion bundles from the floor where they have fallen from my purse. I leave the car with my purse and Mary's bright colored backpack and a relatively empty soft leather briefcase, which will soon have student work added to its contents. I have all my necessary items for the day with me. I walk toward the fountain, content.

✻   ✻   ✻   ✻

Bradley and I follow Mary around as she dances like a ballerina. He asks me questions about my 'strange experiences', as he calls them. She is dancing and running and skipping and singing quietly, since it is still quite early and she knows to keep her noise within her own space, unlike those obnoxious people in their cars who play their music for anyone within a fifty yard radius to hear. I am not sure Bradley is satisfied with my answers or even done asking me questions, but I am tired of so much focus on myself.

I tell him, "It is my turn now."

He raises an eyebrow, "Meaning?"

I put my finger on his eyebrow to make it relax, which he has never appreciated but I find more than a bit amusing, "It is my turn to hear about your life now."

He has stepped back so he can raise the other eyebrow without interference, "My tale pales miserably in comparison."

I put my hands on my hips, "I told no tale. I gave you facts."

Bradley is now raising one eyebrow and then the other just to annoy me, "Nevertheless, I have nothing of import to share with you." I suggest to him, as I try to get close enough to still his fluctuating eyebrows, that he obviously needs to get out more.

He sits down on the fountain's thick stone wall and looks at me, "I'm being quite serious now, and I tell you honestly 'getting out', as you refer to it, has little to no appeal to me."

I sit down next to him, keeping my eyes on Mary as she strums her fingers through the fountain's bubbling water, and comment, "It has been over two years since Daniel's death. You are still young and have a whole life ahead of you. Do you not want to share it with someone you care about deeply?"

He almost raises his eyebrow but catches himself, "I care deeply about you. Do you think Michael would mind if I moved into your home so I could share life with you?"

I give him my 'I am being serious' look without saying a word, and he sighs, "Fine. Fine. You've obviously deemed this the appropriate time to have this conversation, so we shall. I'll simply ask you a question, and I believe in your answering of it, you'll have my response also." He pauses, frees his hand from mine then uses both of his to hold his eyebrows in place, "Do you believe if Michael died today you would want to find someone to replace him in two years? In ten years? In twenty years? Can you imagine doing so?" He has folded his hands in his lap and is looking into my eyes, "Ah, now you understand, yes?" Bradley looks out over the campus, "Daniel and I did not have a fight and break-up. He died. We weren't done loving each other. He was taken from me. And of course I realize many people find love again even after the death of a partner, but that's not who I am, and I don't believe it's who you are either. I will love Daniel forever, like Elwood loves his wife, an always present tense love, but hopefully I can do it without finding myself naked on the beach. Gay men do not have quite the latitude of social acceptance regarding their behavior as straight men. I'm more than certain I would be arrested and called a pervert, while Elwood is just a kind and somewhat confused widower who occasionally forgets to wear clothing."

I lay my head against his shoulder, "Do you think if your brother and others who share his opinions regarding gays heard you speak of your love for Daniel in such a manner they could doubt the integrity of such a love?"

He lays his head on mine, "Most assuredly and without doubt, my love for Daniel is an abomination to them."

I state the obvious, "But there is a difference between sex and love. They are just hung up on how you express your sexuality. I do not even think they consider how you love."

We both watch Mary chasing a butterfly as he comments, "My brother and others like him are locked into a belief system that has inspired great acts of compassion and equally great acts of intolerance. I will not spend my days or waste my thoughts attempting to debate them on my morality. Live and let live, I say. Legislation and laws that punish me for being gay are of course unjust, but those will change with time. Social injustice can only be changed when how people think changes, and that, to be lasting, is a slow and natural process. Forcing change, even when the change is good, is tyranny, and that's no way to right a wrong. In America violence was used to end slavery, while in England one man led a quiet debate pursuing his goal, peacefully and relentlessly, for decades and slavery was ended without bloodshed. You and I, of course, have always agreed that violence does not justify violence or end it, and the sad state of African Americans for decades after the Civil War proves that fact."

Mary is now smelling flowers, and we turn to follow her with our eyes, as I, for the first time, voice my greatest concern regarding my own recent experiences,

"That's what bothers me most about what happened with Taen, Bradley. I was so sure I would not have to use violence to stop her, but I did."

Bradley is thoughtful for a moment, "Remember the discussion in Lane's office with my brother and his church elders. Could Hitler and his regime have been stopped without using violence?" He pauses then says, "That was not a rhetorical question, Leah."

I stand and call to Mary then say, "Looking back I can think of no way, but that does not mean one did not exist at the time."

Bradley stands and bends down to catch Mary up into his arms, "I think you and I prefer absolutes, but few conditions related to humanity, in this world, are absolutes."

Mary is patting Bradley's cheeks gently and tries to reassure him, "Maybe the next world will be better and have lots of … those absolutes for you and mommy. Mommy went there, ya know." She pauses and whispers into Bradley's ear, but I can hear her words quite clearly, "I want to go for my birthday, but I haven't asked yet if I can."

Bradley and I look at each other as he sets Mary down, and I have to wonder if the birds and the bees talk Michael and I will have with our children will be much easier for us than our much called for intermittent talks with them about that other world mommy visited.

✳   ✳   ✳   ✳

Mild morning has willingly opened her misty arms and relinquished herself to the bright daystar. In other words, it is almost time for lunch and my creative writing-family group. I am hungry for both. Mary and I are passing through the gates of Dayton School to walk to the large yarded house with a small plaque on the gate announcing discreetly 'Dayton Day Care' and its address '101 Dayton Place'. The house neighbors the school and shares the same shaded street. Mary wants to skip and for me to join her, but I am not a skipper. Michael says I am too-most-of-the-damn-time-serious to involve myself in activities like skipping, and he may be correct, but he could be generalizing. Before Mary and I had breakfast with Bradley in the meeting hall cafeteria, which was after our discussion and Mary's playtime at the fountain, I did involve myself in a tickling match, and that does not sound too-damn-serious to me.

I hear a door close and look away from my watching of Mary's exuberant skipping to see Nathan walking down the steps of the porch, a briefcase in one hand

and a folded newspaper in the other. Mary runs ahead of me to open the gate for him as she greets him, "Hello, Mr. Dayton."

Nathan's quick response and warm smile are characteristic of him, "Hello to you, Mary. Mrs. Dayton is just putting lunch on the table, so your timing is perfect, and she has quite the afternoon activity planned for you and your friends."

Mary wonders aloud, "Maybe she'll forget about our after lunch nap time today, so we can have the activity right away."

Nathan replies, "I'm pretty sure that's not going to happen, aren't you?"

Mary sighs, "I'm pretty sure too, but I say things like that so maybe they can happen."

Nathan responds, "It's good to have hopes and make suggestions."

Mary smiles, "I have lots of them. Bye, Mr. Dayton." She hugs me then runs up the stairs to the door as we call out to each other our usual sentiments when we are saying goodbye to each other: I love you, have a good day, see you later. Crystal waves at us after she has answered Mary's knock. The door is closed, and Nathan and I begin walking back to the school together.

Nathan initiates the conversation, "I know I told you part of this when Crystal and I came to the house while you were convalescing, but I want to reassure you again, so you understand and have no doubts about the situation. My father's decisions to leave the school and to move away were not based entirely on what happened with you. That experience influenced him undoubtedly, but he and I … well, our opinions and beliefs differed on a variety of issues involving the school and the town, and since I was going to inherit the responsibilities sooner or later anyway, his decision to leave was not as shocking to my mom or to Crystal and me as it was to others. He and I had a discussion a couple of months ago regarding the changes that would have to be made knowing I refuse to be involved in any aspect of the family business other than the school and the town. I am most definitely not into his type of fundraising. I am not a political animal, if you get my meaning."

I nod and add, "That was somewhat apparent years ago when you chose to become a marine biologist instead of a banker or a lawyer like your father or grandfather."

Nathan stops walking just before we enter the school gates, "Crystal and I were talking about that just last night, and I have to admit, as I told her, I miss the ocean and my work." He pauses shaking his head, "I may be better at dealing with fish than I am with people."

I put my hand on his arm, "You are good at both, but do you have to give up your research entirely?"

We begin walking again as he responds to my question, "For the next few months at least I'm going to be tied to my desk, so to speak, but once I get the operation running smoothly here, I think I can resume my research and field study. Did Michael tell you about the changes I am making?"

Again I nod, "Your idea of creating a town council to oversee Dayton Land Management Company instead of overseeing it yourself seems progressive and more democratic than how the town has been run since its beginning, but Lane and your father and your grandfather were fair minded men. The people who live here have few if any complaints about their leadership."

Nathan and I turn to face each other, "I appreciate you saying that, especially after my father's decision on Joe Danner's church. I know you were involved in that process and not in agreement with my father's handling of it. But I should probably warn you the changes I plan to make at the school and in the overseeing of the town are going to affect you and Michael more than you may realize." I ask him to explain, so he continues, "Michael has already agreed, assuming you have no qualms about it, of course, to be on the town council and to help me create a document to replace the Town Charter written by my grandfather. Hank has agreed to be on the council. I have asked Calvin and Maybe to consider joining us also, which should ensure the meetings will not be dull. In regards to the school, I plan to set up a meeting with you and Bradley next week to share my ideas about dividing my father's responsibilities between the three of us, but-" he holds up his hand to stop me from making any comments, "I can't discuss that with you now. I have three interviews today to try to find a secretary to replace my mom and a meeting later in the afternoon with dad's accountant. I have a temp sitting at the front desk right now answering the phone, but the paperwork is piling up. I had hoped Crystal might want to be my right hand, as it were, but she loves what she is doing, and that's more important to me. I should let you know your sister has applied for the job."

I open my mouth to speak then close it, and Nathan pats me on the shoulder, "Good for you. My increased interaction with people evidences the voicing of initial reactions is not always the best choice. Better to think about what I have shared for a day or two before we begin a discussion. I really must be going, but I'm glad you're back, Leah. The students and staff have missed you."

Nathan begins to take the path to the Administration Building then faces me again, "I have no desire to pry into personal matters, but do you have any way of knowing if this ... situation in which you've been involved ... is completed?"

I respond based on hope more than fact, "I believe my part in the matter is completed."

Nathan nods, "Then I'll resume normal security at the school."

I say 'okay' as he walks away from me then turn and sit on the wall of the fountain. My external surroundings fade from my vision. I see myself running through passageways in my mind checking that doors are closed and wondering if my own normal internal security will suffice.

∗   ∗   ∗   ∗

I like to be in my classroom alone before the students arrive. I like to get a sense of the atmosphere I have created so carefully by a purposeful arrangement and inclusion of the room's contents. After being gone so much lately, I allow myself a leisurely perusal, my eyes taking in the heavy wooded tables and chairs filling the center of the room and the posters of poets and the bright paintings and hanging plants that fill much of the wall space not used by windows and whiteboard. I turn to the area of the room where two couches face each other and my inventory is stopped. Connor sits on the couch facing me, a book in his hand but his eyes on me. He closes the book, sets it down then stands. I walk over to him, and we look at each other without speaking, each of us trying to gauge the other's frame of mind. He has been such an enigma for me, one moment friendly, the next suspicious, but I want to trust him.

I hold out my hand to him, and he takes my hand in both of his then quietly says, "I'm glad you fared well, were not hurt worse than you were, and that your dog is okay. I know he means a lot to you and your family."

I say thank you to him and add, "I have been told Father Tom's service was a perfect combination of celebrating and missing him. It must be difficult for you to be living there without him. He had such a pleasant way of filling a place with his presence."

Connor looks out the window then comments, "I'll be about my duties, a chore in the orchard or the greenhouse, or tending to the altar or the vestments, and forget he is gone, sure that I'll be hearin' him, his step on the stairs, or his voice callin' to me. It will take time to adjust. He was a good man, and even though I didn't agree with many of his choices regardin' our faith, he served our God with all his heart and soul and was a blessing to those who came to him for so many different reasons." Connor looks into my eyes and steps closer, "Did you discover who was in his room that day?"

I do not answer his question immediately but instead ask him if he knows who the man was. He tells me 'no', so I tell him what I know, what I learned from Malick after he and Sean had their last meeting with Lane before he left. "I was told one of Lane's men was sent to search the church for any pertinent information that could be found. No one was to be hurt. Father Tom walked into his room and the man, at first attempting to hide from Father Tom, changed his mind, jumped out of the closet and startled Father Tom. The man told Lane he didn't hang around to see how Father Tom reacted."

Connor lets go of my hands, "Does Lane's or the man's intent excuse the consequences of their actions?"

I sit down on the couch and look up at Connor, "You tell me, Father Connor; you're the priest. What part of the book are you coming from today? An eye for an eye or let he who has not sinned cast the first stone? Malick's father died, Bradley's parents died, three members of my family died, and now Father Tom is dead primarily because Lane gave two orders. How would you like to punish him? What would make you feel better?"

Connor sits down across from me, "It's not about feelin' better, Leah, it's about justice."

I lean back into the soft cushions of the couch, "I am not arguing with you, Connor, but, according to Sean, Lane is just the parlor general who gave the commands, and parlor generals and corporate executives and their type seldom if ever get what they deserve to the extent that justice would be met. The man who broke into Father Tom's room was shot to death as he tried to steal something from Lane. Malick's father died in the fire he accidentally caused that killed my family and others. Lane gave his last command in the clearing by the cabin after his men had turned on each other and few were left. He told them their services were no longer required, they would receive their final compensation in the regular manner within the week, and to make no attempt to contact him again. Now Lane is gone. His own son cannot get in touch with him. Sean and Malick said it would be difficult even for them to find him. He is cut off from all the people who are most important in his life except for the wife he took with him. Think about it, Connor, justice seems to be occurring without us doing a thing."

Connor leans back now too, studying my face as he asks, "You're satisfied then?"

I sit up straight then lean toward him, "Satisfied? No. Father Tom, May, mom and Papa John, and the others alive, that would be satisfying, but I do not look for satisfaction in what has happened. I cannot find it in my own choices and actions, but I can be grateful my husband and children, and my sister survived the situation. I want to live my life well and positively, and to do that I will think of Lane as seldom as possible. I will have to close that door again and again, Connor, but I know how to do that. Lane's betrayal will not make me bitter. I will think of Father Tom's life instead of the self-serving carelessness that caused his death. I will be a good wife and mom and sister and teacher and friend and if I can do those things well, I will be satisfied."

Connor shakes his head and stands, "So you're thinkin' everything is over, that you can shut those doors in your head, keep silent those voices who have called to you? Aidrea and Malick are here; are you believin' they've chosen to stay because they want those doors closed?"

I stand, turn away from him and walk to my desk, but he follows me and says, "I've chosen to stay also, Leah. The church will be reinstated and other ordained priests will come and work with me, and we will watch to see how well you can keep those doors closed, keep those voices silent."

He walks to the door, opening it before he turns to face me, "I'll be hopin' you and your family will attend the first official Catholic mass to be held in this town in over fifteen years. Put it on your calendar, the first Sunday of next month. Three brothers and two sisters from the 'old country' will be joinin' me. I look forward to introducing them to you, and they, of course, can't wait to meet you."

The door closes, and he is gone. I have ten minutes before my students will be arriving, and I have let Connor unsettle me. I take a deep breath then let it out slowly. My eyes do not resume their inventory of the room's contents; my eyes turn inward. I watch myself running after wild thoughts and memories out of control and wonder if even additional internal security will suffice.

∗   ∗   ∗   ∗

"Hey, Mrs. Callaghan, Mr. Danner said you'd be back and here you are," Tucker greets me in his slow Texas style of speaking. He walks to one of the tables, moves a chair back and sets his backpack down on the floor. I ask him how his day has been so far and he replies, "Last night I finished the final graphics for the computer game I'm making, had a swim this morning before classes started, and lunch was good, so I can't complain. Everyone is talking about Mr. Dayton leaving, so I guess we'll be discussing that in family group today, and that could make for some interesting conversation, don't you think?"

I just smile at Tucker in response. I have my lesson plan book open, and I am looking at what I had planned for the day's discussion in family group, but Tucker's comments have caused me to wonder if trying to focus my students' attention on an issue unrelated to Lane's departure will be possible. I look back through the literary prompts that have been used to begin discussions and initiate writing assignments over the last month or so to discern if I can base a new discussion on an old one to establish continuity and make Lane's sudden departure a discussion of human behavior rather than Lane-specific. I imagine the guessing and gossiping that have been occurring and doubt for a moment if I can channel that flood, then wish Bradley and I had discussed school matters rather than personal matters this morning.

I am gathering items from my desk to take with me to the podium when Maddie and Alana enter the classroom.

Alana's backpack is dropped noisily and she rushes over to put her arms around me, "Mrs. C, Mrs. C, Mr. Danner is great, but I'm so glad you're back." My hands are full, but she does not seem to mind that I cannot return her hug.

I tell her and Maddie it is good to see them both and walk to the front of the classroom as Alana and Maddie join Tucker at the center table. Alana wastes no time in asking me about Lane, "So are you going to tell us if Mr. Dayton's leaving and your recent adventures are connected or are we supposed to draw our own conclusions?"

Maddie shakes her head, "Alana, you're too much. This is Mrs. Callaghan's first day back. Give her a break."

Alana shrugs innocently and looks at me, "We're only allowed to discuss this kind of stuff in family group, and this is family group, so I just figured I'd get things started."

I arrange items on my podium as I ask, "Do you think we might wait for the rest of the group to get here before we begin?"

Alana agrees nonchalantly, but I did not buy myself any time, because the other nine students enter together, calling out greetings to me and taking seats around the tables. When Valerie is settled I walk over to her and give Samson, her guide dog, an ear rub then return to the podium.

For a moment I just look at my students who are talking quietly to each other but also watching me so they will be aware when I am ready to begin. An idea comes to me for a possible lead-in to the Lane discussion, so I open the lesson plan book and my corresponding notebook of class notes, then my students, seeing me doing so, become quiet and attentive.

I establish eye contact with each of them as I say, "Thank you for the good work you have done with Mr. Danner. I had a chance to look through some of your assignments, and I am pleased. Also, thank you for coming to visit me while I was resting after the fire. Thank you also for your phone calls and letters to Teri; her mother called me yesterday and let me know Teri is healing nicely and should return to school in a week or two. Now I realize you have questions about the fire and about Mr. Dayton's decision to … retire early, and I promise 'some' of those

questions will be answered, but they will be asked and answered after we complete a focusing activity." I pause for the two or three students who will want to
moan or sigh heavily expressing their displeasure with my plans, but the room is
quiet, and my students are showing no reactions at all.

I ask, "What is going on?"

Angela raises her hand to respond, "You were expecting a few of us to complain about an intro-activity and we didn't, right?" I nod my head and she continues, "I think it's because we're so glad to have you back we probably wouldn't
even complain if you told us you were giving us a pop quiz over last week's reading assignment, but I hope you won't, because I have questions about it."

I tell Angela there is no pop quiz planned in the near future, then I just smile
at them as I say, "I am glad to be back also, and I will try my best not to torture
you too much today since you are being so good to me."

Neil says, "Bring it on, Mrs. C. We're ready for you."

I ask them to take out their journals and turn to a dated entry. When journals
have been opened and eyes are again focused on me I ask Jacy to read the excerpt
from Robert Frost's poem "Reluctance" they have written in their journals: "'Ah,
when to the heart of man was it ever less than treason to go with the drift of
things, to yield with a grace to reason, and bow and accept the end of love or a
season?'"

I suggest they read their interpretations, their personal reactions, plus their
class discussion notes on Frost's poem. The room is quiet as they do so. I reread
my own notes on the poem and the discussion that followed. When each of the
students has completed their reading I ask if anyone would like to offer a sum-
mary of our first experience with the poem.

Shay raises his hand; I nod, and he taps his pencil against the table as he
begins, "We read the poem the first time to get into a discussion about how we
had all judged and talked about something a couple of people did that they
weren't supposed to have done. Then we were supposed to apply the poem to our
own behavior not make the poem's meaning relevant to what ... well, we all
know who I'm talking about, so ... to what Charlie and Neil did. Based on what
I wrote down we all agreed Frost is commenting on the fact that people will often
choose to go against the norm, to not easily give up on something they feel
strongly about, whether it's a feeling or an idea—'love or a season'. After that you
had us apply the lesson of the poem to areas of interest we have. Before that some
of us tied the poem's meaning to lyrics of songs we like. Then, of course, Neil
and Charlie had to be accountable regarding what they had done."

Neil raises his hand; Shay notices and comments he is done, and Neil clears his throat dramatically, "I didn't trust the process, the way the school has set up how we have to behave, so I did my own thing, and got not only myself but also Charlie in trouble. Frost's poem didn't excuse my behavior; it brought it home to me that people have to realize it's part of our natural chemistry to make choices based on our emotions instead of using our reason. If we could always be reasonable we could pretty much always understand the consequences of a choice we are thinking about making. We would have a better than good idea what's going to happen. The problem for me is taking that two minutes I'd need to think before I do something. And Frost's poem also refers to that part of us which makes it next to impossible to stop feeling strongly about something or someone even if the situation is hopeless."

I thank both Shay and Neil for sharing their ideas then ask the students to create a new entry by writing today's date in their journal, "I will read a poem, line by line, and you will write it down in your journals. The poem's title is "The Boundary Commission" and the poet's name is Paul Muldoon. Mr. Muldoon is a contemporary Irish poet, born in 1951, and educated in Belfast." I pause then begin reading the poem line by line so they can write it down:

> "You remember that village where the border ran
> down the middle of the street,
> with the butcher and baker in different states?
> Today he remarked how a shower of rain
> had stopped so cleanly across Golighty's lane
> it might have been a wall of glass
> that had toppled over. He stood there, for ages,
> to wonder which side, if any, he should be on."

When the students have all stopped writing I ask, "Who can offer insight on either the poem's title or a brief description of Belfast?"

Neil and Angela both raise their hands, so I ask if either of them have a preference. Angela comments she can only share information on Belfast.

Neil says 'no problem', and Angela begins speaking slowly, as if she is organizing her thoughts as she speaks, "Belfast is the capitol of Northern Ireland. It's a place that has come to symbolize the conflict between Catholics and Protestants, between the English and the Irish. All over Northern Ireland most Catholics were denied jobs or a place to live simply because of their faith. Violence escalated there in the late 1960s because of it."

Neil waits to begin to make sure Angela is not just pausing, then says, "I could talk about Ireland's history for hours, but I won't; I'll just give you the bare-bone facts. I'll start with Henry VIII and Elizabeth I who ruled England for most of the 1500s, and they pretty much controlled Ireland, but the northern counties of Ulster just wouldn't buy into English rule or the English Protestantism, so James I, in the beginning of the 1600s decided to create what he called the Ulster Plantation. He sent in Scottish and English Protestants and the Irish Catholics were thrown off their land. Laws were passed denying them equal rights. The Northern Ireland of today, which was officially created in 1921, is the Ulster Plantation of the past. In 1925 the Boundary Commission met to reevaluate the Northern Ireland border, but no changes were made because the Unionists, who favored ties to England, and the Nationalists, who believed the whole island was one country and should not be divided at all, could find no compromise. A third of Northern Ireland's population was Catholic, and a line on a map separated them from their fellow Irish Catholics. In the late 1940s Ireland officially broke all ties with the British Commonwealth, and became the Republic of Ireland, its constitution claiming Northern Ireland, but the British Parliament passed the Ireland Act in the late forties and it solidified the border, but it didn't end the prejudice or unfairness Angela referred to." Neil pauses and asks if he can add a couple of additional facts to what he has already shared. The students nod their heads for him to continue.

"If you were a Catholic in Northern Ireland in the 1950s you most likely worked in low-paying jobs because even though the British Constitution guaranteed the rights of all Northern Irish people, Catholics were 'unofficially' denied rights by landlords and businesses. A group of young people, educated but unemployed, began an organization called the Northern Ireland Civil Rights Association, acronym NICRA, in the late '60s. They planned to use peaceful protest to make the world aware of what was going on. They wanted the discrimination to stop. They planned a march from Belfast to Derry in 1968, an idea some believe was based on Dr. Martin Luther King's 1966 protest march from Selma to Montgomery. Six hundred Irish marched peacefully, but at Derry a large group of Protestants threw nails and stones and hit the marchers with crowbars. The marchers were supposed to be protected by the Royal Ulster Constabulary, acronym the RUC, but the mostly Protestant police force did little to nothing to protect the Catholic protesters. When riots broke out in Catholic neighborhoods to protest how the RUC handled the Derry March, the RUC used brutal measures to stop the riots. Since the RUC was not protecting the Catholic citizens of Northern Ireland, the IRA stepped in and became their protectors, but the main goal of the IRA was the same as it was in 1919 when the organization first began: to get the English out of Ireland. The use of violence on both sides, and the fact the struggle between the English and the Irish is centuries old seemed to make reconciliation impossible. From the late 1960s to the 1990s almost four thousand people, mostly civilians, have died in Northern Ireland in what is called the Troubles."

The room is quiet after Neil stops talking. Students seem to either be jotting down notes or rereading the poem. Shay raises his hand, "I watched a film a couple of years ago. The title was *Some Mother's Son*. The film is about the IRA hunger strikes of the early 1980s in Belfast's Maze Prison. Two mothers must decide if they should have their unconscious sons intravenously fed or let them die for their cause. Their sons were members of the IRA and were protesting their criminal status. They believed themselves to be political prisoners not criminals. In real life, Bobby Sands, an IRA leader, led the hunger strike. He believed it was crucial the British/Northern Irish government recognize that the actions of the IRA were political not criminal. He organized the hunger strike in such a way that he was first to start, then every week another man joined the strike, so their deaths would happen week after week. After sixty-six days, Sands died. Close to 100,000 people attended his funeral procession. Nine other strikers died before the prisoners called off the strike. Less than a week later, the British government met most of the IRA prisoners' demands." Shay pauses, looks down at the poem written in his journal and comments, "The idea of someone standing 'for ages' to decide which side he should be on, or if he should even be on a side, relates to the fact Neil stated: the conflict is centuries old. The Irish people have had to ask themselves for hundreds of years if they should continue to fight for what is rightfully theirs. In the poem, even nature, the rain, cannot cross the border, the unnatural man-made line that puts the town's butcher and baker on opposite sides." Shay pauses, turns pages in his journal, "Frost's poem definitely relates. Neither group, the British government nor the IRA, would "yield with grace to reason" or "bow and accept the end of ... a season". Bobby Sands was in prison most of his life. He'd get out and get arrested again. He had a wife and child. He was elected to be a member of Parliament while he was in prison but died, only twenty-seven years old, before he could take his seat at Westminster and have his voice heard. Maybe he thought his voice would be stronger in death. Maybe he's the best known of the men who died because of his poetry. I went on the Internet and found photos of him and read some of his poems, and the photos and his words made me like him, made me think we could have been friends. For me, his death proved he was a soldier and not a criminal. He was a soldier in an undeclared war fighting for his homeland. Nine other 'soldiers' died after him."

Shay's roommate, Morgan, responds, "I'm sorry he had to die, but using violence to achieve a political agenda is terrorism, Shay. He may have written good poetry, and he may have had a wife and a son, and his struggle against a regime that denies equal rights to his people may be valid, but man, where do we draw the line on fighting for our ideals? Does someone else's son get killed to achieve another person's political agenda? Where does it stop?"

Valerie raises her hand, so I call her name, and she comments, "Not to go off subject too far, but the parallels between the Irish and the Native Americans are too obvious not to mention." Other students agree with her, and I am about to refocus the discussion when Aden stands and walks to the window.

Our eyes are focused on him as he turns and speaks quietly, "First I'm more than tired of the big guy picking on the little guy whether the little guy is Irish or Native American or Jewish or overweight or underweight or whatever. 'Might does not make right'; somebody said that or something like it. I'm probably more than tired of it also because in school I was the little guy, the weaker guy, because I was always sick, but that's not why I stood up and walked over here. What I'm wondering is where we are going with all this, Mrs. Callaghan? We all know Mr. Dayton was very much in favor of a unified Ireland. We all noticed, even if they thought we didn't, the men who definitely didn't act like tourists and were in town a couple of weeks ago. This is a small town and a small school. What happens here may not always get talked about, but that doesn't mean we aren't aware. Too many things have been happening lately: you being gone, Father Tom, the fire, the strange fog and the rain that stayed in one place both at your house and in the forest. And the gunshots didn't sound like a bunch of illegal hunters. If you were going to tell us what really happened, I think you'd say all those events are related. I think you'd tell us you and your dog were shot. I think you'd tell us Mr. Dayton leaving is connected, but that's just what I think, and I could be wrong."

*   *   *   *

I listen to them, press my ear up against the windowpane that separates generations; sometimes I feel a need to tap on the glass and gesture as if I can actually communicate meaningfully there is a steep incline just ahead or a sheer drop off, that just possibly they will need to apply a bit of caution to their momentum, but that is just age speaking to youth, and I am only a warning sign in their peripheral vision. My students are in pairs discussing the assignment they were given, which happened after I told Aden he was more or less correct in his thinking, and after we left the tables and moved to the couches and discussed various emotional or school related issues they have had or are having. I played catch-up with them, and they allowed this. No additional references to Lane were made. The only question regarding my experiences was one made by Jacy asking me if I thought my life would get back to normal now. I only nodded and smiled in response. And now I am sitting at my desk listening and watching, which are what generations need to do for each other, what men and women need to do for each other, what people need to do for each other. I sigh and look at the photos on my desk, the smiling faces of my husband and children drawing my attention. I allow the allure of the next moment to draw me. I will pick up John Henry and Mary, and while we are driving they will 'tell me their days', and I will listen to their words and watch for the even more telling expressions of emotions filling their eyes, then we will be home, and Puppy will run to greet us, and Michael should be there, home again after his days of being gone; Michael, my fireman-husband, home. I sigh and rush my leave-school ritual just a bit. I become a young one with her face pressed up against the present moment, impatient for the next moment to reveal itself.

✳   ✳   ✳   ✳

We are home, and he is, door thrown open behind him, on the deck, then down the stairs. Then he is picking up children, ours, in his arms and above their smiling faces, in between kisses, his eyes meet mine. This is home for me: his eyes, his heart, his arms. Mine, all of him during these first moments, before we exchange words and before we have actually touched each other, we touch and we linger here, knowing the swiftness with which the first moment after being parted will pass. It is a spiritual place in a physical world; it is souls communing, and I am earth to his sky when we touch like this, over and over again through time and beyond time. My heart beats his name; his answers over and over again through a panorama of countless years of wind willing clouds and even sometimes stars across a skyscape of dark and light; we are poet warriors, romantic and fierce in how we love each other, and we know we have known each other since before we had shape or sound.

He is standing before me now, John Henry and Mary chasing Puppy, and we are almost lips to lips, only an infinitesimal shimmering sliver of breeze is between us as he breathes into me, "I missed everything about you."

I can only say, "Yes" before we are heartbeat to heartbeat, his arms pressing me closer into him, as if somehow we can truly be one being, drawing breath in unison, relational mouth to mouth resuscitation, the first kiss in four days.

"Are you two ever going to outgrow this kind of freaky romantic behavior? You've been married long enough that the honeymoon should be over, don't you think?" I do not have to open my eyes to put a speaker to the words. Michael and I are just pressing smiles into each other now as we look into each other's eyes. I move back from him, but stay in his arms, and look around his shoulder to see Brian.

I put on my teacher voice to tell him, "The honeymoon will never be over, brother-in-law, and there is nothing freaky about greeting each other warmly."

"It looked more than warm to me," Brian says back to me as he picks up one of Puppy's large rubber bones to throw, which he does as he asks me if I have driven by my old house.

I look at Michael who is looking at Brian. Brian just says 'oops' then, "I think Puppy and I will go inside and see what John Henry and Mary are munching for after school snacks."

I turn to face Michael as he begins to explain, "Well, I had a different way in mind to tell you, but there's a lot to tell you really. I probably should have told you before I went back to work, but you were recuperating and … I'm not sure why, maybe I was just waiting till things were back to normal."

I sit down on the deck steps, pat the place next to me and say, "From small comments people have made to me today, I'm wondering if 'normal' is possible." Michael sits down next to me, and I continue, "Town councils, new responsibilities at school, Aidrea applying for the administrative assistant job, Connor staying on at the church … there must have been quite a few conversations taking place while I was in the hospital and while I was recuperating. And now Brian suggests there is something happening at the 'old house'. Tell me, tell me, husband."

Michael takes my hand in his as we both look out across our yard at the lake, its surface rippled by an afternoon breeze. With his other hand, he pushes his hair back from his face as he says, "I'll start with the house. Nothing has been decided at all. There were just some suggestions made. The excavation has been back-filled, and we thought it might be a good idea to leave Father Tom's … the church's motor home on the property in case anyone wants to maybe build something there again. Connor was agreeable, because he has no plans for the motor home, but nothing final has been decided. We were waiting to talk with you about it."

I take my hand out of his and spread my arms, "Here I am. Tell me. And who are the individuals who comprise the 'we'? Start with that, please."

Michael smiles, "Your family, sweet thing. You have your family around you again, and they want to stay. Sean thought it might be a good idea for Malick and Aidrea to build a house on the property."

Many reactions to Michael's news are having their way with me. I am happy, of course, Aidrea wants to stay, and it is good a home will be built on that land where the rowan tree stands and where May and Papa John and my mom are buried. It seems right and strange at the same time. I feel a distance too between myself and Michael and the others, because of the many conversations I have obviously missed, but I shake my head instead of dwelling on any of those feelings and ask, "And Sean, will he live with them?"

Michael answers, "Connor has hired Sean as groundskeeper at the church. Connor says he won't have time to care for the orchard or the greenhouse. I think Connor likes the idea of keeping all you wild MacBrides, and his old friend Malick, together. That way he can keep an eye on what's happening. Connor also asked Sean to rebuild the cabin, and to plant trees to replace the ones that burned. Sean will stay at the church until the cabin is finished, then move out there permanently."

I sigh then ask, "Will Malick be a stay-at-home husband while Aidrea works?"

Michael puts his arm around my shoulders, "I thought you might know that one since you were at school today. Nathan hired him." Michael does not offer any more information, so I say 'to do what?' and he responds, "First I should let you know our brother-in-law is not as difficult to get along with as I originally thought, and, second, it turns out he had some teaching experience back in Ireland. Since Nathan believes he will need another teacher because you are going to be handling some of the administrative responsibilities for him, Nathan's hiring him."

I stand and turn to face Michael, "I have not agreed to that yet, Michael."

He stands and pulls me into his arms, even though I am reluctant to be held, "But everyone knows you will, Leah, because there are so many reasons why it's a good idea. Nathan will be able to return to his research and field work at least part-time, you and Bradley enjoy working together and the school will benefit from the fact you two will offer continuity while Nathan makes some changes, plus Malick likes the idea of working part-time at the school and part-time at the marina with Cal."

I lean back in Michael's arms so I can see his face as I repeat his last words as a question, "Malick is working part-time at the marina with Cal?"

Michael nods, "He's been there all week. Did I forget to mention that earlier?"

I pat his cheeks as Mary likes to do, "Yes, husband, you did, and I'm sure there are other interesting little tidbits you have somehow forgotten to mention, but I am on information overload, so let go of me. I am going to go inside and do something 'normal' like make dinner for my family, and I am not going to think about any of this now. And maybe I will look up the definition of 'normal' in the dictionary, because I do not believe I even know what the word means."

Michael's arms tighten around me, pulling me close, "I'm not done with you yet, wife."

I push against him as he begins to kiss my neck and rub his face in my hair, "But I am done with you, husband, so stop doing that."

His eyes search mine as he asks, "You're done with me?"

I stop pushing against him and think of all that has happened in the last few weeks; I become aware of how good his body feels against mine, so I say, "For the moment, just for this small moment."

He sighs, kisses my lips then pats my cheeks, "I'll accept that but only because I'm hungry." As I begin to walk up the steps he slaps me on the behind and says, "Feed your man, woman."

I turn to face him at the door, a safe distance from him, "You know I hate it when you do that."

Michael's facial expression changes, "Hate's a strong word, Leah. We've experienced it, you more than me, but we know what it means now, what it really means. I don't want either of us to hate anything."

Images of Taen fill my mind, but I push them back and close that door, leaning against it in my mind like I am leaning against our door now, "I dislike it greatly when you do that."

Michael walks across the deck and joins me, some of the seriousness gone from his eyes, "I can live with that."

I stand back from the door as he opens it but ask, "What are you saying exactly? Are you going to stop doing it then?"

He holds the door open for me, "How long have we been married, and before that how long were we together?"

I sigh, "Sometimes it seems like we have always been together."

Michael smiles, "So I've been slapping your butt forever; do you really think I'm going to stop? It's just an act of endearment, honey-bunches, that's all. I think you should just get used to it."

He walks into the living room after me as I say, "I will not get used to it, Michael Callaghan, and you should be mature enough to be able to stop."

Michael walks into the kitchen, removes a cold bottle of beer from the fridge, just as Brian walks out of the den. Michael takes a long drink, looks at Brian then at me and belches loudly, "I'm the king of this castle, wench. Start making dinner or I'll do it again."

Brian asks, "Do what?"

I shake my head, realize I have left my purse and briefcase in the car and begin walking to the door to go out and get them. As I open the door I look back at both Michael and Brian, "You are both foul beasts and male, and I may not feed you at all."

Brian is protesting by saying he has not done anything foul in the last half hour or so, and then from behind me Maybe's voice states just as loudly as Brian's, "Now, Leah, you understand the dilemma we face as women."

Maybe and Aidrea walk into the room, and I smile at both of them as I ask, "What dilemma?"

Maybe points at Brian and Michael, "You can't live with them, but you can't live without them, and training them is next to impossible."

John Henry and Mary have joined us from the den. John Henry comes to stand next to me, and I put my arm around his shoulders as he asks 'who can't live without what?' as Mary is asking what a 'dilemma' is while Brian is telling Maybe she is a 'vicious feminist'. Aidrea is laughing and taking Mary up into her arms. I look at Michael, who leans against the door of the refrigerator smiling, and he is saying words to me.

It is difficult to hear his words, but I believe he is saying, "We're back to normal, baby."

*   *   *   *

Night vision. That is what I call looking back through my day and gaining a new perspective. This is a perspective brought on by being relaxed, no doubt, but also due to the fact it is dark outside; the sun has distanced itself from us, so moon and stars can have their way with us, whispering magic into us the day disallows. Whispers during the day seem conspiratorial; they lurk and linger like shadows long after the words have flown from mouth to ear. But in the night, whispers are transparent crystal chimes moved by the breath of moonlight and the shimmering of stars.

Tonight my night vision experience is lit by moonlight and shimmering stars, but I am not in my bed. I sit on the shore of the lake with Maybe and Aidrea. We are night visioning together, like women gathered around an album of photographs who add and edit each other's memories as each image is looked into and searched for possible forgotten details. And we are not just rewinding the day; we are casting images from days past out onto the lake's surface then bringing them into focus with our words, so they can be shared.

Aidrea's words describe a childhood experience she had with May's sister, Megan, "She had received a telegram that morning but didn't share the news it brought with me until after supper. Then she had suggested our customary moonlight walk down to the sea's edge. Megan liked to be close enough to the waves to feel their spray on her face, so we would walk far out onto the rocks. She favored a certain place on the rocks where the moon's light cast its silver path across the water and upon the rocks where we sat. That night she would say words to me she would repeat often."

Aidrea pauses then speaks her next words in Irish before she translates them for us, "That is the path that reminds me, little daughter of my niece, that I am spirit and flesh. That path the moon lights, where the waves of the sea touch the rock and sand of the earth, reminds me that the daily paths I take, the ups and the downs of my walking, will all bring me back to this path where I will walk out of this world into the next. Look upon it often so you don't forget who you are, so you cannot be dragged down by the weight of the day-to-day and forget you're as much spirit as flesh." Aidrea turns to look into my eyes, searching to know the emotional reaction I may not choose to express in words, "That night she told of the fire, of the death of her sister, of our mother, and of the others. She asked me to gather up my strength around me and to see you wrapped in that same strength." Aidrea's hand finds mine in the darkness, and she leans close to me, "I didn't know our mother except through photographs and letters she wrote to me that our father would bring to me when he would return from his frequent visits here, but I knew her in my heart, because she filled a place there. After the deaths, Sean didn't bring any more photographs, and of course there could be no more letters, so in my mind you were always that little girl. Even knowing that you and I look the same, you did not age with me. As time passed, you never shared my reflection in the mirror but stayed the little girl. My heart, the place in it my mother filled, hurt, but when I mourned it was for you, who had lost a mother she knew, a mother who had held her close, who had touched her hair, who had laughed and cried with her." Aidrea looks back to the lake but continues speaking, her words quiet but resonating, drawn from the deep echoing well of memory, "That night by the sea, on the rocks, Megan told me to follow the moon's path of light with my eyes until at its greatest distance it became so close I lost all sense of my place on the rock or the waves' spray on my face. She told me to listen to the waves' song until it became only the beating of a heart, and that I must match my heartbeat to the other heart's rhythm. She said in that place that is no place and is before and beyond time, I would see my mother and grandmother and feel arms around me that had not held me since my birth. I did what she said, and I felt what she said I would, and that was the beginning of my training. Megan continued teaching me until her death two years ago. I was in Belfast when she died, but when I returned home I went to that place she and I had shared for so many nights for so many years and I said goodbye to the woman who had raised me and felt her arms around me one last time." Aidrea looks back at me and smiles, "You would have liked Megan. Dad told me she was like your May in many ways, but Megan didn't have to hide who she was or what she could do, so she was a bit more outspoken than May. Dad's actual word was 'eccentric', but I don't think of her that way."

Maybe sighs and says, "I hope this will be the first of many nights where we come together to talk and learn from each other. We'll have to take Aidrea to meet Shadowmaker next time, won't we, Leah, and tell her the story of Grandma Hitaw?"

Before I can answer, I am startled by Puppy's greeting, his head rubbing against my back. I turn and see John Henry standing behind Puppy.

I smile at him as Aidrea says, "Well, well, look at this good old man coming to make sure his womenfolk are safe."

John Henry comes to stand behind me as Puppy moves from me to Maybe in his head rubbing. John Henry comments somewhat shyly, "We watched from the window until Puppy started making noise to go out. I didn't want him to wake Dad or Mary."

Puppy moves to Aidrea, and she scratches his chest and ears but then stops and looks up as an eagle flies over us then turns and flies closer as it passes over us again. She stands and smiles, giving Puppy one last pat, "Another of our men is letting us know the hour is late, and it's time to return home."

I stand and turn to look at John Henry to gauge his reaction to Aidrea's statement. He pats my arms and says, "It's okay, mom. This is how our life is now."

I take his hand in mine and ask, "Do you mind how our life is now?"

He shakes his head and in typical John Henry style comments, "It's real, so I can't mind. I'd rather know the truth than think I know but not know ... ya know?"

Aidrea and Maybe and I all look at each other and nod our agreement to John Henry. Then Maybe walks over to John Henry, bends down so they are at the same eye level, and declares, "Perhaps men aren't impossible."

John Henry looks at each one of us, his expression thoughtful, and replies, "Mom says men and women aren't really that different. We're all just people trying to live life well. Right, mom?"

I just smile and nod in response, thinking to myself we are all just people trying to live life well, trying to comprehend all the nuances and survive all the storms, trying to get handholds and feet placement right, trying to just choose the right damn fork from the place settings of circumstance and situation that continuously offer us more choices than we can sometimes, often times, discern. We are all just surviving one moment as we prepare for the choices and possibilities of the next and the next after that and then the next moment after that ... our eyes taking in the present as the past pulls us back into itself as the future shimmers like distant stars enticing us ... living ... breathing in deeply all that is around us ... exhaling out into the worlds we inhabit all that we are ... over and over again, forever, until our spirits become stronger than our bones and we become dancers moved by the breath of a creator whose heartbeat beats in all of us.

I sigh, say goodbye to my sister and to my friend, pick up my son who is getting too big to pick up and walk with Puppy on a path of light sent by the moon across the lake through the trees and onto our deck. I walk on moonlight to return home and imagine I see a woman I never met watching me as she walks her own moonlit path. I say goodnight to Megan and smile as I breathe in the sweet smell of my son's hair and decide I always want to do more than just survive; I want to live each moment well. Father Tom would approve, and thinking of him, I say goodnight to him too ... and to my mom and Papa John ... and to May. I say to them 'sweet dreams' as I say it into the rooms of my house as I tuck John Henry into his bed. Sweet dreams ... sweet life.

*   *   *   *

Morning is sweet too and a bit shy at times, the way it seeps into the room. This is totally unlike midday's march with its band of bright light playing loud songs. I am in the kitchen making potato salad and spaghettini primavera. John Henry and Mary and Michael are straightening up and cleaning the house, so I do not have much more to do before family and friends arrive. Puppy has already gone out and come in again, taking care of his morning business, and he is quite pleased at the bits of potato I toss to him now and then as he lays on the kitchen floor keeping me company. I am listening as Michael sings a silly, made-up song to John Henry and Mary. They begin giggling loudly, then Puppy seems to give me an apologetic look before he runs to join them. I am about to follow Puppy when I hear someone knocking on the door.

I walk to the door and see my father standing with two cases of Killian Reds in his arms with a package balanced on the top of the cases. He is smiling as he says, "Be a good daughter and tell your kind old father where to put the brew."

I open the door and kiss his cheek before I walk with him to the edge of the deck and point to the side of the stairs where four ice chests sit side by side. "Michael put ice in them already. Do you want help?"

Sean says 'help would be good,' then we are quiet as we both listen to the silly words of Michael's song until it ends abruptly in Michael's laughter and John Henry's and Mary's giggles. Sean sets the package on the edge of the deck, and we load the bottles of beer into the ice chests. We are surrounded by bird song, the water of the lake lapping on its shore, breeze and sunlight passing through the branches of trees. We smile into each other when we have finished our task. Sean puts his arms around me and holds me as he speaks quiet words, "It's grateful I am you still love me after all that happened so long ago and more recently too. Grateful and glad for it, I am. I can't make up to you the loss of Colleen and May and John, but Aidrea and I want to be a part of your family. I can offer you that, Leah. I can offer you today and tomorrow and the day after that if you'll let me, daughter."

My heart feels full the way hearts sometimes can in their safekeeping of emotions. A deep fathomless joy and a smooth bearable sorrow, its sharp edges worn down, bring tears to my eyes. I tell my father I will cherish each day we have together. We step back from each other, and he hands me the package as he shrugs his shoulders, "Do you recognize the writing?"

I look at my name printed on the brown wrapping paper and recognize the handwriting immediately, "It is Lane's." Sean nods and suggests I open it now before we are joined by others. I hesitate, wondering if I should just tuck it away somewhere and open it later, but opening it later will not change what I will find inside, so I do as Sean suggests. The package is heavy but not unmanageable.

After the package has revealed its contents to us we just stand and look at Lane's brief note lying beside the two golden neckrings and the knife with its scabbard cushioned in bubble wrap and tissue paper. Lane's words read: 'I know

now I have no right to these. Forgive me for the harm I've caused.' I fold the tissue paper and bubble wrap back over the package's contents and close the box's lid.

Sean puts his arm around my shoulders and asks, "What do you want to do with them?"

I respond quickly, "I will think about that after the party. We will talk with Michael and Aidrea and Malick about them. Then we can decide what we should do." I pause then speak what I am thinking aloud, "Perhaps I should take them back, bury them under the altar, let the past keep its treasures and its heartache; I believe the two will always be intertwined."

Sean nods his head and repeats 'perhaps'. I look at him to check his expression but sense no ulterior motivation in him. He shakes his head, "I will not disappoint you again, Leah. I understand what's important and maybe even how to achieve it, not only for my family but also for my country. I will be a loving father and a loving patriot. I'll see if I cannot do more good than harm in the last part of my life. You can trust me."

I feel that I can and say, "I do, Sean … dad." Then I walk into the house and into my bedroom. I put the box underneath my shoe rack in my closet and return outside without being seen by my husband or children, who are all in the guest bathroom. Michael begins singing again as I rejoin Sean.

Before Sean and I can begin talking again, John Henry and Mary, followed by Puppy, run out of the door, across the deck, down the deck stairs, and out into the yard where they turn and look back at the door, then all our eyes are focused on Michael, who is standing with an apron that was May's slung low around his hips. He has a shower cap on his head and a long handled toilet bowl brush in his hand, which he waves around jabbing the air menacingly each time his voice rises in a shrill falsetto. He stops when he sees Sean.

Sean opens an ice chest, picks up one of the beers, and walks over to Michael handing it to him. Sean pats Michael on the shoulder, then turns to walk into the house as he comments, "Drink this son, you need it. Housecleaning is women's work, doing it has unhinged your brain. Beer will fix you."

Michael grins at me, drops the toilet bowl cleaning brush on the deck, and turns to follow Sean saying "Thanks, Sean." Then I hear him say, "I think there's a game on."

John Henry and Mary join me. We walk up the deck stairs together as we hear my father speaking to Michael, "You're going to have to take the apron off, Michael. I can handle the plastic thing on your head, but I can't give the game the concentration it's due with you wearing an apron with flowers and … what are those … little bunnies on it. You need to get a manly apron if you're going to wear one. One with hammers on it." The noise of a crowd cheering and a broadcaster's voice drowns out any other comments made by my father and husband, but I do not mind at all, having heard more than enough.

I pick up the brush as John Henry opens the door for Mary, and he comments, "Well, mom, maybe women and men really are different."

He is smiling when I turn to him to respond, "I can only hope that is true, John Henry, I can only hope that is true."

✳   ✳   ✳   ✳

My front deck and yard are full of friends and family and an assortment of coolers and a variety of dogs and trucks and SUVs and lake toys and folding chairs, and even the air is full. There are small and large conversations occurring here and there, and some of the men are shouting as they play volleyball, which of course makes my dog and his visiting dog-friends bark, which makes the kids chase the dogs, and it is all a glorious, loud celebration of life. I sit at the large table on the deck with Katy, Matilda, Katherine, and Sarah. We are watching my children and a collection of friends and cousins at play. Four generations of Callaghans are represented in our gathering.

Matilda sits with her eyes closed for a moment, and then sensing I am watching her as the other women talk quietly, she opens them, their clear sky blue in such contrast with her loosely bound silver hair. Her voice is soft but vibrant as she speaks, "It must do your heart good to have your own family represented here today. Aidrea's Malick seems to be holding his own in the volleyball game, or Michael's just slapping him on the back to be encouraging. Aidrea has been surrounded by children most of the day. She must tell a good story. I'm not sure who is more enthralled, Maybe or the young ones. Of course, Sean has made himself right at home. He and Hank and Patrick haven't moved from their table by the lake, and they seem to be talking more than watching the canoes and sailboats as they usually do. I wonder if Patrick is reminding them of all the pranks they pulled as boys, or if they are finally telling him about all the pranks they pulled they actually got away with."

Matilda puts her hand in her pocket, and whatever it was I was about to say is gone from my mind. She notices I am watching her with my mouth open and reaches over and pats my arm as she reassures me, "No, Leah, I have nothing in my pocket for you this time."

I lean back in my chair and sigh, "Thank goodness."

Matilda smiles then asks, "I was wondering though if I could look at the ring you are wearing. Have you learned its history?"

I take off the ring and hand it to Matilda and answer her by saying, "I was told the pearl was Dagda's first gift to Danu. Then it was given to Jhace to give to Brigid when they married. Jhace had the setting made so Brigid could wear the pearl as a ring." The pearl reminds me of a star as it captures the sun's filtered light falling through the branches of trees. Matilda feels the inside of the band with her finger then hands the ring back to me.

Suddenly I remember what Brigid said about symbols engraved on the inside of the band, and I look to see as I ask Matilda, "Why did you feel the inside of the ring?"

Matilda laughs gently, "Perhaps for no reason at all."

I want more of an answer than that, "No, you did it intentionally."

Matilda leans toward me so she can look directly into my eyes, "It's difficult for you to believe that my only purposes in all this were to bring you the first letter, to remind you of something you had been told but had forgotten, and to pray, of course; that was my biggest responsibility. My duties were small, Leah, but necessary. Not all involved had the privilege or the liability to serve as you did, but we played our parts. Elwood, Bradley, your children, even Lane, and, of course, your Michael were necessary. Every thread in a tapestry completes the image portrayed. After the danger became evident, Father Tom no longer asked me to bring you the letters, and I didn't feel remiss in allowing him to protect me in that way, but when he died I wondered if my agreement didn't lead to his death. May knew though, kind heart that she is, and reassured me in the way she communicates with me. All that happened occurred as it was supposed to happen. So I can miss our dear Father Tom without feeling guilty, and that is a blessing to me. You, I hope, can do the same."

I put the ring back on my finger and take Matilda's hand in mine, "Shame on you, Auntie. All you just told me is important, but you did not answer my question." Even as I am speaking to her my mind is trying to focus on something else, then I realize Elwood is not here. I share my concern with Matilda, "Michael told me he spoke with Elwood, and he was planning to be here, but he is not."

Matilda looks around then stands slowly as I help her, "We shall go find him then, you and I."

I say 'yes' to her, but notice my car and Michael's truck are both blocked by other vehicles in the driveway. I ask Matilda to wait for a moment then walk quickly over to the volleyball game. Michael comes to me as soon as he sees me standing across the court from him. I tell him Elwood is not here, and he agrees we should find Elwood then asks me the question I have been asking myself, "How will we know where to look for him?"

Before I can make a reply, Malick stands next to Michael. Michael explains the situation to him, and Malick volunteers to look for Elwood himself. Michael looks over at the cars in the driveway and says, "That's great, but your car is blocked too." Malick and I exchange glances, then Michael catches on and nods, "Okay, okay, I'm the slow one. Just do me a favor and don't sprout wings right here in the middle of everyone."

Malick shakes his head, "Thanks for the good advice. I would never have considered that." Malick walks away from us, stopping to drop a kiss on the top of Aidrea's head before he walks around to the back of the house.

Aidrea joins us as Michael suggests a break to those involved in the volleyball game. He recommends grabbing a beer, and no one complains. I explain to Aidrea why Malick left and our transportation problem.

Aidrea replies quickly, "Malick brought the car. I rode my bike. We can take my bike."

Michael pats her shoulder, "I'm sure you're in great shape, Aidrea, but the hills around here are going to make riding a bike slow going."

Aidrea turns and walks away then stops indicating we should follow her, so we do. Halfway down the driveway, parked under a tree is a teal and white Harley Davidson Sportster with lots of chrome, a sissy bar and black leather saddlebags. The only reason I can even identify it is Michael has wanted a Harley Davidson Fat Boy ever since we got married and he frequently shows me photographs and explains in great detail the characteristics of each bike. For as long as he has wanted a Fat Boy, he has tried to get me interested in a Sportster. I have no interest at all.

Michael turns and looks at Aidrea, admiration shining out of his eyes, "You'll have no trouble with the hills. Take Leah with you. I'll explain to Matilda why she can't go with you two and play host to our guests. Call me if you need me. If I have to I'll take whoever's car is at the end of the line."

Aidrea is pulling a helmet out of each saddlebag and I have not managed to take a single step closer to the bike. Michael sees my reluctance and puts an arm around my shoulders and moves me to the bike. Michael's words are meant to comfort me as Aidrea hands me a helmet, "You're going to want one after this, Leah. Just concentrate on finding Elwood and forget you're even on a bike."

Aidrea swings her leg over the bike as Michael is adjusting my chin strap. Aidrea pats the seat behind her, "Come on, sister. I've been riding for years. I can outrun—." She stops herself mid-sentence as I see Michael shaking his head 'no' in my peripheral vision.

I climb onto the bike. She turns the key, pushes the starter button, and waves at Michael who is giving us a 'thumbs up'. I am thinking about returning his gesture using a different finger, but it is only a negative thought I choose not to act out. We sit there surrounded by the bike's loudness while I assume she is letting the bike warm up. I am wondering if I have any duties as the person behind the driver, refusing to use the colloquialism for my position on the bike. I tap her shoulder and try to talk over the noise, then suddenly I am hearing her voice in my helmet, "Just talk to me, Leah, I'll hear you just fine. You don't have to yell either. Malick always yells."

I clear my throat for some reason and ask her if there is anything I am supposed to do. She replies, without commenting on my lack of knowledge, "Just put your arms around my waist and hold on. I'll head toward the library then to the shore. I understand he looks for his wife and son there. Malick may already know where he is and if so, he'll find us. Are you ready?"

I say 'yes', and we are off. We are zooming, for lack of a better word. If she were Michael, I would suggest strongly she slow down on the curves, but I do not know her well enough to complain about her driving, so I only hold on. I decide to lean over just a bit and look to see the speedometer. I discover we are not actually going faster than a race car; we are only traveling around forty miles per hour. We have only gone a few miles when a shadow passes over us. Malick, or a real eagle with a death wish, suddenly drops in front of us, and Aidrea slows to around thirty miles per hour. From the roads we are taking I know we are going to the library. I stop thinking about the fact I am on the back of a motorcycle and concentrate on Elwood, praying he is alright. Then without even thinking about what I am doing, I call out to him in the spirit. I tell him I will be with him soon. I repeat those words over and over until I am stopped by an overwhelming feeling of apprehension. Despair becomes physical, dark and looming, pulling at me but without arms or hands. I begin to raise my hands to push against it, but Aidrea holds my arms around her with one of her hands.

I remember then to hold on to her as I listen to her words, "Hold on, Leah. We'll fight this one together, but you have to stay with me for now."

I try to do what she is asking of me, but I am too many places at once. I am on the bike then in another place without physical attributes except I have a sense of light behind me and darkness in front of me. I am aware of the bike slowing and turning. When we stop I do not move because one moment I am aware we are in the library parking lot then suddenly I am back in the other place. Hands hold my arms and lift my leg over the bike. I hear both Malick and Aidrea but cannot understand their words. Then I am being carried. When I return to the other place again I force myself to turn and look around me but my movement is slow, as if I am pushing through quicksand.

When I do finally manage to turn to my left, Elwood stands a short distance from me, but the light surrounding me does not surround him. The darkness is projecting itself into him through his eyes and his heart, and I cannot see his legs below his knees. His hands are also in darkness. I call out to him. Then the shape of a bird's beak and head push against what seems like the fabric of the light. Breaking through, it flies toward us but in slow motion like I move. The darkness seems to gather itself up like a wave of thick black oil poured out but obstructed. The eagle flies against it trying to keep its body between Elwood and the darkness, but the eagle's momentum is almost completely stilled as if it is flying into a relentless wind.

Through the opening the eagle made into the light's surface a giant hand appears, first just fingertips then slowly the whole hand reaches in and wraps around Elwood trying to pull him out with it. I perceive a sound coming from the darkness, but it is so low I feel it more than hear it. The eagle uses its talons as I use my hands, trying to tear through the tentacles binding themselves to Elwood. The darkness' hold on Elwood is stretched so thin it becomes gray instead of black.

I look at Elwood's face and see his eyes are closed. I call his name, telling him to open his eyes, which he does, then I am lying on the lawn in front of the library. Malick, in human form, is breathing hard and on his back, his face flushed. I am on my stomach, my legs sprawled out behind me with one arm bent under my body. Elwood is standing totally still, his eyes closed, his arms out in front of him as if he is reaching for something. Aidrea is sitting with her legs bent under her with her hands folded in her lap. Her eyes are closed but her lips move. She appears to be meditating or praying and quite calm.

I decide to try and place myself into a sitting position, but I feel as though I have just run a marathon for which I did not train. My limbs are not cooperating with me. When I do finally manage to arrange myself, I see that Malick is also sitting. His breathing is more normal as he nods at Aidrea, "She's letting him see his wife and son. It shouldn't be much longer. He can't speak to them, but he is seeing them as they are now, and that should allow him to feel hope again."

I am beyond being surprised, so I just nod my head back at him then sit and wait along with Malick for Aidrea and Elwood to return to us. I watch Elwood's face and see tears fall from his eyes as his lips form a smile. Aidrea's lips have stopped forming their silent words, and Malick has moved to stand behind Elwood. Malick's arms are positioned in such a way I can see he expects to catch Elwood if he falls. I ask if he needs my help, but he shakes his head and tells me to just relax and wait for Aidrea.

She and Elwood open their eyes at the same time. Elwood's body seems to fold forward but Malick holds him, lowering him to the ground slowly. Aidrea stretches her arms over her head then turns her head first one way and then in the opposite direction. She somehow gracefully crawls over to me and sits next to me as she says, "Once you have more understanding you'll be great at all this, Leah."

I look over at Elwood, who seems to be resting in Malick's arms, then look back at Aidrea and reply, "I was under the impression I had fulfilled my obligation, and my life would go back to the way it was, in as much as that is possible."

Aidrea looks at Malick who is listening to what we are saying to each other then asks me, "Is that what you want?"

I am about to answer when Michael drives up in a car belonging to one of his friends and parks next to Aidrea's bike. He comes to me but looks at Malick, who indicates to him that Elwood is fine. He asks me how I am.

I say 'fine' to him. He looks at Aidrea and asks how she is. She answers him but looks at me, "I'm feeling better at the moment than your wife is." He asks her why that is and again she answers him but continues to look at me, "She had another experience in that other place, as she calls it."

Michael decides to speak to me directly, "Did you think it was all over, Leah, that you had opened a door you could close like you have closed doors before?" I say 'yes' to him, and he takes me in his arms. "You've been given a gift I don't think you can return."

I look at Aidrea and try my idea out on her, "Perhaps Connor can sprinkle holy water on me, and I will be cured."

Aidrea leans close to me, "Do you think your gift is evil?"

I close my eyes and lean against Michael as I shake my head 'no' then add, "I know what evil is, and I am not evil. It just all seems incredibly complicated and uncontrollable."

Michael hugs me to him as he says, "Aidrea and Malick are going to help you, Leah. You'll be fine. You'll be great. I promise. Sean says you're amazing for not knowing more than you do."

I stop leaning against him and sit up straight as I comment I am not sure whether I should say 'gee, thanks, dad' or not when I see Sean again. Then I stand up and point my finger at Michael, "And I do not want a bike."

I walk over to Elwood and Malick then sit down next to them, but I hear Michael tell Aidrea, "Baby steps. She's not much into surprises."

I look over at him and point at him again for no reason, "Or skipping."

Aidrea and Michael smile at each other as he restates what I have just said, "It's true; she's not a skipper either, and I can understand that completely, but skipping is a lot more demanding than riding a bike."

Elwood stops our banter by asking, "Have I missed the party?"

Michael answers, "No way, it's just getting started. Dad and Sean were firing up the barbecues, with a great deal of verbal assistance from Grandpa Patrick, when I left. Are you ready to go or do you need some more time?"

Elwood sits up and pats Malick's hand, "Thank you, Malick. I believe if you will help me get my legs under me I will do fine on my own from there." Malick helps Elwood stand, then Elwood turns and thanks me, "Leah, once again you helped me find my way back. Thank you." He walks over to Aidrea and takes her hand, "Seeing them will allow me to have hope for the rest of my days. Thank you, Aidrea." Then he looks at Michael and thanks him.

Michael shakes his head, "I didn't really do anything, Elwood, except ask God to protect each one of you. Of course, Matilda has been praying since we realized you weren't at the party."

Malick shakes his head, "We all play a part, Michael."

Michael raises his hands, "I'm good with that. I'm not complaining."

Aidrea quietly asks me if I am good with my part. I put my arm around her shoulders as we all begin walking back to the parking lot. I think about my words before I say them to her, "I am so glad, so thankful you are a part of my life. And to have Sean here with us is good also, but the other aspect of my new way of living ... I am not sure about that or how I feel about it, but it does not really matter how I feel about it, does it?"

Aidrea puts her arm around my waist, "Yes and no. Destiny is a fluid thing, not words carved in stone. This is your destiny, but within that destiny you still have choices."

I sigh, "That is what I thought you would say."

When we reach her bike she begins to hand me a helmet, but I back away from her and state very clearly, "I am making a choice here. I am choosing to ride with Elwood and Michael in the car. Malick can ride with you."

Malick shakes his whole body, "I hate those damn things. They're too noisy. Let Michael ride with her."

Aidrea says that is fine with her, and Michael throws the car keys to Malick, kisses me on the cheek, and tells Elwood he will see him at the party. I sit in the backseat and lean my head back, closing my eyes. I allow myself to see the shape Taen's hate took. I allow myself to see Elwood's hopelessness. I remember being with Brigid at the altar, and I again see the almost transparent beings surrounding us with their crystalline bodies and pristine voices; I see the people in my life who stand close enough to let me know them, who trust me with their hearts full of their hopes and fears, and I become so aware of what shapes love and faith take. Then I am no longer in the backseat of the car. I am in the meadow. Shal and Brigid stand before me. I can see the altar through their bodies. They are becoming like the others, and their voices when they speak are more like musical notes than words.

Brigid's words embrace me, "Thank you, Leah. Trust the moment."

Shal's says simply, "Be well, Leah. Live well."

Then I am sitting in the car again. I am home. Elwood and Malick no longer sit in the front seat, but I realize Michael is sitting next to me holding my hand. When I look at him I see his eyes are full of wonder.

His words are only a whisper when he speaks, "I came to sit with you, to make sure you came back to us."

I whisper back, "I will always return to you."

He leans closer to me, our lips almost touching, "They let me see this time, Leah. I saw Shal and Brigid. I saw the altar. I heard their voices."

I smile, "Then we share that too now."

Michael breathes his words into me, "We have forever, wife."

I feel the beat of his heart as he kisses my lips. I hear the beat of that other heart offering me an eternal hope, offering me forever illumined by a gentle fire seeking only to cast its light into the opaque fog of wanting more than the moment offers me, that I might come to believe with a sure faith that within a single moment we have the opportunity to love and live well together always … always. I let the perceptions of my thoughts, the discernments of my spirit, and the sensations of my body linger on nothing beyond my awareness of the moment. I let this moment fill me completely. It is more than enough.

References

Antpohler, Werner. <u>Newgrange, Dowth & Knowth</u>. Dublin: Mercier Press, 2000.

Bender, Paul. Interview. Colville, Wa., Februauary 2004. (<u>The Complete Ropes Manual</u>, 2nd Edition. Karl Rohnke, Catherine M. Tait & Jim Wall. Iowa: Kendall/Hunt Co., 1994.)

Blackwell, Amy Hackney & Ryan Hackney. <u>The Everythihng Irish History and Heritage Book</u>. Massachusetts: Adam Media, 2004.

Bouton, Bruce C., Larry E. Cordle and Carl E. Jackson. (Performed by Garth Brooks.) Tennessee: Slide Bar Music.

Doors, The. "Crystal Ships." California: Doors Music Company.

Ehrlich, Gretel. <u>The Solace of Open Spaces</u>. New York, Penguin Books, 1985.

Eliot, T.S. <u>Four Quartets</u>. Florida, Harcourt, Inc., 1943.

Frost, Robert. "Reluctance." Sohn, David A. & Richard Tyre. <u>Frost: The Poet and His Poetry</u>. New York: Bantam Book/Holt, Rhinehart, and Winston, Inc., 1969.

Healy, Sean. "In Memoriam: Bobby Sands." <u>Green Left Weekly</u>. http://greenleft.org.au/back/1991/11/11p8.htm.

Ingersoll, Robert Green. <u>The Works of Robert G. Ingersoll</u>. New York: C.P. Farrell, 1990.

Heaney, Marie. "The Children of Lir." <u>The Names Upon the Harp</u>. New York: Scholastic, Inc., 2000.

Joyce, Timothy. <u>Celtic Christianity</u>. New York: Orbis Books, 1998.

Lowery, John and Brian Hugh Warner. "The Bright Young Things." (Performed by Marilyn Manson.) California: Chrysalis Music/GTR Hack Music.

Mackillop, James. <u>Dictionary of Celtic Mythology</u>. Oxford: Oxford Press, 1998.

McCaffrey, Carmel & Leo Eaton. <u>In Search of Ancient Ireland</u>. Chicago: New Amsterdam Books/Ivan R. Dee, 2002.

Megaw, Ruth and Vincent. <u>Celtic Art</u>. New York: Thames & Hudson, 1989.

Morris, Nick. "All In." California: Good Show Entertainment.

Muldoon, Paul. "The Boundary Commission." <u>Irish Literature—A Reader</u>. Murphy, Maureen O'Rourke and James MacKillop. New York: Syracuse University Press, 1987.

978-0-595-42356-9
0-595-42356-6

Printed in the United States
87632LV00003B/1-18/A